THE SHORT STORIES OF

S A K I

(H. H. MUNRO)

WITH AN INTRODUCTION BY

CHRISTOPHER MORLEY

THE MODERN LIBRARY · NEW YORK

COPYRIGHT, 1930, 1958, BY THE VIKING PRESS, INC.

THE MODERN LIBRARY
is published by RANDOM HOUSE, INC.
BENNETT CERF • DONALD S. KLOPFER

Manufactured in the United States of America by H. Wolff

vi   INTRODUCTION

INTRODUCTION

by CHRISTOPHER MORLEY

THE smiling bitter rubaiyat from which Hector Munro
took his pseudonym were effectively symbolic of his own
gift. The empty glass we turn down for him is the fragile
hollow-stemmed goblet meant for driest champagne; it is of
finest crystal. Occasionally at his table we are aware that he
was also a still wine of elect vintage; but for the most part
he preferred to sparkle and fume with incessant bubbles of
wit; a wit for which such words as satire, cynicism, sophistry,
are all too gassy.

There is something of great encouragement in this renewed
republication of his tales. One might have thought that to
the rising generation he would speak an unassimilable language.
Like certain beverages now almost mythical in the United
States, he is genuinely pre-War; genuinely Scotch too. At least
one reader is taken back by him to the vanished world of an
Oxford common-room when copies of the *Bystander* or the
Westminster Gazette occasionally printed his grave mockeries.
More often, though, it was the *Morning Post*. The faithful
and severe anti-Americanism of that journal caused it to be
read by some Rhodes Scholars as a carminative. It was worth
it, for there one discovered Saki.

In recent revivals of his books distinguished enthusiasts have
spoken handsomely of his urbane malice and charm. But in all
those comments the friendliest critics have shown themselves
instinctively puzzled how to proceed; all have fallen back upon
quotation of Saki's own felicities. This is inevitable. The fact is
there are few writers less profitable to write *about*. Saki exists
only to be read. The exquisite lightness of his work offers
no grasp for the solemnities of earnest criticism. He is of those
brilliant and lucky volatiles who are to be enjoyed, not critic-

handled. He will be instinctively recognized and relished by those capable.

Mr. E. V. Lucas, expert on both mirth and grimness, long ago described the perfect hostess as one who puts by the guest-room bed "a volume either of O. Henry or Saki or both." It is all right to put it there, but one hopes it will be brought down-stairs the next morning, for Saki's most perfect felicity is to be read aloud in a house-party setting. The bracketing with O. Henry is not just casual; though the two are as different as Texas and Surrey, both are instinctive story-tellers dealing perfectly with their chosen material. (Both also did all their best work for newspapers.) The English country-house hostess, chambermaid, or candidate standing for a "bye-election" are creatures as wild and strange to an American reader as O. Henry's ranchman and medicine-show grifters to the London congregation of W. H. Smith. Both Saki and O. Henry are masters of the park-bench setting. Saki was less insistent on twisting the story's tail, but an equal master of surprise when he chose. Let the lover of O. Henry read Saki's *Dusk*, or *The Mouse*, or *The Reticence of Lady Anne*, or *The Open Window*, and see what I mean. The English flapper or Nut of pre-War days was anatomized by Saki as shrewdly as— and less sentimentally than—O. Henry's sheepherder or shop-girl. He could purge the decorous amenities of an English week-end party with blasts of cyclone farce. He could show the conversation of a few ladies at bridge as deadly and quick on the trigger of concealed weapons as a Western bar-room brawl.

There is no greater compliment to be paid the right kind of friend than to hand him Saki, without comment. Particularly to those less familiar with the mysterious jungles of English humour, a savage country with birds of unexpected plumage, Saki's insouciant spoof may be a revelation. Many who believe the famous phrase "no more privacy than a goldfish" to be inalienably American will be surprised to find that Saki used it in 1903 or thereabouts. (Though I dare say it may really date from Alexander Pope.) Delicate, airy, lucid, precise, with the inconspicuous agility of perfect style, he can pass into the uncanny, the tragic, into mocking fairy-tales grimmer than Grimm. His phrases are always urbane and usually final. "His hair and forehead furnished a recessional note in a personality that was in all other respects obtrusive and assertive." Probably more than any writer who ever lived he has made a study of aunts and nephews. His sister's biographical sketch, which tells with moderation of the appalling auntly regime of their childhood, gives us a clue to this. Aunts and werewolves were two of his specialities. Of what other writer can it be said that his Life could not be written until his aunts had died.

There are certain social types whom Saki cooks and serves for us as absolutely as perfect asparagus and hollandaise. Even their names are genius, as every critic has noted. Sir James Beanquest, Mrs. Thropplestance, Ada Spelvexit, Mrs. Quabarl, Clovis Sangrail, Comus Bassington, Blanche Bavvel, Hortensia Bavvel—can you resist the desire to be introduced to these? Clovis, Playboy of the Week-End World, I have always supposed to be so called because he was so appallingly frank.

Saki writes so lightly that you might hardly notice how beautifully also. And here and there, beneath so much enchanting play upon words, you will be startled and embarrassed by play upon hearts. Let me repeat what I once put into the mouth of the "Old Mandarin" in a pseudo-Chinese translation:

> There is something specially Chinese
> In Saki's Tory humour,
> He has the claw of the demon-cat
> Beneath his brilliant robe.
> Suavest comedian, silkiest satirist,
> Smooth as a shave
> With a new razor-blade.

CONTENTS

THE CHRONICLES OF CLOVIS

THE TOYS OF PEACE

THE SQUARE EGG

Reginald

First collected, 1904

These sketches originally appeared in the *Westminster Gazette*. Thanks are due to the Editors for permission to republish them.

REGINALD

I DID it—I should have known better. I persuaded Reginald to go to the McKillops' garden-party against his will.

We all make mistakes occasionally. "They know you're here, and they'll think it so funny if you don't go. And I want particularly to be in with Mrs. McKillop just now."

"I know, you want one of her smoke Persian kittens as a prospective wife for Wumples—or a husband, is it?" (Reginald has a magnificent scorn for details, other than sartorial.) "And I am expected to undergo social martyrdom to suit the connubial exigencies—"

"Reginald! It's nothing of the kind, only I'm sure Mrs. McKillop would be pleased if I brought you. Young men of your brilliant attractions are rather at a premium at her garden-parties."

"Should be at a premium in heaven," remarked Reginald complacently.

"There will be very few of you there, if that is what you mean. But seriously, there won't be any great strain upon your powers of endurance; I promise you that you shan't have to play croquet, or talk to the Archdeacon's wife, or do anything that is likely to bring on physical prostration. You can just wear your sweetest clothes and a moderately amiable expression, and eat chocolate-creams with the appetite of a *blasé* parrot. Nothing more is demanded of you."

Reginald shut his eyes. "There will be the exhaustingly up-to-date young women who will ask me if I have seen *San Toy*; a less progressive grade who will yearn to hear about the Diamond Jubilee—the historic event, not the horse. With a little encouragement, they will inquire if I saw the Allies march into Paris. Why are women so fond of raking up the

3

past? They're as bad as tailors, who invariably remember what you owe them for a suit long after you've ceased to wear it."

"I'll order lunch for one o'clock; that will give you two and a half hours to dress in."

Reginald puckered his brow into a tortured frown, and I knew that my point was gained. He was debating what tie would go with which waistcoat.

Even then I had my misgivings.

.   .   .   .

During the drive to the McKillops' Reginald was possessed with a great peace, which was not wholly to be accounted for by the fact that he had inveigled his feet into shoes a size too small for them. I misgave more than ever, and having once launched Reginald on to the McKillops' lawn, I established him near a seductive dish of *marrons glacés*, and as far from the Archdeacon's wife as possible; as I drifted away to a diplomatic distance I heard with painful distinctness the eldest Mawkby girl asking him if he had seen *San Toy*.

It must have been ten minutes later, not more, and I had been having *quite* an enjoyable chat with my hostess, and had promised to lend her *The Eternal City* and my recipe for rabbit mayonnaise, and was just about to offer a kind home for her third Persian kitten, when I perceived, out of the corner of my eye, that Reginald was not where I had left him, and that the *marrons glacés* were untasted. At the same moment I became aware that old Colonel Mendoza was essaying to tell his classic story of how he introduced golf into India, and that Reginald was in dangerous proximity. There are occasions when Reginald is caviare to the Colonel.

"When I was at Poona in '76—"

"My dear Colonel," purred Reginald, "fancy admitting such a thing! Such a give-away for one's age! I wouldn't admit being on this planet in '76." (Reginald in his wildest lapses into veracity never admits to being more than twenty-two.)

The Colonel went to the colour of a fig that has attained great ripeness, and Reginald, ignoring my efforts to intercept him, glided away to another part of the lawn. I found him a few minutes later happily engaged in teaching the youngest Rampage boy the approved theory of mixing absinthe, within full earshot of his mother. Mrs. Rampage occupies a prominent place in local Temperance movements.

As soon as I had broken up this unpromising *tête-à-tête* and settled Reginald where he could watch the croquet players losing their tempers, I wandered off to find my hostess and renew the kitten negotiations at the point where they had been interrupted. I did not succeed in running her down at once, and eventually it was Mrs. McKillop who sought me out, and her conversation was not of kittens.

"Your cousin is discussing *Zaza* with the Archdeacon's wife; at least, he is discussing, she is ordering her carriage."

She spoke in the dry, staccato tone of one who repeats a French exercise, and I knew that as far as Millie McKillop was concerned, Wumples was devoted to a lifelong celibacy.

"If you don't mind," I said hurriedly, "I think we'd like our carriage ordered too," and I made a forced march in the direction of the croquet ground.

I found every one talking nervously and feverishly of the weather and the war in South Africa, except Reginald, who was reclining in a comfortable chair with the dreamy, far-away look that a volcano might wear just after it had desolated entire villages. The Archdeacon's wife was buttoning up her gloves with a concentrated deliberation that was fearful to behold. I shall have to treble my subscription to her Cheerful Sunday Evenings Fund before I dare set foot in her house again.

At that particular moment the croquet players finished their game, which had been going on without a symptom of finality during the whole afternoon. Why, I ask, should it have stopped precisely when a counter-attraction was so necessary? Every one seemed to drift towards the area of disturbance, of which the chairs of the Archdeacon's wife and Reginald formed the storm-centre. Conversation flagged, and there settled upon the company that expectant hush that precedes the dawn—when your neighbours don't happen to keep poultry.

"What did the Caspian Sea?" asked Reginald, with appalling suddenness.

There were symptoms of a stampede. The Archdeacon's wife looked at me. Kipling or some one has described somewhere the look a foundered camel gives when the caravan moves on and leaves it to its fate. The peptonized reproach in the good lady's eyes brought the passage vividly to my mind.

I played my last card.

"Reginald, it's getting late, and a sea-mist is coming on." I knew that the elaborate curl over his right eyebrow was not guaranteed to survive a sea-mist.

.   .   .   .   .   .

"Never, never again, will I take you to a garden-party. Never. . . . You behaved abominably. . . . What did the Caspian see?"

A shade of genuine regret for misused opportunities passed over Reginald's face.

"After all," he said, "I believe an apricot tie would have gone better with the lilac waistcoat."

REGINALD ON CHRISTMAS PRESENTS

I WISH it to be distinctly understood (said Reginald) that I don't want a "George, Prince of Wales" Prayer-book as a Christmas present. The fact cannot be too widely known.

There ought (he continued) to be technical education classes on the science of present-giving. No one seems to have the faintest notion of what any one else wants, and the prevalent ideas on the subject are not creditable to a civilized community.

There is, for instance, the female relative in the country who "knows a tie is always useful," and sends you some spotted horror that you could only wear in secret or in Tottenham Court Road. It *might* have been useful had she kept it to tie up currant bushes with, when it would have served the double purpose of supporting the branches and frightening away the birds—for it is an admitted fact that the ordinary tomtit of commerce has a sounder æsthetic taste than the average female relative in the country.

Then there are aunts. They are always a difficult class to deal with in the matter of presents. The trouble is that one never catches them really young enough. By the time one has educated them to an appreciation of the fact that one does not wear red woollen mittens in the West End, they die, or quarrel with the family, or do something equally inconsiderate. That is why the supply of trained aunts is always so precarious.

There is my Aunt Agatha, *par exemple*, who sent me a pair of gloves last Christmas, and even got so far as to choose a kind that was being worn and had the correct number of buttons. But—*they were nines!* I sent them to a boy whom I hated intimately: he didn't wear them, of course, but he could have—that was where the bitterness of death came in. It was nearly as consoling as sending white flowers to his funeral. Of course I wrote and told my aunt that they were the one thing that had been wanting to make existence blossom like a rose; I am afraid she thought me frivolous—she comes from the North, where they live in the fear of Heaven and the Earl of Durham. (Reginald affects an exhaustive knowledge of things political, which furnishes an excellent excuse for not discussing them.) Aunts with a dash of foreign extraction in them are the most satisfactory in the way of understanding these things; but if you can't choose your aunt, it is wisest in the long run to choose the present and send her the bill.

Even friends of one's own set, who might be expected to know better, have curious delusions on the subject. I am *not* collecting copies of the cheaper editions of Omar Khayyám. I gave the last four that I received to the lift-boy, and I like to think of him reading them, with FitzGerald's notes, to his aged mother. Lift-boys always have aged mothers; shows such nice feeling on their part, I think.

Personally, I can't see where the difficulty in choosing suitable presents lies. No boy who had brought himself up properly could fail to appreciate one of those decorative bottles of liqueurs that are so reverently staged in Morel's window—and it wouldn't in the least matter if one did get duplicates. And there would always be the supreme moment of dreadful uncertainty whether it was *crême de menthe* or Chartreuse—like the expectant thrill on seeing your partner's hand turned up at bridge. People may say what they like about the decay of Christianity; the religious system that produced green Chartreuse can never really die.

And then, of course, there are liqueur glasses, and crystallized fruits, and tapestry curtains, and heaps of other necessaries of life that make really sensible presents—not to speak of luxuries, such as having one's bills paid, or getting something quite sweet in the way of jewellery. Unlike the alleged Good Woman of the Bible, I'm not above rubies. When found, by the way, she must have been rather a problem at Christmas-time; nothing short of a blank cheque would have fitted the situation. Perhaps it's as well that she's died out.

The great charm about me (concluded Reginald) is that I am so easily pleased. But I draw the line at a "Prince of Wales" Prayer-book.

REGINALD ON THE ACADEMY

"ONE goes to the Academy in self-defence," said Reginald. "It is the one topic one has in common with the Country Cousins."

"It is almost a religious observance with them," said the Other. "A kind of artistic Mecca, and when the good ones die they go—"

"To the Chantrey Bequest. The mystery is *what* they find to talk about in the country."

"There are two subjects of conversation in the country: Servants, and Can fowls be made to pay? The first, I believe, is compulsory, the second optional."

"As a function," resumed Reginald, "the Academy is a failure."

"You think it would be tolerable without the pictures?"

"The pictures are all right, in their way; after all, one can always *look* at them if one is bored with one's surroundings, or wants to avoid an imminent acquaintance."

"Even that doesn't always save one. There is the inevitable female whom you met once in Devonshire, or the Matoppo Hills, or somewhere, who charges up to you with the remark that it's funny how one always meets people one knows at the Academy. Personally, I *don't* think it funny."

"I suffered in that way just now," said Reginald plaintively, "from a woman whose word I had to take that she had met me last summer in Brittany."

"I hope you were not too brutal?"

"I merely told her with engaging simplicity that the art of life was the avoidance of the unattainable."

"Did she try and work it out on the back of her catalogue?"

"Not there and then. She murmured something about being 'so clever.' Fancy coming to the Academy to be clever!"

"To be clever in the afternoon argues that one is dining nowhere in the evening."

"Which reminds me that I can't remember whether I accepted an invitation from you to dine at Kettner's tonight."

"On the other hand, I can remember with startling distinctness not having asked you to."

"So much certainty is unbecoming in the young; so we'll consider that settled. What were you talking about? Oh, pictures. Personally, I rather like them; they are so refreshingly real and probable, they take one away from the unrealities of life."

"One likes to escape from oneself occasionally."

"That is the disadvantage of a portrait; as a rule, one's bitterest friends can find nothing more to ask than the faithful unlikeness that goes down to posterity as oneself. I hate posterity—it's so fond of having the last word. Of course, as regards portraits, there are exceptions."

"For instance?"

"To die before being painted by Sargent is to go to heaven prematurely."

"With the necessary care and impatience, you may avoid that catastrophe."

"If you're going to be rude," said Reginald, "I shall dine with you tomorrow night as well. The chief vice of the Academy," he continued, "is its nomenclature. Why, for instance, should an obvious trout-stream with a palpable rabbit sitting in the foreground be called 'an evening dream of unbeclouded peace,' or something of that sort?"

"You think," said the Other, "that a name should economize description rather than stimulate imagination?"

"Properly chosen, it should do both. There is my lady kitten at home, for instance; I've called it Derry."

"Suggests nothing to my imagination but protracted sieges and religious animosities. Of course, I don't know your kitten—"

"Oh, you're silly. It's a sweet name, and it answers to it—when it wants to. Then, if there are any unseemly noises in the night, they can be explained succinctly: Derry and Toms."

"You might almost charge for the advertisement. But as applied to pictures, don't you think your system would be too subtle, say, for the Country Cousins?"

"Every reformation must have its victims. You can't expect the fatted calf to share the enthusiasm of the angels over the prodigal's return. Another darling weakness of the Academy is that none of its luminaries must 'arrive' in a hurry. You can see them coming for years, like a Balkan trouble or a street improvement, and by the time they have painted a thousand or so square yards of canvas, their work begins to be recognized."

"Some one who Must Not be Contradicted said that a man must be a success by the time he's thirty, or never."

"To have reached thirty," said Reginald, "is to have failed in life."

REGINALD AT THE THEATRE

"AFTER all," said the Duchess vaguely, "there are certain things you can't get away from. Right and wrong, good conduct and moral rectitude, have certain well-defined limits."

"So, for the matter of that," replied Reginald, "has the Russian Empire. The trouble is that the limits are not always in the same place."

Reginald and the Duchess regarded each other with mutual distrust, tempered by a scientific interest. Reginald considered that the Duchess had much to learn; in particular, not to hurry out of the Carlton as though afraid of losing one's last 'bus. A woman, he said, who is careless of disappearances is capable of leaving town before Goodwood, and dying at the wrong moment of an unfashionable disease.

The Duchess thought that Reginald did not exceed the ethical standard which circumstances demanded.

"Of course," she resumed combatively, "it's the prevailing fashion to believe in perpetual change and mutability, and all that sort of thing, and to say we are all merely an improved form of primeval ape—of course you subscribe to that doctrine?"

"I think it decidedly premature; in most people I know the process is far from complete."

"And equally of course you are quite irreligious?"

"Oh, by no means. The fashion just now is a Roman Catholic frame of mind with an Agnostic conscience: you get the mediæval picturesqueness of the one with the modern conveniences of the other."

The Duchess suppressed a sniff. She was one of those people who regard the Church of England with patronizing affection, as if it were something that had grown up in their kitchen garden.

"But there are other things," she continued, "which I suppose are to a certain extent sacred even to you. Patriotism, for instance, and Empire, and Imperial responsibility, and blood-is-thicker-than-water, and all that sort of thing."

Reginald waited for a couple of minutes before replying, while the Lord of Rimini temporarily monopolized the acoustic possibilities of the theatre.

"That is the worst of a tragedy," he observed, "one can't always hear oneself talk. Of course I accept the Imperial idea and the responsibility. After all, I would just as soon think in Continents as anywhere else. And some day, when the season is over and we have the time, you shall explain to me the exact blood-brotherhood and all that sort of thing that exists between a French Canadian and a mild Hindoo and a Yorkshireman, for instance."

"Oh, well, 'dominion over palm and pine,' you know," quoted the Duchess hopefully; "of course we mustn't forget that we're all part of the great Anglo-Saxon Empire."

"Which for its part is rapidly becoming a suburb of Jerusalem. A very pleasant suburb, I admit, and quite a charming Jerusalem. But still a suburb."

"Really, to be told one's living in a suburb when one is conscious of spreading the benefits of civilization all over the world! Philanthropy—I suppose you will say *that* is a comfortable delusion; and yet even you must admit that whenever want or misery or starvation is known to exist, however distant or difficult of access, we instantly organize relief on the most generous scale, and distribute it, if need be, to the uttermost ends of the earth."

The Duchess paused, with a sense of ultimate triumph. She had made the same observation at a drawing-room meeting, and it had been extremely well received.

"I wonder," said Reginald, "if you have ever walked down the Embankment on a winter night?"

"Gracious, no, child! Why do you ask?"

"I didn't; I only wondered. And even your philanthropy, practised in a world where everything is based on competition, must have a debit as well as a credit account. The young ravens cry for food."

"And are fed."

"Exactly. Which presupposes that something else is fed upon."

"Oh, you're simply exasperating. You've been reading Nietzsche till you haven't got any sense of moral proportion left. May I ask if you are governed by *any* laws of conduct whatever?"

"There are certain fixed rules that one observes for one's own comfort. For instance, never be flippantly rude to any inoffensive, grey-bearded stranger that you may meet in pine forests or hotel smoking-rooms on the Continent. It always turns out to be the King of Sweden."

"The restraint must be dreadfully irksome to you. When I was younger, boys of your age used to be nice and innocent."

"Now we are only nice. One must specialize in these days. Which reminds me of the man I read of in some sacred book who was given a choice of what he most desired. And because he didn't ask for titles and honours and dignities, but only for immense wealth, these other things came to him also."

"I am sure you didn't read about him in any sacred book."

"Yes; I fancy you will find him in Debrett."

REGINALD'S PEACE POEM

"I'M writing a poem on Peace," said Reginald, emerging from a sweeping operation through a tin of mixed biscuits, in whose depths a macaroon or two might yet be lurking.

"Something of the kind seems to have been attempted already," said the Other.

"Oh, I know; but I may never have the chance again. Besides, I've got a new fountain pen. I don't pretend to have gone on any very original lines; in writing about Peace the thing is to say what everybody else is saying, only to say it better. It begins with the usual ornithological emotion:

'When the widgeon westward winging
        Heard the folk Vereeniginging,
        Heard the shouting and the singing—' "

"Vereeninginging is good, but why widgeon?"

"Why not? Anything that winged westward would naturally begin with a *w*."

"Need it wing westward?"

"The bird must go somewhere. You wouldn't have it hang
around and look foolish. Then I've brought in something
about the heedless hartebeest galloping over the deserted
veldt."

"Of course you know it's practically extinct in those
regions?"

"I can't help *that*, it gallops so nicely. I make it have all
sorts of unexpected yearnings:

> 'Mother, may I go and maffick,
>   Tear around and hinder traffic?'

Of course you'll say there would be no traffic worth bothering
about on the bare and sun-scorched veldt, but there's no other
word that rhymes with maffick."

"Seraphic?"

Reginald considered. "It might do, but I've got a lot
about angels later on. You must have angels in a Peace poem;
I know dreadfully little about their habits."

"They can do unexpected things, like the hartebeest."

"Of course. Then I turn on London, the City of Dreadful Nocturnes, resonant with hymns of joy and thanksgiving:

> 'And the sleeper, eye unlidding,
>   Heard a voice for ever bidding
>   Much farewell to Dolly Gray;
>   Turning weary on his truckle-
>   Bed he heard the honey-suckle
>   Lauded in apiarian lay.'

Longfellow at his best wrote nothing like that."

"I agree with you."

"I wish you wouldn't. I've a sweet temper, but I can't
stand being agreed with. And I'm so worried about the aasvogel."

Reginald stared dismally at the biscuit-tin, which now presented an unattractive array of rejected cracknels.

"I believe," he murmured, "if I could find a woman with an unsatisfied craving for cracknels, I should marry her."

"What is the tragedy of the aasvogel?" asked the Other sympathetically.

"Oh, simply that there's no rhyme for it. I thought about it all the time I was dressing—it's dreadfully bad for one to think whilst one's dressing—and all lunch-time, and I'm still hung up over it. I feel like those unfortunate automobilists who achieve an unenviable motoriety by coming to a hopeless stop with their cars in the most crowded thoroughfares. I'm afraid I shall have to drop the aasvogel, and it did give such lovely local colour to the thing."

"Still you've got the heedless hartebeest."

"And quite a decorative bit of moral admonition—when you've worried the meaning out—

'Cease, War, thy bubbling madness that the wine shares,
And bid thy legions turn their swords to mine shares.'

Mine shares seems to fit the case better than ploughshares. There's lots more about the blessings of Peace, shall I go on reading it?"

"If I must make a choice, I think I would rather they went on with the war."

REGINALD'S CHOIR TREAT

"NEVER," wrote Reginald to his most darling friend "be a pioneer. It's the Early Christian that gets the fattest lion."

Reginald, in his way, was a pioneer.

None of the rest of his family had anything approaching Titian hair or a sense of humour, and they used primroses as a table decoration.

It follows that they never understood Reginald, who came down late to breakfast, and nibbled toast, and said disrespectful things about the universe. The family ate porridge, and believed in everything, even the weather forecast.

Therefore the family was relieved when the vicar's daughter undertook the reformation of Reginald. Her name was Amabel; it was the vicar's one extravagance. Amabel was accounted a beauty and intellectually gifted; she never played tennis, and was reputed to have read Maeterlinck's *Life of the Bee*. If you abstain from tennis *and* read Maeterlinck in a small country village, you are of necessity intellectual. Also she had been twice to Fécamp to pick up a good French accent from the Americans staying there; consequently she had a knowledge of the world which might be considered useful in dealings with a worldling.

Hence the congratulations in the family when Amabel undertook the reformation of its wayward member.

Amabel commenced operations by asking her unsuspecting pupil to tea in the vicarage garden; she believed in the healthy influence of natural surroundings, never having been in Sicily, where things are different.

And like every woman who has ever preached repentance to unregenerate youth, she dwelt on the sin of an empty life, which always seems so much more scandalous in the country, where people rise early to see if a new strawberry has happened during the night.

Reginald recalled the lilies of the field, "which simply sat and looked beautiful, and defied competition."

"But that is not an example for us to follow," gasped Amabel.

"Unfortunately, we can't afford to. You don't know what a world of trouble I take in trying to rival the lilies in their artistic simplicity."

"You are really indecently vain of your appearance. A good life is infinitely preferable to good looks."

"You agree with me that the two are incompatible. I always say beauty is only sin deep."

Amabel began to realize that the battle is not always to the strong-minded. With the immemorial resource of her sex, she abandoned the frontal attack and laid stress on her unassisted labours in parish work, her mental loneliness, her discouragements—and at the right moment she produced strawberries and cream. Reginald was obviously affected by the latter, and when his preceptress suggested that he might begin the strenuous life by helping her to supervise the annual outing of the bucolic infants who composed the local choir, his eyes shone with the dangerous enthusiasm of a convert.

Reginald entered on the strenuous life alone, as far as Amabel was concerned. The most virtuous women are not proof against damp grass, and Amabel kept her bed with a cold. Reginald called it a dispensation; it had been the dream of his life to stage-manage a choir outing. With strategic insight, he led his shy, bullet-headed charges to the nearest woodland stream and allowed them to bathe; then he seated himself on their discarded garments and discoursed on their immediate future, which, he decreed, was to embrace a Bacchanalian procession through the village. Forethought had provided the occasion with a supply of tin whistles, but the introduction of a he-goat from a neighbouring orchard was a brilliant afterthought. Properly, Reginald explained, there should have been an outfit of panther skins; as it was, those who had spotted handkerchiefs were allowed to wear them, which they did with thankfulness. Reginald recognized the impossibility, in the time at his disposal, of teaching his shivering neophytes a chant in honour of Bacchus, so he started them off with a more familiar, if less appropriate, temperance hymn. After all, he said, it is the spirit of the thing that counts. Following the etiquette of dramatic authors on first nights, he remained discreetly in the background while the procession, with extreme diffidence and the goat, wound its way lugubriously towards the village. The singing had died down long before the main street was reached, but the miserable wailing of pipes brought the inhabitants to their doors. Reginald said he had seen something like it in pictures; the villagers had seen nothing like it in their lives, and remarked as much freely.

Reginald's family never forgave him. They had no sense of humour.

REGINALD ON WORRIES

I HAVE (said Reginald) an aunt who worries. She's not really an aunt—a sort of amateur one, and they aren't really worries. She is a social success, and has no domestic tragedies worth speaking of, so she adopts any decorative sorrows that are going, myself included. In that way she's the antithesis, or whatever you call it, to those sweet, uncomplaining women one knows who have seen trouble, and worn blinkers ever since. Of course, one just loves them for it, but I must confess they make me uncomfy; they remind one so of a duck that goes flapping about with forced cheerfulness long after its head's been cut off. Ducks have *no* repose. Now, my aunt has a shade of hair that suits her, and a cook who quarrels with the other servants, which is always a hopeful sign, and a conscience that's absentee for about eleven months of the year, and only turns up at Lent to annoy her husband's people, who are considerably Lower than the angels, so to speak: with all these natural advantages—she says her particular tint of bronze is a natural advantage, and there can be no two opinions as to the advantage—of course she has to send out for her afflictions, like those restaurants where they haven't got a licence. The system has this advantage, that you can fit your unhappinesses in with your other engagements, whereas real worries have a way of arriving at meal-times, and when you're dressing, or other solemn moments. I knew a canary once that had been trying for months and years to hatch out a family, and every one looked upon it as a blameless infatuation, like the sale of Delagoa Bay, which would be an annual loss to the Press agencies if it ever came to pass; and one day the bird really did bring it off, in the middle of family prayers. I say the middle, but it was also the end: you can't go on being thankful for daily bread when you are wondering what on earth very new canaries expect to be fed on.

At present she's rather in a Balkan state of mind about the treatment of the Jews in Roumania. Personally, I think the

18

Jews have estimable qualities; they're so kind to their poor—
and to our rich. I daresay in Roumania the cost of living
beyond one's income isn't so great. Over here the trouble is
that so many people who have money to throw about seem to
have such vague ideas where to throw it. That fund, for instance, to relieve the victims of sudden disasters—what is a
sudden disaster? There's Marion Mulciber, who *would* think
she could play bridge, just as she would think she could ride
down a hill on a bicycle; on that occasion she went to a hospital, now she's gone into a Sisterhood—lost all she had, you
know, and gave the rest to Heaven. Still, you can't call it a
sudden calamity; *that* occurred when poor dear Marion was
born. The doctors said at the time that she couldn't live more
than a fortnight, and she's been trying ever since to see if she
could. Women are so opinionated.

And then there's the Education Question—not that I can
see that there's anything to worry about in that direction. To
my mind, education is an absurdly overrated affair. At least,
one never took it very seriously at school, where everything
was done to bring it prominently under one's notice. Anything
that is worth knowing one practically teaches oneself, and the
rest obtrudes itself sooner or later. The reason one's elders
know so comparatively little is because they have to unlearn
so much that they acquired by way of education before we
were born. Of course I'm a believer in Nature-study; as I said
to Lady Beauwhistle, if you want a lesson in elaborate arti-
ficiality, just watch the studied unconcern of a Persian cat entering a crowded salon, and then go and practise it for a fortnight. The Beauwhistles weren't born in the Purple, you
know, but they're getting there on the instalment system—so
much down, and the rest when you feel like it. They have
kind hearts, and they never forget birthdays. I forget what
he was, something in the City, where the patriotism comes
from; and she—oh, well, her frocks are built in Paris, but
she wears them with a strong English accent. So public-
spirited of her. I think she must have been very strictly brought
up, she's so desperately anxious to do the wrong thing cor-

rectly. Not that it really matters nowadays, as I told her: I know some perfectly virtuous people who are received everywhere.

REGINALD ON HOUSE-PARTIES

THE drawback is, one never really *knows* one's hosts and hostesses. One gets to know their fox-terriers and their chrysanthemums, and whether the story about the go-cart can be turned loose in the drawing-room, or must be told privately to each member of the party, for fear of shocking public opinion; but one's host and hostess are a sort of human hinterland that one never has the time to explore.

There was a fellow I stayed with once in Warwickshire who farmed his own land, but was otherwise quite steady. Should never have suspected him of having a soul, yet not very long afterwards he eloped with a lion-tamer's widow and set up as a golf-instructor somewhere on the Persian Gulf; dreadfully immoral, of course, because he was only an indifferent player, but still, it showed imagination. His wife was really to be pitied, because he had been the only person in the house who understood how to manage the cook's temper, and now she has to put "D.V." on her dinner invitations. Still, that's better than a domestic scandal; a woman who leaves her cook never wholly recovers her position in Society.

I suppose the same thing holds good with the hosts; they seldom have more than a superficial acquaintance with their guests, and so often just when they do get to know you a bit better, they leave off knowing you altogether. There was *rather* a breath of winter in the air when I left those Dorsetshire people. You see, they had asked me down to shoot, and I'm not particularly immense at that sort of thing. There's such a deadly sameness about partridges; when you've missed one, you've missed the lot—at least, that's been my experience. And they tried to rag me in the smoking-room about not being able to hit a bird at five yards, a sort of bovine ragging that suggested cows buzzing round a gadfly and thinking they

were teasing it. So I got up the next morning at early dawn—
I know it was dawn, because there were lark-noises in the sky,
and the grass looked as if it had been left out all night—and
hunted up the most conspicuous thing in the bird line that I
could find, and measured the distance, as nearly as it would
let me, and shot away all I knew. They said afterwards that
it was a tame bird; that's simply *silly*, because it was awfully
wild at the first few shots. Afterwards it quieted down a bit,
and when its legs had stopped waving farewells to the landscape I got a gardener-boy to drag it into the hall, where
everybody must see it on their way to the breakfast-room. I
breakfasted upstairs myself. I gathered afterwards that the
meal was tinged with a very unchristian spirit. I suppose it's
unlucky to bring peacock's feathers into a house; anyway, there
was a blue-pencilly look in my hostess's eye when I took my
departure.

Some hostesses, of course, will forgive anything, even unto
pavonicide (is there such a word?), as long as one is nice-
looking and sufficiently unusual to counterbalance some of the
others; and there *are* others—the girl, for instance, who reads
Meredith, and appears at meals with unnatural punctuality in
a frock that's made at home and repented at leisure. She
eventually finds her way to India and gets married, and comes
home to admire the Royal Academy, and to imagine that an
indifferent prawn curry is for ever an effective substitute for
all that we have been taught to believe is luncheon. It's then
that she is really dangerous; but at her worst she is never quite
so bad as the woman who fires *Exchange and Mart* questions at
you without the least provocation. Imagine the other day, just
when I was doing my best to understand half the things I was
saying, being asked by one of those seekers after country home
truths how many fowls she could keep in a run ten feet by
six, or whatever it was! I told her whole crowds, as long as
she kept the door shut, and the idea didn't seem to have struck
her before; at least, she brooded over it for the rest of dinner.

Of course, as I say, one never really *knows* one's ground,
and one may make mistakes occasionally. But then one's mistakes sometimes turn out assets in the long-run: if we had

never bungled away our American colonies we might never have had the boy from the States to teach us how to wear our hair and cut our clothes, and we must get our ideas from somewhere, I suppose. Even the Hooligan was probably invented in China centuries before we thought of him. England must wake up, as the Duke of Devonshire said the other day, wasn't it? Oh, well, it was some one else. Not that I ever indulge in despair about the Future; there always have been men who have gone about despairing of the Future, and when the Future arrives it says nice, superior things about their having acted according to their lights. It is dreadful to think that other people's grandchildren may one day rise up and call one amiable.

There are moments when one sympathizes with Herod.

REGINALD AT THE CARLTON

"A MOST variable climate," said the Duchess; "and how unfortunate that we should have had that very cold weather at a time when coal was so dear! So distressing for the poor."

"Some one has observed that Providence is always on the side of the big dividends," remarked Reginald.

The Duchess ate an anchovy in a shocked manner; she was sufficiently old-fashioned to dislike irreverence towards dividends.

Reginald had left the selection of a feeding-ground to her womanly intuition, but he chose the wine himself, knowing that womanly intuition stops short at claret. A woman will cheerfully choose husbands for her less attractive friends, or take sides in a political controversy without the least knowledge of the issues involved—but no woman ever cheerfully chose a claret.

"Hors d'œuvres have always a pathetic interest for me," said Reginald: "they remind me of one's childhood that one goes through, wondering what the next course is going to be

like—and during the rest of the menu one wishes one had
eaten more of the hors d'œuvres. Don't you love watching the
different ways people have of entering a restaurant? There is
the woman who races in as though her whole scheme of life
were held together by a one-pin despotism which might abdicate
its functions at any moment; it's really a relief to see her
reach her chair in safety. Then there are the people who troop
in with an-unpleasant-duty-to-perform air, as if they were
angels of Death entering a plague city. You see that type of
Briton very much in hotels abroad. And nowadays there are
always the Johannes-bourgeois, who bring a Cape-to-Cairo
atmosphere with them—what may be called the Rand Manner, I suppose."

"Talking about hotels abroad," said the Duchess, "I am
preparing notes for a lecture at the Club on the educational
effects of modern travel, dealing chiefly with the moral side
of the question. I was talking to Lady Beauwhistle's aunt the
other day—she's just come back from Paris, you know. Such
a sweet woman—"

"And so silly. In these days of the overeducation of women
she's quite refreshing. They say some people went through
the siege of Paris without knowing that France and Germany
were at war; but the Beauwhistle aunt is credited with having
passed the whole winter in Paris under the impression that the
Humberts were a kind of bicycle. . . . Isn't there a bishop
or somebody who believes we shall meet all the animals we
have known on earth in another world? How frightfully embarrassing to meet a whole shoal of whitebait you had last
known at Prince's! I'm sure in my nervousness I should talk
of nothing but lemons. Still, I daresay they would be quite as
offended if one hadn't eaten them. I know if I were served up
at a cannibal feast I should be dreadfully annoyed if any one
found fault with me for not being tender enough, or having
been kept too long."

"My idea about the lecture," resumed the Duchess hurriedly, "is to inquire whether promiscuous Continental travel
doesn't tend to weaken the moral fibre of the social conscience.
There are people one knows, quite nice people when they are

in England, who are so *different* when they are anywhere the other side of the Channel."

"The people with what I call Tauchnitz morals," observed Reginald. "On the whole, I think they get the best of two very desirable worlds. And, after all, they charge so much for excess luggage on some of those foreign lines that it's really an economy to leave one's reputation behind one occasionally."

"A scandal, my dear Reginald, is as much to be avoided at Monaco or any of those places as at Exeter, let us say."

"Scandal, my dear Irene——I may call you Irene, mayn't I?"

"I don't know that you have known me long enough for that."

"I've known you longer than your god-parents had when they took the liberty of calling you that name. Scandal is merely the compassionate allowance which the gay make to the humdrum. Think how many blameless lives are brightened by the blazing indiscretions of other people. Tell me, who is the woman with the old lace at the table on our left? Oh, *that* doesn't matter; it's quite the thing nowadays to stare at people as if they were yearlings at Tattersall's."

"Mrs. Spelvexit? Quite a charming woman; separated from her husband——"

"Incompatibility of income?"

"Oh, nothing of that sort. By miles of frozen ocean, I was going to say. He explores ice-floes and studies the movements of herrings, and has written a most interesting book on the home-life of the Esquimaux; but naturally he has very little home-life of his own."

"A husband who comes home with the Gulf Stream *would* be rather a tied-up asset."

"His wife is exceedingly sensible about it. She collects postage-stamps. Such a resource. Those people with her are the Whimples, very old acquaintances of mine; they're always having trouble, poor things."

"Trouble is not one of those fancies you can take up and drop at any moment; it's like a grouse-moor or the opium-habit —once you start it you've got to keep it up."

"Their eldest son was such a disappointment to them; they wanted him to be a linguist, and spent no end of money on having him taught to speak—oh, dozens of languages!—and then he became a Trappist monk. And the youngest, who was intended for the American marriage market, has developed political tendencies, and writes pamphlets about the housing of the poor. Of course it's a most important question, and I devote a good deal of time to it myself in the mornings; but, as Laura Whimple says, it's as well to have an establishment of one's own before agitating about other people's. She feels it very keenly, but she always maintains a cheerful appetite, which I think is so unselfish of her."

"There are different ways of taking disappointment. There was a girl I knew who nursed a wealthy uncle through a long illness, borne by her with Christian fortitude, and then he died and left his money to a swine-fever hospital. She found she'd about cleared stock in fortitude by that time, and now she gives drawing-room recitations. That's what I call being vindictive."

"Life is full of its disappointments," observed the Duchess, "and I suppose the art of being happy is to disguise them as illusions. But that, my dear Reginald, becomes more difficult as one grows older."

"I think it's more generally practised than you imagine. The young have aspirations that never come to pass, the old have reminiscences of what never happened. It's only the middle-aged who are really conscious of their limitations— that is why one should be so patient with them. But one never is."

"After all," said the Duchess, "the disillusions of life may depend on our way of assessing it. In the minds of those who come after us we may be remembered for qualities and successes which we quite left out of the reckoning."

"It's not always safe to depend on the commemorative tendencies of those who come after us. There may have been disillusionments in the lives of the mediæval saints, but they would scarcely have been better pleased if they could have foreseen that their names would be associated nowadays chiefly with racehorses and the cheaper clarets. And now, if you can tear yourself away from the salted almonds, we'll go and have coffee under the palms that are so necessary for our discomfort."

REGINALD ON BESETTING SINS

THE WOMAN WHO TOLD THE TRUTH

THERE was once (said Reginald) a woman who told the truth. Not all at once, of course, but the habit grew upon her gradually, like lichen on an apparently healthy tree. She had no children—otherwise it might have been different. It began with little things, for no particular reason except that her life was a rather empty one, and it is so easy to slip into the habit of telling the truth in little matters. And then it became difficult to draw the line at more important things, until at last she took to telling the truth about her age; she said she was forty-two and five months—by that time, you see, she was veracious even to months. It may have been pleasing to the angels, but her elder sister was not gratified. On the Woman's birthday, instead of the opera-tickets which she had hoped for, her sister gave her a view of Jerusalem from the Mount of Olives, which is not quite the same thing. The revenge of an elder sister may be long in coming, but, like a South-Eastern express, it arrives in its own good time.

The friends of the Woman tried to dissuade her from over-indulgence in the practice, but she said she was wedded to the truth; whereupon it was remarked that it was scarcely logical to be so much together in public. (No really provident woman lunches regularly with her husband if she wishes to burst upon him as a revelation at dinner. He must have time to forget; an afternoon is not enough.) And after a while her friends began to thin out in patches. Her passion for the truth was not compatible with a large visiting-list. For instance, she told Miriam

Klopstock *exactly* how she looked at the Ilexes' ball. Certainly Miriam had asked for her candid opinion, but the Woman prayed in church every Sunday for peace in our time, and it was not consistent.

It was unfortunate, every one agreed, that she had no family; with a child or two in the house, there is an unconscious check upon too free an indulgence in the truth. Children are given us to discourage our better emotions. That is why the stage, with all its efforts, can never be as artificial as life; even in an Ibsen drama one must reveal to the audience things that one would suppress before the children or servants.

Fate may have ordained the truth-telling from the commencement and should justly bear some of the blame; but in having no children the Woman was guilty, at least, of contributory negligence.

Little by little she felt she was becoming a slave to what had once been merely an idle propensity; and one day she knew. Every woman tells ninety per cent. of the truth to her dressmaker; the other ten per cent. is the irreducible minimum of deception beyond which no self-respecting client trespasses. Madame Draga's establishment was a meeting-ground for naked truths and overdressed fictions, and it was here, the Woman felt, that she might make a final effort to recall the artless mendacity of past days. Madame herself was in an inspiring mood, with the air of a sphinx who knew all things and preferred to forget most of them. As a War Minister she might have been celebrated, but she was content to be merely rich.

"If I take it in here, and—Miss Howard, one moment, if you please—and there, and round like this—so—I really think you will find it quite easy."

The Woman hesitated; it seemed to require such a small effort to simply acquiesce in Madame's views. But habit had become too strong. "I'm afraid," she faltered, "it's just the least little bit in the world too—"

And by that least little bit she measured the deeps and eternities of her thraldom to fact. Madame was not best

pleased at being contradicted on a professional matter, and
when Madame lost her temper you usually found it afterwards in the bill.

And at last the dreadful thing came, as the Woman had
foreseen all along that it must; it was one of those paltry
little truths with which she harried her waking hours. On a
raw Wednesday morning, in a few ill-chosen words, she told
the cook that she drank. She remembered the scene afterwards
as vividly as though it had been painted in her mind by Abbey.
The cook was a good cook, as cooks go; and as cooks go she
went.

Miriam Klopstock came to lunch the next day. Women and
elephants never forget an injury.

REGINALD'S DRAMA

REGINALD closed his eyes with the elaborate weariness
of one who has rather nice eyelashes and thinks it useless to conceal the fact.

"One of these days," he said, "I shall write a really great
drama. No one will understand the drift of it, but every one
will go back to their homes with a vague feeling of dissatisfaction with their lives and surroundings. Then they will put
up new wall-papers and forget."

"But how about those that have oak panelling all over the
house?" said the Other.

"They can always put down new stair-carpets," pursued
Reginald, "and, anyhow, I'm not responsible for the audience
having a happy ending. The play would be quite sufficient
strain on one's energies. I should get a bishop to say it was immoral and beautiful—no dramatist has thought of that before,
and every one would come to condemn the bishop, and they
would stay on out of sheer nervousness. After all, it requires
a great deal of moral courage to leave in a marked manner
in the middle of the second act, when your carriage isn't
ordered till twelve. And it would commence with wolves

worrying something on a lonely waste—you wouldn't see them, of course; but you would hear them snarling and scrunching, and I should arrange to have a wolfy fragrance suggested across the footlights. It would look so well on the programmes, 'Wolves in the first act, by Jamrach.' And old Lady Whortleberry, who never misses a first night, would scream. She's always been nervous since she lost her first husband. He died quite abruptly while watching a county cricket match; two and a half inches of rain had fallen for seven runs, and it was supposed that the excitement killed him. Anyhow, it gave her quite a shock; it was the first husband she'd lost, you know, and now she always screams if anything thrilling happens too soon after dinner. And after the audience had heard the Whortleberry scream the thing would be fairly launched."

"And the plot?"

"The plot," said Reginald, "would be one of those little everyday tragedies that one sees going on all round one. In my mind's eye there is the case of the Mudge-Jervises, which in an unpretentious way has quite an Enoch Arden intensity underlying it. They'd only been married some eighteen months or so, and circumstances had prevented their seeing much of each other. With him there was always a foursome or something that had to be played and replayed in different parts of the country, and she went in for slumming quite as seriously as if it was a sport. With her, I suppose, it was. She belonged to the Guild of the Poor Dear Souls, and they hold the record for having nearly reformed a washerwoman. No one has ever really reformed a washerwoman, and that is why the competition is so keen. You can rescue charwomen by fifties with a little tea and personal magnetism, but with washerwomen it's different; wages are too high. This particular laundress, who came from Bermondsey or some such place, was really rather a hopeful venture, and they thought at last that she might be safely put in the window as a specimen of successful work. So they had her paraded at a drawing-room "At Home" at Agatha Camelford's; it was sheer bad luck that some liqueur chocolates had been turned loose by mistake among the refreshments—really liqueur chocolates, with very little chocolate. And of course the old soul found them out, and cornered the entire stock. It was like finding a whelk-stall in a desert, as she afterwards partially expressed herself. When the liqueurs began to take effect, she started to give them imitations of farmyard animals as they know them in Bermondsey. She began with a dancing bear, and you know Agatha doesn't approve of dancing, except at Buckingham Palace under proper supervision. And then she got up on the piano and gave them an organ monkey; I gather she went in for realism rather than a Maeterlinckian treatment of the subject. Finally, she fell into the piano and said she was a parrot in a cage, and for an impromptu performance I believe she was very word-perfect; no one had heard anything like it, except Baroness Boobelstein who has attended sittings of the Austrian Reichsrath. Agatha is trying the Rest-cure at Buxton."

"But the tragedy?"

"Oh, the Mudge-Jervises. Well, they were getting along quite happily, and their married life was one continuous exchange of picture-postcards; and then one day they were thrown together on some neutral ground where foursomes and washerwomen overlapped, and discovered that they were hopelessly divided on the Fiscal Question. They have thought it best to separate, and she is to have the custody of the Persian kittens for nine months in the year—they go back to him for the winter, when she is abroad. There you have the material for a tragedy drawn straight from life—and the piece could be called 'The Price They Paid for Empire.' And of course one would have to work in studies of the struggle of hereditary tendency against environment and all that sort of thing. The woman's father could have been an Envoy to some of the smaller German Courts; that's where she'd get her passion for visiting the poor, in spite of the most careful upbringing. *C'est le premier pa qui compte*, as the cuckoo said when it swallowed its foster-parent. That, I think, is quite clever."

"And the wolves?"

"Oh, the wolves would be a sort of elusive undercurrent in the background that would never be satisfactorily explained.

After all, life teems with things that have no earthly reason. And whenever the characters could think of nothing brilliant to say about marriage or the War Office, they could open a window and listen to the howling of the wolves. But that would be very seldom."

REGINALD ON TARIFFS

I'M not going to discuss the Fiscal Question (said Reginald); I wish to be original. At the same time, I think one suffers more than one realizes from the system of free imports. I should like, for instance, a really prohibitive duty put upon the partner who declares on a weak red suit and hopes for the best. Even a free outlet for compressed verbiage doesn't balance matters. And I think there should be a sort of bounty-fed export (is that the right expression?) of the people who impress on you that you ought to take life seriously. There are only two classes that really can't help taking life seriously—school-girls of thirteen and Hohenzollerns; they might be exempt. Albanians come under another heading; they take life whenever they get the opportunity. The one Albanian that I was ever on speaking terms with was rather a decadent example. He was a Christian and a grocer, and I don't fancy he had ever killed anybody. I didn't like to question him on the sub-ject—that showed my delicacy. Mrs. Nicorax says I have no delicacy; she hasn't forgiven me about the mice. You see, when I was staying down there, a mouse used to cake-walk about my room half the night, and none of their silly patent traps seemed to take its fancy as a bijou residence, so I deter-mined to appeal to the better side of it—which with mice is the inside. So I called it Percy, and put little delicacies down near its hole every night, and that kept it quiet while I read Max Nordau's *Degeneration* and other reproving literature, and went to sleep. And now she says there is a whole colony of mice in that room.

That isn't where the indelicacy comes in. She went out

riding with me, which was entirely her own suggestion, and as we were coming home through some meadows she made a quite unnecessary attempt to see if her pony would jump a rather messy sort of brook that was there. It wouldn't. It went with her as far as the water's edge, and from that point Mrs. Nicorax went on alone. Of course I had to fish her out from the bank, and my riding-breeches are not cut with a view to salmon-fishing—it's rather an art even to ride in them. Her habit-skirt was one of those open questions that need not be adhered to in emergencies, and on this occasion it remained behind in some water-weeds. She wanted me to fish about for that too, but I felt I had done enough Pharaoh's daughter business for an October afternoon, and I was beginning to want my tea. So I bundled her up on to her pony, and gave her a lead towards home as fast as I cared to go. What with the wet and the unusual responsibility, her abridged costume did not stand the pace particularly well, and she got quite querulous when I shouted back that I had no pins with me—and no string. Some women expect so much from a fellow. When we got into the drive she wanted to go up the back way to the stables, but the ponies *know* they always get sugar at the front door, and I never attempt to hold a pulling pony; as for Mrs. Nicorax it took her all she knew to keep a firm hand on her seceding garments, which, as her maid remarked afterwards, were more *tout* than *ensemble*. Of course nearly the whole house-party were out on the lawn watching the sunset—the only day this month that it's occurred to the sun to show itself, as Mrs. Nic. viciously observed—and I shall never forget the expression on her husband's face as we pulled up. "My darling, this is too much!" was his first spoken comment; taking into consideration the state of her toilet, it was the most brilliant thing I had ever heard him say, and I went into the library to be alone and scream. Mrs. Nicorax says I have no delicacy.

Talking about tariffs, the lift-boy, who reads extensively between the landings, says it won't do to tax raw commodities. What, exactly, is a raw commodity? Mrs. Van Challaby says men are raw commodities till you marry them; after they've struck Mrs. Van C., I can fancy they pretty soon become a finished article. Certainly she's had a good deal of experience to support her opinion. She lost one husband in a railway accident, and mislaid another in the Divorce Court, and the current one has just got himself squeezed in a Beef Trust. "What was he doing in a Beef Trust, anyway?" she asked tearfully, and I suggested that perhaps he had an unhappy home. I only said it for the sake of making conversation; which it did. Mrs. Van Challaby said things about me which in her calmer moments she would have hesitated to spell. It's a pity people can't discuss fiscal matters without getting wild. However, she wrote next day to ask if I could get her a Yorkshire terrier of the size and shade that's being worn now, and that's as near as a woman can be expected to get to owning herself in the wrong. And she will tie a salmon-pink bow to its collar, and call it "Reggie," and take it with her everywhere—like poor Miriam Klopstock, who *would* take her Chow with her to the bathroom, and while she was bathing it was playing at she-bears with her garments. Miriam is always late for breakfast, and she wasn't really missed till the middle of lunch.

However, I'm not going any further into the Fiscal Question. Only I should like to be protected from the partner with a weak red tendency.

REGINALD'S CHRISTMAS REVEL

THEY say (said Reginald) that there's nothing sadder than victory except defeat. If you've ever stayed with dull people during what is alleged to be the festive season, you can probably revise that saying. I shall never forget putting in a Christmas at the Babwolds'. Mrs. Babwold is some relation of my father's—a sort of to-be-left-till-called-for cousin—and that was considered sufficient reason for my having to accept her invitation at about the sixth time of asking; though why the sins of the father should be visited by the children—you won't find any notepaper in that drawer; that's where I keep old menus and first-night programmes.

Mrs. Babwold wears a rather solemn personality, and has never been known to smile, even when saying disagreeable things to her friends or making out the Stores list. She takes her pleasures sadly. A state elephant at a Durbar gives one a very similar impression. Her husband gardens in all weathers. When a man goes out in the pouring rain to brush caterpillars off rose trees, I generally imagine his life indoors leaves something to be desired; anyway, it must be very unsettling for the caterpillars.

Of course there were other people there. There was a Major Somebody who had shot things in Lapland, or somewhere of that sort; I forget what they were, but it wasn't for want of reminding. We had them cold with every meal almost, and he was continually giving us details of what they measured from tip to tip, as though he thought we were going to make them warm under-things for the winter. I used to listen to him with a rapt attention that I thought rather suited me, and then one day I quite modestly gave the dimensions of an okapi I had shot in the Lincolnshire fens. The Major turned a beautiful Tyrian scarlet (I remember thinking at the time that I should like my bathroom hung in that colour), and I think that at that moment he almost found it in his heart to dislike me. Mrs. Babwold put on a first-aid-to-the-injured expression, and asked him why he didn't publish a book of his sporting reminiscences; it would be so interesting. She didn't remember till afterwards that he had given her two fat volumes on the subject, with his portrait and autograph as a frontispiece and an appendix on the habits of the Arctic mussel.

It was in the evening that we cast aside the cares and distractions of the day and really lived. Cards were thought to be too frivolous and empty a way of passing the time, so most of them played what they called a book game. You went out into the hall—to get an inspiration, I suppose—then you came in again with a muffler tied round your neck and looked silly, and the others were supposed to guess that you were *Wee MacGreegor*. I held out against the inanity as long as I decently could, but at last, in a lapse of good-nature, I consented to masquerade as a book, only I warned them that it would take some time to carry out. They waited for the best part of forty minutes while I went and played wineglass skittles with the page-boy in the pantry; you play it with a champagne cork, you know, and the one who knocks down the most glasses without breaking them wins. I won, with four unbroken out of seven; I think William suffered from over-anxiousness. They were rather mad in the drawing-room at my not having come back, and they weren't a bit pacified when I told them afterwards that I was *At the end of the passage*.

"I never did like Kipling," was Mrs. Babwold's comment, when the situation dawned upon her. "I couldn't see anything clever in *Earthworms out of Tuscany*—or is that by Darwin?"

Of course these games are very educational, but, personally, I prefer bridge.

On Christmas evening we were supposed to be specially festive in the Old English fashion. The hall was horribly draughty, but it seemed to be the proper place to revel in, and it was decorated with Japanese fans and Chinese lanterns, which gave it a very Old English effect. A young lady with a confidential voice favoured us with a long recitation about a little girl who died or did something equally hackneyed, and then the Major gave us a graphic account of a struggle he had with a wounded bear. I privately wished that the bears would win sometimes on these occasions; at least they wouldn't go vapouring about it afterwards. Before we had time to recover our spirits, we were indulged with some thought-reading by a young man whom one knew instinctively had a good mother and an indifferent tailor—the sort of young man who talks unflaggingly through the thickest soup, and smooths his hair dubiously as though he thought it might hit back. The thought-reading was rather a success; he announced that the hostess was thinking about poetry, and she admitted that her mind was dwelling on one of Austin's odes. Which was near enough. I fancy she had been really wondering whether a scrag-end of mutton and some cold plum-pudding would do for the kitchen dinner next day. As a crowning dissipation, they all sat down to play progressive halma, with milk-chocolate for prizes. I've been carefully brought up, and I don't like to play games of skill for milk-chocolate, so I invented a headache and retired from the scene. I had been preceded a few minutes earlier by Miss Langshan-Smith, a rather formidable lady, who always got up at some uncomfortable hour in the morning, and gave you the impression that she had been in communication with most of the European Governments before breakfast. There was a paper pinned on her door with a signed request that she might be called particularly early on the morrow. Such an opportunity does not come twice in a lifetime. I covered up everything except the signature with another notice, to the effect that before these words should meet the eye she would have ended a misspent life, was sorry for the trouble she was giving, and would like a military funeral. A few minutes later I violently exploded an air-filled paper bag on the landing, and gave a stage moan that could have been heard in the cellars. Then I pursued my original intention and went to bed. The noise those people made in forcing open the good lady's door was positively indecorous; she resisted gallantly, but I believe they searched her for bullets for about a quarter of an hour, as if she had been a historic battlefield.

I hate travelling on Boxing Day, but one must occasionally do things that one dislikes.

REGINALD'S RUBAIYAT

THE other day (confided Reginald), when I was killing time in the bathroom and making bad resolutions for the New Year, it occurred to me that I would like to be a poet. The chief qualification, I understand, is that you must be born. Well, I hunted up my birth certificate, and found that I was all right on that score, and then I got to work on a Hymn to the New Year, which struck me as having possibilities. It suggested extremely unusual things to absolutely unlikely people, which I believe is the art of first-class cater-

ing in any department. Quite the best verse in it went something like this:

> "Have you heard the groan of a gravelled grouse,
>   Or the snarl of a snaffled snail
>   (Husband or mother, like me, or spouse),
>   Have you lain a-creep in the darkened house
>   Where the wounded wombats wail?"

It was quite improbable that any one had, you know, and
that's where it stimulated the imagination and took people
out of their narrow, humdrum selves. No one has ever called
me narrow or humdrum, but even I felt worked up now and
then at the thought of that house with the stricken wombats
in it. It simply wasn't nice. But the editors were unanimous
in leaving it alone; they said the thing had been done before
and done worse, and that the market for that sort of work
was extremely limited.

It was just on the top of that discouragement that the
Duchess wanted me to write something in her album—something Persian, you know, and just a little bit decadent—and I
thought a quatrain on an unwholesome egg would meet the
requirements of the case. So I started in with:

> "Cackle, cackle, little hen,
>   How I wonder if and when
>   Once you laid the egg that I
>   Met, alas! too late. Amen."

The Duchess objected to the Amen, which I thought gave
an air of forgiveness and *chose jugée* to the whole thing; also
she said it wasn't Persian enough, as though I were trying to
sell her a kitten whose mother had married for love rather
than pedigree. So I recast it entirely, and the new version
read:

> "The hen that laid thee moons ago, who knows
>   In what Dead Yesterday her shades repose;
>   To some election turn thy waning span
>   And rain thy rottenness on fiscal foes."

I thought there was enough suggestion of decay in that to
satisfy a jackal, and to me there was something infinitely

pathetic and appealing in the idea of the egg having a sort of St. Luke's summer of commercial usefulness. But the Duchess begged me to leave out any political allusions; she's the president of a Women's Something or other, and she said it might be taken as an endorsement of deplorable methods. I never can remember which Party Irene discourages with her support, but I shan't forget an occasion when I was staying at her place and she gave me a pamphlet to leave at the house of a doubtful voter, and some grapes and things for a woman who was suffering from a chill on the top of a patent medicine. I thought it much cleverer to give the grapes to the former and the political literature to the sick woman, and the Duchess was quite absurdly annoyed about it afterwards. It seems the leaflet was addressed "To those about to wobble" —I wasn't responsible for the silly title of the thing—and the woman never recovered; anyway, the voter was completely won over by the grapes and jellies, and I think that should have balanced matters. The Duchess called it bribery, and said it might have compromised the candidate she was supporting; he was expected to subscribe to church funds and chapel funds, and football and cricket clubs and regattas, and bazaars and beanfeasts and bell-ringers, and poultry shows and ploughing matches, and reading-rooms and choir outings, and shooting trophies and testimonials, and anything of that sort; but bribery would not have been tolerated.

I fancy I have perhaps more talent for electioneering than for poetry, and I was really getting extended over this quatrain business. The egg began to be unmanageable, and the Duchess suggested something with a French literary ring about it. I hunted back in my mind for the most familiar French classic that I could take liberties with, and after a little exercise of memory I turned out the following:

> "Hast thou the pen that once the gardener had?
> I have it not; and know, these pears are bad.
> Oh, larger than the horses of the Prince
> Are those the general drives in Kaikobad."

Even that didn't altogether satisfy Irene; I fancy the geography of it puzzled her. She probably thought Kaikobad

was an unfashionable German spa, where you'd meet matrimonial bargain-hunters and emergency Servian kings. My
temper was beginning to slip its moorings by that time. I look
rather nice when I lose my temper. (I hoped you would say
I lose it very often. I mustn't monopolize the conversation.)

"Of course, if you want something really Persian and passionate, with red wine and bulbuls in it," I went on to suggest; but she grabbed the book from me.

"Not for worlds. Nothing with red wine or passion in it.
Dear Agatha gave me the album, and she would be mortified
to the quick—"

I said I didn't believe Agatha had a quick, and we got
quite heated in arguing the matter. Finally, the Duchess declared I shouldn't write anything nasty in her book, and I
said I shouldn't write anything in her nasty book, so there
wasn't a very wide point of difference between us. For the
rest of the afternoon I pretended to be sulking, but I was
really working back to that quatrain, like a fox-terrier that's
buried a deferred lunch in a private flower-bed. When I got
an opportunity I hunted up Agatha's autograph, which had
the front page all to itself, and, copying her prim handwriting
as well as I could, I inserted above it the following Thibetan
fragment:

> "With Thee, oh, my Beloved, to do a dâk
> (a dâk I believe is a sort of uncomfortable post-journey)
>   On the pack-saddle of a grunting yak,
>   With never room for chilling chaperon,
>   'Twere better than a Panhard in the Park."

That Agatha would get on to a yak in company with a
lover even in the comparative seclusion of Thibet is unthinkable. I very much doubt if she'd do it with her own husband
in the privacy of the Simplon tunnel. But poetry, as I've remarked before, should always stimulate the imagination.

By the way, when you asked me the other day to dine with
you on the 14th, I said I was dining with the Duchess. Well,
I'm not. I'm dining with you.

THE INNOCENCE OF REGINALD

REGINALD slid a carnation of the newest shade into the buttonhole of his latest lounge coat, and surveyed the result with approval. "I am just in the mood," he observed, "to have my portrait painted by some one with an unmistakable future. So comforting to go down to posterity as 'Youth with a Pink Carnation' in catalogue-company with 'Child with Bunch of Primroses,' and all that crowd."

"Youth," said the Other, "should suggest innocence."

"But never act on the suggestion. I don't believe the two ever really go together. People talk vaguely about the innocence of a little child, but they take mighty good care not to let it out of their sight for twenty minutes. The watched pot never boils over. I knew a boy once who really was innocent; his parents were in Society, but they never gave him a moment's anxiety from his infancy. He believed in company prospectuses, and in the purity of elections, and in women marrying for love, and even in a system for winning at roulette. He never quite lost his faith in it, but he dropped more money than his employers could afford to lose. When last I heard of him, he was believing in his innocence; the jury weren't. All the same, I really am innocent just now of something every one accuses me of having done, and so far as I can see, their accusations will remain unfounded."

"Rather an unexpected attitude for you."

"I love people who do unexpected things. Didn't you always adore the man who slew a lion in a pit on a snowy day? But about this unfortunate innocence. Well, quite long ago, when I'd been quarrelling with more people than usual, you among the number—it must have been in November, I never quarrel with you too near Christmas—I had an idea that I'd like to write a book. It was to be a book of personal reminiscences, and was to leave out nothing."

"Reginald!"

"Exactly what the Duchess said when I mentioned it to her. I was provoking and said nothing, and the next thing, of course, was that every one heard that I'd written the book and got it in the press. After that, I might have been a gold-fish in a glass bowl for all the privacy I got. People attacked me about it in the most unexpected places, and implored or commanded me to leave out things that I'd forgotten had ever happened. I sat behind Miriam Klopstock one night in the dress-circle at His Majesty's, and she began at once about the incident of the Chow dog in the bathroom, which she in-sisted must be struck out. We had to argue it in a disjointed fashion, because some of the people wanted to listen to the play, and Miriam takes nines in voices. They had to stop her playing in the 'Macaws' Hockey Club because you could hear what she thought when her shins got mixed up in a scrim-mage for half a mile on a still day. They are called the Macaws because of their blue-and-yellow costumes, but I understand there was nothing yellow about Miriam's language. I agreed to make one alteration, as I pretended I had got it a Spitz instead of a Chow, but beyond that I was firm. She megaphoned back two minutes later, 'You promised you would never mention it; don't you ever keep a promise?' When people had stopped glaring in our direction, I replied that I'd as soon think of keeping white mice. I saw her tear-ing little bits out of her programme for a minute or two, and then she leaned back and snorted, 'You're not the boy I took you for,' as though she were an eagle arriving at Olym-pus with the wrong Ganymede. That was her last audible remark, but she went on tearing up her programme and scat-tering the pieces around her, till one of her neighbours asked with immense dignity whether she should send for a waste-paper-basket. I didn't stay for the last act.

"Then there is Mrs.—oh, I never can remember her name; she lives in a street that the cabmen have never heard of, and is at home on Wednesdays. She frightened me horribly once at a private view by saying mysteriously, 'I oughtn't to be here, you know; this is one of my days.' I thought that she meant that she was subject to periodical outbreaks and was expecting an attack at any moment. So embarrassing if she had suddenly taken it into her head that she was Cesare Borgia or St. Elizabeth of Hungary. That sort of thing would make one unpleasantly conspicuous even at a private view. However, she merely meant to say that it was Wednesday, which at the moment was incontrovertible. Well, she's on quite a different tack to the Klopstock. She doesn't visit anywhere very extensively, and, of course, she's awfully keen for me to drag in an incident that occurred at one of the Beauwhistle garden-parties, when she says she accidentally hit the shins of a Serene Somebody or other with a croquet mallet and that he swore at her in German. As a matter of fact, he went on discoursing on the Gordon-Bennett affair in French. (I never can remember if it's a new submarine or a divorce. Of course, how stupid of me!) To be disagreeably exact, I fancy she missed him by about two inches—over-anxiousness, probably—but she likes to think she hit him. I've felt that way with a partridge which I always imagine keeps on flying strong, out of false pride, till it's the other side of the hedge. She said she could tell me everything she was wearing on the occasion. I said I didn't want my book to read like a laundry list, but she explained that she didn't mean those sort of things.

"And there's the Chilworth boy, who can be charming as long as he's content to be stupid and wear what he's told to; but he gets the idea now and then that he'd like to be epigrammatic, and the result is like watching a rook trying to build a nest in a gale. Since he got wind of the book, he's been persecuting me to work in something of his about the Russians and the Yalu Peril, and is quite sulky because I won't do it.

"Altogether, I think it would be rather a brilliant inspiration if you were to suggest a fortnight in Paris."

Reginald in Russia
First Collected, 1910

"The Baker's Dozen" originally appeared in the *Journal of the Leinster Regiment*. The other sketches have appeared from time to time in the *Westminster Gazette*. To the Editors of these publications the author is indebted for permission to re-publish them.

REGINALD IN RUSSIA

REGINALD sat in a corner of the Princess's salon and tried to forgive the furniture, which started out with an obvious intention of being Louis Quinze, but relapsed at frequent intervals into Wilhelm II.

He classified the Princess with that distinct type of woman that looks as if it habitually went out to feed hens in the rain.

Her name was Olga; she kept what she hoped and believed to be a fox-terrier, and professed what she thought were Socialist opinions. It is not necessary to be called Olga if you are a Russian Princess; in fact, Reginald knew quite a number who were called Vera; but the fox-terrier and the Socialism are essential.

"The Countess Lomshen keeps a bull-dog," said the Princess suddenly. "In England is it more chic to have a bull-dog than a fox-terrier?"

Reginald threw his mind back over the canine fashions of the last ten years and gave an evasive answer.

"Do you think her handsome, the Countess Lomshen?" asked the Princess.

Reginald thought the Countess's complexion suggested an exclusive diet of macaroons and pale sherry. He said so.

"But that cannot be possible," said the Princess triumphantly; "I've seen her eating fish-soup at Donon's."

The Princess always defended a friend's complexion if it was really bad. With her, as with a great many of her sex, charity began at homeliness and did not generally progress much farther.

Reginald withdrew his macaroon and sherry theory, and became interested in a case of miniatures.

"That?" said the Princess; "that is the old Princess Lorikoff. She lived in Millionaya Street, near the Winter Palace, and was one of the Court ladies of the Old Russian school. Her knowledge of people and events was extremely limited; but she used to patronize every one who came in contact with her. There was a story that when she died and left the Millionaya for Heaven she addressed St. Peter in her formal staccato French: 'Je suis la Princesse Lor-i-koff. Il me donne grand plaisir à faire votre connaissance. Je vous en prie me présenter au Bon Dieu.' St. Peter made the desired introduction, and the Princess addressed le Bon Dieu: 'Je suis la Princesse Lor-i-koff. Il me donne grand plaisir à faire votre connaissance. On a souvent parlé de vous à l'église de la rue Million.' "

"Only the old and the clergy of Established churches know how to be flippant gracefully," commented Reginald; "which reminds me that in the Anglican Church in a certain foreign capital, which shall be nameless, I was present the other day when one of the junior chaplains was preaching in aid of distressed somethings or other, and he brought a really eloquent passage to a close with the remark, 'The tears of the afflicted, to what shall I liken them—to diamonds?' The other junior chaplain, who had been dozing out of professional jealousy, awoke with a start and asked hurriedly, 'Shall I play to diamonds, partner?' It didn't improve matters when the senior chaplain remarked dreamily but with painful distinctness, 'Double diamonds.' Every one looked at the preacher, half expecting him to redouble, but he contented himself with scoring what points he could under the circumstances."

"You English are always so frivolous," said the Princess. "In Russia we have too many troubles to permit of our being light-hearted."

Reginald gave a delicate shiver, such as an Italian greyhound might give in contemplating the approach of an ice age of which he personally disapproved, and resigned himself to the inevitable political discussion.

"Nothing that you hear about us in England is true," was the Princess's hopeful beginning.

"I always refused to learn Russian geography at school,"

observed Reginald; "I was certain some of the names must be wrong."

"Everything is wrong with our system of government," continued the Princess placidly. "The Bureaucrats think only of their pockets, and the people are exploited and plundered in every direction, and everything is mismanaged."

"With us," said Reginald, "a Cabinet usually gets the credit of being depraved and worthless beyond the bounds of human conception by the time it has been in office about four years."

"But if it is a bad Government you can turn it out at the election," argued the Princess.

"As far as I remember, we generally do," said Reginald.

"But here it is dreadful, every one goes to such extremes. In England you never go to extremes."

"We go to the Albert Hall," explained Reginald.

"There is always a see-saw with us between repression and violence," continued the Princess; "and the pity of it is the people are really not in the least inclined to be anything but peaceable. Nowhere will you find people more good-natured, or family circles where there is more affection."

"There I agree with you," said Reginald. "I know a boy who lives somewhere on the French Quay who is a case in point. His hair curls naturally, especially on Sundays, and he plays bridge well, even for a Russian, which is saying much. I don't think he has any other accomplishments, but his family affection is really of a very high order. When his maternal grandmother died he didn't go as far as to give up bridge altogether but he declared on nothing but black suits for the next three months. That, I think, was really beautiful."

The Princess was not impressed.

"I think you must be very self-indulgent and live only for amusement," she said. "A life of pleasure-seeking and card-playing and dissipation brings only dissatisfaction. You will find that out some day."

"Oh, I know it turns out that way sometimes," assented Reginald. "Forbidden fizz is often the sweetest."

But the remark was wasted on the Princess, who preferred champagne that had at least a suggestion of dissolved barley-sugar.

"I hope you will come and see me again," she said in a tone that prevented the hope from becoming too infectious, adding as a happy after-thought, "you must come to stay with us in the country."

Her particular part of the country was a few hundred versts the other side of Tamboff, with some fifteen miles of agrarian disturbance between her and the nearest neighbour. Reginald felt that there is some privacy which should be sacred from intrusion.

THE RETICENCE OF LADY ANNE

EGBERT came into the large, dimly lit drawing-room with the air of a man who is not certain whether he is entering a dovecote or a bomb factory, and is prepared for either eventuality. The little domestic quarrel over the luncheon-table had not been fought to a definite finish, and the question was how far Lady Anne was in a mood to renew or forgo hostilities. Her pose in the arm-chair by the tea-table was rather elaborately rigid; in the gloom of a December afternoon Egbert's pince-nez did not materially help him to discern the expression of her face.

By way of breaking whatever ice might be floating on the surface he made a remark about a dim religious light. He or Lady Anne were accustomed to make that remark between 4.30 and 6 on winter and late autumn evenings; it was a part of their married life. There was no recognized rejoinder to it, and Lady Anne made none.

Don Tarquinio lay astretch on the Persian rug, basking in the firelight with superb indifference to the possible ill-humour of Lady Anne. His pedigree was as flawlessly Persian as the rug, and his ruff was coming into the glory of its second winter. The page-boy, who had Renaissance tendencies.

had christened him Don Tarquinio. Left to themselves, Egbert and Lady Anne would unfailingly have called him Fluff, but they were not obstinate.

Egbert poured himself out some tea. As the silence gave no sign of breaking on Lady Anne's initiative, he braced himself for another Yermak effort.

"My remark at lunch had a purely academic application," he announced; "you seem to put an unnecessarily personal significance into it."

Lady Anne maintained her defensive barrier of silence. The bullfinch lazily filled in the interval with an air from *Iphigénie en Tauride*. Egbert recognized it immediately, because it was the only air the bullfinch whistled, and he had come to them with the reputation for whistling it. Both Egbert and Lady Anne would have preferred something from *The Yeoman of the Guard*, which was their favourite opera. In matters artistic they had a similarity of taste. They leaned towards the honest and explicit in art, a picture, for instance, that told its own story, with generous assistance from its title. A riderless warhorse with harness in obvious disarray, staggering into a courtyard full of pale swooning women, and marginally noted "Bad News," suggested to their minds a distinct interpretation of some military catastrophe. They could see what it was meant to convey, and explain it to friends of duller intelligence.

The silence continued. As a rule Lady Anne's displeasure became articulate and markedly voluble after four minutes of introductory muteness. Egbert seized the milk-jug and poured some of its contents into Don Tarquinio's saucer; as the saucer was already full to the brim an unsightly overflow was the result. Don Tarquinio looked on with a surprised interest that evanesced into elaborate unconsciousness when he was appealed to by Egbert to come and drink up some of the spilt matter. Don Tarquinio was prepared to play many rôles in life, but a vacuum carpet-cleaner was not one of them.

"Don't you think we're being rather foolish?" said Egbert cheerfully.

If Lady Anne thought so she didn't say so.

"I daresay the fault has been partly on my side," continued Egbert, with evaporating cheerfulness. "After all, I'm only human, you know. You seem to forget that I'm only human."

He insisted on the point, as if there had been unfounded suggestions that he was built on Satyr lines, with goat continuations where the human left off.

The bullfinch recommenced its air from *Iphigénie en Tauride*. Egbert began to feel depressed. Lady Anne was not drinking her tea. Perhaps she was feeling unwell. But when Lady Anne felt unwell she was not wont to be reticent on the subject. "No one knows what I suffer from indigestion" was one of her favourite statements; but the lack of knowledge can only have been caused by defective listening; the amount of information available on the subject would have supplied material for a monograph.

Evidently Lady Anne was not feeling unwell.

Egbert began to think he was being unreasonably dealt with; naturally he began to make concessions.

"I daresay," he observed, taking as central a position on the hearth-rug as Don Tarquinio could be persuaded to concede him, "I may have been to blame. I am willing, if I can thereby restore things to a happier standpoint, to undertake to lead a better life."

He wondered vaguely how it would be possible. Temptations came to him, in middle age, tentatively and without insistence, like a neglected butcher-boy who asks for a Christmas box in February for no more hopeful reason than that he didn't get one in December. He had no more idea of succumbing to them than he had of purchasing the fish-knives and fur boas that ladies are impelled to sacrifice through the medium of advertisement columns during twelve months of the year. Still, there was something impressive in this unasked-for renunciation of possibly latent enormities.

Lady Anne showed no sign of being impressed.

Egbert looked at her nervously through his glasses. To get the worst of an argument with her was no new experience. To get the worst of a monologue was a humiliating novelty.

"I shall go and dress for dinner," he announced in a voice into which he intended some shade of sternness to creep.

At the door a final access of weakness impelled him to make a further appeal,

"Aren't we being very silly?"

"A fool," was Don Tarquinio's mental comment as the door closed on Egbert's retreat. Then he lifted his velvet forepaws in the air and leapt lightly on to a bookshelf immediately under the bullfinch's cage. It was the first time he had seemed to notice the bird's existence, but he was carrying out a long-formed theory of action with the precision of mature deliberation. The bullfinch, who had fancied himself something of a despot, depressed himself of a sudden into a third of his normal displacement; then he fell to a helpless wing-beating and shrill cheeping. He had cost twenty-seven shillings without the cage, but Lady Anne made no sign of interfering. She had been dead for two hours.

THE LOST SANJAK

THE prison Chaplain entered the condemned's cell for the last time, to give such consolation as he might.

"The only consolation I crave for," said the condemned, "is to tell my story in its entirety to some one who will at least give it a respectful hearing."

"We must not be too long over it," said the Chaplain, looking at his watch.

The condemned repressed a shiver and commenced.

"Most people will be of opinion that I am paying the penalty of my own violent deeds. In reality I am a victim to a lack of specialization in my education and character."

"Lack of specialization!" said the Chaplain.

"Yes. If I had been known as one of the few men in England familiar with the fauna of the Outer Hebrides, or able to repeat stanzas of Camoëns' poetry in the original, I should have had no difficulty in proving my identity in the crisis when my identity became a matter of life and death for me. But my education was merely a moderately good one, and my temperament was of the general order that avoids specialization. I know a little in a general way about gardening and history and old masters, but I could never tell you off-hand whether 'Stella van der Loopen' was a chrysanthemum or a heroine of the American War of Independence, or something by Romney in the Louvre."

The Chaplain shifted uneasily in his seat. Now that the alternatives had been suggested they all seemed dreadfully possible.

"I fell in love, or thought I did, with the local doctor's wife," continued the condemned. "Why I should have done so, I cannot say, for I do not remember that she possessed any particular attractions of mind or body. On looking back at past events it seems to me that she must have been distinctly ordinary, but I suppose the doctor had fallen in love with her once, and what man has done man can do. She appeared to be pleased with the attentions which i paid her, and to that extent I suppose I might say she encouraged me, but I think she was honestly unaware that I meant anything more than a little neighbourly interest. When one is face to face with Death one wishes to be just."

The Chaplain murmured approval. "At any rate, she was genuinely horrified when I took advantage of the doctor's absence one evening to declare what I believed to be my passion. She begged me to pass out of her life and I could scarcely do otherwise than agree, though I hadn't the dimmest idea of how it was to be done. In novels and plays I knew it was a regular occurrence, and if you mistook a lady's sentiments or intentions you went off to India and did things on the frontier as a matter of course. As I stumbled along the doctor's carriage-drive I had no very clear idea as to what my line of action was to be, but I had a vague feeling that I must look at the *Times* Atlas before going to bed. Then, on the dark and lonely highway, I came suddenly on a dead body."

The Chaplain's interest in the story visibly quickened.

"Judging by the clothes it wore the corpse was that of a

Salvation Army captain. Some shocking accident seemed to have struck him down, and the head was crushed and battered out of all human semblance. Probably, I thought, a motor-car fatality; and then, with a sudden overmastering insistence, came another thought, that here was a remarkable opportunity for losing my identity and passing out of the life of the doctor's wife for ever. No tiresome and risky voyage to distant lands, but a mere exchange of clothes and identity with the unknown victim of an unwitnessed accident. With considerable difficulty I undressed the corpse, and clothed it anew in my own garments. Any one who has valeted a dead Salvation Army captain in an uncertain light will appreciate the difficulty. With the idea, presumably, of inducing the doctor's wife to leave her husband's roof-tree for some habitation which would be run at my expense, I had crammed my pockets with a store of banknotes, which represented a good deal of my immediate worldly wealth. When, therefore, I stole away into the world in the guise of a nameless Salvationist, I was not without resources which would easily support so humble a rôle for a considerable period. I tramped to a neighbouring market-town, and, late as the hour was, the production of a few shillings procured me supper and a night's lodging in a cheap coffee-house. The next day I started forth on an aimless course of wandering from one small town to another. I was already somewhat disgusted with the upshot of my sudden freak; in a few hours' time I was considerably more so. In the contents-bill of a local news sheet I read the announcement of my own murder at the hands of some person unknown; on buying a copy of the paper for a detailed account of the tragedy, which at first had aroused in me a certain grim amusement, I found that the deed was ascribed to a wandering Salvationist of doubtful antecedents, who had been seen lurking in the roadway near the scene of the crime. I was no longer amused. The matter promised to be embarrassing. What I had mistaken for a motor accident was evidently a case of savage assault and murder, and, until the real culprit was found, I should have much difficulty in explaining my intrusion into the affair. Of course I could establish my own identity; but how, without disagreeably involving the doctor's wife, could I give any adequate reason for changing clothes with the murdered man? While my brain worked feverishly at this problem, I subconsciously obeyed a secondary instinct—to get as far away as possible from the scene of the crime, and to get rid at all costs of my incriminating uniform. There I found a difficulty. I tried two or three obscure clothes shops, but my entrance invariably aroused an attitude of hostile suspicion in the proprietors, and on one excuse or another they avoided serving me with the now ardently desired change of clothing. The uniform that I had so thoughtlessly donned seemed as difficult to get out of as the fatal shirt of— You know, I forget the creature's name."

"Yes, yes," said the Chaplain hurriedly. "Go on with your story."

"Somehow, until I could get out of those compromising garments, I felt it would not be safe to surrender myself to the police. The thing that puzzled me was why no attempt was made to arrest me, since there was no question as to the suspicion which followed me, like an inseparable shadow, wherever I went. Stares, nudgings, whisperings, and even loud-spoken remarks of 'that's 'im' greeted my every appearance, and the meanest and most deserted eating-house that I patronized soon became filled with a crowd of furtively watching customers. I began to sympathize with the feelings of Royal personages trying to do a little private shopping under the unsparing scrutiny of an irrepressible public. And still, with all this inarticulate shadowing, which weighed on my nerves almost worse than open hostility would have done, no attempt was made to interfere with my liberty. Later on I discovered the reason. At the time of the murder on the lonely highway a series of important blood-hound trials had been taking place in the near neighbourhood, and some dozen and a half couples of trained animals had been put on the track of the supposed murderer— on my track. One of our most public-spirited London dailies had offered a princely prize to the owner of the pair that should first track me down, and betting on the chances of the respective competitors became rife throughout the land. The dogs ranged far and wide over about thirteen counties, and though my own movements had become by this time perfectly well known to police and public alike, the sporting instincts of the nation stepped in to prevent my premature arrest. 'Give the dogs a chance,' was the prevailing sentiment, whenever some ambitious local constable wished to put an end to my drawn-out evasion of justice. My final capture by the winning pair was not a very dramatic episode, in fact, I'm not sure that they would have taken any notice of me if I hadn't spoken to them and patted them, but the event gave rise to an extraordinary amount of partisan excitement. The owner of the pair who were next nearest up at the finish was an American, and he lodged a protest on the ground that an otterhound had married into the family of the winning pair six generations ago, and that the prize had been offered to the first pair of bloodhounds to capture the murderer, and that a dog that had one sixty-fourth part of otterhound blood in it couldn't technically be considered a bloodhound. I forget how the matter was ultimately settled, but it aroused a tremendous amount of acrimonious discussion on both sides of the Atlantic. My own contribution to the controversy consisted in pointing out that the whole dispute was beside the mark, as the actual murderer had not yet been captured; but I soon discovered that on this point there was not the least divergence of public or expert opinion. I had looked forward apprehensively to the proving of my identity and the establishment of my motives as a disagreeable necessity; I speedily found out that the most disagreeable part of the business was that it couldn't be done. When I saw in the glass the haggard and hunted expression which the experiences of the past few weeks had stamped on my erstwhile placid countenance, I could scarcely feel surprised that the few friends and relations I possessed refused to recognize me in my altered guise, and persisted in their obstinate but widely shared belief that it was I who had been done to death on the highway. To make matters worse, infinitely worse, an aunt of the really murdered man, an appalling female of an obviously low order of intelligence, identified me as her nephew, and gave the authorities a lurid account of my depraved youth and of her laudable but un-availing efforts to spank me into a better way. I believe it was even proposed to search me for finger-prints."

"But," said the Chaplain, "surely your educational attainments—"

"That was just the crucial point," said the condemned; "that was where my lack of specialization told so fatally against me. The dead Salvationist, whose identity I had so lightly and so disastrously adopted, had possessed a veneer of cheap modern education. It should have been easy to demonstrate that my learning was on altogether another plane to his, but in my nervousness I bungled miserably over test after test that was put to me The little French I had ever known deserted me; I could not render a simple phrase about the gooseberry of the gardener into that language, because I had forgotten the French for gooseberry."

The Chaplain again wriggled uneasily in his seat. "And then," resumed the condemned, "came the final discomfiture. In our village we had a modest little debating club, and I remembered having promised, chiefly, I suppose, to please and impress the doctor's wife, to give a sketchy kind of lecture on the Balkan Crisis. I had relied on being able to get up my facts from one or two standard works, and the back-numbers of certain periodicals. The prosecution had made a careful note of the circumstance that the man whom I claimed to be —and actually was—had posed locally as some sort of second-hand authority on Balkan affairs, and, in the midst of a string of questions on indifferent topics, the examining counsel asked me with a diabolical suddenness if I could tell the Court the whereabouts of Novibazar. I felt the question to be a crucial one; something told me that the answer was St. Petersburg or Baker Street. I hesitated, looked helplessly round at the sea of tensely expectant faces, pulled myself together, and chose Baker Street. And then I knew that everything was lost. The prosecution had no difficulty in demonstrating that an individual, even moderately versed in the affairs of the Near East, could never have so unceremoniously dislocated Novibazar from its accustomed corner of the map. It was an answer which the Salvation Army captain might conceivably have made—and I had made it. The circumstantial evidence connecting the Salvationist with the crime was overwhelmingly convincing, and I had inextricably identified myself with the Salvationist. And thus it comes to pass that in ten minutes' time I shall be hanged by the neck until I am dead in expiation of the murder of myself, which murder never took place, and of which, in any case, I am necessarily innocent."

.   .   .   .

When the Chaplain returned to his quarters, some fifteen minutes later, the black flag was floating over the prison tower. Breakfast was waiting for him in the dining-room, but he first passed into his library, and, taking up the *Times* Atlas, consulted a map of the Balkan Peninsula. "A thing like that," he observed, closing the volume with a snap, "might happen to any one."

THE SEX THAT DOESN'T SHOP

THE opening of a large new centre for West End shopping, particularly feminine shopping, suggests the reflection, Do women ever really shop? Of course, it is a well-attested fact that they go forth shopping as assiduously as a bee goes flower-visiting, but do they shop in the practical sense of the word? Granted the money, time, and energy, a resolute course of shopping transactions would naturally result in having one's ordinary domestic needs unfailingly supplied, whereas it is notorious that women servants (and housewives of all classes) make it almost a point of honour not to be supplied with everyday necessities. "We shall be out of starch by Thursday," they say with fatalistic foreboding, and by Thursday they are out of starch. They have predicted almost to a minute the moment when their supply would give out, and if Thursday happens to be early closing day their triumph is complete. A shop where starch is stored for retail purposes possibly stands at their very door, but the feminine mind has rejected such an obvious source for replenishing a dwindling stock. "We don't deal there" places it at once beyond the pale of human resort. And it is noteworthy that just as a sheep-worrying dog seldom molests the flocks in his near neighbourhood, so a woman rarely deals with shops in her immediate vicinity. The more remote the source of supply the more fixed seems to be the resolve to run short of the commodity. The Ark had probably not quitted its last moorings five minutes before some feminine voice gloatingly recorded a shortage of bird-seed. A few days ago two lady acquaintances of mine were confessing to some mental uneasiness because a friend had called just before lunch-time, and they had been unable to ask her to stop and share their meal, as (with a touch of legitimate pride) "there was nothing in the house." I pointed out that they lived in a street that bristled with provision shops and that it would have been easy to mobilize a very passable luncheon in less than five minutes. "That," they said, with quiet dignity, "would not have occurred to us," and I felt that I had suggested something bordering on the indecent.

But it is in catering for her literary wants that a woman's shopping capacity breaks down most completely. If you have perchance produced a book which has met with some little measure of success, you are certain to get a letter from some lady whom you scarcely know to bow to, asking you "how it can be got." She knows the name of the book, its author, and who published it, but how to get into actual contact with it is still an unsolved problem to her. You write back pointing out that to have recourse to an ironmonger or a corn-dealer will only entail delay and disappointment, and suggest an application to a bookseller as the most hopeful thing you can think of. In a day or two she writes again: "It is all right; I have borrowed it from your aunt." Here, of course, we have an example of the Beyond-Shopper, one who has learned the Better Way, but the helplessness exists even when such bypaths of relief are closed. A lady who lives in the West End was expressing to me the other day her interest in West Highland terriers, and her desire to know more about the breed, so when, a few days later, I came across an exhaustive article on that subject in the current number of one of our best known outdoor-weeklies, I mentioned the circumstance in a letter, giving the date of that number. "I cannot get the paper," was her telephoned response. And she couldn't. She lived in a city where news-agents are numbered, I suppose, by the thousand, and she must have passed dozens of such shops in her daily shopping excursions, but as far as she was concerned that article on West Highland terriers might as well have been written in a missal stored away in some Buddhist monastery in Eastern Thibet.

The brutal directness of the masculine shopper arouses a certain combative derision in the feminine onlooker. A cat that spreads one shrew-mouse over the greater part of a long summer afternoon, and then possibly loses him, doubtless feels the same contempt for the terrier who compresses his rat into ten seconds of the strenuous life. I was finishing off a short list of purchases a few afternoons ago when I was discovered by a lady of my acquaintance whom, swerving aside from the lead given us by her god-parents thirty years ago, we will call Agatha.

"You're surely not buying blotting-paper *here?*" she exclaimed in an agitated whisper, and she seemed so genuinely concerned that I stayed my hand.

"Let me take you to Winks and Pinks," she said as soon as we were out of the building: "they've got such lovely shades of blotting-paper—pearl and heliotrope and *momie* and crushed—"

"But I want ordinary white blotting-paper," I said.

"Never mind. They know me at Winks and Pinks," she replied inconsequently. Agatha apparently has an idea that blotting-paper is only sold in small quantities to persons of known reputation, who may be trusted not to put it to dangerous or improper uses. After walking some two hundred yards she began to feel that her tea was of more immediate importance than my blotting-paper.

"What do you want blotting-paper for?" she asked suddenly. I explained patiently.

"I use it to dry up the ink of wet manuscript without smudging the writing. Probably a Chinese invention of the second century before Christ, but I'm not sure. The only other use for it that I can think of is to roll it into a ball for a kitten to play with."

"But you haven't got a kitten," said Agatha, with a feminine desire for stating the entire truth on most occasions.

"A stray one might come in at any moment," I replied.

Anyway I didn't get the blotting-paper.

THE BLOOD-FEUD OF TOAD-WATER

A WEST-COUNTRY EPIC

THE Cricks lived at Toad-Water; and in the same lonely upland spot Fate had pitched the home of the Saunderses, and for miles around these two dwellings there was never a neighbour or a chimney or even a burying-ground to bring a sense of cheerful communion or social intercourse. Nothing but fields and spinneys and barns, lanes and waste-lands. Such was Toad-Water; and, even so, Toad-Water had its history. Thrust away in the benighted hinterland of a scattered market district, it might have been supposed that these two detached items of the Great Human Family would have leaned towards one another in a fellowship begotten of kindred circumstances and a common isolation from the outer world. And perhaps it had been so once, but the way of things had brought it otherwise. Indeed, otherwise. Fate, which had linked the two families in such unavoidable association of habitat, had ordained that the Crick household should nourish and maintain among its earthly possessions sundry head of domestic fowls, while to the Saunderses was given a disposition towards the cultivation of garden crops. Herein lay the material, ready to hand, for the coming of feud and ill-blood. For the grudge between the man of herbs and the man of live stock is no new thing; you will find traces of it in the fourth chapter of

Genesis. And one sunny afternoon in late spring-time the feud came—came, as such things mostly do come, with seeming aimlessness and triviality. One of the Crick hens, in obedience to the nomadic instincts of her kind, wearied of her legitimate scratching-grounds, and flew over the low wall that divided the holdings of the neighbours. And there, on the yonder side, with a hurried consciousness that her time and opportunities might be limited, the misguided bird scratched and scraped and beaked and delved in the soft yielding bed that had been prepared for the solace and well-being of a colony of seedling onions. Little showers of earth-mould and root-fibres went spraying before the hen and behind her, and every minute the area of her operations widened. The onions suffered considerably. Mrs. Saunders, sauntering at this luckless moment down the garden path, in order to fill her soul with reproaches at the iniquity of the weeds, which grew faster than she or her good man cared to remove them, stopped in mute discomfiture before the presence of a more magnificent grievance. And then, in the hour of her calamity, she turned instinctively to the Great Mother, and gathered in her capacious hands large clods of the hard brown soil that lay at her feet. With a terrible sincerity of purpose, though with a contemptible inadequacy of aim, she rained her earth bolts at the marauder, and the bursting pellets called forth a flood of cackling protest and panic from the hastily departing fowl. Calmness under misfortune is not an attribute of either hen-folk or women-kind, and while Mrs. Saunders declaimed over her onion bed such portions of the slang dictionary as are permitted by the Nonconformist conscience to be said or sung, the Vasco da Gama fowl was waking the echoes of Toad-Water with crescendo bursts of throat music which compelled attention to her griefs. Mrs. Crick had a long family, and was therefore licensed, in the eyes of her world, to have a short temper, and when some of her ubiquitous offspring had informed her, with the authority of eye-witnesses, that her neighbour had so far forgotten herself as to heave stones at her hen—her best hen, the best layer in the countryside—her thoughts clothed themselves in language "unbecoming to a Christian woman"

—so at least said Mrs. Saunders, to whom most of the language was applied. Nor was she, on her part, surprised at Mrs. Crick's conduct in letting her hens stray into other body's gardens, and then abusing of them, seeing as how she remembered things against Mrs. Crick—and the latter simultaneously had recollections of lurking episodes in the past of Susan Saunders that were nothing to her credit. "Fond memory, when all things fade we fly to thee," and in the paling light of an April afternoon the two women confronted each other from their respective sides of the party wall, recalling with shuddering breath the blots and blemishes of their neighbour's family record. There was that aunt of Mrs. Crick's who had died a pauper in Exeter workhouse—every one knew that Mrs. Saunders' uncle on her mother's side drank himself to death—then there was that Bristol cousin of Mrs. Crick's! From the shrill triumph with which his name was dragged in, his crime must have been pilfering from a cathedral at least, but as both remembrancers were speaking at once it was difficult to distinguish his infamy from the scandal which beclouded the memory of Mrs. Saunders' brother's wife's mother—who may have been a regicide, and was certainly not a nice person as Mrs. Crick painted her. And then, with an air of accumulating and irresistible conviction, each belligerent informed the other that she was no lady—after which they withdrew in a great silence, feeling that nothing further remained to be said. The chaffinches clinked in the apple trees and the bees droned round the berberis bushes, and the waning sunlight slanted pleasantly across the garden plots, but between the neighbour households had sprung up a barrier of hate, permeating and permanent.

The male heads of the families were necessarily drawn into the quarrel, and the children on either side were forbidden to have anything to do with the unhallowed offspring of the other party. As they had to travel a good three miles along the same road to school every day, this was awkward, but such things have to be. Thus all communication between the households was sundered. Except the cats. Much as Mrs. Saunders might deplore it, rumour persistently pointed to the Crick he-cat as the presumable father of sundry kittens of which the Saunders she-cat was indisputably the mother. Mrs. Saunders drowned the kittens, but the disgrace remained.

Summer succeeded spring, and winter summer, but the feud outlasted the waning seasons. Once, indeed, it seemed as though the healing influences of religion might restore to Toad-Water its erstwhile peace; the hostile families found themselves side by side in the soul-kindling atmosphere of a Revival Tea, where hymns were blended with a beverage that came of tea-leaves and hot water and took after the latter parent, and where ghostly counsel was tempered by garnishings of solidly fashioned buns—and here, wrought up by the environment of festive piety, Mrs. Saunders so far unbent as to remark guardedly to Mrs. Crick that the evening had been a fine one. Mrs. Crick, under the influence of her ninth cup of tea and her fourth hymn, ventured on the hope that it might continue fine, but a maladroit allusion on the part of the Saunders good man to the backwardness of garden crops brought the Feud stalking forth from its corner with all its old bitterness. Mrs. Saunders joined heartily in the singing of the final hymn, which told of peace and joy and archangels and golden glories; but her thoughts were dwelling on the pauper aunt of Exeter.

Years have rolled away, and some of the actors in this wayside drama have passed into the Unknown; other onions have arisen, have flourished, have gone their way, and the offending hen has long since expiated her misdeeds and lain with trussed feet and look of ineffable peace under the arched roof of Barnstaple market.

But the Blood-feud of Toad-Water survives to this day.

A YOUNG TURKISH CATASTROPHE

THE Minister for Fine Arts (to whose Department had been lately added the new subsection of Electoral Engineering) paid a business visit to the Grand Vizier. According to Eastern etiquette they discoursed for a while on indifferent subjects. The Minister only checked himself in time from making a passing reference to the Marathon Race, remembering that the Vizier had a Persian grandmother and might consider any allusion to Marathon as somewhat tactless. Presently the Minister touched the subject of his interview.

"Under the new Constitution are women to have votes?" he asked suddenly.

"To have votes? Women?" exclaimed the Vizier in some astonishment. "My dear Pasha, the New Departure has a flavour of the absurd as it is; don't let's try and make it altogether ridiculous. Women have no souls and no intelligence; why on earth should they have votes?"

"I know it sounds absurd," said the Minister, "but they are seriously considering the idea in the West."

"Then they must have a larger equipment of seriousness than I gave them credit for. After a lifetime of specialized effort in maintaining my gravity I can scarcely restrain an inclination to smile at the suggestion. Why, our womenfolk in most cases don't know how to read or write. How could they perform the operation of voting?"

"They could be shown the names of the candidates and where to make their cross."

"I beg your pardon?" interrupted the Vizier.

"Their crescent, I mean," corrected the Minister. "It would be to the liking of the Young Turkish Party," he added.

"Oh, well," said the Vizier, "if we are to do the thing at all we may as well go the whole h—" he pulled up just as he was uttering the name of an unclean animal, and continued, "the complete camel. I will issue instructions that womenfolk are to have votes."

. . . . . .

The poll was drawing to a close in the Lakoumistan division. The candidate of the Young Turkish Party was known to be three or four hundred votes ahead, and he was already drafting his address, returning thanks to the electors. His victory had been almost a foregone conclusion, for he had set in motion all the approved electioneering machinery of the West. He had even employed motor-cars. Few of his supporters had gone to the poll in these vehicles, but, thanks to the intelligent driving of his chauffeurs, many of his opponents had gone to their graves or to the local hospitals, or otherwise abstained from voting. And then something unlooked-for happened. The rival candidate, Ali the Blest, arrived on the scene with his wives and womenfolk, who numbered, roughly, six hundred. Ali had wasted little effort on election literature, but had been heard to remark that every vote given to his opponent meant another sack thrown into the Bosporus. The Young Turkish candidate, who had conformed to the Western custom of one wife and hardly any mistresses, stood by helplessly while his adversary's poll swelled to a triumphant majority.

"Cristabel Columbus!" he exclaimed, invoking in some confusion the name of a distinguished pioneer; "who would have thought it?"

"Strange," mused Ali, "that one who harangued so clamorously about the Secret Ballot should have overlooked the Veiled Vote."

And, walking homeward with his constituents, he murmured in his beard an improvisation on the heretic poet of Persia:

> "One, rich in metaphors, his Cause contrives
> To urge with edgèd words, like Kabul knives;
> And I, who worst him in this sorry game,
> Was never rich in anything but—wives."

JUDKIN OF THE PARCELS

A FIGURE in an indefinite tweed suit, carrying brown-paper parcels. That is what we met suddenly, at the bend of a muddy Dorsetshire lane, and the roan mare stared and obviously thought of a curtsy. The mare is road-shy, with intervals of stolidity, and there is no telling what she will pass and what she won't. We call her Redford. That was my first meeting with Judkin, and the next time the circumstances were the same; the same muddy lane, the same rather apologetic figure in the tweed suit, the same—or very similar —parcels. Only this time the roan looked straight in front of her.

Whether I asked the groom or whether he advanced the information, I forget; but someway I gradually reconstructed the life-history of this trudger of the lanes. It was much the same, no doubt, as that of many others who are from time to time pointed out to one as having been aforetime in crack cavalry regiments and noted performers in the saddle; men who have breathed into their lungs the wonder of the East, have romped through life as through a cotillon, have had a thrust perhaps at the Viceroy's Cup, and done fantastic horsefleshy things around the Gulf of Aden. And then a golden stream has dried up, the sunlight has faded suddenly out of things, and the gods have nodded "Go." And they have not gone. They have turned instead to the muddy lanes and cheap villas and the marked-down ills of life, to watch pear trees growing and to encourage hens for their eggs. And Judkin was even as these others; the wine had been suddenly spilt from his cup of life, and he had stayed to suck at the dregs which the wise throw away. In the days of his scorn for most things he would have stared the roan mare and her turn-out out of all pretension to smartness, as he would have frozen a cheap claret behind its cork, or a plain woman behind her veil; and now he was walking stoically through the mud, in a tweed suit that would eventually go on to the gardener's boy, and would perhaps fit him. The dear gods, who know the end before the beginning, were perhaps growing a gardener's boy somewhere to fit the garments, and Judkin was only a care-taker, inhabiting a portion of them. That is what I like to think, and I am probably wrong. And Judkin, whose clothes had been to him once more than a religion, scarcely less sacred than a family quarrel, would carry those parcels back to his villa and to the wife who awaited him and them—a wife who may, for all we know to the contrary, have had a figure once, and perhaps has yet a heart of gold—of nine-carat gold, let us say at the least—but assuredly a soul of tape. And he that has fetched and carried will explain how it had fared with him in his dealings, and if he has brought the wrong sort of sugar or thread he will wheedle away the displeasure from that leaden face as a pastrycook girl will drive bluebottles off a stale bun. And that man has known what it was to coax the fret of a thoroughbred, to soothe its toss and sweat as it danced beneath him in the glee and chafe of its pulses and the glory of its thews. He has been in the raw places of the earth, where the desert beasts have whimpered their unthinkable psalmody, and their eyes have shone back the reflex of the midnight stars—and he can immerse himself in the tending of an incubator. It is horrible and wrong, and yet when I have met him in the lanes his face has worn a look of tedious cheerfulness that might pass for happiness. Has Judkin of the Parcels found something in the lees of life that I have missed in going to and fro over many waters? Is there more wisdom in his perverseness than in the madness of the wise? The dear gods know.

I don't think I saw Judkin more than three times all told, and always the lane was our point of contact; but as the roan mare was taking me to the station one heavy, cloud-smeared day, I passed a dull-looking villa that the groom, or instinct, told me was Judkin's home. From beyond a hedge of ragged elder-bushes could be heard the thud, thud of a spade, with an occasional clink and pause, as if some one had picked out a stone and thrown it to a distance, and I knew that *he* was doing nameless things to the roots of a pear tree. Near by him, I felt sure, would be lying a large and late vegetable marrow, and its largeness and lateness would be a theme of conversation at luncheon. It would be suggested that it should grace the harvest thanksgiving service; the harvest having been so generally unsatisfactory, it would be unfair to let the farmers supply all the material for rejoicing.

And while I was speeding townwards along the rails Judkin would be plodding his way to the vicarage bearing a vegetable marrow and a basketful of dahlias. The basket to be returned.

GABRIEL-ERNEST

"THERE is a wild beast in your woods," said the artist Cunningham, as he was being driven to the station. It was the only remark he had made during the drive, but as Van Cheele had talked incessantly his companion's silence had not been noticeable.

"A stray fox or two and some resident weasels. Nothing more formidable," said Van Cheele. The artist said nothing.

"What did you mean about a wild beast?" said Van Cheele later, when they were on the platform.

"Nothing. My imagination. Here is the train," said Cunningham.

That afternoon Van Cheele went for one of his frequent rambles through his woodland property. He had a stuffed bittern in his study, and knew the names of quite a number of wild flowers, so his aunt had possibly some justification in describing him as a great naturalist. At any rate, he was a great walker. It was his custom to take mental notes of everything he saw during his walks, not so much for the purpose of assisting contemporary science as to provide topics for conversation afterwards. When the bluebells began to show themselves in flower he made a point of informing every one of the fact; the season of the year might have warned his hearers of the likelihood of such an occurrence, but at least they felt that he was being absolutely frank with them.

What Van Cheele saw on this particular afternoon was, however, something far removed from his ordinary range of experience. On a shelf of smooth stone overhanging a deep pool in the hollow of an oak coppice a boy of about sixteen lay asprawl, drying his wet brown limbs luxuriously in the sun. His wet hair, parted by a recent dive, lay close to his head, and his light-brown eyes, so light that there was an almost tigerish gleam in them, were turned towards Van Cheele with a certain lazy watchfulness. It was an unexpected apparition, and Van Cheele found himself engaged in the novel process of thinking before he spoke. Where on earth could this wild-looking boy hail from? The miller's wife had lost a child some two months ago, supposed to have been swept away by the mill-race, but that had been a mere baby, not a half-grown lad.

"What are you doing there?" he demanded.

"Obviously, sunning myself," replied the boy.

"Where do you live?"

"Here, in these woods."

"You can't live in the woods," said Van Cheele.

"They are very nice woods," said the boy, with a touch of patronage in his voice.

"But where do you sleep at night?"

"I don't sleep at night; that's my busiest time."

Van Cheele began to have an irritated feeling that he was grappling with a problem that was eluding him.

"What do you feed on?" he asked.

"Flesh," said the boy, and he pronounced the word with slow relish, as though he were tasting it.

"Flesh! What flesh?"

"Since it interests you, rabbits, wild-fowl, hares, poultry, lambs in their season, children when I can get any; they're usually too well locked in at night, when I do most of my hunting. It's quite two months since I tasted child-flesh."

Ignoring the chaffing nature of the last remark Van Cheele tried to draw the boy on the subject of possible poaching operations.

"You're talking rather through your hat when you speak of feeding on hares." (Considering the nature of the boy's toilet the simile was hardly an apt one.) "Our hillside hares aren't easily caught."

"At night I hunt on four feet," was the somewhat cryptic response.

"I suppose you mean that you hunt with a dog?" hazarded Van Cheele.

The boy rolled slowly over on to his back, and laughed a weird low laugh, that was pleasantly like a chuckle and disagreeably like a snarl.

"I don't fancy any dog would be very anxious for my company, especially at night."

Van Cheele began to feel that there was something positively uncanny about the strange-eyed, strange-tongued youngster.

"I can't have you staying in these woods," he declared authoritatively.

"I fancy you'd rather have me here than in your house," said the boy.

The prospect of this wild, nude animal in Van Cheele's primly ordered house was certainly an alarming one.

"If you don't go I shall have to make you," said Van Cheele.

The boy turned like a flash, plunged into the pool, and in a moment had flung his wet and glistening body half-way up the bank where Van Cheele was standing. In an otter the movement would not have been remarkable; in a boy Van Cheele found it sufficiently startling. His foot slipped as he made an involuntary backward movement, and he found himself almost prostrate on the slippery weed-grown bank, with those tigerish yellow eyes not very far from his own. Almost instinctively he half raised his hand to his throat. The boy laughed again, a laugh in which the snarl had nearly driven out the chuckle, and then, with another of his astonishing lightning movements, plunged out of view into a yielding tangle of weed and fern.

"What an extraordinary wild animal!" said Van Cheele as he picked himself up. And then he recalled Cunningham's remark, "There is a wild beast in your woods."

Walking slowly homeward, Van Cheele began to turn over in his mind various local occurrences which might be traceable to the existence of this astonishing young savage.

Something had been thinning the game in the woods lately, poultry had been missing from the farms, hares were growing unaccountably scarcer, and complaints had reached him of lambs being carried off bodily from the hills. Was it possible that this wild boy was really hunting the countryside in company with some clever poacher dog? He had spoken of hunting "four-footed" by night, but then, again, he had hinted strangely at no dog caring to come near him, "especially at night." It was certainly puzzling. And then, as Van Cheele ran his mind over the various depredations that had been committed during the last month or two, he came suddenly to a dead stop, alike in his walk and his speculations. The child missing from the mill two months ago—the accepted theory was that it had tumbled into the mill-race and been swept away; but the mother had always declared she had heard a shriek on the hill side of the house, in the opposite direction from the water. It was unthinkable, of course, but he wished that the boy had not made that uncanny remark about child-flesh eaten two months ago. Such dreadful things should not be said even in fun.

Van Cheele, contrary to his usual wont, did not feel disposed to be communicative about his discovery in the wood. His position as a parish councillor and justice of the peace seemed somehow compromised by the fact that he was harbouring a personality of such doubtful repute on his property; there was even a possibility that a heavy bill of damages for raided lambs and poultry might be laid at his door. At dinner that night he was quite unusually silent.

"Where's your voice gone to?" said his aunt. "One would think you had seen a wolf."

Van Cheele, who was not familiar with the old saying, thought the remark rather foolish; if he *had* seen a wolf on his property his tongue would have been extraordinarily busy with the subject.

At breakfast next morning Van Cheele was conscious that his feeling of uneasiness regarding yesterday's episode had not wholly disappeared, and he resolved to go by train to the neighbouring cathedral town, hunt up Cunningham, and learn from him what he had really seen that had prompted the remark about a wild beast in the woods. With this resolution taken, his usual cheerfulness partially returned, and he hummed a bright little melody as he sauntered to the morning-room for his customary cigarette. As he entered the room the melody made way abruptly for a pious invocation. Gracefully asprawl on the ottoman, in an attitude of almost exaggerated repose, was the boy of the woods. He was drier than when Van Cheele had last seen him, but no other alteration was noticeable in his toilet.

"How dare you come here?" asked Van Cheele furiously.

"You told me I was not to stay in the woods," said the boy calmly.

"But not to come here. Supposing my aunt should see you!"

And with a view to minimizing that catastrophe Van Cheele hastily obscured as much of his unwelcome guest as possible under the folds of a *Morning Post*. At that moment his aunt entered the room.

"This is a poor boy who has lost his way—and lost his memory. He doesn't know who he is or where he comes from," explained Van Cheele desperately, glancing apprehensively at the waif's face to see whether he was going to add inconvenient candour to his other savage propensities.

Miss Van Cheele was enormously interested.

"Perhaps his underlinen is marked," she suggested.

"He seems to have lost most of that, too," said Van Cheele, making frantic little grabs at the *Morning Post* to keep it in its place.

A naked homeless child appealed to Miss Van Cheele as warmly as a stray kitten or derelict puppy would have done.

"We must do all we can for him," she decided, and in a very short time a messenger, dispatched to the rectory, where a page-boy was kept, had returned with a suit of pantry clothes, and the necessary accessories of shirt, shoes, collar, etc. Clothed, clean, and groomed, the boy lost none of his uncanniness in Van Cheele's eyes, but his aunt found him sweet.

"We must call him something till we know who he really is," she said. "Gabriel-Ernest, I think; those are nice suitable names."

Van Cheele agreed, but he privately doubted whether they were being grafted on to a nice suitable child. His misgivings were not diminished by the fact that his staid and elderly spaniel had bolted out of the house at the first incoming of the boy, and now obstinately remained shivering and yapping at the farther end of the orchard, while the canary, usually as vocally industrious as Van Cheele himself, had put itself on an allowance of frightened cheeps. More than ever he was resolved to consult Cunningham without loss of time.

As he drove off to the station his aunt was arranging that Gabriel-Ernest should help her to entertain the infant members of her Sunday-school class at tea that afternoon.

Cunningham was not at first disposed to be communicative.

"My mother died of some brain trouble," he explained, "so you will understand why I am averse to dwelling on anything of an impossibly fantastic nature that I may see or think that I have seen."

"But what *did* you see?" persisted Van Cheele.

"What I thought I saw was something so extraordinary that no really sane man could dignify it with the credit of having actually happened. I was standing, the last evening I was with you, half-hidden in the hedgegrowth by the orchard gate, watching the dying glow of the sunset. Suddenly I became aware of a naked boy, a bather from some neighbouring pool, I took him to be, who was standing out on the bare hillside also watching the sunset. His pose was so suggestive of some wild faun of Pagan myth that I instantly wanted to engage him as a model, and in another moment I think I should have hailed him. But just then the sun dipped out of view, and all the orange and pink slid out of the landscape, leaving it cold and grey. And at the same moment an astounding thing happened—the boy vanished too!"

"What! vanished away into nothing?" asked Van Cheele excitedly.

"No; that is the dreadful part of it," answered the artist; "on the open hillside where the boy had been standing a second ago, stood a large wolf, blackish in colour, with gleaming fangs and cruel, yellow eyes. You may think—"

But Van Cheele did not stop for anything as futile as thought. Already he was tearing at top speed towards the station. He dismissed the idea of a telegram. "Gabriel-Ernest is a werewolf" was a hopelessly inadequate effort at conveying the situation, and his aunt would think it was a code message to which he had omitted to give her the key. His one hope was that he might reach home before sundown. The cab which he chartered at the other end of the railway journey bore him with what seemed exasperating slowness along the country roads, which were pink and mauve with the flush of the sinking sun. His aunt was putting away some unfinished jams and cake when he arrived.

"Where is Gabriel-Ernest?" he almost screamed.

"He is taking the little Toop child home," said his aunt. "It was getting so late, I thought it wasn't safe to let it go back alone. What a lovely sunset, isn't it?"

But Van Cheele, although not oblivious of the glow in the western sky, did not stay to discuss its beauties. At a speed for which he was scarcely geared he raced along the narrow lane that led to the home of the Toops. On one side ran the swift current of the mill-stream, on the other rose the stretch of bare hillside. A dwindling rim of red sun showed still on the skyline, and the next turning must bring him in view of the ill-assorted couple he was pursuing. Then the colour went suddenly out of things, and a grey light settled itself with a quick shiver over the landscape. Van Cheele heard a shrill wail of fear, and stopped running.

Nothing was ever seen again of the Toop child or Gabriel-Ernest, but the latter's discarded garments were found lying in the road, so it was assumed that the child had fallen into the water, and that the boy had stripped and jumped in, in a vain endeavour to save it. Van Cheele and some workmen who were near by at the time testified to having heard a child scream loudly just near the spot where the clothes were found. Mrs. Toop, who had eleven other children, was decently resigned to her bereavement, but Miss Van Cheele sincerely mourned her lost foundling. It was on her initiative that a memorial brass was put up in the parish church to "Gabriel-Ernest, an unknown boy, who bravely sacrificed his life for another."

Van Cheele gave way to his aunt in most things, but he flatly refused to subscribe to the Gabriel-Ernest memorial.

THE SAINT AND THE GOBLIN

THE little stone Saint occupied a retired niche in a side aisle of the old cathedral. No one quite remembered who he had been, but that in a way was a guarantee of respectability. At least so the Goblin said. The Goblin was a very fine specimen of quaint stone carving, and lived up in the corbel on the wall opposite the niche of the little Saint. He was connected with some of the best cathedral folk, such as the queer carvings in the choir stalls and chancel screen, and even the gargoyles high up on the roof. All the fantastic beasts and manikins that sprawled and twisted in wood or stone or lead overhead in the arches or away down in the crypt were in some way akin to him; consequently he was a person of recognized importance in the cathedral world.

The little stone Saint and the Goblin got on very well together, though they looked at most things from different points of view. The Saint was a philanthropist in an old-fashioned way; he thought the world, as he saw it, was good, but might be improved. In particular he pitied the church mice, who were miserably poor. The Goblin, on the other hand, was of opinion that the world, as he knew it, was bad, but had better be let alone. It was the function of the church mice to be poor.

"All the same," said the Saint, "I feel very sorry for them."

"Of course you do," said the Goblin; "it's *your* function to feel sorry for them. If they were to leave off being poor you couldn't fulfil your functions. You'd be a sinecure."

He rather hoped that the Saint would ask him what a sinecure meant, but the latter took refuge in a stony silence. The Goblin might be right, but still, he thought, he would like to do something for the church mice before winter came on; they were so very poor.

Whilst he was thinking the matter over he was startled by something falling between his feet with a hard metallic clatter. It was a bright new thaler; one of the cathedral jack-daws, who collected such things, had flown in with it to a stone cornice just above his niche, and the banging of the sacristy door had startled him into dropping it. Since the invention of gun powder the family nerves were not what they had been.

"What have you got there?" asked the Goblin.

"A silver thaler," said the Saint. "Really," he continued, "it is most fortunate; now I can do something for the church mice."

"How will you manage it?" asked the Goblin.

The Saint considered.

"I will appear in a vision to the vergeress who sweeps the floors. I will tell her that she will find a silver thaler between my feet, and that she must take it and buy a measure of corn and put it on my shrine. When she finds the money she will know that it was a true dream, and she will take care to follow my directions. Then the mice will have food all the winter."

"Of course *you* can do that," observed the Goblin. "Now, *I* can only appear to people after they have had a heavy supper of indigestible things. My opportunities with the vergeress would be limited. There is some advantage in being a saint after all."

All this while the coin was lying at the Saint's feet. It was clean and glittering and had the Elector's arms beautifully stamped upon it. The Saint began to reflect that such an op-portunity was too rare to be hastily disposed of. Perhaps indiscriminate charity might be harmful to the church mice. After all, it was their function to be poor; the Goblin had said so, and the Goblin was generally right.

"I've been thinking," he said to that personage, "that perhaps it would be really better if I ordered a thaler's worth of candles to be placed on my shrine instead of the corn."

He often wished, for the look of the thing, that people would sometimes burn candles at his shrine; but as they had forgotten who he was it was not considered a profitable speculation to pay him that attention.

"Candles would be more orthodox," said the Goblin.

"More orthodox, certainly," agreed the Saint, "and the mice could have the ends to eat; candle-ends are most fattening."

The Goblin was too well bred to wink; besides, being a stone goblin, it was out of the question.

.   .   .   .   .   .   ‘

"Well, if it ain't there, sure enough!" said the vergeress next morning. She took the shining coin down from the gusty niche and turned it over and over in her grimy hands. Then she put it to her mouth and bit it.

"She can't be going to eat it," thought the Saint, and fixed her with his stoniest stare.

"Well," said the woman, in a somewhat shriller key, "who'd have thought it! A saint, too!"

Then she did an unaccountable thing. She hunted an old piece of tape out of her pocket, and tied it crosswise, with a big loop, round the thaler, and hung it round the neck of the little Saint.

Then she went away.

"The only possible explanation," said the Goblin, "is that it's a bad one."

.   .   .   .

"What is that decoration your neighbour is wearing?" asked a wyvern that was wrought into the capital of an adjacent pillar.

The Saint was ready to cry with mortification, only, being of stone, he couldn't.

"It's a coin of—ahem!—fabulous value," replied the Goblin tactfully.

And the news went round the Cathedral that the shrine of the little stone Saint had been enriched by a priceless offering.

"After all, it's something to have the conscience of a goblin," said the Saint to himself.

The church mice were as poor as ever. But that was their function.

THE SOUL OF LAPLOSHKA

LAPLOSHKA was one of the meanest men I have ever met, and quite one of the most entertaining. He said horrid things about other people in such a charming way that one forgave him for the equally horrid things he said about oneself behind one's back. Hating anything in the way of ill-natured gossip ourselves, we are always grateful to those who do it for us and do it well. And Laploshka did it really well.

Naturally Laploshka had a large circle of acquaintances, and as he exercised some care in their selection it followed that an appreciable proportion were men whose bank balances enabled them to acquiesce indulgently in his rather one-sided views on hospitality. Thus, although possessed of only moderate means, he was able to live comfortably within his income, and still more comfortably within those of various tolerantly disposed associates.

But towards the poor or to those of the same limited resources as himself his attitude was one of watchful anxiety; he seemed to be haunted by a besetting fear lest some fraction of a shilling or franc, or whatever the prevailing coinage might be, should be diverted from his pocket or service into that of a hard-up companion. A two-franc cigar would be cheerfully offered to a wealthy patron, on the principle of doing evil that good may come, but I have known him indulge in agonies of perjury rather than admit the incriminating possession of a copper coin when change was needed to tip a waiter. The coin would have been duly returned at the earliest opportunity—he would have taken means to ensure against forgetfulness on the part of the borrower—but accidents might happen, and even the temporary estrangement from his penny or sou was a calamity to be avoided.

The knowledge of this amiable weakness offered a perpetual temptation to play upon Laploshka's fears of involuntary generosity. To offer him a lift in a cab and pretend not to have enough money to pay the fare, to fluster him with a request for a sixpence when his hand was full of silver just received in change, these were a few of the petty torments that ingenuity prompted as occasion afforded. To do justice to Laploshka's resourcefulness it must be admitted that he always emerged somehow or other from the most embarrassing dilemma without in any way compromising his reputation for saying "No." But the gods send opportunities at some time to most men, and mine came one evening when Laploshka and I were supping together in a cheap boulevard restaurant. (Except when he was the bidden guest of some one with an irreproachable income, Laploshka was wont to curb his appetite for high living; on such fortunate occasions he let it go on an easy snaffle.) At the conclusion of the meal a somewhat urgent message called me away, and without heeding my companion's agitated protest, I called back cruelly, "Pay my share; I'll settle with you tomorrow." Early on the morrow Laploshka hunted me down by instinct as I walked along a side street that I hardly ever frequented. He had the air of a man who had not slept.

"You owe me two francs from last night," was his breathless greeting.

I spoke evasively of the situation in Portugal, where more trouble seemed brewing. But Laploshka listened with the abstraction of the deaf adder, and quickly returned to the subject of the two francs.

"I'm afraid I must owe it to you," I said lightly and brutally. "I haven't a sou in the world," and I added mendaciously, "I'm going away for six months or perhaps longer."

Laploshka said nothing, but his eyes bulged a little and his cheeks took on the mottled hues of an ethnographical map of the Balkan Peninsula. That same day, at sundown, he died. "Failure of the heart's action" was the doctor's verdict; but I, who knew better, knew that he had died of grief.

There arose the problem of what to do with his two francs. To have killed Laploshka was one thing; to have kept his beloved money would have argued a callousness of feeling of which I am not capable. The ordinary solution, of giving it to the poor, would by no means fit the present situation, for nothing would have distressed the dead man more than such a misuse of his property. On the other hand, the bestowal of two francs on the rich was an operation which called for some tact. An easy way out of the difficulty seemed, however, to present itself the following Sunday, as I was wedged into the cosmopolitan crowd which filled the side-aisle of one of the most popular Paris churches. A collecting-bag, for "the poor of Monsieur le Curé," was buffeting its tortuous way across the seemingly impenetrable human sea, and a German in front of me, who evidently did not wish his appreciation of the magnificent music to be marred by a suggestion of payment, made audible criticisms to his companion on the claims of the said charity.

"They do not want money," he said; "they have too much money. They have no poor. They are all pampered."

If that were really the case my way seemed clear. I dropped Laploshka's two francs into the bag with a murmured blessing on the rich of Monsieur le Curé.

Some three weeks later chance had taken me to Vienna, and I sat one evening regaling myself in a humble but excellent little Gasthaus up in the Währinger quarter. The appointments were primitive, but the Schnitzel, the beer, and the cheese could not have been improved on. Good cheer brought good custom, and with the exception of one small table near the door every place was occupied. Half-way through my meal I happened to glance in the direction of that empty seat, and saw that it was no longer empty. Poring over the bill of fare with the absorbed scrutiny of one who seeks the cheapest among the cheap was Laploshka. Once he looked across at me, with a comprehensive glance at my repast, as though to say, "It is my two francs you are eating," and then looked swiftly away. Evidently the poor of Monsieur le Curé had been genuine poor. The Schnitzel turned to leather in my mouth, the beer seemed tepid; I left the Emmenthaler untasted. My one idea was to get away from the room, away from the table where *that* was seated; and as I fled I felt Laploshka's reproachful eyes watching the amount that I gave to the piccolo—out of his two francs. I lunched next day at an expensive restaurant which I felt sure that the living Laploshka would never have entered on his own account, and I hoped that the dead Laploshka would observe the same barriers. I was not mistaken, but as I came out I found him miserably studying the bill of fare stuck up on the portals. Then he slowly made his way over to a milk-hall. For the first time in my experience I missed the charm and gaiety of Vienna life.

After that, in Paris or London or wherever I happened to be, I continued to see a good deal of Laploshka. If I had a seat in a box at a theatre I was always conscious of his eyes furtively watching me from the dim recesses of the gallery. As I turned into my club on a rainy afternoon I would see him taking inadequate shelter in a doorway opposite. Even if I indulged in the modest luxury of a penny chair in the Park he generally confronted me from one of the free benches, never staring at me, but always elaborately conscious of my presence. My friends began to comment on my changed looks, and advised me to leave off heaps of things. I should have liked to have left off Laploshka.

On a certain Sunday—it was probably Easter, for the crush was worse than ever—I was again wedged into the crowd listening to the music in the fashionable Paris church, and again the collection-bag was buffeting its way across the human sea. An English lady behind me was making ineffectual efforts to convey a coin into the still distant bag, so I took the money at her request and helped it forward to its destination. It was a two-franc piece. A swift inspiration came to me, and I merely dropped my own sou into the bag and slid the silver coin into my pocket. I had withdrawn Laploshka's two francs from the poor, who should never have had that legacy. As I backed away from the crowd I heard a woman's voice say, "I don't believe he put my money in the bag. There are swarms of people in Paris like that!" But my mind was lighter than it had been for a long time.

The delicate mission of bestowing the retrieved sum on the deserving rich still confronted me. Again I trusted to the inspiration of accident, and again fortune favoured me. A shower drove me, two days later, into one of the historic churches on the left bank of the Seine, and there I found, peering at the old wood-carvings, the Baron R., one of the wealthiest and most shabbily dressed men in Paris. It was now or never. Putting a strong American inflection into the French which I usually talked with an unmistakable British accent, I catechized the Baron as to the date of the church's building, its dimensions, and other details which an American tourist would be certain to want to know. Having acquired such information as the Baron was able to impart on short notice, I solemnly placed the two-franc piece in his hand, with the hearty assurance that it was "pour vous," and turned to go. The Baron was slightly taken aback, but accepted the situation with a good grace. Walking over to a small box fixed in the wall, he dropped Laploshka's two francs into the slot. Over the box was the inscription, "Pour les pauvres de M. le Curé."

That evening, at the crowded corner by the Café de la Paix, I caught a fleeting glimpse of Laploshka. He smiled, slightly raised his hat, and vanished. I never saw him again. After all, the money had been *given* to the deserving rich, and the soul of Laploshka was at peace.

THE BAG

"THE Major is coming in to tea," said Mrs. Hoopington to her niece. "He's just gone round to the stables with his horse. Be as bright and lively as you can; the poor man's got a fit of the glooms."

Major Pallaby was a victim of circumstances, over which he had no control, and of his temper, over which he had very little. He had taken on the Mastership of the Pexdale Hounds in succession to a highly popular man who had fallen foul of his committee, and the Major found himself confronted with the overt hostility of at least half the hunt, while his lack of tact and amiability had done much to alienate the remainder. Hence subscriptions were beginning to fall off, foxes grew provokingly scarcer, and wire obtruded itself with increasing frequency. The Major could plead reasonable excuse for his fit of the glooms.

In ranging herself as a partisan on the side of Major Pallaby Mrs. Hoopington had been largely influenced by the fact that she had made up her mind to marry him at an early date. Against his notorious bad temper she set his three thousand a year, and his prospective succession to a baronetcy gave a casting vote in his favour. The Major's plans on the subject of matrimony were not at present in such an advanced stage as Mrs. Hoopington's, but he was beginning to find his way over to Hoopington Hall with a frequency that was already being commented on.

"He had a wretchedly thin field out again yesterday," said Mrs. Hoopington. "Why you didn't bring one or two hunting men down with you, instead of that stupid Russian boy, I can't think."

"Vladimir isn't stupid," protested her niece; "he's one of the most amusing boys I ever met. Just compare him for a moment with some of your heavy hunting men——"

"Anyhow, my dear Norah, he can't ride."

"Russians never can; but he shoots."

"Yes; and what does he shoot? Yesterday he brought home a woodpecker in his game-bag."

"But he'd shot three pheasants and some rabbits as well."

"That's no excuse for including a woodpecker in his game-bag."

"Foreigners go in for mixed bags more than we do. A Grand Duke pots a vulture just as seriously as we should stalk a bustard. Anyhow, I've explained to Vladimir that certain birds are beneath his dignity as a sportsman. And as he's only nineteen, of course, his dignity is a sure thing to appeal to."

Mrs. Hoopington sniffed. Most people with whom Vladimir came in contact found his high spirits infectious, but his present hostess was guaranteed immune against infection of that sort.

"I hear him coming in now," she observed. "I shall go and get ready for tea. We're going to have it here in the hall. Entertain the Major if he comes in before I'm down, and, above all, be bright."

Norah was dependent on her aunt's good graces for many little things that made life worth living, and she was conscious of a feeling of discomfiture because the Russian youth whom she had brought down as a welcome element of change in the country-house routine was not making a good impression. That young gentleman, however, was supremely unconscious of any shortcomings, and burst into the hall, tired, and less sprucely groomed than usual, but distinctly radiant. His game-bag looked comfortably full.

"Guess what I have shot," he demanded.

"Pheasants, wood-pigeons, rabbits," hazarded Norah.

"No; a large beast; I don't know what you call it in English. Brown, with a darkish tail." Norah changed colour.

"Does it live in a tree and eat nuts?" she asked, hoping that the use of the adjective "large" might be an exaggeration.

Vladimir laughed.

"Oh, no; not a *biyelka*."

"Does it swim and eat fish?" asked Norah, with a fervent prayer in her heart that it might turn out to be an otter.

"No," said Vladimir, busy with the straps of his game-bag; "it lives in the woods, and eats rabbits and chickens."

Norah sat down suddenly, and hid her face in her hands.

"Merciful Heaven!" she wailed; "he's shot a fox!"

Vladimir looked up at her in consternation. In a torrent of agitated words she tried to explain the horror of the situation. The boy understood nothing, but was thoroughly alarmed.

"Hide it, hide it!" said Norah frantically, pointing to the

still unopened bag. "My aunt and the Major will be here in a moment. Throw it on the top of that chest; they won't see it there."

Vladimir swung the bag with fair aim; but the strap caught in its flight on the outstanding point of an antler fixed in the wall, and the bag, with its terrible burden, remained suspended just above the alcove where tea would presently be laid. At that moment Mrs. Hoopington and the Major entered the hall.

"The Major is going to draw our covers tomorrow," announced the lady, with a certain heavy satisfaction. "Smithers is confident that we'll be able to show him some sport; he swears he's seen a fox in the nut copse three times this week."

"I'm sure I hope so; I hope so," said the Major moodily. "I must break this sequence of blank days. One hears so often that a fox has settled down as a tenant for life in certain covers, and then when you go to turn him out there isn't a trace of him. I'm certain a fox was shot or trapped in Lady Widden's woods the very day before we drew them."

"Major, if any one tried that game on in my woods they'd get short shrift," said Mrs. Hoopington.

Norah found her way mechanically to the tea-table and made her fingers frantically busy in rearranging the parsley round the sandwich dish. On one side of her loomed the morose countenance of the Major, on the other she was conscious of the scared, miserable eyes of Vladimir. And above it all hung *that*. She dared not raise her eyes above the level of the tea-table, and she almost expected to see a spot of accusing vulpine blood drip down and stain the whiteness of the cloth. Her aunt's manner signalled to her the repeated message to "be bright"; for the present she was fully occupied in keeping her teeth from chattering.

"What did you shoot today?" asked Mrs. Hoopington suddenly of the unusually silent Vladimir.

"Nothing—nothing worth speaking of," said the boy.

Norah's heart, which had stood still for a space, made up for lost time with a most disturbing bound.

"I wish you'd find something that was worth speaking about," said the hostess; "every one seems to have lost their tongues."

"When did Smithers last see that fox?" said the Major.

"Yesterday morning; a fine dog-fox, with a dark brush," confided Mrs. Hoopington.

"Aha, we'll have a good gallop after that brush tomorrow," said the Major, with a transient gleam of good humour. And then gloomy silence settled again round the tea-table, a silence broken only by despondent munchings and the occasional feverish rattle of a teaspoon in its saucer. A diversion was at last afforded by Mrs. Hoopington's fox-terrier, which had jumped on to a vacant chair, the better to survey the delicacies of the table, and was now sniffing in an upward direction at something apparently more interesting than cold tea-cake.

"What is exciting him?" asked his mistress, as the dog suddenly broke into short, angry barks, with a running accompaniment of tremulous whines.

"Why," she continued, "it's your game-bag, Vladimir! What *have* you got in it?"

"By Gad," said the Major, who was now standing up; "there's a pretty warm scent!"

And then a simultaneous idea flashed on himself and Mrs. Hoopington. Their faces flushed to distinct but harmonious tones of purple, and with one accusing voice they screamed, "You've shot the fox!"

Norah tried hastily to palliate Vladimir's misdeed in their eyes, but it is doubtful whether they heard her. The Major's fury clothed and reclothed itself in words as frantically as a woman up in town for one day's shopping tries on a succession of garments. He reviled and railed at fate and the general scheme of things, he pitied himself with a strong, deep pity too poignant for tears, he condemned every one with whom he had ever come in contact to endless and abnormal punishments. In fact, he conveyed the impression that if a destroying angel had been lent to him for a week it would have had very little time for private study. In the lulls of his outcry could be heard the querulous monotone of Mrs. Hoopington and the sharp staccato barking of the fox-terrier. Vladimir, who did not understand a tithe of what was being said, sat fondling a cigarette and repeating under his breath from time to time a vigorous English adjective which he had long ago taken affectionately into his vocabulary. His mind strayed back to the youth in the old Russian folk-tale who shot an enchanted bird with dramatic results. Meanwhile, the Major, roaming round the hall like an imprisoned cyclone, had caught sight of and joyfully pounced on the telephone apparatus, and lost no time in ringing up the hunt secretary and announcing his resignation of the Mastership. A servant had by this time brought his horse round to the door, and in a few seconds Mrs. Hoopington's shrill monotone had the field to itself. But after the Major's display her best efforts at vocal violence missed their full effect; it was as though one had come straight out from a Wagner opera into a rather tame thunderstorm. Realizing, perhaps, that her tirades were something of an anticlimax, Mrs. Hoopington broke suddenly into some rather necessary tears and marched out of the room, leaving behind her a silence almost as terrible as the turmoil which had preceded it.

"What shall I do with—*that?*" asked Vladimir at last.

"Bury it," said Norah.

"Just plain burial?" said Vladimir, rather relieved. He had almost expected that some of the local clergy would have insisted on being present, or that a salute might have to be fired over the grave.

And thus it came to pass that in the dusk of a November evening the Russian boy, murmuring a few of the prayers of his Church for luck, gave hasty but decent burial to a large polecat under the lilac trees at Hoopington.

THE STRATEGIST

M RS. JALLATT'S young people's parties were severely exclusive; it came cheaper that way, because you could ask fewer to them. Mrs. Jallatt didn't study cheapness, but somehow she generally attained it.

"There'll be about ten girls," speculated Rollo, as he drove to the function, "and I suppose four fellows, unless the Wrotsleys bring their cousin, which Heaven forbid. That would mean Jack and me against three of them."

Rollo and the Wrotsley brethren had maintained an undying feud almost from nursery days. They only met now and then in the holidays, and the meeting was usually tragic for whichever happened to have the fewest backers on hand. Rollo was counting tonight on the presence of a devoted and muscular partisan to hold an even balance. As he arrived he heard his prospective champion's sister apologizing to the hostess for the unavoidable absence of her brother; a moment later he noted that the Wrotsleys *had* brought their cousin.

Two against three would have been exciting and possibly unpleasant; one against three promised to be about as amusing as a visit to a dentist. Rollo ordered his carriage for as early as was decently possible, and faced the company with a smile that he imagined the better sort of aristocrat would have worn when mounting to the guillotine.

"So glad you were able to come," said the elder Wrotsley heartily.

"Now, you children will like to play games, I suppose," said Mrs. Jallatt, by way of giving things a start, and as they were too well-bred to contradict her there only remained the question of what they were to play at.

"I know of a good game," said the elder Wrotsley innocently. "The fellows leave the room and think of a word; then they come back again, and the girls have to find out what the word is."

Rollo knew that game. He would have suggested it himself if his faction had been in the majority.

"It doesn't promise to be very exciting," sniffed the superior Dolores Sneep as the boys filed out of the room. Rollo thought differently. He trusted to Providence that Wrotsley had nothing worse than knotted handkerchiefs at his disposal.

The word-choosers locked themselves in the library to ensure that their deliberations should not be interrupted. Providence turned out to be not even decently neutral; on a rack on the library wall were a dog-whip and a whalebone riding switch. Rollo thought it criminal negligence to leave such weapons of precision lying about. He was given a choice of evils, and chose the dog-whip; the next minute or so he spent in wondering how he could have made such a stupid selection. Then they went back to the languidly expectant females.

"The word's 'camel,'" announced the Wrotsley cousin blunderingly.

"You stupid!" screamed the girls, "we've got to *guess* the word. Now you'll have to go back and think of another."

"Not for worlds," said Rollo; "I mean, the word isn't really camel; we were rotting. Pretend it's dromedary!" he whispered to the others.

"I heard them say 'dromedary'! I heard them. I don't care what you say; I heard them," squealed the odious Dolores. "With ears as long as hers one would hear anything," thought Rollo savagely.

"We shall have to go back, I suppose," said the elder Wrotsley resignedly.

The conclave locked itself once more into the library. "Look here, I'm not going through that dog-whip business again," protested Rollo.

"Certainly not, dear," said the elder Wrotsley; "we'll try the whalebone switch this time, and then you'll know which hurts most. It's only by personal experience that one finds out these things."

It was swiftly borne in upon Rollo that his earlier selection of the dog-whip had been a really sound one. The conclave gave his under-lip time to steady itself while it debated the choice of the necessary word. "Mustang" was no good, as half the girls wouldn't know what it meant; finally "quagga" was pitched on.

"You must come and sit down over here," chorused the investigating committee on their return; but Rollo was obdurate in insisting that the questioned person always stood up. On the whole, it was a relief when the game was ended and supper was announced.

Mrs. Jallatt did not stint her young guests, but the more expensive delicacies of her supper-table were never unnecessarily duplicated, and it was usually good policy to take what you wanted while it was still there. On this occasion she had provided sixteen peaches to "go round" among fourteen children; it was really not her fault that the two Wrotsleys and their cousin, foreseeing the long foodless drive home, had each quietly pocketed an extra peach, but it was distinctly trying for Dolores and the fat and good-natured Agnes Blaik to be left with one peach between them.

"I suppose we had better halve it," said Dolores sourly.

But Agnes was fat first and good-natured afterwards; those were her guiding principles in life. She was profuse in her sympathy for Dolores, but she hastily devoured the peach, explaining that it would spoil it to divide it; the juice ran out so.

"Now what would you all like to do?" demanded Mrs. Jallatt by way of a diversion. "The professional conjurer whom I had engaged has failed me at the last moment. Can any of you recite?"

There were symptoms of a general panic. Dolores was known to recite "Locksley Hall" on the least provocation. There had been occasions when her opening line, "Comrades, leave me here a little," had been taken as a literal injunction by a large section of her hearers. There was a murmur of relief when Rollo hastily declared that he could do a few conjuring tricks. He had never done one in his life, but those two visits to the library had goaded him to unusual recklessness.

"You've seen conjuring chaps take coins and cards out of people," he announced; "well, I'm going to take more interesting things out of some of you. Mice, for instance."

"Not mice!"

A shrill protest rose, as he had foreseen, from the majority of his audience.

"Well, fruit, then."

The amended proposal was received with approval. Agnes positively beamed.

Without more ado Rollo made straight for his trio of enemies, plunged his hand successively into their breast-pockets, and produced three peaches. There was no applause, but no amount of hand-clapping would have given the performer as much pleasure as the silence which greeted his coup.

"Of course, we were in the know," said the Wrotsley cousin lamely.

"That's done it," chuckled Rollo to himself.

"If they *had* been confederates they would have sworn they knew nothing about it," said Dolores, with piercing conviction.

"Do you know any more tricks?" asked Mrs. Jallatt hurriedly.

Rollo did not. He hinted that he might have changed the three peaches into something else, but Agnes had already converted one into girl-food, so nothing more could be done in that direction.

"I know a game," said the elder Wrotsley heavily, "where the fellows go out of the room, and think of some character in history; then they come back and act him, and the girls have to guess who it's meant for."

"I'm afraid I must be going," said Rollo to his hostess.

"Your carriage won't be here for another twenty minutes," said Mrs. Jallatt.

"It's such a fine evening I think I'll walk and meet it."

"It's raining rather steadily at present. You've just time to play that historical game."

"We haven't heard Dolores recite," said Rollo desperately; as soon as he had said it he realized his mistake. Confronted with the alternative of "Locksley Hall," public opinion declared unanimously for the history game.

Rollo played his last card. In an undertone meant apparently for the Wrotsley boy, but carefully pitched to reach Agnes, he observed:

"All right, old man; we'll go and finish those chocolates we left in the library."

"I think it's only fair that the girls should take their turn in going out," exclaimed Agnes briskly. She was great on fairness.

"Nonsense," said the others; "there are too many of us."

"Well, four of us can go. I'll be one of them."

And Agnes darted off towards the library, followed by three less eager damsels.

Rollo sank into a chair and smiled ever so faintly at the Wrotsleys, just a momentary baring of the teeth; an otter, escaping from the fangs of the hounds into the safety of a deep pool, might have given a similar demonstration of its feelings.

From the library came the sound of moving furniture. Agnes was leaving nothing unturned in her quest for the mythical chocolates. And then came a more blessed sound, wheels crunching wet gravel.

"It has been a most enjoyable evening," said Rollo to his hostess.

CROSS CURRENTS

VANESSA PENNINGTON had a husband who was poor, with few extenuating circumstances, and an admirer who, though comfortably rich, was cumbered with a sense of honour. His wealth made him welcome in Vanessa's eyes, but his code of what was right impelled him to go away and forget her, or at the most to think of her in the intervals of doing a great many other things. And although Alaric Clyde loved Vanessa, and thought he should always go on loving her, he gradually and unconsciously allowed himself to be wooed and won by a more alluring mistress; he fancied that his continued shunning of the haunts of men was a self-imposed exile, but his heart was caught in the spell of the

Wilderness, and the Wilderness was kind and beautiful to him. When one is young and strong and unfettered the wild earth can be very kind and very beautiful. Witness the legion of men who were once young and unfettered and now eat out their souls in dustbins, because, having erstwhile known and loved the Wilderness, they broke from her thrall and turned aside into beaten paths.

In the high waste places of the world Clyde roamed and hunted and dreamed, death-dealing and gracious as some god of Hellas, moving with his horses and servants and four-footed camp followers from one dwelling ground to another, a welcome guest among wild primitive village folk and nomads, a friend and slayer of the fleet, shy beasts around him. By the shores of misty upland lakes he shot the wild fowl that had winged their way to him across half the old world; beyond Bokhara he watched the wild Aryan horsemen at their gambols; watched, too, in some dim-lit tea-house one of those beautiful uncouth dances that one can never wholly forget; or, making a wide cast down to the valley of the Tigris, swam and rolled in its snow-cooled racing waters. Vanessa, meanwhile, in a Bayswater back street, was making out the weekly laundry list, attending bargain sales, and, in her more adventurous moments, trying new ways of cooking whiting. Occasionally she went to bridge parties, where, if the play was not illuminating, at least one learned a great deal about the private life of some of the Royal and Imperial Houses. Vanessa, in a way, was glad that Clyde had done the proper thing. She had a strong natural bias towards respectability, though she would have preferred to have been respectable in smarter surroundings, where her example would have done more good. To be beyond reproach was one thing, but it would have been nicer to have been nearer to the Park.

And then of a sudden her regard for respectability and Clyde's sense of what was right were thrown on the scrap-heap of unnecessary things. They had been useful and highly important in their time, but the death of Vanessa's husband made them of no immediate moment.

The news of the altered condition of things followed Clyde

with leisurely persistence from one place of call to another, and at last ran him to a standstill somewhere in the Orenburg Steppe. He would have found it exceedingly difficult to analyze his feelings on receipt of the tidings. The Fates had unexpectedly (and perhaps just a little officiously) removed an obstacle from his path. He supposed he was overjoyed, but he missed the feeling of elation which he had experienced some four months ago when he had bagged a snow-leopard with a lucky shot after a day's fruitless stalking. Of course he would go back and ask Vanessa to marry him, but he was determined on enforcing a condition: on no account would he desert his newer love. Vanessa would have to agree to come out into the Wilderness with him.

The lady hailed the return of her lover with even more relief than had been occasioned by his departure. The death of John Pennington had left his widow in circumstances which were more straitened than ever, and the Park had receded even from her notepaper, where it had long been retained as a courtesy title on the principle that addresses are given to us to conceal our whereabouts. Certainly she was more independent now than heretofore, but independence, which means so much to many women, was of little account to Vanessa, who came under the heading of the mere female. She made little ado about accepting Clyde's condition, and announced herself ready to follow him to the end of the world; as the world was round she nourished a complacent idea that in the ordinary course of things one would find oneself in the neighbourhood of Hyde Park Corner sooner or later no matter how far afield one wandered.

East of Budapest her complacency began to filter away, and when she saw her husband treating the Black Sea with a familiarity which she had never been able to assume towards the English Channel, misgivings began to crowd in upon her. Adventures which would have presented an amusing and enticing aspect to a better-bred woman aroused in Vanessa only the twin sensations of fright and discomfort. Flies bit her, and she was persuaded that it was only sheer boredom that prevented camels from doing the same. Clyde did his best, and a very good best it was, to infuse something of the banquet into their prolonged desert picnics, but even snow-cooled Heidsieck lost its flavour when you were convinced that the dusky cupbearer who served it with such reverent elegance was only waiting a convenient opportunity to cut your throat. It was useless for Clyde to give Yussuf a character for devotion such as is rarely found in any Western servant. Vanessa was well enough educated to know that all dusky-skinned people take human life as unconcernedly as Bayswater folk take singing lessons.

And with a growing irritation and querulousness on her part came a further disenchantment, born of the inability of husband and wife to find a common ground of interest. The habits and migrations of the sand grouse, the folklore and customs of Tartars and Turkomans, the points of a Cossack pony—these were matters which evoked only a bored indifference in Vanessa. On the other hand, Clyde was not thrilled on being informed that the Queen of Spain detested mauve, or that a certain Royal duchess, for whose tastes he was never likely to be called on to cater, nursed a violent but perfectly respectable passion for beef olives.

Vanessa began to arrive at the conclusion that a husband who added a roving disposition to a settled income was a mixed blessing. It was one thing to go to the end of the world; it was quite another thing to make oneself at home there. Even respectability seemed to lose some of its virtue when one practised it in a tent.

Bored and disillusioned with the drift of her new life, Vanessa was undisguisedly glad when distraction offered itself in the person of Mr. Dobrinton, a chance acquaintance whom they had first run against in the primitive hostelry of a benighted Caucasian town. Dobrinton was elaborately British, in deference perhaps to the memory of his mother, who was said to have derived part of her origin from an English governess who had come to Lemberg a long way back in the last century. If you had called him Dobrinski when off his guard he would probably have responded readily enough; holding, no doubt, that the end crowns all, he had taken a slight liberty with the family patronymic. To look at, Mr. Dobrinton was not a very attractive specimen of masculine humanity, but in Vanessa's eyes he was a link with that civilization which Clyde seemed so ready to ignore and forgo. He could sing "Yip-I-Addy" and spoke of several duchesses as if he knew them—in his more inspired moments almost as if they knew him. He even pointed out blemishes in the cuisine or cellar departments of some of the more august London restaurants, a species of Higher Criticism which was listened to by Vanessa in awe-stricken admiration. And, above all, he sympathized, at first discreetly, afterwards with more latitude, with her fretful discontent at Clyde's nomadic instincts. Business connected with oil-wells had brought Dobrinton to the neighbourhood of Baku; the pleasure of appealing to an appreciative female audience induced him to deflect his return journey so as to coincide a good deal with his new acquaintances' line of march. And while Clyde trafficked with Persian horse-dealers or hunted the wild grey pigs in their lairs and added to his notes on Central Asian game-fowl, Dobrinton and the lady discussed the ethics of desert respectability from points of view that showed a daily tendency to converge. And one evening Clyde dined alone, reading between the courses a long letter from Vanessa, justifying her action in flitting to more civilized lands with a more congenial companion.

It was distinctly evil luck for Vanessa, who really was thoroughly respectable at heart, that she and her lover should run into the hands of Kurdish brigands on the first day of their flight. To be mewed up in a squalid Kurdish village in close companionship with a man who was only your husband by adoption, and to have the attention of all Europe drawn to your plight, was about the least respectable thing that could happen. And there were international complications, which made things worse. "English lady and her husband, of foreign nationality, held by Kurdish brigands who demand ransom" had been the report of the nearest Consul. Although Dobrinton was British at heart, the other portions of him belonged to the Habsburgs, and though the Habsburgs took no great pride or pleasure in this particular unit of their wide and varied possessions, and would gladly have exchanged him for some interesting bird or mammal for the Schoenbrunn Park, the code of international dignity demanded that they should display a decent solicitude for his restoration. And while the Foreign Offices of the two countries were taking the usual steps to secure the release of their respective subjects a further horrible complication ensued. Clyde, following on the track of the fugitives, not with any special desire to overtake them, but with a dim feeling that it was expected of him, fell into the hands of the same community of brigands. Diplomacy, while anxious to do its best for a lady in misfortune, showed signs of becoming restive at this expansion of its task; as a frivolous young gentleman in Downing Street remarked, "Any husband of Mrs. Dobrinton's we shall be glad to extricate, but let us know how many there are of them." For a woman who valued respectability Vanessa really had no luck.

Meanwhile the situation of the captives was not free from embarrassment. When Clyde explained to the Kurdish headmen the nature of his relationship with the runaway couple they were gravely sympathetic, but vetoed any idea of summary vengeance, since the Habsburgs would be sure to insist on the delivery of Dobrinton alive, and in a reasonably undamaged condition. They did not object to Clyde administering a beating to his rival for half an hour every Monday and Thursday, but Dobrinton turned such a sickly green when he heard of this arrangement that the chief was obliged to withdraw the concession.

And so, in the cramped quarters of a mountain hut, the ill-assorted trio watched the insufferable hours crawl slowly by. Dobrinton was too frightened to be conversational, Vanessa was too mortified to open her lips, and Clyde was moodily silent. The little Lemberg *négociant* plucked up heart once to give a quavering rendering of "Yip-I-Addy," but when he reached the statement "home was never like this" Vanessa tearfully begged him to stop. And silence fastened itself with growing insistence on the three captives who were so tragically herded together; thrice a day they drew near to one another swallow the meal that had been prepared for them, like desert beasts meeting in mute suspended hostility at the drinking-pool, and then drew back to resume the vigil of waiting.

Clyde was less carefully watched than the others. "Jealousy will keep him to the woman's side," thought his Kurdish captors. They did not know that his wilder, truer love was calling to him with a hundred voices from beyond the village bounds. And one evening, finding that he was not getting the attention to which he was entitled, Clyde slipped away down the mountain side and resumed his study of Central Asian game-fowl. The remaining captives were guarded henceforth with greater rigour, but Dobrinton at any rate scarcely regretted Clyde's departure.

The long arm, or perhaps one might better say the long purse, of diplomacy at last effected the release of the prisoners, but the Habsburgs were never to enjoy the guerdon of their outlay. On the quay of the little Black Sea Port, where the rescued pair came once more into contact with civilization, Dobrinton was bitten by a dog which was assumed to be mad, though it may only have been indiscriminating. The victim did not wait for symptoms of rabies to declare themselves, but died forthwith of fright, and Vanessa made the homeward journey alone, conscious somehow of a sense of slightly restored respectability. Clyde, in the intervals of correcting the proofs of his book on the game-fowl of Central Asia, found time to press a divorce suit through the Courts, and as soon as possible hied him away to the congenial solitudes of the Gobi Desert to collect material for a work on the fauna of that region. Vanessa, by virtue perhaps of her earlier intimacy with the cooking rites of the whiting, obtained a place on the kitchen staff of a West End Club. It was not brilliant, but at least it was within two minutes of the Park.

THE BAKER'S DOZEN

Characters:

MAJOR RICHARD DUMBARTON
MRS. CAREWE
MRS. PALY-PAGET

Scene—Deck of eastward-bound steamer. Major Dumbarton seated on deck-chair, another chair by his side, with the name "Mrs. Carewe" painted on it, a third near by.

(Enter, R., Mrs. Carewe, seats herself leisurely in her deck-chair, the Major affecting to ignore her presence.)

Major (turning suddenly): Emily! After all these years! This is fate!

Em.: Fate! Nothing of the sort; it's only me. You men are always such fatalists. I deferred my departure three whole weeks, in order to come out in the same boat that I saw you were travelling by. I bribed the steward to put our chairs side by side in an unfrequented corner, and I took enormous pains to be looking particularly attractive this morning, and then you say, "This is fate." I *am* looking particularly attractive, am I not?

Maj.: More than ever. Time has only added a ripeness to your charms.

Em.: I knew you'd put it exactly in those words. The phraseology of love-making is awfully limited, isn't it? After all, the chief charm is in the fact of being made love to. You *are* making love to me, aren't you?

Maj.: Emily dearest, I had already begun making advances, even before you sat down here. I also bribed the steward to put our seats together in a secluded corner. "You may consider it done, sir," was his reply. That was immediately after breakfast.

Em.: How like a man to have his breakfast first. I attended to the seat business as soon as I left my cabin.

Maj.: Don't be unreasonable. It was only at breakfast that I discovered your blessed presence on the boat. I paid violent and unusual attention to a flapper all through the meal in order to make you jealous. She's probably in her cabin writing reams about me to a fellow-flapper at this very moment.

Em.: You needn't have taken all that trouble to make me jealous, Dickie. You did that years ago, when you married another woman.

Maj.: Well, you had gone and married another man—a widower, too, at that.

Em.: Well, there's no particular harm in marrying a widower, I suppose. I'm ready to do it again, if I meet a really nice one.

Maj.: Look here, Emily, it's not fair to go at that rate. You're a lap ahead of me the whole time. It's my place to propose to you; all you've got to do is to say "Yes."

Em.: Well, I've practically said it already, so we needn't dawdle over that part.

Maj.: Oh, well—

(They look at each other, then suddenly embrace with considerable energy.)

Maj.: We dead-heated it that time. (Suddenly jumping to his feet.) Oh, d—— I'd forgotten!

Em.: Forgotten what?

Maj.: The children. I ought to have told you. Do you mind children?

Em.: Not in moderate quantities. How many have you got?

Maj. (counting hurriedly on his fingers): Five.

Em.: Five!

Maj. (anxiously): Is that too many?

Em.: It's rather a number. The worst of it is, I've some myself.

Maj.: Many?

Em.: Eight.

Maj.: Eight in six years! Oh, Emily!

Em.: Only four were my own. The other four were by my husband's first marriage. Still, that practically makes eight.

Maj.: And eight and five make thirteen. We can't start our married life with thirteen children; it would be most unlucky. (Walks up and down in agitation.) Some way must

be found out of this. If we could only bring them down te
twelve. Thirteen is so horribly unlucky.

Em.: Isn't there some way by which we could part with
one or two? Don't the French want more children? I've often
seen articles about it in the *Figaro*.

Maj.: I fancy they want French children. Mine don't even
speak French.

Em.: There's always a chance that one of them might turn
out depraved and vicious, and then you could disown him.
I've heard of that being done.

Maj.: But, good gracious, you've got to educate him first.
You can't expect a boy to be vicious till he's been to a good
school.

Em.: Why couldn't he be naturally depraved? Lots of boys
are.

Maj.: Only when they inherit it from depraved parents.
You don't suppose there's any depravity in me, do you?

Em.: It sometimes skips a generation, you know. Weren't
any of your family bad?

Maj.: There was an aunt who was never spoken of.

Em.: There you are!

Maj.: But one can't build too much on that. In mid-Vic-
torian days they labelled all sorts of things as unspeakable that
we should speak about quite tolerantly. I daresay this particular aunt had only married a Unitarian, or rode to hounds
on both sides of her horse, or something of that sort. Anyhow, we can't wait indefinitely for one of the children to
take after a doubtfully depraved great aunt. Something else
must be thought of.

Em.: Don't people ever adopt children from other families?

Maj.: I've heard of it being done by childless couples, and
those sort of people—

Em.: Hush! Some one's coming. Who is it?

Maj.: Mrs. Paly-Paget.

Em.: The very person!

Maj.: What, to adopt a child? Hasn't she got any?

Em.: Only one miserable hen-baby.

Maj.: Let's sound her on the subject.

(*Enter* Mrs. Paly-Paget, R.)

Ah, good morning, Mrs. Paly-Paget. I was just wondering at breakfast where did we meet last?

Mrs. P.-P.: At the Criterion, wasn't it? (*Drops into vacant chair.*)

Maj.: At the Criterion, of course.

Mrs. P.-P.: I was dining with Lord and Lady Slugford. Charming people, but so mean. They took us afterwards to the Velodrome, to see some dancer interpreting Mendelssohn's "songs without clothes." We were all packed up in a little box near the roof, and you may imagine how hot it was. It was like a Turkish bath. And, of course, one couldn't see anything.

Maj.: Then it was not like a Turkish bath.

Mrs. P.-P.: Major!

Em.: We were just talking of you when you joined us.

Mrs. P.-P.: Really! Nothing very dreadful, I hope.

Em.: Oh, dear, no! It's too early on the voyage for that sort of thing. We were feeling rather sorry for you.

Mrs. P.-P.: Sorry for me? Whatever for?

Maj.: Your childless hearth and all that, you know. No little pattering feet.

Mrs. P.-P.: Major! How dare you? I've got my little girl, I suppose you know. Her feet can patter as well as other children's.

Maj.: Only one pair of feet.

Mrs. P.-P.: Certainly. My child isn't a centipede. Considering the way they move us about in those horrid jungle stations, without a decent bungalow to set one's foot in, I consider I've got a hearthless child, rather than a childless hearth. Thank you for your sympathy all the same. I daresay it was well meant. Impertinence often is.

Em.: Dear Mrs. Paly-Paget, we were only feeling sorry for your sweet little girl when she grows older, you know. No little brothers and sisters to play with.

Mrs. P.-P.: Mrs. Carewe, this conversation strikes me as being indelicate, to say the least of it. I've only been married two and a half years, and my family is naturally a small one.

Maj.: Isn't it rather an exaggeration to talk of one little female child as a family? A family suggests numbers.

Mrs. P.-P.: Really, Major, your language is extraordinary. I daresay I've only got a little female child, as you call it, at present—

Maj.: Oh, it won't change into a boy later on, if that's what you're counting on. Take our word for it; we've had so much more experience in these affairs than you have. Once a female, always a female. Nature is not infallible, but she always abides by her mistakes.

Mrs. P.-P. (rising): Major Dumbarton, these boats are uncomfortably small, but I trust we shall find ample accommodation for avoiding each other's society during the rest of the voyage. The same wish applies to you, Mrs. Carewe.

(Exit Mrs. Paly-Paget, L.)

Maj.: What an unnatural mother! (Sinks into chair.)

Em.: I wouldn't trust a child with any one who had a temper like hers. Oh, Dickie, why did you go and have such a large family? You always said you wanted me to be the mother of your children.

Maj.: I wasn't going to wait while you were founding and fostering dynasties in other directions. Why you couldn't be content to have children of your own, without collecting them like batches of postage stamps I can't think. The idea of marrying a man with four children!

Em.: Well, you're asking me to marry one with five.

Maj.: Five! (Springing to his feet.) Did I say five?

Em.: You certainly said five.

Maj.: Oh, Emily, supposing I've miscounted them! Listen now, keep count with me. Richard—that's after me, of course.

Em.: One.

Maj.: Albert-Victor—that must have been in Coronation year.

Em.: Two!

Maj.: Maud. She's called after—

Em.: Never mind who she's called after. Three!

Maj.: And Gerald.

Em.: Four!

Maj.: That's the lot.

Em.: Are you sure?

Maj.: I swear that's the lot. I must have counted Albert-Victor as two.

Em.: Richard!

Maj.: Emily!

(They embrace.)

THE MOUSE

THEODORIC VOLER had been brought up, from infancy to the confines of middle age, by a fond mother whose chief solicitude had been to keep him screened from what she called the coarser realities of life. When she died she left Theodoric alone in a world that was as real as ever, and a good deal coarser than he considered it had any need to be. To a man of his temperament and upbringing even a simple railway journey was crammed with petty annoyances and minor discords, and as he settled himself down in a second-class compartment one September morning he was conscious of ruffled feelings and general mental discomposure. He had been staying at a country vicarage, the inmates of which had been certainly neither brutal nor bacchanalian, but their supervision of the domestic establishment had been of that lax order which invites disaster. The pony carriage that was to take him to the station had never been properly ordered, and when the moment for his departure drew near the handyman who should have produced the required article was nowhere to be found. In this emergency Theodoric, to his mute but very intense disgust, found himself obliged to collaborate with the vicar's daughter in the task of harnessing the pony, which necessitated groping about in an ill-lighted outhouse called a stable, and smelling very like one—except in patches where it smelt of mice. Without being actually afraid of mice, Theodoric classed them among the coarser incidents of life, and considered that Providence, with a little exercise of moral courage, might long ago have recognized that they were not indispensable, and have withdrawn them from circulation. As the train glided out of the station Theodoric's nervous imagination accused himself of exhaling a weak odour of stable-yard, and possibly of displaying a mouldy straw or two on his usually well-brushed garments. Fortunately the only other occupant of the compartment, a lady of about the same age as himself, seemed inclined for slumber rather than scrutiny; the train was not due to stop till the terminus was reached, in about an hour's time, and the carriage was of the old-fashioned sort, that held no communication with a corridor, therefore no further travelling companions were likely to intrude on Theodoric's semi-privacy. And yet the train had scarcely attained its normal speed before he became reluctantly but vividly aware that he was not alone with the slumbering lady; he was not even alone in his own clothes. A warm, creeping movement over his flesh betrayed the unwelcome and highly resented presence, unseen but poignant, of a strayed mouse, that had evidently dashed into its present retreat during the episode of the pony harnessing. Furtive stamps and shakes and wildly directed pinches failed to dislodge the intruder, whose motto, indeed, seemed to be Excelsior; and the lawful occupant of the clothes lay back against the cushions and endeavoured rapidly to evolve some means for putting an end to the dual ownership. It was unthinkable that he should continue for the space of a whole hour in the horrible position of a Rowton House for vagrant mice (already his imagination had at least doubled the numbers of the alien invasion). On the other hand, nothing less drastic than partial disrobing would ease him of his tormentor, and to undress in the presence of a lady, even for so laudable a purpose, was an idea that made his eartips tingle in a blush of abject shame. He had never been able to bring himself even to the mild exposure of open-work socks in the presence of the fair sex. And yet —the lady in this case was to all appearances soundly and securely asleep; the mouse, on the other hand, seemed to be trying to crowd a Wanderjahr into a few strenuous minutes. If there is any truth in the theory of transmigration, this particular mouse must certainly have been in a former state a member of the Alpine Club. Sometimes in its eagerness it lost its footing and slipped for half an inch or so; and then, in fright, or more probably temper, it bit. Theodoric was goaded into the most audacious undertaking of his life. Crimsoning to the hue of a beetroot and keeping an agonized watch on his slumbering fellow-traveller, he swiftly and noiselessly secured the ends of his railway-rug to the racks on either side of the carriage, so that a substantial curtain hung athwart the compartment. In the narrow dressing-room that he had thus improvised he proceeded with violent haste to extricate himself partially and the mouse entirely from the surrounding casings of tweed and half-wool. As the unravelled mouse gave a wild leap to the floor, the rug, slipping its fastening at either end, also came down with a heart-curdling flop, and almost simultaneously the awakened sleeper opened her eyes. With a movement almost quicker than the mouse's, Theodoric pounced on the rug, and hauled its ample folds chin-high over his dismantled person as he collapsed into the further corner of the carriage. The blood raced and beat in the veins of his neck and forehead, while he waited dumbly for the communication-cord to be pulled. The lady, however, contented herself with a silent stare at her strangely muffled companion. How much had she seen, Theodoric queried to himself, and in any case what on earth must she think of his present posture?

"I think I have caught a chill," he ventured desperately.

"Really, I'm sorry," she replied. "I was just going to ask you if you would open this window."

"I fancy it's malaria," he added, his teeth chattering slightly, as much from fright as from a desire to support his theory.

"I've got some brandy in my hold-all, if you'll kindly reach it down for me," said his companion.

"Not for worlds—I mean, I never take anything for it," he assured her earnestly.

"I suppose you caught it in the Tropics?"

Theodoric, whose acquaintance with the Tropics was limited

to an annual present of a chest of tea from an uncle in Ceylon, felt that even the malaria was slipping from him. Would it be possible, he wondered, to disclose the real state of affairs to her in small instalments?

"Are you afraid of mice?" he ventured, growing, if possible, more scarlet in the face.

"Not unless they came in quantities, like those that ate up Bishop Hatto. Why do you ask?"

"I had one crawling inside my clothes just now," said Theodoric in a voice that hardly seemed his own. "It was a most awkward situation."

"It must have been, if you wear your clothes at all tight," she observed; "but mice have strange ideas of comfort."

"I had to get rid of it while you were asleep," he continued; then, with a gulp, he added, "it was getting rid of it that brought me to—to this."

"Surely leaving off one small mouse wouldn't bring on a chill," she exclaimed, with a levity that Theodoric accounted abominable.

Evidently she had detected something of his predicament, and was enjoying his confusion. All the blood in his body seemed to have mobilized in one concentrated blush, and an agony of abasement, worse than a myriad mice, crept up and down over his soul. And then, as reflection began to assert itself, sheer terror took the place of humiliation. With every minute that passed the train was rushing nearer to the crowded and bustling terminus where dozens of prying eyes would be exchanged for the one paralyzing pair that watched him from the further corner of the carriage. There was one slender despairing chance, which the next few minutes must decide. His fellow-traveller might relapse into a blessed slumber. But as the minutes throbbed by that chance ebbed away. The furtive glance which Theodoric stole at her from time to time disclosed only an unwinking wakefulness.

"I think we must be getting near now," she presently observed.

Theodoric had already noted with growing terror the recurring stacks of small, ugly dwellings that heralded the journey's end. The words acted as a signal. Like a hunted beast breaking cover and dashing madly towards some other haven of momentary safety he threw aside his rug, and struggled frantically into his dishevelled garments. He was conscious of dull suburban stations racing past the window, of a choking, hammering sensation in his throat and heart, and of an icy silence in that corner towards which he dared not look. Then as he sank back in his seat, clothed and almost delirious, the train slowed down to a final crawl, and the woman spoke.

"Would you be so kind," she asked, "as to get me a porter to put me into a cab? It's a shame to trouble you when you're feeling unwell, but being blind makes one so helpless at a railway station."

The Chronicles of Clovis

First Collected, 1911

TO THE LYNX KITTEN,
WITH HIS RELUCTANTLY GIVEN CONSENT,
THIS BOOK IS AFFECTIONATELY
DEDICATED

H. H. M.
August, 1911

"THE Background" originally appeared in the *Leinsters' Magazine;* "The Stampeding of Lady Bastable" in the *Daily Mail;* "Mrs. Packletide's Tiger," "The Chaplet," "The Peace Offering," "Filboid Studge" and "Ministers of Grace" (in an abbreviated form) in the *Bystander;* and the remainder of the stories (with the exception of "The Music on the Hill," "The Story of St. Vespaluus," "The Secret Sin of Septimus Brope," "The Remoulding of Groby Lington," and "The Way to the Dairy," which have never previously been published) in the *Westminster Gazette.* To the Editors of these papers I am indebted for courteous permission to reprint them.

H. H. M.

ESMÉ

"ALL hunting stories are the same," said Clovis; "just as all Turf stories are the same, and all—"

"My hunting story isn't a bit like any you've ever heard," said the Baroness. "It happened quite a while ago, when I was about twenty-three. I wasn't living apart from my husband then; you see, neither of us could afford to make the other a separate allowance. In spite of everything that proverbs may say, poverty keeps together more homes than it breaks up. But we always hunted with different packs. All this has nothing to do with the story."

"We haven't arrived at the meet yet. I suppose there was a meet," said Clovis.

"Of course there was a meet," said the Baroness; "all the usual crowd were there, especially Constance Broddle. Constance is one of those strapping florid girls that go so well with autumn scenery or Christmas decorations in church. 'I feel a presentiment that something dreadful is going to happen,' she said to me; 'am I looking pale?'

"She was looking about as pale as a beetroot that has suddenly heard bad news.

"'You're looking nicer than usual,' I said, 'but that's so easy for you.' Before she had got the right bearings of this remark we had settled down to business; hounds had found a fox lying out in some gorse-bushes."

"I knew it," said Clovis; "in every fox-hunting story that I've ever heard there's been a fox and some gorse-bushes."

"Constance and I were well mounted," continued the Baroness serenely, "and we had no difficulty in keeping ourselves in the first flight, though it was a fairly stiff run. Towards the finish, however, we must have held rather too independent a line, for we lost the hounds, and found ourselves plodding aimlessly along miles away from anywhere. It was fairly exasperating, and my temper was beginning to let itself go by inches, when on pushing our way through an accommodating hedge we were gladdened by the sight of hounds in full cry in a hollow just beneath us.

" 'There they go,' cried Constance, and then added in a gasp, 'In Heaven's name, what are they hunting?'

"It was certainly no mortal fox. It stood more than twice as high, had a short, ugly head, and an enormous thick neck.

" 'It's a hyæna,' I cried; 'it must have escaped from Lord Pabham's Park.'

"At that moment the hunted beast turned and faced its pursuers, and the hounds (there were only about six couple of them) stood round in a half-circle and looked foolish. Evidently they had broken away from the rest of the pack on the trail of this alien scent, and were not quite sure how to treat their quarry now they had got him.

"The hyæna hailed our approach with unmistakable relief and demonstrations of friendliness. It had probably been accustomed to uniform kindness from humans, while its first experience of a pack of hounds had left a bad impression. The hounds looked more than ever embarrassed as their quarry paraded its sudden intimacy with us, and the faint toot of a horn in the distance was seized on as a welcome signal for unobtrusive departure. Constance and I and the hyæna were left alone in the gathering twilight.

" 'What are we to do?' asked Constance.

" 'What a person you are for questions,' I said.

" 'Well, we can't stay here all night with a hyæna,' she retorted.

" 'I don't know what your ideas of comfort are,' I said; 'but I shouldn't think of staying here all night even without a hyæna. My home may be an unhappy one, but at least it has hot and cold water laid on, and domestic service, and other conveniences which we shouldn't find here. We had better make for that ridge of trees to the right; I imagine the Crowley road is just beyond.'

"We trotted off slowly along a faintly marked cart-track, with the beast following cheerfully at our heels.

" 'What on earth are we to do with the hyæna?' came the inevitable question.

" 'What does one generally do with hyænas?' I asked crossly.

" 'I've never had anything to do with one before,' said Constance.

" 'Well, neither have I. If we even knew its sex we might give it a name. Perhaps we might call it Esmé. That would do in either case.'

"There was still sufficient daylight for us to distinguish wayside objects, and our listless spirits gave an upward perk as we came upon a small half-naked gipsy brat picking blackberries from a low-growing bush. The sudden apparition of two horsewomen and a hyæna set it off crying, and in any case we should scarcely have gleaned any useful geographical information from that source; but there was a probability that we might strike a gipsy encampment somewhere along our route. We rode on hopefully but uneventfully for another mile or so.

" 'I wonder what that child was doing there,' said Constance presently.

" 'Picking blackberries. Obviously.'

" 'I don't like the way it cried,' pursued Constance; 'somehow its wail keeps ringing in my ears.'

"I did not chide Constance for her morbid fancies; as a matter of fact the same sensation, of being pursued by a persistent fretful wail, had been forcing itself on my rather overtired nerves. For company's sake I hullooed to Esmé, who had lagged somewhat behind. With a few springy bounds he drew up level, and then shot past us.

"The wailing accompaniment was explained. The gipsy child was firmly, and I expect painfully, held in his jaws.

" 'Merciful Heaven!' screamed Constance, 'what on earth shall we do? What are we to do?'

"I am perfectly certain that at the Last Judgment Constance will ask more questions than any of the examining Seraphs.

" 'Can't we do something?' she persisted tearfully, as Esmé cantered easily along in front of our tired horses.

"Personally I was doing everything that occurred to me at the moment. I stormed and scolded and coaxed in English and French and gamekeeper language; I made absurd, ineffectual cuts in the air with my thongless hunting-crop; I hurled my sandwich case at the brute; in fact, I really don't know what more I could have done. And still we lumbered on through the deepening dusk, with that dark uncouth shape lumbering ahead of us, and a drone of lugubrious music floating in our ears. Suddenly Esmé bounded aside into some thick bushes, where we could not follow; the wail rose to a shriek and then stopped altogether. This part of the story I always hurry over, because it is really rather horrible. When the beast joined us again, after an absence of a few minutes, there was an air of patient understanding about him, as though he knew that he had done something of which we disapproved, but which he felt to be thoroughly justifiable.

" 'How can you let that ravening beast trot by your side?' asked Constance. She was looking more than ever like an albino beetroot.

" 'In the first place, I can't prevent it,' I said; 'and in the second place, whatever else he may be, I doubt if he's ravening at the present moment.'

"Constance shuddered. 'Do you think the poor little thing suffered much?' came another of her futile questions.

" 'The indications were all that way,' I said; 'on the other hand, of course, it may have been crying from sheer temper. Children sometimes do.'

"It was nearly pitch-dark when we emerged suddenly into the high road. A flash of lights and the whir of a motor went past us at the same moment at uncomfortably close quarters. A thud and a sharp screeching yell followed a second later. The car drew up, and when I had ridden back to the spot I found a young man bending over a dark motionless mass lying by the roadside.

" 'You have killed my Esmé,' I exclaimed bitterly.

" 'I'm so awfully sorry,' said the young man; 'I keep dogs myself, so I know what you must feel about it. I'll do anything I can in reparation.'

" 'Please bury him at once,' I said; 'that much I think I may ask of you.'

" 'Bring the spade, William,' he called to the chauffeur. Evidently hasty roadside interments were contingencies that had been provided against.

"The digging of a sufficiently large grave took some little time. 'I say, what a magnificent fellow,' said the motorist as the corpse was rolled over into the trench. 'I'm afraid he must have been rather a valuable animal.'

" 'He took second in the puppy class at Birmingham last year,' I said resolutely.

"Constance snorted loudly.

" 'Don't cry, dear,' I said brokenly; 'it was all over in a moment. He couldn't have suffered much.'

" 'Look here,' said the young fellow desperately, 'you simply must let me do something by way of reparation.'

"I refused sweetly, but as he persisted I let him have my address.

"Of course, we kept our own counsel as to the earlier episodes of the evening. Lord Pabham never advertised the loss of his hyæna; when a strictly fruit-eating animal strayed from his park a year or two previously he was called upon to give compensation in eleven cases of sheep-worrying and practically to re-stock his neighbours' poultry-yards, and an escaped hyæna would have mounted up to something on the scale of a Government grant. The gipsies were equally unobtrusive over their missing offspring; I don't suppose in large encampments they really know to a child or two how many they've got."

The Baroness paused reflectively, and then continued:

"There was a sequel to the adventure, though. I got through the post a charming little diamond brooch, with the name Esmé set in a sprig of rosemary. Incidentally, too, I lost the friendship of Constance Broddle. You see, when I sold the brooch

I quite properly refused to give her any share of the proceeds. I pointed out that the Esmé part of the affair was my own invention, and the hyæna part of it belonged to Lord Pabham, if it really was his hyæna, of which, of course, I've no proof."

THE MATCH-MAKER

THE grill-room clock struck eleven with the respectful unobtrusiveness of one whose mission in life is to be ignored. When the flight of time should really have rendered abstinence and migration imperative the lighting apparatus would signal the fact in the usual way.

Six minutes later Clovis approached the supper-table, in the blessed expectancy of one who has dined sketchily and long ago.

"I'm starving," he announced, making an effort to sit down gracefully and read the menu at the same time.

"So I gathered," said his host, "from the fact that you were nearly punctual. I ought to have told you that I'm a Food Reformer. I've ordered two bowls of bread-and-milk and some health biscuits. I hope you don't mind."

Clovis pretended afterwards that he didn't go white above the collar-line for the fraction of a second.

"All the same," he said, "you ought not to joke about such things. There really are such people. I've known people who've met them. To think of all the adorable things there are to eat in the world, and then to go through life munching sawdust and being proud of it."

"They're like the Flagellants of the Middle Ages, who went about mortifying themselves."

"They had some excuse," said Clovis. "They did it to save their immortal souls, didn't they? You needn't tell me that a man who doesn't love oysters and asparagus and good wines has got a soul, or a stomach either. He's simply got the instinct for being unhappy highly developed."

Clovis relapsed for a few golden moments into tender inmacies with a succession of rapidly disappearing oysters.

"I think oysters are more beautiful than any religion," he resumed presently. "They not only forgive our unkindness to them; they justify it, they incite us to go on being perfectly horrid to them. Once they arrive at the supper-table they seem to enter thoroughly into the spirit of the thing. There's nothing in Christianity or Buddhism that quite matches the sympathetic unselfishness of an oyster. Do you like my new waistcoat? I'm wearing it for the first time tonight."

"It looks like a great many others you've had lately, only worse. New dinner waistcoats are becoming a habit with you."

"They say one always pays for the excesses of one's youth; mercifully that isn't true about one's clothes. My mother is thinking of getting married."

"Again!"

"It's the first time."

"Of course, you ought to know. I was under the impression that she'd been married once or twice at least."

"Three times, to be mathematically exact. I meant that it was the first time she'd thought about getting married; the other times she did it without thinking. As a matter of fact, it's really I who am doing the thinking for her in this case. You see, it's quite two years since her last husband died."

"You evidently think that brevity is the soul of widowhood."

"Well, it struck me that she was getting moped, and beginning to settle down, which wouldn't suit her a bit. The first symptom that I noticed was when she began to complain that we were living beyond our income. All decent people live beyond their incomes nowadays, and those who aren't respectable live beyond other people's. A few gifted individuals manage to do both."

"It's hardly so much a gift as an industry."

"The crisis came," returned Clovis, "when she suddenly started the theory that late hours were bad for one, and wanted me to be in by one o'clock every night. Imagine that sort of thing for me, who was eighteen on my last birthday."

"On your last two birthdays, to be mathematically exact."

"Oh, well, that's not my fault. I'm not going to arrive at nineteen as long as my mother remains at thirty-seven. One must have some regard for appearances."

"Perhaps your mother would age a little in the process of settling down."

"That's the last thing she'd think of. Feminine reformations always start in on the failings of other people. That's why I was so keen on the husband idea."

"Did you go as far as to select the gentleman, or did you merely throw out a general idea, and trust to the force of suggestion?"

"If one wants a thing done in a hurry one must see to it oneself. I found a military Johnny hanging round on a loose end at the club, and took him home to lunch once or twice. He'd spent most of his life on the Indian frontier, building roads, and relieving famines and minimizing earthquakes, and all that sort of thing that one does do on frontiers. He could talk sense to a peevish cobra in fifteen native languages, and probably knew what to do if you found a rogue elephant on your croquet-lawn; but he was shy and diffident with women. I told my mother privately that he was an absolute woman-hater; so, of course, she laid herself out to flirt all she knew, which isn't a little."

"And was the gentleman responsive?"

"I hear he told some one at the club that he was looking out for a Colonial job, with plenty of hard work, for a young friend of his, so I gather that he has some idea of marrying into the family."

"You seem destined to be the victim of the reformation, after all."

Clovis wiped the trace of Turkish coffee and the beginnings of a smile from his lips, and slowly lowered his dexter eyelid. Which, being interpreted, probably meant, "I *don't* think!"

TOBERMORY

IT was a chill, rain-washed afternoon of a late August day,
that indefinite season when partridges are still in security
or cold storage, and there is nothing to hunt—unless one is
bounded on the north by the Bristol Channel, in which case
one may lawfully gallop after fat red stags. Lady Blemley's
house-party was not bounded on the north by the Bristol Channel, hence there was a full gathering of her guests round the
tea-table on this particular afternoon. And, in spite of the
blankness of the season and the triteness of the occasion, there
was no trace in the company of that fatigued restlessness which
means a dread of the pianola and a subdued hankering for
auction bridge. The undisguised open-mouthed attention of
the entire party was fixed on the homely negative personality
of Mr. Cornelius Appin. Of all her guests, he was the one
who had come to Lady Blemley with the vaguest reputation.
Some one had said he was "clever," and he had got his invitation in the moderate expectation, on the part of his hostess,
that some portion at least of his cleverness would be contributed to the general entertainment. Until tea-time that day
she had been unable to discover in what direction, if any, his
cleverness lay. He was neither a wit nor a croquet champion,
a hypnotic force nor a begetter of amateur theatricals. Neither
did his exterior suggest the sort of man in whom women are
willing to pardon a generous measure of mental deficiency.
He had subsided into mere Mr. Appin, and the Cornelius
seemed a piece of transparent baptismal bluff. And now he
was claiming to have launched on the world a discovery beside which the invention of gunpowder, of the printing-press,
and of steam locomotion were inconsiderable trifles. Science
had made bewildering strides in many directions during recent
decades, but this thing seemed to belong to the domain of
miracle rather than to scientific achievement.

"And do you really ask us to believe," Sir Wilfrid was
saying, "that you have discovered a means for instructing

animals in the art of human speech, and that dear old Tobermory has proved your first successful pupil?"

"It is a problem at which I have worked for the last seventeen years," said Mr. Appin, "but only during the last eight or nine months have I been rewarded with glimmerings of success. Of course I have experimented with thousands of animals, but latterly only with cats, those wonderful creatures which have assimilated themselves so marvellously with our civilization while retaining all their highly developed feral instincts. Here and there among cats one comes across an outstanding superior intellect, just as one does among the ruck of human beings, and when I made the acquaintance of Tobermory a week ago I saw at once that I was in contact with a 'Beyond-cat' of extraordinary intelligence. I had gone far along the road to success in recent experiments; with Tobermory, as you call him, I have reached the goal."

Mr. Appin concluded his remarkable statement in a voice which he strove to divest of a triumphant inflection. No one said "Rats," though Clovis's lips moved in a monosyllabic contortion which probably invoked those rodents of disbelief.

"And do you mean to say," asked Miss Resker, after a slight pause, "that you have taught Tobermory to say and understand easy sentences of one syllable?"

"My dear Miss Resker," said the wonder-worker patiently, "one teaches little children and savages and backward adults in that piecemeal fashion; when one has once solved the problem of making a beginning with an animal of highly developed intelligence one has no need for those halting methods. Tobermory can speak our language with perfect correctness."

This time Clovis very distinctly said, "Beyond-rats!" Sir Wilfrid was more polite, but equally sceptical.

"Hadn't we better have the cat in and judge for ourselves?" suggested Lady Blemley.

Sir Wilfrid went in search of the animal, and the company settled themselves down to the languid expectation of witnessing some more or less adroit drawing-room ventriloquism.

In a minute Sir Wilfrid was back in the room, his face

white beneath its tan and his eyes dilated with excitement.

"By Gad, it's true!"

His agitation was unmistakably genuine, and his hearers started forward in a thrill of awakened interest.

Collapsing into an armchair he continued breathlessly: "I found him dozing in the smoking-room, and called out to him to come for his tea. He blinked at me in his usual way, and I said, 'Come on, Toby; don't keep us waiting'; and, by Gad! he drawled out in a most horribly natural voice that he'd come when he dashed well pleased! I nearly jumped out of my skin!"

Appin had preached to absolutely incredulous hearers; Sir Wilfrid's statement carried instant conviction. A Babel-like chorus of startled exclamation arose, amid which the scientist sat mutely enjoying the first fruit of his stupendous discovery.

In the midst of the clamour Tobermory entered the room and made his way with velvet tread and studied unconcern across to the group seated round the tea-table.

A sudden hush of awkwardness and constraint fell on the company. Somehow there seemed an element of embarrassment in addressing on equal terms a domestic cat of acknowledged dental ability.

"Will you have some milk, Tobermory?" asked Lady Blemley in a rather strained voice.

"I don't mind if I do," was the response, couched in a tone of even indifference. A shiver of suppressed excitement went through the listeners, and Lady Blemley might be excused for pouring out the saucerful of milk rather unsteadily.

"I'm afraid I've spilt a good deal of it," she said apologetically.

"After all, it's not my Axminster," was Tobermory's rejoinder.

Another silence fell on the group, and then Miss Resker, in her best district-visitor manner, asked if the human language had been difficult to learn. Tobermory looked squarely at her for a moment and then fixed his gaze serenely on the middle distance. It was obvious that boring questions lay outside his scheme of life.

"What do you think of human intelligence?" asked Mavis Pellington lamely.

"Of whose intelligence in particular?" asked Tobermory coldly.

"Oh, well, mine for instance," said Mavis, with a feeble laugh.

"You put me in an embarrassing position," said Tobermory, whose tone and attitude certainly did not suggest a shred of embarrassment. "When your inclusion in this house-party was suggested Sir Wilfrid protested that you were the most brainless woman of his acquaintance, and that there was a wide distinction between hospitality and the care of the feeble-minded. Lady Blemley replied that your lack of brain-power was the precise quality which had earned you your invitation, as you were the only person she could think of who might be idiotic enough to buy their old car. You know, the one they call 'The Envy of Sisyphus,' because it goes quite nicely up-hill if you push it."

Lady Blemley's protestations would have had greater effect if she had not casually suggested to Mavis only that morning that the car in question would be just the thing for her down at her Devonshire home.

Major Barfield plunged in heavily to effect a diversion.

"How about your carryings-on with the tortoise-shell puss up at the stables, eh?"

The moment he had said it every one realized the blunder.

"One does not usually discuss these matters in public," said Tobermory frigidly. "From a slight observation of your ways since you've been in this house I should imagine you'd find it inconvenient if I were to shift the conversation on to your own little affairs."

The panic which ensued was not confined to the Major.

"Would you like to go and see if cook has got your dinner ready?" suggested Lady Blemley hurriedly, affecting to ignore the fact that it wanted at least two hours to Tobermory's dinner-time.

"Thanks," said Tobermory, "not quite so soon after my tea. I don't want to die of indigestion."

"Cats have nine lives, you know," said Sir Wilfrid heartily.

"Possibly," answered Tobermory; "but only one liver."

"Adelaide!" said Mrs. Cornett, "do you mean to encourage that cat to go out and gossip about us in the servants' hall?"

The panic had indeed become general. A narrow ornamental balustrade ran in front of most of the bedroom windows at the Towers, and it was recalled with dismay that this had formed a favourite promenade for Tobermory at all hours, whence he could watch the pigeons—and heaven knew what else besides. If he intended to become reminiscent in his present outspoken strain the effect would be something more than disconcerting. Mrs. Cornett, who spent much time at her toilet table, and whose complexion was reputed to be of a nomadic though punctual disposition, looked as ill at ease as the Major. Miss Scrawen, who wrote fiercely sensuous poetry and led a blameless life, merely displayed irritation; if you are methodical and virtuous in private you don't necessarily want every one to know it. Bertie van Tahn, who was so depraved at seventeen that he had long ago given up trying to be any worse, turned a dull shade of gardenia white, but he did not commit the error of dashing out of the room like Odo Finsberry, a young gentleman who was understood to be reading for the Church and who was possibly disturbed at the thought of scandals he might hear concerning other people. Clovis had the presence of mind to maintain a composed exterior; privately he was calculating how long it would take to procure a box of fancy mice through the agency of the *Exchange and Mart* as a species of hush-money.

Even in a delicate situation like the present, Agnes Resker could not endure to remain too long in the background.

"Why did I ever come down here?" she asked dramatically.

Tobermory immediately accepted the opening.

"Judging by what you said to Mrs. Cornett on the croquet-lawn yesterday, you were out for food. You described the Blemleys as the dullest people to stay with that you knew, but said they were clever enough to employ a first-rate cook; otherwise they'd find it difficult to get any one to come down a second time."

"There's not a word of truth in it! I appeal to Mrs. Cornett—" exclaimed the discomfited Agnes.

"Mrs. Cornett repeated your remark afterwards to Bertie van Tahn," continued Tobermory, "and said, 'That woman is a regular Hunger Marcher; she'd go anywhere for four square meals a day,' and Bertie van Tahn said—"

At this point the chronicle mercifully ceased. Tobermory had caught a glimpse of the big yellow Tom from the Rectory working his way through the shrubbery towards the stable wing. In a flash he had vanished through the open French window.

With the disappearance of his too brilliant pupil Cornelius Appin found himself beset by a hurricane of bitter upbraiding, anxious inquiry, and frightened entreaty. The responsibility for the situation lay with him, and he must prevent matters from becoming worse. Could Tobermory impart his dangerous gift to other cats? was the first question he had to answer. It was possible, he replied, that he might have initiated his intimate friend the stable puss into his new accomplishment, but it was unlikely that his teaching could have taken a wider range as yet.

"Then," said Mrs. Cornett, "Tobermory may be a valuable cat and a great pet; but I'm sure you'll agree, Adelaide, that both he and the stable cat must be done away with without delay."

"You don't suppose I've enjoyed the last quarter of an hour, do you?" said Lady Blemley bitterly. "My husband and I are very fond of Tobermory—at least, we were before this horrible accomplishment was infused into him; but now, of course, the only thing is to have him destroyed as soon as possible."

"We can put some strychnine in the scraps he always gets at dinner-time," said Sir Wilfrid, "and I will go and drown the stable cat myself. The coachman will be very sore at losing his pet, but I'll say a very catching form of mange has broken out in both cats and we're afraid of it spreading to the kennels."

"But my great discovery!" expostulated Mr. Appin; "after all my years of research and experiment—"

"You can go and experiment on the short-horns at the farm, who are under proper control," said Mrs. Cornett, "or the elephants at the Zoological Gardens. They're said to be highly intelligent, and they have this recommendation, that they don't come creeping about our bedrooms and under chairs, and so forth."

An archangel ecstatically proclaiming the Millennium, and then finding that it clashed unpardonably with Henley and would have to be indefinitely postponed, could hardly have felt more crestfallen than Cornelius Appin at the reception of his wonderful achievement. Public opinion, however, was against him—in fact, had the general voice been consulted on the subject it is probable that a strong minority vote would have been in favour of including him in the strychnine diet.

Defective train arrangements and a nervous desire to see matters brought to a finish prevented an immediate dispersal of the party, but dinner that evening was not a social success. Sir Wilfrid had had rather a trying time with the stable cat and subsequently with the coachman. Agnes Resker ostentatiously limited her repast to a morsel of dry toast, which she bit as though it were a personal enemy; while Mavis Pellington maintained a vindictive silence throughout the meal. Lady Blemley kept up a flow of what she hoped was conversation, but her attention was fixed on the doorway. A plateful of carefully dosed fish scraps was in readiness on the sideboard, but sweets and savoury and dessert went their way, and no Tobermory appeared either in the dining-room or kitchen.

The sepulchral dinner was cheerful compared with the subsequent vigil in the smoking-room. Eating and drinking had at least supplied a distraction and cloak to the prevailing embarrassment. Bridge was out of the question in the general tension of nerves and tempers, and after Odo Finsberry had given a lugubrious rendering of "Mélisande in the Wood" to a frigid audience, music was tacitly avoided. At eleven the servants went to bed, announcing that the small window in the pantry had been left open as usual for Tobermory's private use. The guests read steadily through the current batch of magazines, and fell back gradually on the "Badminton Library" and bound volumes of *Punch*. Lady Blemley made periodic visits to the pantry, returning each time with an expression of listless depression which forestalled questioning.

At two o'clock Clovis broke the dominating silence.

"He won't turn up tonight. He's probably in the local newspaper office at the present moment, dictating the first instalment of his reminiscences. Lady What's-her-name's book won't be in it. It will be the event of the day."

Having made this contribution to the general cheerfulness, Clovis went to bed. At long intervals the various members of the house-party followed his example.

The servants taking round the early tea made a uniform announcement in reply to a uniform question. Tobermory had not returned.

Breakfast was, if anything, a more unpleasant function than dinner had been, but before its conclusion the situation was relieved. Tobermory's corpse was brought in from the shrubbery, where a gardener had just discovered it. From the bites on his throat and the yellow fur which coated his claws it was evident that he had fallen in unequal combat with the big Tom from the Rectory.

By midday most of the guests had quitted the Towers, and after lunch Lady Blemley had sufficiently recovered her spirits to write an extremely nasty letter to the Rectory about the loss of her valuable pet.

Tobermory had been Appin's one successful pupil, and he was destined to have no successor. A few weeks later an elephant in the Dresden Zoological Garden, which had shown no previous signs of irritability, broke loose and killed an Englishman who had apparently been teasing it. The victim's name was variously reported in the papers as Oppin and Eppelin, but his front name was faithfully rendered Cornelius.

"If he was trying German irregular verbs on the poor beast," said Clovis, "he deserved all he got."

MRS. PACKLETIDE'S TIGER

IT was Mrs. Packletide's pleasure and intention that she should shoot a tiger. Not that the lust to kill had suddenly descended on her, or that she felt that she would leave India safer and more wholesome than she had found it, with one fraction less of wild beast per million of inhabitants. The compelling motive for her sudden deviation towards the footsteps of Nimrod was the fact that Loona Bimberton had recently been carried eleven miles in an aeroplane by an Algerian aviator, and talked of nothing else; only a personally procured tiger-skin and a heavy harvest of Press photographs could successfully counter that sort of thing. Mrs. Packletide had already arranged in her mind the lunch she would give at her house in Curzon Street, ostensibly in Loona Bimberton's honour, with a tiger-skin rug occupying most of the foreground and all of the conversation. She had also already designed in her mind the tiger-claw brooch that she was going to give Loona Bimberton on her next birthday. In a world that is supposed to be chiefly swayed by hunger and by love Mrs. Packletide was an exception; her movements and motives were largely governed by dislike of Loona Bimberton.

Circumstances proved propitious. Mrs. Packletide had offered a thousand rupees for the opportunity of shooting a tiger without overmuch risk or exertion, and it so happened that a neighbouring village could boast of being the favoured rendezvous of an animal of respectable antecedents, which had been driven by the increasing infirmities of age to abandon game-killing and confine its appetite to the smaller domestic animals. The prospect of earning the thousand rupees had stimulated the sporting and commercial instinct of the villagers; children were posted night and day on the outskirts of the local jungle to head the tiger back in the unlikely event of his attempting to roam away to fresh hunting-grounds, and the cheaper kinds of goats were left about with elaborate carelessness to keep him satisfied with his present quarters. The one great anxiety was lest he should die of old age before the date appointed for the memsahib's shoot. Mothers carrying their babies home through the jungle after the day's work in the fields hushed their singing lest they might curtail the restful sleep of the venerable herd-robber.

The great night duly arrived, moonlit and cloudless. A platform had been constructed in a comfortable and conveniently placed tree, and thereon crouched Mrs. Packletide and her paid companion, Miss Mebbin. A goat, gifted with a particularly persistent bleat, such as even a partially deaf tiger might be reasonably expected to hear on a still night, was tethered at the correct distance. With an accurately sighted rifle and a thumb-nail pack of patience cards the sportswoman awaited the coming of the quarry.

"I suppose we are in some danger?" said Miss Mebbin.

She was not actually nervous about the wild beast, but she had a morbid dread of performing an atom more service than she had been paid for.

"Nonsense," said Mrs. Packletide; "it's a very old tiger. It couldn't spring up here even if it wanted to."

"If it's an old tiger I think you ought to get it cheaper. A thousand rupees is a lot of money."

Louisa Mebbin adopted a protective elder-sister attitude towards money in general, irrespective of nationality or denomination. Her energetic intervention had saved many a rouble from dissipating itself in tips in some Moscow hotel, and francs and centimes clung to her instinctively under circumstances which would have driven them headlong from less sympathetic hands. Her speculations as to the market depreciation of tiger remnants were cut short by the appearance on the scene of the animal itself. As soon as it caught sight of the tethered goat it lay flat on the earth, seemingly less from a desire to take advantage of all available cover than for the purpose of snatching a short rest before commencing the grand attack.

"I believe it's ill," said Louisa Mebbin, loudly in Hindustani, for the benefit of the village headman, who was in ambush in a neighbouring tree.

"Hush!" said Mrs. Packletide, and at that moment the tiger commenced ambling towards his victim.

"Now, now!" urged Miss Mebbin with some excitement; "if he doesn't touch the goat we needn't pay for it." (The bait was an extra.)

The rifle flashed out with a loud report, and the great tawny beast sprang to one side and then rolled over in the stillness of death. In a moment a crowd of excited natives had swarmed on to the scene, and their shouting speedily carried the glad news to the village, where a thumping of tom-toms took up the chorus of triumph. And their triumph and rejoicing found a ready echo in the heart of Mrs. Packletide; already that luncheon-party in Curzon Street seemed immeasurably nearer.

It was Louisa Mebbin who drew attention to the fact that the goat was in death-throes from a mortal bullet-wound, while no trace of the rifle's deadly work could be found on the tiger. Evidently the wrong animal had been hit, and the beast of prey had succumbed to heart-failure, caused by the sudden report of the rifle, accelerated by senile decay. Mrs. Packletide was pardonably annoyed at the discovery; but, at any rate, she was the possessor of a dead tiger, and the villagers, anxious for their thousand rupees, gladly connived at the fiction that she had shot the beast. And Miss Mebbin was a paid companion. Therefore did Mrs. Packletide face the cameras with a light heart, and her pictured fame reached from the pages of the *Texas Weekly Snapshot* to the illustrated Monday supplement of the *Novoe Vremya*. As for Loona Bimberton, she refused to look at an illustrated paper for weeks, and her letter of thanks for the gift of a tiger-claw brooch was a model of repressed emotions. The luncheon-party she declined; there are limits beyond which repressed emotions become dangerous.

From Curzon Street the tiger-skin rug travelled down to the Manor House, and was duly inspected and admired by the county, and it seemed a fitting and appropriate thing when Mrs. Packletide went to the County Costume Ball in the character of Diana. She refused to fall in, however, with Clovis's tempt‹ing suggestion of a primeval dance party, at which every one should wear the skins of beasts they had recently slain. "I should be in rather a Baby Bunting condition," confessed Clovis, "with a miserable rabbit-skin or two to wrap up in, but then," he added, with a rather malicious glance at Diana's pro‐portions, "my figure is quite as good as that Russian dancing boy's."

"How amused every one would be if they knew what really happened," said Louisa Mebbin a few days after the ball.

"What do you mean?" asked Mrs. Packletide quickly.

"How you shot the goat and frightened the tiger to death," said Miss Mebbin, with her disagreeably pleasant laugh.

"No one would believe it," said Mrs. Packletide, her face changing colour as rapidly as though it were going through a book of patterns before post-time.

"Loona Bimberton would," said Miss Mebbin. Mrs. Packle‐tide's face settled on an unbecoming shade of greenish white.

"You surely wouldn't give me away?" she asked.

"I've seen a week-end cottage near Dorking that I should rather like to buy," said Miss Mebbin with seeming irrel‐evance. "Six hundred and eighty, freehold. Quite a bargain, only I don't happen to have the money."

.   .   .   .

Louisa Mebbin's pretty week-end cottage, christened by her "Les Fauves," and gay in summer-time with its garden borders of tiger-lilies, is the wonder and admiration of her friends.

"It is a marvel how Louisa manages to do it," is the gen‐eral verdict.

Mrs. Packletide indulges in no more big-game shooting.

"The incidental expenses are so heavy," she confides to in‐quiring friends.

THE STAMPEDING OF LADY BASTABLE

"IT would be rather nice if you would put Clovis up for another six days while I go up north to the MacGregors'," said Mrs. Sangrail sleepily across the breakfast-table. It was her invariable plan to speak in a sleepy, comfortable voice whenever she was unusually keen about anything; it put people off their guard, and they frequently fell in with her wishes before they had realized that she was really asking for anything. Lady Bastable, however, was not so easily taken unawares; possibly she knew that voice and what it betokened—at any rate, she knew Clovis.

She frowned at a piece of toast and ate it very slowly, as though she wished to convey the impression that the process hurt her more than it hurt the toast; but no extension of hospitality on Clovis's behalf rose to her lips.

"It would be a great convenience to me," pursued Mrs. Sangrail, abandoning the careless tone. "I particularly don't want to take him to the MacGregors', and it will only be for six days."

"It will seem longer," said Lady Bastable dismally. "The last time he stayed here for a week—"

"I know," interrupted the other hastily, "but that was nearly two years ago. He was younger then."

"But he hasn't improved," said her hostess; "it's no use growing older if you only learn new ways of misbehaving yourself."

Mrs. Sangrail was unable to argue the point; since Clovis had reached the age of seventeen she had never ceased to bewail his irrepressible waywardness to all her circle of acquaintances, and a polite scepticism would have greeted the slightest hint at a prospective reformation. She discarded the fruitless effort at cajolery and resorted to undisguised bribery.

"If you'll have him here for these six days I'll cancel that outstanding bridge account."

It was only for forty-nine shillings, but Lady Bastable loved shillings with a great, strong love. To lose money at bridge and not to have to pay it was one of those rare experiences which gave the card-table a glamour in her eyes which it could never otherwise have possessed. Mrs. Sangrail was almost equally devoted to her card winnings, but the prospect of conveniently warehousing her offspring for six days, and incidentally saving his railway fare to the north, reconciled her to the sacrifice; when Clovis made a belated appearance at the breakfast-table the bargain had been struck.

"Just think," said Mrs. Sangrail sleepily; "Lady Bastable has very kindly asked you to stay on here while I go to the MacGregors'."

Clovis said suitable things in a highly unsuitable manner, and proceeded to make punitive expeditions among the breakfast dishes with a scowl on his face that would have driven the purr out of a peace conference. The arrangement that had been concluded behind his back was doubly distasteful to him. In the first place, he particularly wanted to teach the Mac-Gregor boys, who could well afford the knowledge, how to play poker-patience; secondly, the Bastable catering was of the kind that is classified as a rude plenty, which Clovis translated as a plenty that gives rise to rude remarks. Watching him from behind ostentatiously sleepy lids, his mother realized, in the light of long experience, that any rejoicing over the success of her manœuvre would be distinctly premature. It was one thing to fit Clovis into a convenient niche of the domestic jig-saw puzzle; it was quite another matter to get him to stay there.

Lady Bastable was wont to retire in state to the morning-room immediately after breakfast and spend a quiet hour in skimming through the papers; they were there, so she might as well get their money's worth out of them. Politics did not greatly interest her, but she was obsessed with a favourite foreboding that one of these days there would be a great social upheaval, in which everybody would be killed by everybody else. "It will come sooner than we think," she would observe darkly; a mathematical expert of exceptionally high powers would have been puzzled to work out the approximate date from the slender and confusing groundwork which this assertion afforded.

On this particular morning the sight of Lady Bastable enthroned among her papers gave Clovis the hint towards which his mind had been groping all breakfast time. His mother had gone upstairs to supervise packing operations, and he was alone on the ground-floor with his hostess—and the servants. The latter were the key to the situation. Bursting wildly into the kitchen quarters, Clovis screamed a frantic though strictly non-committal summons: "Poor Lady Bastable! In the morning-room! Oh, quick!" The next moment the butler, cook, page-boy, two or three maids, and a gardener who had happened to be in one of the outer kitchens were following in a hot scurry after Clovis as he headed back for the morning-room. Lady Bastable was roused from the world of newspaper lore by hearing a Japanese screen in the hall go down with a crash. Then the door leading from the hall flew open and her young guest tore madly through the room, shrieked at her in passing, "The jacquerie! They're on us!" and dashed like an escaping hawk out through the French window. The scared mob of servants burst in on his heels, the gardener still clutching the sickle with which he had been trimming hedges, and the impetus of their headlong haste carried them, slipping and sliding, over the smooth parquet flooring towards the chair where their mistress sat in panic-stricken amazement. If she had had a moment granted her for reflection she would have behaved, as she afterwards explained, with considerable dignity. It was probably the sickle which decided her, but anyway she followed the lead that Clovis had given her through the French window, and ran well and far across the lawn before the eyes of her astonished retainers.

· · · · ·

Lost dignity is not a possession which can be restored at a moment's notice, and both Lady Bastable and the butler found the process of returning to normal conditions almost as painful as a slow recovery from drowning. A jacquerie, even if carried out with the most respectful of intentions, cannot fail to leave some traces of embarrassment behind it. By lunch-time, however, decorum had reasserted itself with enhanced rigour as a natural rebound from its recent overthrow, and the meal was served in a frigid stateliness that might have been framed on a Byzantine model. Half-way through its duration Mrs. Sangrail was solemnly presented with an envelope lying on a silver salver. It contained a cheque for forty-nine shillings.

The MacGregor boys learned how to play poker-patience; after all, they could afford to.

THE BACKGROUND

"THAT woman's art-jargon tires me," said Clovis to his journalist friend. "She's so fond of talking of certain pictures as 'growing on one,' as though they were a sort of fungus."

"That reminds me," said the journalist, "of the story of Henri Deplis. Have I ever told it you?"

Clovis shook his head.

"Henri Deplis was by birth a native of the Grand Duchy of Luxemburg. On maturer reflection he became a commercial traveller. His business activities frequently took him beyond the limits of the Grand Duchy, and he was stopping in a small town of Northern Italy when news reached him from home that a legacy from a distant and deceased relative had fallen to his share.

"It was not a large legacy, even from the modest standpoint of Henri Deplis, but it impelled him towards some seemingly harmless extravagances. In particular it led him to patronize local art as represented by the tattoo-needles of Signor Andreas Pincini. Signor Pincini was, perhaps, the most brilliant master of tattoo craft that Italy had ever known, but his circumstances were decidedly impoverished, and for the sum of six hundred francs he gladly undertook to cover his client's back, from the collar-bone down to the waist-line, with a glowing representation of the Fall of Icarus. The design, when finally developed, was a slight disappointment to Monsieur Deplis, who had suspected Icarus of being a fortress taken by Wallenstein in the Thirty Years' War, but he was more than satisfied with the execution of the work, which was acclaimed by all who had the privilege of seeing it as Pincini's masterpiece.

"It was his greatest effort, and his last. Without even waiting to be paid, the illustrious craftsman departed this life, and was buried under an ornate tombstone, whose winged cherubs would have afforded singularly little scope for the exercise of his favourite art. There remained, however, the widow Pincini, to whom the six hundred francs were due. And thereupon arose the great crisis in the life of Henri Deplis, traveller of commerce. The legacy, under the stress of numerous little calls on its substance, had dwindled to very insignificant proportions, and when a pressing wine bill and sundry other current accounts had been paid, there remained little more than 430 francs to offer to the widow. The lady was properly indignant, not wholly, as she volubly explained, on account of the suggested writing-off of 170 francs, but also at the attempt to depreciate the value of her late husband's acknowledged masterpiece. In a week's time Deplis was obliged to reduce his offer to 405 francs, which circumstance fanned the widow's indignation into a fury. She cancelled the sale of the work of art, and a few days later Deplis learned with a sense of consternation that she had presented it to the municipality of Bergamo, which had gratefully accepted it. He left the neighbourhood as unobtrusively as possible, and was genuinely relieved when his business commands took him to Rome, where he hoped his identity and that of the famous picture might be lost sight of.

"But he bore on his back the burden of the dead man's genius. On presenting himself one day in the steaming corridor of a vapour bath, he was at once hustled back into his clothes by the proprietor, who was a North Italian, and who emphatically refused to allow the celebrated Fall of Icarus to be publicly on view without the permission of the municipality of Bergamo. Public interest and official vigilance increased as the matter became more widely known, and Deplis was unable to take a simple dip in the sea or river on the hottest afternoon unless clothed up to the collar-bone in a substantial bathing garment. Later on the authorities of Bergamo conceived the idea that salt water might be injurious to the masterpiece, and a perpetual injunction was obtained which debarred the muchly harassed commercial traveller from sea bathing under any circumstances. Altogether, he was fervently thankful when his firm of employers found him a new range of activities in the neighbourhood of Bordeaux. His thankfulness, however, ceased abruptly at the Franco-Italian frontier. An imposing array of official force barred his departure, and he was sternly reminded of the stringent law which forbids the exportation of Italian works of art.

"A diplomatic parley ensued between the Luxemburgian and Italian Governments, and at one time the European situation became overcast with the possibilities of trouble. But the Italian Government stood firm; it declined to concern itself in the least with the fortunes or even the existence of Henri Deplis, commercial traveller, but was immovable in its decision that the Fall of Icarus (by the late Pincini, Andreas) at present the property of the municipality of Bergamo, should not leave the country.

"The excitement died down in time, but the unfortunate Deplis, who was of a constitutionally retiring disposition, found himself a few months later once more the storm-centre of a furious controversy. A certain German art expert, who had obtained from the municipality of Bergamo permission to inspect the famous masterpiece, declared it to be a spurious Pincini, probably the work of some pupil whom he had employed in his declining years. The evidence of Deplis on the subject was obviously worthless, as he had been under the influence of the customary narcotics during the long process of pricking in the design. The editor of an Italian art journal refuted the contentions of the German expert and undertook to prove that his private life did not conform to any modern standard of decency. The whole of Italy and Germany were drawn into the dispute, and the rest of Europe was soon involved in the quarrel. There were stormy scenes in the Spanish Parliament, and the University of Copenhagen bestowed a gold medal on the German expert (afterwards sending a commission to examine his proofs on the spot), while two Polish schoolboys in Paris committed suicide to show what *they* thought of the matter.

"Meanwhile, the unhappy human background fared no better than before, and it was not surprising that he drifted into the ranks of Italian anarchists. Four times at least he was escorted to the frontier as a dangerous and undesirable foreigner, but he was always brought back as the Fall of Icarus (attributed to Pincini, Andreas, early Twentieth Century). And then one day, at an anarchist congress at Genoa, a fellow-worker, in the heat of debate, broke a phial full of corrosive liquid over his back. The red shirt that he was wearing mitigated the effects, but the Icarus was ruined beyond recognition. His assailant was severely reprimanded for assaulting a fellow-anarchist and received seven years' imprisonment for defacing a national art treasure. As soon as he was able to leave the hospital Henri Deplis was put across the frontier as an undesirable alien.

"In the quieter streets of Paris, especially in the neighbourhood of the Ministry of Fine Arts, you may sometimes meet a depressed, anxious-looking man, who, if you pass him the time of day, will answer you with a slight Luxemburgian accent. He nurses the illusion that he is one of the lost arms of the Venus de Milo, and hopes that the French Government may be persuaded to buy him. On all other subjects I believe he is tolerably sane."

HERMANN THE IRASCIBLE—A STORY OF THE GREAT WEEP

IT was in the second decade of the Twentieth Century, after the Great Plague had devastated England, that Hermann the Irascible, nicknamed also the Wise, sat on the British throne. The Mortal Sickness had swept away the entire Royal Family, unto the third and fourth generations, and thus it came to pass that Hermann the Fourteenth of Saxe-Drachsen-Wachtelstein, who had stood thirtieth in the order of succession, found himself one day ruler of the British dominions within and beyond the seas. He was one of the unexpected things that happen in politics, and he happened with great thoroughness. In many ways he was the most progressive monarch who had sat on an important throne; before people knew where they were, they were somewhere else. Even his Ministers, progressive though they were by tradition, found it difficult to keep pace with his legislative suggestions.

"As a matter of fact," admitted the Prime Minister, "we are hampered by these votes-for-women creatures; they disturb our meetings throughout the country, and they try to turn Downing Street into a sort of political picnic-ground."

"They must be dealt with," said Hermann.

"Dealt with," said the Prime Minister; "exactly, just so; but how?"

"I will draft you a Bill," said the King, sitting down at his typewriting machine, "enacting that women shall vote at all future elections. *Shall* vote, you observe; or, to put it plainer, must. Voting will remain optional, as before, for male electors; but every woman between the ages of twenty-one and seventy will be obliged to vote, not only at elections for Parliament, county councils, district boards, parish councils, and municipalities, but for coroners, school inspectors, churchwardens, curators of museums, sanitary authorities, police-court interpreters, swimming-bath instructors, contractors, choir-masters, market superintendents, art-school teachers, cathedral vergers, and other local functionaries whose names I will add as they occur to me. All these offices will become elective, and failure to vote at any election falling within her area of residence will involve the female elector in a penalty of £10. Absence, unsupported by an adequate medical certificate, will not be accepted as an excuse. Pass this Bill through the two Houses of Parliament and bring it to me for signature the day after tomorrow."

From the very outset the Compulsory Female Franchise produced little or no elation even in circles which had been loudest in demanding the vote. The bulk of the women of the country had been indifferent or hostile to the franchise agitation, and the most fanatical Suffragettes began to wonder what they had found so attractive in the prospect of putting ballot-papers into a box. In the country districts the task of carrying out the provisions of the new Act was irksome enough; in the towns and cities it became an incubus. There seemed no end to the elections. Laundresses and seamstresses had to hurry away from their work to vote, often for a candidate whose name they hadn't heard before, and whom they selected at haphazard; female clerks and waitresses got up extra early to get their voting done before starting off to their places of business. Society women found their arrangements impeded and upset by the continual necessity for attending the polling stations, and week-end parties and summer holidays became gradually a masculine luxury. As for Cairo and the Riviera, they were possible only for genuine invalids or people of enormous wealth, for the accumulation of £10 fines during a prolonged absence was a contingency that even ordinarily wealthy folk could hardly afford to risk.

It was not wonderful that the female disfranchisement agitation became a formidable movement. The No-Votes-for-Women League numbered its feminine adherents by the million; its colours, citron and old Dutch-madder, were flaunted everywhere, and its battle hymn, "We Don't Want to Vote," became a popular refrain. As the Government showed no signs of being impressed by peaceful persuasion, more violent methods came into vogue. Meetings were disturbed, Ministers were mobbed, policemen were bitten, and ordinary prison fare rejected, and on the eve of the anniversary of Trafalgar women bound themselves in tiers up the entire length of the Nelson column so that its customary floral decoration had to be abandoned. Still the Government obstinately adhered to its conviction that women ought to have the vote.

Then, as a last resort, some woman wit hit upon an expedient which it was strange that no one had thought of before.

The Great Weep was organized. Relays of women, ten thousand at a time, wept continuously in the public places of the Metropolis. They wept in railway stations, in tubes and omnibuses, in the National Gallery, at the Army and Navy Stores, in St. James's Park, at ballad concerts, at Prince's and in the Burlington Arcade. The hitherto unbroken success of the brilliant farcical comedy "Henry's Rabbit" was imperilled by the presence of drearily weeping women in stalls and circle and gallery, and one of the brightest divorce cases that had been tried for many years was robbed of much of its sparkle by the lachrymose behaviour of a section of the audience.

"What are we to do?" asked the Prime Minister, whose cook had wept into all the breakfast dishes and whose nursemaid had gone out, crying quietly and miserably, to take the children for a walk in the Park.

"There is a time for everything," said the King; "there is a time to yield. Pass a measure through the two Houses depriving women of the right to vote, and bring it to me for the Royal assent the day after tomorrow."

As the Minister withdrew, Hermann the Irascible, who was also nicknamed the Wise, gave a profound chuckle.

"There are more ways of killing a cat than by choking it with cream," he quoted, "but I'm not sure," he added, "that it's not the best way."

THE UNREST-CURE

ON the rack in the railway carriage immediately opposite Clovis was a solidly wrought travelling bag, with a carefully written label, on which was inscribed, "J. P. Huddle, The Warren, Tilfield, near Slowborough." Immediately below the rack sat the human embodiment of the label, a solid, sedate individual, sedately dressed, sedately conversational. Even without his conversation (which was addressed to a friend seated by his side, and touched chiefly on such topics as the backwardness of Roman hyacinths and the prevalence of measles at the Rectory), one could have gauged fairly accurately the temperament and mental outlook of the travelling bag's owner. But he seemed unwilling to leave anything to the imagination of a casual observer, and his talk grew presently personal and introspective.

"I don't know how it is," he told his friend, "I'm not much over forty, but I seem to have settled down into a deep groove of elderly middle-age. My sister shows the same tendency. We like everything to be exactly in its accustomed place; we like things to happen exactly at their appointed times; we like everything to be usual, orderly, punctual, methodical, to a hair's breadth, to a minute. It distresses and upsets us if it is not so. For instance, to take a very trifling matter, a thrush has built its nest year after year in the catkin-tree on the lawn; this year, for no obvious reason, it is building in the ivy on the garden wall. We have said very little about it, but I think we both feel that the change is unnecessary, and just a little irritating."

"Perhaps," said the friend, "it is a different thrush."

"We have suspected that," said J. P. Huddle, "and I think it gives us even more cause for annoyance. We don't feel that we want a change of thrush at our time of life; and yet, as I have said, we have scarcely reached an age when these things should make themselves seriously felt."

"What you want," said the friend, "is an Unrest-cure."

"An Unrest-cure? I've never heard of such a thing."

"You've heard of Rest-cures for people who've broken down under stress of too much worry and strenuous living; well, you're suffering from overmuch repose and placidity, and you need the opposite kind of treatment."

"But where would one go for such a thing?"

"Well, you might stand as an Orange candidate for Kilkenny, or do a course of district visiting in one of the Apache quarters of Paris, or give lectures in Berlin to prove that most of Wagner's music was written by Gambetta; and there's always the interior of Morocco to travel in. But, to be really effective, the Unrest-cure ought to be tried in the home. How you would do it I haven't the faintest idea."

It was at this point in the conversation that Clovis became galvanized into alert attention. After all, his two days' visit to an elderly relative at Slowborough did not promise much excitement. Before the train had stopped he had decorated his sinister shirt-cuff with the inscription, "J. P. Huddle, The Warren, Tilfield, near Slowborough."

. . . .

Two mornings later Mr. Huddle broke in on his sister's privacy as she sat reading *Country Life* in the morning room. It was her day and hour and place for reading *Country Life*, and the intrusion was absolutely irregular; but he bore in his hand a telegram, and in that household telegrams were recognized as happening by the hand of God. This particular telegram partook of the nature of a thunderbolt. "Bishop examining confirmation class in neighbourhood unable stay rectory on account measles invokes your hospitality sending secretary arrange."

"I scarcely know the Bishop; I've only spoken to him once," exclaimed J. P. Huddle, with the exculpating air of one who realizes too late the indiscretion of speaking to strange Bishops. Miss Huddle was the first to rally; she disliked thunderbolts as fervently as her brother did, but the womanly instinct in her told her that thunderbolts must be fed.

"We can curry the cold duck," she said. It was not the appointed day for curry, but the little orange envelope involved a certain departure from rule and custom. Her brother said nothing, but his eyes thanked her for being brave.

"A young gentleman to see you," announced the parlourmaid.

"The secretary!" murmured the Huddles in unison; they instantly stiffened into a demeanour which proclaimed that, though they held all strangers to be guilty, they were willing to hear anything they might have to say in their defence. The young gentleman, who came into the room with a certain elegant haughtiness, was not at all Huddle's idea of a bishop's secretary; he had not supposed that the episcopal establishment could have afforded such an expensively upholstered article when there were so many other claims on its resources. The face was fleetingly familiar; if he had bestowed more attention on the fellow-traveller sitting opposite him in the railway carriage two days before he might have recognized Clovis in his present visitor.

"You are the Bishop's secretary?" asked Huddle, becoming consciously deferential.

"His confidential secretary," answered Clovis. "You may call me Stanislaus; my other name doesn't matter. The Bishop and Colonel Alberti may be here to lunch. I shall be here in any case."

It sounded rather like the programme of a Royal visit.

"The Bishop is examining a confirmation class in the neighbourhood, isn't he?" asked Miss Huddle.

"Ostensibly," was the dark reply, followed by a request for a large-scale map of the locality.

Clovis was still immersed in a seemingly profound study of the map when another telegram arrived. It was addressed to "Prince Stanislaus, care of Huddle, The Warren, etc." Clovis glanced at the contents and announced: "The Bishop and Alberti won't be here till late in the afternoon." Then he returned to his scrutiny of the map.

The luncheon was not a very festive function. The princely secretary ate and drank with fair appetite, but severely discouraged conversation. At the finish of the meal he broke suddenly into a radiant smile, thanked his hostess for a charming repast, and kissed her hand with deferential rapture. Miss Huddle was unable to decide in her mind whether the action savoured of Louis Quatorzian courtliness or the reprehensible Roman attitude towards the Sabine women. It was not her day for having a headache, but she felt that the circumstances excused her, and retired to her room to have as much headache as was possible before the Bishop's arrival. Clovis, having asked the way to the nearest telegraph office, disappeared presently down the carriage drive. Mr. Huddle met him in the hall some two hours later, and asked when the Bishop would arrive.

"He is in the library with Alberti," was the reply.

"But why wasn't I told? I never knew he had come!" exclaimed Huddle.

"No one knows he is here," said Clovis; "the quieter we can keep matters the better. And on no account disturb him in the library. Those are his orders."

"But what is all this mystery about? And who is Alberti? And isn't the Bishop going to have tea?"

"The Bishop is out for blood, not tea."

"Blood!" gasped Huddle, who did not find that the thunderbolt improved on acquaintance.

"Tonight is going to be a great night in the history of Christendom," said Clovis. "We are going to massacre every Jew in the neighbourhood."

"To massacre the Jews!" said Huddle indignantly. "Do you mean to tell me there's a general rising against them?"

"No, it's the Bishop's own idea. He's in there arranging all the details now."

"But—the Bishop is such a tolerant, humane man."

"That is precisely what will heighten the effect of his action. The sensation will be enormous."

That at least Huddle could believe.

"He will be hanged!" he exclaimed with conviction.

"A motor is waiting to carry him to the coast, where a steam yacht is in readiness."

"But there aren't thirty Jews in the whole neighbourhood," protested Huddle, whose brain, under the repeated shocks of the day, was operating with the uncertainty of a telegraph wire during earthquake disturbances.

"We have twenty-six on our list," said Clovis, referring to a bundle of notes. "We shall be able to deal with them all the more thoroughly."

"Do you mean to tell me that you are meditating violence against a man like Sir Leon Birberry," stammered Huddle; "he's one of the most respected men in the country."

"He's down on our list," said Clovis carelessly; "after all, we've got men we can trust to do our job, so we shan't have to rely on local assistance. And we've got some Boy-scouts helping us as auxiliaries."

"Boy-scouts!"

"Yes; when they understood there was real killing to be done they were even keener than the men."

"This thing will be a blot on the Twentieth Century!"

"And your house will be the blotting-pad. Have you realized that half the papers of Europe and the United States will publish pictures of it? By the way, I've sent some photographs of you and your sister, that I found in the library, to the *Matin* and *Die Woche*; I hope you don't mind. Also a sketch of the staircase; most of the killing will probably be done on the staircase."

The emotions that were surging in J. P. Huddle's brain were almost too intense to be disclosed in speech, but he managed to gasp out: "There aren't any Jews in this house."

"Not at present," said Clovis.

"I shall go to the police," shouted Huddle with sudden energy.

"In the shrubbery," said Clovis, "are posted ten men, who have orders to fire on any one who leaves the house without my signal of permission. Another armed picquet is in ambush near the front gate. The Boy-scouts watch the back premises."

At this moment the cheerful hoot of a motor-horn was heard from the drive. Huddle rushed to the hall door with the feeling of a man half-awakened from a nightmare, and beheld Sir Leon Birberry, who had driven himself over in his car. "I got your telegram," he said; "what's up?"

Telegram? It seemed to be a day of telegrams.

"Come here at once. Urgent. James Huddle," was the purport of the message displayed before Huddle's bewildered eyes.

"I see it all!" he exclaimed suddenly in a voice shaken with agitation, and with a look of agony in the direction of the shrubbery he hauled the astonished Birberry into the house. Tea had just been laid in the hall, but the now thoroughly panic-stricken Huddle dragged his protesting guest upstairs, and in a few minutes' time the entire household had been summoned to that region of momentary safety. Clovis alone graced the tea-table with his presence; the fanatics in the library were evidently too immersed in their monstrous machinations to dally with the solace of teacup and hot toast. Once the youth rose, in answer to the summons of the front-door bell, and admitted Mr. Paul Isaacs, shoemaker and parish councillor, who had also received a pressing invitation to The Warren. With an atrocious assumption of courtesy, which a Borgia could hardly have outdone, the secretary escorted this new captive of his net to the head of the stairway, where his involuntary host awaited him.

And then ensued a long ghastly vigil of watching and waiting. Once or twice Clovis left the house to stroll across to the shrubbery, returning always to the library, for the purpose evidently of making a brief report. Once he took in the letters from the evening postman, and brought them to the top of the stairs with punctilious politeness. After his next absence he came half-way up the stairs to make an announcement.

"The Boy-scouts mistook my signal, and have killed the postman. I've had very little practice in this sort of thing, you see. Another time I shall do better."

The housemaid, who was engaged to be married to the evening postman, gave way to clamorous grief.

"Remember that your mistress has a headache," said J. P. Huddle. (Miss Huddle's headache was worse.)

Clovis hastened downstairs, and after a short visit to the library returned with another message:

"The Bishop is sorry to hear that Miss Huddle has a headache. He is issuing orders that as far as possible no firearms shall be used near the house; any killing that is necessary on the premises will be done with cold steel. The Bishop does not see why a man should not be a gentleman as well as a Christian."

That was the last they saw of Clovis; it was nearly seven o'clock, and his elderly relative liked him to dress for dinner. But, though he had left them for ever, the lurking suggestion of his presence haunted the lower regions of the house during the long hours of the wakeful night, and every creak of the stairway, every rustle of wind through the shrubbery, was fraught with horrible meaning. At about seven next morning the gardener's boy and the early postman finally convinced the watchers that the Twentieth Century was still unblotted.

"I don't suppose," mused Clovis, as an early train bore him townwards, "that they will be in the least grateful for the Unrest-cure."

THE JESTING OF ARLINGTON STRINGHAM

ARLINGTON STRINGHAM made a joke in the House of Commons. It was a thin House, and a very thin joke; something about the Anglo-Saxon race having a great many angles. It is possible that it was unintentional, but a fellow-member, who did not wish it to be supposed that he was asleep because his eyes were shut, laughed. One or two of the papers noted "a laugh" in brackets, and another, which was notorious for the carelessness of its political news, mentioned "laughter." Things often begin in that way.

"Arlington made a joke in the House last night," said Eleanor Stringham to her mother; "in all the years we've been married neither of us has made jokes, and I don't like it now. I'm afraid it's the beginning of the rift in the lute."

"What lute?" said her mother.

"It's a quotation," said Eleanor.

To say that anything was a quotation was an excellent method, in Eleanor's eyes, for withdrawing it from discussion, just as you could always defend indifferent lamb late in the season by saying "It's mutton."

And, of course, Arlington Stringham continued to tread the thorny path of conscious humour into which Fate had beckoned him.

"The country's looking very green, but, after all, that's what it's there for," he remarked to his wife two days later.

"That's very modern, and I daresay very clever, but I'm afraid it's wasted on me," she observed coldly. If she had known how much effort it had cost him to make the remark she might have greeted it in a kinder spirit. It is the tragedy of human endeavour that it works so often unseen and un-guessed.

Arlington said nothing, not from injured pride, but because he was thinking hard for something to say. Eleanor mistook his silence for an assumption of tolerant superiority, and her anger prompted her to a further gibe.

"You had better tell it to Lady Isobel. I've no doubt she would appreciate it."

Lady Isobel was seen everywhere with a fawn-coloured collie at a time when every one else kept nothing but Pekinese, and she had once eaten four green apples at an afternoon tea in the Botanical Gardens, so she was widely credited with a rather unpleasant wit. The censorious said she slept in a ham-mock and understood Yeats's poems, but her family denied both stories.

"The rift is widening to an abyss," said Eleanor to her mother that afternoon.

"I should not tell that to any one," remarked her mother, after long reflection.

"Naturally, I should not talk about it very much," said Eleanor, "but why shouldn't I mention it to any one?"

"Because you can't have an abyss in a lute. There isn't room."

Eleanor's outlook on life did not improve as the afternoon wore on. The page-boy had brought from the library *By Mere and Wold* instead of *By Mere Chance*, the book which every one denied having read. The unwelcome substitute appeared to be a collection of nature notes contributed by the author to the pages of some Northern weekly, and when one had been prepared to plunge with disapproving mind into a regrettable chronicle of ill-spent lives it was intensely irritating to read "the dainty yellow-hammers are now with us, and flaunt their jaundiced livery from every bush and hillock." Besides, the thing was so obviously untrue; either there must be hardly any bushes or hillocks in those parts or the country must be fear-fully overstocked with yellow-hammers. The thing scarcely seemed worth telling such a lie about. And the page-boy stood there, with his sleekly brushed and parted hair, and his air of chaste and callous indifference to the desires and passions of the world. Eleanor hated boys, and she would have liked to have whipped this one long and often. It was perhaps the yearning of a woman who had no children of her own.

She turned at random to another paragraph. "Lie quietly concealed in the fern and bramble in the gap by the old rowan tree, and you may see, almost every evening during early summer, a pair of lesser whitethroats creeping up and down the nettles and hedge-growth that mask their nesting-place."

The insufferable monotony of the proposed recreation! Eleanor would not have watched the most brilliant performance at His Majesty's Theatre for a single evening under such uncomfortable circumstances, and to be asked to watch lesser whitethroats creeping up and down a nettle "almost every evening" during the height of the season struck her as an imputation on her intelligence that was positively offensive. Impatiently she transferred her attention to the dinner menu, which the boy had thoughtfully brought in as an alternative to the more solid literary fare. "Rabbit curry," met her eye, and the lines of disapproval deepened on her already puckered brow. The cook was a great believer in the influence of environment, and nourished an obstinate conviction that if you brought rabbit and curry-powder together in one dish a rabbit curry would be the result. And Clovis and the odious Bertie van Tahn were coming to dinner. Surely, thought Eleanor, if Arlington knew how much she had had that day to try her, he would refrain from joke-making.

At dinner that night it was Eleanor herself who mentioned the name of a certain statesman, who may be decently covered under the disguise of X.

"X.," said Arlington Stringham, "has the soul of a meringue."

It was a useful remark to have on hand, because it applied equally well to four prominent statesmen of the day, which quadrupled the opportunities for using it.

"Meringues haven't got souls," said Eleanor's mother.

"It's a mercy that they haven't," said Clovis; "they would

be always losing them, and people like my aunt would get up missions to meringues, and say it was wonderful how much one could teach them and how much more one could learn from them."

"What could you learn from a meringue?" asked Eleanor's mother.

"My aunt has been known to learn humility from an ex-Viceroy," said Clovis.

"I wish cook would learn to make curry, or have the sense to leave it alone," said Arlington, suddenly and savagely.

Eleanor's face softened. It was like one of his old remarks in the days when there was no abyss between them.

It was during the debate on the Foreign Office vote that Stringham made his great remark that "the people of Crete unfortunately make more history than they can consume locally." It was not brilliant, but it came in the middle of a dull speech, and the House was quite pleased with it. Old gentlemen with bad memories said it reminded them of Disraeli.

It was Eleanor's friend, Gertrude Ilpton, who drew her attention to Arlington's newest outbreak. Eleanor in these days avoided the morning papers.

"It's very modern, and I suppose very clever," she observed.

"Of course it's clever," said Gertrude; "all Lady Isobel's sayings are clever, and luckily they bear repeating."

"Are you sure it's one of her sayings?" asked Eleanor.

"My dear, I've heard her say it dozens of times."

"So that is where he gets his humour," said Eleanor slowly, and the hard lines deepened round her mouth.

The death of Eleanor Stringham from an overdose of chloral, occurring at the end of a rather uneventful season, excited a certain amount of unobtrusive speculation. Clovis, who perhaps exaggerated the importance of curry in the home, hinted at domestic sorrow.

And of course Arlington never knew. It was the tragedy of his life that he should miss the fullest effect of his jesting.

SREDNI VASHTAR

CONRADIN was ten years old, and the doctor had pronounced his professional opinion that the boy would not
live another five years. The doctor was silky and effete, and
counted for little, but his opinion was endorsed by Mrs. De
Ropp, who counted for nearly everything. Mrs. De Ropp
was Conradin's cousin and guardian, and in his eyes she represented those three-fifths of the world that are necessary and
disagreeable and real; the other two-fifths, in perpetual antagonism to the foregoing, were summed up in himself and his
imagination. One of these days Conradin supposed he would
succumb to the mastering pressure of wearisome necessary
things—such as illnesses and coddling restrictions and drawn-
out dulness. Without his imagination, which was rampant
under the spur of loneliness, he would have succumbed long
ago.

Mrs. De Ropp would never, in her honestest moments, have
confessed to herself that she disliked Conradin, though she
might have been dimly aware that thwarting him "for his
good" was a duty which she did not find particularly irksome.
Conradin hated her with a desperate sincerity which he was
perfectly able to mask. Such few pleasures as he could contrive for himself gained an added relish from the likelihood
that they would be displeasing to his guardian, and from the
realm of his imagination she was locked out—an unclean
thing, which should find no entrance.

In the dull, cheerless garden, overlooked by so many windows that were ready to open with a message not to do this
or that, or a reminder that medicines were due, he found little
attraction. The few fruit-trees that it contained were set
jealously apart from his plucking, as though they were rare
specimens of their kind blooming in an arid waste; it would
probably have been difficult to find a market-gardener who
would have offered ten shillings for their entire yearly produce.
In a forgotten corner, however, almost hidden behind a dismal
shrubbery, was a disused tool-shed of respectable proportions.

and within its walls Conradin found a haven, something that took on the varying aspects of a playroom and a cathedral. He had peopled it with a legion of familiar phantoms, evoked partly from fragments of history and partly from his own brain, but it also boasted two inmates of flesh and blood. In one corner lived a ragged-plumaged Houdan hen, on which the boy lavished an affection that had scarcely another outlet. Further back in the gloom stood a large hutch, divided into two compartments, one of which was fronted with close iron bars. This was the abode of a large polecat-ferret, which a friendly butcher-boy had once smuggled, cage and all, into its present quarters, in exchange for a long-secreted hoard of small silver. Conradin was dreadfully afraid of the lithe, sharp-fanged beast, but it was his most treasured possession. Its very presence in the tool-shed was a secret and fearful joy, to be kept scrupulously from the knowledge of the Woman, as he privately dubbed his cousin. And one day, out of Heaven knows what material, he spun the beast a wonderful name, and from that moment it grew into a god and a religion. The Woman indulged in religion once a week at a church near by, and took Conradin with her, but to him the church service was an alien rite in the House of Rimmon. Every Thursday, in the dim and musty silence of the tool-shed, he 'worshipped with mystic and elaborate ceremonial before the wooden hutch where dwelt Sredni Vashtar, the great ferret. Red flowers in their season and scarlet berries in the winter-time were offered at his shrine, for he was a god who laid some special stress on the fierce impatient side of things, as opposed to the Woman's religion, which, as far as Conradin could observe, went to great lengths in the contrary direction. And on great festivals powdered nutmeg was strewn in front of his hutch, an important feature of the offering being that the nutmeg had to be stolen. These festivals were of irregular occurrence, and were chiefly appointed to celebrate some passing event. On one occasion, when Mrs. De Ropp suffered from acute toothache for three days, Conradin kept up the festival during the entire three days, and almost succeeded in persuading himself that Sredni Vashtar was personally responsible for the toothache.

If the malady had lasted for another day the supply of nutmeg would have given out.

The Houdan hen was never drawn into the cult of Sredni Vashtar. Conradin had long ago settled that she was an Anabaptist. He did not pretend to have the remotest knowledge as to what an Anabaptist was, but he privately hoped that it was dashing and not very respectable. Mrs. De Ropp was the ground plan on which he based and detested all respectability.

After a while Conradin's absorption in the tool-shed began to attract the notice of his guardian. "It is not good for him to be pottering down there in all weathers," she promptly decided, and at breakfast one morning she announced that the Houdan hen had been sold and taken away overnight. With her short-sighted eyes she peered at Conradin, waiting for an outbreak of rage and sorrow, which she was ready to rebuke with a flow of excellent precepts and reasoning. But Conradin said nothing: there was nothing to be said. Something perhaps in his white set face gave her a momentary qualm, for at tea that afternoon there was toast on the table, a delicacy which she usually banned on the ground that it was bad for him; also because the making of it "gave trouble," a deadly offence in the middle-class feminine eye.

"I thought you liked toast," she exclaimed, with an injured air, observing that he did not touch it.

"Sometimes," said Conradin.

In the shed that evening there was an innovation in the worship of the hutch-god. Conradin had been wont to chant his praises, tonight he asked a boon.

"Do one thing for me, Sredni Vashtar."

The thing was not specified. As Sredni Vashtar was a god he must be supposed to know. And choking back a sob as he looked at that other empty corner, Conradin went back to the world he so hated.

And every night, in the welcome darkness of his bedroom, and every evening in the dusk of the tool-shed, Conradin's bitter litany went up: "Do one thing for me, Sredni Vashtar."

Mrs. De Ropp noticed that the visits to the shed did not cease, and one day she made a further journey of inspection.

"What are you keeping in that locked hutch?" she asked. "I believe it's guinea-pigs. I'll have them all cleared away."

Conradin shut his lips tight, but the Woman ransacked his bedroom till she found the carefully hidden key, and forthwith marched down to the shed to complete her discovery. It was a cold afternoon, and Conradin had been bidden to keep to the house. From the furthest window of the dining-room the door of the shed could just be seen beyond the corner of the shrubbery, and there Conradin stationed himself. He saw the Woman enter, and then he imagined her opening the door of the sacred hutch and peering down with her short-sighted eyes into the thick straw bed where his god lay hidden. Perhaps she would prod at the straw in her clumsy impatience. And Conradin fervently breathed his prayer for the last time. But he knew as he prayed that he did not believe. He knew that the Woman would come out presently with that pursed smile he loathed so well on her face, and that in an hour or two the gardener would carry away his wonderful god, a god no longer, but a simple brown ferret in a hutch. And he knew that the Woman would triumph always as she triumphed now, and that he would grow ever more sickly under her pestering and domineering and superior wisdom, till one day nothing would matter much more with him, and the doctor would be proved right. And in the sting and misery of his defeat, he began to chant loudly and defiantly the hymn of his threatened idol:

> Sredni Vashtar went forth,
> His thoughts were red thoughts and his teeth were white.
> His enemies called for peace, but he brought them death.
> Sredni Vashtar the Beautiful.

And then of a sudden he stopped his chanting and drew closer to the window-pane. The door of the shed still stood ajar as it had been left, and the minutes were slipping by. They were long minutes, but they slipped by nevertheless. He watched the starlings running and flying in little parties across the lawn; he counted them over and over again, with one eye always on that swinging door. A sour-faced maid came in to lay the table for tea, and still Conradin stood and waited and watched. Hope had crept by inches into his heart, and now a look of triumph began to blaze in his eyes that had only known the wistful patience of defeat. Under his breath, with a furtive exultation, he began once again the pæan of victory and devastation. And presently his eyes were rewarded: out through that doorway came a long, low, yellow-and-brown beast, with eyes a-blink at the waning daylight, and dark wet stains around the fur of jaws and throat. Conradin dropped on his knees. The great polecat-ferret made its way down to a small brook at the foot of the garden, drank for a moment, then crossed a little plank bridge and was lost to sight in the bushes. Such was the passing of Sredni Vashtar.

"Tea is ready," said the sour-faced maid; "where is the mistress?"

"She went down to the shed some time ago," said Conradin.

And while the maid went to summon her mistress to tea, Conradin fished a toasting-fork out of the sideboard drawer and proceeded to toast himself a piece of bread. And during the toasting of it and the buttering of it with much butter and the slow enjoyment of eating it, Conradin listened to the noises and silences which fell in quick spasms beyond the dining-room door. The loud foolish screaming of the maid, the answering chorus of wondering ejaculations from the kitchen region, the scuttering footsteps and hurried embassies for outside help, and then, after a lull, the scared sobbings and the shuffling tread of those who bore a heavy burden into the house.

"Whoever will break it to the poor child? I couldn't for the life of me!" exclaimed a shrill voice. And while they debated the matter among themselves, Conradin made himself another piece of toast.

ADRIAN

A CHAPTER IN ACCLIMATIZATION

HIS baptismal register spoke of him pessimistically as John Henry, but he had left that behind with the other maladies of infancy, and his friends knew him under the front-name of Adrian. His mother lived in Bethnal Green, which was not altogether his fault; one can discourage too much history in one's family, but one cannot always prevent geography. And, after all, the Bethnal Green habit has this virtue—that it is seldom transmitted to the next generation. Adrian lived in a roomlet which came under the auspicious constellation of W.

How he lived was to a great extent a mystery even to himself; his struggle for existence probably coincided in many material details with the rather dramatic accounts he gave of it to sympathetic acquaintances. All that is definitely known is that he now and then emerged from the struggle to dine at the Ritz or Carlton, correctly garbed and with a correctly critical appetite. On these occasions he was usually the guest of Lucas Croyden, an amiable worldling, who had three thousand a year and a taste for introducing impossible people to irreproachable cookery. Like most men who combine three thousand a year with an uncertain digestion, Lucas was a Socialist, and he argued that you cannot hope to elevate the masses until you have brought plovers' eggs into their lives and taught them to appreciate the difference between coupe Jacques and Macédoine de fruits. His friends pointed out that it was a doubtful kindness to initiate a boy from behind a drapery counter into the blessedness of the higher catering, to which Lucas invariably replied that all kindnesses were doubtful. Which was perhaps true.

It was after one of his Adrian evenings that Lucas met his aunt, Mrs. Mebberley, at a fashionable teashop, where the lamp of family life is still kept burning and you meet relatives who might otherwise have slipped your memory.

"Who was that good-looking boy who was dining with you last night?" she asked. "He looked much too nice to be thrown away upon you."

Susan Mebberley was a charming woman, but she was also an aunt.

"Who are his people?" she continued, when the protégé's name (revised version) had been given her.

"His mother lives at Beth—"

Lucas checked himself on the threshold of what was perhaps a social indiscretion.

"Beth? Where is it? It sounds like Asia Minor. Is she mixed up with Consular people?"

"Oh, no. Her work lies among the poor."

This was a side-slip into truth. The mother of Adrian was employed in a laundry.

"I see," said Mrs. Mebberley, "mission work of some sort. And meanwhile the boy has no one to look after him. It's obviously my duty to see that he doesn't come to harm. Bring him to call on me."

"My dear Aunt Susan," expostulated Lucas, "I really know very little about him. He may not be at all nice, you know, on further acquaintance."

"He has delightful hair and a weak mouth. I shall take him with me to Homburg or Cairo."

"It's the maddest thing I ever heard of," said Lucas angrily.

"Well, there is a strong strain of madness in our family. If you haven't noticed it yourself all your friends must have."

"One is so dreadfully under everybody's eyes at Homburg. At least you might give him a preliminary trial at Etretat."

"And be surrounded by Americans trying to talk French? No, thank you. I love Americans, but not when they try to talk French. What a blessing it is that they never try to talk English. Tomorrow at five you can bring your young friend to call on me."

And Lucas, realizing that Susan Mebberley was a woman as well as an aunt, saw that she would have to be allowed to have her own way.

Adrian was duly carried abroad under the Mebberley wing; but as a reluctant concession to sanity Homburg and other inconveniently fashionable resorts were given a wide berth, and the Mebberley establishment planted itself down in the best hotel at Dohledorf, an Alpine townlet somewhere at the back of the Engadine. It was the usual kind of resort, with the usual type of visitors, that one finds over the greater part of Switzerland during the summer season, but to Adrian it was all unusual. The mountain air, the certainty of regular and abundant meals, and in particular the social atmosphere, affected him much as the indiscriminating fervour of a forcing-house might affect a weed that had strayed within its limits. He had been brought up in a world where breakages were regarded as crimes and expiated as such; it was something new and altogether exhilarating to find that you were considered rather amusing if you smashed things in the right manner and at the recognized hours. Susan Mebberley had expressed the intention of showing Adrian a bit of the world; the particular bit of the world represented by Dohledorf began to be shown a good deal of Adrian.

Lucas got occasional glimpses of the Alpine sojourn, not from his aunt or Adrian, but from the industrious pen of Clovis, who was also moving as a satellite in the Mebberley constellation.

"The entertainment which Susan got up last night ended in disaster. I thought it would. The Grobmayer child, a particularly loathsome five-year-old, had appeared as 'Bubbles' during the early part of the evening, and been put to bed during the interval. Adrian watched his opportunity and kidnapped it when the nurse was downstairs, and introduced it during the second half of the entertainment, thinly disguised as a performing pig. It certainly *looked* very like a pig, and grunted and slobbered just like the real article; no one knew exactly what it was, but every one said it was awfully clever, especially the Grobmayers. At the third curtain Adrian pinched it too hard, and it yelled 'Marmar'! I am supposed to be good at descriptions, but don't ask me to describe the sayings and doings of the Grobmayers at that moment; it was like one of the angrier Psalms set to Strauss's music. We have moved to an hotel higher up the valley."

Clovis's next letter arrived five days later, and was written from the Hotel Steinbock.

"We left the Hotel Victoria this morning. It was fairly comfortable and quiet—at least there was an air of repose about it when we arrived. Before we had been in residence twenty-four hours most of the repose had vanished 'like a dutiful bream,' as Adrian expressed it. However, nothing unduly outrageous happened till last night, when Adrian had a fit of insomnia and amused himself by unscrewing and transposing all the bedroom numbers on his floor. He transferred the bathroom label to the adjoining bedroom door, which happened to be that of Frau Hofrath Schilling, and this morning from seven o'clock onwards the old lady had a stream of involuntary visitors; she was too horrified and scandalized it seems to get up and lock her door. The would-be bathers flew back in confusion to their rooms, and, of course, the change of numbers led them astray again, and the corridor gradually filled with panic-stricken, scantily robed humans, dashing wildly about like rabbits in a ferret-infested warren. It took nearly an hour before the guests were all sorted into their respective rooms, and the Frau Hofrath's condition was still causing some anxiety when we left. Susan is beginning to look a little worried. She can't very well turn the boy adrift, as he hasn't got any money, and she can't send him to his people as she doesn't know where they are. Adrian says his mother moves about a good deal and he's lost her address. Probably, if the truth were known, he's had a row at home. So many boys nowadays seem to think that quarrelling with one's family is a recognized occupation."

Lucas's next communication from the travellers took the form of a telegram from Mrs. Mebberley herself. It was sent "reply prepaid," and consisted of a single sentence: "In Heaven's name, where is Beth?"

THE CHAPLET

A STRANGE stillness hung over the restaurant; it was one of those rare moments when the orchestra was not discoursing the strains of the Ice-cream Sailor waltz.

"Did I ever tell you," asked Clovis of his friend, "the tragedy of music at mealtimes?

"It was a gala evening at the Grand Sybaris Hotel, and a special dinner was being served in the Amethyst dining-hall. The Amethyst dining-hall had almost a European reputation, especially with that section of Europe which is historically identified with the Jordan Valley. Its cooking was beyond reproach, and its orchestra was sufficiently highly salaried to be above criticism. Thither came in shoals the intensely musical and the almost intensely musical, who are very many, and in still greater numbers the merely musical, who know how Tschaikowsky's name is pronounced and can recognize several of Chopin's nocturnes if you give them due warning; these eat in the nervous, detached manner of roebuck feeding in the open, and keep anxious ears cocked towards the orchestra for the first hint of a recognizable melody.

" 'Ah, yes, Pagliacci,' they murmur, as the opening strains follow hot upon the soup, and if no contradiction is forthcoming from any better-informed quarter they break forth into subdued humming by way of supplementing the efforts of the musicians. Sometimes the melody starts on level terms with the soup, in which case the banqueters contrive somehow to hum between the spoonfuls; the facial expression of enthusiasts who are punctuating potage St. Germain with Pagliacci is not beautiful, but it should be seen by those who are bent on observing all sides of life. One cannot discount the unpleasant things of this world merely by looking the other way.

"In addition to the aforementioned types the restaurant was patronized by a fair sprinkling of the absolutely non-musical; their presence in the dining-hall could only be explained on the supposition that they had come there to dine

"The earlier stages of the dinner had worn off. The wine

lists had been consulted, by some with the blank embarrassment of a schoolboy suddenly called on to locate a Minor
Prophet in the tangled hinterland of the Old Testament, by
others with the severe scrutiny which suggests that they have
visited most of the higher-priced wines in their own homes and
probed their family weaknesses. The diners who chose their
wine in the latter fashion always gave their orders in a pene-
trating voice, with a plentiful garnishing of stage directions.
By insisting on having your bottle pointing to the north when
the cork is being drawn, and calling the waiter Max, you may
induce an impression on your guests which hours of laboured
boasting might be powerless to achieve. For this purpose, however, the guests must be chosen as carefully as the wine.

"Standing aside from the revellers in the shadow of a
massive pillar was an interested spectator who was assuredly of
the feast, and yet not in it. Monsieur Aristide Saucourt was
the *chef* of the Grand Sybaris Hotel, and if he had an equal
in his profession he had never acknowledged the fact. In his
own domain he was a potentate, hedged around with the cold
brutality that Genius expects rather than excuses in her children; he never forgave, and those who served him were
careful that there should be little to forgive. In the outer
world, the world which devoured his creations, he was an
influence; how profound or how shallow an influence he never
attempted to guess. It is the penalty and the safeguard of
genius that it computes itself by troy weight in a world that
measures by vulgar hundredweights.

"Once in a way the great man would be seized with a desire
to watch the effect of his master-efforts, just as the guiding
brain of Krupp's might wish at a supreme moment to intrude
into the firing line of an artillery duel. And such an occasion
was the present. For the first time in the history of the Grand
Sybaris Hotel, he was presenting to its guests the dish which
he had brought to that pitch of perfection which almost
amounts to scandal. Canetons à la mode d'Amblève. In thin
gilt lettering on the creamy white of the menu how little those
words conveyed to the bulk of the imperfectly educated diners.
And yet how much specialized effort had been lavished. how

much carefully treasured lore had been ungarnered, before those six words could be written. In the Department of Deux-Sèvres ducklings had lived peculiar and beautiful lives and died in the odour of satiety to furnish the main theme of the dish; champignons, which even a purist for Saxon English would have hesitated to address as mushrooms, had contributed their languorous atrophied bodies to the garnishing, and a sauce devised in the twilight reign of the Fifteenth Louis had been summoned back from the imperishable past to take its part in the wonderful confection. Thus far had human effort laboured to achieve the desired result; the rest had been left to human genius—the genius of Aristide Saucourt.

"And now the moment had arrived for the serving of the great dish, the dish which world-weary Grand Dukes and market-obsessed money magnates counted among their happiest memories. And at the same moment something else happened. The leader of the highly salaried orchestra placed his violin caressingly against his chin, lowered his eyelids, and floated into a sea of melody.

" 'Hark!' said most of the diners, 'he is playing "The Chaplet." '

"They knew it was 'The Chaplet' because they had heard it played at luncheon and afternoon tea, and at supper the night before, and had not had time to forget.

" 'Yes, he is playing "The Chaplet," ' they reassured one another. The general voice was unanimous on the subject. The orchestra had already played it eleven times that day, four times by desire and seven times from force of habit, but the familiar strains were greeted with the rapture due to a revelation. A murmur of much humming rose from half the tables in the room, and some of the more overwrought listeners laid down knife and fork in order to be able to burst in with loud clappings at the earliest permissible moment.

"And the Canetons à la mode d'Amblève? In stupefied, sickened wonder Aristide watched them grow cold in total neglect, or suffer the almost worse indignity of perfunctory pecking and listless munching while the banqueters lavished their approval and applause on the music-makers. Calves' liver and bacon, with parsley sauce, could hardly have figured more ignominiously in the evening's entertainment. And while the master of culinary art leaned back against the sheltering pillar, choking with a horrible brain-searing rage that could find no outlet for its agony, the orchestra leader was bowing his acknowledgments of the hand-clappings that rose in a storm around him. Turning to his colleagues he nodded the signal for an encore. But before the violin had been lifted anew into position there came from the shadow of the pillar an explosive negative.

" 'Noh! Noh! You do not play thot again!'

"The musician turned in furious astonishment. Had he taken warning from the look in the other man's eyes he might have acted differently. But the admiring plaudits were ringing in his ears, and he snarled out sharply, 'That is for me to decide.'

" 'Noh! You play thot never again,' shouted the *chef*, and the next moment he had flung himself violently upon the loathed being who had supplanted him in the world's esteem. A large metal tureen, filled to the brim with steaming soup, had just been placed on a side table in readiness for a late party of diners; before the waiting staff or the guests had time to realize what was happening, Aristide had dragged his struggling victim up to the table and plunged his head deep down into the almost boiling contents of the tureen. At the further end of the room the diners were still spasmodically applauding in view of an encore.

"Whether the leader of the orchestra died from drowning by soup, or from the shock to his professional vanity, or was scalded to death, the doctors were never wholly able to agree. Monsieur Aristide Saucourt, who now lives in complete retirement, always inclined to the drowning theory."

THE QUEST

AN unwonted peace hung over the Villa Elsinore, broken, however, at frequent intervals, by clamorous lamentations suggestive of bewildered bereavement. The Momebys had lost their infant child; hence the peace which its absence entailed; they were looking for it in wild, undisciplined fashion, giving tongue the whole time, which accounted for the outcry which swept through house and garden whenever they returned to try the home coverts anew. Clovis, who was temporarily and unwillingly a paying guest at the villa, had been dozing in a hammock at the far end of the garden when Mrs. Momeby had broken the news to him.

"We've lost Baby," she screamed.

"Do you mean that it's dead, or stampeded, or that you staked it at cards and lost it that way?" asked Clovis lazily.

"He was toddling about quite happily on the lawn," said Mrs. Momeby tearfully, "and Arnold had just come in, and I was asking him what sort of sauce he would like with the asparagus—"

"I hope he said hollandaise," interrupted Clovis, with a show of quickened interest, "because if there's anything I hate—"

"And all of a sudden I missed Baby," continued Mrs. Momeby in a shriller tone. "We've hunted high and low, in house and garden and outside the gates, and he's nowhere to be seen."

"Is he anywhere to be heard?" asked Clovis; "if not, he must be at least two miles away."

"But where? And how?" asked the distracted mother.

"Perhaps an eagle or a wild beast has carried him off," suggested Clovis.

"There aren't eagles and wild beasts in Surrey," said Mrs. Momeby, but a note of horror had crept into her voice.

"They escape now and then from travelling shows. Sometimes I think they let them get loose for the sake of the advertisement. Think what a sensational headline it would make

164

in the local papers: 'Infant son of prominent Nonconformist devoured by spotted hyæna.' Your husband isn't a prominent Nonconformist, but his mother came of Wesleyan stock, and you must allow the newspapers some latitude."

"But we should have found his remains," sobbed Mrs. Momeby.

"If the hyæna was really hungry and not merely toying with his food there wouldn't be much in the way of remains. It would be like the small-boy-and-apple story—there ain't going to be no core."

Mrs. Momeby turned away hastily to seek comfort and counsel in some other direction. With the selfish absorption of young motherhood she entirely disregarded Clovis's obvious anxiety about the asparagus sauce. Before she had gone a yard, however, the click of the side gate caused her to pull up sharp. Miss Gilpet, from the Villa Peterhof, had come over to hear details of the bereavement. Clovis was already rather bored with the story, but Mrs. Momeby was equipped with that merciless faculty which finds as much joy in the ninetieth time of telling as in the first.

"Arnold had just come in; he was complaining of rheumatism—"

"There are so many things to complain of in this household that it would never have occurred to me to complain of rheumatism," murmured Clovis.

"He was complaining of rheumatism," continued Mrs. Momeby, trying to throw a chilling inflection into a voice that was already doing a good deal of sobbing and talking at high pressure as well.

She was again interrupted.

"There is no such thing as rheumatism," said Miss Gilpet. She said it with the conscious air of defiance that a waiter adopts in announcing that the cheapest-priced claret in the wine-list is no more. She did not proceed, however, to offer the alternative of some more expensive malady, but denied the existence of them all.

Mrs. Momeby's temper began to shine out through her grief.

"I suppose you'll say next that Baby hasn't really disappeared."

"He has disappeared," conceded Miss Gilpet, "but only because you haven't sufficient faith to find him. It's only lack of faith on your part that prevents him from being restored to you safe and well."

"But if he's been eaten in the meantime by a hyæna and partly digested," said Clovis, who clung affectionately to his wild beast theory, "surely some ill-effects would be noticeable?"

Miss Gilpet was rather staggered by this complication of the question.

"I feel sure that a hyæna has not eaten him," she said lamely.

"The hyæna may be equally certain that it has. You see, it may have just as much faith as you have, and more special knowledge as to the present whereabouts of the baby."

Mrs. Momeby was in tears again. "If you have faith," she sobbed, struck by a happy inspiration, "won't you find our little Erik for us? I am sure you have powers that are denied to us."

Rose-Marie Gilpet was thoroughly sincere in her adherence to Christian Science principles; whether she understood or correctly expounded them the learned in such manners may best decide. In the present case she was undoubtedly confronted with a great opportunity, and as she started forth on her vague search she strenuously summoned to her aid every scrap of faith that she possessed. She passed out into the bare and open high road, followed by Mrs. Momeby's warning, "It's no use going there, we've searched there a dozen times." But Rose-Marie's ears were already deaf to all things save self-congratulation; for sitting in the middle of the highway, playing contentedly with the dust and some faded buttercups, was a white-pinafored baby with a mop of tow-coloured hair tied over one temple with a pale-blue ribbon. Taking first the usual feminine precaution of looking to see that no motor-car was on the distant horizon, Rose-Marie dashed at the child and bore it, despite its vigorous opposition, in through the portals of Elsinore. The child's furious screams had already announced the fact of its discovery, and the almost hysterical parents raced down the lawn to meet their restored offspring. The æsthetic value of the scene was marred in some degree by Rose-Marie's difficulty in holding the struggling infant, which was borne wrong-end foremost towards the agitated bosom of its family. "Our own little Erik come back to us," cried the Momebys in unison; as the child had rammed its fists tightly into its eye-sockets and nothing could be seen of its face but a widely gaping mouth, the recognition was in itself almost an act of faith.

"Is he glad to get back to Daddy and Mummy again?" crooned Mrs. Momeby; the preference which the child was showing for its dust and buttercup distractions was so marked that the question struck Clovis as being unnecessarily tactless.

"Give him a ride on the roly-poly," suggested the father brilliantly, as the howls continued with no sign of early abatement. In a moment the child had been placed astride the big garden roller and a preliminary tug was given to set it in motion. From the hollow depths of the cylinder came an ear-splitting roar, drowning even the vocal efforts of the squalling baby, and immediately afterwards there crept forth a white-pinafored infant with a mop of tow-coloured hair tied over one temple with a pale blue ribbon. There was no mistaking either the features or the lung-power of the new arrival.

"Our own little Erik," screamed Mrs. Momeby, pouncing on him and nearly smothering him with kisses; "did he hide in the roly-poly to give us all a big fright?"

This was the obvious explanation of the child's sudden disappearance and equally abrupt discovery. There remained, however, the problem of the interloping baby, which now sat whimpering on the lawn in a disfavour as chilling as its previous popularity had been unwelcome. The Momebys glared at it as though it had wormed its way into their short-lived affections by heartless and unworthy pretences. Miss Gilpet's face took on an ashen tinge as she stared helplessly at the bunched-up figure that had been such a gladsome sight to her eyes a few moments ago.

"When love is over, how little of love even the lover understands," quoted Clovis to himself.

Rose-Marie was the first to break the silence.

"If that is Erik you have in your arms, who is—that?"

"That, I think, is for you to explain," said Mrs. Momeby stiffly.

"Obviously," said Clovis, "it's a duplicate Erik that your powers of faith called into being. The question is: What are you going to do with him?"

The ashen pallor deepened in Rose-Marie's cheeks. Mrs. Momeby clutched the genuine Erik closer to her side, as though she feared that her uncanny neighbour might out of sheer pique turn him into a bowl of gold-fish.

"I found him sitting in the middle of the road," said Rose-Marie weakly.

"You can't take him back and leave him there," said Clovis; "the highway is meant for traffic, not to be used as a lumber-room for disused miracles."

Rose-Marie wept. The proverb "Weep and you weep alone," broke down as badly on application as most of its kind. Both babies were wailing lugubriously, and the parent Momebys had scarcely recovered from their earlier lachrymose condition. Clovis alone maintained an unruffled cheerfulness.

"Must I keep him always?" asked Rose-Marie dolefully.

"Not always," said Clovis consolingly; "he can go into the Navy when he's thirteen." Rose-Marie wept afresh.

"Of course," added Clovis, "there may be no end of a bother about his birth certificate. You'll have to explain matters to the Admiralty, and they're dreadfully hidebound."

It was rather a relief when a breathless nursemaid from the Villa Charlottenburg over the way came running across the lawn to claim little Percy, who had slipped out of the front gate and disappeared like a twinkling from the high road.

And even then Clovis found it necessary to go in person to the kitchen to make sure about the asparagus sauce.

WRATISLAV

THE Gräfin's two elder sons had made deplorable marriages. It was, observed Clovis, a family habit. The youngest boy, Wratislav, who was the black sheep of a rather greyish family, had as yet made no marriage at all.

"There is certainly this much to be said for viciousness," said the Gräfin, "it keeps boys out of mischief."

"Does it?" asked the Baroness Sophie, not by way of questioning the statement, but with a painstaking effort to talk intelligently. It was the one matter in which she attempted to override the decrees of Providence, which had obviously never intended that she should talk otherwise than inanely.

"I don't know why I shouldn't talk cleverly," she would complain; "my mother was considered a brilliant conversationalist."

"These things have a way of skipping one generation," said the Gräfin.

"That seems so unjust," said Sophie; "one doesn't object to one's mother having outshone one as a clever talker, but I must admit that I should be rather annoyed if my daughters talked brilliantly."

"Well, none of them do," said the Gräfin consolingly.

"I don't know about that," said the Baroness, promptly veering round in defence of her offspring. "Elsa said something quite clever on Thursday about the Triple Alliance. Something about it being like a paper umbrella, that was all right as long as you didn't take it out in the rain. It's not every one who could say that."

"Every one has said it; at least every one that I know. But then I know very few people."

"I don't think you're particularly agreeable today."

"I never am. Haven't you noticed that women with a really perfect profile like mine are seldom even moderately agreeable?"

"I don't think your profile is so perfect as all that," said the Baroness.

"It would be surprising if it wasn't. My mother was one of the most noted classical beauties of her day."

"These things sometimes skip a generation, you know," put in the Baroness, with the breathless haste of one to whom repartee comes as rarely as the finding of a gold-handled umbrella.

"My dear Sophie," said the Gräfin sweetly, "that isn't in the least bit clever; but you do try so hard that I suppose I oughtn't to discourage you. Tell me something: has it ever occurred to you that Elsa would do very well for Wratislav? It's time he married somebody, and why not Elsa?"

"Elsa marry that dreadful boy!" gasped the Baroness.

"Beggars can't be choosers," observed the Gräfin.

"Elsa isn't a beggar!"

"Not financially, or I shouldn't have suggested the match. But she's getting on, you know, and has no pretensions to brains or looks or anything of that sort."

"You seem to forget that she's my daughter."

"That shows my generosity. But, seriously, I don't see what there is against Wratislav. He has no debts—at least, nothing worth speaking about."

"But think of his reputation! If half the things they say about him are true—"

"Probably three-quarters of them are. But what of it? You don't want an archangel for a son-in-law."

"I don't want Wratislav. My poor Elsa would be miserable with him."

"A little misery wouldn't matter very much with her; it would go so well with the way she does her hair, and if she couldn't get on with Wratislav she could always go and do good among the poor."

The Baroness picked up a framed photograph from the table.

"He certainly is very handsome," she said doubtfully; adding even more doubtfully. "I dare say dear Elsa might reform him."

The Gräfin had the presence of mind to laugh in the right key.

. . . .

Three weeks later the Gräfin bore down upon the Baroness Sophie in a foreign bookseller's shop in the Graben, where she was, possibly, buying books of devotion, though it was the wrong counter for them.

"I've just left the dear children at the Rodenstahls'," was the Gräfin's greeting.

"Were they looking very happy?" asked the Baroness.

"Wratislav was wearing some new English clothes, so, of course, he was quite happy. I overheard him telling Toni a rather amusing story about a nun and a mousetrap, which won't bear repetition. Elsa was telling every one else a witticism about the Triple Alliance being like a paper umbrella—which seems to bear repetition with Christian fortitude."

"Did they seem much wrapped up in each other?"

"To be candid, Elsa looked as if she were wrapped up in a horse-rug. And why let her wear saffron colour?"

"I always think it goes with her complexion."

"Unfortunately it doesn't. It stays with it. Ugh. Don't forget, you're lunching with me on Thursday."

The Baroness was late for her luncheon engagement the following Thursday.

"Imagine what has happened!" she screamed as she burst into the room.

"Something remarkable, to make you late for a meal," said the Gräfin.

"Elsa has run away with the Rodenstahls' chauffeur!"

"Kolossal!"

"Such a thing as that no one in our family has ever done," gasped the Baroness.

"Perhaps he didn't appeal to them in the same way," suggested the Gräfin judicially.

The Baroness began to feel that she was not getting the astonishment and sympathy to which her catastrophe entitled her.

"At any rate," she snapped, "now she can't marry Wratislav."

"She couldn't in any case," said the Gräfin; "he left suddenly for abroad last night."

"For abroad! Where?"

"For Mexico, I believe."

"Mexico! But what for? Why Mexico?"

"The English have a proverb, 'Conscience makes cowboys of us all.'"

"I didn't know Wratislav had a conscience."

"My dear Sophie, he hasn't. It's other people's consciences that send one abroad in a hurry. Let's go and eat."

THE EASTER EGG

IT was distinctly hard lines for Lady Barbara, who came of good fighting stock, and was one of the bravest women of her generation, that her son should be so undisguisedly a coward. Whatever good qualities Lester Slaggby may have possessed, and he was in some respects charming, courage could certainly never be imputed to him. As a child he had suffered from childish timidity, as a boy from unboyish funk, and as a youth he had exchanged unreasoning fears for others which were more formidable from the fact of having a carefully-thought-out basis. He was frankly afraid of animals, nervous with firearms, and never crossed the Channel without mentally comparing the numerical proportion of life belts to passengers. On horseback he seemed to require as many hands as a Hindu god, at least four for clutching the reins, and two more for patting the horse soothingly on the neck. Lady Barbara no longer pretended not to see her son's prevailing weakness; with her usual courage she faced the knowledge of it squarely, and, mother-like, loved him none the less.

Continental travel, anywhere away from the great tourist tracks, was a favoured hobby with Lady Barbara, and Lester joined her as often as possible. Eastertide usually found her at Knobaltheim, an upland township in one of those small princedoms that make inconspicuous freckles on the map of Central Europe.

A long-standing acquaintanceship with the reigning family made her a personage of due importance in the eyes of her old friend the Burgomaster, and she was anxiously consulted by that worthy on the momentous occasion when the Prince made known his intention of coming in person to open a sanatorium outside the town. All the usual items in a programme of welcome, some of them fatuous and commonplace, others quaint and charming, had been arranged for, but the Burgomaster hoped that the resourceful English lady might have something new and tasteful to suggest in the way of loyal greeting. The Prince was known to the outside world, if at all, as an old-fashioned reactionary, combating modern progress, as it were, with a wooden sword; to his own people he was known as a kindly old gentleman with a certain endearing stateliness which had nothing of standoffishness about it. Knobaltheim was anxious to do its best. Lady Barbara discussed the matter with Lester and one or two acquaintances in her little hotel, but ideas were difficult to come by.

"Might I suggest something to the gnädige Frau?" asked a sallow high-cheek-boned lady to whom the Englishwoman had spoken once or twice, and whom she had set down in her mind as probably a Southern Slav.

"Might I suggest something for the Reception Fest?" she went on, with a certain shy eagerness. "Our little child here, our baby, we will dress him in little white coat, with small wings, as an Easter angel, and he will carry a large white Easter egg, and inside shall be a basket of plover eggs, of which the Prince is so fond, and he shall give it to his Highness as Easter offering. It is so pretty an idea; we have seen it done once in Styria."

Lady Barbara looked dubiously at the proposed Easter angel, a fair, wooden-faced child of about four years old. She had noticed it the day before in the hotel, and wondered rather how such a tow-headed child could belong to such a dark-visaged couple as the woman and her husband; probably, she thought, an adopted baby, especially as the couple were not young.

"Of course Gnädige Frau will escort the little child up to the Prince," pursued the woman; "but he will be quite good, and do as he is told."

"We haf some pluffers' eggs shall come fresh from Wien," said the husband.

The small child and Lady Barbara seemed equally unenthusiastic about the pretty idea; Lester was openly discouraging, but when the Burgomaster heard of it he was enchanted. The combination of sentiment and plovers' eggs appealed strongly to his Teutonic mind.

On the eventful day the Easter angel, really quite prettily and quaintly dressed, was a centre of kindly interest to the gala crowd marshalled to receive his Highness. The mother was unobtrusive and less fussy than most parents would have been under the circumstances, merely stipulating that she should place the Easter egg herself in the arms that had been carefully schooled how to hold the precious burden. Then Lady Barbara moved forward, the child marching stolidly and with grim determination at her side. It had been promised cakes and sweeties galore if it gave the egg well and truly to the kind old gentleman who was waiting to receive it. Lester had tried to convey to it privately that horrible smackings would attend any failure in its share of the proceedings, but it is doubtful if his German caused more than an immediate distress. Lady Barbara had thoughtfully provided herself with an emergency supply of chocolate sweetmeats; children may sometimes be time-servers, but they do not encourage long accounts. As they approached nearer to the princely daïs Lady Barbara stood discreetly aside, and the stolid-faced infant walked forward alone, with staggering but steadfast gait, encouraged by a murmur of elderly approval. Lester, standing in the front row of the onlookers, turned to scan the crowd for the beaming faces of the happy parents. In a side-road which led to the railway station he saw a cab; entering the cab with every appearance of furtive haste were the dark-visaged couple who had been so plausibly eager for the "pretty idea." The sharpened instinct of cowardice lit up the situation to him in one swift flash. The blood roared and surged to his head as though thousands of floodgates had been opened in his veins and arteries, and his brain was the common sluice in which all the torrents met. He saw nothing but a blur around him. Then the blood ebbed away in quick waves, till his very heart seemed drained and empty, and he stood nervelessly, helplessly, dumbly watching the child, bearing its accursed burden with slow, relentless steps nearer and nearer to the group that waited sheep-like to receive him. A fascinated curiosity compelled Lester to turn his head towards the fugitives; the cab had started at hot pace in the direction of the station.

The next moment Lester was running, running faster than any of those present had ever seen a man run, and—he was not running away. For that stray fraction of his life some unwonted impulse beset him, some hint of the stock he came from, and he ran unflinchingly towards danger. He stooped and clutched at the Easter egg as one tries to scoop up the ball in Rugby football. What he meant to do with it he had not considered, the thing was to get it. But the child had been promised cakes and sweetmeats if it safely gave the egg into the hands of the kindly old gentleman; it uttered no scream, but it held to its charge with limpet grip. Lester sank to his knees, tugging savagely at the tightly clasped burden, and angry cries rose from the scandalized onlookers. A questioning, threatening ring formed round him, then shrank back in recoil as he shrieked out one hideous word. Lady Barbara heard the word and saw the crowd race away like scattered sheep, saw the Prince forcibly hustled away by his attendants; also she saw her son lying prone in an agony of overmastering terror, his spasm of daring shattered by the child's unexpected resistance, still clutching frantically, as though for safety, at that white-satin gew-gaw, unable to crawl even from its deadly neighbourhood, able only to scream and scream and scream. In her brain she was dimly conscious of balancing, or striving to balance, the abject shame which had him now in thrall against the one compelling act of courage which had flung him grandly and madly on to the point of danger. It was only for the fraction of a minute that she stood watching the two entangled figures, the infant with its woodenly obstinate face and body tense with dogged resistance, and the boy limp and already nearly dead with a terror that almost stifled his screams; and over them the long gala streamers flapping gaily in the sunshine. She never forgot the scene; but then, it was the last she ever saw.

Lady Barbara carries her scarred face with its sightless eyes as bravely as ever in the world, but at Eastertide her friends are careful to keep from her ears any mention of the children's Easter symbol.

FILBOID STUDGE, THE STORY OF A MOUSE THAT HELPED

"I WANT to marry your daughter," said Mark Spayley with faltering eagerness. "I am only an artist with an income of two hundred a year, and she is the daughter of an enormously wealthy man, so I suppose you will think my offer a piece of presumption."

Duncan Dullamy, the great company inflator, showed no outward sign of displeasure. As a matter of fact, he was secretly relieved at the prospect of finding even a two-hundred-a-year husband for his daughter Leonore. A crisis was rapidly rushing upon him, from which he knew he would emerge with neither money nor credit; all his recent ventures had fallen flat, and flattest of all had gone the wonderful new breakfast food, Pipenta, on the advertisement of which he had sunk such huge sums. It could scarcely be called a drug in the market; people bought drugs, but no one bought Pipenta.

"Would you marry Leonore if she were a poor man's daughter?" asked the man of phantom wealth.

"Yes," said Mark, wisely avoiding the error of over-protestation. And to his astonishment Leonore's father not only gave his consent, but suggested a fairly early date for the wedding.

"I wish I could show my gratitude in some way," said Mark with genuine emotion. "I'm afraid it's rather like the mouse proposing to help the lion."

"Get people to buy that beastly muck," said Dullamy, nodding savagely at a poster of the despised Pipenta, "and you'll have done more than any of my agents have been able to accomplish."

"It wants a better name," said Mark reflectively, "and something distinctive in the poster line. Anyway, I'll have a shot at it."

Three weeks later the world was advised of the coming of a new breakfast food, heralded under the resounding name of "Filboid Studge." Spayley put forth no pictures of massive babies springing up with fungus-like rapidity under its forcing influence, or of representatives of the leading nations of the world scrambling with fatuous eagerness for its possession. One huge sombre poster depicted the Damned in Hell suffering a new torment from their inability to get at the Filboid Studge which elegant young fiends held in transparent bowls just beyond their reach. The scene was rendered even more gruesome by a subtle suggestion of the features of leading men and women of the day in the portrayal of the Lost Souls; prominent individuals of both political parties, Society hostesses, well-known dramatic authors and novelists, and distinguished aeroplanists were dimly recognizable in that doomed throng; noted lights of the musical-comedy stage flickered wanly in the shades of the Inferno, smiling still from force of habit, but with the fearsome smiling rage of baffled effort. The poster bore no fulsome allusions to the merits of the new breakfast food, but a single grim statement ran in bold letters along its base: "They cannot buy it now."

Spayley had grasped the fact that people will do things from a sense of duty which they would never attempt as a pleasure. There are thousands of respectable middle-class men who, if you found them unexpectedly in a Turkish bath, would explain in all sincerity that a doctor had ordered them to take Turkish baths; if you told them in return that you went there because you liked it, they would stare in pained wonder at the frivolity of your motive. In the same way, whenever a massacre of Armenians is reported from Asia Minor, every one assumes that it has been carried out "under orders" from somewhere or another; no one seems to think that there are people who might *like* to kill their neighbours now and then.

And so it was with the new breakfast food. No one would have eaten Filboid Studge as a pleasure, but the grim austerity of its advertisement drove housewives in shoals to the grocers' shops to clamour for an immediate supply. In small kitchens solemn pig-tailed daughters helped depressed mothers to perform the primitive ritual of its preparation. On the breakfast-tables of cheerless parlours it was partaken of in silence. Once the womenfolk discovered that it was thoroughly unpalatable, their zeal in forcing it on their households knew no bounds. "You haven't eaten your Filboid Studge!" would be screamed at the appetiteless clerk as he hurried weariedly from the breakfast-table, and his evening meal would be prefaced by a warmed-up mess which would be explained as "your Filboid Studge that you didn't eat this morning." Those strange fanatics who ostentatiously mortify themselves, inwardly and outwardly, with health biscuits and health garments, battened aggressively on the new food. Earnest spectacled young men devoured it on the steps of the National Liberal Club. A bishop who did not believe in a future state preached against the poster, and a peer's daughter died from eating too much of the compound. A further advertisement was obtained when an infantry regiment mutinied and shot its officers rather than eat the nauseous mess; fortunately, Lord Birrell of Blatherstone, who was War Minister at the moment, saved the situation by his happy epigram, that "Discipline to be effective must be optional."

Filboid Studge had become a household word, but Dullamy wisely realized that it was not necessarily the last word in breakfast dietary; its supremacy would be challenged as soon as some yet more unpalatable food should be put on the market. There might even be a reaction in favour of something tasty and appetizing, and the Puritan austerity of the moment might be banished from domestic cookery. At an opportune moment, therefore, he sold out his interests in the article which had brought him in colossal wealth at a critical juncture, and placed his financial reputation beyond the reach of cavil. As for Leonore, who was now an heiress on a far greater scale than ever before, he naturally found her something a vast deal higher in the husband market than a two-hundred-a-year poster designer. Mark Spayley, the brainmouse who had helped the financial lion with such untoward effect, was left to curse the day he produced the wonder-working poster.

"After all," said Clovis, meeting him shortly afterwards at his club, "you have this doubtful consolation, that 'tis not in mortals to countermand success."

THE MUSIC ON THE HILL

SYLVIA SELTOUN ate her breakfast in the morning-room at Yessney with a pleasant sense of ultimate victory, such as a fervent Ironside might have permitted himself on the morrow of Worcester fight. She was scarcely pugnacious by temperament, but belonged to that more successful class of fighters who are pugnacious by circumstance. Fate had willed that her life should be occupied with a series of small struggles, usually with the odds slightly against her, and usually she had just managed to come through winning. And now she felt that she had brought her hardest and certainly her most important struggle to a successful issue. To have married Mortimer Seltoun, "Dead Mortimer" as his more intimate enemies called him, in the teeth of the cold hostility of his family, and in spite of his unaffected indifference to women, was indeed an achievement that had needed some determination and adroitness to carry through; yesterday she had brought her victory to its concluding stage by wrenching her husband away from Town and its group of satellite watering-places and "settling him down," in the vocabulary of her kind, in this remote wood-girt manor farm which was his country house.

"You will never get Mortimer to go," his mother had said carpingly, "but if he once goes he'll stay; Yessney throws almost as much a spell over him as Town does. One can understand what holds him to Town, but Yessney—" and the dowager had shrugged her shoulders.

There was a sombre almost savage wildness about Yessney that was certainly not likely to appeal to town-bred tastes, and Sylvia, notwithstanding her name, was accustomed to nothing much more sylvan than "leafy Kensington." She looked on the country as something excellent and wholesome in its way, which was apt to become troublesome if you encouraged it overmuch. Distrust of town-life had been a new thing with her, born of her marriage with Mortimer, and she had watched with satisfaction the gradual fading of what she called "the Jermyn-Street-look" in his eyes as the woods and heather of Yessney had closed in on them yesternight. Her will-power and strategy had prevailed; Mortimer would stay.

Outside the morning-room windows was a triangular slope of turf, which the indulgent might call a lawn, and beyond its low hedge of neglected fuschia bushes a steeper slope of heather and bracken dropped down into cavernous combes overgrown with oak and yew. In its wild open savagery there seemed a stealthy linking of the joy of life with the terror of unseen things. Sylvia smiled complacently as she gazed with a School-of-Art appreciation at the landscape, and then of a sudden she almost shuddered.

"It is very wild," she said to Mortimer, who had joined her; "one could almost think that in such a place the worship of Pan had never quite died out."

"The worship of Pan never has died out," said Mortimer. "Other newer gods have drawn aside his votaries from time to time, but he is the Nature-God to whom all must come back at last. He has been called the Father of all the Gods, but most of his children have been stillborn."

Sylvia was religious in an honest, vaguely devotional kind of way, and did not like to hear her beliefs spoken of as mere aftergrowths, but it was at least something new and hopeful

to hear Dead Mortimer speak with such energy and conviction on any subject.

"You don't really believe in Pan?" she asked incredulously.

"I've been a fool in most things," said Mortimer quietly,
"but I'm not such a fool as not to believe in Pan when I'm
down here. And if you're wise you won't disbelieve in him too
boastfully while you're in his country."

It was not till a week later, when Sylvia had exhausted the
attractions of the woodland walks round Yessney, that she
ventured on a tour of inspection of the farm buildings. A
farmyard suggested in her mind a scene of cheerful bustle,
with churns and flails and smiling dairymaids, and teams of
horses drinking knee-deep in duck-crowded ponds. As she
wandered among the gaunt grey buildings of Yessney manor
farm her first impression was one of crushing stillness and
desolation, as though she had happened on some lone deserted
homestead long given over to owls and cobwebs; then came
a sense of furtive watchful hostility, the same shadow of unseen things that seemed to lurk in the wooded combes and
coppices. From behind heavy doors and shuttered windows
came the restless stamp of hoof or rasp of chain halter, and
at times a muffled bellow from some stalled beast. From a distant corner a shaggy dog watched her with intent unfriendly
eyes; as she drew near it slipped quietly into its kennel, and
slipped out again as noiselessly when she had passed by. A few
hens, questing for food under a rick, stole away under a gate
at her approach. Sylvia felt that if she had come across any
human beings in this wilderness of barn and byre they would
have fled wraith-like from her gaze. At last, turning a corner
quickly, she came upon a living thing that did not fly from
her. Astretch in a pool of mud was an enormous sow, gigantic
beyond the town-woman's wildest computation of swine-flesh,
and speedily alert to resent and if necessary repel the unwonted
intrusion. It was Sylvia's turn to make an unobtrusive retreat.
As she threaded her way past rickyards and cowsheds and long
blank walls, she started suddenly at a strange sound—the echo
of a boy's laughter, golden and equivocal. Jan, the only boy

employed on the farm, a tow-headed, wizen-faced yokel, was visibly at work on a potato clearing half-way up the nearest hill-side, and Mortimer, when questioned, knew of no other probable or possible begetter of the hidden mockery that had ambushed Sylvia's retreat. The memory of that untraceable echo was added to her other impressions of a furtive sinister "something" that hung around Yessney.

Of Mortimer she saw very little; farm and woods and trout-streams seemed to swallow him up from dawn till dusk. Once, following the direction she had seen him take in the morning, she came to an open space in a nut copse, further shut in by huge yew trees, in the centre of which stood a stone pedestal surmounted by a small bronze figure of a youthful Pan. It was a beautiful piece of workmanship, but her attention was chiefly held by the fact that a newly cut bunch of grapes had been placed as an offering at its feet. Grapes were none too plentiful at the manor house, and Sylvia snatched the bunch angrily from the pedestal. Contemptuous annoyance dominated her thoughts as she strolled slowly homeward, and then gave way to a sharp feeling of something that was very near fright; across a thick tangle of undergrowth a boy's face was scowling at her, brown and beautiful, with unutterably evil eyes. It was a lonely pathway, all pathways round Yessney were lonely for the matter of that, and she sped forward without waiting to give a closer scrutiny to this sudden apparition. It was not till she had reached the house that she discovered that she had dropped the bunch of grapes in her flight.

"I saw a youth in the wood today," she told Mortimer that evening, "brown-faced and rather handsome, but a scoundrel to look at. A gipsy lad, I suppose."

"A reasonable theory," said Mortimer, "only there aren't any gipsies in these parts at present."

"Then who was he?" asked Sylvia, and as Mortimer appeared to have no theory of his own, she passed on to recount her finding of the votive offering.

"I suppose it was your doing," she observed; "it's a harmless piece of lunacy, but people would think you dreadfully silly if they knew of it."

"Did you meddle with it in any way?" asked Mortimer.

"I—I threw the grapes away. It seemed so silly," said Sylvia, watching Mortimer's impassive face for a sign of annoyance.

"I don't think you were wise to do that," he said reflectively. "I've heard it said that the Wood Gods are rather horrible to those who molest them."

"Horrible perhaps to those that believe in them, but you see I don't," retorted Sylvia.

"All the same," said Mortimer in his even, dispassionate tone, "I should avoid the woods and orchards if I were you, and give a wide berth to the horned beasts on the farm."

It was all nonsense, of course, but in that lonely wood-girt spot nonsense seemed able to rear a bastard brood of uneasiness.

"Mortimer," said Sylvia suddenly, "I think we will go back to Town some time soon."

Her victory had not been so complete as she had supposed; it had carried her on to ground that she was already anxious to quit.

"I don't think you will ever go back to Town," said Mortimer. He seemed to be paraphrasing his mother's prediction as to himself.

Sylvia noted with dissatisfaction and some self-contempt that the course of her next afternoon's ramble took her instinctively clear of the network of woods. As to the horned cattle, Mortimer's warning was scarcely needed, for she had always regarded them as of doubtful neutrality at the best: her imagination unsexed the most matronly dairy cows and turned them into bulls liable to "see red" at any moment. The ram who fed in the narrow paddock below the orchards she had adjudged, after ample and cautious probation, to be of docile temper; today, however, she decided to leave his docility untested, for the usually tranquil beast was roaming with every sign of restlessness from corner to corner of his meadow. A low, fitful piping, as of some reedy flute, was coming from the depth of a neighbouring copse, and there seemed to be some subtle connection between the animal's restless pacing and the wild music from the wood. Sylvia turned her steps in an upward direction and climbed the heather-clad slopes that stretched in rolling shoulders high above Yessney. She had left the piping notes behind her, but across the wooded combes at her feet the wind brought her another kind of music, the straining bay of hounds in full chase. Yessney was just on the outskirts of the Devon-and-Somerset country, and the hunted deer sometimes came that way. Sylvia could presently see a dark body, breasting hill after hill, and sinking again and again out of sight as he crossed the combes, while behind him steadily swelled that relentless chorus, and she grew tense with the excited sympathy that one feels for any hunted thing in whose capture one is not directly interested. And at last he broke through the outermost line of oak scrub and fern and stood panting in the open, a fat September stag carrying a well-furnished head. His obvious course was to drop down to the brown pools of Undercombe, and thence make his way towards the red deer's favoured sanctuary, the sea. To Sylvia's surprise, however, he turned his head to the upland slope and came lumbering resolutely onward over the heather. "It will be dreadful," she thought, "the hounds will pull him down under my very eyes." But the music of the pack seemed to have died away for a moment, and in its place she heard again that wild piping, which rose now on this side, now on that, as though urging the failing stag to a final effort. Sylvia stood well aside from his path, half hidden in a thick growth of whortle bushes, and watched him swing stiffly upward, his flanks dark with sweat, the coarse hair on his neck showing light by contrast. The pipe music shrilled suddenly around her, seeming to come from the bushes at her very feet, and at the same moment the great beast slewed round and bore directly down upon her. In an instant her pity for the hunted animal was changed to wild terror at her own danger; the thick heather roots mocked her scrambling efforts at flight, and she looked frantically downward for a glimpse of oncoming hounds. The huge antler spikes were within a few yards of her,

and in a flash of numbing fear she remembered Mortimer's
warning, to beware of horned beasts on the farm. And then
with a quick throb of joy she saw that she was not alone; a
human figure stood a few paces aside, knee-deep in the whortle
bushes.

"Drive it off!" she shrieked. But the figure made no answering movement.

The antlers drove straight at her breast, the acrid smell of
the hunted animal was in her nostrils, but her eyes were filled
with the horror of something she saw other than her oncoming
death. And in her ears rang the echo of a boy's laughter, golden
and equivocal.

THE STORY OF ST. VESPALUUS

"TELL me a story," said the Baroness, staring out despairingly at the rain; it was that light, apologetic sort of
rain that looks as if it was going to leave off every minute and
goes on for the greater part of the afternoon.

"What sort of story?" asked Clovis, giving his croquet
mallet a valedictory shove into retirement.

"One just true enough to be interesting and not true enough
to be tiresome," said the Baroness.

Clovis rearranged several cushions to his personal solace and
satisfaction; he knew that the Baroness liked her guests to be
comfortable, and he thought it right to respect her wishes in
that particular.

"Have I ever told you the story of St. Vespaluus?" he
asked.

"You've told me stories about grand-dukes and lion-tamers
and financiers' widows and a postmaster in Herzegovina,"
said the Baroness, "and about an Italian jockey and an amateur
governess who went to Warsaw, and several about your
mother, but certainly never anything about a saint."

"This story happened a long while ago," he said, "in those
uncomfortable piebald times when a third of the people were

Pagan, and a third Christian, and the biggest third of all just followed whichever religion the Court happened to profess. There was a certain king called Hkrikros, who had a fearful temper and no immediate successor in his own family; his married sister, however, had provided him with a large stock of nephews from which to select his heir. And the most eligible and royally-approved of all these nephews was the sixteen-year-old Vespaluus. He was the best looking, and the best horseman and javelin-thrower, and had that priceless princely gift of being able to walk past a supplicant with an air of not having seen him, but would certainly have given something if he had. My mother has that gift to a certain extent; she can go smilingly and financially unscathed through a charity bazaar, and meet the organizers next day with a solicitous 'had I but known you were in need of funds' air that is really rather a triumph in audacity. Now Hkrikros was a Pagan of the first water, and kept the worship of the sacred serpents, who lived in a hallowed grove on a hill near the royal palace, up to a high pitch of enthusiasm. The common people were allowed to please themselves, within certain discreet limits, in the matter of private religion, but any official in the service of the Court who went over to the new cult was looked down on, literally as well as metaphorically, the looking down being done from the gallery that ran round the royal bear-pit. Consequently there was considerable scandal and consternation when the youthful Vespaluus appeared one day at a Court function with a rosary tucked into his belt, and announced in reply to angry questionings that he had decided to adopt Christianity, or at any rate to give it a trial. If it had been any of the other nephews the king would possibly have ordered something drastic in the way of scourging and banishment, but in the case of the favoured Vespaluus he determined to look on the whole thing much as a modern father might regard the announced intention of his son to adopt the stage as a profession. He sent accordingly for the Royal Librarian. The royal library in those days was not a very extensive affair, and the keeper of the king's books had a great deal of leisure on his hands. Consequently he was in frequent demand for the settlement of other people's affairs when these strayed beyond normal limits and got temporarily unmanageable.

" 'You must reason with Prince Vespaluus,' said the king, 'and impress on him the error of his ways. We cannot have the heir to the throne setting such a dangerous example.'

" 'But where shall I find the necessary arguments?' asked the Librarian.

" 'I give you free leave to pick and choose your arguments in the royal woods and coppices,' said the king; 'if you cannot get together some cutting observations and stinging retorts suitable to the occasion you are a person of very poor resource.'

"So the Librarian went into the woods and gathered a goodly selection of highly argumentative rods and switches, and then proceeded to reason with Vespaluus on the folly and iniquity and above all the unseemliness of his conduct. His reasoning left a deep impression on the young prince, an impression which lasted for many weeks, during which time nothing more was heard about the unfortunate lapse into Christianity. Then a further scandal of the same nature agitated the Court. At a time when he should have been engaged in audibly invoking the gracious protection and patronage of the holy serpents, Vespaluus was heard singing a chant in honour of St. Odilo of Cluny. The king was furious at this new outbreak, and began to take a gloomy view of the situation; Vespaluus was evidently going to show a dangerous obstinacy in persisting in his heresy. And yet there was nothing in his appearance to justify such perverseness; he had not the pale eye of the fanatic or the mystic look of the dreamer. On the contrary, he was quite the best-looking boy at Court; he had an elegant, well-knit figure, a healthy complexion, eyes the colour of very ripe mulberries, and dark hair, smooth and very well cared for."

"It sounds like a description of what you imagine yourself to have been like at the age of sixteen," said the Baroness.

"My mother has probably been showing you some of my early photographs," said Clovis. Having turned the sarcasm into a compliment, he resumed his story.

"The king had Vespaluus shut up in a dark tower for three

days, with nothing but bread and water to live on, the squealing and fluttering of bats to listen to, and drifting clouds to
watch through one little window slit. The anti-Pagan section
of the community began to talk portentously of the boy-
martyr. The martyrdom was mitigated, as far as the food was
concerned, by the carelessness of the tower warden, who once
or twice left a portion of his own supper of broiled meat and
fruit and wine by mistake in the prince's cell. After the punishment was over, Vespaluus was closely watched for any
further symptom of religious perversity, for the king was
determined to stand no more opposition on so important a
matter, even from a favourite nephew. If there was any more
of this nonsense, he said, the succession to the throne would
have to be altered.

"For a time all went well; the festival of summer sports
was approaching, and the young Vespaluus was too engrossed
in wrestling and foot-running and javelin-throwing competi-
tions to bother himself with the strife of conflicting religious
systems. Then, however, came the great culminating feature
of the summer festival, the ceremonial dance round the grove
of the sacred serpents, and Vespaluus, as we should say, 'sat it
out.' The affront to the State religion was too public and
ostentatious to be overlooked, even if the king had been so
minded, and he was not in the least so minded. For a day and
a half he sat apart and brooded, and every one thought he was
debating within himself the question of the young prince's
death or pardon; as a matter of fact he was merely thinking
out the manner of the boy's death. As the thing had to be done,
and was bound to attract an enormous amount of public attention in any case, it was as well to make it as spectacular and
impressive as possible.

" 'Apart from his unfortunate taste in religions,' said the
king, 'and his obstinacy in adhering to it, he is a sweet and
pleasant youth, therefore it is meet and fitting that he should
be done to death by the winged envoys of sweetness.'

" 'Your Majesty means——?' said the Royal Librarian.

" 'I mean,' said the king, 'that he shall be stung to death
by bees. By the royal bees, of course.'

" 'A most elegant death,' said the Librarian.

" 'Elegant and spectacular, and decidedly painful,' said the king; 'it fulfils all the conditions that could be wished for.'

"The king himself thought out all the details of the execution ceremony. Vespaluus was to be stripped of his clothes, his hands were to be bound behind him, and he was then to be slung in a recumbent position immediately above three of the largest of the royal beehives, so that the least movement of his body would bring him in jarring contact with them. The rest could be safely left to the bees. The death throes, the king computed, might last anything from fifteen to forty minutes, though there was division of opinion and considerable wagering among the other nephews as to whether death might not be almost instantaneous, or, on the other hand, whether it might not be deferred for a couple of hours. Anyway, they all agreed, it was vastly preferable to being thrown down into an evil smelling bear-pit and being clawed and mauled to death by imperfectly carnivorous animals.

"It so happened, however, that the keeper of the royal hives had leanings towards Christianity himself, and moreover, like most of the Court officials, he was very much attached to Vespaluus. On the eve of the execution, therefore, he busied himself with removing the stings from all the royal bees; it was a long and delicate operation, but he was an expert bee-master, and by working hard nearly all night he succeeded in disarming all, or almost all, of the hive inmates."

"I didn't know you could take the sting from a live bee," said the Baroness incredulously.

"Every profession has its secrets," replied Clovis; "if it hadn't it wouldn't be a profession. Well, the moment for the execution arrived; the king and Court took their places, and accommodation was found for as many of the populace as wished to witness the unusual spectacle. Fortunately the royal bee-yard was of considerable dimensions, and was commanded, moreover, by the terraces that ran round the royal gardens; with a little squeezing and the erection of a few platforms room was found for everybody. Vespaluus was carried into the open space in front of the hives, blushing and slightly embarrassed, but not at all displeased at the attention which was being centred on him."

"He seems to have resembled you in more things than in appearance," said the Baroness.

"Don't interrupt at a critical point in the story," said Clovis. "As soon as he had been carefully adjusted in the prescribed position over the hives, and almost before the gaolers had time to retire to a safe distance, Vespaluus gave a lusty and well-aimed kick, which sent all three hives toppling one over another. The next moment he was wrapped from head to foot in bees; each individual insect nursed the dreadful and humiliating knowledge that in this supreme hour of catastrophe it could not sting, but each felt that it ought to pretend to. Vespaluus squealed and wriggled with laughter, for he was being tickled nearly to death, and now and again he gave a furious kick and used a bad word as one of the few bees that had escaped disarmament got its protest home. But the spectators saw with amazement that he showed no signs of approaching death agony, and as the bees dropped wearily away in clusters from his body his flesh was seen to be as white and smooth as before the ordeal, with a shiny glaze from the honey-smear of innumerable bee-feet, and here and there a small red spot where one of the rare stings had left its mark. It was obvious that a miracle had been performed in his favour, and one loud murmur, of astonishment or exultation, rose from the onlooking crowd. The king gave orders for Vespaluus to be taken down to await further orders, and stalked silently back to his midday meal, at which he was careful to eat heartily and drink copiously as though nothing unusual had happened. After dinner he sent for the Royal Librarian.

"'What is the meaning of this fiasco?' he demanded.

"'Your Majesty,' said that official, 'either there is something radically wrong with the bees—'

"'There is nothing wrong with my bees,' said the king haughtily, 'they are the best bees.'

"'Or else,' said the Librarian, 'there is something irremediably right about Prince Vespaluus.'

"'If Vespaluus is right I must be wrong,' said the king

"The Librarian was silent for a moment. Hasty speech has been the downfall of many; ill-considered silence was the undoing of the luckless Court functionary.

"Forgetting the restraint due to his dignity, and the golden rule which imposes repose of mind and body after a heavy meal, the king rushed upon the keeper of the royal books and hit him repeatedly and promiscuously over the head with an ivory chessboard, a pewter wine-flagon, and a brass candlestick; he knocked him violently and often against an iron torch sconce, and kicked him thrice round the banqueting chamber with rapid, energetic kicks. Finally, he dragged him down a long passage by the hair of his head and flung him out of a window into the courtyard below."

"Was he much hurt?" asked the Baroness.

"More hurt than surprised," said Clovis. "You see, the king was notorious for his violent temper. However, this was the first time he had let himself go so unrestrainedly on the top of a heavy meal. The Librarian lingered for many days—in fact, for all I know, he may have ultimately recovered, but Hkrikros died that same evening. Vespaluus had hardly finished getting the honey stains off his body before a hurried deputation came to put the coronation oil on his head. And what with the publicly-witnessed miracle and the accession of a Christian sovereign, it was not surprising that there was a general scramble of converts to the new religion. A hastily consecrated bishop was overworked with a rush of baptisms in the hastily improvised Cathedral of St. Odilo. And the boy-martyr-that-might-have-been was transposed in the popular imagination into a royal boy-saint, whose fame attracted throngs of curious and devout sightseers to the capital. Vespaluus, who was busily engaged in organizing the games and athletic contests that were to mark the commencement of his reign, had no time to give heed to the religious fervour which was effervescing round his personality; the first indication he had of the existing state of affairs was when the Court Chamberlain (a recent and very ardent addition to the Christian community) brought for his approval the outlines of a projected ceremonial cutting-down of the idolatrous serpent-grove.

" 'Your Majesty will be graciously pleased to cut down the first tree with a specially consecrated axe,' said the obsequious official.

" 'I'll cut off your head first, with any axe that comes handy,' said Vespaluus indignantly; 'do you suppose that I'm going to begin my reign by mortally affronting the sacred serpents? It would be most unlucky.'

" 'But your Majesty's Christian principles?' exclaimed the bewildered Chamberlain.

" 'I never had any,' said Vespaluus; 'I used to pretend to be a Christian convert just to annoy Hkrikros. He used to fly into such delicious tempers. And it was rather fun being whipped and scolded and shut up in a tower all for nothing. But as to turning Christian in real earnest, like you people seem to do, I couldn't think of such a thing. And the holy and esteemed serpents have always helped me when I've prayed to them for success in my running and wrestling and hunting, and it was through their distinguished intercession that the bees were not able to hurt me with their stings. It would be black ingratitude to turn against their worship at the very outset of my reign. I hate you for suggesting it.'

"The Chamberlain wrung his hands despairingly.

" 'But, your Majesty,' he wailed, 'the people are reverencing you as a saint, and the nobles are being Christianized in batches, and neighbouring potentates of that Faith are sending special envoys to welcome you as a brother. There is some talk of making you the patron saint of beehives, and a certain shade of honey-yellow has been christened Vespaluusian gold at the Emperor's Court. You can't surely go back on all this.'

" 'I don't mind being reverenced and greeted and honoured,' said Vespaluus; 'I don't even mind being sainted in moderation, as long as I'm not expected to be saintly as well. But I wish you clearly and finally to understand that I will *not* give up the worship of the august and auspicious serpents.'

"There was a world of unspoken bear-pit in the way he uttered those last words, and the mulberry-dark eyes flashed dangerously.

" 'A new reign,' said the Chamberlain to himself, 'but the same old temper.'

"Finally, as a State necessity, the matter of the religions was compromised. At stated intervals the king appeared before his subjects in the national cathedral in the character of St. Vespaluus, and the idolatrous grove was gradually pruned and lopped away till nothing remained of it. But the sacred and esteemed serpents were removed to a private shrubbery in the royal gardens, where Vespaluus the Pagan and certain members of his household devoutly and decently worshipped them. That possibly is the reason why the boy-king's success in sports and hunting never deserted him to the end of his days, and that is also the reason why, in spite of the popular veneration for his sanctity, he never received official canonization."

"It has stopped raining," said the Baroness.

THE WAY TO THE DAIRY

THE Baroness and Clovis sat in a much-frequented corner of the Park exchanging biographical confidences about the long succession of passers-by.

"Who are those depressed-looking young women who have just gone by?" asked the Baroness; "they have the air of people who have bowed to destiny and are not quite sure whether the salute will be returned."

"Those," said Clovis, "are the Brimley Bomefields. I dare say you would look depressed if you had been through their experiences."

"I'm always having depressing experiences," said the Baroness, "but I never give them outward expression. It's as bad as looking one's age. Tell me about the Brimley Bomefields."

"Well," said Clovis, "the beginning of their tragedy was that they found an aunt. The aunt had been there all the time, but they had very nearly forgotten her existence until a distant relative refreshed their memory by remembering her very distinctly in his will; it is wonderful what the force of example will accomplish. The aunt, who had been unobtrusively poor, became quite pleasantly rich, and the Brimley Bomefields grew suddenly concerned at the loneliness of her life and took her under their collective wings. She had as many wings around her at this time as one of those beast-things in Revelation."

"So far I don't see any tragedy from the Brimley Bomefields' point of view," said the Baroness.

"We haven't got to it yet," said Clovis. "The aunt had been used to living very simply, and had seen next to nothing of what we should consider life, and her nieces didn't encourage her to do much in the way of making a splash with her money. Quite a good deal of it would come to them at her death, and she was a fairly old woman, but there was one circumstance which cast a shadow of gloom over the satisfaction they felt in the discovery and acquisition of this desirable aunt: she openly acknowledged that a comfortable slice of her little fortune would go to a nephew on the other side of her family. He was rather a deplorable thing in rotters, and quite hopelessly top-hole in the way of getting through money, but he had been more or less decent to the old lady in her unremembered days, and she wouldn't hear anything against him. At least, she wouldn't pay any attention to what she did hear, but her nieces took care that she should have to listen to a good deal in that line. It seemed such a pity, they said among themselves, that good money should fall into such worthless hands. They habitually spoke of their aunt's money as 'good money,' as though other people's aunts dabbled for the most part in spurious currency.

"Regularly after the Derby, St. Leger, and other notable racing events they indulged in audible speculations as to how much money Roger had squandered in unfortunate betting transactions.

"'His travelling expenses must come to a big sum,' said the eldest Brimley Bomefield one day; 'they say he attends every race-meeting in England, besides others abroad. I shouldn't wonder if he went all the way to India to see the race for the Calcutta Sweepstake that one hears so much about.'

"'Travel enlarges the mind, my dear Christine,' said her aunt.

"'Yes, dear aunt, travel undertaken in the right spirit,' agreed Christine; 'but travel pursued merely as a means towards gambling and extravagant living is more likely to contract the purse than to enlarge the mind. However, as long as Roger enjoys himself, I suppose he doesn't care how fast or unprofitably the money goes, or where he is to find more. It seems a pity, that's all.'

"The aunt by that time had begun to talk of something else, and it was doubtful if Christine's moralizing had been even accorded a hearing. It was her remark, however—the aunt's remark, I mean—about travel enlarging the mind, that gave the youngest Brimley Bomefield her great idea for the showing-up of Roger.

"'If aunt could only be taken somewhere to see him gambling and throwing away money,' she said, 'it would open her eyes to his character more effectually than anything we can say.'

"'My dear Veronique,' said her sisters, 'we can't go following him to race-meetings.'

"'Certainly not to race-meetings,' said Veronique, 'but we might go to some place where one can look on at gambling without taking part in it.'

"'Do you mean Monte Carlo?' they asked her, beginning to jump rather at the idea.

"'Monte Carlo is a long way off, and has a dreadful reputation,' said Veronique; 'I shouldn't like to tell our friends that we were going to Monte Carlo. But I believe Roger usually goes to Dieppe about this time of year, and some quite respectable English people go there, and the journey wouldn't be expensive. If aunt could stand the Channel crossing the change of scene might do her a lot of good.'

"And that was how the fateful idea came to the Brimley Bomefields.

"From the very first set-off disaster hung over the expedition, as they afterwards remembered. To begin with, all the Brimley Bomefields were extremely unwell during the crossing, while the aunt enjoyed the sea air and made friends with all manner of strange travelling companions. Then, although it was many years since she had been on the Continent, she had served a very practical apprenticeship there as a paid companion, and her knowledge of colloquial French beat theirs to a standstill. It became increasingly difficult to keep under their collective wings a person who knew what she wanted and was able to ask for it and to see that she got it. Also, as far as Roger was concerned, they drew Dieppe blank; it turned out that he was staying at Pourville, a little watering-place a mile or two further west. The Brimley Bomefields discovered that Dieppe was too crowded and frivolous, and persuaded the old lady to migrate to the comparative seclusion of Pourville.

" 'You won't find it dull, you know,' they assured her; 'there is a little casino attached to the hotel, and you can watch the people dancing and throwing away their money at *petits chevaux*.'

"It was just before *petits chevaux* had been supplanted by *boule*.

"Roger was not staying in the same hotel, but they knew that the casino would be certain of his patronage on most afternoons and evenings.

"On the first evening of their visit they wandered into the casino after a fairly early dinner, and hovered near the tables. Bertie van Tahn was staying there at the time, and he described the whole incident to me. The Brimley Bomefields kept a furtive watch on the doors as though they were expecting some one to turn up, and the aunt got more and more amused and interested watching the little horses whirl round and round the board.

" 'Do you know, poor little number eight hasn't won for the last thirty-two times,' she said to Christine; 'I've been keeping count. I shall really have to put five francs on him to encourage him.'

" 'Come and watch the dancing, dear,' said Christine

nervously. It was scarcely a part of their strategy that Roger should come in and find the old lady backing her fancy at the *petits chevaux* table.

" 'Just wait while I put five francs on number eight,' said the aunt, and in another moment her money was lying on the table. The horses commenced to move round; it was a slow race this time, and number eight crept up at the finish like some crafty demon and placed his nose just a fraction in front of number three, who had seemed to be winning easily. Recourse had to be had to measurement, and the number eight was proclaimed the winner. The aunt picked up thirty-five francs. After that the Brimley Bomefields would have had to have used concerted force to get her away from the tables. When Roger appeared on the scene she was fifty-two francs to the good; her nieces were hovering forlornly in the background, like chickens that have been hatched out by a duck and are despairingly watching their parent disporting herself in a dangerous and uncongenial element. The supper-party which Roger insisted on standing that night in honour of his aunt and the three Miss Brimley Bomefields was remarkable for the unrestrained gaiety of two of the participants and the funereal mirthlessness of the remaining guests.

" 'I do not think,' Christine confided afterwards to a friend, who re-confided it to Bertie van Tahn, 'that I shall ever be able to touch *pâté de foie gras* again. It would bring back memories of that awful evening.'

"For the next two or three days the nieces made plans for returning to England or moving on to some other resort where there was no casino. The aunt was busy making a system for winning at *petits chevaux*. Number eight, her first love, had been running rather unkindly for her, and a series of plunges on number five had turned out even worse.

" 'Do you know, I dropped over seven hundred francs at the tables this afternoon,' she announced cheerfully at dinner on the fourth evening of their visit.

" 'Aunt! Twenty-eight pounds! And you were losing last night too.'

" 'Oh, I shall get it all back,' she said optimistically; 'but not here. These silly little horses are no good. I shall go somewhere where one can play comfortably at roulette. You needn't look so shocked. I've always felt that, given the opportunity, I should be an inveterate gambler, and now you darlings have put the opportunity in my way. I must drink your very good healths. Waiter, a bottle of *Pontet Canet*. Ah, it's number seven on the wine list; I shall plunge on number seven to-night. It won four times running this afternoon when I was backing that silly number five.'

"Number seven was not in a winning mood that evening. The Brimley Bomefields, tired of watching disaster from a distance, drew near to the table where their aunt was now an honoured habituée, and gazed mournfully at the successive victories of one and five and eight and four, which swept 'good money' out of the purse of seven's obstinate backer. The day's losses totalled something very near two thousand francs.

"'You incorrigible gamblers,' said Roger chaffingly to them, when he found them at the tables.

"'We are not gambling,' said Christine freezingly; 'we are looking on.'

"'I *don't* think,' said Roger knowingly; 'of course you're a syndicate and aunt is putting the stakes on for all of you. Any one can tell by your looks when the wrong horse wins that you've got a stake on.'

"Aunt and nephew had supper alone that night, or at least they would have if Bertie hadn't joined them; all the Brimley Bomefields had headaches.

"The aunt carried them all off to Dieppe the next day and set cheerily about the task of winning back some of her losses. Her luck was variable; in fact, she had some fair streaks of good fortune, just enough to keep her thoroughly amused with her new distraction; but on the whole she was a loser. The Brimley Bomefields had a collective attack of nervous prostration on the day when she sold out a quantity of shares in Argentine rails. 'Nothing will ever bring that money back,' they remarked lugubriously to one another.

"Veronique at last could bear it no longer, and went home; you see, it had been her idea to bring the aunt on this disastrous expedition, and though the others did not cast the fact verbally in her face, there was a certain lurking reproach in their eyes which was harder to meet than actual upbraidings. The other two remained behind, forlornly mounting guard over their aunt until such time as the waning of the Dieppe season should at last turn her in the direction of home and safety. They made anxious calculations as to how little 'good money' might, with reasonable luck, be squandered in the meantime. Here, however, their reckoning went far astray; the close of the Dieppe season merely turned their aunt's thoughts in search of some other convenient gambling resort. 'Show a cat the way to the dairy—' I forget how the proverb goes on, but it summed up the situation as far as the Brimley Bomefields' aunt was concerned. She had been introduced to unexplored pleasures, and found them greatly to her liking, and she was in no hurry to forgo the fruits of her newly acquired knowledge. You see, for the first time in her life the old thing was thoroughly enjoying herself; she was losing money, but she had plenty of fun and excitement over the process, and she had enough left to do very comfortably on. Indeed, she was only just learning to understand the art of doing oneself well. She was a popular hostess, and in return her fellow-gamblers were always ready to entertain her to dinners and suppers when their luck was in. Her nieces, who still remained in attendance on her, with the pathetic unwillingness of a crew to leave a foundering treasure ship which might yet be steered into port, found little pleasure in these Bohemian festivities; to see 'good money' lavished on good living for the entertainment of a nondescript circle of acquaintances who were not likely to be in any way socially useful to them, did not attune them to a spirit of revelry. They contrived, whenever possible, to excuse themselves from participation in their aunt's deplored gaieties; the Brimley Bomefield headaches became famous.

"And one day the nieces came to the conclusion that, as they would have expressed it, 'no useful purpose would be served' by their continued attendance on a relative who had so thoroughly emancipated herself from the sheltering protection of their wings. The aunt bore the announcement of their departure with a cheerfulness that was almost disconcerting.

" 'It's time you went home and had those headaches seen to by a specialist,' was her comment on the situation.

"The homeward journey of the Brimley Bomefields was a veritable retreat from Moscow, and what made it the more bitter was the fact that the Moscow, in this case, was not overwhelmed with fire and ashes, but merely extravagantly over-illuminated.

"From mutual friends and acquaintances they sometimes get glimpses of their prodigal relative, who has settled down into a confirmed gambling maniac, living on such salvage of income as obliging moneylenders have left at her disposal.

"So you need not be surprised," concluded Clovis, "if they do wear a depressed look in public."

"Which is Veronique?" asked the Baroness.

"The most depressed-looking of the three," said Clovis.

THE PEACE OFFERING

"I WANT you to help me in getting up a dramatic entertainment of some sort," said the Baroness to Clovis. "You see, there's been an election petition down here, and a member unseated and no end of bitterness and ill-feeling, and the County is socially divided against itself. I thought a play of some kind would be an excellent opportunity for bringing people together again, and giving them something to think of besides tiresome political squabbles."

The Baroness was evidently ambitious of reproducing beneath her own roof the pacifying effects traditionally ascribed to the celebrated Reel of Tullochgorum.

"We might do something on the lines of Greek tragedy," said Clovis, after due reflection; "the Return of Agamemnon, for instance."

The Baroness frowned.

"It sounds rather reminiscent of an election result, doesn't it?"

"It wasn't that sort of return," explained Clovis; "it was a home-coming."

"I thought you said it was a tragedy."

"Well, it was. He was killed in his bathroom, you know."

"Oh, now I know the story, of course. Do you want me to take the part of Charlotte Corday?"

"That's a different story and a different century," said Clovis; "the dramatic unities forbid one to lay a scene in more than one century at a time. The killing in this case has to be done by Clytemnestra."

"Rather a pretty name. I'll do that part. I suppose you want to be Aga—whatever his name is?"

"Dear no. Agamemnon was the father of grown-up children, and probably wore a beard and looked prematurely aged I shall be his charioteer or bath-attendant, or something decorative of that kind. We must do everything in the Sumurun manner, you know."

"I don't know," said the Baroness; "at least, I should know better if you would explain exactly what you mean by the Sumurun manner."

Clovis obliged: "Weird music, and exotic skippings and flying leaps, and lots of drapery and undrapery. Particularly undrapery."

"I think I told you the County are coming. The County won't stand anything very Greek."

"You can get over any objection by calling it Hygiene, or limb-culture, or something of that sort. After all, every one exposes their insides to the public gaze and sympathy nowadays, so why not one's outside?"

"My dear boy, I can ask the County to a Greek play, or to a costume play, but to a Greek-costume play, never. It doesn't do to let the dramatic instinct carry one too far; one must consider one's environment. When one lives among greyhounds one should avoid giving life-like imitations of a rabbit, unless one wants one's head snapped off. Remember, I've got this place on a seven years' lease. And then," continued the Baroness, "as to skippings and flying leaps; I must ask Emily Dushford to take a part. She's a dear good thing, and will do anything she's told, or try to; but can you imagine her doing a flying leap under any circumstances?"

"She can be Cassandra, and she need only take flying leaps into the future, in a metaphorical sense."

"Cassandra; rather a pretty name. What kind of character is she?"

"She was a sort of advance-agent for calamities. To know her was to know the worst. Fortunately for the gaiety of the age she lived in, no one took her very seriously. Still, it must have been fairly galling to have her turning up after every catastrophe with a conscious air of 'perhaps another time you'll believe what I say.'"

"I should have wanted to kill her."

"As Clytemnestra I believe you gratify that very natural wish."

"Then it has a happy ending, in spite of it being a tragedy?"

"Well, hardly," said Clovis; "you see, the satisfaction of putting a violent end to Cassandra must have been considerably damped by the fact that she had foretold what was going to happen to her. She probably dies with an intensely irritating 'what-did-I-tell-you' smile on her lips. By the way, of course all the killing will be done in the Sumurun manner."

"Please explain again," said the Baroness, taking out a note-book and pencil.

"Little and often, you know, instead of one sweeping blow. You see, you are at your own home, so there's no need to hurry over the murdering as though it were some disagreeable but necessary duty."

"And what sort of end do I have? I mean, what curtain do I get?"

"I suppose you rush into your lover's arms. That is where one of the flying leaps will come in."

The getting-up and rehearsing of the play seemed likely to cause, in a restricted area, nearly as much heart-burning and ill-feeling as the election petition. Clovis, as adapter and stage-manager, insisted, as far as he was able, on the charioteer being quite the most prominent character in the play, and his panther-skin tunic caused almost as much trouble and discussion as Clytemnestra's spasmodic succession of lovers, who broke down on probation with alarming uniformity. When the cast was at length fixed beyond hope of reprieve matters went scarcely more smoothly. Clovis and the Baroness rather overdid the Sumurun manner, while the rest of the company could hardly be said to attempt it at all. As for Cassandra, who was expected to improvise her own prophecies, she appeared to be as incapable of taking flying leaps into futurity as of executing more than a severely plantigrade walk across the stage.

"Woe! Trojans, woe to Troy!" was the most inspired remark she could produce after several hours of conscientious study of all the available authorities.

"It's no earthly use foretelling the fall of Troy," expostulated Clovis, "because Troy has fallen before the action of the play begins. And you mustn't say too much about your own impending doom either, because that will give things away too much to the audience."

After several minutes of painful brain-searching, Cassandra smiled reassuringly.

"I know. I'll predict a long and happy reign for George the Fifth."

"My dear girl," protested Clovis, "have you reflected that Cassandra specialized in foretelling calamities?"

There was another prolonged pause and another triumphant issue.

"I know. I'll foretell a most disastrous season for the fox-hounds."

"On no account," entreated Clovis; "do remember that all Cassandra's predictions came true. The M.F.H. and the Hunt Secretary are both awfully superstitious, and they are both going to be present."

Cassandra retreated hastily to her bedroom to bathe her eyes before appearing at tea.

The Baroness and Clovis were by this time scarcely on speaking terms. Each sincerely wished their respective rôle to be the pivot round which the entire production should revolve, and each lost no opportunity for furthering the cause they had at heart. As fast as Clovis introduced some effective bit of busi-

ness for the charioteer (and he introduced a great many), the
Baroness would remorselessly cut it out, or more often dove-
tail it into her own part, while Clovis retaliated in a similar
fashion whenever possible. The climax came when Clytemnestra annexed some highly complimentary lines, which were
to have been addressed to the charioteer by a bevy of admiring
Greek damsels, and put them into the mouth of her lover.
Clovis stood by in apparent unconcern while the words:

"Oh, lovely stripling, radiant as the dawn," were transposed into:

"Oh, Clytemnestra, radiant as the dawn," but there was a
dangerous glitter in his eye that might have given the Baroness
warning. He had composed the verse himself, inspired and
thoroughly carried away by his subject; he suffered, therefore,
a double pang in beholding his tribute deflected from its
destined object, and his words mutilated and twisted into what
became an extravagant panegyric on the Baroness's personal
charms. It was from this moment that he became gentle and
assiduous in his private coaching of Cassandra.

The County, forgetting its dissensions, mustered in full
strength to witness the much-talked-of production. The protective Providence that looks after little children and amateur
theatricals made good its traditional promise that everything
should be right on the night. The Baroness and Clovis seemed
to have sunk their mutual differences, and between them dominated the scene to the partial eclipse of all the other characters,
who, for the most part, seemed well content to remain in the
shadow. Even Agamemnon, with ten years of strenuous life
around Troy standing to his credit, appeared to be an unobtrusive personality compared with his flamboyant charioteer.
But the moment came for Cassandra (who had been excused
from any very definite outpourings during rehearsals) to support her rôle by delivering herself of a few well-chosen anticipations of pending misfortune. The musicians obliged with
appropriately lugubrious wailings and thumpings, and the
Baroness seized the opportunity to make a dash to the dressing-
room to effect certain repairs in her make-up. Cassandra
nervous but resolute, came down to the footlight. and, like one

repeating a carefully learned lesson, flung her remarks straight at the audience:

"I see woe for this fair country if the brood of corrupt, self-seeking, unscrupulous, unprincipled politicians" (here she named one of the two rival parties in the State) "continue to infest and poison our local councils and undermine our Parliamentary representation; if they continue to snatch votes by nefarious and discreditable means—"

A humming as of a great hive of bewildered and affronted bees drowned her further remarks and wore down the droning of the musicians. The Baroness, who should have been greeted on her return to the stage with the pleasing invocation, "Oh, Clytemnestra, radiant as the dawn," heard instead the imperious voice of Lady Thistledale ordering her carriage, and something like a storm of open discord going on at the back of the room.

.   .   .   .

The social divisions in the County healed themselves after their own fashion; both parties found common ground in condemning the Baroness's outrageously bad taste and tactlessness.

She has been fortunate in sub-letting for the greater part of her seven years' lease.

THE PEACE OF MOWSLE BARTON

CREFTON LOCKYER sat at his ease, an ease alike of body and soul, in the little patch of ground, half-orchard and half-garden, that abutted on the farmyard at Mowsle Barton. After the stress and noise of long years of city life, the repose and peace of the hill-begirt homestead struck on his senses with an almost dramatic intensity. Time and space seemed to lose their meaning and their abruptness; the minutes slid away into hours, and the meadows and fallows sloped away into middle distance, softly and imperceptibly. Wild weeds of the hedgerow straggled into the flower-garden, and wallflowers and garden bushes made counter-raids into farmyard and lane. Sleepy-looking hens and solemn preoccupied ducks were equally at home in yard, orchard, or roadway; nothing seemed to belong definitely to anywhere; even the gates were not necessarily to be found on their hinges. And over the whole scene brooded the sense of a peace that had almost a quality of magic in it. In the afternoon you felt that it had always been afternoon, and must always remain afternoon; in the twilight you knew that it could never have been anything else but twilight. Crefton Lockyer sat at his ease in the rustic seat beneath an old medlar tree, and decided that here was the life-anchorage that his mind had so fondly pictured and that latterly his tired and jarred senses had so often pined for. He would make a permanent lodging-place among these simple friendly people, gradually increasing the modest comforts with which he would like to surround himself, but falling in as much as possible with their manner of living.

As he slowly matured this resolution in his mind an elderly woman came hobbling with uncertain gait through the orchard. He recognized her as a member of the farm household, the mother or possibly the mother-in-law of Mrs. Spurfield, his present landlady, and hastily formulated some pleasant remark to make to her. She forestalled him.

"There's a bit of writing chalked up on the door over yonder. What is it?"

She spoke in a dull impersonal manner, as though the question had been on her lips for years and had best be got rid of. Her eyes, however, looked impatiently over Crefton's head at the door of a small barn which formed the outpost of a straggling line of farm buildings.

"Martha Pillamon is an old witch" was the announcement that met Crefton's inquiring scrutiny, and he hesitated a moment before giving the statement wider publicity. For all he knew to the contrary, it might be Martha herself to whom he was speaking. It was possible that Mrs. Spurfield's maiden name had been Pillamon. And the gaunt, withered old dame at his side might certainly fulfil local conditions as to the outward aspect of a witch.

"It's something about some one called Martha Pillamon," he explained cautiously.

"What does it say?"

"It's very disrespectful," said Crefton; "it says she's a witch. Such things ought not to be written up."

"It's true, every word of it," said his listener with considerable satisfaction, adding as a special descriptive note of her own, "the old toad."

And as she hobbled away through the farmyard she shrilled out in her cracked voice, "Martha Pillamon is an old witch!"

"Did you hear what she said?" mumbled a weak, angry voice somewhere behind Crefton's shoulder. Turning hastily, he beheld another old crone, thin and yellow and wrinkled, and evidently in a high state of displeasure. Obviously this was Martha Pillamon in person. The orchard seemed to be a favourite promenade for the aged women of the neighbourhood.

"'Tis lies, 'tis sinful lies," the weak voice went on. "'Tis Betsy Croot is the old witch. She an' her daughter, the dirty rat. I'll put a spell on 'em, the old nuisances."

As she limped slowly away her eye caught the chalk inscription on the barn door.

"What's written up there?" she demanded, wheeling round on Crefton.

"Vote for Soarker," he responded, with the craven boldness of the practised peacemaker.

The old woman grunted, and her mutterings and her faded red shawl lost themselves gradually among the tree-trunks. Crefton rose presently and made his way towards the farmhouse. Somehow a good deal of the peace seemed to have slipped out of the atmosphere.

The cheery bustle of tea-time in the old farm kitchen, which Crefton had found so agreeable on previous afternoons, seemed to have soured today into a certain uneasy melancholy. There was a dull, dragging silence around the board, and the tea itself, when Crefton came to taste it, was a flat, lukewarm concoction that would have driven the spirit of revelry out of a carnival.

"It's no use complaining of the tea," said Mrs. Spurfield hastily, as her guest stared with an air of polite inquiry at his cup. "The kettle won't boil, that's the truth of it."

Crefton turned to the hearth, where an unusually fierce fire was banked up under a big black kettle, which sent a thin wreath of steam from its spout, but seemed otherwise to ignore the action of the roaring blaze beneath it.

"It's been there more than an hour, an' boil it won't," said Mrs. Spurfield, adding, by way of complete explanation, "we're bewitched."

"It's Martha Pillamon as has done it," chimed in the old mother; "I'll be even with the old toad. I'll put a spell on her."

"It must boil in time," protested Crefton, ignoring the suggestions of foul influences. "Perhaps the coal is damp."

"It won't boil in time for supper, nor for breakfast to-morrow morning, not if you was to keep the fire a-going all night for it," said Mrs. Spurfield. And it didn't. The household subsisted on fried and baked dishes, and a neighbour obligingly brewed tea and sent it across in a moderately warm condition.

"I suppose you'll be leaving us, now that things has turned up uncomfortable," Mrs. Spurfield observed at breakfast; "there are folks as deserts one as soon as trouble comes."

Crefton hurriedly disclaimed any immediate change of plans; he observed, however, to himself that the earlier heartiness of manner had in a large measure deserted the household. Suspicious looks, sulky silences, or sharp speeches had become the order of the day. As for the old mother, she sat about the kitchen or the garden all day, murmuring threats and spells against Martha Pillamon. There was something alike terrifying and piteous in the spectacle of these frail old morsels of humanity consecrating their last flickering energies to the task of making each other wretched. Hatred seemed to be the one faculty which had survived in undiminished vigour and intensity where all else was dropping into ordered and symmetrical decay. And the uncanny part of it was that some horrid unwholesome power seemed to be distilled from their spite and their cursings. No amount of sceptical explanation could remove the undoubted fact that neither kettle nor saucepan would come to boiling-point over the hottest fire. Crefton clung as long as possible to the theory of some defect in the coals, but a wood fire gave the same result, and when a small spirit-lamp kettle, which he ordered out by carrier, showed the same obstinate refusal to allow its contents to boil he felt that he had come suddenly into contact with some unguessed-at and very evil aspect of hidden forces. Miles away, down through an opening in the hills, he could catch glimpses of a road where motor-cars sometimes passed, and yet here, so little removed from the arteries of the latest civilization, was a bat-haunted old homestead, where something unmistakably like witchcraft seemed to hold a very practical sway.

Passing out through the farm garden on his way to the lanes beyond, where he hoped to recapture the comfortable sense of peacefulness that was so lacking around house and hearth—especially hearth—Crefton came across the old mother, sitting mumbling to herself in the seat beneath the medlar tree. "Let un sink as swims, let un sink as swims," she was repeating over and over again, as a child repeats a half-learned lesson. And now and then she would break off into a shrill laugh, with a note of malice in it that was not pleasant to hear. Crefton was glad when he found himself out of earshot, in the quiet and seclusion of the deep overgrown lanes that seemed to lead away to nowhere; one, narrower and deeper than the rest, attracted his footsteps, and he was almost annoyed when he found that it really did act as a miniature roadway to a human dwelling. A forlorn-looking cottage with a scrap of ill-tended cabbage garden and a few aged apple trees stood at an angle where a swift-flowing stream widened out for a space into a decent-sized pond before hurrying away again through the willows that had checked its course. Crefton leaned against a tree-trunk and looked across the swirling eddies of the pond at the humble little homestead opposite him; the only sign of life came from a small procession of dingy-looking ducks that marched in single file down to the water's edge. There is always something rather taking in the way a duck changes itself in an instant from a slow, clumsy waddler of the earth to a graceful, buoyant swimmer of the waters, and Crefton waited with a certain arrested attention to watch the leader of the file launch itself on to the surface of the pond. He was aware at the same time of a curious warning instinct that something strange and unpleasant was about to happen. The duck flung itself confidently forward into the water, and rolled immediately under the surface. Its head appeared for a moment and went under again, leaving a train of bubbles in its wake, while wings and legs churned the water in a helpless swirl of flapping and kicking. The bird was obviously drowning. Crefton thought at first that it had caught itself in some weeds, or was being attacked from below by a pike or water-rat. But no blood floated to the surface, and the wildly bobbing body made the circuit of the pond current without hindrance from any entanglement. A second duck had by this time launched itself into the pond, and a second struggling body rolled and twisted under the surface. There was something peculiarly piteous in the sight of the gasping beaks that showed now and again above the water, as though in terrified protest at this treachery of a trusted and familiar element. Crefton gazed with something like horror as a third duck poised itself on the bank and splashed in, to share the fate of the other two. He felt almost relieved when the remainder of the flock, taking tardy alarm from the commotion of the slowly drowning bodies, drew themselves up with tense outstretched necks, and sidled away from the scene of danger, quacking a deep note of disquietude as they went. At the same moment Crefton became aware that he was not the only human witness of the scene; a bent and withered old woman, whom he recognized at once as Martha Pillamon, of sinister reputation, had limped down the cottage path to the water's edge, and was gazing fixedly at the gruesome whirligig of dying birds that went in horrible procession round the pool. Presently her voice rang out in a shrill note of quavering rage:

" 'Tis Betsy Croot adone it, the old rat. I'll put a spell on her, see if I don't."

Crefton slipped quietly away, uncertain whether or no the old woman had noticed his presence. Even before she had proclaimed the guiltiness of Betsy Croot, the latter's muttered incantation "Let un sink as swims" had flashed uncomfortably across his mind. But it was the final threat of a retaliatory spell which crowded his mind with misgiving to the exclusion of all other thoughts or fancies. His reasoning powers could no longer afford to dismiss these old-wives' threats as empty bickerings. The household at Mowsle Barton lay under the displeasure of a vindictive old woman who seemed able to materialize her personal spites in a very practical fashion, and there was no saying what form her revenge for three drowned ducks might not take. As a member of the household Crefton might find himself involved in some general and highly disagreeable visitation of Martha Pillamon's wrath. Of course he knew that he was giving way to absurd fancies, but the behaviour of the spirit-lamp kettle and the subsequent scene at the pond had considerably unnerved him. And the vagueness of his alarm added to its terrors; when once you have taken the Impossible into your calculations its possibilities become practically limitless.

Crefton rose at his usual early hour the next morning, after one of the least restful nights he had spent at the farm. His sharpened senses quickly detected that subtle atmosphere of things-being-not-altogether well that hangs over a stricken household. The cows had been milked, but they stood huddled about in the yard, waiting impatiently to be driven out afield, and the poultry kept up an importunate querulous reminder of deferred feeding-time; the yard pump, which usually made discordant music at frequent intervals during the early morning, was today ominously silent. In the house itself there was a coming and going of scuttering footsteps, a rushing and dying away of hurried voices, and long, uneasy stillnesses. Crefton finished his dressing and made his way to the head of a narrow staircase. He could hear a dull, complaining voice, a voice into which an awed hush had crept, and recognized the speaker as Mrs. Spurfield.

"He'll go away, for sure," the voice was saying; "there are those as runs away from one as soon as real misfortune shows itself."

Crefton felt that he probably was one of "those," and that there were moments when it was advisable to be true to type.

He crept back to his room, collected and packed his few belongings, placed the money due for his lodgings on a table, and made his way out by a back door into the yard. A mob of poultry surged expectantly towards him; shaking off their interested attentions he hurried along under cover of cow-stall, piggery, and hayricks till he reached the lane at the back of the farm. A few minutes' walk, which only the burden of his portmanteaux restrained from developing into an un-disguised run, brought him to a main road, where the early carrier soon overtook him and sped him onward to the neigh-bouring town. At a bend of the road he caught a last glimpse of the farm; the old gabled roofs and thatched barns, the straggling orchard, and the medlar tree, with its wooden seat, stood out with an almost spectral clearness in the early morn-ing light, and over it all brooded that air of magic possession which Crefton had once mistaken for peace.

The bustle and roar of Paddington Station smote on his ears with a welcome protective greeting.

"Very bad for our nerves, all this rush and hurry," said a fellow-traveller; "give me the peace and quiet of the country."

Crefton mentally surrendered his share of the desired com-modity. A crowded, brilliantly over-lighted music-hall, where an exuberant rendering of "1812" was being given by a strenuous orchestra, came nearest to his ideal of a nerve seda-tive.

THE TALKING-OUT OF TARRINGTON

"HEAVENS!" exclaimed the aunt of Clovis, "here's some one I know bearing down on us. I can't remember his name, but he lunched with us once in Town. Tarrington—

yes, that's it. He's heard of the picnic I'm giving for the Princess, and he'll cling to me like a lifebelt till I give him an invitation; then he'll ask if he may bring all his wives and mothers and sisters with him. That's the worst of these small watering-places; one can't escape from anybody."

"I'll fight a rearguard action for you if you like to do a bolt now," volunteered Clovis; "you've a clear ten yards start if you don't lose time."

The aunt of Clovis responded gamely to the suggestion, and churned away like a Nile steamer, with a long brown ripple of Pekingese spaniel trailing in her wake.

"Pretend you don't know him," was her parting advice, tinged with the reckless courage of the non-combatant.

The next moment the overtures of an affably disposed gentleman were being received by Clovis with a "silent-upon-a-peak-in-Darien" stare which denoted an absence of all previous acquaintance with the object scrutinized.

"I expect you don't know me with my moustache," said the new-comer; "I've only grown it during the last two months."

"On the contrary," said Clovis, "the moustache is the only thing about you that seemed familiar to me. I felt certain that I had met it somewhere before."

"My name is Tarrington," resumed the candidate for recognition.

"A very useful kind of name," said Clovis; "with a name of that sort no one would blame you if you did nothing in particular heroic or remarkable, would they? And yet if you were to raise a troop of light horse in a moment of national emergency, 'Tarrington's Light Horse' would sound quite appropriate and pulse-quickening; whereas if you were called Spoopin, for instance, the thing would be out of the question. No one, even in a moment of national emergency, could possibly belong to Spoopin's Horse."

The new-comer smiled weakly, as one who is not to be put off by mere flippancy, and began again with patient persistence:

"I think you ought to remember my name——"

"I shall," said Clovis, with an air of immense sincerity.

"My aunt was asking me only this morning to suggest names for four young owls she's just had sent her as pets. I shall call them all Tarrington; then if one or two of them die or fly away, or leave us in any of the ways that pet owls are prone to, there will be always one or two left to carry on your name. And my aunt won't *let* me forget it; she will always be asking 'Have the Tarringtons had their mice?' and questions of that sort. She says if you keep wild creatures in captivity you ought to see after their wants, and of course she's quite right there."

"I met you at luncheon at your aunt's house once—" broke in Mr. Tarrington, pale but still resolute.

"My aunt never lunches," said Clovis; "she belongs to the National Anti-Luncheon League, which is doing quite a lot of good work in a quiet, unobtrusive way. A subscription of half a crown per quarter entitles you to go without ninety-two luncheons."

"This must be something new," exclaimed Tarrington.

"It's the same aunt that I've always had," said Clovis coldly.

"I perfectly well remember meeting you at a luncheon-party given by your aunt," persisted Tarrington, who was beginning to flush an unhealthy shade of mottled pink.

"What was there for lunch?" asked Clovis.

"Oh, well, I don't remember that—"

"How nice of you to remember my aunt when you can no longer recall the names of the things you ate. Now my memory works quite differently. I can remember a menu long after I've forgotten the hostess that accompanied it. When I was seven years old I recollect being given a peach at a garden-party by some Duchess or other; I can't remember a thing about her, except that I imagine our acquaintance must have been of the slightest, as she called me a 'nice little boy,' but I have unfading memories of that peach. It was one of those exuberant peaches that meet you halfway, so to speak, and are all over you in a moment. It was a beautiful unspoiled product of a hothouse, and yet it managed quite successfully to give itself the airs of a compote. You had to bite it and imbibe it at the same time. To me there has always been something charming and mystic in the thought of that delicate velvet

globe of fruit, slowly ripening and warming to perfection
through the long summer days and perfumed nights, and then
coming suddenly athwart my life in the supreme moment of
its existence. I can never forget it, even if I wished to. And
when I had devoured all that was edible of it, there still remained the stone, which a heedless, thoughtless child would
doubtless have thrown away; I put it down the neck of a young
friend who was wearing a very *décolleté* sailor suit. I told
him it was a scorpion, and from the way he wriggled and
screamed he evidently believed it, though where the silly kid
imagined I could procure a live scorpion at a garden-party I
don't know. Altogether, that peach is for me an unfading and
happy memory—"

The defeated Tarrington had by this time retreated out of
ear-shot, comforting himself as best he might with the reflection that a picnic which included the presence of Clovis might
prove a doubtfully agreeable experience.

"I shall certainly go in for a Parliamentary career," said
Clovis to himself as he turned complacently to rejoin his aunt.
"As a talker-out of inconvenient bills I should be invaluable."

THE HOUNDS OF FATE

IN the fading light of a close dull autumn afternoon Martin
Stoner plodded his way along muddy lanes and rut-seamed
cart tracks that led he knew not exactly whither. Somewhere
in front of him, he fancied, lay the sea, and towards the sea
his footsteps seemed persistently turning; why he was struggling wearily forward to that goal he could scarcely have explained, unless he was possessed by the same instinct that turns
a hard-pressed stag cliffward in its last extremity. In his case
the hounds of Fate were certainly pressing him with unrelenting insistence; hunger, fatigue, and despairing hopelessness
had numbed his brain, and he could scarcely summon sufficient
energy to wonder what underlying impulse was driving him
onward. Stoner was one of those unfortunate individuals who

seem to have tried everything; a natural slothfulness and improvidence had always intervened to blight any chance of even moderate success, and now he was at the end of his tether, and there was nothing more to try. Desperation had not awakened in him any dormant reserve of energy; on the contrary, a mental torpor grew up round the crisis of his fortunes. With the clothes he stood up in, a halfpenny in his pocket, and no single friend or acquaintance to turn to, with no prospect either of a bed for the night or a meal for the morrow, Martin Stoner trudged stolidly forward, between moist hedgerows and beneath dripping trees, his mind almost a blank, except that he was subconsciously aware that somewhere in front of him lay the sea. Another consciousness obtruded itself now and then—the knowledge that he was miserably hungry. Presently he came to a halt by an open gateway that led into a spacious and rather neglected farm-garden; there was little sign of life about, and the farm-house at the further end of the garden looked chill and inhospitable. A drizzling rain, however, was setting in, and Stoner thought that here perhaps he might obtain a few minutes' shelter and buy a glass of milk with his last remaining coin. He turned slowly and wearily into the garden and followed a narrow, flagged path up to a side door. Before he had time to knock the door opened and a bent, withered-looking old man stood aside in the doorway as though to let him pass in.

"Could I come in out of the rain?" Stoner began, but the old man interrupted him.

"Come in, Master Tom. I knew you would come back one of these days."

Stoner lurched across the threshold and stood staring uncomprehendingly at the other.

"Sit down while I put you out a bit of supper," said the old man with quavering eagerness. Stoner's legs gave way from very weariness, and he sank inertly into the arm-chair that had been pushed up to him. In another minute he was devouring the cold meat, cheese, and bread, that had been placed on the table at his side.

"You'm little changed these four years," went on the old man, in a voice that sounded to Stoner as something in a dream, far away and inconsequent; "but you'll find us a deal changed, you will. There's no one about the place same as when you left; nought but me and your old Aunt. I'll go and tell her that you'm come; she won't be seeing you, but she'll let you stay right enough. She always did say if you was to come back you should stay, but she'd never set eyes on you or speak to you again."

The old man placed a mug of beer on the table in front of Stoner and then hobbled away down a long passage. The drizzle of rain had changed to a furious lashing downpour, which beat violently against door and windows. The wanderer thought with a shudder of what the sea-shore must look like under this drenching rainfall, with night beating down on all sides. He finished the food and beer and sat numbly waiting for the return of his strange host. As the minutes ticked by on the grandfather clock in the corner a new hope began to flicker and grow in the young man's mind; it was merely the expansion of his former craving for food and a few minutes' rest into a longing to find a night's shelter under this seemingly hospitable roof. A clattering of footsteps down the passage heralded the old farm servant's return.

"The old missus won't see you, Master Tom, but she says you are to stay. 'Tis right enough, seeing the farm will be yours when she be put under earth. I've had a fire lit in your room, Master Tom, and the maids has put fresh sheets on to the bed. You'll find nought changed up there. Maybe you'm tired and would like to go there now."

Without a word Martin Stoner rose heavily to his feet and followed his ministering angel along a passage, up a short creaking stair, along another passage, and into a large room lit with a cheerfully blazing fire. There was but little furniture, plain, old-fashioned, and good of its kind; a stuffed squirrel in a case and a wall-calendar of four years ago were about the only symptoms of decoration. But Stoner had eyes for little else than the bed, and could scarce wait to tear his clothes off him before rolling in a luxury of weariness into its comfortable depths. The hounds of Fate seemed to have checked for a brief moment.

In the cold light of morning Stoner laughed mirthlessly as he slowly realized the position in which he found himself. Perhaps he might snatch a bit of breakfast on the strength of his likeness to this other missing ne'er-do-well, and get safely away before any one discovered the fraud that had been thrust on him. In the room downstairs he found the bent old man ready with a dish of bacon and fried eggs for "Master Tom's" breakfast, while a hard-faced elderly maid brought in a teapot and poured him out a cup of tea. As he sat at the table a small spaniel came up and made friendly advances.

" 'Tis old Bowker's pup," explained the old man, whom the hard-faced maid had addressed as George. "She was main fond of you; never seemed the same after you went away to Australee. She died 'bout a year agone. 'Tis her pup."

Stoner found it difficult to regret her decease; as a witness for identification she would have left something to be desired.

"You'll go for a ride, Master Tom?" was the next startling proposition that came from the old man. "We've a nice little roan cob that goes well in saddle. Old Biddy is getting a bit up in years, though 'er goes well still, but I'll have the little roan saddled and brought round to door."

"I've got no riding things," stammered the castaway, almost laughing as he looked down at his one suit of well-worn clothes.

"Master Tom," said the old man earnestly, almost with an offended air, "all your things is just as you left them. A bit of airing before the fire an' they'll be all right. 'Twill be a bit of a distraction like, a little riding and wild-fowling now and agen. You'll find the folk around here has hard and bitter minds towards you. They hasn't forgotten nor forgiven. No one'll come nigh you, so you'd best get what distraction you can with horse and dog. They'm good company, too."

Old George hobbled away to give his orders, and Stoner, feeling more than ever like one in a dream, went upstairs to inspect "Master Tom's" wardrobe. A ride was one of the pleasures dearest to his heart, and there was some protection against immediate discovery of his imposture in the thought that none of Tom's aforetime companions were likely to favour him with a close inspection. As the interloper thrust himself into some tolerably well-fitting riding cords he wondered vaguely what manner of misdeed the genuine Tom had committed to set the whole countryside against him. The thud of quick, eager hoofs on damp earth cut short his speculations. The roan cob had been brought up to the side door.

"Talk of beggars on horseback," thought Stoner to himself, as he trotted rapidly along the muddy lanes where he had tramped yesterday as a down-at-heel outcast; and then he flung reflection indolently aside and gave himself up to the pleasure of a smart canter along the turf-grown side of a level stretch of road. At an open gateway he checked his pace to allow two carts to turn into a field. The lads driving the carts found time to give him a prolonged stare, and as he passed on he heard an excited voice call out, " 'Tis Tom Prike! I knowed him at once; showing hisself here agen, is he?"

Evidently the likeness which had imposed at close quarters on a doddering old man was good enough to mislead younger eyes at a short distance.

In the course of his ride he met with ample evidence to confirm the statement that local folk had neither forgotten nor forgiven the bygone crime which had come to him as a legacy from the absent Tom. Scowling looks, mutterings, and nudgings greeted him whenever he chanced upon human beings; "Bowker's pup," trotting placidly by his side, seemed the one element of friendliness in a hostile world.

As he dismounted at the side door he caught a fleeting glimpse of a gaunt, elderly woman peering at him from behind the curtain of an upper window. Evidently this was his aunt by adoption.

Over the ample midday meal that stood in readiness for him Stoner was able to review the possibilities of his extraordinary situation. The real Tom, after four years of absence, might suddenly turn up at the farm, or a letter might come from him at any moment. Again, in the character of heir to the farm, the false Tom might be called on to sign documents, which would be an embarrassing predicament. Or a relative might arrive who would not imitate the aunt's attitude of aloofness. All these things would mean ignominious exposure. On the other hand, the alternative was the open sky and the muddy lanes that led down to the sea. The farm offered him, at any rate, a temporary refuge from destitution; farming was one of the many things he had "tried," and he would be able to do a certain amount of work in return for the hospitality to which he was so little entitled.

"Will you have cold pork for your supper," asked the hard-faced maid, as she cleared the table, "or will you have it hotted up?"

"Hot, with onions," said Stoner. It was the only time in his life that he had made a rapid decision. And as he gave the order he knew that he meant to stay.

Stoner kept rigidly to those portions of the house which seemed to have been allotted to him by a tacit treaty of de-limitation. When he took part in the farm-work it was as one who worked under orders and never initiated them. Old George, the roan cob, and Bowker's pup were his sole companions in a world that was otherwise frostily silent and hostile. Of the mistress of the farm he saw nothing. Once, when he knew she had gone forth to church, he made a furtive visit to the farm parlour in an endeavour to glean some frag-mentary knowledge of the young man whose place he had usurped, and whose ill-repute he had fastened on himself. There were many photographs hung on the walls, or stuck in prim frames, but the likeness he sought for was not among them. At last, in an album thrust out of sight, he came across what he wanted. There was a whole series, labelled "Tom," a podgy child of three, in a fantastic frock, an awkward boy of about twelve, holding a cricket bat as though he loathed it, a rather good-looking youth of eighteen with very smooth, evenly parted hair, and, finally, a young man with a somewhat surly dare-devil expression. At this last portrait Stoner looked with particular interest; the likeness to himself was unmis-takable.

From the lips of old George, who was garrulous enough on most subjects, he tried again and again to learn something of the nature of the offence which shut him off as a creature to be shunned and hated by his fellow-men.

"What do the folk around here say about me?" he asked one day as they were walking home from an outlying field.

The old man shook his head.

"They be bitter agen you, mortal bitter. Ay, 'tis a sad business, a sad business."

And never could he be got to say anything more enlightening.

On a clear frosty evening, a few days before the festival of Christmas, Stoner stood in a corner of the orchard which commanded a wide view of the countryside. Here and there he could see the twinkling dots of lamp or candle glow which told of human homes where the goodwill and jollity of the season held their sway. Behind him lay the grim, silent farmhouse, where no one ever laughed, where even a quarrel would have seemed cheerful. As he turned to look at the long grey front of the gloom-shadowed building, a door opened and old George came hurriedly forth. Stoner heard his adopted name called in a tone of strained anxiety. Instantly he knew that something untoward had happened, and with a quick revulsion of outlook his sanctuary became in his eyes a place of peace and contentment, from which he dreaded to be driven.

"Master Tom," said the old man in a hoarse whisper, "you must slip away quiet from here for a few days. Michael Ley is back in the village, an' he swears to shoot you if he can come across you. He'll do it, too, there's murder in the look of him. Get away under cover of night, 'tis only for a week or so, he won't be here longer."

"But where am I to go?" stammered Stoner, who had caught the infection of the old man's obvious terror.

"Go right away along the coast to Punchford and keep hid there. When Michael's safe gone I'll ride the roan over to the Green Dragon at Punchford; when you see the cob stabled at the Green Dragon 'tis a sign you may come back agen."

"But—" began Stoner hesitatingly.

" 'Tis all right for money," said the other; "the old Missus agrees you'd best do as I say, and she's given me this."

The old man produced three sovereigns and some odd silver.

Stoner felt more of a cheat than ever as he stole away that night from the back gate of the farm with the old woman's money in his pocket. Old George and Bowker's pup stood watching him a silent farewell from the yard. He could scarcely fancy that he would ever come back, and he felt a throb of compunction for those two humble friends who would wait wistfully for his return. Some day perhaps the real Tom would come back, and there would be wild wonderment among those simple farm folks as to the identity of the shadowy guest they had harboured under their roof. For his own fate he felt no immediate anxiety; three pounds goes but little way in the world when there is nothing behind it, but to a man who has counted his exchequer in pennies it seems a good starting-point. Fortune had done him a whimsically kind turn when last he trod these lanes as a hopeless adventurer, and there might yet be a chance of his finding some work and making a fresh start; as he got further from the farm his spirits rose higher. There was a sense of relief in regaining once more his lost identity and ceasing to be the uneasy ghost of another. He scarcely bothered to speculate about the implacable enemy who had dropped from nowhere into his life; since that life was now behind him one unreal item the more made little difference. For the first time for many months he began to hum a careless light-hearted refrain. Then there stepped out from the shadow of an overhanging oak tree a man with a gun. There was no need to wonder who he might be; the moonlight falling on his white set face revealed a glare of human hate such as Stoner in the ups and downs of his wanderings had never seen before. He sprang aside in a wild effort to break through the hedge that bordered the lane, but the tough branches held him fast. The hounds of Fate had waited for him in those narrow lanes, and this time they were not to be denied.

THE RECESSIONAL

CLOVIS sat in the hottest zone but two of a Turkish bath, alternately inert in statuesque contemplation and rapidly manœuvring a fountain-pen over the pages of a note-book.

"Don't interrupt me with your childish prattle," he observed to Bertie van Tahn, who had slung himself languidly into a neighbouring chair and looked conversationally inclined; "I'm writing deathless verse."

Bertie looked interested.

"I say, what a boon you would be to portrait painters if you really got to be notorious as a poetry writer. If they couldn't get your likeness hung in the Academy as 'Clovis Sangrail, Esq., at work on his latest poem,' they could slip you in as a Study of the Nude or Orpheus descending into Jermyn Street. They always complain that modern dress handicaps them, whereas a towel and a fountain-pen—"

"It was Mrs. Packletide's suggestion that I should write this thing," said Clovis, ignoring the bypaths to fame that Bertie van Tahn was pointing out to him. "You see, Loona Bimberton had a Coronation Ode accepted by the *New Infancy*, a paper that has been started with the idea of making the *New Age* seem elderly and hidebound. 'So clever of you, dear Loona,' the Packletide remarked when she had read it; 'of course, any one could write a Coronation Ode, but no one else would have thought of doing it.' Loona protested that these things were extremely difficult to do, and gave us to understand that they were more or less the province of a gifted few. Now the Packletide has been rather decent to me in many ways, a sort of financial ambulance, you know, that carries you off the field when you're hard hit, which is a frequent occurrence with me, and I've no use whatever for Loona Bimberton, so I chipped in and said I could turn out that sort of stuff by the square yard if I gave my mind to it. Loona said I couldn't, and we got bets on, and between you and me I think the money's fairly safe. Of course, one of the conditions of the wager is that the thing has to be published in something or other, local newspapers barred; but Mrs. Packletide has endeared herself by many little acts of thoughtfulness to the editor of the *Smoky Chimney*, so if I can hammer out anything at all approaching the level of the usual Ode output we ought to be all right. So far I'm getting along so comfortably that I begin to be afraid that I must be one of the gifted few."

"It's rather late in the day for a Coronation Ode, isn't it?" said Bertie.

"Of course," said Clovis; "this is going to be a Durbar Recessional, the sort of thing that you can keep by you for all time if you want to."

"Now I understand your choice of a place to write it in," said Bertie van Tahn, with the air of one who has suddenly unravelled a hitherto obscure problem; "you want to get the local temperature."

"I came here to get freedom from the inane interruptions of the mentally deficient," said Clovis, "but it seems I asked too much of fate."

Bertie van Tahn prepared to use his towel as a weapon of precision, but reflecting that he had a good deal of unprotected coast-line himself, and that Clovis was equipped with a fountain-pen as well as a towel, he relapsed pacifically into the depths of his chair.

"May one hear extracts from the immortal work?" he asked. "I promise that nothing that I hear now shall prejudice me against borrowing a copy of the *Smoky Chimney* at the right moment."

"It's rather like casting pearls into a trough," remarked Clovis pleasantly, "but I don't mind reading you bits of it. It begins with a general dispersal of the Durbar participants:

" 'Back to their homes in Himalayan heights
    The stale pale elephants of Cutch Behar
    Roll like great galleons on a tideless sea—' "

"I don't believe Cutch Behar is anywhere near the Himalayan region," interrupted Bertie. "You ought to have an atlas on hand when you do this sort of thing; and why stale and pale?"

"After the late hours and the excitement, of course," said Clovis; "and I said their *homes* were in the Himalayas. You can have Himalayan elephants in Cutch Behar, I suppose, just as you have Irish-bred horses running at Ascot."

"You said they were going back to the Himalayas," objected Bertie.

"Well, they would naturally be sent home to recuperate. It's the usual thing out there to turn elephants loose in the hills, just as we put horses out to grass in this country."

Clovis could at least flatter himself that he had infused some of the reckless splendour of the East into his mendacity.

"Is it all going to be in blank verse?" asked the critic.

"Of course not; 'Durbar' comes at the end of the fourth line."

"That seems so cowardly; however, it explains why you pitched on Cutch Behar."

"There is more connection between geographical place-names and poetical inspiration than is generally recognized; one of the chief reasons why there are so few really great poems about Russia in our language is that you can't possibly get a rhyme to names like Smolensk and Tobolsk and Minsk."

Clovis spoke with the authority of one who has tried.

"Of course, you could rhyme Omsk with Tomsk," he continued; "in fact, they seem to be there for that purpose, but the public wouldn't stand that sort of thing indefinitely."

"The public will stand a good deal," said Bertie malevolently, "and so small a proportion of it knows Russian that you could always have an explanatory footnote asserting that the last three letters in Smolensk are not pronounced. It's quite as believable as your statement about putting elephants out to grass in the Himalayan range."

"I've got rather a nice bit," resumed Clovis with unruffled serenity, "giving an evening scene on the outskirts of a jungle village:

> " 'Where the coiled cobra in the gloaming gloats,
> And prowling panthers stalk the wary goats.' "

"There is practically no gloaming in tropical countries," said Bertie indulgently; "but I like the masterly reticence with which you treat the cobra's motive for gloating. The unknown is proverbially the uncanny. I can picture nervous readers of the *Smoky Chimney* keeping the light turned on in their bedrooms all night out of sheer sickening uncertainty as to *what* the cobra might have been gloating about."

"Cobras gloat naturally," said Clovis, "just as wolves are always ravening from mere force of habit, even after they've hopelessly overeaten themselves. I've got a fine bit of colour painting later on," he added, "where I describe the dawn coming up over the Brahma-putra river:

> " 'The amber dawn-drenched East with sun-shafts kissed,
>   Stained sanguine apricot and amethyst,
>   O'er the washed emerald of the mango groves
>   Hangs in a mist of opalescent mauves,
>   While painted parrot-flights impinge the haze
>   With scarlet, chalcedon and chrysoprase.' "

"I've never seen the dawn come up over the Brahma-putra river," said Bertie, "so I can't say if it's a good description of the event, but it sounds more like an account of an extensive jewel robbery. Anyhow, the parrots give a good useful touch of local colour. I suppose you've introduced some tigers into the scenery? An Indian landscape would have rather a bare, unfinished look without a tiger or two in the middle distance."

"I've got a hen-tiger somewhere in the poem," said Clovis, hunting through his notes. "Here she is:

> " 'The tawny tigress 'mid the tangled teak
>   Drags to her purring cubs' enraptured ears
>   The harsh death-rattle in the pea-fowl's beak,
>   A jungle lullaby of blood and tears.' "

Bertie van Tahn rose hurriedly from his recumbent position and made for the glass door leading into the next compartment.

"I think your idea of home life in the jungle is perfectly horrid," he said. "The cobra was sinister enough, but the improvised rattle in the tiger-nursery is the limit. If you're going to make me turn hot and cold all over I may as well go into the steam room at once."

"Just listen to this line," said Clovis; "it would make the reputation of any ordinary poet:

> " 'and overhead
> The pendulum-patient Punkah, parent of stillborn breeze.' "

"Most of your readers will think 'punkah' is a kind of iced drink or half-time at polo," said Bertie, and disappeared into the steam.

.   .   .   .

The *Smoky Chimney* duly published the "Recessional," but it proved to be its swan song, for the paper never attained to another issue.

Loona Bimberton gave up her intention of attending the Durbar and went into a nursing-home on the Sussex Downs. Nervous breakdown after a particularly strenuous season was the usually accepted explanation, but there are three or four people who know that she never really recovered from the dawn breaking over the Brahma-putra river.

A MATTER OF SENTIMENT

IT was the eve of the great race, and scarcely a member of Lady Susan's house-party had as yet a single bet on. It was one of those unsatisfactory years when one horse held a commanding market position, not by reason of any general belief in its crushing superiority, but because it was extremely difficult to pitch on any other candidate to whom to pin one's faith. Peradventure II was the favourite, not in the sense of being a popular fancy, but by virtue of a lack of confidence in any one of his rather undistinguished rivals. The brains of clubland were much exercised in seeking out possible merit where none was very obvious to the naked intelligence, and the house-party at Lady Susan's was possessed by the same uncertainty and irresolution that infected wider circles.

"It is just the time for bringing off a good coup," said Bertie van Tahn.

"Undoubtedly. But with what?" demanded Clovis for the twentieth time.

The women of the party were just as keenly interested in the matter, and just as helplessly perplexed; even the mother of Clovis, who usually got good racing information from her dressmaker, confessed herself fancy free on this occasion. Colonel Drake, who was professor of military history at a minor cramming establishment, was the only person who had a definite selection for the event, but as his choice varied every three hours he was worse than useless as an inspired guide. The crowning difficulty of the problem was that it could only be fitfully and furtively discussed. Lady Susan disapproved of racing. She disapproved of many things; some people went as far as to say that she disapproved of most things. Disapproval was to her what neuralgia and fancy needlework are to many other women. She disapproved of early morning tea and auction bridge, of ski-ing and the two-step, of the Russian ballet and the Chelsea Arts Club ball, of the French policy in Morocco and the British policy everywhere. It was not that she was particularly strict or narrow in her views of life, but she had been the eldest sister of a large family of self-indulgent children, and her particular form of indulgence had consisted in openly disapproving of the foibles of the others. Unfortunately the hobby had grown up with her. As she was rich, influential, and very, very kind, most people were content to count their early tea as well lost on her behalf. Still, the necessity for hurriedly dropping the discussion of an enthralling topic, and suppressing all mention of it during her presence on the scene, was an affliction at a moment like the present, when time was slipping away and indecision was the prevailing note.

After a lunch-time of rather strangled and uneasy conversation, Clovis managed to get most of the party together at the further end of the kitchen gardens, on the pretext of admiring the Himalayan pheasants. He had made an important discovery. Motkin, the butler, who (as Clovis expressed it) had grown prematurely grey in Lady Susan's service, added to his other excellent qualities an intelligent interest in matters connected with the Turf. On the subject of the forthcoming race he was not illuminating, except in so far that he shared the prevailing unwillingness to see a winner in Peradventure II. But where he outshone all the members of the house-party was in the fact that he had a second cousin who was head stable-lad at a neighbouring racing establishment, and usually gifted with much inside information as to private form and possibilities. Only the fact of her ladyship having taken it into her head to invite a house-party for the last week of May had prevented Mr. Motkin from paying a visit of consultation to his relative with respect to the big race; there was still time to cycle over if he could get leave of absence for the afternoon on some specious excuse.

"Let's jolly well hope he does," said Bertie van Tahn; "under the circumstances a second cousin is almost as useful as second sight."

"That stable ought to know something, if knowledge is to be found anywhere," said Mrs. Packletide hopefully.

"I expect you'll find he'll echo my fancy for Motorboat," said Colonel Drake.

At this moment the subject had to be hastily dropped. Lady Susan bore down upon them, leaning on the arm of Clovis's mother, to whom she was confiding the fact that she disapproved of the craze for Pekingese spaniels. It was the third thing she had found time to disapprove of since lunch, without counting her silent and permanent disapproval of the way Clovis's mother did her hair.

"We have been admiring the Himalayan pheasants," said Mrs. Packletide suavely.

"They went off to a bird-show at Nottingham early this morning," said Lady Susan, with the air of one who disapproves of hasty and ill-considered lying.

"Their house, I mean; such perfect roosting arrangements, and all so clean," resumed Mrs. Packletide, with an increased glow of enthusiasm. The odious Bertie van Tahn was murmuring audible prayers for Mrs. Packletide's ultimate estrangement from the paths of falsehood.

"I hope you don't mind dinner being a quarter of an hour late tonight," said Lady Susan; "Motkin has had an urgent summons to go and see a sick relative this afternoon. He wanted to bicycle there, but I am sending him in the motor."

"How very kind of you! Of course we don't mind dinner being put off." The assurances came with unanimous and hearty sincerity.

At the dinner-table that night an undercurrent of furtive curiosity directed itself towards Motkin's impassive countenance. One or two of the guests almost expected to find a slip of paper concealed in their napkins, bearing the name of the second cousin's selection. They had not long to wait. As the butler went round with the murmured question, "Sherry?" he added in an even lower tone the cryptic words, "Better not." Mrs. Packletide gave a start of alarm, and refused the sherry; there seemed some sinister suggestion in the butler's warning, as though her hostess had suddenly become addicted to the Borgia habit. A moment later the explanation flashed on her that "Better Not" was the name of one of the runners in the big race. Clovis was already pencilling it on his cuff, and Colonel Drake, in his turn, was signalling to every one in hoarse whispers and dumb-show the fact that he had all along fancied "B.N."

Early next morning a sheaf of telegrams went Townward, representing the market commands of the house-party and servants' hall.

It was a wet afternoon, and most of Lady Susan's guests hung about the hall, waiting apparently for the appearance of tea, though it was scarcely yet due. The advent of a telegram quickened every one into a flutter of expectancy; the page who brought the telegram to Clovis waited with unusual alertness to know if there might be an answer.

Clovis read the message and gave an exclamation of annoyance.

"No bad news, I hope," said Lady Susan. Every one else knew that the news was not good.

"It's only the result of the Derby," he blurted out; "Sadowa won; an utter outsider."

"Sadowa!" exclaimed Lady Susan; "you don't say so! How remarkable! It's the first time I've ever backed a horse; in fact

I disapprove of horse-racing, but just for once in a way I put money on this horse, and it's gone and won."

"May I ask," said Mrs. Packletide, amid the general silence, "why you put your money on this particular horse? None of the sporting prophets mentioned it as having an outside chance."

"Well," said Lady Susan, "you may laugh at me, but it was the name that attracted me. You see, I was always mixed up with the Franco-German war; I was married on the day that the war was declared, and my eldest child was born the day that peace was signed, so anything connected with the war has always interested me. And when I saw there was a horse running in the Derby called after one of the battles in the Franco-German war, I said I *must* put some money on it, for once in a way, though I disapprove of racing. And it's actually won."

There was a general groan. No one groaned more deeply than the professor of military history.

THE SECRET SIN OF SEPTIMUS BROPE

"WHO and what is Mr. Brope?" demanded the aunt of Clovis suddenly.

Mrs. Riversedge, who had been snipping off the heads of defunct roses, and thinking of nothing in particular, sprang hurriedly to mental attention. She was one of those old-fashioned hostesses who consider that one ought to know something about one's guests, and that the something ought to be to their credit.

"I believe he comes from Leighton Buzzard," she observed by way of preliminary explanation.

"In these days of rapid and convenient travel," said Clovis, who was dispersing a colony of green-fly with visitations of cigarette smoke, "to come from Leighton Buzzard does not necessarily denote any great strength of character. It might only mean mere restlessness. Now if he had left it under a cloud, or as a protest against the incurable and heartless frivolity of its inhabitants, that would tell us something about the man and his mission in life."

"What does he do?" pursued Mrs. Troyle magisterially.

"He edits the *Cathedral Monthly*," said her hostess, "and he's enormously learned about memorial brasses and transepts and the influence of Byzantine worship on modern liturgy, and all those sort of things. Perhaps he is just a little bit heavy and immersed in one range of subjects, but it takes all sorts to make a good house-party, you know. You don't find him *too* dull, do you?"

"Dulness I could overlook," said the aunt of Clovis: "what I cannot forgive is his making love to my maid."

"My dear Mrs. Troyle," gasped the hostess, "what an extraordinary idea! I assure you Mr. Brope would not dream of doing such a thing."

"His dreams are a matter of indifference to me; for all I care his slumbers may be one long indiscretion of unsuitable erotic advances, in which the entire servants' hall may be involved. But in his waking hours he shall not make love to my maid. It's no use arguing about it, I'm firm on the point."

"But you must be mistaken," persisted Mrs. Riversedge; "Mr. Brope would be the last person to do such a thing."

"He is the first person to do such a thing, as far as my information goes, and if I have any voice in the matter he certainly shall be the last. Of course, I am not referring to respectably-intentioned lovers."

"I simply cannot think that a man who writes so charmingly and informingly about transepts and Byzantine influences would behave in such an unprincipled manner," said Mrs. Riversedge; "what evidence have you that he's doing anything of the sort? I don't want to doubt your word, of course, but we mustn't be too ready to condemn him unheard, must we?"

"Whether we condemn him or not, he has certainly not been unheard. He has the room next to my dressing-room, and on two occasions, when I dare say he thought I was absent, I have plainly heard him announcing through the wall, 'I love you, Florrie.' Those partition walls upstairs are very thin; one can almost hear a watch ticking in the next room."

"Is your maid called Florence?"

"Her name is Florinda."

"What an extraordinary name to give a maid!"

"I did not give it to her; she arrived in my service already christened."

"What I mean is," said Mrs. Riversedge, "that when I get maids with unsuitable names I call them Jane; they soon get used to it."

"An excellent plan," said the aunt of Clovis coldly; "unfortunately I have got used to being called Jane myself. It happens to be my name."

She cut short Mrs. Riversedge's flood of apologies by abruptly remarking:

"The question is not whether I'm to call my maid Florinda, but whether Mr. Brope is to be permitted to call her Florrie. I am strongly of opinion that he shall not."

"He may have been repeating the words of some song," said Mrs. Riversedge hopefully; "there are lots of those sorts of silly refrains with girls' names," she continued, turning to Clovis as a possible authority on the subject. " 'You mustn't call me Mary——' "

"I shouldn't think of doing so," Clovis assured her; "in the first place, I've always understood that your name was Henrietta; and then I hardly know you well enough to take such a liberty."

"I mean there's a *song* with that refrain," hurriedly explained Mrs. Riversedge, "and there's 'Rhoda, Rhoda kept a pagoda,' and 'Maisie is a daisy,' and heaps of others. Certainly it doesn't sound like Mr. Brope to be singing such songs, but I think we ought to give him the benefit of the doubt."

"I had already done so," said Mrs. Troyle, "until further evidence came my way."

She shut her lips with the resolute finality of one who enjoys the blessed certainty of being implored to open them again.

"Further evidence!" exclaimed her hostess; "do tell me!"

"As I was coming upstairs after breakfast Mr. Brope was just passing my room. In the most natural way in the world a piece of paper dropped out of a packet that he held in his hand and fluttered to the ground just at my door. I was going to call out to him 'You've dropped something,' and then for some reason I held back and didn't show myself till he was safely in his room. You see it occurred to me that I was very seldom in my room just at that hour, and that Florinda was almost always there tidying up things about that time. So I picked up that innocent-looking piece of paper."

Mrs. Troyle paused again, with the self-applauding air of one who has detected an asp lurking in an apple-charlotte.

Mrs. Riversedge snipped vigorously at the nearest rose bush, incidentally decapitating a Viscountess Folkestone that was just coming into bloom.

"What was on the paper?" she asked.

"Just the words in pencil, 'I love you, Florrie,' and then underneath, crossed out with a faint line, but perfectly plain to read, 'Meet me in the garden by the yew.'"

"There *is* a yew tree at the bottom of the garden," admitted Mrs. Riversedge.

"At any rate he appears to be truthful," commented Clovis.

"To think that a scandal of this sort should be going on under my roof!" said Mrs. Riversedge indignantly.

"I wonder why it is that scandal seems so much worse under a roof," observed Clovis; "I've always regarded it as a proof of the superior delicacy of the cat tribe that it conducts most of its scandals above the slates."

"Now I come to think of it," resumed Mrs. Riversedge, "there are things about Mr. Brope that I've never been able to account for. His income, for instance: he only gets two hundred a year as editor of the *Cathedral Monthly*, and I know that his people are quite poor, and he hasn't any private means. Yet he manages to afford a flat somewhere in Westminster, and he goes abroad to Bruges and those sorts of places every year, and always dresses well, and gives quite nice luncheon-parties in the season. You can't do all that on two hundred a year, can you?"

"Does he write for any other papers?" queried Mrs. Troyle.

"No, you see he specializes so entirely on liturgy and ecclesiastical architecture that his field is rather restricted. He once tried the *Sporting and Dramatic* with an article on church edifices in famous fox-hunting centres, but it wasn't considered of sufficient general interest to be accepted. No, I don't see how he can support himself in his present style merely by what he writes."

"Perhaps he sells spurious transepts to American enthusiasts," suggested Clovis.

"How could you sell a transept?" said Mrs. Riversedge; "such a thing would be impossible."

"Whatever he may do to eke out his income," interrupted Mrs. Troyle, "he is certainly not going to fill in his leisure moments by making love to my maid."

"Of course not," agreed her hostess; "that must be put a stop to at once. But I don't quite know what we ought to do."

"You might put a barbed wire entanglement round the yew tree as a precautionary measure," said Clovis.

"I don't think that the disagreeable situation that has arisen is improved by flippancy," said Mrs. Riversedge; "a good maid is a treasure—"

"I am sure I don't know what I should do without Florinda," admitted Mrs. Troyle; "she understands my hair. I've long ago given up trying to do anything with it myself. I regard one's hair as I regard husbands: as long as one is seen together in public one's private divergences don't matter. Surely that was the luncheon gong."

Septimus Brope and Clovis had the smoking-room to themselves after lunch. The former seemed restless and preoccupied, the latter quietly observant.

"What is a lorry?" asked Septimus suddenly; "I don't mean the thing on wheels, of course I know what that is, but isn't there a bird with a name like that, the larger form of a lorikeet?"

"I fancy it's a lory, with one 'r,'" said Clovis lazily, "in which case it's no good to you."

Septimus Brope stared in some astonishment.

"How do you mean, no good to me?" he asked, with more than a trace of uneasiness in his voice.

"Won't rhyme with Florrie," explained Clovis briefly.

Septimus sat upright in his chair, with unmistakable alarm on his face.

"How did you find out? I mean how did you know I was trying to get a rhyme to Florrie?" he asked sharply.

"I didn't know," said Clovis, "I only guessed. When you wanted to turn the prosaic lorry of commerce into a feathered poem flitting through the verdure of a tropical forest, I knew you must be working up a sonnet, and Florrie was the only female name that suggested itself as rhyming with lorry."

Septimus still looked uneasy.

"I believe you know more," he said.

Clovis laughed quietly, but said nothing.

"How much do you know?" Septimus asked desperately.

"The yew tree in the garden," said Clovis.

"There! I felt certain I'd dropped it somewhere. But you must have guessed something before. Look here, you have surprised my secret. You won't give me away, will you? It is nothing to be ashamed of, but it wouldn't do for the editor of the *Cathedral Monthly* to go in openly for that sort of thing, would it?"

"Well, I suppose not," admitted Clovis.

"You see," continued Septimus, "I get quite a decent lot of money out of it. I could never live in the style I do on what I get as editor of the *Cathedral Monthly*."

Clovis was even more startled than Septimus had been earlier in the conversation, but he was better skilled in repressing surprise.

"Do you mean to say you get money out of—Florrie?" he asked.

"Not out of Florrie, as yet," said Septimus; "in fact, I don't mind saying that I'm having a good deal of trouble over Florrie. But there are a lot of others."

Clovis's cigarette went out.

"This is *very* interesting," he said slowly. And then, with Septimus Brope's next words, illumination dawned on him.

"There are heaps of others; for instance:

> " 'Cora with the lips of coral,
>   You and I will never quarrel.' "

That was one of my earliest successes, and it still brings me
in royalties. And then there is—'Esmeralda, when I first beheld her,' and 'Fair Teresa, how I love to please her,' both of
those have been fairly popular. And there is one rather dreadful one," continued Septimus, flushing deep carmine, "which
has brought me in more money than any of the others:

> " 'Lively little Lucie
>   With her naughty nez retrousse.' "

Of course, I loathe the whole lot of them; in fact, I'm
rapidly becoming something of a woman-hater under their influence, but I can't afford to disregard the financial aspect of
the matter. And at the same time you can understand that my
position as an authority on ecclesiastical architecture and litur-
gical subjects would be weakened, if not altogether ruined, if
it once got about that I was the author of 'Cora with the lips
of coral' and all the rest of them."

Clovis had recovered sufficiently to ask in a sympathetic, if
rather unsteady, voice what was the special trouble with
"Florrie."

"I can't get her into lyric shape, try as I will," said Septimus mournfully. "You see, one has to work in a lot of
sentimental, sugary compliment with a catchy rhyme, and a
certain amount of personal biography or prophecy. They've
all of them got to have a long string of past successes recorded
about them, or else you've got to foretell blissful things about
them and yourself in the future. For instance, there is:

> " 'Dainty little girlie Mavis,
>   She is such a rara avis,
>   All the money I can save is
>   All to be for Mavis mine.' "

It goes to a sickening namby-pamby waltz tune, and for
months nothing else was sung and hummed in Blackpool and
other popular centres."

This time Clovis's self-control broke down badly.

"Please excuse me," he gurgled, "but I can't help it when I remember the awful solemnity of that article of yours that you so kindly read us last night, on the Coptic Church in its relation to early Christian worship."

Septimus groaned.

"You see how it would be," he said; "as soon as people knew me to be the author of that miserable sentimental twaddle, all respect for the serious labours of my life would be gone. I dare say I know more about memorial brasses than any one living, in fact I hope one day to publish a monograph on the subject, but I should be pointed out everywhere as the man whose ditties were in the mouths of nigger minstrels along the entire coast-line of our Island home. Can you wonder that I positively hate Florrie all the time that I'm trying to grind out sugar-coated rhapsodies about her?"

"Why not give free play to your emotions, and be brutally abusive? An uncomplimentary refrain would have an instant success as a novelty if you were sufficiently outspoken."

"I've never thought of that," said Septimus, "and I'm afraid I couldn't break away from the habit of fulsome adulation and suddenly change my style."

"You needn't change your style in the least," said Clovis; "merely reverse the sentiment and keep to the inane phraseology of the thing. If you'll do the body of the song I'll knock off the refrain, which is the thing that principally matters, I believe. I shall charge half-shares in the royalties, and throw in my silence as to your guilty secret. In the eyes of the world you shall still be the man who has devoted his life to the study of transepts and Byzantine ritual; only sometimes, in the long winter evenings, when the wind howls drearily down the chimney and the rain beats against the windows, I shall think of you as the author of 'Cora with the lips of coral.' Of course, if in sheer gratitude at my silence you like to take me for a much-needed holiday to the Adriatic or somewhere equally interesting, paying all expenses, I shouldn't dream of refusing."

Later in the afternoon Clovis found his aunt and Mrs.

Riversedge indulging in gentle exercise in the Jacobean garden.

"I've spoken to Mr. Brope about F.," he announced.

"How splendid of you! What did he say?" came in a quick chorus from the two ladies.

"He was quite frank and straightforward with me when he saw that I knew his secret," said Clovis, "and it seems that his intentions were quite serious, if slightly unsuitable. I tried to show him the impracticability of the course that he was following. He said he wanted to be understood, and he seemed to think that Florinda would excel in that requirement, but I pointed out that there were probably dozens of delicately nurtured, pure-hearted young English girls who would be capable of understanding him, while Florinda was the only person in the world who understood my aunt's hair. That rather weighed with him, for he's not really a selfish animal, if you take him in the right way, and when I appealed to the memory of his happy childish days, spent amid the daisied fields of Leighton Buzzard (I suppose daisies do grow there), he was obviously affected. Anyhow, he gave me his word that he would put Florinda absolutely out of his mind, and he has agreed to go for a short trip abroad as the best distraction for his thoughts. I am going with him as far as Ragusa. If my aunt should wish to give me a really nice scarf-pin (to be chosen by myself), as a small recognition of the very considerable service I have done her, I shouldn't dream of refusing. I'm not one of those who think that because one is abroad one can go about dressed anyhow."

A few weeks later in Blackpool and places where they sing, the following refrain held undisputed sway:

> "How you bore me, Florrie,
>   With those eyes of vacant blue;
> You'll be very sorry, Florrie,
>   If I marry you.
> Though I'm easy-goin', Florrie,
>   This I swear is true,
> I'll throw you down a quarry, Florrie,
>   If I marry you."

"MINISTERS OF GRACE"

ALTHOUGH he was scarcely yet out of his teens, the Duke of Scaw was already marked out as a personality widely differing from others of his caste and period. Not in externals; therein he conformed correctly to type. His hair was faintly reminiscent of Houbigant, and at the other end of him his shoes exhaled the right *soupçon* of harness-room; his socks compelled one's attention without losing one's respect; and his attitude in repose had just that suggestion of Whistler's mother, so becoming in the really young. It was within that the trouble lay, if trouble it could be accounted, which marked him apart from his fellows. The Duke was religious. Not in any of the ordinary senses of the word; he took small heed of High Church or Evangelical standpoints, he stood outside of all the movements and missions and cults and crusades of the day, uncaring and uninterested. Yet in a mystical-practical way of his own, which had served him unscathed and unshaken through the fickle years of boyhood, he was intensely and intensively religious. His family were naturally, though unobtrusively, distressed about it. "I am so afraid it may affect his bridge," said his mother.

The Duke sat in a pennyworth of chair in St. James's Park, listening to the pessimisms of Belturbet, who reviewed the existing political situation from the gloomiest of standpoints.

"Where I think you political spade-workers are so silly," said the Duke, "is in the misdirection of your efforts. You spend thousands of pounds of money, and Heaven knows how much dynamic force of brain power and personal energy, in trying to elect or displace this or that man, whereas you could gain your ends so much more simply by making use of the men as you find them. If they don't suit your purpose as they are, transform them into something more satisfactory."

"Do you refer to hypnotic suggestion?" asked Belturbet, with the air of one who is being trifled with.

"Nothing of the sort. Do you understand what I mean by

the verb to koepenick? That is to say, to replace an authority by a spurious imitation that would carry just as much weight for the moment as the displaced original; the advantage, of course, being that the koepenick replica would do what you wanted, whereas the original does what seems best in its own eyes."

"I suppose every public man has a double, if not two or three," said Belturbet; "but it would be a pretty hard task to koepenick a whole bunch of them and keep the originals out of the way."

"There have been instances in European history of highly successful koepenickery," said the Duke dreamily.

"Oh, of course, there have been False Dimitris and Perkin Warbecks, who imposed on the world for a time," assented Belturbet, "but they personated people who were dead or safely out of the way. That was a comparatively simple matter. It would be far easier to pass oneself off as dead Hannibal than as living Haldane, for instance."

"I was thinking," said the Duke, "of the most famous case of all, the angel who koepenicked King Robert of Sicily with such brilliant results. Just imagine what an advantage it would be to have angels deputizing, to use a horrible but convenient word, for Quinston and Lord Hugo Sizzle, for example. How much smoother the Parliamentary machine would work than at present!"

"Now you're talking nonsense," said Belturbet; "angels don't exist nowadays, at least, not in that way, so what is the use of dragging them into a serious discussion? It's merely silly."

"If you talk to me like that I shall just *do* it," said the Duke.

"Do what?" asked Belturbet. There were times when his young friend's uncanny remarks rather frightened him.

"I shall summon angelic forces to take over some of the more troublesome personalities of our public life, and I shall send the ousted originals into temporary retirement in suitable animal organisms. It's not every one who would have the knowledge or the power necessary to bring such a thing off—"

"Oh, stop that inane rubbish," said Belturbet angrily; "it's getting wearisome. Here's Quinston coming," he added, as there approached along the almost deserted path the well-known figure of a young Cabinet Minister, whose personality evoked a curious mixture of public interest and unpopularity.

"Hurry along, my dear man," said the young Duke to the Minister, who had given him a condescending nod; "your time is running short," he continued in a provocative strain; "the whole inept crowd of you will shortly be swept away into the world's waste-paper basket."

"You poor little strawberry-leafed nonentity," said the Minister, checking himself for a moment in his stride and rolling out his words spasmodically; "who is going to sweep us away, I should like to know? The voting masses are on our side, and all the ability and administrative talent is on our side too. No power of earth or Heaven is going to move us from our place till we choose to quit it. No power of earth or——"

Belturbet saw, with bulging eyes, a sudden void where a moment earlier had been a Cabinet Minister; a void emphasized rather than relieved by the presence of a puffed-out bewildered-looking sparrow, which hopped about for a moment in a dazed fashion and then fell to a violent cheeping and scolding.

"If we could understand sparrow-language," said the Duke serenely, "I fancy we should hear something infinitely worse than 'strawberry-leafed nonentity.'"

"But good Heavens, Eugène," said Belturbet hoarsely, "what has become of—— Why, there he is! How on earth did he get there?" And he pointed with a shaking finger towards a semblance of the vanished Minister, which approached once more along the unfrequented path.

The Duke laughed.

"It is Quinston to all outward appearance," he said composedly, "but I fancy you will find, on closer investigation, that it is an angel under-study of the real article."

The Angel-Quinston greeted them with a friendly smile.

"How beastly happy you two look sitting there!" he said wistfully.

"I don't suppose you'd care to change places with poor little us," replied the Duke chaffingly.

"How about poor little me?" said the Angel modestly. "I've got to run about behind the wheels of popularity, like a spotted dog behind a carriage, getting all the dust and trying to look as if I was an important part of the machine. I must seem a perfect fool to you onlookers sometimes."

"I think you are a perfect angel," said the Duke.

The Angel-that-had-been-Quinston smiled and passed on his way, pursued across the breadth of the Horse Guards Parade by a tiresome little sparrow that cheeped incessantly and furiously at him.

"That's only the beginning," said the Duke complacently; "I've made it operative with all of them, irrespective of parties."

Belturbet made no coherent reply; he was engaged in feeling his pulse. The Duke fixed his attention with some interest on a black swan that was swimming with haughty, stiff-necked aloofness amid the crowd of lesser water-fowl that dotted the ornamental water. For all its pride of bearing, something was evidently ruffling and enraging it; in its way it seemed as angry and amazed as the sparrow had been.

At the same moment a human figure came along the pathway. Belturbet looked up apprehensively.

"Kedzon," he whispered briefly.

"An Angel-Kedzon, if I am not mistaken," said the Duke. "Look, he is talking affably to a human being. That settles it."

A shabbily dressed lounger had accosted the man who had been Viceroy in the splendid East, and who still reflected in his mien some of the cold dignity of the Himalayan snow-peaks.

"Could you tell me, sir, if them white birds is storks or halbatrosses? I had an argyment——"

The cold dignity thawed at once into genial friendliness. "Those are pelicans, my dear sir. Are you interested in birds? If you would join me in a bun and a glass of milk at the stall yonder, I could tell you some interesting things about Indian birds. Right oh! Now the hill-mynah, for instance—"

The two men disappeared in the direction of the bun stall, chatting volubly as they went, and shadowed from the other side of the railed enclosure by a black swan, whose temper seemed to have reached the limit of inarticulate rage.

Belturbet gazed in an open-mouthed wonder after the retreating couple, then transferred his attention to the infuriated swan, and finally turned with a look of scared comprehension at his young friend lolling unconcernedly in his chair. There was no longer any room to doubt what was happening. The "silly talk" had been translated into terrifying action.

"I think a prairie oyster on the top of a stiffish brandy-and-soda might save my reason," said Belturbet weakly, as he limped towards his club.

It was late in the day before he could steady his nerves sufficiently to glance at the evening papers. The Parliamentary report proved significant reading, and confirmed the fears that he had been trying to shake off. Mr. Ap Dave, the Chancellor, whose lively controversial style endeared him to his supporters and embittered him, politically speaking, to his opponents, had risen in his place to make an unprovoked apology for having alluded in a recent speech to certain protesting taxpayers as "skulkers." He had realized on reflection that they were in all probability perfectly honest in their inability to understand certain legal technicalities of the new finance laws. The House had scarcely recovered from this sensation when Lord Hugo Sizzle caused a further flutter of astonishment by going out of his way to indulge in an outspoken appreciation of the fairness, loyalty, and straightforwardness not only of the Chancellor, but of all the members of the Cabinet. A wit had gravely suggested moving the adjournment of the House in view of the unexpected circumstances that had arisen.

Belturbet anxiously skimmed over a further item of news printed immediately below the Parliamentary report: "Wild cat found in an exhausted condition in Palace Yard."

"Now I wonder which of them—" he mused, and then an appalling idea came to him. "Supposing he's put them both into the same beast!" He hurriedly ordered another prairie oyster.

Belturbet was known in his club as a strictly moderate drinker; his consumption of alcoholic stimulants that day gave rise to considerable comment.

The events of the next few days were piquantly bewildering to the world at large; to Belturbet, who knew dimly what was happening, the situation was fraught with recurring alarms. The old saying that in politics it's the unexpected that always happens received a justification that it had hitherto somewhat lacked, and the epidemic of startling personal changes of front was not wholly confined to the realm of actual politics. The eminent chocolate magnate, Sadbury, whose antipathy to the Turf and everything connected with it was a matter of general knowledge, had evidently been replaced by an Angel-Sadbury, who proceeded to electrify the public by blossoming forth as an owner of race-horses, giving as a reason his matured conviction that the sport was, after all, one which gave healthy open-air recreation to large numbers of people drawn from all classes of the community, and incidentally stimulated the important industry of horse-breeding. His colours, chocolate and cream hoops spangled with pink stars, promised to become as popular as any on the Turf. At the same time, in order to give effect to his condemnation of the evils resulting from the spread of the gambling habit among wage-earning classes, who lived for the most part from hand to mouth, he suppressed all betting news and tipsters' forecasts in the popular evening paper that was under his control. His action received instant recognition and support from the Angel-proprietor of the *Evening Views*, the principal rival evening halfpenny paper, who forthwith issued an ukase decreeing a similar ban on betting news, and in a short while the regular evening Press was purged of all mention of starting prices and probable winners. A considerable drop in the circulation of all these papers was the immediate result, accompanied, of course, by a falling-off in advertisement value, while a crop of special betting broadsheets sprang up to supply the newly created want. Under their influence the betting habit became if anything rather more widely diffused than before. The Duke had possibly overlooked the futility of koepenick-ing the leaders of the nation with excellently intentioned angel under-studies, while leaving the mass of the people in its original condition.

Further sensation and dislocation was caused in the Press world by the sudden and dramatic *rapprochement* which took place between the Angel-Editor of the *Scrutator* and the Angel-Editor of the *Anglian Review*, who not only ceased to criticize and disparage the tone and tendencies of each other's publication, but agreed to exchange editorships for alternating periods. Here again public support was not on the side of the angels; constant readers of the *Scrutator* complained bitterly of the strong meat which was thrust upon them at fitful intervals in place of the almost vegetarian diet to which they had become confidently accustomed; even those who were not mentally averse to strong meat as a separate course were pardonably annoyed at being supplied with it in the pages of the *Scrutator*. To be suddenly confronted with a pungent herring salad when one had attuned oneself to tea and toast, or to discover a richly truffled segment of *pâté de foie* dissembled in a bowl of bread and milk, would be an experience that might upset the equanimity of the most placidly disposed mortal. An equally vehement outcry arose from the regular subscribers of the *Anglian Review*, who protested against being served from time to time with literary fare which no young person of sixteen could possibly want to devour in secret. To take infinite precautions, they complained, against the juvenile perusal of such eminently innocuous literature was like reading the Riot Act on an uninhabited island. Both reviews suffered a serious falling-off in circulation and influence. Peace hath its devastations as well as war.

The wives of noted public men formed another element of discomfiture which the young Duke had almost entirely left out of his calculations. It is sufficiently embarrassing to keep abreast of the possible wobblings and veerings-round of a human husband, who, from the strength or weakness of his personal character, may leap over or slip through the barriers which divide the parties; for this reason a merciful politician usually marries late in life, when he has definitely made up his mind on which side he wishes his wife to be socially valuable. But these trials were as nothing compared to the bewilderment caused by the Angel-husbands who seemed in some cases to have revolutionized their outlook on life in the interval between breakfast and dinner, without premonition or preparation of any kind, and apparently without realizing the least need for subsequent explanation. The temporary peace which brooded over the Parliamentary situation was by no means reproduced in the home circles of the leading statesmen and politicians. It had been frequently and extensively remarked of Mrs. Exe that she would try the patience of an angel; now the tables were reversed, and she unwittingly had an opportunity for discovering that the capacity for exasperating behaviour was not all on one side.

And then, with the introduction of the Navy Estimates, Parliamentary peace suddenly dissolved. It was the old quarrel between Ministers and the Opposition as to the adequacy or the reverse of the Government's naval programme. The Angel-Quinston and the Angel-Hugo-Sizzle contrived to keep the debates free from personalities and pinpricks, but an enormous sensation was created when the elegant lackadaisical Halfan Halfour threatened to bring up fifty thousand stalwarts to wreck the House if the Estimates were not forthwith revised on a Two-Power basis. It was a memorable scene when he rose in his place, in response to the scandalized shouts of his opponents, and thundered forth, "Gentlemen, I glory in the name of Apache."

Belturbet, who had made several fruitless attempts to ring up his young friend since the fateful morning in St. James's Park, ran him to earth one afternoon at his club, smooth and spruce and unruffled as ever.

"Tell me, what on earth have you turned Cocksley Coxon into?" Belturbet asked anxiously, mentioning the name of one of the pillars of unorthodoxy in the Anglican Church. "I don't fancy he *believes* in angels, and if he finds an angel preaching orthodox sermons from his pulpit while he's been turned into a fox-terrier, he'll develop rabies in less than no time."

"I rather think it was a fox-terrier," said the Duke lazily.

Belturbet groaned heavily, and sank into a chair.

"Look here, Eugène," he whispered hoarsely, having first looked well round to see that no one was within hearing range, "you've got to stop it. Consols are jumping up and down like bronchos, and that speech of Halfour's in the House last night has simply startled everybody out of their wits. And then on the top of it, Thistlebery——"

"What has he been saying?" asked the Duke quickly.

"Nothing. That's just what's so disturbing. Every one thought it was simply inevitable that he should come out with a great epoch-making speech at this juncture, and I've just seen on the tape that he has refused to address any meetings at present, giving as a reason his opinion that something more than mere speech-making was wanted."

The young Duke said nothing, but his eyes shone with quiet exultation.

"It's so unlike Thistlebery," continued Belturbet; "at least," he said suspiciously, "it's unlike the *real* Thistlebery——"

"The real Thistlebery is flying about somewhere as a vocally industrious lapwing," said the Duke calmly; "I expect great things of the Angel-Thistlebery," he added.

At this moment there was a magnetic stampede of members towards the lobby, where the tape-machines were ticking out some news of more than ordinary import.

"*Coup d'état* in the North. Thistlebery seizes Edinburgh Castle. Threatens civil war unless Government expands naval programme."

In the babel which ensued Belturbet lost sight of his young friend. For the best part of the afternoon he searched one likely haunt after another, spurred on by the sensational posters which the evening papers were displaying broadcast over the West End. "General Baden-Baden mobilizes Boy-Scouts. Another *coup d'état* feared. Is Windsor Castle safe?" This was one of the earlier posters, and was followed by one of even more sinister purport: "Will the Test-match have to be postponed?" It was this disquietening question which brought home the real seriousness of the situation to the London public, and made people wonder whether one might not pay too high a price for the advantages of party government. Belturbet, questing round in the hope of finding the originator of the trouble, with a vague idea of being able to induce him to restore matters to their normal human footing, came across an elderly club acquaintance who dabbled extensively in some of the more sensitive market securities. He was pale with indignation, and his pallor deepened as a breathless newsboy dashed past with a poster inscribed: "Premier's constituency harried by moss-troopers. Halfour sends encouraging telegram to rioters. Letchworth Garden City threatens reprisals. Foreigners taking refuge in Embassies and National Liberal Club."

"This is devils' work!" he said angrily.

Belturbet knew otherwise.

At the bottom of St. James's Street a newspaper motor-cart, which had just come rapidly along Pall Mall, was surrounded by a knot of eagerly talking people, and for the first time that afternoon Belturbet heard expressions of relief and congratulation.

It displayed a placard with the welcome announcement: "Crisis ended. Government gives way. Important expansion of naval programme."

There seemed to be no immediate necessity for pursuing the quest of the errant Duke, and Belturbet turned to make his way homeward through St. James's Park. His mind, attuned to the alarums and excursions of the afternoon, became dimly aware that some excitement of a detached nature was going on around him. In spite of the political ferment which reigned in the streets, quite a large crowd had gathered to watch the unfolding of a tragedy that had taken place on the shore of the ornamental water. A large black swan, which had recently shown signs of a savage and dangerous disposition, had suddenly attacked a young gentleman who was walking by the water's edge, dragged him down under the surface, and drowned him before any one could come to his assistance.

At the moment when Belturbet arrived on the spot several park-keepers were engaged in lifting the corpse into a punt. Belturbet stooped to pick up a hat that lay near the scene of the struggle. It was a smart soft felt hat, faintly reminiscent of Houbigant.

More than a month elapsed before Belturbet had sufficiently recovered from his attack of nervous prostration to take an interest once more in what was going on in the world of politics. The Parliamentary Session was still in full swing, and a General Election was looming in the near future. He called for a batch of morning papers and skimmed rapidly through the speeches of the Chancellor, Quinston, and other Ministerial leaders, as well as those of the principal Opposition champions, and then sank back in his chair with a sigh of relief. Evidently the spell had ceased to act after the tragedy which had overtaken its invoker. There was no trace of angel anywhere.

THE REMOULDING OF
GROBY LINGTON

"A man is known by the company he keeps."

IN the morning-room of his sister-in-law's house Groby Lington fidgeted away the passing minutes with the demure restlessness of advanced middle age. About a quarter of an hour would have to elapse before it would be time to say his good-byes and make his way across the village green to the station, with a selected escort of nephews and nieces. He was a good-natured, kindly dispositioned man, and in theory he was delighted to pay periodical visits to the wife and children of his dead brother William; in practice, he infinitely preferred the comfort and seclusion of his own house and garden, and the companionship of his books and his parrot to these rather meaningless and tiresome incursions into a family circle with which he had little in common. It was not so much the spur of his own conscience that drove him to make the occasional short journey by rail to visit his relatives, as an obedient concession to the more insistent but vicarious conscience of his brother, Colonel John, who was apt to accuse him of neglecting poor old William's family. Groby usually forgot or ignored the existence of his neighbour kinsfolk until such time as he was threatened with a visit from the Colonel, when he would put matters straight by a hurried pilgrimage across the few miles of intervening country to renew his acquaintance with the young people and assume a kindly if rather forced interest in the well-being of his sister-in-law. On this occasion he had cut matters so fine between the timing of his exculpatory visit and the coming of Colonel John, that he would scarcely be home before the latter was due to arrive. Anyhow, Groby had got it over, and six or seven months might decently elapse before he need again sacrifice his comforts and inclinations on the altar of family sociability. He was inclined to be distinctly cheerful as he hopped about the room, picking up first one object, then another, and subjecting each to a brief bird-like scrutiny.

Presently his cheerful listlessness changed sharply to an attitude of vexed attention. In a scrap-book of drawings and caricatures belonging to one of his nephews he had come across an unkindly clever sketch of himself and his parrot, solemnly confronting each other in postures of ridiculous gravity and repose, and bearing a likeness to one another that the artist had done his utmost to accentuate. After the first flush of annoyance had passed away, Groby laughed good-naturedly and admitted to himself the cleverness of the drawing. Then the feeling of resentment repossessed him, resentment not against the caricaturist who had embodied the idea in pen and ink, but against the possible truth that the idea represented. Was it really the case that people grew in time to resemble the animals they kept as pets, and had he unconsciously become more and more like the comically solemn bird that was his constant companion? Groby was unusually silent as he walked to the train with his escort of chattering nephews and nieces, and during the short railway journey his mind was more and more possessed with an introspective conviction that

he had gradually settled down into a sort of parrot-like existence. What, after all, did his daily routine amount to but
a sedate meandering and pecking and perching, in his garden,
among his fruit trees, in his wicker chair on the lawn, or by
the fireside in his library? And what was the sum total of his
conversation with chance-encountered neighbours? "Quite a
spring day, isn't it?" "It looks as though we should have some
rain." "Glad to see you about again; you must take care of
yourself." "How the young folk shoot up, don't they?" Strings
of stupid, inevitable perfunctory remarks came to his mind,
remarks that were certainly not the mental exchange of human
intelligences, but mere empty parrot-talk. One might really
just as well salute one's acquaintances with "Pretty Polly. Puss,
puss, miaow!" Groby began to fume against the picture of
himself as a foolish feathered fowl which his nephew's sketch
had first suggested, and which his own accusing imagination
was filling in with such unflattering detail.

"I'll give the beastly bird away," he said resentfully; though
he knew at the same time that he would do no such thing.
It would look so absurd after all the years that he had kept
the parrot and made much of it suddenly to try and find it a
new home.

"Has my brother arrived?" he asked of the stable-boy, who
had come with the pony-carriage to meet him.

"Yessir, came down by the two-fifteen. Your parrot's dead."
The boy made the latter announcement with the relish which
his class finds in proclaiming a catastrophe.

"My parrot dead?" said Groby. "What caused its death?"

"The ipe," said the boy briefly.

"The ipe?" queried Groby. "Whatever's that?"

"The ipe what the Colonel brought down with him," came
the rather alarming answer.

"Do you mean to say my brother is ill?" asked Groby. "Is
it something infectious?"

"Th' Colonel's so well as ever he was," said the boy; and
as no further explanation was forthcoming Groby had to possess himself in mystified patience till he reached home. His
brother was waiting for him at the hall door.

"Have you heard about the parrot?" he asked at once. " 'Pon my soul I'm awfully sorry. The moment he saw the monkey I'd brought down as a surprise for you he squawked out, 'Rats to you, sir!' and the blessed monkey made one spring at him, got him by the neck and whirled him round like a rattle. He was as dead as mutton by the time I'd got him out of the little beggar's paws. Always been such a friendly little beast, the monkey has, should never have thought he'd got it in him to see red like that. Can't tell you how sorry I feel about it, and now of course you'll hate the sight of the monkey."

"Not at all," said Groby sincerely. A few hours earlier the tragic end which had befallen his parrot would have presented itself to him as a calamity; now it arrived almost as a polite attention on the part of the Fates.

"The bird was getting old, you know," he went on, in explanation of his obvious lack of decent regret at the loss of his pet. "I was really beginning to wonder if it was an unmixed kindness to let him go on living till he succumbed to old age. What a charming little monkey!" he added, when he was introduced to the culprit.

The new-comer was a small, long-tailed monkey from the Western Hemisphere, with a gentle, half-shy, half-trusting manner that instantly captured Groby's confidence; a student of simian character might have seen in the fitful red light in its eyes some indication of the underlying temper which the parrot had so rashly put to the test with such dramatic consequences for itself. The servants, who had come to regard the defunct bird as a regular member of the household, and one who gave really very little trouble, were scandalized to find his bloodthirsty aggressor installed in his place as an honoured domestic pet.

"A nasty heathen ipe what don't never say nothing sensible and cheerful, same as pore Polly did," was the unfavourable verdict of the kitchen quarters.

.   .   .   .

One Sunday morning, some twelve or fourteen months after the visit of Colonel John and the parrot-tragedy, Miss Wepley sat decorously in her pew in the parish church, immediately in front of that occupied by Groby Lington. She was, comparatively speaking, a new-comer in the neighbourhood, and was not personally acquainted with her fellowworshipper in the seat behind, but for the past two years the Sunday morning service had brought them regularly within each other's sphere of consciousness. Without having paid particular attention to the subject, she could probably have given a correct rendering of the way in which he pronounced certain words occurring in the responses, while he was well aware of the trivial fact that, in addition to her prayer book and handkerchief, a small paper packet of throat lozenges always reposed on the seat beside her. Miss Wepley rarely had recourse to her lozenges, but in case she should be taken with a fit of coughing she wished to have the emergency duly provided for. On this particular Sunday the lozenges occasioned an unusual diversion in the even tenor of her devotions, far more disturbing to her personally than a prolonged attack of coughing would have been. As she rose to take part in the singing of the first hymn, she fancied that she saw the hand of her neighbour, who was alone in the pew behind her, make a furtive downward grab at the packet lying on the seat; on turning sharply round she found that the packet had certainly disappeared, but Mr. Lington was to all outward seeming serenely intent on his hymn-book. No amount of interrogatory glaring on the part of the despoiled lady could bring the least shade of conscious guilt to his face.

"Worse was to follow," as she remarked afterwards to a scandalized audience of friends and acquaintances. "I had scarcely knelt in prayer when a lozenge, one of *my* lozenges, came whizzing into the pew, just under my nose. I turned round and stared, but Mr. Lington had his eyes closed and his lips moving as though engaged in prayer. The moment I resumed my devotions another lozenge came rattling in, and then another. I took no notice for a while, and then turned round suddenly just as the dreadful man was about to flip another one at me. He hastily pretended to be turning over the leaves of his book, but I was not to be taken in that time.

He saw that he had been discovered and no more lozenges came. Of course I have changed my pew."

"No gentleman would have acted in such a disgraceful manner," said one of her listeners; "and yet Mr. Lington used to be so respected by everybody. He seems to have behaved like a little ill-bred schoolboy."

"He behaved like a monkey," said Miss Wepley.

Her unfavourable verdict was echoed in other quarters about the same time. Groby Lington had never been a hero in the eyes of his personal retainers, but he had shared the approval accorded to his defunct parrot as a cheerful, well-disposioned body, who gave no particular trouble. Of late months, however, this character would hardly have been endorsed by the members of his domestic establishment. The stolid stable-boy, who had first announced to him the tragic end of his feathered pet, was one of the first to give voice to the murmurs of disapproval which became rampant and general in the servants' quarters, and he had fairly substantial grounds for his disaffection. In a burst of hot summer weather he had obtained permission to bathe in a modest-sized pond in the orchard, and thither one afternoon Groby had bent his steps, attracted by loud imprecations of anger mingled with the shriller chattering of monkey-language. He beheld his plump diminutive servitor, clad only in a waistcoat and a pair of socks, storming ineffectually at the monkey which was seated on a low branch of an apple tree, abstractedly fingering the remainder of the boy's outfit, which he had removed just out of his reach.

"The ipe's been an' took my clothes," whined the boy, with the passion of his kind for explaining the obvious. His incomplete toilet effect rather embarrassed him, but he hailed the arrival of Groby with relief, as promising moral and material support in his efforts to get back his raided garments. The monkey had ceased its defiant jabbering, and doubtless with a little coaxing from its master it would hand back the plunder.

"If I lift you up," suggested Groby, "you will just be able to reach the clothes."

The boy agreed, and Groby clutched him firmly by the waistcoat, which was about all there was to catch hold of, and lifted him clear of the ground. Then, with a deft swing he sent him crashing into a clump of tall nettles, which closed receptively round him. The victim had not been brought up in a school which teaches one to repress one's emotions—if a fox had attempted to gnaw at his vitals he would have flown to complain to the nearest hunt committee rather than have affected an attitude of stoical indifference. On this occasion the volume of sound which he produced under the stimulus of pain and rage and astonishment was generous and sustained, but above his bellowings he could distinctly hear the triumphant chattering of his enemy in the tree, and a peal of shrill laughter from Groby.

When the boy had finished an improvised St. Vitus caracole, which would have brought him fame on the boards of the Coliseum, and which indeed met with ready appreciation and applause from the retreating figure of Groby Lington, he found that the monkey had also discreetly retired, while his clothes were scattered on the grass at the foot of the tree.

"They'm two ipes, that's what they be," he muttered angrily, and if his judgment was severe, at least he spoke under the sting of considerable provocation.

It was a week or two later that the parlour-maid gave notice, having been terrified almost to tears by an outbreak of sudden temper on the part of the master anent some underdone cutlets. "'E gnashed 'is teeth at me, 'e did reely," she informed a sympathetic kitchen audience.

"I'd like to see 'im talk like that to me, I would," said the cook defiantly, but her cooking from that moment showed a marked improvement.

It was seldom that Groby Lington so far detached himself from his accustomed habits as to go and form one of a house-party, and he was not a little piqued that Mrs. Glenduff should have stowed him away in the musty old Georgian wing of the house, in the next room, moreover, to Leonard Spabbink, the eminent pianist.

"He plays Liszt like an angel," had been the hostess's enthusiastic testimonial.

"He may play him like a trout for all I care," had been Groby's mental comment, "but I wouldn't mind betting that he snores. He's just the sort and shape that would. And if I hear him snoring through those ridiculous thin-panelled walls, there'll be trouble."

He did, and there was.

Groby stood it for about two and a quarter minutes, and then made his way through the corridor into Spabbink's room. Under Groby's vigorous measures the musician's flabby, redundant figure sat up in bewildered semi-consciousness like an ice-cream that has been taught to beg. Groby prodded him into complete wakefulness, and then the pettish self-satisfied pianist fairly lost his temper and slapped his domineering visitant on the hand. In another moment Spabbink was being nearly stifled and very effectually gagged by a pillow-case tightly bound round his head, while his plump pyjama'd limbs were hauled out of bed and smacked, pinched, kicked, and bumped in a catch-as-catch-can progress across the floor, towards the flat shallow bath in whose utterly inadequate depths Groby perseveringly strove to drown him. For a few moments the room was almost in darkness: Groby's candle had overturned in an early stage of the scuffle, and its flicker scarcely reached to the spot where splashings, smacks, muffled cries, and splutterings, and a chatter of ape-like rage told of the struggle that was being waged round the shores of the bath. A few instants later the one-sided combat was brightly lit up by the flare of blazing curtains and rapidly kindling panelling.

When the hastily aroused members of the house-party stampeded out on to the lawn, the Georgian wing was well alight and belching forth masses of smoke, but some moments elapsed before Groby appeared with the half-drowned pianist in his arms, having just bethought him of the superior drowning facilities offered by the pond at the bottom of the lawn. The cool night air sobered his rage, and when he found that he was innocently acclaimed as the heroic rescuer of poor Leonard

Spabbink, and loudly commended for his presence of mind in tying a wet cloth round his head to protect him from smoke suffocation, he accepted the situation, and subsequently gave a graphic account of his finding the musician asleep with an overturned candle by his side and the conflagration well started. Spabbink gave *his* version some days later, when he had partially recovered from the shock of his midnight castigation and immersion, but the gentle pitying smiles and evasive comments with which his story was greeted warned him that the public ear was not at his disposal. He refused, however, to attend the ceremonial presentation of the Royal Humane Society's life-saving medal.

It was about this time that Groby's pet monkey fell a victim to the disease which attacks so many of its kind when brought under the influence of a northern climate. Its master appeared to be profoundly affected by its loss, and never quite recovered the level of spirits that he had recently attained. In company with the tortoise, which Colonel John presented to him on his last visit, he potters about his lawn and kitchen garden, with none of his erstwhile sprightliness; and his nephews and nieces are fairly well justified in alluding to him as "Old Uncle Groby."

Beasts and Super-Beasts

First Collected, 1914

"The Open Window," "The Schartz-Metterklume Method," and "Clovis on Parental Responsibilities," originally appeared in the *Westminster Gazette;* "The Elk" in the *Bystander,* and the remaining stories in the *Morning Post.* To the Editors of these papers I am indebted for their courtesy in allowing me to reprint them. H. H. M.

THE SHE-WOLF

LEONARD BILSITER was one of those people who have failed to find this world attractive or interesting, and who have sought compensation in an "unseen world" of their own experience or imagination—or invention. Children do that sort of thing successfully, but children are content to convince themselves, and do not vulgarize their beliefs by trying to convince other people. Leonard Bilsiter's beliefs were for "the few," that is to say, any one who would listen to him.

His dabblings in the unseen might not have carried him beyond the customary platitudes of the drawing-room visionary if accident had not reinforced his stock-in-trade of mystical lore. In company with a friend, who was interested in a Ural mining concern, he had made a trip across Eastern Europe at a moment when the great Russian railway strike was developing from a threat to a reality; its outbreak caught him on the return journey, somewhere on the further side of Perm, and it was while waiting for a couple of days at a wayside station in a state of suspended locomotion that he made the acquaintance of a dealer in harness and metalware, who profitably whiled away the tedium of the long halt by initiating his English travelling companion in a fragmentary system of folk-lore that he had picked up from Trans-Baikal traders and natives. Leonard returned to his home circle garrulous about his Russian strike experiences, but oppressively reticent about certain dark mysteries, which he alluded to under the resounding title of Siberian Magic. The reticence wore off in a week or two under the influence of an entire lack of general curiosity, and Leonard began to make more detailed allusions to the enormous powers which this new esoteric force, to use his own description of it, conferred on the initiated few who knew how to wield it. His aunt, Cecilia Hoops, who loved sensation perhaps rather better than she loved the truth, gave him as clamorous an advertisement as any one could wish for by retailing an account of how he had turned a vegetable marrow into a wood-pigeon before her very eyes. As a manifestation of the possession of supernatural powers, the story was discounted in some quarters by the respect accorded to Mrs. Hoops' powers of imagination.

However divided opinion might be on the question of Leonard's status as a wonder-worker or a charlatan, he certainly arrived at Mary Hampton's house-party with a reputation for pre-eminence in one or other of those professions, and he was not disposed to shun such publicity as might fall to his share. Esoteric forces and unusual powers figured largely in whatever conversation he or his aunt had a share in, and his own performances, past and potential, were the subject of mysterious hints and dark avowals.

"I wish you would turn me into a wolf, Mr. Bilsiter," said his hostess at luncheon the day after his arrival.

"My dear Mary," said Colonel Hampton, "I never knew you had a craving in that direction."

"A she-wolf, of course," continued Mrs. Hampton; "it would be too confusing to change one's sex as well as one's species at a moment's notice."

"I don't think one should jest on these subjects," said Leonard.

"I'm not jesting, I'm quite serious, I assure you. Only don't do it today; we have only eight available bridge players, and it would break up one of our tables. Tomorrow we shall be a larger party. Tomorrow night, after dinner—"

"In our present imperfect understanding of these hidden forces I think one should approach them with humbleness rather than mockery," observed Leonard, with such severity that the subject was forthwith dropped.

Clovis Sangrail had sat unusually silent during the discussion on the possibilities of Siberian magic; after lunch he side-tracked Lord Pabham into the comparative seclusion of the billiard-room and delivered himself of a searching question.

"Have you such a thing as a she-wolf in your collection of wild animals? A she-wolf of moderately good temper?"

Lord Pabham considered. "There is Louisa," he said, "a rather fine specimen of the timber-wolf. I got her two years ago in exchange for some Arctic foxes. Most of my animals get to be fairly tame before they've been with me very long; I think I can say Louisa has an angelic temper, as she-wolves go. Why do you ask?"

"I was wondering whether you would lend her to me for tomorrow night," said Clovis, with the careless solicitude of one who borrows a collar stud or a tennis racquet.

"Tomorrow night?"

"Yes, wolves are nocturnal animals, so the late hours won't hurt her," said Clovis, with the air of one who has taken everything into consideration; "one of your men could bring her over from Pabham Park after dusk, and with a little help he ought to be able to smuggle her into the conservatory at the same moment that Mary Hampton makes an unobtrusive exit."

Lord Pabham stared at Clovis for a moment in pardonable bewilderment; then his face broke into a wrinkled network of laughter.

"Oh, that's your game, is it? You are going to do a little Siberian magic on your own account. And is Mrs. Hampton willing to be a fellow-conspirator?"

"Mary is pledged to see me through with it, if you will guarantee Louisa's temper."

"I'll answer for Louisa," said Lord Pabham.

By the following day the house-party had swollen to larger proportions, and Bilsiter's instinct for self-advertisement expanded duly under the stimulant of an increased audience. At dinner that evening he held forth at length on the subject of unseen forces and untested powers, and his flow of impressive eloquence continued unabated while coffee was being served in the drawing-room preparatory to a general migration to the card-room. His aunt ensured a respectful hearing for his utterances, but her sensation-loving soul hankered after something more dramatic than mere vocal demonstration.

"Won't you do something to *convince* them of your powers,

Leonard?" she pleaded. "Change something into another shape. He can, you know, if he only chooses to," she informed the company.

"Oh, do," said Mavis Pellington earnestly, and her request was echoed by nearly every one present. Even those who were not open to conviction were perfectly willing to be entertained by an exhibition of amateur conjuring.

Leonard felt that something tangible was expected of him.

"Has any one present," he asked, "got a three-penny bit or some small object of no particular value—?"

"You're surely not going to make coins disappear, or something primitive of that sort?" said Clovis contemptuously.

"I think it very unkind of you not to carry out my suggestion of turning me into a wolf," said Mary Hampton, as she crossed over to the conservatory to give her macaws their usual tribute from the dessert dishes.

"I have already warned you of the danger of treating these powers in a mocking spirit," said Leonard solemnly.

"I don't believe you can do it," laughed Mary provocatively from the conservatory; "I dare you to do it if you can. I defy you to turn me into a wolf."

As she said this she was lost to view behind a clump of azaleas.

"Mrs. Hampton—" began Leonard with increased solemnity, but he got no further. A breath of chill air seemed to rush across the room, and at the same time the macaws broke forth into ear-splitting screams.

"What on earth is the matter with those confounded birds, Mary?" exclaimed Colonel Hampton; at the same moment an even more piercing scream from Mavis Pellington stampeded the entire company from their seats. In various attitudes of helpless horror or instinctive defence they confronted the evil-looking grey beast that was peering at them from amid a setting of fern and azalea.

Mrs. Hoops was the first to recover from the general chaos of fright and bewilderment.

"Leonard!" she screamed shrilly to her nephew, "turn it

back into Mrs. Hampton at once! It may fly at us at any moment. Turn it back!"

"I—I don't know how to," faltered Leonard, who looked more scared and horrified than any one.

"What!" shouted Colonel Hampton, "you've taken the abominable liberty of turning my wife into a wolf, and now you stand there calmly and say you can't turn her back again!"

To do strict justice to Leonard, calmness was not a distinguishing feature of his attitude at the moment.

"I assure you I didn't turn Mrs. Hampton into a wolf; nothing was farther from my intentions," he protested.

"Then where is she, and how came that animal into the conservatory?" demanded the Colonel.

"Of course we must accept your assurance that you didn't turn Mrs. Hampton into a wolf," said Clovis politely, "but you will agree that appearances are against you."

"Are we to have all these recriminations with that beast standing there ready to tear us to pieces?" wailed Mavis indignantly.

"Lord Pabham, you know a good deal about wild beasts—" suggested Colonel Hampton.

"The wild beasts that I have been accustomed to," said Lord Pabham, "have come with proper credentials from well-known dealers, or have been bred in my own menagerie. I've never before been confronted with an animal that walks unconcernedly out of an azalea bush, leaving a charming and popular hostess unaccounted for. As far as one can judge from *outward* characteristics," he continued, "it has the appearance of a well-grown female of the North American timber-wolf, a variety of the common species *canis lupus*."

"Oh, never mind its Latin name," screamed Mavis, as the beast came a step or two further into the room; "can't you entice it away with food, and shut it up where it can't do any harm?"

"If it is really Mrs. Hampton, who has just had a very good dinner, I don't suppose food will appeal to it very strongly," said Clovis.

"Leonard," beseeched Mrs. Hoops tearfully, "even if this *is* none of your doing can't you use your great powers to turn this dreadful beast into something harmless before it bites us all—a rabbit or something?"

"I don't suppose Colonel Hampton would care to have his wife turned into a succession of fancy animals as though we were playing a round game with her," interposed Clovis.

"I absolutely forbid it," thundered the Colonel.

"Most wolves that I've had anything to do with have been inordinately fond of sugar," said Lord Pabham; "if you like I'll try the effect on this one."

He took a piece of sugar from the saucer of his coffee cup and flung it to the expectant Louisa, who snapped it in mid-air. There was a sigh of relief from the company; a wolf that ate sugar when it might at the least have been employed in tearing macaws to pieces had already shed some of its terrors. The sigh deepened to a gasp of thanksgiving when Lord Pabham decoyed the animal out of the room by a pretended largesse of further sugar. There was an instant rush to the vacated conservatory. There was no trace of Mrs. Hampton except the plate containing the macaws' supper.

"The door is locked on the inside!" exclaimed Clovis, who had deftly turned the key as he affected to test it.

Every one turned towards Bilsiter.

"If you haven't turned my wife into a wolf," said Colonel Hampton, "will you kindly explain where she has disappeared to, since she obviously could not have gone through a locked door? I will not press you for an explanation of how a North American timber-wolf suddenly appeared in the conservatory, but I think I have some right to inquire what has become of Mrs. Hampton."

Bilsiter's reiterated disclaimer was met with a general murmur of impatient disbelief.

"I refuse to stay another hour under this roof," declared Mavis Pellington.

"If our hostess has really vanished out of human form," said Mrs. Hoops, "none of the ladies of the party can very well remain. I absolutely decline to be chaperoned by a wolf!"

"It's a she-wolf," said Clovis soothingly.

The correct etiquette to be observed under the unusual circumstances received no further elucidation. The sudden entry of Mary Hampton deprived the discussion of its immediate interest.

"Some one has mesmerized me," she exclaimed crossly; "I found myself in the game larder, of all places, being fed with sugar by Lord Pabham. I hate being mesmerized, and the doctor has forbidden me to touch sugar."

The situation was explained to her, as far as it permitted of anything that could be called explanation.

"Then you *really* did turn me into a wolf, Mr. Bilsiter?" she exclaimed excitedly.

But Leonard had burned the boat in which he might now have embarked on a sea of glory. He could only shake his head feebly.

"It was I who took that liberty," said Clovis; "you see, I happen to have lived for a couple of years in North-eastern Russia, and I have more than a tourist's acquaintance with the magic craft of that region. One does not care to speak about these strange powers, but once in a way, when one hears a lot of nonsense being talked about them, one is tempted to show what Siberian magic can accomplish in the hands of some one who really understands it. I yielded to that temptation. May I have some brandy? the effort has left me rather faint."

If Leonard Bilsiter could at that moment have transformed Clovis into a cockroach and then have stepped on him he would gladly have performed both operations.

LAURA

"YOU are not really dying, are you?" asked Amanda. "I have the doctor's permission to live till Tuesday," said Laura.

"But today is Saturday; this is serious!" gasped Amanda

"I don't know about it being serious; it is certainly Saturday," said Laura.

"Death is always serious," said Amanda.

"I never said I was going to die. I am presumably going to leave off being Laura, but I shall go on being something. An animal of some kind, I suppose. You see, when one hasn't been very good in the life one has just lived, one reincarnates in some lower organism. And I haven't been very good, when one comes to think of it. I've been petty and mean and vindictive and all that sort of thing when circumstances have seemed to warrant it."

"Circumstances never warrant that sort of thing," said Amanda hastily.

"If you don't mind my saying so," observed Laura, "Egbert is a circumstance that would warrant any amount of that sort of thing. You're married to him—that's different; you've sworn to love, honour, and endure him: I haven't."

"I don't see what's wrong with Egbert," protested Amanda.

"Oh, I dare say the wrongness has been on my part," admitted Laura dispassionately; "he has merely been the extenuating circumstance. He made a thin, peevish kind of fuss, for instance, when I took the collie puppies from the farm out for a run the other day."

"They chased his young broods of speckled Sussex and drove two sitting hens off their nests, besides running all over the flower beds. You know how devoted he is to his poultry and garden."

"Anyhow, he needn't have gone on about it for the entire evening and then have said, 'Let's say no more about it' just when I was beginning to enjoy the discussion. That's where one of my petty vindictive revenges came in," added Laura with an unrepentant chuckle; "I turned the entire family of speckled Sussex into his seedling shed the day after the puppy episode."

"How could you?" exclaimed Amanda.

"It came quite easy," said Laura; "two of the hens pretended to be laying at the time, but I was firm."

"And we thought it was an accident!"

"You see," resumed Laura, "I really *have* some grounds for supposing that my next incarnation will be in a lower organism. I shall be an animal of some kind. On the other hand, I haven't been a bad sort in my way, so I think I may count on being a nice animal, something elegant and lively, with a love of fun. An otter, perhaps."

"I can't imagine you as an otter," said Amanda.

"Well, I don't suppose you can imagine me as an angel, if it comes to that," said Laura.

Amanda was silent. She couldn't.

"Personally I think an otter life would be rather enjoyable," continued Laura; "salmon to eat all the year round, and the satisfaction of being able to fetch the trout in their own homes without having to wait for hours till they condescend to rise to the fly you've been dangling before them; and an elegant svelte figure——"

"Think of the otter hounds," interposed Amanda; "how dreadful to be hunted and harried and finally worried to death!"

"Rather fun with half the neighbourhood looking on, and anyhow not worse than this Saturday-to-Tuesday business of dying by inches; and then I should go on into something else. If I had been a moderately good otter I suppose I should get back into human shape of some sort; probably something rather primitive—a little brown, unclothed Nubian boy, I should think."

"I wish you would be serious," sighed Amanda; "you really ought to be if you're only going to live till Tuesday."

As a matter of fact Laura died on Monday.

"So dreadfully upsetting," Amanda complained to her uncle-in-law, Sir Lulworth Quayne. "I've asked quite a lot of people down for golf and fishing, and the rhododendrons are just looking their best."

"Laura always was inconsiderate," said Sir Lulworth; "she was born during Goodwood week, with an Ambassador staying in the house who hated babies."

"She had the maddest kind of ideas," said Amanda; "do you know if there was any insanity in her family?"

"Insanity? No, I never heard of any. Her father lives in West Kensington, but I believe he's sane on all other subjects."

"She had an idea that she was going to be reincarnated as an otter," said Amanda.

"One meets with those ideas of reincarnation so frequently, even in the West," said Sir Lulworth, "that one can hardly set them down as being mad. And Laura was such an unaccountable person in this life that I should not like to lay down definite rules as to what she might be doing in an after state."

"You think she really might have passed into some animal form?" asked Amanda. She was one of those who shape their opinions rather readily from the standpoint of those around them.

Just then Egbert entered the breakfast-room, wearing an air of bereavement that Laura's demise would have been insufficient, in itself, to account for.

"Four of my speckled Sussex have been killed," he exclaimed; "the very four that were to go to the show on Friday. One of them was dragged away and eaten right in the middle of that new carnation bed that I've been to such trouble and expense over. My best flower bed and my best fowls singled out for destruction; it almost seems as if the brute that did the deed had special knowledge how to be as devastating as possible in a short space of time."

"Was it a fox, do you think?" asked Amanda.

"Sounds more like a polecat," said Sir Lulworth.

"No," said Egbert, "there were marks of webbed feet all over the place, and we followed the tracks down to the stream at the bottom of the garden; evidently an otter."

Amanda looked quickly and furtively across at Sir Lulworth.

Egbert was too agitated to eat any breakfast, and went out to superintend the strengthening of the poultry yard defences.

"I think she might at least have waited till the funeral was over," said Amanda in a scandalized voice.

"It's her own funeral, you know," said Sir Lulworth; "it's a nice point in etiquette how far one ought to show respect to one's own mortal remains."

Disregard for mortuary convention was carried to further lengths next day; during the absence of the family at the funeral ceremony the remaining survivors of the speckled Sussex were massacred. The marauder's line of retreat seemed to have embraced most of the flower beds on the lawn, but the strawberry beds in the lower garden had also suffered.

"I shall get the otter hounds to come here at the earliest possible moment," said Egbert savagely.

"On no account! You can't dream of such a thing!" exclaimed Amanda. "I mean, it wouldn't do, so soon after a funeral in the house."

"It's a case of necessity," said Egbert; "once an otter takes to that sort of thing it won't stop."

"Perhaps it will go elsewhere now that there are no more fowls left," suggested Amanda.

"One would think you wanted to shield the beast," said Egbert.

"There's been so little water in the stream lately," objected Amanda; "it seems hardly sporting to hunt an animal when it has so little chance of taking refuge anywhere."

"Good gracious!" fumed Egbert, "I'm not thinking about sport. I want to have the animal killed as soon as possible."

Even Amanda's opposition weakened when, during church time on the following Sunday, the otter made its way into the house, raided half a salmon from the larder and worried it into scaly fragments on the Persian rug in Egbert's studio.

"We shall have it hiding under our beds and biting pieces out of our feet before long," said Egbert, and from what Amanda knew of this particular otter she felt that the possibility was not a remote one.

On the evening preceding the day fixed for the hunt Amanda spent a solitary hour walking by the banks of the stream, making what she imagined to be hound noises. It was charitably supposed by those who overheard her performance, that she was practising for farmyard imitations at the forthcoming village entertainment.

It was her friend and neighbour, Aurora Burret, who brought her news of the day's sport.

"Pity you weren't out; we had quite a good day. We found at once, in the pool just below your garden."

"Did you—kill?" asked Amanda.

"Rather. A fine she-otter. Your husband got rather badly bitten in trying to 'tail it.' Poor beast, I felt quite sorry for it, it had such a human look in its eyes when it was killed. You'll call me silly, but do you know who the look reminded me of? My dear woman, what is the matter?"

When Amanda had recovered to a certain extent from her attack of nervous prostration Egbert took her to the Nile Valley to recuperate. Change of scene speedily brought about the desired recovery of health and mental balance. The escapades of an adventurous otter in search of a variation of diet were viewed in their proper light. Amanda's normally placid temperament reasserted itself. Even a hurricane of shouted curses, coming from her husband's dressing-room, in her husband's voice, but hardly in his usual vocabulary, failed to disturb her serenity as she made a leisurely toilet one evening in a Cairo hotel.

"What is the matter? What has happened?" she asked in amused curiosity.

"The little beast has thrown all my clean shirts into the bath! Wait till I catch you, you little—"

"What little beast?" asked Amanda, suppressing a desire to laugh; Egbert's language was so hopelessly inadequate to express his outraged feelings.

"A little beast of a naked brown Nubian boy." spluttered Egbert.

And now Amanda is seriously ill.

THE BOAR-PIG

"THERE is a back way on to the lawn," said Mrs. Philidore Stossen to her daughter, "through a small grass paddock and then through a walled fruit garden full of gooseberry bushes. I went all over the place last year when the family were away. There is a door that opens from the fruit garden into a shrubbery, and once we emerge from there we can mingle with the guests as if we had come in by the ordinary way. It's much safer than going in by the front entrance and running the risk of coming bang up against the hostess; that would be so awkward when she doesn't happen to have invited us."

"Isn't it a lot of trouble to take for getting admittance to a garden party?"

"To a garden party, yes; to *the* garden party of the season, certainly not. Every one of any consequence in the county, with the exception of ourselves, has been asked to meet the Princess, and it would be far more troublesome to invent explanations as to why we weren't there than to get in by a roundabout way. I stopped Mrs. Cuvering in the road yesterday and talked very pointedly about the Princess. If she didn't choose to take the hint and send me an invitation it's not my fault, is it? Here we are: we just cut across the grass and through that little gate into the garden."

Mrs. Stossen and her daughter, suitably arrayed for a county garden party function with an infusion of Almanack de Gotha, sailed through the narrow grass paddock and the ensuing gooseberry garden with the air of state barges making an unofficial progress along a rural trout stream. There was a certain amount of furtive haste mingled with the stateliness of their advance as though hostile searchlights might be turned on them at any moment; and, as a matter of fact, they were not unobserved. Matilda Cuvering, with the alert eyes of thirteen years and the added advantage of an exalted position in the branches of a medlar tree, had enjoyed a good view of the Stossen flanking movement and had foreseen exactly where it would break down in execution.

"They'll find the door locked, and they'll jolly well have to go back the way they came," she remarked to herself. "Serves them right for not coming in by the proper entrance. What a pity Tarquin Superbus isn't loose in the paddock. After all, as every one else is enjoying themselves, I don't see why Tarquin shouldn't have an afternoon out."

Matilda was of an age when thought is action; she slid
down from the branches of the medlar tree, and when she
clambered back again, Tarquin, the huge white Yorkshire
boar-pig, had exchanged the narrow limits of his sty for the
wider range of the grass paddock. The discomfited Stossen expedition, returning in recriminatory but otherwise orderly retreat from the unyielding obstacle of the locked door, came to
a sudden halt at the gate dividing the paddock from the gooseberry garden.

"What a villainous-looking animal," exclaimed Mrs. Stossen; "it wasn't there when we came in."

"It's there now, anyhow," said her daughter. "What on
earth are we to do? I wish we had never come."

The boar-pig had drawn nearer to the gate for a closer
inspection of the human intruders, and stood champing his
jaws and blinking his small red eyes in a manner that was
doubtless intended to be disconcerting, and, as far as the Stos-
sens were concerned, thoroughly achieved that result.

"Shoo! Hish! Hish! Shoo!" cried the ladies in chorus.

"If they think they're going to drive him away by reciting
lists of the kings of Israel and Judah they're laying themselves out for disappointment," observed Matilda from her
seat in the medlar tree. As she made the observation aloud
Mrs. Stossen became for the first time aware of her presence.
A moment or two earlier she would have been anything but
pleased at the discovery that the garden was not as deserted
as it looked, but now she hailed the fact of the child's presence on the scene with absolute relief.

"Little girl, can you find some one to drive away—" she
began hopefully.

"Comment? Comprends pas," was the response.

"Oh, are you French? Êtes vous française?"

"Pas de tous. 'Suis anglaise."

"Then why not talk English? I want to know if—"

"Permettez-moi expliquer. You see, I'm rather under a
cloud," said Matilda. "I'm staying with my aunt, and I was
told I must behave particularly well today, as lots of people
were coming for a garden party, and I was told to imitate

Claude, that's my young cousin, who never does anything wrong except by accident, and then is always apologetic about it. It seems they thought I ate too much raspberry trifle at lunch, and they said Claude never eats too much raspberry trifle. Well, Claude always goes to sleep for half an hour after lunch, because he's told to, and I waited till he was asleep, and tied his hands and started forcible feeding with a whole bucketful of raspberry trifle that they were keeping for the garden-party. Lots of it went on to his sailor-suit and some of it on to the bed, but a good deal went down Claude's throat, and they can't say again that he has never been known to eat too much raspberry trifle. That is why I am not allowed to go to the party, and as an additional punishment I must speak French all the afternoon. I've had to tell you all this in English, as there were words like 'forcible feeding' that I didn't know the French for; of course I could have invented them, but if I had said *nourriture obligatoire* you wouldn't have had the least idea what I was talking about. *Mais maintenant, nous parlons français.*"

"Oh, very well, *très bien*," said Mrs. Stossen reluctantly; in moments of flurry such French as she knew was not under very good control. "*Là, à l'autre côté de la porte, est un cochon—*"

"*Un cochon? Ah, le petit charmant!*" exclaimed Matilda with enthusiasm.

"*Mais non, pas du tout petit, et pas du tout charmant; un bête féroce—*"

"*Une bête*," corrected Matilda; "a pig is masculine as long as you call it a pig, but if you lose your temper with it and call it a ferocious beast it becomes one of us at once. French is a dreadfully unsexing language."

"For goodness' sake let us talk English then," said Mrs. Stossen. "Is there any way out of this garden except through the paddock where the pig is?"

"I always go over the wall, by way of the plum tree," said Matilda.

"Dressed as we are we could hardly do that," said Mrs. Stossen; it was difficult to imagine her doing it in any costume.

"Do you think you could go and get some one who would drive the pig away?" asked Miss Stossen.

"I promised my aunt I would stay here till five o'clock; it's not four yet."

"I am sure, under the circumstances, your aunt would per-mit—"

"My conscience would not permit," said Matilda with cold dignity.

"We can't stay here till five o'clock," exclaimed Mrs. Stossen with growing exasperation.

"Shall I recite to you to make the time pass quicker?" asked Matilda obligingly. " 'Belinda, the little Breadwinner,' is considered my best piece, or, perhaps, it ought to be something in French. Henri Quatre's address to his soldiers is the only thing I really know in that language."

"If you will go and fetch some one to drive that animal away I will give you something to buy yourself a nice present," said Mrs. Stossen.

Matilda came several inches lower down the medlar tree.

"That is the most practical suggestion you have made yet for getting out of the garden," she remarked cheerfully; "Claude and I are collecting money for the Children's Fresh Air Fund, and we are seeing which of us can collect the biggest sum."

"I shall be very glad to contribute half a crown, very glad indeed," said Mrs. Stossen, digging that coin out of the depths of a receptacle which formed a detached outwork of her toilet.

"Claude is a long way ahead of me at present," continued Matilda, taking no notice of the suggested offering; "you see, he's only eleven, and has golden hair, and those are enormous advantages when you're on the collecting job. Only the other day a Russian lady gave him ten shillings. Russians understand the art of giving far better than we do. I expect Claude will net quite twenty-five shillings this afternoon; he'll have the field to himself, and he'll be able to do the pale, fragile, not-long-for-this-world business to perfection after his raspberry trifle experience. Yes, he'll be quite two pounds ahead of me by now."

With much probing and plucking and many regretful murmurs the beleaguered ladies managed to produce seven-and-sixpence between them.

"I am afraid this is all we've got," said Mrs. Stossen.

Matilda showed no sign of coming down either to the earth or to their figure.

"I could not do violence to my conscience for anything less than ten shillings," she announced stiffly.

Mother and daughter muttered certain remarks under their breath, in which the word "beast" was prominent, and probably had no reference to Tarquin.

"I find I *have* got another half-crown," said Mrs. Stossen in a shaking voice; "here you are. Now please fetch some one quickly."

Matilda slipped down from the tree, took possession of the donation, and proceeded to pick up a handful of over-ripe medlars from the grass at her feet. Then she climbed over the gate and addressed herself affectionately to the boar-pig.

"Come, Tarquin, dear old boy; you know you can't resist medlars when they're rotten and squashy."

Tarquin couldn't. By dint of throwing the fruit in front of him at judicious intervals Matilda decoyed him back to his sty, while the delivered captives hurried across the paddock.

"Well, I never! The little minx!" exclaimed Mrs. Stossen when she was safely on the high road. "The animal wasn't savage at all, and as for the ten shillings, I don't believe the Fresh Air Fund will see a penny of it!"

There she was unwarrantably harsh in her judgment. If you examine the books of the fund you will find the acknowledgment: "Collected by Miss Matilda Cuvering, 2s. 6d."

THE BROGUE

THE hunting season had come to an end, and the Mullets had not succeeded in selling the Brogue. There had been a kind of tradition in the family for the past three or four, years, a sort of fatalistic hope, that the Brogue would find a purchaser before the hunting was over; but seasons came and went without anything happening to justify such ill-founded optimism. The animal had been named Berserker in the earlier stages of its career; it had been rechristened the Brogue later on, in recognition of the fact that, once acquired, it was extremely difficult to get rid of. The unkinder wits of the neighbourhood had been known to suggest that the first letter of its name was superfluous. The Brogue had been variously described in sale catalogues as a light-weight hunter, a lady's hack, and, more simply, but still with a touch of imagination, as a useful brown gelding, standing 15.1. Toby Mullet had ridden him for four seasons with the West Wessex; you can ride almost any sort of horse with the West Wessex as long as it is an animal that knows the country. The Brogue knew the country intimately, having personally created most of the gaps that were to be met with in banks and hedges for many miles round. His manners and characteristics were not ideal in the hunting field, but he was probably rather safer to ride to hounds than he was as a hack on country roads. According to the Mullet family, he was not really road-shy, but there were one or two objects of dislike that brought on sudden attacks of what Toby called swerving sickness. Motors and cycles he treated with tolerant disregard, but pigs, wheelbarrows, piles of stones by the roadside, perambulators in a village street, gates painted too aggressively white, and sometimes, but not always, the newer kind of beehives, turned him aside from his tracks in vivid imitation of the zigzag course of forked lightning. If a pheasant rose noisily from the other side of a hedgerow the Brogue would spring into the air at the same moment, but this may have been due to a desire to be companionable. The Mullet family contradicted the widely prevalent report that the horse was a confirmed crib-biter.

It was about the third week in May that Mrs. Mullet, relict of the late Sylvester Mullet, and mother of Toby and a bunch of daughters, assailed Clovis Sangrail on the outskirts of the village with a breathless catalogue of local happenings.

"You know our new neighbour, Mr. Penricarde?" she

vociferated; "awfully rich, owns tin mines in Cornwall, middle-aged and rather quiet. He's taken the Red House on a long lease and spent a lot of money on alterations and improvements. Well, Toby's sold him the Brogue!"

Clovis spent a moment or two in assimilating the astonishing news; then he broke out into unstinted congratulation. If he had belonged to a more emotional race he would probably have kissed Mrs. Mullet.

"How wonderful lucky to have pulled it off at last! Now you can buy a decent animal. I've always said that Toby was clever. Ever so many congratulations."

"Don't congratulate me. It's the most unfortunate thing that could have happened!" said Mrs. Mullet dramatically.

Clovis stared at her in amazement.

"Mr. Penricarde," said Mrs. Mullet, sinking her voice to what she imagined to be an impressive whisper, though it rather resembled a hoarse, excited squeak, "Mr. Penricarde has just begun to pay attentions to Jessie. Slight at first, but now unmistakable. I was a fool not to have seen it sooner. Yesterday, at the Rectory garden party, he asked her what her favourite flowers were, and she told him carnations, and today a whole stack of carnations has arrived, clove and malmaison and lovely dark red ones, regular exhibition blooms, and a box of chocolates that he must have got on purpose from London. And he's asked her to go round the links with him tomorrow. And now, just at this critical moment, Toby has sold him that animal. It's a calamity!"

"But you've been trying to get the horse off your hands for years," said Clovis.

"I've got a houseful of daughters," said Mrs. Mullet, "and I've been trying—well, not to get them off my hands, of course, but a husband or two wouldn't be amiss among the lot of them; there are six of them, you know."

"I don't know," said Clovis, "I've never counted, but I expect you're right as to the number; mothers generally know these things."

"And now," continued Mrs. Mullet, in her tragic whisper, "when there's a rich husband-in-prospect imminent on the horizon Toby goes and sells him that miserable animal. It will probably kill him if he tries to ride it; anyway it will kill any affection he might have felt towards any member of our family. What is to be done? We can't very well ask to have the horse back; you see, we praised it up like anything when we thought there was a chance of his buying it, and said it was just the animal to suit him."

"Couldn't you steal it out of his stable and send it to grass at some farm miles away?" suggested Clovis. "Write 'Votes for Women' on the stable door, and the thing would pass for a Suffragette outrage. No one who knew the horse could possibly suspect you of wanting to get it back again."

"Every newspaper in the country would ring with the affair," said Mrs. Mullet; "can't you imagine the headline, 'Valuable Hunter Stolen by Suffragettes'? The police would scour the countryside till they found the animal."

"Well, Jessie must try and get it back from Penricarde on the plea that it's an old favourite. She can say it was only sold because the stable had to be pulled down under the terms of an old repairing lease, and that now it has been arranged that the stable is to stand for a couple of years longer."

"It sounds a queer proceeding to ask for a horse back when you've just sold him," said Mrs. Mullet, "but something must be done, and done at once. The man is not used to horses, and I believe I told him it was as quiet as a lamb. After all, lambs go kicking and twisting about as if they were demented, don't they?"

"The lamb has an entirely unmerited character for sedateness," agreed Clovis.

Jessie came back from the golf links next day in a state of mingled elation and concern.

"It's all right about the proposal," she announced, "he came out with it at the sixth hole. I said I must have time to think it over. I accepted him at the seventh."

"My dear," said her mother, "I think a little more maidenly reserve and hesitation would have been advisable, as you've known him so short a time. You might have waited till the ninth hole."

"The seventh is a very long hole," said Jessie; "besides, the tension was putting us both off our game. By the time we'd got to the ninth hole we'd settled lots of things. The honeymoon is to be spent in Corsica, with perhaps a flying visit to Naples if we feel like it, and a week in London to wind up with. Two of his nieces are to be asked to be bridesmaids, so with our lot there will be seven, which is rather a lucky number. You are to wear your pearl grey, with any amount of Honiton lace jabbed into it. By the way, he's coming over this evening to ask your consent to the whole affair. So far all's well, but about the Brogue it's a different matter. I told him the legend about the stable, and how keen we were about buying the horse back, but he seems equally keen on keeping it. He said he must have horse exercise now that he's living in the country, and he's going to start riding tomorrow. He's ridden a few times in the Row on an animal that was accustomed to carry octogenarians and people undergoing rest cures, and that's about all his experience in the saddle—oh, and he rode a pony once in Norfolk, when he was fifteen and the pony twenty-four; and tomorrow he's going to ride the Brogue! I shall be a widow before I'm married, and I do so want to see what Corsica's like; it looks so silly on the map."

Clovis was sent for in haste, and the developments of the situation put before him.

"Nobody can ride that animal with any safety," said Mrs. Mullet, "except Toby, and he knows by long experience what it is going to shy at, and manages to swerve at the same time."

"I did hint to Mr. Penricarde—to Vincent, I should say—that the Brogue didn't like white gates," said Jessie.

"White gates!" exclaimed Mrs. Mullet; "did you mention what effect a pig has on him? He'll have to go past Lockyer's farm to get to the high road, and there's sure to be a pig or two grunting about in the lane."

"He's taken rather a dislike to turkeys lately," said Toby.

"It's obvious that Penricarde mustn't be allowed to go out on that animal," said Clovis, "at least not till Jessie has married him, and tired of him. I tell you what: ask him to a picnic tomorrow, starting at an early hour; he's not the sort to go out for a ride before breakfast. The day after I'll get the rector to drive him over to Crowleigh before lunch, to see the new cottage hospital they're building there. The Brogue will be standing idle in the stable and Toby can offer to exercise it; then it can pick up a stone or something of the sort and go conveniently lame. If you hurry on the wedding a bit the lameness fiction can be kept up till the ceremony is safely over."

Mrs. Mullet belonged to an emotional race, and she kissed Clovis.

It was nobody's fault that the rain came down in torrents the next morning, making a picnic a fantastic impossibility. It was also nobody's fault, but sheer ill-luck, that the weather cleared up sufficiently in the afternoon to tempt Mr. Penricarde to make his first essay with the Brogue. They did not get as far as the pigs at Lockyer's farm; the rectory gate was painted a dull unobtrusive green, but it had been white a year or two ago, and the Brogue never forgot that he had been in the habit of making a violent curtsey, a back-pedal and a swerve at this particular point of the road. Subsequently, there being apparently no further call on his services, he broke his way into the rectory orchard, where he found a hen turkey in a coop; later visitors to the orchard found the coop almost intact, but very little left of the turkey.

Mr. Penricarde, a little stunned and shaken, and suffering from a bruised knee and some minor damages, good-naturedly ascribed the accident to his own inexperience with horses and country roads, and allowed Jessie to nurse him back into complete recovery and golf-fitness within something less than a week.

In the list of wedding presents which the local newspaper published a fortnight or so later appeared the following item:

"Brown saddle-horse, 'The Brogue,' bridegroom's gift to bride."

"Which shows," said Toby Mullet, "that he knew nothing."

"Or else," said Clovis, "that he has a very pleasing wit."

THE HEN

"DORA BITTHOLZ is coming on Thursday," said Mrs. Sangrail.

"This next Thursday?" asked Clovis.

His mother nodded.

"You've rather done it, haven't you?" he chuckled. "Jane Martlet has only been here five days, and she never stays less than a fortnight, even when she's asked definitely for a week. You'll never get her out of the house by Thursday."

"Why should I?" asked Mrs. Sangrail. "She and Dora are good friends, aren't they? They used to be, as far as I remember."

"They used to be; that's what makes them all the more bitter now. Each feels that she has nursed a viper in her bosom. Nothing fans the flame of human resentment so much as the discovery that one's bosom has been utilized as a snake sanatorium."

"But what has happened? Has some one been making mischief?"

"Not exactly," said Clovis; "a hen came between them."

"A hen? What hen?"

"It was a bronze Leghorn or some such exotic breed, and Dora sold it to Jane at a rather exotic price. They both go in for prize poultry, you know, and Jane thought she was going to get her money back in a large family of pedigree chickens. The bird turned out to be an abstainer from the egg habit, and I'm told that the letters which passed between the two women were a revelation as to how much invective could be got on to a sheet of notepaper."

"How ridiculous!" said Mrs. Sangrail. "Couldn't some of their friends compose the quarrel?"

"People tried," said Clovis, "but it must have been rather like composing the storm music of the 'Fliegende Holländer.' Jane was willing to take back some of her most libellous remarks if Dora would take back the hen, but Dora said that would be owning herself in the wrong, and you know she'd as soon think of owning slum property in Whitechapel as do that."

"It's a most awkward situation," said Mrs. Sangrail. "Do you suppose they won't speak to one another?"

"On the contrary, the difficulty will be to get them to leave off. Their remarks on each other's conduct and character have hitherto been governed by the fact that only four ounces of plain speaking can be sent through the post for a penny."

"I can't put Dora off," said Mrs. Sangrail. "I've already postponed her visit once, and nothing short of a miracle would make Jane leave before her self-allotted fortnight is over."

"Miracles are rather in my line," said Clovis. "I don't pretend to be very hopeful in this case, but I'll do my best."

"As long as you don't drag me into it—" stipulated his mother.

.   .   .   .

"Servants are a bit of a nuisance," muttered Clovis, as he sat in the smoking-room after lunch, talking fitfully to Jane Martlet in the intervals of putting together the materials of a cocktail, which he had irreverently patented under the name of an Ella Wheeler Wilcox. It was partly compounded of old brandy and partly of curaçoa; there were other ingredients, but they were never indiscriminately revealed.

"Servants a nuisance!" exclaimed Jane, bounding into the topic with the exuberant plunge of a hunter when it leaves the high road and feels turf under its hoofs; "I should think they were! The trouble I've had in getting suited this year you would hardly believe. But I don't see what you have to complain of—your mother is so wonderfully lucky in her servants. Sturridge, for instance—he's been with you for years, and I'm sure he's a paragon as butlers go."

"That's just the trouble," said Clovis. "It's when servants have been with you for years that they become a really serious nuisance. The 'here today and gone tomorrow' sort don't matter—you've simply got to replace them; it's the stayers and the paragons that are the real worry."

"But if they give satisfaction——"

"That doesn't prevent them from giving trouble. Now, you've mentioned Sturridge—it was Sturridge I was particularly thinking of when I made the observation about servants being a nuisance."

"The excellent Sturridge a nuisance! I can't believe it."

"I know he's excellent, and we just couldn't get along without him; he's the one reliable element in this rather haphazard household. But his very orderliness has had an effect on him. Have you ever considered what it must be like to go on unceasingly doing the correct thing in the correct manner in the same surroundings for the greater part of a lifetime? To know and ordain and superintend exactly what silver and glass and table linen shall be used and set out on what occasions, to have cellar and pantry and plate-cupboard under a minutely devised and undeviating administration, to be noise-less, impalpable, omnipresent, and, as far as your own department is concerned, omniscient?"

"I should go mad," said Jane with conviction.

"Exactly," said Clovis thoughtfully, swallowing his completed Ella Wheeler Wilcox.

"But Sturridge hasn't gone mad," said Jane with a flutter of inquiry in her voice.

"On most points he's thoroughly sane and reliable," said Clovis, "but at times he is subject to the most obstinate delusions, and on those occasions he becomes not merely a nuisance but a decided embarrassment."

"What sort of delusions?"

"Unfortunately they usually centre round one of the guests of the house party, and that is where the awkwardness comes in. For instance, he took it into his head that Matilda Shering-ham was the Prophet Elijah, and as all that he remembered about Elijah's history was the episode of the ravens in the wilderness he absolutely declined to interfere with what he imagined to be Matilda's private catering arrangements, wouldn't allow any tea to be sent up to her in the morning, and if he was waiting at table he passed her over altogether in handing round the dishes."

"How very unpleasant. Whatever did you do about it?"

"Oh, Matilda got fed, after a fashion, but it was judged to be best for her to cut her visit short. It was really the only thing to be done," said Clovis with some emphasis.

"I shouldn't have done that," said Jane, "I should have humoured him in some way. I certainly shouldn't have gone away."

Clovis frowned.

"It is not always wise to humour people when they get these ideas into their heads. There's no knowing to what lengths they may go if you encourage them."

"You don't mean to say he might be dangerous, do you?" asked Jane with some anxiety.

"One can never be certain," said Clovis; "now and then he gets some idea about a guest which *might* take an unfortunate turn. That is precisely what is worrying me at the present moment."

"What, has he taken a fancy about some one here now?" asked Jane excitedly. "How thrilling! Do tell me who it is."

"You," said Clovis briefly.

"Me?"

Clovis nodded.

"Who on earth does he think I am?"

"Queen Anne," was the unexpected answer.

"Queen Anne! What an idea. But, anyhow, there's nothing dangerous about her; she's such a colourless personality."

"What does posterity chiefly say about Queen Anne?" asked Clovis rather sternly.

"The only thing that I can remember about her," said Jane, "is the saying 'Queen Anne's dead.'"

"Exactly," said Clovis, staring at the glass that had held the Ella Wheeler Wilcox, "dead."

"Do you mean he takes me for the ghost of Queen Anne?" asked Jane.

"Ghost? Dear no. No one ever heard of a ghost that came down to breakfast and ate kidneys and toast and honey with a healthy appetite. No, it's the fact of you being so very much alive and flourishing that perplexes and annoys him. All his life he has been accustomed to look on Queen Anne as the personification of everything that is dead and done with, 'as dead as Queen Anne,' you know; and now he has to fill your glass at lunch and dinner and listen to your accounts of the gay time you had at the Dublin Horse Show, and naturally he feels that something's very wrong with you."

"But he wouldn't be downright hostile to me on that account, would he?" Jane asked anxiously.

"I didn't get really alarmed about it till lunch today," said Clovis; "I caught him glowering at you with a very sinister look and muttering: 'Ought to be dead long ago, she ought, and some one should see to it.' That's why I mentioned the matter to you."

"This is awful," said Jane; "your mother must be told about it at once."

"My mother mustn't hear a word about it," said Clovis earnestly; "it would upset her dreadfully. She relies on Sturridge for everything."

"But he might kill me at any moment," protested Jane.

"Not at any moment; he's busy with the silver all the afternoon."

"You'll have to keep a sharp look-out all the time and be on your guard to frustrate any murderous attack," said Jane, adding in a tone of weak obstinacy: "It's a dreadful situation to be in, with a mad butler dangling over you like the sword of What's-his-name, but I'm certainly not going to cut my visit short."

Clovis swore horribly under his breath; the miracle was an obvious misfire.

It was in the hall the next morning after a late breakfast that Clovis had his final inspiration as he stood engaged in coaxing rust spots from an old putter.

"Where is Miss Martlet?" he asked the butler, who was at that moment crossing the hall.

"Writing letters in the morning-room, sir," said Sturridge, announcing a fact of which his questioner was already aware.

"She wants to copy the inscription on that old basket-hilted sabre," said Clovis, pointing to a venerable weapon hanging on the wall. "I wish you'd take it to her; my hands are all over oil. Take it without the sheath, it will be less trouble."

The butler drew the blade, still keen and bright in its well-cared-for old age, and carried it into the morning-room. There was a door near the writing-table leading to a back stairway; Jane vanished through it with such lightning rapidity that the butler doubted whether she had seen him come in. Half an hour later Clovis was driving her and her hastily packed luggage to the station.

"Mother will be awfully vexed when she comes back from her ride and finds you have gone," he observed to the departing guest, "but I'll make up some story about an urgent wire having called you away. It wouldn't do to alarm her unnecessarily about Sturridge."

Jane sniffed slightly at Clovis' ideas of unnecessary alarm, and was almost rude to the young man who came round with thoughtful inquiries as to luncheon-baskets.

The miracle lost some of its usefulness from the fact that Dora wrote the same day postponing the date of her visit, but, at any rate, Clovis holds the record as the only human being who ever hustled Jane Martlet out of the time-table of her migrations.

THE OPEN WINDOW

"MY aunt will be down presently, Mr. Nuttel," said a very self-possessed young lady of fifteen; "in the meantime you must try and put up with me."

Framton Nuttel endeavoured to say the correct something which should duly flatter the niece of the moment without unduly discounting the aunt that was to come. Privately he doubted more than ever whether these formal visits on a succession of total strangers would do much towards helping the nerve cure which he was supposed to be undergoing.

"I know how it will be," his sister had said when he was preparing to migrate to this rural retreat; "you will bury yourself down there and not speak to a living soul, and your nerves will be worse than ever from moping. I shall just give you letters of introduction to all the people I know there. Some of them, as far as I can remember, were quite nice."

Framton wondered whether Mrs. Sappleton, the lady to whom he was presenting one of the letters of introduction, came into the nice division.

"Do you know many of the people round here?" asked the niece, when she judged that they had had sufficient silent communion.

"Hardly a soul," said Framton. "My sister was staying here, at the rectory, you know, some four years ago, and she gave me letters of introduction to some of the people here."

He made the last statement in a tone of distinct regret.

"Then you know practically nothing about my aunt?" pursued the self-possessed young lady.

"Only her name and address," admitted the caller. He was wondering whether Mrs. Sappleton was in the married or widowed state. An undefinable something about the room seemed to suggest masculine habitation.

"Her great tragedy happened just three years ago," said the child; "that would be since your sister's time."

"Her tragedy?" asked Framton; somehow in this restful country spot tragedies seemed out of place.

"You may wonder why we keep that window wide open on an October afternoon," said the niece, indicating a large French window that opened on to a lawn.

"It is quite warm for the time of the year," said Framton; "but has that window got anything to do with the tragedy?"

"Out through that window, three years ago to a day, her husband and her two young brothers went off for their day's shooting. They never came back. In crossing the moor to their favourite snipe-shooting ground they were all three engulfed in a treacherous piece of bog. It had been that dreadful wet summer, you know, and places that were safe in other years gave way suddenly without warning. Their bodies were never recovered. That was the dreadful part of it." Here the child's voice lost its self-possessed note and became falteringly human. "Poor aunt always thinks that they will come back some day, they and the little brown spaniel that was lost with them, and walk in at that window just as they used to do. That is why the window is kept open every evening till it is quite dusk. Poor dear aunt, she has often told me how they went out, her husband with his white waterproof coat over his arm, and Ronnie, her youngest brother, singing, 'Bertie, why do you bound?' as he always did to tease her, because she said it got on her nerves. Do you know, sometimes on still, quiet evenings like this, I almost get a creepy feeling that they will all walk in through that window——"

She broke off with a little shudder. It was a relief to Framton when the aunt bustled into the room with a whirl of apologies for being late in making her appearance.

"I hope Vera has been amusing you?" she said.

"She has been very interesting," said Framton.

"I hope you don't mind the open window," said Mrs. Sappleton briskly; "my husband and brothers will be home directly from shooting, and they always come in this way. They've been out for snipe in the marshes today, so they'll make a fine mess over my poor carpets. So like you men-folk, isn't it?"

She rattled on cheerfully about the shooting and the scarcity of birds, and the prospects for duck in the winter. To Framton it was all purely horrible. He made a desperate but only partially successful effort to turn the talk on to a less ghastly topic; he was conscious that his hostess was giving him only a fragment of her attention, and her eyes were constantly straying past him to the open window and the lawn beyond. It was certainly an unfortunate coincidence that he should have paid his visit on this tragic anniversary.

"The doctors agree in ordering me complete rest, an absence of mental excitement, and avoidance of anything in the nature of violent physical exercise," announced Framton, who laboured under the tolerably wide-spread delusion that total strangers and chance acquaintances are hungry for the least detail of one's ailments and infirmities, their cause and cure. "On the matter of diet they are not so much in agreement," he continued.

"No?" said Mrs. Sappleton, in a voice which only replaced a yawn at the last moment. Then she suddenly brightened into alert attention—but not to what Framton was saying.

"Here they are at last!" she cried. "Just in time for tea, and don't they look as if they were muddy up to the eyes!"

Framton shivered slightly and turned towards the niece with a look intended to convey sympathetic comprehension. The child was staring out through the open window with dazed horror in her eyes. In a chill shock of nameless fear Framton swung round in his seat and looked in the same direction.

In the deepening twilight three figures were walking across the lawn towards the window; they all carried guns under their arms, and one of them was additionally burdened with a white coat hung over his shoulders. A tired brown spaniel kept close at their heels. Noiselessly they neared the house, and then a hoarse young voice chanted out of the dusk: "I said, Bertie, why do you bound?"

Framton grabbed wildly at his stick and hat; the hall-door, the gravel-drive, and the front gate were dimly noted stages in his headlong retreat. A cyclist coming along the road had to run into the hedge to avoid imminent collision.

"Here we are, my dear," said the bearer of the white mackintosh, coming in through the window; "fairly muddy, but most of it's dry. Who was that who bolted out as we came up?"

"A most extraordinary man, a Mr. Nuttel," said Mrs. Sappleton; "could only talk about his illnesses, and dashed off without a word of good-bye or apology when you arrived. One would think he had seen a ghost."

"I expect it was the spaniel," said the niece calmly; "he told me he had a horror of dogs. He was once hunted into a cemetery somewhere on the banks of the Ganges by a pack of pariah dogs, and had to spend the night in a newly dug grave with the creatures snarling and grinning and foaming just above him. Enough to make any one lose their nerve."

Romance at short notice was her speciality.

THE TREASURE-SHIP

THE great galleon lay in semi-retirement under the sand weed and water of the northern bay where the fortune of war and weather had long ago ensconced it. Three and a quarter centuries had passed since the day when it had taken the high seas as an important unit of a fighting squadron—precisely which squadron the learned were not agreed. The galleon had brought nothing into the world, but it had, according to tradition and report, taken much out of it. But how much? There again the learned were in disagreement. Some were as generous in their estimate as an income-tax assessor, others applied a species of higher criticism to the submerged treasure chests, and debased their contents to the currency of goblin gold. Of the former school was Lulu, Duchess of Dulverton.

The Duchess was not only a believer in the existence of a sunken treasure of alluring proportions; she also believed that she knew of a method by which the said treasure might be precisely located and cheaply disembedded. An aunt on her mother's side of the family had been Maid of Honour at the Court of Monaco, and had taken a respectful interest in the deep-sea researches in which the Throne of that country, impatient perhaps of its terrestrial restrictions, was wont to immerse itself. It was through the instrumentality of this relative that the Duchess learned of an invention, perfected and very nearly patented by a Monegaskan savant, by means of which the home-life of the Mediterranean sardine might be studied at a depth of many fathoms in a cold white light of more than ball-room brilliancy. Implicated in this invention (and, in the Duchess's eyes, the most attractive part of it) was an electric suction dredge, specially designed for dragging to the surface such objects of interest and value as might be found in the more accessible levels of the ocean-bed. The rights of the invention were to be acquired for a matter of eighteen hundred francs, and the apparatus for a few thousand more. The Duchess of Dulverton was rich, as the world

counted wealth: she nursed the hope of being one day rich
at her own computation. Companies had been formed and
efforts had been made again and again during the course of
three centuries to probe for the alleged treasures of the interesting galleon; with the aid of this invention she considered
that she might go to work on the wreck privately and inde-
pendently. After all, one of her ancestors on her mother's
side was descended from Medina Sidonia, so she was of opinion that she had as much right to the treasure as any one. She
acquired the invention and bought the apparatus.

Among other family ties and encumbrances, Lulu possessed
a nephew, Vasco Honiton, a young gentleman who was blessed
with a small income and a large circle of relatives, and lived
impartially and precariously on both. The name Vasco had
been given him possibly in the hope that he might live up to
its adventurous tradition, but he limited himself strictly to
the home industry of adventurer, preferring to exploit the
assured rather than to explore the unknown. Lulu's intercourse
with him had been restricted of recent years to the negative
processes of being out of town when he called on her, and
short of money when he wrote to her. Now, however, she bethought herself of his eminent suitability for the direction of
a treasure-seeking experiment; if any one could extract gold
from an unpromising situation it would certainly be Vasco—
of course, under the necessary safeguards in the way of supervision. Where money was in question Vasco's conscience was
liable to fits of obstinate silence.

Somewhere on the west coast of Ireland the Dulverton
property included a few acres of shingle, rock, and heather,
too barren to support even an agrarian outrage, but embracing
a small and fairly deep bay where the lobster yield was good in
most seasons. There was a bleak little house on the property,
and for those who liked lobsters and solitude, and were able
to accept an Irish cook's ideas as to what might be perpetrated
in the name of mayonnaise, Innisgluther was a tolerable exile
during the summer months. Lulu seldom went there herself,
but she lent the house lavishly to friends and relations. She
put it now at Vasco's disposal.

"It will be the very place to practise and experiment with the salvage apparatus," she said; "the bay is quite deep in places, and you will be able to test everything thoroughly before starting on the treasure hunt."

In less than three weeks Vasco turned up in town to report progress.

"The apparatus works beautifully," he informed his aunt; "the deeper one got the clearer everything grew. We found something in the way of a sunken wreck to operate on, too!"

"A wreck in Innisgluther Bay!" exclaimed Lulu.

"A submerged motor-boat, the *Sub-Rosa*," said Vasco.

"No! really?" said Lulu; "poor Billy Yuttley's boat. I remember it went down somewhere off that coast some three years ago. His body was washed ashore at the Point. People said at the time that the boat was capsized intentionally—a case of suicide, you know. People always say that sort of thing when anything tragic happens."

"In this case they were right," said Vasco.

"What do you mean?" asked the Duchess hurriedly. "What makes you think so?"

"I know," said Vasco simply.

"Know? How can you know? How can any one know? The thing happened three years ago."

"In a locker of the *Sub-Rosa* I found a water-tight strong-box. It contained papers." Vasco paused with dramatic effect and searched for a moment in the inner breast-pocket of his coat. He drew out a folded slip of paper. The Duchess snatched at it in almost indecent haste and moved appreciably nearer the fireplace.

"Was this in the *Sub-Rosa's* strong-box?" she asked.

"Oh, no," said Vasco carelessly, "that is a list of the well-known people who would be involved in a very disagreeable scandal if the *Sub-Rosa's* papers were made public. I've put you at the head of it, otherwise it follows alphabetical order."

The Duchess gazed helplessly at the string of names, which seemed for the moment to include nearly every one she knew.

As a matter of fact, her own name at the head of the list exercised an almost paralyzing effect on her thinking faculties.

"Of course you have destroyed the papers?" she asked, when she had somewhat recovered herself. She was conscious that she made the remark with an entire lack of conviction.

Vasco shook his head.

"But you should have," said Lulu angrily; "if, as you say, they are highly compromising—"

"Oh, they are, I assure you of that," interposed the young man.

"Then you should put them out of harm's way at once. Supposing anything should leak out, think of all these poor, unfortunate people who would be involved in the disclosures," and Lulu tapped the list with an agitated gesture.

"Unfortunate, perhaps, but not poor," corrected Vasco; "if you read the list carefully you'll notice that I haven't troubled to include any one whose financial standing isn't above question."

Lulu glared at her nephew for some moments in silence. Then she asked hoarsely: "What are you going to do?"

"Nothing—for the remainder of my life," he answered meaningly. "A little hunting, perhaps," he continued, "and I shall have a villa at Florence. The Villa Sub-Rosa would sound rather quaint and picturesque, don't you think, and quite a lot of people would be able to attach a meaning to the name. And I suppose I must have a hobby; I shall probably collect Raeburns."

Lulu's relative, who lived at the Court of Monaco, got quite a snappish answer when she wrote recommending some further invention in the realm of marine research.

THE COBWEB

THE farmhouse kitchen probably stood where it did as a matter of accident or haphazard choice; yet its situation might have been planned by a master-strategist in farmhouse architecture. Dairy and poultry-yard, and herb garden, and all the busy places of the farm seemed to lead by easy access into its wide flagged haven, where there was room for everything and where muddy boots left traces that were easily swept away. And yet, for all that it stood so well in the centre of human bustle, its long, latticed window, with the wide window-seat, built into an embrasure beyond the huge fireplace, looked out on a wild spreading view of hill and heather and wooded combe. The window nook made almost a little room in itself, quite the pleasantest room in the farm as far as situation and capabilities went. Young Mrs. Ladbruk, whose husband had just come into the farm by way of inheritance, cast covetous eyes on this snug corner, and her fingers itched to make it bright and cozy with chintz curtains and bowls of flowers, and a shelf or two of old china. The musty farm parlour, looking out to a prim, cheerless garden imprisoned within high, blank walls, was not a room that lent itself readily either to comfort or decoration.

"When we are more settled I shall work wonders in the way of making the kitchen habitable," said the young woman to her occasional visitors. There was an unspoken wish in those words, a wish which was unconfessed as well as unspoken. Emma Ladbruk was the mistress of the farm; jointly with her husband she might have her say, and to a certain extent her way, in ordering its affairs. But she was not mistress of the kitchen.

On one of the shelves of an old dresser, in company with chipped sauce-boats, pewter jugs, cheese-graters, and paid bills, rested a worn and ragged Bible, on whose front page was the record, in faded ink, of a baptism dated ninety-four years ago. "Martha Crale" was the name written on that yellow page. The yellow, wrinkled old dame who hobbled and muttered about the kitchen, looking like a dead autumn leaf which the winter winds still pushed hither and thither, had once been Martha Crale; for seventy odd years she had been Martha Mountjoy. For longer than any one could remember she had pattered to and fro between oven and wash-house and dairy, and out to chicken-run and garden, grumbling and muttering and scolding, but working unceasingly. Emma Ladbruk, of whose coming she took as little notice as she would of a bee wandering in at a window on a summer's day, used at first to watch her with a kind of frightened curiosity. She was so old and so much a part of the place, it was difficult to think of her exactly as a living thing. Old Shep, the white-nozzled, stiff-limbed collie, waiting for his time to die, seemed almost more human than the withered, dried-up old woman. He had been a riotous, roystering puppy, mad with the joy of life, when she was already a tottering, hobbling dame; now he was just a blind, breathing carcase, nothing more, and she still worked with frail energy, still swept and baked and washed, fetched and carried. If there were something in these wise old dogs that did not perish utterly with death, Emma used to think to herself, what generations of ghost-dogs there must be out on those hills, that Martha had reared and fed and tended and spoken a last good-bye word to in that old kitchen. And what memories she must have of human generations that had passed away in her time. It was difficult for any one, let alone a stranger like Emma, to get her to talk of the days that had been; her shrill, quavering speech was of doors that had been left unfastened, pails that had got mislaid, calves whose feeding-time was overdue, and the various little faults and lapses that chequer a farmhouse routine. Now and again, when election time came round, she would unstore her recollections of the old names round which the fight had waged in the days gone by. There had been a Palmerston, that had been a name down Tiverton way; Tiverton was not a far journey as the crow flies, but to Martha it was almost a foreign country. Later there had been Northcotes and Aclands, and many other newer names that she had forgotten; the names changed, but it was always Libruls and Toories, Yellows and Blues. And they always quarrelled and shouted as to who was right and who was wrong. The one they quarrelled about most was a fine old gentleman with an angry face—she had seen his picture on the walls. She had seen it on the floor too, with a rotten apple squashed over it, for the farm had changed its politics from time to time. Martha had never been on one side or the other;

none of "they" had ever done the farm a stroke of good. Such was her sweeping verdict, given with all a peasant's distrust of the outside world.

When the half-frightened curiosity had somewhat faded away, Emma Ladbruk was uncomfortably conscious of another feeling towards the old woman. She was a quaint old tradition, lingering about the place, she was part and parcel of the farm itself, she was something at once pathetic and picturesque—but she was dreadfully in the way. Emma had come to the farm full of plans for little reforms and improvements, in part the result of training in the newest ways and methods, in part the outcome of her own ideas and fancies. Reforms in the kitchen region, if those deaf old ears could have been induced to give them even a hearing, would have met with short shrift and scornful rejection, and the kitchen region spread over the zone of dairy and market business and half the work of the household. Emma, with the latest science of dead-poultry dressing at her fingertips, sat by, an unheeded watcher, while old Martha trussed the chickens for the market-stall as she had trussed them for nearly four-score years—all leg and no breast. And the hundred hints anent effective cleaning and labour-lightening and the things that make for wholesomeness which the young woman was ready to impart or to put into action dropped away into nothingness before that wan, muttering, unheeding presence. Above all, the coveted window corner, that was to be a dainty, cheerful oasis in the gaunt old kitchen, stood now choked and lumbered with a litter of odds and ends that Emma, for all her nominal authority, would not have dared or cared to displace; over them seemed to be spun the protection of something that was like a human cobweb. Decidedly Martha was in the way. It would have been an unworthy meanness to have wished to see the span of that brave old life shortened by a few paltry months, but as the days sped by Emma was conscious that the wish was there, disowned though it might be, lurking at the back of her mind.

She felt the meanness of the wish come over her with a qualm of self-reproach one day when she came into the kitchen

and found an unaccustomed state of things in that usually
busy quarter. Old Martha was not working. A basket of corn
was on the floor by her side, and out in the yard the poultry
were beginning to clamour a protest of overdue feeding-time.
But Martha sat huddled in a shrunken bunch on the window
seat, looking out with her dim old eyes as though she saw
something stranger than the autumn landscape.

"Is anything the matter, Martha?" asked the young woman.

" 'Tis death, 'tis death a-coming," answered the quavering
voice; "I knew 'twere coming. I knew it. 'Tweren't for nothing that old Shep's been howling all morning. An' last night I
heard the screech-owl give the death-cry, and there were something white as run across the yard yesterday; 'tweren't a cat
nor a stoat, 'twere something. The fowls knew 'twere something; they all drew off to one side. Ay, there's been warnings. I knew it were a-coming."

The young woman's eyes clouded with pity. The old thing
sitting there so white and shrunken had once been a merry,
noisy child, playing about in lanes and hay-lofts and farmhouse garrets; that had been eighty odd years ago, and now she
was just a frail old body cowering under the approaching chill
of the death that was coming at last to take her. It was not
probable that much could be done for her, but Emma hastened
away to get assistance and counsel. Her husband, she knew, was
down at a tree-felling some little distance off, but she might
find some other intelligent soul who knew the old woman
better than she did. The farm, she soon found out, had that
faculty common to farmyards of swallowing up and losing
its human population. The poultry followed her in interested
fashion, and swine grunted interrogations at her from behind
the bars of their sties, but barnyard and rickyard, orchard and
stables and dairy, gave no reward to her search. Then, as she
retraced her steps towards the kitchen, she came suddenly on
her cousin, young Mr. Jim, as every one called him, who
divided his time between amateur horse-dealing, rabbit-shooting, and flirting with the farm maids.

"I'm afraid old Martha is dying," said Emma. Jim was not

the sort of person to whom one had to break news gently.

"Nonsense," he said; "Martha means to live to a hundred. She told me so, and she'll do it."

"She may be actually dying at this moment, or it may just be the beginning of the break-up," persisted Emma, with a feeling of contempt for the slowness and dulness of the young man.

A grin spread over his good-natured features.

"It don't look like it," he said, nodding towards the yard. Emma turned to catch the meaning of his remark. Old Martha stood in the middle of a mob of poultry scattering handfuls of grain around her. The turkey-cock, with the bronzed sheen of his feathers and the purple-red of his wattles, the game-cock with the glowing metallic lustre of his Eastern plumage, the hens, with their ochres and buffs and umbers and their scarlet combs, and the drakes, with their bottle-green heads, made a medley of rich colour, in the centre of which the old woman looked like a withered stalk standing amid the riotous growth of gaily-hued flowers. But she threw the grain deftly amid the wilderness of beaks, and her quavering voice carried as far as the two people who were watching her. She was still harping on the theme of death coming to the farm.

"I knew 'twere a-coming. There's been signs an' warnings."

"Who's dead, then, old Mother?" called out the young man.

"'Tis young Mister Ladbruk," she shrilled back; "they've just a-carried his body in. Run out of the way of a tree that was coming down an' ran hisself on to an iron post. Dead when they picked un up. Ay, I knew 'twere coming."

And she turned to fling a handful of barley at a belated group of guinea-fowl that came racing toward her.

. . . .

The farm was a family property, and passed to the rabbit-shooting cousin as the next-of-kin. Emma Ladbruk drifted out of its history as a bee that had wandered in at an open window might flit its way out again. On a cold grey morning she stood waiting with her boxes already stowed in the farm cart, till the last of the market produce should be ready, for the train she was to catch was of less importance than the chickens and butter and eggs that were to be offered for sale. From where she stood she could see an angle of the long latticed window that was to have been cozy with curtains and gay with bowls of flowers. Into her mind came the thought that for months, perhaps for years, long after she had been utterly forgotten, a white, unheeding face would be seen peering out through those latticed panes, and a weak muttering voice would be heard quavering up and down those flagged passages. She made her way to a narrow barred casement that opened into the farm larder. Old Martha was standing at a table trussing a pair of chickens for the market stall as she had trussed them for nearly fourscore years.

THE LULL

"I'VE asked Latimer Springfield to spend Sunday with us and stop the night," announced Mrs. Durmot at the breakfast-table.

"I thought he was in the throes of an election," remarked her husband.

"Exactly; the poll is on Wednesday, and the poor man will have worked himself to a shadow by that time. Imagine what electioneering must be like in this awful soaking rain, going along slushy country roads and speaking to damp audiences in draughty schoolrooms, day after day for a fortnight. He'll have to put in an appearance at some place of worship on Sunday morning, and he can come to us immediately afterwards and have a thorough respite from everything connected with politics. I won't let him even think of them. I've had the picture of Cromwell dissolving the Long Parliament taken down from the staircase, and even the portrait of Lord Rosebery's 'Ladas' removed from the smoking-room. And, Vera," added Mrs. Durmot, turning to her sixteen-year-old niece, "be careful what colour ribbon you wear in your hair; not blue or yellow on any account; those are the rival party colours, and emerald green or orange would be almost as bad, with this Home Rule business to the fore."

"On state occasions I always wear a black ribbon in my hair," said Vera with crushing dignity.

Latimer Springfield was a rather cheerless, oldish young man, who went into politics somewhat in the spirit in which other people might go into half mourning. Without being an enthusiast, however, he was a fairly strenuous plodder, and Mrs. Durmot had been reasonably near the mark in asserting that he was working at high pressure over this election. The restful lull which his hostess enforced on him was decidedly welcome, and yet the nervous excitement of the contest had too great a hold on him to be totally banished.

"I know he's going to sit up half the night working up points for his final speeches," said Mrs. Durmot regretfully; "however, we've kept politics at arm's length all the afternoon and evening. More than that we cannot do."

"That remains to be seen," said Vera, but she said it to herself.

Latimer had scarcely shut his bedroom door before he was immersed in a sheaf of notes and pamphlets, while a fountain-pen and pocket-book were brought into play for the due marshalling of useful facts and discreet fictions. He had been at work for perhaps thirty-five minutes, and the house was seemingly consecrated to the healthy slumber of country life, when a stifled squealing and scuffling in the passage was followed by a loud tap at his door. Before he had time to answer, a much-encumbered Vera burst into the room with the question: "I say, can I leave these here?"

"These" were a small black pig and a lusty specimen of black-red gamecock.

Latimer was moderately fond of animals, and particularly interested in small livestock rearing from the economic point of view; in fact, one of the pamphlets on which he was at that moment engaged warmly advocated the further development of the pig and poultry industry in our rural districts; but he

was pardonably unwilling to share even a commodious bedroom
with samples of henroost and sty products.

"Wouldn't they be happier somewhere outside?" he asked,
tactfully expressing his own preference in the matter in an
apparent solicitude for theirs.

"There is no outside," said Vera impressively, "nothing
but a waste of dark, swirling waters. The reservoir at Brinkley
has burst."

"I didn't know there was a reservoir at Brinkley," said
Latimer.

"Well, there isn't now, it's jolly well all over the place,
and as we stand particularly low we're the centre of an inland
sea just at present. You see the river has overflowed its banks
as well."

"Good gracious! Have any lives been lost?"

"Heaps, I should say. The second housemaid has already
identified three bodies that have floated past the billiard-room
window as being the young man she's engaged to. Either she's
engaged to a large assortment of the population round here or
else she's very careless at identification. Of course it may be the
same body coming round again and again in a swirl; I hadn't
thought of that."

"But we ought to go out and do rescue work, oughtn't we?"
said Latimer, with the instinct of a Parliamentary candidate
for getting into the local limelight.

"We can't," said Vera decidedly, "we haven't any boats
and we're cut off by a raging torrent from any human habitation. My aunt particularly hoped you would keep to your room
and not add to the confusion, but she thought it would be so
kind of you if you would take in Hartlepool's Wonder, the
gamecock, you know, for the night. You see, there are eight
other gamecocks, and they fight like furies if they get together,
so we're putting one in each bedroom. The fowl-houses are all
flooded out, you know. And then I thought perhaps you
wouldn't mind taking in this wee piggie; he's rather a little
love, but he has a vile temper. He gets that from his mother—
not that I like to say things against her when she's lying dead
and drowned in her sty, poor thing. What he really wants is a

man's firm hand to keep him in order. I'd try and grapple
with him myself, only I've got my chow in my room, you
know, and he goes for pigs wherever he finds them."

"Couldn't the pig go in the bathroom?" asked Latimer
faintly, wishing that he had taken up as determined a stand
on the subject of bedroom swine as the chow had.

"The bathroom?" Vera laughed shrilly. "It'll be full of
Boy Scouts till morning if the hot water holds out."

"Boy Scouts?"

"Yes, thirty of them came to rescue us while the water was
only waist-high; then it rose another three feet or so and we
had to rescue them. We're giving them hot baths in batches
and drying their clothes in the hot-air cupboard, but, of course
drenched clothes don't dry in a minute, and the corridor and
staircase are beginning to look like a bit of coast scenery by
Tuke. Two of the boys are wearing your Melton overcoat; I
hope you don't mind."

"It's a new overcoat," said Latimer, with every indication
of minding dreadfully.

"You'll take every care of Hartlepool's Wonder, won't
you?" said Vera. "His mother took three firsts at Birmingham,
and he was second in the cockerel class last year at Gloucester.
He'll probably roost on the rail at the bottom of your bed.
I wonder if he'd feel more at home if some of his wives
were up here with him? The hens are all in the pantry, and
I think I could pick out Hartlepool Helen; she's his favourite."

Latimer showed a belated firmness on the subject of Hartlepool Helen, and Vera withdrew without pressing the point,
having first settled the gamecock on his extemporized perch
and taken an affectionate farewell of the pigling. Latimer undressed and got into bed with all due speed, judging that the
pig would abate its inquisitorial restlessness once the light was
turned out. As a substitute for a cozy, straw-bedded sty the
room offered, at first inspection, few attractions, but the dis-
consolate animal suddenly discovered an appliance in which
the most luxuriously contrived piggeries were notably deficient.
The sharp edge of the underneath part of the bed was pitched

at exactly the right elevation to permit the pigling to scrape himself ecstatically backwards and forwards, with an artistic humping of the back at the crucial moment and an accompanying gurgle of long-drawn delight. The gamecock, who may have fancied that he was being rocked in the branches of a pine-tree, bore the motion with greater fortitude than Latimer was able to command. A series of slaps directed at the pig's body were accepted more as an additional and pleasing irritant than as a criticism of conduct or a hint to desist; evidently something more than a man's firm hand was needed to deal with the case. Latimer slipped out of bed in search of a weapon of dissuasion. There was sufficient light in the room to enable the pig to detect this manœuvre, and the vile temper, inherited from the drowned mother, found full play. Latimer bounded back into bed, and his conqueror, after a few threatening snorts and champings of its jaws, resumed its massage operations with renewed zeal. During the long wakeful hours which ensued Latimer tried to distract his mind from his own immediate troubles by dwelling with decent sympathy on the second housemaid's bereavement, but he found himself more often wondering how many Boy Scouts were sharing his Melton overcoat. The rôle of Saint Martin *malgré lui* was not one which appealed to him.

Towards dawn the pigling fell into a happy slumber, and Latimer might have followed its example, but at about the same time Stupor Hartlepooli gave a rousing crow, clattered down to the floor and forthwith commenced a spirited combat with his reflection in the wardrobe mirror. Remembering that the bird was more or less under his care Latimer performed Hague Tribunal offices by draping a bath-towel over the provocative mirror, but the ensuing peace was local and short-lived. The deflected energies of the gamecock found new outlet in a sudden and sustained attack on the sleeping and temporarily inoffensive pigling, and the duel which followed was desperate and embittered beyond any possibility of effective intervention. The feathered combatant had the advantage of being able, when hard pressed, to take refuge on the bed, and freely availed himself of this circumstance; the pigling never quite succeeded in hurling himself on to the same eminence, but it was not from want of trying.

Neither side could claim any decisive success, and the struggle had been practically fought to a standstill by the time that the maid appeared with the early morning tea.

"Lor, sir," she exclaimed in undisguised astonishment, "do you want those animals in your room?"

Want!

The pigling, as though aware that it might have outstayed its welcome, dashed out at the door, and the gamecock followed it at a more dignified pace.

"If Miss Vera's dog sees that pig—!" exclaimed the maid, and hurried off to avert such a catastrophe.

A cold suspicion was stealing over Latimer's mind; he went to the window and drew up the blind. A light, drizzling rain was falling, but there was not the faintest trace of any inundation.

Some half-hour later he met Vera on the way to the breakfast-room.

"I should not like to think of you as a deliberate liar," he observed coldly, "but one occasionally has to do things one does not like."

"At any rate I kept your mind from dwelling on politics all the night," said Vera.

Which was, of course, perfectly true.

THE UNKINDEST BLOW

THE season of strikes seemed to have run itself to a standstill. Almost every trade and industry and calling in which a dislocation could possibly be engineered had indulged in that luxury. The last and least successful convulsion had been the strike of the World's Union of Zoological Garden attendants, who, pending the settlement of certain demands, refused to minister further to the wants of the animals committed to their charge or to allow any other keepers to take their place. In this case the threat of the Zoological Gardens authorities that if the men "came out" the animals should come out also had intensified and precipitated the crisis. This imminent prospect of the larger carnivores, to say nothing of rhinoceroses and bull bison, roaming at large and unfed in the heart of London, was not one which permitted of prolonged conferences. The Government of the day, which from its tendency to be a few hours behind the course of events had been nicknamed the Government of the afternoon, was obliged to intervene with promptitude and decision. A strong force of Blue-jackets was despatched to Regent's Park to take over the temporarily abandoned duties of the strikers. Blue-jackets were chosen in preference to land forces, partly on account of the traditional readiness of the British Navy to go anywhere and do anything, partly by reason of the familiarity of the average sailor with monkeys, parrots, and other tropical fauna, but chiefly at the urgent request of the First Lord of the Admiralty, who was keenly desirous of an opportunity for performing some personal act of unobtrusive public service within the province of his department.

"If he insists on feeding the infant jaguar himself, in defiance of its mother's wishes, there may be another by-election in the north," said one of his colleagues, with a hopeful inflection in his voice. "By-elections are not very desirable at present, but we must not be selfish."

As a matter of fact the strike collapsed peacefully without any outside intervention. The majority of the keepers had become so attached to their charges that they returned to work of their own accord.

And then the nation and the newspapers turned with a sense of relief to happier things. It seemed as if a new era of contentment was about to dawn. Everybody had struck who could possibly want to strike or who could possibly be cajoled or bullied into striking, whether they wanted to or not. The lighter and brighter side of life might now claim some attention. And conspicuous among the other topics that sprang into sudden prominence was the pending Falvertoon divorce suit.

The Duke of Falvertoon was one of those human *hors*

d'œuvres that stimulate the public appetite for sensation without giving it much to feed on. As a mere child he had been precociously brilliant; he had declined the editorship of the *Anglian Review* at an age when most boys are content to have declined *mensa*, a table, and though he could not claim to have originated the Futurist movement in literature, his "Letters to a Possible Grandson," written at the age of fourteen, had attracted considerable notice. In later days his brilliancy had been less conspicuously displayed. During a debate in the House of Lords on affairs in Morocco, at a moment when that country, for the fifth time in seven years, had brought half Europe to the verge of war, he had interpolated the remark "a little Moor and how much it is," but in spite of the encouraging reception accorded to this one political utterance he was never tempted to a further display in that direction. It began to be generally understood that he did not intend to supplement his numerous town and country residences by living overmuch in the public eye.

And then had come the unlooked-for tidings of the imminent proceedings for divorce. And such a divorce! There were cross-suits and allegations and counter-allegations, charges of cruelty and desertion, everything in fact that was necessary to make the case one of the most complicated and sensational of its kind. And the number of distinguished people involved or cited as witnesses not only embraced both political parties in the realm and several Colonial governors, but included an exotic contingent from France, Hungary, the United States of North America, and the Grand Duchy of Baden. Hotel accommodation of the more expensive sort began to experience a strain on its resources. "It will be quite like the Durbar without the elephants," exclaimed an enthusiastic lady who, to do her justice, had never seen a Durbar. The general feeling was one of thankfulness that the last of the strikes had been got over before the date fixed for the hearing of the great suit.

As a reaction from the season of gloom and industrial strife that had just passed away the agencies that purvey and stage-manage sensations laid themselves out to do their level best on this momentous occasion. Men who had made their reputations as special descriptive writers were mobilized from distant corners of Europe and the further side of the Atlantic in order to enrich with their pens the daily printed records of the case; one word-painter, who specialized in descriptions of how witnesses turn pale under cross-examination, was summoned hurriedly back from a famous and prolonged murder trial in Sicily, where indeed his talents were being decidedly wasted. Thumb-nail artists and expert kodak manipulators were retained at extravagant salaries, and special dress reporters were in high demand. An enterprising Paris firm of costume builders presented the defendant Duchess with three special creations, to be worn, marked, learned, and extensively reported at various critical stages of the trial; and as for the cinematograph agents, their industry and persistence was untiring. Films representing the Duke saying good-bye to his favourite canary on the eve of the trial were in readiness weeks before the event was due to take place; other films depicted the Duchess holding imaginary consultations with fictitious lawyers or making a light repast off specially advertised vegetarian sandwiches during a supposed luncheon interval. As far as human foresight and human enterprise could go nothing was lacking to make the trial a success.

Two days before the case was down for hearing the advance reporter of an important syndicate obtained an interview with the Duke for the purpose of gleaning some final grains of information concerning his Grace's personal arrangements during the trial.

"I suppose I may say this will be one of the biggest affairs of its kind during the lifetime of a generation," began the reporter as an excuse for the unsparing minuteness of detail that he was about to make quest for.

"I suppose so—if it comes off," said the Duke lazily.

"If?" queried the reporter, in a voice that was something between a gasp and a scream.

"The Duchess and I are both thinking of going on strike," said the Duke.

"Strike!"

The baleful word flashed out in all its old hideous familiarity. Was there to be no end to its recurrence?

"Do you mean," faltered the reporter, "that you are contemplating a mutual withdrawal of the charges?"

"Precisely," said the Duke.

"But think of the arrangements that have been made, the special reporting, the cinematographs, the catering for the distinguished foreign witnesses, the prepared music-hall allusions; think of all the money that has been sunk—"

"Exactly," said the Duke coldly, "the Duchess and I have realized that it is we who provide the material out of which this great far-reaching industry has been built up. Widespread employment will be given and enormous profits made during the duration of the case, and we, on whom all the stress and racket falls, will get—what? An unenviable notoriety and the privilege of paying heavy legal expenses whichever way the verdict goes. Hence our decision to strike. We don't wish to be reconciled; we fully realize that it is a grave step to take, but unless we get some reasonable consideration out of this vast stream of wealth and industry that we have called into being we intend coming out of court and staying out. Good afternoon."

The news of this latest strike spread universal dismay. Its inaccessibility to the ordinary methods of persuasion made it peculiarly formidable. If the Duke and Duchess persisted in being reconciled the Government could hardly be called on to interfere. Public opinion in the shape of social ostracism might be brought to bear on them, but that was as far as coercive measures could go. There was nothing for it but a conference, with powers to propose liberal terms. As it was, several of the foreign witnesses had already departed and others had telegraphed cancelling their hotel arrangements.

The conference, protracted, uncomfortable, and occasionally acrimonious, succeeded at last in arranging for a resumption of litigation, but it was a fruitless victory. The Duke, with a touch of his earlier precocity, died of premature decay a fortnight before the date fixed for the new trial.

THE ROMANCERS

IT was autumn in London, that blessed season between the harshness of winter and the insincerities of summer; a trustful season when one buys bulbs and sees to the registration of one's vote, believing perpetually in spring and a change of Government.

Morton Crosby sat on a bench in a secluded corner of Hyde Park, lazily enjoying a cigarette and watching the slow grazing promenade of a pair of snow-geese, the male looking rather like an albino edition of the russet-hued female. Out of the corner of his eye Crosby also noted with some interest the hesitating hoverings of a human figure, which had passed and repassed his seat two or three times at shortening intervals, like a wary crow about to alight near some possibly edible morsel. Inevitably the figure came to an anchorage on the bench, within easy talking distance of its original occupant. The uncared-for clothes, the aggressive, grizzled beard, and the furtive, evasive eye of the new-comer bespoke the professional cadger, the man who would undergo hours of humiliating tale-spinning and rebuff rather than adventure on half a day's decent work.

For a while the new-comer fixed his eyes straight in front of him in a strenuous, unseeing gaze; then his voice broke out with the insinuating inflection of one who has a story to retail well worth any loiterer's while to listen to.

"It's a strange world," he said.

As the statement met with no response he altered it to the form of a question.

"I dare say you've found it to be a strange world mister?"

"As far as I am concerned," said Crosby, "the strangeness has worn off in the course of thirty-six years."

"Ah," said the greybeard, "I could tell you things that you'd hardly believe. Marvellous things that have really happened to me."

"Nowadays there is not demand for marvellous things that have really happened," said Crosby discouragingly; "the professional writers of fiction turn these things out so much better. For instance, my neighbours tell me wonderful, incredible things that their Aberdeens and chows and borzois have done; I never listen to them. On the other hand, I have read *The Hound of the Baskervilles* three times."

The greybeard moved uneasily in his seat; then he opened up new country.

"I take it that you are a professing Christian," he observed.

"I am a prominent and I think I may say an influential member of the Mussulman community of Eastern Persia," said Crosby, making an excursion himself into the realms of fiction.

The greybeard was obviously disconcerted at this new check of introductory conversation, but the defeat was only momentary.

"Persia. I should never have taken you for a Persian," he remarked, with a somewhat aggrieved air.

"I am not," said Crosby; "my father was an Afghan."

"An Afghan!" said the other, smitten into bewildered silence for a moment. Then he recovered himself and renewed his attack.

"Afghanistan. Ah! We've had some wars with that country; now, I dare say, instead of fighting it we might have learned something from it. A very wealthy country, I believe. No real poverty there."

He raised his voice on the word "poverty" with a suggestion of intense feeling. Crosby saw the opening and avoided it.

"It possesses, nevertheless, a number of highly talented and ingenious beggars," he said; "if I had not spoken so disparagingly of marvellous things that have really happened I would tell you the story of Ibrahim and the eleven camel-loads of blotting-paper. Also I have forgotten exactly how it ended."

"My own life-story is a curious one," said the stranger, apparently stifling all desire to hear the history of Ibrahim; "I was not always as you see me now."

"We are supposed to undergo complete change in the course of every seven years," said Crosby, as an explanation of the foregoing announcement.

"I mean I was not always in such distressing circumstances as I am at present," pursued the stranger doggedly.

"That sounds rather rude," said Crosby stiffly, "considering that you are at present talking to a man reputed to be one of the most gifted conversationalists of the Afghan border."

"I don't mean in that way," said the greybeard hastily; "I've been very much interested in your conversation. I was alluding to my unfortunate financial situation. You mayn't hardly believe it, but at the present moment I am absolutely without a farthing. Don't see any prospect of getting any money, either, for the next few days. I don't suppose you've ever found yourself in such a position," he added.

"In the town of Yom," said Crosby, "which is in Southern Afghanistan, and which also happens to be my birthplace, there was a Chinese philosopher who used to say that one of the three chiefest human blessings was to be absolutely without money. I forget what the other two were."

"Ah, I dare say," said the stranger, in a tone that betrayed no enthusiasm for the philosopher's memory; "and did he practise what he preached? That's the test."

"He lived happily with very little money or resources," said Crosby.

"Then I expect he had friends who would help him liberally whenever he was in difficulties, such as I am in at present."

"In Yom," said Crosby, "it is not necessary to have friends in order to obtain help. Any citizen of Yom would help a stranger as a matter of course."

The greybeard was now genuinely interested. The conversation had at last taken a favourable turn.

"If some one, like me, for instance, who was in undeserved difficulties, asked a citizen of that town you speak of for a small loan to tide over a few days' impecuniosity—five shillings, or perhaps a rather larger sum—would it be given to him as a matter of course?"

"There would be a certain preliminary," said Crosby; "one would take him to a wine-shop and treat him to a measure of wine, and then, after a little high-flown conversation, one would put the desired sum in his hand and wish him good-day. It is a roundabout way of performing a simple transaction, but in the East all ways are roundabout."

The listener's eyes were glittering.

"Ah," he exclaimed, with a thin sneer ringing meaningly through his words, "I suppose you've given up all those generous customs since you left your town. Don't practise them now, I expect."

"No one who has lived in Yom," said Crosby fervently, "and remembers its green hills covered with apricot and almond trees, and the cold water that rushes down like a caress from the upland snows and dashes under the little wooden bridges, no one who remembers these things and treasures the memory of them would ever give up a single one of its unwritten laws and customs. To me they are as binding as though I still lived in that hallowed home of my youth."

"Then if I was to ask you for a small loan——" began the greybeard fawningly, edging nearer on the seat and hurriedly wondering how large he might safely make his request, "if I was to ask you for, say——"

"At any other time, certainly," said Crosby; "in the months of November and December, however, it is absolutely forbidden for any one of our race to give or receive loans or gifts; in fact, one does not willingly speak of them. It is considered unlucky. We will therefore close this discussion."

"But it is still October!" exclaimed the adventurer with an eager, angry whine, as Crosby rose from his seat; "wants eight days to the end of the month!"

"The Afghan November began yesterday," said Crosby severely, and in another moment he was striding across the Park, leaving his recent companion scowling and muttering furiously on the seat.

"I don't believe a word of his story," he chattered to himself; "pack of nasty lies from beginning to end. Wish I'd told him so to his face. Calling himself an Afghan!"

The snorts and snarls that escaped from him for the next quarter of an hour went far to support the truth of the old saying that two of a trade never agree.

THE SCHARTZ-METTERKLUME
METHOD

LADY CARLOTTA stepped out on to the platform of the small wayside station and took a turn or two up and down its uninteresting length, to kill time till the train should be pleased to proceed on its way. Then, in the roadway beyond, she saw a horse struggling with a more than ample load, and a carter of the sort that seems to bear a sullen hatred against the animal that helps him to earn a living. Lady Carlotta promptly betook her to the roadway, and put rather a different complexion on the struggle. Certain of her acquaintances were wont to give her plentiful admonition as to the undesirability of interfering on behalf of a distressed animal, such interference being "none of her business." Only once had she put the doctrine of non-interference into practice, when one of its most eloquent exponents had been besieged for nearly three hours in a small and extremely uncomfortable may-tree by an angry boar-pig, while Lady Carlotta, on the other side of the fence, had proceeded with the water-colour sketch she was engaged on, and refused to interfere between the boar and his prisoner. It is to be feared that she lost the friendship of the ultimately rescued lady. On this occasion she merely lost the train, which gave way to the first sign of impatience it had shown throughout the journey, and steamed off without her. She bore the desertion with philosophical indifference; her friends and relations were thoroughly well used to the fact of her luggage arriving without her. She wired a vague non-committal message to her destination to say that she was coming on "by another train." Before she had time to think what her next move might be she was confronted by an imposingly attired lady, who seemed to be taking a prolonged mental inventory of her clothes and looks.

"You must be Miss Hope, the governess I've come to meet," said the apparition, in a tone that admitted of very little argument.

"Very well, if I must I must," said Lady Carlotta to herself with dangerous meekness.

"I am Mrs. Quabarl," continued the lady; "and where, pray, is your luggage?"

"It's gone astray," said the alleged governess, falling in with the excellent rule of life that the absent are always to blame; the luggage had, in point of fact, behaved with perfect correctitude. "I've just telegraphed about it," she added, with a nearer approach to truth.

"How provoking," said Mrs. Quabarl; "these railway companies are so careless. However, my maid can lend you things for the night," and she led the way to her car.

During the drive to the Quabarl mansion Lady Carlotta was impressively introduced to the nature of the charge that had been thrust upon her; she learned that Claude and Wilfrid were delicate, sensitive young people, that Irene had the artistic temperament highly developed, and that Viola was something or other else of a mould equally commonplace among children of that class and type in the twentieth century.

"I wish them not only to be *taught*," said Mrs. Quabarl, "but *interested* in what they learn. In their history lessons, for instance, you must try to make them feel that they are being introduced to the life-stories of men and women who really lived, not merely committing a mass of names and dates to memory. French, of course, I shall expect you to talk at meal-times several days in the week."

"I shall talk French four days of the week and Russian in the remaining three."

"Russian? My dear Miss Hope, no one in the house speaks or understands Russian."

"That will not embarrass me in the least," said Lady Carlotta coldly.

Mrs. Quabarl, to use a colloquial expression, was knocked off her perch. She was one of those imperfectly self-assured individuals who are magnificent and autocratic as long as they are not seriously opposed. The least show of unexpected resistance goes a long way towards rendering them cowed and apologetic. When the new governess failed to express wondering admiration of the large newly purchased and expensive car, and lightly alluded to the superior advantages of one or two makes which had just been put on the market, the discomfiture of her patroness became almost abject. Her feelings were those which might have animated a general of ancient warfaring days, on beholding his heaviest battle-elephant ignominiously driven off the field by slingers and javelin throwers.

At dinner that evening, although reinforced by her husband, who usually duplicated her opinions and lent her moral support generally, Mrs. Quabarl regained none of her lost ground. The governess not only helped herself well and truly to wine, but held forth with considerable show of critical knowledge on various vintage matters, concerning which the Quabarls were in no wise able to pose as authorities. Previous governesses had limited their conversation on the wine topic to a respectful and doubtless sincere expression of a preference for water. When this one went as far as to recommend a wine firm in whose hands you could not go very far wrong Mrs. Quabarl thought it time to turn the conversation into more usual channels.

"We got very satisfactory references about you from Canon Teep," she observed; "a very estimable man, I should think."

"Drinks like a fish and beats his wife, otherwise a very lovable character," said the governess imperturbably.

"My *dear* Miss Hope! I trust you are exaggerating," exclaimed the Quabarls in unison.

"One must in justice admit that there is some provocation," continued the romancer. "Mrs. Teep is quite the most irritating bridge-player that I have ever sat down with; her leads and declarations would condone a certain amount of brutality in her partner, but to souse her with the contents of the only soda-water syphon in the house on a Sunday afternoon, when one couldn't get another, argues an indifference to the comfort of others which I cannot altogether overlook. You may think me hasty in my judgments, but it was practically on account of the syphon incident that I left."

"We will talk of this some other time," said Mrs. Quabarl hastily.

"I shall never allude to it again," said the governess with decision.

Mr. Quabarl made a welcome diversion by asking what studies the new instructress proposed to inaugurate on the morrow.

"History to begin with," she informed him.

"Ah, history," he observed sagely; "now in teaching them history you must take care to interest them in what they learn. You must make them feel that they are being introduced to the life-stories of men and women who really lived—"

"I've told her all that," interposed Mrs. Quabarl.

"I teach history on the Schartz-Metterklume method," said the governess loftily.

"Ah, yes," said her listeners, thinking it expedient to assume an acquaintance at least with the name.

"What are you children doing out here?" demanded Mrs. Quabarl the next morning, on finding Irene sitting rather glumly at the head of the stairs, while her sister was perched in an attitude of depressed discomfort on the window-seat behind her, with a wolf-skin rug almost covering her.

"We are having a history lesson," came the unexpected reply. "I am supposed to be Rome, and Viola up there is the she-wolf; not a real wolf, but the figure of one that the Romans used to set store by—I forget why. Claude and Wilfrid have gone to fetch the shabby women."

"The shabby women?"

"Yes, they've got to carry them off. They didn't want to, but Miss Hope got one of father's fives-bats and said she'd give them a number nine spanking if they didn't, so they've gone to do it."

A loud, angry screaming from the direction of the lawn drew Mrs. Quabarl thither in hot haste, fearful lest the threatened castigation might even now be in process of infliction. The outcry, however, came principally from the two small daughters of the lodge-keeper, who were being hauled and rushed towards the house by the panting and dishevelled Claude and Wilfrid, whose task was rendered even more arduous by the incessant, if not very effectual, attacks of the captured maidens' small brother. The governess, fives-bat in hand, sat negligently on the stone balustrade, presiding over the scene with the cold impartiality of a Goddess of Battles. A furious and repeated chorus of "I'll tell muvver" rose from the lodge children, but the lodge-mother, who was hard of hearing, was for the moment immersed in the preoccupation of her washtub. After an apprehensive glance in the direction of the lodge (the good woman was gifted with the highly militant temper which is sometimes the privilege of deafness) Mrs. Quabarl flew indignantly to the rescue of the struggling captives.

"Wilfrid! Claude! Let those children go at once. Miss Hope, what on earth is the meaning of this scene?"

"Early Roman history; the Sabine women, don't you know? It's the Schartz-Metterklume method to make children understand history by acting it themselves; fixes it in their memory, you know. Of course, if, thanks to your interference, your boys go through life thinking that the Sabine women ultimately escaped, I really cannot be held responsible."

"You may be very clever and modern, Miss Hope," said Mrs. Quabarl firmly, "but I should like you to leave here by the next train. Your luggage will be sent after you as soon as it arrives."

"I'm not certain exactly where I shall be for the next few days," said the dismissed instructress of youth; "you might keep my luggage till I wire my address. There are only a couple of trunks and some golf-clubs and a leopard cub."

"A leopard cub!" gasped Mrs. Quabarl. Even in her departure this extraordinary person seemed destined to leave a trail of embarrassment behind her.

"Well, it's rather left off being a cub; it's more than half-grown, you know. A fowl every day and a rabbit on Sundays is what it usually gets. Raw beef makes it too excitable. Don't trouble about getting the car for me, I'm rather inclined for a walk."

And Lady Carlotta strode out of the Quabarl horizon.

The advent of the genuine Miss Hope, who had made a

mistake as to the day on which she was due to arrive, caused a turmoil which that good lady was quite unused to inspiring. Obviously the Quabarl family had been woefully befooled, but a certain amount of relief came with the knowledge.

"How tiresome for you, dear Carlotta," said her hostess, when the overdue guest ultimately arrived; "how very tiresome losing your train and having to stop overnight in a strange place."

"Oh, dear, no," said Lady Carlotta; "not at all tiresome —for me."

THE SEVENTH PULLET

"IT'S not the daily grind that I complain of," said Blenkinthrope resentfully; "it's the dull grey sameness of my life outside of office hours. Nothing of interest comes my way, nothing remarkable or out of the common. Even the little things that I do try to find some interest in don't seem to interest other people. Things in my garden, for instance."

"The potato that weighed just over two pounds," said his friend Gorworth.

"Did I tell you about that?" said Blenkinthrope; "I was telling the others in the train this morning. I forgot if I'd told you."

"To be exact you told me that it weighed just under two pounds, but I took into account the fact that abnormal vegetables and freshwater fish have an after-life, in which growth is not arrested."

"You're just like the others," said Blenkinthrope sadly, "you only make fun of it."

"The fault is with the potato, not with us," said Gorworth; "we are not in the least interested in it because it is not in the least interesting. The men you go up in the train with every day are just in the same case as yourself; their lives are commonplace and not very interesting to themselves, and they certainly are not going to wax enthusiastic over the commonplace events in other men's lives. Tell them something startling, dramatic, piquant, that has happened to yourself or to some one in your family, and you will capture their interest at once. They will talk about you with a certain personal pride to all their acquaintances. 'Man I know intimately, fellow called Blenkinthrope, lives down my way, had two of his fingers clawed clean off by a lobster he was carrying home to supper. Doctor says entire hand may have to come off.' Now that is conversation of a very high order. But imagine walking into a tennis club with the remark: 'I know a man who has grown a potato weighing two and a quarter pounds.'"

"But hang it all, my dear fellow," said Blenkinthrope impatiently, "haven't I just told you that nothing of a remarkable nature ever happens to me?"

"Invent something," said Gorworth. Since winning a prize for excellence in Scriptural knowledge at a preparatory school he had felt licensed to be a little more unscrupulous than the circle he moved in. Much might surely be excused to one who in early life could give a list of seventeen trees mentioned in the Old Testament.

"What sort of thing?" asked Blenkinthrope, somewhat snappishly.

"A snake got into your hen-run yesterday morning and killed six out of seven pullets, first mesmerizing them with its eyes and then biting them as they stood helpless. The seventh pullet was one of that French sort, with feathers all over its eyes, so it escaped the mesmeric snare, and just flew at what it could see of the snake and pecked it to pieces."

"Thank you," said Blenkinthrope stiffly; "it's a very clever invention. If such a thing had really happened in my poultry-run I admit I should have been proud and interested to tell people about it. But I'd rather stick to fact, even if it is plain fact." All the same his mind dwelt wistfully on the story of the Seventh Pullet. He could picture himself telling it in the train amid the absorbed interest of his fellow-passengers. Unconsciously all sorts of little details and improvements began to suggest themselves.

Wistfulness was till his dominant mood when he took his seat in the railway carriage the next morning. Opposite him sat Stevenham, who had attained to a recognized brevet of importance through the fact of an uncle having dropped dead in the act of voting at a Parliamentary election. That had happened three years ago, but Stevenham was still deferred to on all questions of home and foreign politics.

"Hullo, how's the giant mushroom, or whatever it was?" was all the notice Blenkinthrope got from his fellow travellers.

Young Duckby, whom he mildly disliked, speedily monopolized the general attention by an account of a domestic bereavement.

"Had four young pigeons carried off last night by a whacking big rat. Oh, a monster he must have been; you could tell by the size of the hole he made breaking into the loft."

No moderate-sized rat ever seemed to carry out any predatory operations in these regions; they were all enormous in their enormity.

"Pretty hard lines that," continued Duckby, seeing that he had secured the attention and respect of the company; "four squeakers carried off at one swoop. You'd find it rather hard to match that in the way of unlooked-for bad luck."

"I had six pullets out of a pen of seven killed by a snake yesterday afternoon," said Blenkinthrope, in a voice which he hardly recognized as his own.

"By a snake?" came in excited chorus.

"It fascinated them with its deadly, glittering eyes, one after the other, and struck them down while they stood helpless. A bedridden neighbour, who wasn't able to call for assistance, witnessed it all from her bedroom window."

"Well, I never!" broke in the chorus, with variations.

"The interesting part of it is about the seventh pullet, the one that didn't get killed," resumed Blenkinthrope, slowly lighting a cigarette. His diffidence had left him, and he was beginning to realize how safe and easy depravity can seem once one has the courage to begin. "The six dead birds were Minorcas; the seventh was a Houdan with a mop of feathers all over its eyes. It could hardly see the snake at all, so of course it wasn't mesmerized like the others. It just could see something wriggling on the ground, and went for it and pecked it to death."

"Well, I'm blessed!" exclaimed the chorus.

In the course of the next few days Blenkinthrope discovered how little the loss of one's self-respect affects one when one has gained the esteem of the world. His story found its way into one of the poultry papers, and was copied thence into a daily news-sheet as a matter of general interest. A lady wrote from the North of Scotland recounting a similar episode which she had witnessed as occurring between a stoat and a blind grouse. Somehow a lie seems so much less reprehensible when one can call it a lee.

For a while the adapter of the Seventh Pullet story enjoyed to the full his altered standing as a person of consequence, one who had had some share in the strange events of his times. Then he was thrust once again into the cold grey background by the sudden blossoming into importance of Smith-Paddon, a daily fellow-traveller, whose little girl had been knocked down and nearly hurt by a car belonging to a musical-comedy actress. The actress was not in the car at the time, but she was in numerous photographs which appeared in the illustrated papers of Zoto Dobreen inquiring after the well-being of Maisie, daughter of Edmund Smith-Paddon, Esq. With this new human interest to absorb them the travelling companions were almost rude when Blenkinthrope tried to explain his contrivance for keeping vipers and peregrine falcons out of his chicken-run.

Gorworth, to whom he unburdened himself in private, gave him the same counsel as theretofore.

"Invent something."

"Yes, but what?"

The ready affirmative coupled with the question betrayed a significant shifting of the ethical standpoint.

It was a few days later that Blenkinthrope revealed a chapter of family history to the customary gathering in the railway carriage.

"Curious thing happened to my aunt, the one who lives in

Paris," he began. He had several aunts, but they were all geographically distributed over Greater London.

"She was sitting on a seat in the Bois the other afternoon, after lunching at the Roumanian Legation."

Whatever the story gained in picturesqueness for the dragging-in of diplomatic "atmosphere." it ceased from that moment to command any acceptance as a record of current events. Gorworth had warned his neophyte that this would be the case, but the traditional enthusiasm of the neophyte had triumphed over discretion.

"She was feeling rather drowsy, the effect probably of the champagne, which she's not in the habit of taking in the middle of the day."

A subdued murmur of admiration went round the company. Blenkinthrope's aunts were not used to taking champagne in the middle of the year, regarding it exclusively as a Christmas and New Year accessory.

"Presently a rather portly gentleman passed by her seat and paused an instant to light a cigar. At that moment a youngish man came up behind him, drew the blade from a swordstick, and stabbed him half a dozen times through and through. 'Scoundrel,' he cried to his victim, 'you do not know me. My name is Henri Leturc.' The elder man wiped away some of the blood that was spattering his clothes, turned to his assailant, and said: 'And since when has an attempted assassination been considered an introduction?' Then he finished lighting his cigar and walked away. My aunt had intended screaming for the police, but seeing the indifference with which the principal in the affair treated the matter she felt that it would be an impertinence on her part to interfere. Of course I need hardly say she put the whole thing down to the effects of a warm, drowsy afternoon and the Legation champagne. Now comes the astonishing part of my story. A fortnight later a bank manager was stabbed to death with a swordstick in that very part of the Bois. His assassin was the son of a charwoman formerly working at the bank, who had been dismissed from her job by the manager on account of chronic intemperance. His name was Henri Leturc."

From that moment Blenkinthrope was tacitly accepted as the Munchausen of the party. No effort was spared to draw him out from day to day in the exercise of testing their powers of credulity, and Blenkinthrope, in the false security of an assured and receptive audience, waxed industrious and ingenious in supplying the demand for marvels. Duckby's satirical story of a tame otter that had a tank in the garden to swim in, and whined restlessly whenever the water-rate was overdue, was scarcely an unfair parody of some of Blenkinthrope's wilder efforts. And then one day came Nemesis.

Returning to his villa one evening Blenkinthrope found his wife sitting in front of a pack of cards, which she was scrutinizing with unusual concentration.

"The same old patience-game?" he asked carelessly.

"No, dear; this is the Death's Head patience, the most difficult of them all. I've never got it to work out, and somehow I should be rather frightened if I did. Mother only got it out once in her life; she was afraid of it, too. Her great-aunt had done it once and fallen dead from excitement the next moment, and mother always had a feeling that she would die if she ever got it out. She died the same night that she did it. She was in bad health at the time, certainly, but it was a strange coincidence."

"Don't do it if it frightens you," was Blenkinthrope's practical comment as he left the room. A few minutes later his wife called to him.

"John, it gave me such a turn, I nearly got it out. Only the five of diamonds held me up at the end. I really thought I'd done it."

"Why, you can do it," said Blenkinthrope, who had come back to the room; "if you shift the eight of clubs on to that open nine the five can be moved on to the six."

His wife made the suggested move with hasty, trembling fingers, and piled the outstanding cards on to their respective packs. Then she followed the example of her mother and great-grand-aunt.

Blenkinthrope had been genuinely fond of his wife, but in the midst of his bereavement one dominant thought obtruded itself. Something sensational and real had at last come into his life; no longer was it a grey, colourless record. The head-lines which might appropriately describe his domestic tragedy kept shaping themselves in his brain. "Inherited presentiment comes true." "The Death's Head patience: Card-game that justified its sinister name in three generations." He wrote out a full story of the fatal occurrence for the *Essex Vedette*, the editor of which was a friend of his, and to another friend he gave a condensed account, to be taken up to the office of one of the halfpenny dailies. But in both cases his reputation as a romancer stood fatally in the way of the fulfilment of his ambitions. "Not the right thing to be Munchausening in a time of sorrow," agreed his friends among themselves, and a brief note of regret at the "sudden death of the wife of our respected neighbour, Mr. John Blenkinthrope, from heart failure," appearing in the news column of the local paper was the forlorn outcome of his visions of widespread publicity.

Blenkinthrope shrank from the society of his erstwhile travelling companions and took to travelling townwards by an earlier train. He sometimes tries to enlist the sympathy and attention of a chance acquaintance in details of the whistling prowess of his best canary or the dimensions of his largest beet-root; he scarcely recognizes himself as the man who was once spoken about and pointed out as the owner of the Seventh Pullet.

THE BLIND SPOT

"YOU'VE just come back from Adelaide's funeral, haven't you?" said Sir Lulworth to his nephew; "I suppose it was very like most other funerals?"

"I'll tell you all about it at lunch," said Egbert.

"You'll do nothing of the sort. It wouldn't be respectful either to your great-aunt's memory or to the lunch. We begin with Spanish olives, then a borsch, then more olives and a bird of some kind, and a rather enticing Rhenish wine, not at all expensive as wines go in this country, but still quite laud-

able in its way. Now there's absolutely nothing in that menu
that harmonizes in the least with the subject of your great-
aunt Adelaide or her funeral. She was a charming woman,
and quite as intelligent as she had any need to be, but somehow she always reminded me of an English cook's idea of a
Madras curry."

"She used to say you were frivolous," said Egbert. Something in his tone suggested that he rather endorsed the verdict.

"I believe I once considerably scandalized her by declaring
that clear soup was a more important factor in life than a
clear conscience. She had very little sense of proportion. By
the way, she made you her principal heir, didn't she?"

"Yes," said Egbert, "and executor as well. It's in that connection that I particularly want to speak to you."

"Business is not my strong point at any time," said Sir Lulworth, "and certainly not when we're on the immediate threshold of lunch."

"It isn't exactly business," explained Egbert, as he followed
his uncle into the dining-room. "It's something rather serious.
Very serious."

"Then we can't possibly speak about it now," said Sir Lulworth; "no one could talk seriously during a borsch. A beautifully constructed borsch, such as you are going to experience
presently, ought not only to banish conversation but almost to
annihilate thought. Later on, when we arrive at the second
stage of olives, I shall be quite ready to discuss that new book
on Borrow, or, if you prefer it, the present situation in the
Grand Duchy of Luxemburg. But I absolutely decline to talk
anything approaching business till we have finished with the
bird."

For the greater part of the meal Egbert sat in an abstracted
silence, the silence of a man whose mind is focussed on one
topic. When the coffee stage had been reached he launched
himself suddenly athwart his uncle's reminiscences of the
Court of Luxemburg.

"I think I told you that great-aunt Adelaide had made me
her executor. There wasn't very much to be done in the way
of legal matters, but I had to go through her papers."

"That would be a fairly heavy task in itself. I should imagine there were reams of family letters."

"Stacks of them, and most of them highly uninteresting. There was one packet, however, which I thought might repay a careful perusal. It was a bundle of correspondence from her brother Peter."

"The Canon of tragic memory," said Lulworth.

"Exactly, of tragic memory, as you say; a tragedy that has never been fathomed."

"Probably the simplest explanation was the correct one," said Sir Lulworth; "he slipped on the stone staircase and fractured his skull in falling."

Egbert shook his head. "The medical evidence all went to prove that the blow on the head was struck by some one coming up behind him. A wound caused by violent contact with the steps could not possibly have been inflicted at that angle of the skull. They experimented with a dummy figure falling in every conceivable position."

"But the motive?" exclaimed Sir Lulworth; "no one had any interest in doing away with him, and the number of people who destroy Canons of the Established Church for the mere fun of killing must be extremely limited. Of course there are individuals of weak mental balance who do that sort of thing, but they seldom conceal their handiwork; they are more generally inclined to parade it."

"His cook was under suspicion," said Egbert shortly.

"I know he was," said Sir Lulworth, "simply because he was about the only person on the premises at the time of the tragedy. But could anything be sillier than trying to fasten a charge of murder on to Sebastien? He had nothing to gain, in fact, a good deal to lose, from the death of his employer. The Canon was paying him quite as good wages as I was able to offer him when I took him over into my service. I have since raised them to something a little more in accordance with his real worth, but at the time he was glad to find a new place without troubling about an increase of wages. People were fighting rather shy of him, and he had no friends in this country. No; if any one in the world was interested in the prolonged life and unimpaired digestion of the Canon it would certainly be Sebastien."

"People don't always weigh the consequences of their rash acts," said Egbert, "otherwise there would be very few murders committed. Sebastien is a man of hot temper."

"He is a southerner," admitted Sir Lulworth; "to be geographically exact I believe he hails from the French slopes of the Pyrenees. I took that into consideration when he nearly killed the gardener's boy the other day for bringing him a spurious substitute for sorrel. One must always make allowances for origin and locality and early environment; 'Tell me your longitude and I'll know what latitude to allow you,' is my motto."

"There, you see," said Egbert, "he nearly killed the gardener's boy."

"My dear Egbert, between nearly killing a gardener's boy and altogether killing a Canon there is a wide difference. No doubt you have often felt a temporary desire to kill a gardener's boy; you have never given way to it, and I respect you for your self-control. But I don't suppose you have ever wanted to kill an octogenarian Canon. Besides, as far as we know, there had never been any quarrel or disagreement between the two men. The evidence at the inquest brought that out very clearly."

"Ah!" said Egbert, with the air of a man coming at last into a deferred inheritance of conversational importance, "that is precisely what I want to speak to you about."

He pushed away his coffee cup and drew a pocket-book from his inner breast-pocket. From the depths of the pocket-book he produced an envelope, and from the envelope he extracted a letter, closely written in a small, neat handwriting.

"One of the Canon's numerous letters to Aunt Adelaide," he explained, "written a few days before his death. Her memory was already failing when she received it, and I dare say she forgot the contents as soon as she had read it; otherwise, in the light of what subsequently happened, we should have heard something of this letter before now. If it had been produced at the inquest I fancy it would have made some difference in the course of affairs. The evidence, as you remarked just now, choked off suspicion against Sebastien by disclosing an utter absence of anything that could be considered a motive or provocation for the crime, if crime there was."

"Oh, read the letter," said Sir Lulworth impatiently.

"It's a long rambling affair, like most of his letters in his later years," said Egbert. "I'll read the part that bears immediately on the mystery.

"'I very much fear I shall have to get rid of Sebastien. He cooks divinely, but he has the temper of a fiend or an anthropoid ape, and I am really in bodily fear of him. We had a dispute the other day as to the correct sort of lunch to be served on Ash Wednesday, and I got so irritated and annoyed at his conceit and obstinacy that at last I threw a cupful of coffee in his face and called him at the same time an impudent jackanapes. Very little of the coffee went actually in his face, but I have never seen a human being show such deplorable lack of self-control. I laughed at the threat of killing me that he spluttered out in his rage, and thought the whole thing would blow over, but I have several times since caught him scowling and muttering in a highly unpleasant fashion, and lately I have fancied that he was dogging my footsteps about the grounds, particularly when I walk of an evening in the Italian Garden.'

"It was on the steps in the Italian Garden that the body was found," commented Egbert, and resumed reading.

"'I dare say the danger is imaginary; but I shall feel more at ease when he has quitted my service.'"

Egbert paused for a moment at the conclusion of the extract; then, as his uncle made no remark, he added: "If lack of motive was the only factor that saved Sebastien from prosecution I fancy this letter will put a different complexion on matters."

"Have you shown it to any one else?" asked Sir Lulworth, reaching out his hand for the incriminating piece of paper.

"No," said Egbert, handing it across the table, "I thought I would tell you about it first. Heavens, what are you doing?"

Egbert's voice rose almost to a scream. Sir Lulworth had

flung the paper well and truly into the glowing centre of the grate. The small, neat handwriting shrivelled into black flaky nothingness.

"What on earth did you do that for?" gasped Egbert. "That letter was our one piece of evidence to connect Sebastien with the crime."

"That is why I destroyed it," said Sir Lulworth.

"But why should you want to shield him?" cried Egbert; "the man is a common murderer."

"A common murderer, possibly, but a very uncommon cook."

DUSK

NORMAN GORTSBY sat on a bench in the Park, with his back to a strip of bush-planted sward, fenced by the park railings, and the Row fronting him across a wide stretch of carriage drive. Hyde Park Corner, with its rattle and hoot of traffic, lay immediately to his right. It was some thirty minutes past six on an early March evening, and dusk had fallen heavily over the scene, dusk mitigated by some faint moonlight and many street lamps. There was a wide emptiness over road and sidewalk, and yet there were many unconsidered figures moving silently through the half-light or dotted unobtrusively on bench and chair, scarcely to be distinguished from the shadowed gloom in which they sat.

The scene pleased Gortsby and harmonized with his present mood. Dusk, to his mind, was the hour of the defeated. Men and women, who had fought and lost, who hid their fallen fortunes and dead hopes as far as possible from the scrutiny of the curious, came forth in this hour of gloaming, when their shabby clothes and bowed shoulders and unhappy eyes might pass unnoticed, or, at any rate, unrecognized.

> A king that is conquered must see strange looks,
> So bitter a thing is the heart of man.

The wanderers in the dusk did not choose to have strange looks fasten on them, therefore they came out in this bat-fashion,

taking their pleasure sadly in a pleasure-ground that had emptied of its rightful occupants. Beyond the sheltering screen of
bushes and palings came a realm of brilliant lights and noisy,
rushing traffic. A blazing, many-tiered stretch of windows
shone through the dusk and almost dispersed it, marking the
haunts of those other people, who held their own in life's
struggle, or at any rate had not had to admit failure. So
Gortsby's imagination pictured things as he sat on his bench
in the almost deserted walk. He was in the mood to count
himself among the defeated. Money troubles did not press
on him; had he so wished he could have strolled into the
thoroughfares of light and noise, and taken his place among
the jostling ranks of those who enjoyed prosperity or struggled
for it. He had failed in a more subtle ambition, and for the
moment he was heart sore and disillusionized, and not disinclined to take a certain cynical pleasure in observing and label-
ling his fellow wanderers as they went their ways in the dark
stretches between the lamp-lights.

On the bench by his side sat an elderly gentleman with a
drooping air of defiance that was probably the remaining
vestige of self-respect in an individual who had ceased to
defy successfully anybody or anything. His clothes could
scarcely be called shabby, at least they passed muster in the
half-light, but one's imagination could not have pictured the
wearer embarking on the purchase of a half-crown box of
chocolates or laying out ninepence on a carnation buttonhole.
He belonged unmistakably to that forlorn orchestra to whose
piping no one dances; he was one of the world's lamenters
who induces no responsive weeping. As he rose to go Gortsby
imagined him returning to a home circle where he was snubbed
and of no account, or to some bleak lodging where his ability
to pay a weekly bill was the beginning and end of the interest
he inspired. His retreating figure vanished slowly into the
shadows, and his place on the bench was taken almost immediately by a young man, fairly well dressed but scarcely more
cheerful of mien than his predecessor. As if to emphasize the
fact that the world went badly with him the new-comer un-

burdened himself of an angry and very audible expletive as he flung himself into the seat.

"You don't seem in a very good temper," said Gortsby, judging that he was expected to take due notice of the demonstration.

The young man turned to him with a look of disarming frankness which put him instantly on his guard.

"You wouldn't be in a good temper if you were in the fix I'm in," he said; "I've done the silliest thing I've ever done in my life."

"Yes?" said Gortsby dispassionately.

"Came up this afternoon, meaning to stay at the Patagonian Hotel in Berkshire Square," continued the young man; "when I got there I found it had been pulled down some weeks ago and a cinema theatre run up on the site. The taxi driver recommended me to another hotel some way off and I went there. I just sent a letter to my people, giving them the address, and then I went out to buy some soap—I'd forgotten to pack any and I hate using hotel soap. Then I strolled about a bit, had a drink at a bar and looked at the shops, and when I came to turn my steps back to the hotel I suddenly realized that I didn't remember its name or even what street it was in. There's a nice predicament for a fellow who hasn't any friends or connections in London! Of course I can wire to my people for the address, but they won't have got my letter till to-morrow; meantime I'm without any money, came out with about a shilling on me, which went in buying the soap and getting the drink, and here I am, wandering about with twopence in my pocket and nowhere to go for the night."

There was an eloquent pause after the story had been told. "I suppose you think I've spun you rather an impossible yarn," said the young man presently, with a suggestion of resentment in his voice.

"Not at all impossible," said Gortsby judicially; "I remember doing exactly the same thing once in a foreign capital, and on that occasion there were two of us, which made it more remarkable. Luckily we remembered that the hotel was on a sort of canal, and when we struck the canal we were able to find our way back to the hotel."

The youth brightened at the reminiscence. "In a foreign city I wouldn't mind so much," he said; "one could go to one's Consul and get the requisite help from him. Here in one's own land one is far more derelict if one gets into a fix. Unless I can find some decent chap to swallow my story and lend me some money I seem likely to spend the night on the Embankment. I'm glad, anyhow, that you don't think the story outrageously improbable."

He threw a good deal of warmth into the last remark, as though perhaps to indicate his hope that Gortsby did not fall far short of the requisite decency.

"Of course," said Gortsby slowly, "the weak point of your story is that you can't produce the soap."

The young man sat forward hurriedly, felt rapidly in the pockets of his overcoat, and then jumped to his feet.

"I must have lost it," he muttered angrily.

"To lose an hotel and a cake of soap on one afternoon suggests wilful carelessness," said Gortsby, but the young man scarcely waited to hear the end of the remark. He flitted away down the path, his head held high, with an air of somewhat jaded jauntiness.

"It was a pity," mused Gortsby; "the going out to get one's own soap was the one convincing touch in the whole story, and yet it was just that little detail that brought him to grief. If he had had the brilliant forethought to provide himself with a cake of soap, wrapped and sealed with all the solicitude of the chemist's counter, he would have been a genius in his particular line. In his particular line genius certainly consists of an infinite capacity for taking precautions."

With that reflection Gortsby rose to go; as he did so an exclamation of concern escaped him. Lying on the ground by the side of the bench was a small oval packet, wrapped and sealed with the solicitude of a chemist's counter. It could be nothing else but a cake of soap, and it had evidently fallen out of the youth's overcoat pocket when he flung himself down on the seat. In another moment Gortsby was scudding along

the dusk-shrouded path in anxious quest for a youthful figure
in a light overcoat. He had nearly given up the search when
he caught sight of the object of his pursuit standing irresolutely
on the border of the carriage drive, evidently uncertain
whether to strike across the Park or make for the bustling
pavements of Knightsbridge. He turned round sharply with
an air of defensive hostility when he found Gortsby hailing
him.

"The important witness to the genuineness of your story has
turned up," said Gortsby, holding out the cake of soap; "it
must have slid out of your overcoat pocket when you sat down
on the seat. I saw it on the ground after you left. You must
excuse my disbelief, but appearances were really rather against
you, and now, as I appealed to the testimony of the soap I
think I ought to abide by its verdict. If the loan of a sovereign
is any good to you—"

The young man hastily removed all doubt on the subject
by pocketing the coin.

"Here is my card with my address," continued Gortsby;
"any day this week will do for returning the money, and
here is the soap—don't lose it again; it's been a good friend
to you."

"Lucky thing your finding it," said the youth, and then,
with a catch in his voice, he blurted out a word or two of
thanks and fled headlong in the direction of Knightsbridge.

"Poor boy, he as nearly as possible broke down," said
Gortsby to himself. "I don't wonder either; the relief from
his quandary must have been acute. It's a lesson to me not
to be too clever in judging by circumstances."

As Gortsby retraced his steps past the seat where the little
drama had taken place he saw an elderly gentleman poking
and peering beneath it and on all sides of it, and recognized
his earlier fellow occupant.

"Have you lost anything, sir?" he asked.

"Yes, sir, a cake of soap."

"I HOPE you've come full of suggestions for Christmas," said Lady Blonze to her latest arrived guest; "the old-fashioned Christmas and the up-to-date Christmas are both so played out. I want to have something really original this year."

"I was staying with the Mathesons last month," said Blanche Boveal eagerly, "and we had such a good idea. Every one in the house-party had to be a character and behave consistently all the time, and at the end of the visit one had to guess what every one's character was. The one who was voted to have acted his or her character best got a prize."

"It sounds amusing," said Lady Blonze.

"I was St. Francis of Assisi," continued Blanche; "we hadn't got to keep to our right sexes. I kept getting up in the middle of a meal and throwing out food to the birds; you see, the chief thing that one remembers of St. Francis is that he was fond of the birds. Every one was so stupid about it, and thought that I was the old man who feeds the sparrows in the Tuileries Gardens. Then Colonel Pentley was the Jolly Miller on the banks of Dee."

"How on earth did he do that?" asked Bertie van Tahn.

"'He laughed and sang from morn till night,'" explained Blanche.

"How dreadful for the rest of you," said Bertie; "and anyway he wasn't on the banks of Dee."

"One had to imagine that," said Blanche.

"If you could imagine all that you might as well imagine cattle on the further bank and keep on calling them home, Mary-fashion, across the sands of Dee. Or you might change the river to the Yarrow and imagine it was on the top of you, and say you were Willie, or whoever it was, drowned in Yarrow."

"Of course it's easy to make fun of it," said Blanche sharply, "but it was extremely interesting and amusing. The prize was rather a fiasco, though. You see, Millie Matheson said her character was Lady Bountiful, and as she was our hostess, of course we all had to vote that she carried out her character better than any one. Otherwise I ought to have got the prize."

"It's quite an idea for a Christmas party," said Lady Blonze; "we must certainly do it here."

Sir Nicholas was not so enthusiastic. "Are you quite sure, my dear, that you're wise in doing this thing?" he said to his wife when they were alone together. "It might do very well at the Mathesons', where they had rather a staid, elderly house-party, but here it will be a different matter. There is the Durmot flapper, for instance, who simply stops at nothing, and you know what Van Tahn is like. Then there is Cyril Skatterly; he has madness on one side of his family and a Hungarian grandmother on the other."

"I don't see what they could do that would matter," said Lady Blonze.

"It's the unknown that is to be dreaded," said Sir Nicholas. "If Skatterly took it into his head to represent a Bull of Bashan, well, I'd rather not be here."

"Of course we shan't allow any Bible characters. Besides, I don't know what the Bulls of Bashan really did that was so very dreadful; they just came round and gaped, as far as I remember."

"My dear, you don't know what Skatterly's Hungarian imagination mightn't read into the part; it would be small satisfaction to say to him afterwards: 'You've behaved as no Bull of Bashan would have behaved.'"

"Oh, you're an alarmist," said Lady Blonze; "I particularly want to have this idea carried out. It will be sure to be talked about a lot."

"That is quite possible," said Sir Nicholas.

.   .   .   .

Dinner that evening was not a particularly lively affair; the strain of trying to impersonate a self-imposed character or to glean hints of identity from other people's conduct acted as a check on the natural festivity of such a gathering. There was a general feeling of gratitude and acquiescence when good-natured Rachel Klammerstein suggested that there should be an hour or two's respite from "the game" while they all listened to a little piano-playing after dinner. Rachel's love of piano music was not indiscriminate, and concentrated itself chiefly on selections rendered by her idolized offspring, Moritz and Augusta, who, to do them justice, played remarkably well.

The Klammersteins were deservedly popular as Christmas guests; they gave expensive gifts lavishly on Christmas Day and New Year, and Mrs. Klammerstein had already dropped hints of her intention to present the prize for the best enacted character in the game competition. Every one had brightened at this prospect; if it had fallen to Lady Blonze, as hostess, to provide the prize, she would have considered that a little souvenir of some twenty or twenty-five shillings' value would meet the case, whereas coming from a Klammerstein source it would certainly run to several guineas.

The close time for impersonation efforts came to an end with the final withdrawal of Moritz and Augusta from the piano. Blanche Boveal retired early, leaving the room in a series of laboured leaps that she hoped might be recognized as a tolerable imitation of Pavlova. Vera Durmot, the sixteen-year-old flapper, expressed her confident opinion that the performance was intended to typify Mark Twain's famous jumping frog, and her diagnosis of the case found general acceptance. Another guest to set an example of early bed-going was Waldo Plubley, who conducted his life on a minutely regulated system of time-tables and hygienic routine. Waldo was a plump, indolent young man of seven-and-twenty, whose mother had early in his life decided for him that he was unusually delicate, and by dint of much coddling and home-keeping had succeeded in making him physically soft and mentally peevish. Nine hours' unbroken sleep, preceded by elaborate breathing exercises and other hygienic ritual, was among the indispensable regulations which Waldo imposed on himself, and there were innumerable small observances which he exacted from those who were in any way obliged to minister to his requirements; a special teapot for the decoction

of his early tea was always solemnly handed over to the bedroom staff of any house in which he happened to be staying.
No one had ever quite mastered the mechanism of this precious
vessel, but Bertie van Tahn was responsible for the legend that
its spout had to be kept facing north during the process of
infusion.

On this particular night the irreducible nine hours were
severely mutilated by the sudden and by no means noiseless
incursion of a pyjama-clad figure into Waldo's room at an
hour midway between midnight and dawn.

"What is the matter? What are you looking for?" asked
the awakened and astonished Waldo, slowly recognizing Van
Tahn, who appeared to be searching hastily for something he
had lost.

"Looking for sheep," was the reply.

"Sheep?" exclaimed Waldo.

"Yes, sheep. You don't suppose I'm looking for giraffes,
do you?"

"I don't see why you should expect to find either in my
room," retorted Waldo furiously.

"I can't argue the matter at this hour of the night," said
Bertie, and began hastily rummaging in the chest of drawers.
Shirts and underwear went flying on to the floor.

"There are no sheep here, I tell you," screamed Waldo.

"I've only got your word for it," said Bertie, whisking
most of the bedclothes on to the floor; "if you weren't concealing something you wouldn't be so agitated."

Waldo was by this time convinced that Van Tahn was raving mad, and made an anxious effort to humour him.

"Go back to bed like a dear fellow," he pleaded, "and
your sheep will turn up all right in the morning."

"I dare say," said Bertie gloomily, "without their tails.
Nice fool I shall look with a lot of Manx sheep."

And by way of emphasizing his annoyance at the prospect
he sent Waldo's pillows flying to the top of the wardrobe.

"But *why* no tails?" asked Waldo, whose teeth were chattering with fear and rage and lowered temperature.

"My dear boy, have you never heard the ballad of Little Bo-Peep?" said Bertie with a chuckle. "It's my character in the Game, you know. If I didn't go hunting about for my lost sheep no one would be able to guess who I was; and now go to sleepy weeps like a good child or I shall be cross with you."

"I leave you to imagine," wrote Waldo in the course of a long letter to his mother, "how much sleep I was able to recover that night, and you know how essential nine uninterrupted hours of slumber are to my health."

On the other hand he was able to devote some wakeful hours to exercises in breathing wrath and fury against Bertie van Tahn.

Breakfast at Blonzecourt was a scattered meal, on the "come when you please" principle, but the house-party was supposed to gather in full strength at lunch. On the day after the "Game" had been started there were, however, some notable absentees. Waldo Plubley, for instance, was reported to be nursing a headache. A large breakfast and an "A.B.C." had been taken up to his room, but he had made no appearance in the flesh.

"I expect he's playing up to some character," said Vera Durmot; "isn't there a thing of Molière's, 'Le Malade Imaginaire'? I expect he's that."

Eight or nine lists came out, and were duly pencilled with the suggestion.

"And where are the Klammersteins?" asked Lady Blonze; "they're usually so punctual."

"Another character pose, perhaps," said Bertie van Tahn; "'the Lost Ten Tribes.'"

"But there are only three of them. Besides, they'll want their lunch. Hasn't any one seen anything of them?"

"Didn't you take them out in your car?" asked Blanche Boveal, addressing herself to Cyril Skatterly.

"Yes, took them out to Slogberry Moor immediately after breakfast. Miss Durmot came too."

"I saw you and Vera come back," said Lady Blonze, "but

I didn't see the Klammersteins. Did you put them down in the village?"

"No," said Skatterly shortly.

"But where are they? Where did you leave them?"

"We left them on Slogberry Moor," said Vera calmly.

"On Slogberry Moor? Why, it's more than thirty miles away! How are they going to get back?"

"We didn't stop to consider that," said Skatterly; "we asked them to get out for a moment, on the pretence that the car had stuck, and then we dashed off full speed and left them there."

"But how dare you do such a thing? It's most inhuman! Why, it's been snowing for the last hour."

"I expect there'll be a cottage or farmhouse somewhere if they walk a mile or two."

"But why on earth have you done it?"

The question came in a chorus of indignant bewilderment.

"*That* would be telling what our characters are meant to be," said Vera.

"Didn't I warn you?" said Sir Nicholas tragically to his wife.

"It's something to do with Spanish history; we don't mind giving you that clue," said Skatterly, helping himself cheerfully to salad, and then Bertie van Tahn broke forth into peals of joyous laughter.

"I've got it! Ferdinand and Isabella deporting the Jews! Oh, lovely! Those two have certainly won the prize; we shan't get anything to beat that for thoroughness."

Lady Blonze's Christmas party was talked about and written about to an extent that she had not anticipated in her most ambitious moments. The letters from Waldo's mother would alone have made it memorable.

COUSIN TERESA

BASSET HARROWCLUFF returned to the home of his fathers, after an absence of four years, distinctly well pleased with himself. He was only thirty-one, but he had put in some useful service in an out-of-the-way, though not unimportant, corner of the world. He had quieted a province, kept open a trade route, enforced the tradition of respect which is worth the ransom of many kings in out-of-the-way regions, and done the whole business on rather less expenditure than would be requisite for organizing a charity in the home country. In Whitehall and places where they think, they doubtless thought well of him. It was not inconceivable, his father allowed himself to imagine, that Basset's name might figure in the next list of Honours.

Basset was inclined to be rather contemptuous of his half-brother, Lucas, whom he found feverishly engrossed in the same medley of elaborate futilities that had claimed his whole time and energies, such as they were, four years ago, and almost as far back before that as he could remember. It was the contempt of the man of action for the man of activities, and it was probably reciprocated. Lucas was an over-well nourished individual, some nine years Basset's senior, with a colouring that would have been accepted as a sign of intensive culture in an asparagus, but probably meant in this case mere abstention from exercise. His hair and forehead furnished a recessional note in a personality that was in all other respects obtrusive and assertive. There was certainly no Semitic blood in Lucas's parentage, but his appearance contrived to convey at least a suggestion of Jewish extraction. Clovis Sangrail, who knew most of his associates by sight, said it was undoubtedly a case of protective mimicry.

Two days after Basset's return, Lucas frisked in to lunch in a state of twittering excitement that could not be restrained even for the immediate consideration of soup, but had to be verbally discharged in spluttering competition with mouthfuls of vermicelli.

"I've got hold of an idea for something immense," he babbled, "something that is simply It."

Basset gave a short laugh that would have done equally well as a snort, if one had wanted to make the exchange. His half-brother was in the habit of discovering futilities that were "simply It" at frequently recurring intervals. The discovery generally meant that he flew up to town, preceded by glowingly worded telegrams, to see some one connected with the stage or the publishing world, got together one or two momentous luncheon parties, flitted in and out of "Gambrinus" for one or two evenings, and returned home with an air of subdued importance and the asparagus tint slightly intensified. The great idea was generally forgotten a few weeks later in the excitement of some new discovery.

"The inspiration came to me whilst I was dressing," announced Lucas; "it will be *the* thing in the next music-hall *revue*. All London will go mad over it. It's just a couplet; of course there will be other words, but they won't matter. Listen:

> Cousin Teresa takes out Cæsar,
> Fido, Jock, and the big borzoi.

A lilting, catchy sort of refrain, you see, and big-drum business on the two syllables of bor-zoi. It's immense. And I've thought out all the business of it; the singer will sing the first verse alone, then during the second verse Cousin Teresa will walk through, followed by four wooden dogs on wheels; Cæsar will be an Irish terrier, Fido a black poodle, Jock a fox-terrier, and the borzoi, of course, will be a borzoi. During the third verse Cousin Teresa will come on alone, and the dogs will be drawn across by themselves from the opposite wing; then Cousin Teresa will catch on to the singer and go off-stage in one direction, while dogs' procession goes off in the other, crossing *en route*, which is always very effective. There'll be a lot of applause there, and for the fourth verse Cousin Teresa will come on in sables and the dogs will all have coats on. Then I've got a great idea for the fifth verse; each of the dogs will be led on by a Nut, and Cousin Teresa will come on from the opposite side, crossing *en route*, always effective, and then she turns round and leads the whole lot of them off on a string, and all the time every one singing like mad:

> Cousin Teresa takes out Cæsar,
> Fido, Jock, and the big borzoi.

Tum-Tum! Drum business on the two last syllables. I'm so excited, I shan't sleep a wink tonight. I'm off tomorrow by the ten-fifteen. I've wired to Hermanova to lunch with me."

If any of the rest of the family felt any excitement over the creation of Cousin Teresa, they were signally successful in concealing the fact.

"Poor Lucas does take his silly little ideas seriously," said Colonel Harrowcluff afterwards in the smoking-room.

"Yes," said his younger son, in a slightly less tolerant tone, "in a day or two he'll come back and tell us that his sensational masterpiece is above the heads of the public, and in about three weeks' time he'll be wild with enthusiasm over a scheme to dramatize the poems of Herrick or something equally promising."

And then an extraordinary thing befell. In defiance of all precedent Lucas's glowing anticipations were justified and endorsed by the course of events. If Cousin Teresa was above the heads of the public, the public heroically adapted itself to her altitude. Introduced as an experiment at a dull moment in a new *revue*, the success of the item was unmistakable; the calls were so insistent and uproarious that even Lucas's ample devisings of additional "business" scarcely sufficed to keep pace with the demand. Packed houses on successive evenings confirmed the verdict of the first night audience, stalls and boxes filled significantly just before the turn came on, and emptied significantly after the last *encore* had been given. The manager tearfully acknowledged that Cousin Teresa was It. Stage hands and supers and programme sellers acknowledged it to one another without the least reservation. The name of the *revue* dwindled to secondary importance, and vast letters of electric blue blazoned the words "Cousin Teresa" from the front of the great palace of pleasure. And of course, the magic of the famous refrain laid its spell all over the Metropolis. Restaurant proprietors were obliged to provide the members of their orchestras with painted wooden dogs on wheels, in order that the much-demanded and always conceded melody should be rendered with the necessary spectacular effects, and the crash of bottles and forks on the tables at the mention of the big borzoi usually drowned the sincerest efforts of drum or cymbals. Nowhere and at no time could one get away from the double thump that brought up the rear of the refrain; revellers reeling home at night banged it on doors and hoardings, milkmen clashed their cans to its cadence, messenger boys hit smaller messenger boys resounding double smacks on the same principle. And the more thoughtful circles of the great city were not deaf to the claims and significance of the popular melody. An enterprising and emancipated preacher discoursed from his pulpit on the inner meaning of "Cousin Teresa," and Lucas Harrowcluff was invited to lecture on the subject of his great achievement to members of the Young Men's Endeavour League, the Nine Arts Club, and other learned and willing-to-learn bodies. In Society it seemed to be the one thing people really cared to talk about; men and women of middle age and average education might be seen together in corners earnestly discussing, not the question whether Servia should have an outlet on the Adriatic, or the possibilities of a British success in international polo contests, but the more absorbing topic of the problematic Aztec or Nilotic origin of the Teresa *motif*.

"Politics and patriotism are so boring and so out of date," said a revered lady who had some pretensions to oracular utterance; "we are too cosmopolitan nowadays to be really moved by them. That is why one welcomes an intelligible production like 'Cousin Teresa,' that has a genuine message for one. One can't understand the message all at once, of course, but one felt from the very first that it was there. I've been to see it eighteen times and I'm going again tomorrow and on Thursday. One can't see it often enough."

.　　　.　　　.　　　.　　　.　　　.　　　.

"It would be rather a popular move if we gave this Harrowcluff person a knighthood or something of the sort," said the Minister reflectively.

"Which Harrowcluff?" asked his secretary.

"Which? There is only one, isn't there?" said the Minister; "the 'Cousin Teresa' man, of course. I think every one would be pleased if we knighted him. Yes, you can put him down on the list of certainties—under the letter L."

"The letter L," said the secretary, who was new to his job: "does that stand for Liberalism or liberality?"

Most of the recipients of Ministerial favour were expected to qualify in both of those subjects.

"Literature," explained the Minister.

And thus, after a fashion, Colonel Harrowcluff's expectation of seeing his son's name in the list of Honours was gratified.

THE YARKAND MANNER

SIR LULWORTH QUAYNE was making a leisurely progress through the Zoological Society's Gardens in company with his nephew, recently returned from Mexico. The latter was interested in comparing and contrasting allied types of animals occurring in the North American and Old World fauna.

"One of the most remarkable things in the wanderings of species," he observed, "is the sudden impulse to trek and migrate that breaks out now and again, for no apparent reason, in communities of hitherto stay-at-home animals."

"In human affairs the same phenomenon is occasionally noticeable," said Sir Lulworth; "perhaps the most striking instance of it occurred in this country while you were away in the wilds of Mexico. I mean the wander fever which suddenly displayed itself in the managing and editorial staffs of certain London newspapers. It began with the stampede of the entire staff of one of our most brilliant and enterprising weeklies to the banks of the Seine and the heights of Montmartre. The migration was a brief one, but it heralded an era of restlessness in the Press world which lent quite a new meaning to the phrase 'newspaper circulation.' Other editorial staffs were not slow to imitate the example that had been set them. Paris soon dropped out of fashion as being too near home; Nürnberg, Seville, and Salonica became more favoured as planting-out grounds for the personnel of not only weekly but daily papers as well. The localities were perhaps not always well chosen; the fact of a leading organ of Evangelical thought being edited for two successive fortnights from Trouville and Monte Carlo was generally admitted to have been a mistake. And even when enterprising and adventurous editors took themselves and their staffs further afield there were some unavoidable clashings. For instance, the *Scrutator, Sporting Bluff* and *The Damsels' Own Paper* all pitched on Khartoum for the same week. It was, perhaps, a desire to out-distance all possible competition that influenced the management of the *Daily Intelligencer*, one of the most solid and respected organs of Liberal opinion, in its decision to transfer its offices for three or four weeks from Fleet Street to Eastern Turkestan, allowing, of course, a necessary margin of time for the journey there and back. This was, in many respects, the most remarkable of all the Press stampedes that were experienced at this time. There was no make-believe about the undertaking; proprietor, manager, editor, sub-editors, leader-writers, principal reporters, and so forth, all took part in what was popularly alluded to as the *Drang nach Osten;* an intelligent and efficient office-boy was all that was left in the deserted hive of editorial industry."

"That was doing things rather thoroughly, wasn't it?" said the nephew.

"Well, you see," said Sir Lulworth, "the migration idea was falling somewhat into disrepute from the half-hearted manner in which it was occasionally carried out. You were

not impressed by the information that such and such a paper
was being edited and brought out at Lisbon or Innsbruck if
you chanced to see the principal leader-writer or the art editor
lunching as usual at their accustomed restaurants. The *Daily
Intelligencer* was determined to give no loophole for cavil at
the genuineness of its pilgrimage, and it must be admitted
that to a certain extent the arrangements made for transmit-
ting copy and carrying on the usual features of the paper during the long outward journey worked smoothly and well. The
series of articles which commenced at Baku on 'What Cob-
denism might do for the camel industry' ranks among the
best of the recent contributions to Free Trade literature, while
the views on foreign policy enunciated 'from a roof in
Yarkand' showed at least as much grasp of the international
situation as those that had germinated within half a mile of
Downing Street. Quite in keeping, too, with the older and better traditions of British journalism was the manner of the
home-coming; no bombast, no personal advertisement, no
flamboyant interviews. Even a complimentary luncheon at the
Voyagers' Club was courteously declined. Indeed, it began to
be felt that the self-effacement of the returned pressmen was
being carried to a pedantic length. Foreman compositors, advertisement clerks, and other members of the non-editorial
staff, who had, of course, taken no part in the great trek, found
it as impossible to get into direct communication with the editor and his satellites now that they had returned as when they
had been excusably inaccessible in Central Asia. The sulky,
overworked office-boy, who was the one connecting link between the editorial brain and the business departments of the
paper, sardonically explained the new aloofness as the 'Yark-
and manner.' Most of the reporters and sub-editors seemed to
have been dismissed in autocratic fashion since their return and
new ones engaged by letter; to these the editor and his immediate associates remained an unseen presence, issuing its instructions solely through the medium of curt type-written notes.
Something mystic and Tibetan and forbidden had replaced the
human bustle and democratic simplicity of pre-migration days,
and the same experience was encountered by those who made

social overtures to the returned wanderers. The most brilliant hostess of Twentieth Century London flung the pearl of her hospitality into the unresponsive trough of the editorial letter-box; it seemed as if nothing short of a Royal command would drag the hermit-souled *revenants* from their self-imposed seclusion. People began to talk unkindly of the effect of high altitudes and Eastern atmosphere on minds and temperaments unused to such luxuries. The Yarkand manner was not popular."

"And the contents of the paper," said the nephew, "did they show the influence of the new style?"

"Ah!" said Sir Lulworth, "that was the exciting thing. In home affairs, social questions, and the ordinary events of the day not much change was noticeable. A certain Oriental carelessness seemed to have crept into the editorial department, and perhaps a note of lassitude not unnatural in the work of men who had returned from what has been a fairly arduous journey. The aforetime standard of excellence was scarcely maintained, but at any rate the general lines of policy and outlook were not departed from. It was in the realm of foreign affairs that a startling change took place. Blunt, forcible, outspoken articles appeared, couched in language which nearly turned the autumn manœuvres of six important Powers into mobilizations. Whatever else the *Daily Intelligencer* had learned in the East, it had not acquired the art of diplomatic ambiguity. The man in the street enjoyed the articles and bought the paper as he had never bought it before; the men in Downing Street took a different view. The Foreign Secretary, hitherto accounted a rather reticent man, became positively garrulous in the course of perpetually disavowing the sentiments expressed in the *Daily Intelligencer's* leaders; and then one day the Government came to the conclusion that something definite and drastic must be done. A deputation, consisting of the Prime Minister, the Foreign Secretary, four leading financiers, and a well-known Nonconformist divine, made its way to the offices of the paper. At the door leading to the editorial department the way was barred by a nervous but defiant office-boy.

" 'You can't see the editor nor any of the staff,' he announced.

" 'We insist on seeing the editor or some responsible person,' said the Prime Minister, and the deputation forced its way in. The boy had spoken truly; there was no one to be seen. In the whole suite of rooms there was no sign of human life.

" 'Where is the editor?' 'Or the foreign editor?' 'Or the chief leader-writer?' 'Or anybody?'

"In answer to the shower of questions the boy unlocked a drawer and produced a strange-looking envelope, which bore a Khokand postmark, and a date of some seven or eight months back. It contained a scrap of paper on which was written the following message:

" 'Entire party captured by brigand tribe on homeward journey. Quarter of million demanded as ransom, but would probably take less. Inform Government, relations, and friends.'

"There followed the signatures of the principal members of the party and instructions as to how and where the money was to be paid.

"The letter had been directed to the office-boy-in-charge, who had quietly suppressed it. No one is a hero to one's own office-boy, and he evidently considered that a quarter of a million was an unwarrantable outlay for such a doubtfully advantageous object as the repatriation of an errant newspaper staff. So he drew the editorial and other salaries, forged what signatures were necessary, engaged new reporters, did what sub-editing he could, and made as much use as possible of the large accumulation of special articles that was held in reserve for emergencies. The articles on foreign affairs were entirely his own composition.

"Of course the whole thing had to be kept as quiet as possible; an interim staff, pledged to secrecy, was appointed to keep the paper going till the pining captives could be sought out, ransomed, and brought home, in twos and threes to escape notice, and gradually things were put back on their old footing. The articles on foreign affairs reverted to the wonted traditions of the paper."

"But," interposed the nephew, "how on earth did the boy account to the relatives all those months for the non-appearance—"

"That," said Sir Lulworth, "was the most brilliant stroke of all. To the wife or nearest relative of each of the missing men he forwarded a letter, copying the handwriting of the supposed writer as well as he could, and making excuses about vile pens and ink; in each letter he told the same story, varying only the locality, to the effect that the writer, alone of the whole party, was unable to tear himself away from the wild liberty and allurements of Eastern life, and was going to spend several months roaming in some selected region. Many of the wives started off immediately in pursuit of their errant husbands, and it took the Government a considerable time and much trouble to reclaim them from their fruitless quests along the banks of the Oxus, the Gobi Desert, the Orenburg steppe, and other outlandish places. One of them, I believe, is still lost somewhere in the Tigris Valley."

"And the boy?"

"Is still in journalism."

THE BYZANTINE OMELETTE

SOPHIE CHATTEL-MONKHEIM was a Socialist by conviction and a Chattel-Monkheim by marriage. The particular member of that wealthy family whom she had married was rich, even as his relatives counted riches. Sophie had very advanced and decided views as to the distribution of money: it was a pleasing and fortunate circumstance that she also had the money. When she inveighed eloquently against the evils of capitalism at drawing-room meetings and Fabian conferences she was conscious of a comfortable feeling that the system, with all its inequalities and iniquities, would probably last her time. It is one of the consolations of middle-aged reformers that the good they inculcate must live after them if it is to live at all.

On a certain spring evening, somewhere towards the dinner-hour, Sophie sat tranquilly between her mirror and her maid, undergoing the process of having her hair built into an elaborate reflection of the prevailing fashion. She was hedged round with a great peace, the peace of one who has attained a desired end with much effort and perseverance, and who has found it still eminently desirable in its attainment. The Duke of Syria had consented to come beneath her roof as a guest, was even now installed beneath her roof, and would shortly be sitting at her dining-table. As a good Socialist, Sophie disapproved of social distinctions, and derided the idea of a princely caste, but if there were to be these artificial gradations of rank and dignity she was pleased and anxious to have an exalted specimen of an exalted order included in her house-party. She was broad-minded enough to love the sinner while hating the sin——not that she entertained any warm feeling of personal affection for the Duke of Syria, who was a comparative stranger, but still, as Duke of Syria, he was very, very welcome beneath her roof. She could not have explained why, but no one was likely to ask her for an explanation, and most hostesses envied her.

"You must surpass yourself tonight, Richardson," she said complacently to her maid; "I must be looking my very best. We must all surpass ourselves."

The maid said nothing, but from the concentrated look in her eyes and the deft play of her fingers it was evident that she was beset with the ambition to surpass herself.

A knock came at the door, a quiet but peremptory knock, as of some one who would not be denied.

"Go and see who it is," said Sophie; "it may be something about the wine."

Richardson held a hurried conference with an invisible messenger at the door; when she returned there was noticeable a curious listlessness in place of her hitherto alert manner.

"What is it?" asked Sophie.

"The household servants have 'downed tools,' madame," said Richardson.

"Downed tools!" exclaimed Sophie; "do you mean to say they've gone on strike?"

"Yes, madame," said Richardson, adding the information: "It's Gaspare that the trouble is about."

"Gaspare?" said Sophie wonderingly; "the emergency chef! The omelette specialist!"

"Yes, madame. Before he became an omelette specialist he was a valet, and he was one of the strike-breakers in the great strike at Lord Grimford's two years ago. As soon as the household staff here learned that you had engaged him they resolved to 'down tools' as a protest. They haven't got any grievance against you personally, but they demand that Gaspare should be immediately dismissed."

"But," protested Sophie, "he is the only man in England who understands how to make a Byzantine omelette. I engaged him specially for the Duke of Syria's visit, and it would be impossible to replace him at short notice. I should have to send to Paris, and the Duke loves Byzantine omelettes. It was the one thing we talked about coming from the station."

"He was one of the strike-breakers at Lord Grimford's," reiterated Richardson.

"This is too awful," said Sophie; "a strike of servants at a moment like this, with the Duke of Syria staying in the house. Something must be done immediately. Quick, finish my hair and I'll go and see what I can do to bring them round."

"I can't finish your hair, madame," said Richardson quietly, but with immense decision. "I belong to the union and I can't do another half-minute's work till the strike is settled. I'm sorry to be disobliging."

"But this is inhuman!" exclaimed Sophie tragically; "I've always been a model mistress and I've refused to employ any but union servants, and this is the result. I can't finish my hair myself; I don't know how to. What am I to do? It's wicked!"

"Wicked is the word," said Richardson; "I'm a good Conservative, and I've no patience with this Socialist foolery, asking your pardon. It's tyranny, that's what it is, all along the line, but I've my living to make, same as other people, and I've got to belong to the union. I couldn't touch another hair-pin without a strike permit, not if you was to double my wages."

The door burst open and Catherine Malsom raged into the room.

"Here's a nice affair," she screamed, "a strike of household servants without a moment's warning, and I'm left like this! I can't appear in public in this condition."

After a very hasty scrutiny Sophie assured her that she could not.

"Have they *all* struck?" she asked her maid.

"Not the kitchen staff," said Richardson, "they belong to a different union."

"Dinner at least will be assured," said Sophie, "that is something to be thankful for."

"Dinner!" snorted Catherine, "what on earth is the good of dinner when none of us will be able to appear at it? Look at your hair—and look at me! or rather, don't."

"I know it's difficult to manage without a maid; can't your husband be any help to you?" asked Sophie despairingly.

"Henry? He's in worse case than any of us. His man is the only person who really understands that ridiculous new-fangled Turkish bath that he insists on taking with him every-where."

"Surely he could do without a Turkish bath for one eve-ning," said Sophie; "I can't appear without hair, but a Turk-ish bath is a luxury."

"My good woman," said Catherine, speaking with a fear-ful intensity, "Henry was *in* the bath when the strike started. *In* it, do you understand? He's there now."

"Can't he get out?"

"He doesn't know how to. Every time he pulls the lever marked 'release' he only releases hot steam. There are two kinds of steam in the bath, 'bearable' and 'scarcely bearable';

he has released them both. By this time I'm probably a widow."

"I simply can't send away Gaspare," wailed Sophie; "I should never be able to secure another omelette specialist."

"Any difficulty that I may experience in securing another husband is of course a trifle beneath any one's consideration," said Catherine bitterly.

Sophie capitulated. "Go," she said to Richardson, "and tell the Strike Committee, or whoever are directing this affair, that Gaspare is herewith dismissed. And ask Gaspare to see me presently in the library, when I will pay him what is due to him and make what excuses I can; and then fly back and finish my hair."

Some half an hour later Sophie marshalled her guests in the Grand Salon preparatory to the formal march to the dining-room. Except that Henry Malsom was of the ripe raspberry tint that one sometimes sees at private theatricals representing the human complexion, there was little outward sign among those assembled of the crisis that had just been encountered and surmounted. But the tension had been too stupefying while it lasted not to leave some mental effects behind it. Sophie talked at random to her illustrious guest, and found her eyes straying with increasing frequency towards the great doors through which would presently come the blessed announcement that dinner was served. Now and again she glanced mirror-ward at the reflection of her wonderfully coiffed hair, as an insurance underwriter might gaze thankfully at an overdue vessel that had ridden safely into harbour in the wake of a devastating hurricane. Then the doors opened and the welcome figure of the butler entered the room. But he made no general announcement of a banquet in readiness, and the doors closed behind him; his message was for Sophie alone.

"There is no dinner, madame," he said gravely; "the kitchen staff have 'downed tools.' Gaspare belongs to the Union of Cooks and Kitchen Employés, and as soon as they heard of his summary dismissal at a moment's notice they struck work. They demand his instant reinstatement and an apology to the union. I may add, madame, that they are very firm; I've been obliged even to hand back the dinner rolls that were already on the table."

After the lapse of eighteen months Sophie Chattel-Monk-heim is beginning to go about again among her old haunts and associates, but she still has to be very careful. The doctors will not let her attend anything at all exciting, such as a drawing-room meeting or a Fabian conference; it is doubtful, indeed, whether she wants to.

THE FEAST OF NEMESIS

"IT'S a good thing that Saint Valentine's Day has dropped out of vogue," said Mrs. Thackenbury; "what with Christmas and New Year and Easter, not to speak of birth-days, there are quite enough remembrance days as it is. I tried to save myself trouble at Christmas by just sending flowers to all my friends, but it wouldn't work; Gertrude has eleven hot-houses and about thirty gardeners, so it would have been ridiculous to send flowers to her, and Milly has just started a florist's shop, so it was equally out of the question there. The stress of having to decide in a hurry what to give to Gertrude and Milly just when I thought I'd got the whole question nicely off my mind completely ruined my Christmas, and then the awful monotony of the letters of thanks: 'Thank you so much for your lovely flowers. It was so good of you to think of me.' Of course in the majority of cases I hadn't thought about the recipients at all; their names were down in my list of 'people who must not be left out.' If I trusted to remembering them there would be some awful sins of omission."

"The trouble is," said Clovis to his aunt, "all these days of intrusive remembrance harp so persistently on one aspect of human nature and entirely ignore the other; that is why they become so perfunctory and artificial. At Christmas and New Year you are emboldened and encouraged by convention to send gushing messages of optimistic goodwill and servile affec-

tion to people whom you would scarcely ask to lunch unless
some one else had failed you at the last moment; if you are
supping at a restaurant on New Year's Eve you are permitted
and expected to join hands and sing 'For Auld Lang Syne'
with strangers whom you have never seen before and never
want to see again. But no licence is allowed in the opposite
direction."

"Opposite direction; what opposite direction?" queried Mrs.
Thackenbury.

"There is no outlet for demonstrating your feelings towards
people whom you simply loathe. That is really the crying
need of our modern civilization. Just think how jolly it would
be if a recognized day were set apart for the paying off of old
scores and grudges, a day when one could lay oneself out to
be gracefully vindictive to a carefully treasured list of 'people who must not be let off.' I remember when I was at a
private school we had one day, the last Monday of the term I
think it was, consecrated to the settlement of feuds and
grudges; of course we did not appreciate it as much as it deserved, because after all, any day of the term could be used
for that purpose. Still, if one had chastised a smaller boy for
being cheeky weeks before, one was always permitted on that
day to recall the episode to his memory by chastising him again.
That is what the French call reconstructing the crime."

"I should call it reconstructing the punishment," said Mrs.
Thackenbury; "and, anyhow, I don't see how you could introduce a system of primitive school-boy vengeance into civilized adult life. We haven't outgrown our passions, but we are
supposed to have learned how to keep them within strictly
decorous limits."

"Of course the thing would have to be done furtively and
politely," said Clovis; "the charm of it would be that it would
never be perfunctory like the other thing. Now, for instance,
you say to yourself: 'I must show the Webleys some attention
at Christmas, they were kind to dear Bertie at Bournemouth,'
and you send them a calendar, and daily for six days after
Christmas the male Webley asks the female Webley if she has
remembered to thank you for the calendar you sent them.

Well, transplant that idea to the other and more human side of your nature, and say to yourself: 'Next Thursday is Nemesis Day; what on earth can I do to those odious people next door who made such an absurd fuss when Ping Yang bit their youngest child?' Then you'd get up awfully early on the allotted day and climb over into their garden and dig for truffles on their tennis court with a good gardening fork, choosing, of course, that part of the court that was screened from observation by the laurel bushes. You wouldn't find any truffles but you would find a great peace, such as no amount of present-giving could ever bestow."

"I shouldn't," said Mrs. Thackenbury, though her air of protest sounded a bit forced; "I should feel rather a worm for doing such a thing."

"You exaggerate the power of upheaval which a worm would be able to bring into play in the limited time available," said Clovis; "if you put in a strenuous ten minutes with a really useful fork, the result ought to suggest the operations of an unusually masterful mole or a badger in a hurry."

"They might guess I had done it," said Mrs. Thackenbury.

"Of course they would," said Clovis; "that would be half the satisfaction of the thing, just as you like people at Christmas to know what presents or cards you've sent them. The thing would be much easier to manage, of course, when you were on outwardly friendly terms with the object of your dislike. That greedy little Agnes Blaik, for instance, who thinks of nothing but her food, it would be quite simple to ask her to a picnic in some wild woodland spot and lose her just before lunch was served; when you found her again every morsel of food could have been eaten up."

"It would require no ordinary human strategy to lose Agnes Blaik when luncheon was imminent: in fact, I don't believe it could be done."

"Then have all the other guests, people whom you dislike, and lose the luncheon. It could have been sent by accident in the wrong direction."

"It would be a ghastly picnic," said Mrs. Thackenbury.

"For them, but not for you," said Clovis; "you would have

had an early and comforting lunch before you started, and you could improve the occasion by mentioning in detail the items of the missing banquet—the lobster Newburg and the egg mayonnaise, and the curry that was to have been heated in a chafing-dish. Agnes Blaik would be delirious long before you got to the list of wines, and in the long interval of waiting before they had quite abandoned hope of the lunch turning up, you could induce them to play silly games, such as that idiotic one of 'the Lord Mayor's dinner-party,' in which every one has to choose the name of a dish and do something futile when it is called out. In this case they would probably burst into tears when their dish is mentioned. It would be a heavenly picnic."

Mrs. Thackenbury was silent for a moment; she was probably making a mental list of the people she would like to invite to the Duke Humphrey picnic. Presently she asked: "And that odious young man, Waldo Plubley, who is always coddling himself—have you thought of anything that one could do to him?" Evidently she was beginning to see the possibilities of Nemesis Day.

"If there was anything like a general observance of the festival," said Clovis, "Waldo would be in such demand that you would have to bespeak him weeks beforehand, and even then, if there were an east wind blowing or a cloud or two in the sky he might be too careful of his precious self to come out. It would be rather jolly if you could lure him into a hammock in the orchard, just near the spot where there is a wasps' nest every summer. A comfortable hammock on a warm afternoon would appeal to his indolent tastes, and then, when he was getting drowsy, a lighted fusee thrown into the nest would bring the wasps out in an indignant mass. and they would soon find a 'home away from home' on Waldo's fat body. It takes some doing to get out of a hammock in a hurry."

"They might sting him to death," protested Mrs. Thackenbury.

"Waldo is one of those people who would be enormously improved by death," said Clovis; "but if you didn't want to go as far as that, you could have some wet straw ready to hand, and set it alight under the hammock at the same time that the fusee was thrown into the nest; the smoke would keep all but the most militant of the wasps just outside the stinging line, and as long as Waldo remained within its protection he would escape serious damage, and could be eventually restored to his mother, kippered all over and swollen in places, but still perfectly recognizable."

"His mother would be my enemy for life," said Mrs. Thackenbury.

"That would be one greeting less to exchange at Christmas," said Clovis.

THE DREAMER

IT was the season of sales. The august establishment of Walpurgis and Nettlepink had lowered its prices for an entire week as a concession to trade observances, much as an Archduchess might protestingly contract an attack of influenza for the unsatisfactory reason that influenza was locally prevalent. Adela Chemping, who considered herself in some measure superior to the allurements of an ordinary bargain sale, made a point of attending the reduction week at Walpurgis and Nettlepink's.

"I'm not a bargain hunter," she said, "but I like to go
~~~ ~~~ ~~~ are."

dhat beneath her surface strength of char-
..owed a gracious undercurrent of human weakness.

With a view to providing herself with a male escort Mrs. Chemping had invited her youngest nephew to accompany her on the first day of the shopping expedition, throwing in the additional allurement of a cinematograph theatre and the prospect of light refreshment. As Cyprian was not yet eighteen, she hoped he might not have reached that stage in masculine development when parcel-carrying is looked on as a thing abhorrent.

"Meet me just outside the floral department," she wrote to him, "and don't be a moment later than eleven."

Cyprian was a boy who carried with him through early life the wondering look of a dreamer, the eyes of one who sees things that are not visible to ordinary mortals, and invests the commonplace things of this world with qualities unsuspected by plainer folk—the eyes of a poet or a house agent. He was quietly dressed—that sartorial quietude which frequently accompanies early adolescence, and is usually attributed by novel-writers to the influence of a widowed mother. His air was brushed back in a smoothness as of ribbon seaweed and seamed with a narrow furrow that scarcely aimed at being a parting. His aunt particularly noted this item of his toilet when they met at the appointed rendezvous, because he was standing waiting for her bareheaded.

"Where is your hat?" she asked.

"I didn't bring one with me," he replied.

Adela Chemping was slightly scandalized.

"You are not going to be what they call a Nut, are you?" she inquired with some anxiety, partly with the idea that a Nut would be an extravagance which her sister's small household would scarcely be justified in incurring, partly, perhaps, with the instinctive apprehension that a Nut, even in its embryo stage, would refuse to carry parcels.

Cyprian looked at her with his wondering, dreamy eyes.

"I didn't bring a hat," he said, "because it is such a nuisance when one is shopping; I mean it is so awkward if one meets any one one knows and has to take one's hat off when one's hands are full of parcels. If one hasn't got a hat on one can't take it off."

Mrs. Chemping sighed with great relief; her worst fear had been laid at rest.

"It is more orthodox to wear a hat," she observed, and then turned her attention briskly to the business in hand.

"We will go first to the table-linen counter," she said, leading the way in that direction; "I should like to look at some napkins."

The wondering look deepened in Cyprian's eyes as he followed his aunt; he belonged to a generation that is supposed to be over-fond of the rôle of mere spectator, but looking at napkins that one did not mean to buy was a pleasure beyond his comprehension. Mrs. Chemping held one or two napkins up to the light and stared fixedly at them, as though she half expected to find some revolutionary cypher written on them in scarcely visible ink; then she suddenly broke away in the direction of the glassware department.

"Millicent asked me to get her a couple of decanters if there were any going really cheap," she explained on the way, "and I really do want a salad bowl. I can come back to the napkins later on."

She handled and scrutinized a large number of decanters and a long series of salad bowls, and finally bought seven chrysanthemum vases.

"No one uses that kind of vase nowadays," she informed Cyprian, "but they will do for presents next Christmas."

Two sunshades that were marked down to a price that Mrs. Chemping considered absurdly cheap were added to her purchases.

"One of them will do for Ruth Colson; she is going out to the Malay States, and a sunshade will always be useful there. And I must get her some thin writing paper. It takes up no room in one's baggage."

Mrs. Chemping bought stacks of writing paper; it was so cheap, and it went so flat in a trunk or portmanteau. She also bought a few envelopes—envelopes somehow seemed rather an extravagance compared with notepaper.

"Do you think Ruth will like blue or grey paper?" she asked Cyprian.

"Grey," said Cyprian, who had never met the lady in question.

"Have you any mauve notepaper of this quality?" Adela asked the assistant.

"We haven't any mauve," said the assistant, "but we've two shades of green and a darker shade of grey."

Mrs. Chemping inspected the greens and the darker grey, and chose the blue.

"Now we can have some lunch," she said.

Cyprian behaved in an exemplary fashion in the refreshment department, and cheerfully accepted a fish cake and a mince pie and a small cup of coffee as adequate restoratives after two hours of concentrated shopping. He was adamant, however, in resisting his aunt's suggestion that a hat should be bought for him at the counter where men's head-wear was being disposed of at temptingly reduced prices.

"I've got as many hats as I want at home," he said, "and besides, it rumples one's hair so, trying them on."

Perhaps he was going to develop into a Nut after all. It was a disquieting symptom that he left all the parcels in charge of the cloak-room attendant.

"We shall be getting more parcels presently," he said, "so we need not collect these till we have finished our shopping."

His aunt was doubtfully appeased; some of the pleasure and excitement of a shopping expedition seemed to evaporate when one was deprived of immediate personal contact with one's purchases.

"I'm going to look at those napkins again," she said, as they descended the stairs to the ground floor. "You need not come," she added, as the dreaming look in the boy's eyes changed for a moment into one of mute protest, "you can meet me afterwards in the cutlery department; I've just remembered that I haven't a corkscrew in the house that can be depended on."

Cyprian was not to be found in the cutlery department when his aunt in due course arrived there, but in the crush and bustle of anxious shoppers and busy attendants it was an easy matter to miss any one. It was in the leather goods department some quarter of an hour later that Adela Chemping caught sight of her nephew, separated from her by a rampart of suitcases and portmanteaux and hemmed in by the jostling crush of human beings that now invaded every corner of the great shopping emporium. She was just in time to witness a pardonable but rather embarrassing mistake on the part of a lady who had wriggled her way with unstayable determination towards the bareheaded Cyprian, and was now breathlessly demanding the sale price of a handbag which had taken her fancy.

"There now," exclaimed Adela to herself, "she takes him

for one of the shop assistants because he hasn't got a hat on.
I wonder it hasn't happened before."

Perhaps it had. Cyprian, at any rate, seemed neither startled
nor embarrassed by the error into which the good lady had
fallen. Examining the ticket on the bag, he announced in a
clear, dispassionate voice:

"Black seal, thirty-four shillings marked down to twenty-
eight. As a matter of fact, we are clearing them out at a
special reduction price of twenty-six shillings. They are going
off rather fast."

"I'll take it," said the lady, eagerly digging some coins out
of her purse.

"Will you take it as it is?" asked Cyprian; "it will be a
matter of a few minutes to get it wrapped up, there is such
a crush."

"Never mind, I'll take it as it is," said the purchaser, clutching her treasure and counting the money into Cyprian's palm.

Several kind strangers helped Adela into the open air.

"It's the crush and the heat," said one sympathizer to another; "it's enough to turn any one giddy."

When she next came across Cyprian he was standing in the
crowd that pushed and jostled around the counters of the
book department. The dream look was deeper than ever in
his eyes. He had just sold two books of devotion to an elderly
Canon.

THE QUINCE TREE

"I'VE just been to see old Betsy Mullen," announced Vera
to her aunt, Mrs. Bebberly Cumble; "she seems in rather
a bad way about her rent. She owes about fifteen weeks of it,
and says she doesn't know where any of it is to come from."

"Betsy Mullen always is in difficulties with her rent, and
the more people help her with it the less she troubles about it,"
said the aunt. "I certainly am not going to assist her any more.
The fact is, she will have to go into a smaller and cheaper
cottage; there are several to be had at the other end of the

village for half the rent that she is paying, or supposed to be paying, now. I told her a year ago that she ought to move."

"But she wouldn't get such a nice garden anywhere else," protested Vera, "and there's such a jolly quince tree in the corner. I don't suppose there's another quince tree in the whole parish. And she never makes any quince jam; I think to have a quince tree and not to make quince jam shows such strength of character. Oh, she can't possibly move away from that garden."

"When one is sixteen," said Mrs. Bebberly Cumble severely, "one talks of things being impossible which are merely uncongenial. It is not only possible but it is desirable that Betsy Mullen should move into smaller quarters; she has scarcely enough furniture to fill that big cottage."

"As far as value goes," said Vera after a short pause, "there is more in Betsy's cottage than in any other house for miles round."

"Nonsense," said the aunt; "she parted with whatever old china ware she had long ago."

"I'm not talking about anything that belongs to Betsy herself," said Vera darkly; "but of course, you don't know what I know, and I don't suppose I ought to tell you."

"You must tell me at once," exclaimed the aunt, her senses leaping into alertness like those of a terrier suddenly exchanging a bored drowsiness for the lively anticipation of an immediate rat hunt.

"I'm perfectly certain that I oughtn't to tell you anything about it," said Vera, "but, then, I often do things that I oughtn't to do."

"I should be the last person to suggest that you should do anything that you ought not to do——" began Mrs. Bebberly Cumble impressively.

"And I am always swayed by the last person who speaks to me," admitted Vera, "so I'll do what I ought not to do and tell you."

Mrs. Bebberly Cumble thrust a very pardonable sense of exasperation into the background of her mind and demanded impatiently:

"What is there in Betsy Mullen's cottage that you are making such a fuss about?"

"It's hardly fair to say that *I've* made a fuss about it," said Vera; "this is the first time I've mentioned the matter, but there's been no end of trouble and mystery and newspaper speculation about it. It's rather amusing to think of the columns of conjecture in the Press and the police and detectives hunting about everywhere at home and abroad, and all the while that innocent-looking little cottage has held the secret."

"You don't mean to say it's the Louvre picture, La Something or other, the woman with the smile, that disappeared about two years ago?" exclaimed the aunt with rising excitement.

"Oh, no, not that," said Vera, "but something quite as important and just as mysterious—if anything, rather more scandalous."

"Not the Dublin—?"

Vera nodded.

"The whole jolly lot of them."

"In Betsy's cottage? Incredible!"

"Of course Betsy hasn't an idea as to what they are," said Vera; "she just knows that they are something valuable and that she must keep quiet about them. I found out quite by accident what they were and how they came to be there. You see, the people who had them were at their wits' end to know where to stow them away for safe keeping, and some one who was motoring through the village was struck by the snug loneliness of the cottage and thought it would be just the thing. Mrs. Lamper arranged the matter with Betsy and smuggled the things in."

"Mrs. Lamper?"

"Yes; she does a lot of district visiting, you know."

"I am quite aware that she takes soup and flannel and improving literature to the poorer cottages," said Mrs. Bebberly Cumble, "but that is hardly the same sort of thing as disposing of stolen goods, and she must have known something about their history; any one who reads the papers, even casually, must have been aware of the theft, and I should think the things were not hard to recognize. Mrs. Lamper has always had the reputation of being a very conscientious woman."

"Of course she was screening some one else," said Vera. "A remarkable feature of the affair is the extraordinary number of quite respectable people who have involved themselves in its meshes by trying to shield others. You would be really astonished if you knew some of the names of the individuals mixed up in it, and I don't suppose a tithe of them knew who the original culprits were; and now I've got you entangled in the mess by letting you into the secret of the cottage."

"You most certainly have not entangled me," said Mrs. Bebberly Cumble indignantly. "I have no intention of shielding anybody. The police must know about it at once; a theft is a theft, whoever is involved. If respectable people choose to turn themselves into receivers and disposers of stolen goods, well, they've ceased to be respectable, that's all. I shall telephone immediately—"

"Oh, aunt," said Vera reproachfully, "it would break the poor Canon's heart if Cuthbert were to be involved in a scandal of this sort. You know it would."

"Cuthbert involved! How can you say such things when you know how much we all think of him?"

"Of course I know you think a lot of him, and that he's engaged to marry Beatrice, and that it will be a frightfully good match, and that he's your ideal of what a son-in-law ought to be. All the same, it was Cuthbert's idea to stow the things away in the cottage, and it was his motor that brought them. He was only doing it to help his friend Pegginson, you know—the Quaker man, who is always agitating for a smaller Navy. I forget how he got involved in it. I warned you that there were lots of quite respectable people mixed up in it, didn't I? That's what I meant when I said it would be impossible for old Betsy to leave the cottage; the things take up a good bit of room, and she couldn't go carrying them about with her other goods and chattels without attracting notice. Of course if she were to fall ill and die it would be equally unfortunate. Her mother lived to be over ninety, she tells me, so with due care and an absence of worry she ought to last for another dozen years at least. By that time perhaps some other arrangements will have been made for disposing of the wretched things."

"I shall speak to Cuthbert about it—after the wedding," said Mrs. Bebberly Cumble.

. . . .

"The wedding isn't till next year," said Vera, in recounting the story to her best girl friend, "and meanwhile old Betsy is living rent free, with soup twice a week and my aunt's doctor to see her whenever she has a finger ache."

"But how on earth did you get to know about it all?" asked her friend, in admiring wonder.

"It was a mystery—" said Vera.

"Of course it was a mystery, a mystery that baffled everybody. What beats me is how you found out—"

"Oh, about the jewels? I invented that part," explained Vera; "I mean the mystery was where old Betsy's arrears of rent were to come from; and she would have hated leaving that jolly quince tree."

THE FORBIDDEN BUZZARDS

"IS matchmaking at all in your line?"

Hugo Peterby asked the question with a certain amount of personal interest.

"I don't specialize in it," said Clovis; "it's all right while you're doing it, but the after-effects are sometimes so disconcerting—the mute reproachful looks of the people you've aided and abetted in matrimonial experiments. It's as bad as selling a man a horse with half a dozen latent vices and watching him discover them piecemeal in the course of the hunting season. I suppose you're thinking of the Coulterneb girl. She's certainly jolly, and quite all right as far as looks go, and I believe a certain amount of money adheres to her. What I don't see is how you will ever manage to propose to her. In all the time I've known her I don't remember her to have stopped talking for three consecutive minutes. You'll have to race her six times round the grass paddock for a bet, and then blurt your proposal out before she's got her wind back. The paddock is laid up for hay, but if you're really in love with her you won't let a consideration of that sort stop you, especially as it's not your hay."

"I think I could manage the proposing part right enough," said Hugo, "if I could count on being left alone with her for four or five hours. The trouble is that I'm not likely to get anything like that amount of grace. That fellow Lanner is showing signs of interesting himself in the same quarter. He's quite heartbreakingly rich and is rather a swell in his way; in fact, our hostess is obviously a bit flattered at having him here. If she gets wind of the fact that he's inclined to be attracted by Betty Coulterneb she'll think it a splendid match and throw them into each other's arms all day long, and then where will my opportunities come in? My one anxiety is to keep him out of the girl's way as much as possible, and if you could help me—"

"If you want me to trot Lanner round the countryside, inspecting alleged Roman remains and studying local methods of bee culture and crop raising, I'm afraid I can't oblige you," said Clovis. "You see, he's taken something like an aversion to me since the other night in the smoking-room."

"What happened in the smoking-room?"

"He trotted out some well-worn chestnut as the latest thing in good stories, and I remarked, quite innocently, that I never could remember whether it was George II. or James II. who was so fond of that particular story, and now he regards me with politely draped dislike. I'll do my best for you, if the opportunity arises, but it will have to be in a roundabout, impersonal manner."

.   .   .   .   .   .

"It's so nice having Mr. Lanner here," confided Mrs. Olston to Clovis the next afternoon; "he's always been engaged when I've asked him before. Such a nice man; he really ought to be married to some nice girl. Between you and me, I have an idea that he came down here for a certain reason."

"I've had much the same idea," said Clovis, lowering his voice; "in fact, I'm almost certain of it."

"You mean he's attracted by—" began Mrs. Olston eagerly.

"I mean he's here for what he can get," said Clovis.

"For what he can *get?*" said the hostess with a touch of indignation in her voice; "what do you mean? He's a very rich man. What should he want to get here?"

"He has one ruling passion," said Clovis, "and there's something he can get here that is not to be had for love nor for money anywhere else in the country, as far as I know."

"But what? Whatever do you mean? What is his ruling passion?"

"Egg-collecting," said Clovis. "He has agents all over the world getting rare eggs for him, and his collection is one of the finest in Europe; but his great ambition is to collect his treasures personally. He stops at no expense nor trouble to achieve that end."

"Good heavens! The buzzards, the rough-legged buzzards!" exclaimed Mrs. Olston; "you don't think he's going to raid their nest?"

"What do you think yourself?" asked Clovis; "the only pair of rough-legged buzzards known to breed in this country are nesting in your woods. Very few people know about them, but as a member of the league for protecting rare birds that information would be at his disposal. I came down in the train with him, and I noticed that a bulky volume of Dresser's *Birds of Europe* was one of the requisites that he had packed in his travelling-kit. It was the volume dealing with short-winged hawks and buzzards."

Clovis believed that if a lie was worth telling it was worth telling well.

"This is appalling," said Mrs. Olston; "my husband would never forgive me if anything happened to those birds. They've been seen about the woods for the last year or two, but this is the first time they've nested. As you say, they are almost the only pair known to be breeding in the whole of Great Britain; and now their nest is going to be harried by a guest staying under my roof. I must do something to stop it. Do you think if I appealed to him——?"

Clovis laughed.

"There is a story going about, which I fancy is true in most of its details, of something that happened not long ago somewhere on the coast of the Sea of Marmora, in which our friend had a hand. A Syrian nightjar, or some such bird, was known to be breeding in the olive gardens of a rich Armenian, who for some reason or other wouldn't allow Lanner to go in and take the eggs though he offered cash down for the permission. The Armenian was found beaten nearly to death a day or two later, and his fences levelled. It was assumed to be a case of Mussulman aggression, and noted as such in all the Consular reports, but the eggs are in the Lanner collection. No, I don't think I should appeal to his better feelings if I were you."

"I must do something," said Mrs. Olston tearfully; "my husband's parting words when he went off to Norway were an injunction to see that those birds were not disturbed, and he's asked about them every time he's written. Do suggest something."

"I was going to suggest picketing," said Clovis.

"Picketing! You mean setting guards round the birds?"

"No; round Lanner. He can't find his way through those woods by night, and you could arrange that you or Evelyn or Jack or the German governess should be by his side in relays all day long. A fellow guest he could get rid of, but he couldn't very well shake off members of the household, and even the most determined collector would hardly go climbing after forbidden buzzards' eggs with a German governess hanging round his neck, so to speak."

Lanner, who had been lazily watching for an opportunity for prosecuting his courtship of the Coulterneb girl, found presently that his chances of getting her to himself for ten minutes even were non-existent. If the girl was ever alone he never was. His hostess had changed suddenly, as far as he was concerned, from the desirable type that lets her guests do nothing in the way that best pleases them, to the sort that drags them over the ground like so many harrows. She showed him the herb garden and the greenhouses, the village church, some water-colour sketches that her sister had done in Corsica, and the place where it was hoped that celery would grow later in the year. He was shown all the Aylesbury ducklings and the row of wooden hives where there would have been bees if there had not been bee disease. He was also taken to the end of a long lane and shown a distant mound whereon local tradition reported that the Danes had once pitched a camp. And when his hostess had to desert him temporarily for other duties he would find Evelyn walking solemnly by his side. Evelyn was fourteen and talked chiefly about good and evil, and of how much one might accomplish in the way of regenerating the world if one was thoroughly determined to do one's utmost. It was generally rather a relief when she was displaced by Jack, who was nine years old, and talked exclusively about the Balkan War without throwing any fresh light on its political or military history. The German governess told Lanner more about Schiller than he had ever heard in his life about any one person; it was perhaps his own fault for having told her that he was not interested in Goethe. When the governess went off picket duty the hostess was again on hand with a not-to-be-gainsaid invitation to visit the cottage of an old woman who remembered Charles James Fox; the woman had been dead for two or three years, but the cottage was still there. Lanner was called back to town earlier than he had originally intended.

Hugo did not bring off his affair with Betty Coulterneb. Whether she refused him or whether, as was more generally supposed, he did not get a chance of saying three consecutive words, has never been exactly ascertained. Anyhow, she is still the jolly Coulterneb girl.

The buzzards successfully reared two young ones, which were shot by a local hairdresser.

THE STAKE

"RONNIE is a great trial to me," said Mrs. Attray plaintively. "Only eighteen years old last February and already a confirmed gambler. I am sure I don't know where he inherits it from; his father never touched cards, and you know how little I play—a game of bridge on Wednesday afternoons in the winter, for threepence a hundred, and even that I shouldn't do if it wasn't that Edith always wants a fourth and would be certain to ask that detestable Jenkinham woman if she couldn't get me. I would much rather sit and talk any day than play bridge; cards are such a waste of time, I think. But as to Ronnie, bridge and baccarat and poker-patience are positively all that he thinks about. Of course I've done my best to stop it; I've asked the Norridrums not to let him play cards when he's over there, but you might as well ask the Atlantic Ocean to keep quiet for a crossing as expect them to bother about a mother's natural anxieties."

"Why do you let him go there?" asked Eleanor Saxelby.

"My dear," said Mrs. Attray, "I don't want to offend them. After all, they are my landlords and I have to look to them for anything I want done about the place; they were very accommodating about the new roof for the orchid house. And they lend me one of their cars when mine is out of order; you know how often it gets out of order."

"I don't know how often," said Eleanor, "but it must happen very frequently. Whenever I want you to take me anywhere in your car I am always told that there is something wrong with it, or else that the chauffeur has got neuralgia and you don't like to ask him to go out."

"He suffers quite a lot from neuralgia," said Mrs. Attray hastily. "Anyhow," she continued, "you can understand that I don't want to offend the Norridrums. Their household is the most rackety one in the county, and I believe no one ever knows to an hour or two when any particular meal will appear on the table or what it will consist of when it does appear."

Eleanor Saxelby shuddered. She liked her meals to be of regular occurrence and assured proportions.

"Still," pursued Mrs. Attray, "whatever their own home life may be, as landlords and neighbours they are considerate and obliging, so I don't want to quarrel with them. Besides, if Ronnie didn't play cards there he'd be playing somewhere else."

"Not if you were firm with him," said Eleanor; "I believe in being firm."

"Firm? I am firm," exclaimed Mrs. Attray; "I am more than firm—I am farseeing. I've done everything I can think of it to prevent Ronnie from playing for money. I've stopped his allowance for the rest of the year, so he can't even gamble on credit, and I've subscribed a lump sum to the church offertory in his name instead of giving him instalments of small silver to put in the bag on Sundays. I wouldn't even let him have the money to tip the hunt servants with, but sent it by postal order. He was furiously sulky about it, but I reminded him of what happened to the ten shillings that I gave him for the Young Men's Endeavour League 'Self-Denial Week.'"

"What did happen to it?" asked Eleanor.

"Well, Ronnie did some preliminary endeavouring with it, on his own account, in connection with the Grand National. If it had come off, as he expressed it, he would have given the League twenty-five shillings and netted a comfortable commission for himself; as it was, that ten shillings was one of the things the League had to deny itself. Since then I've been careful not to let him have a penny piece in his hands."

"He'll get round that in some way," said Eleanor with quiet conviction; "he'll sell things."

"My dear, he's done all that is to be done in that direction already. He's got rid of his wrist-watch and his hunting flask and both his cigarette cases, and I shouldn't be surprised if he's wearing imitation-gold sleeve links instead of those his Aunt Rhoda gave him on his seventeenth birthday. He can't sell his clothes, of course, except his winter overcoat, and I've locked that up in the camphor cupboard on the pretext of preserving it from moth. I really don't see what else he can raise money on. I consider that I've been both firm and farseeing."

"Has he been at the Norridrums lately?" asked Eleanor.

"He was there yesterday afternoon and stayed to dinner," said Mrs. Attray. "I don't quite know when he came home, but I fancy it was late."

"Then depend on it he was gambling," said Eleanor, with the assured air of one who has few ideas and makes the most of them. "Late hours in the country always mean gambling."

"He can't gamble if he has no money and no chance of getting any," argued Mrs. Attray; "even if one plays for small stakes one must have a decent prospect of paying one's losses."

"He may have sold some of the Amherst pheasant chicks," suggested Eleanor; "they would fetch about ten or twelve shillings each, I dare say."

"Ronnie wouldn't do such a thing," said Mrs. Attray; "and anyhow I went and counted them this morning and they're all there. No," she continued, with the quiet satisfaction that comes from a sense of painstaking and merited achievement, "I fancy that Ronnie had to content himself with the rôle of onlooker last night, as far as the card-table was concerned."

"Is that clock right?" asked Eleanor, whose eyes had been straying restlessly towards the mantelpiece for some little time; "lunch is usually so punctual in your establishment."

"Three minutes past the half-hour," exclaimed Mrs. Attray; "cook must be preparing something unusually sumptuous in your honour. I am not in the secret; I've been out all the morning, you know."

Eleanor smiled forgivingly. A special effort by Mrs. Attray's cook was worth waiting a few minutes for.

As a matter of fact, the luncheon fare, when it made its tardy appearance, was distinctly unworthy of the reputation which the justly treasured cook had built up for herself. The soup alone would have sufficed to cast a gloom over any meal that it had inaugurated, and it was not redeemed by anything that followed. Eleanor said little, but when she spoke there was a hint of tears in her voice that was far more eloquent than outspoken denunciation would have been, and even the insouciant Ronald showed traces of depression when he tasted the rognons Saltikoff.

"Not quite the best luncheon I've enjoyed in your house," said Eleanor at last, when her final hope had flickered out with the savoury.

"My dear, it's the worst meal I've sat down to for years," said her hostess; "that last dish tasted principally of red pepper and wet toast. I'm awfully sorry. Is anything the matter in the kitchen, Pellin?" she asked of the attendant maid.

"Well, ma'am, the new cook hadn't hardly time to see to things properly, coming in so sudden—" commenced Pellin by way of explanation.

"The *new* cook!" screamed Mrs. Attray.

"Colonel Norridrum's cook, ma'am," said Pellin.

"What on earth do you mean? What is Colonel Norridrum's cook doing in my kitchen—and where is *my* cook?"

"Perhaps I can explain better than Pellin can," said Ronald hurriedly; "the fact is, I was dining at the Norridrum's yesterday, and they were wishing they had a swell cook like yours, just for today and tomorrow, while they've got some gourmet staying with them; their own cook is no earthly good—well, you've seen what she turns out when she's at all flurried. So I thought it would be rather sporting to play them at baccarat for the loan of our cook against a money stake, and I lost, that's all. I have had rotten luck at baccarat all this year."

The remainder of his explanation, of how he had assured the cooks that the temporary transfer had his mother's sanction, and had smuggled the one out and the other in during the maternal absence, was drowned in the outcry of scandalized upbraiding.

"If I had sold the woman into slavery there couldn't have been a bigger fuss about it," he confided afterwards to Bertie Norridrum, "and Eleanor Saxelby raged and ramped the louder of the two. I tell you what, I'll bet you two of the Amherst pheasants to five shillings that she refuses to have me as a partner at the croquet tournament. We're drawn together, you know."

This time he won his bet.

CLOVIS ON PARENTAL RESPONSIBILITIES

MARION EGGELBY sat talking to Clovis on the only subject that she ever willingly talked about—her offspring and their varied perfections and accomplishments. Clovis was not in what could be called a receptive mood; the younger generation of Eggelby, depicted in the glowing improbable colours of parent impressionism, aroused in him no enthusiasm. Mrs. Eggelby, on the other hand, was furnished with enthusiasm enough for two.

"You would like Eric," she said, argumentatively rather than hopefully. Clovis had intimated very unmistakably that he was unlikely to care extravagantly for either Amy or Willie. "Yes, I feel sure you would like Eric. Every one takes to him at once. You know, he always reminds me of that famous picture of the youthful David—I forget who it's by, but it's very well known."

"That would be sufficient to set me against him, if I saw much of him," said Clovis. "Just imagine at auction bridge, for instance, when one was trying to concentrate one's mind on what one's partner's original declaration had been, and to remember what suits one's opponents had originally discarded, what it would be like to have some one persistently reminding one of a picture of the youthful David. It would be simply maddening. If Eric did that I should detest him."

"Eric doesn't play bridge," said Mrs. Eggelby with dignity.

"Doesn't he?" asked Clovis; "why not?"

"None of my children have been brought up to play card games," said Mrs. Eggelby; "draughts and halma and those sorts of games I encourage. Eric is considered quite a wonderful draughts-player."

"You are strewing dreadful risks in the path of your family," said Clovis; "a friend of mine who is a prison chaplain told me that among the worst criminal cases that have come under his notice, men condemned to death or to long periods of penal servitude, there was not a single bridge-player. On the other hand, he knew at least two expert draughts-players among them."

"I really don't see what my boys have got to do with the criminal classes," said Mrs. Eggelby resentfully. "They have been most carefully brought up, I can assure you that."

"That shows that you were nervous as to how they would turn out," said Clovis. "Now, my mother never bothered about bringing me up. She just saw to it that I got whacked at decent intervals and was taught the difference between right and wrong; there is some difference, you know, but I've forgotten what it is."

"Forgotten the difference between right and wrong!" exclaimed Mrs. Eggelby.

"Well, you see, I took up natural history and a whole lot of other subjects at the same time, and one can't remember everything, can one? I used to know the difference between the Sardinian dormouse and the ordinary kind, and whether the wryneck arrives at our shores earlier than the cuckoo, or the other way round, and how long the walrus takes in growing to maturity; I dare say you knew all those sorts of things once, but I bet you've forgotten them."

"Those things are not important," said Mrs. Eggelby, "but—"

"The fact that we've both forgotten them proves that they *are* important," said Clovis; "you must have noticed that it's always the important things that one forgets, while the trivial, unnecessary facts of life stick in one's memory. There's my cousin, Editha Clubberly, for instance; I can never forget that her birthday is on the 12th of October. It's a matter of utter indifference to me on what date her birthday falls, or whether she was born at all; either fact seems to me absolutely trivial, or unnecessary—I've heaps of other cousins to go on with. On the other hand, when I'm staying with Hildegarde

Shrubley I can never remember the important circumstance whether her first husband got his unenviable reputation on the Turf or the Stock Exchange, and that uncertainty rules Sport and Finance out of the conversation at once. One can never mention travel, either, because her second husband had to live permanently abroad."

"Mrs. Shrubley and I move in very different circles," said Mrs. Eggelby stiffly.

"No one who knows Hildegarde could possibly accuse her of moving in a circle," said Clovis; "her view of life seems to be a non-stop run with an inexhaustible supply of petrol. If she can get some one else to pay for the petrol so much the better. I don't mind confessing to you that she has taught me more than any other woman I can think of."

"What kind of knowledge?" demanded Mrs. Eggelby, with the air a jury might collectively wear when finding a verdict without leaving the box.

"Well, among other things, she's introduced me to at least four different ways of cooking lobster," said Clovis gratefully. "That, of course, wouldn't appeal to you; people who abstain from the pleasures of the card-table never really appreciate the finer possibilities of the dining-table. I suppose their powers of enlightened enjoyment get atrophied from disuse."

"An aunt of mine was very ill after eating a lobster," said Mrs. Eggelby.

"I dare say, if we knew more of her history, we should find out that she'd often been ill before eating the lobster. Aren't you concealing the fact that she'd had measles and influenza and nervous headache and hysteria, and other things that aunts do have, long before she ate the lobster? Aunts that have never known a day's illness are very rare; in fact, I don't personally know of any. Of course if she ate it as a child of two weeks old it might have been her first illness— and her last. But if that was the case I think you should have said so."

"I must be going," said Mrs. Eggelby, in a tone which had been thoroughly sterilized of even perfunctory regret.

Clovis rose with an air of graceful reluctance.

"I have so enjoyed our little talk about Eric," he said; "I quite look forward to meeting him some day."

"Good-bye," said Mrs. Eggelby frostily; the supplementary remark which she made at the back of her throat was—

"I'll take care that you never shall!"

A HOLIDAY TASK

KENELM JERTON entered the dining-hall of the Golden Galleon Hotel in the full crush of the luncheon hour. Nearly every seat was occupied, and small additional tables had been brought in, where floor space permitted, to accommodate late-comers, with the result that many of the tables were almost touching each other. Jerton was beckoned by a waiter to the only vacant table that was discernible, and took his seat with the uncomfortable and wholly groundless idea that nearly every one in the room was staring at him. He was a youngish man of ordinary appearance, quiet of dress and unobtrusive of manner, and he could never wholly rid himself of the idea that a fierce light of public scrutiny beat on him as though he had been a notability or a super-nut. After he had ordered his lunch there came the unavoidable interval of waiting, with nothing to do but to stare at the flower-vase on his table and to be stared at (in imagination) by several flappers, some maturer beings of the same sex, and a satirical-looking Jew. In order to carry off the situation with some appearance of unconcern he became spuriously interested in the contents of the flower-vase.

"What is the name of those roses, d'you know?" he asked the waiter. The waiter was ready at all times to conceal his ignorance concerning items of the wine-list or *menu*; he was frankly ignorant as to the specific name of the roses.

"*Amy Silvester Partington*," said a voice at Jerton's elbow. The voice came from a pleasant-faced, well-dressed young woman who was sitting at a table that almost touched Jerton's.

He thanked her hurriedly and nervously for the information, and made some inconsequent remark about the flowers.

"It is a curious thing," said the young woman, "that I should be able to tell you the name of those roses without an effort of memory, because if you were to ask me my name I should be utterly unable to give it to you."

Jerton had not harboured the least intention of extending his thirst for name-labels to his neighbour. After her rather remarkable announcement, however, he was obliged to say something in the way of polite inquiry.

"Yes," answered the lady, "I suppose it is a case of partial loss of memory. I was in the train coming down here; my ticket told me that I had come from Victoria and was bound for this place. I had a couple of five-pound notes and a sovereign on me, no visiting cards or any other means of identification, and no idea as to who I am. I can only hazily recollect that I have a title; I am Lady Somebody—beyond that my mind is a blank."

"Hadn't you any luggage with you?" asked Jerton.

"That is what I didn't know. I knew the name of this hotel and made up my mind to come here, and when the hotel porter who meets the trains asked if I had any luggage I had to invent a dressing-bag and dress-basket; I could always pretend that they had gone astray. I gave him the name of Smith, and presently he emerged from a confused pile of luggage and passengers with a dressing-bag and dress-basket labelled Kestrel-Smith. I had to take them; I don't see what else I could have done."

Jerton said nothing, but he rather wondered what the lawful owner of the baggage would do.

"Of course it was dreadful arriving at a strange hotel with the name of Kestrel-Smith, but it would have been worse to have arrived without luggage. Anyhow, I hate causing trouble."

Jerton had visions of harassed railway officials and distraught Kestrel-Smiths, but he made no attempt to clothe his mental picture in words. The lady continued her story.

"Naturally, none of my keys would fit the things, but I

told an intelligent page boy that I had lost my key-ring, and he had the locks forced in a twinkling. Rather too intelligent, that boy; he will probably end in Dartmoor. The Kestrel-Smith toilet tools aren't up to much, but they are better than nothing."

"If you feel sure that you have a title," said Jerton, "why not get hold of a peerage and go right through it?"

"I tried that. I skimmed through the list of the House of Lords in 'Whitaker,' but a mere printed string of names conveys awfully little to one, you know. If you were an army officer and had lost your identity you might pore over the Army List for months without finding out who you were. I'm going on another tack; I'm trying to find out by various little tests who I am *not*—that will narrow the range of uncertainty down a bit. You may have noticed, for instance, that I'm lunching principally off lobster Newburg."

Jerton had not ventured to notice anything of the sort.

"It's an extravagance, because it's one of the most expensive dishes on the *menu*, but at any rate it proves that I'm not Lady Starping; she never touches shell-fish, and poor Lady Braddleshrub has no digestion at all; if I am *her* I shall certainly die in agony in the course of the afternoon, and the duty of finding out who I am will devolve on the press and the police and those sort of people; I shall be past caring. Lady Knewford doesn't know one rose from another and she hates men, so she wouldn't have spoken to you in any case; and Lady Mousehilton flirts with every man she meets—I haven't flirted with you, have I?"

Jerton hastily gave the required assurance.

"Well, you see," continued the lady, "that knocks four off the list at once."

"It'll be rather a lengthy process bringing the list down to one," said Jerton.

"Oh, but, of course, there are heaps of them that I couldn't possibly be—women who've got grandchildren or sons old enough to have celebrated their coming of age. I've only got to consider the ones about my own age. I tell you how you might help me this afternoon, if you don't mind; go through any of the back numbers of *Country Life* and those sort of papers that you can find in the smoking-room, and see if you come across my portrait with infant son or anything of that sort. It won't take you ten minutes. I'll meet you in the lounge about tea-time. Thanks awfully."

And the Fair Unknown, having graciously pressed Jerton into the search for her lost identity, rose and left the room. As she passed the young man's table she halted for a moment and whispered:

"Did you notice that I tipped the waiter a shilling? We can cross Lady Ulwight off the list; she would have died rather than do that."

At five o'clock Jerton made his way to the hotel lounge; he had spent a diligent but fruitless quarter of an hour among the illustrated weeklies in the smoking-room. His new acquaintance was seated at a small tea-table, with a waiter hovering in attendance.

"China tea or Indian?" she asked as Jerton came up.

"China, please, and nothing to eat. Have you discovered anything?"

"Only negative information. I'm not Lady Befnal. She disapproves dreadfully at any form of gambling, so when I recognized a well-known book-maker in the hotel lobby I went and put a tenner on an unnamed filly by William the Third out of Mitrovitza for the three-fifteen race. I suppose the fact of the animal being nameless was what attracted me."

"Did it win?" asked Jerton.

"No, came in fourth, the most irritating thing a horse can do when you've backed it win or place. Anyhow, I know now that I'm not Lady Befnal."

"It seems to me that the knowledge was rather dearly bought," commented Jerton.

"Well, yes, it has rather cleared me out," admitted the identity-seeker; "a florin is about all I've got left on me. The lobster Newburg made my lunch rather an expensive one, and, of course, I had to tip that boy for what he did to the Kestrel-Smith locks. I've got rather a useful idea, though. I feel certain that I belong to the Pivot Club; I'll go back to town and ask the hall porter there if there are any letters for me. He knows all the members by sight, and if there are any letters or telephone messages waiting for me, of course that will solve the problem. If he says there aren't any, I shall say: 'You know who I am, don't you?' so I'll find out anyway."

The plan seemed a sound one; a difficulty in its execution suggested itself to Jerton.

"Of course," said the lady, when he hinted at the obstacle, "there's my fare back to town, and my bill here and cabs and things. If you lend me three pounds that ought to see me through comfortably. Thanks ever so. Then there is the question of that luggage: I don't want to be saddled with that for the rest of my life. I'll have it brought down to the hall and you can pretend to mount guard over it while I'm writing a letter. Then I shall just slip away to the station, and you can wander off to the smoking-room, and they can do what they like with the things. They'll advertise them after a bit and the owner can claim them."

Jerton acquiesced in the manœuvre, and duly mounted guard over the luggage while its temporary owner slipped unobtrusively out of the hotel. Her departure was not, however, altogether unnoticed. Two gentlemen were strolling past Jerton, and one of them remarked to the other:

"Did you see that tall young woman in grey who went out just now? She is the Lady—"

His promenade carried him out of earshot at the critical moment when he was about to disclose the elusive identity. The Lady Who? Jerton could scarcely run after a total stranger, break into his conversation, and ask him for information concerning a chance passer-by. Besides, it was desirable that he should keep up the appearance of looking after the luggage. In a minute or two, however, the important personage, the man who knew, came strolling back alone. Jerton summoned up all his courage and waylaid him.

"I think I heard you say you knew the lady who went out of the hotel a few minutes ago, a tall lady, dressed in grey. Excuse me for asking if you could tell me her name; I've been talking to her for half an hour; she—er—she knows all my people and seems to know me, so I suppose I've met her somewhere before, but I'm blest if I can put a name to her. Could you—?"

"Certainly. She's a Mrs. Stroope."

"*Mrs.?*" queried Jerton.

"Yes, she's the Lady Champion at golf in my part of the world. An awful good sort, and goes about a good deal in Society, but she has an awkward habit of losing her memory every now and then, and gets into all sorts of fixes. She's furious, too, if you make any allusion to it afterwards. Good day, sir."

The stranger passed on his way, and before Jerton had had time to assimilate his information he found his whole attention centred on an angry-looking lady who was making loud and fretful-seeming inquiries of the hotel clerks.

"Has any luggage been brought here from the station by mistake, a dress-basket and dressing-case, with the name Kestrel-Smith? It can't be traced anywhere. I saw it put in at Victoria, that I'll swear. Why—there *is* my luggage! and the locks have been tampered with!"

Jerton heard no more. He fled down to the Turkish bath, and stayed there for hours.

THE STALLED OX

THEOPHIL ESHLEY was an artist by profession, a cattle painter by force of environment. It is not to be supposed that he lived on a ranch or a dairy farm, in an atmosphere pervaded with horn and hoof, milking-stool, and branding-iron. His home was in a park-like, villa-dotted district that only just escaped the reproach of being suburban. On one side of his garden there abutted a small, picturesque meadow, in which an enterprising neighbour pastured some small picturesque cows of the Channel Island persuasion. At noonday in summertime the cows stood knee-deep in tall meadow-grass under the shade of a group of walnut trees, with the sunlight falling in dappled patches on their mouse-sleek coats. Eshley had conceived and executed a dainty picture of two reposeful milch-cows in a setting of walnut tree and meadow-grass and filtered sunbeam, and the Royal Academy had duly exposed the same on the walls of its Summer Exhibition. The Royal Academy encourages orderly, methodical habits in its children. Eshley had painted a successful and acceptable picture of cattle drowsing picturesquely under walnut trees, and as he had begun, so, of necessity, he went on. His "Noontide Peace," a study of two dun cows under a walnut tree, was followed by "A Mid-day Sanctuary," a study of a walnut tree, with two dun cows under it. In due succession there came "Where the Gad-Flies Cease from Troubling," "The Haven of the Herd," and "A Dream in Dairyland," studies of walnut trees and dun cows. His two attempts to break away from his own tradition were signal failures: "Turtle Doves Alarmed by Sparrow-hawk" and "Wolves on the Roman Campagna" came back to his studio in the guise of abominable heresies, and Eshley climbed back into grace and the public gaze with "A Shaded Nook Where Drowsy Milkers Dream."

On a fine afternoon in late autumn he was putting some finishing touches to a study of meadow weeds when his neighbour, Adela Pingsford, assailed the outer door of his studio with loud peremptory knockings.

"There is an ox in my garden," she announced, in explanation of the tempestuous intrusion.

"An ox," said Eshley blankly, and rather fatuously; "what kind of ox?"

"Oh, I don't know what kind," snapped the lady. "A common or garden ox, to use the slang expression. It is the garden part of it that I object to. My garden has just been put straight for the winter, and an ox roaming about in it won't improve matters. Besides, there are the chrysanthemums just coming into flower."

"How did it get into the garden?" asked Eshley.

"I imagine it came in by the gate," said the lady impatiently; "it couldn't have climbed the walls, and I don't suppose any one dropped it from an aeroplane as a Bovril advertisement. The immediately important question is not how it got in, but how to get it out."

"Won't it go?" said Eshley.

"If it was anxious to go," said Adela Pingsford rather angrily, "I should not have come here to chat with you about it. I'm practically all alone; the housemaid is having her afternoon out and the cook is lying down with an attack of neuralgia. Anything that I may have learned at school or in after life about how to remove a large ox from a small garden seems to have escaped from my memory now. All I could think of was that you were a near neighbour and a cattle painter, presumably more or less familiar with the subjects that you painted, and that you might be of some slight assistance. Possibly I was mistaken."

"I paint dairy cows, certainly," admitted Eshley, "but I cannot claim to have had any experience in rounding up stray oxen. I've seen it done on a cinema film, of course, but there were always horses and lots of other accessories; besides, one never knows how much of those pictures are faked."

Adela Pingsford said nothing, but led the way to her garden. It was normally a fair-sized garden, but it looked small in comparison with the ox, a huge mottled brute, dull red about the head and shoulders, passing to dirty white on the flanks and hind-quarters, with shaggy ears and large blood-shot eyes. It bore about as much resemblance to the dainty paddock heifers that Eshley was accustomed to paint as the chief of a Kurdish nomad clan would to a Japanese tea-shop girl. Eshley stood very near the gate while he studied the animal's appearance and demeanour. Adela Pingsford continued to say nothing.

"It's eating a chrysanthemum," said Eshley at last, when the silence had become unbearable.

"How observant you are," said Adela bitterly. "You seem to notice everything. As a matter of fact, it has got six chrysanthemums in its mouth at the present moment."

The necessity for doing something was becoming imperative. Eshley took a step or two in the direction of the animal, clapped his hands, and made noises of the "Hish" and "Shoo" variety. If the ox heard them it gave no outward indication of the fact.

"If any hens should ever stray into my garden," said Adela, "I should certainly send for you to frighten them out. You 'shoo' beautifully. Meanwhile, do you mind trying to drive that ox away? That is a *Mademoiselle Louise Bichot* that he's begun on now," she added in icy calm, as a glowing orange head was crushed into the huge munching mouth.

"Since you have been so frank about the variety of the chrysanthemum," said Eshley, "I don't mind telling you that this is an Ayrshire ox."

The icy calm broke down; Adela Pingsford used language that sent the artist instinctively a few feet nearer to the ox. He picked up a pea-stick and flung it with some determination against the animal's mottled flanks. The operation of mashing *Mademoiselle Louise Bichot* into a petal salad was suspended for a long moment, while the ox gazed with concentrated inquiry at the stick-thrower. Adela gazed with equal concentration and more obvious hostility at the same focus. As the beast neither lowered its head nor stamped its feet Eshley ventured on another javelin exercise with another pea-stick. The ox seemed to realize at once that it was to go; it gave a hurried final pluck at the bed where the chrysanthemums had been, and strode swiftly up the garden. Eshley ran to head it towards the gate, but only succeeded in quickening its pace from a walk to a lumbering trot. With an air of inquiry, but with no real hesitation, it crossed the tiny strip of turf that the charitable called the croquet lawn, and pushed its way through the open French window into the morning-room. Some chrysanthemums and other autumn herbage stood about the room in vases, and the animal resumed its browsing operations; all the same, Eshley fancied that the beginnings of a hunted look had come into its eyes, a look that counselled respect. He discontinued his attempt to interfere with its choice of surroundings.

"Mr. Eshley," said Adela in a shaking voice, "I asked you to drive that beast out of my garden, but I did not ask you to drive it into my house. If I must have it anywhere on the premises I prefer the garden to the morning-room."

"Cattle drives are not in my line," said Eshley; "if I remember I told you so at the outset."

"I quite agree," retorted the lady, "painting pretty pictures of pretty little cows is what you're suited for. Perhaps you'd like to do a nice sketch of that ox making itself at home in my morning-room?"

This time it seemed as if the worm had turned; Eshley began striding away.

"Where are you going?" screamed Adela.

"To fetch implements," was the answer.

"Implements? I won't have you use a lasso. The room will be wrecked if there's a struggle."

But the artist marched out of the garden. In a couple of minutes he returned, laden with easel, sketching-stool, and painting materials.

"Do you mean to say that you're going to sit quietly down and paint that brute while it's destroying my morning-room?" gasped Adela.

"It was your suggestion," said Eshley, setting his canvas in position.

"I forbid it; I absolutely forbid it!" stormed Adela.

"I don't see what standing you have in the matter," said the artist; "you can hardly pretend that it's your ox, even by adoption."

"You seem to forget that it's in my morning-room, eating my flowers," came the raging retort.

"You seem to forget that the cook has neuralgia," said Eshley; "she may be just dozing off into a merciful sleep and your outcry will waken her. Consideration for others should be the guiding principle of people in our station of life."

"The man is mad!" exclaimed Adela tragically. A moment later it was Adela herself who appeared to go mad. The ox had finished the vase-flowers and the cover of *Israel Kalisch,* and appeared to be thinking of leaving its rather restricted quarters. Eshley noticed its restlessness and promptly flung it some bunches of Virginia creeper leaves as an inducement to continue the sitting.

"I forget how the proverb runs," he observed; "something about 'better a dinner of herbs than a stalled ox where hate is.' We seem to have all the ingredients for the proverb ready to hand."

"I shall go to the Public Library and get them to telephone for the police," announced Adela, and, raging audibly, she departed.

Some minutes later the ox, awakening probably to the suspicion that oil cake and chopped mangold was waiting for it in some appointed byre, stepped with much precaution out of the morning-room, stared with grave inquiry at the no longer obtrusive and pea-stick-throwing human, and then lumbered heavily but swiftly out of the garden. Eshley packed up his tools and followed the animal's example and "Larkdene" was left to neuralgia and the cook.

The episode was the turning-point in Eshley's artistic career. His remarkable picture, "Ox in a Morning-room, Late Autumn," was one of the sensations and successes of the next Paris Salon, and when it was subsequently exhibited at Munich it was bought by the Bavarian Government, in the teeth of the spirited bidding of three meat-extract firms. From that moment his success was continuous and assured, and the Royal Academy was thankful, two years later, to give a conspicuous position on its walls to his large canvas "Barbary Apes Wrecking a Boudoir."

Eshley presented Adela Pingsford with a new copy of *Israel Kalisch*, and a couple of finely flowering plants of *Madame André Blusset*, but nothing in the nature of a real reconciliation has taken place between them.

THE STORY-TELLER

IT was a hot afternoon, and the railway carriage was correspondingly sultry, and the next stop was at Templecombe, nearly an hour ahead. The occupants of the carriage were a small girl, and a smaller girl, and a small boy. An aunt belonging to the children occupied one corner seat, and the further corner seat on the opposite side was occupied by a bachelor who was a stranger to their party, but the small girls and the small boy emphatically occupied the compartment. Both the aunt and the children were conversational in a limited, persistent way, reminding one of the attentions of a housefly that refused to be discouraged. Most of the aunt's remarks seemed to begin with "Don't," and nearly all of the children's remarks began with "Why?" The bachelor said nothing out loud.

"Don't, Cyril, don't," exclaimed the aunt, as the small boy began smacking the cushions of the seat, producing a cloud of dust at each blow.

"Come and look out of the window," she added.

The child moved reluctantly to the window. "Why are those sheep being driven out of that field?" he asked.

"I expect they are being driven to another field where there is more grass," said the aunt weakly.

"But there is lots of grass in that field," protested the boy; "there's nothing else but grass there. Aunt, there's lots of grass in that field."

"Perhaps the grass in the other field is better," suggested the aunt fatuously.

"Why is it better?" came the swift, inevitable question.

"Oh, look at those cows!" exclaimed the aunt. Nearly every field along the line had contained cows or bullocks, but she spoke as though she were drawing attention to a rarity.

"Why is the grass in the other field better?" persisted Cyril.

The frown on the bachelor's face was deepening to a scowl. He was a hard, unsympathetic man, the aunt decided in her mind. She was utterly unable to come to any satisfactory decision about the grass in the other field.

The smaller girl created a diversion by beginning to recite "On the Road to Mandalay." She only knew the first line, but she put her limited knowledge to the fullest possible use. She repeated the line over and over again in a dreamy but resolute and very audible voice; it seemed to the bachelor as though some one had had a bet with her that she could not repeat the line aloud two thousand times without stopping. Whoever it was who had made the wager was likely to lose his bet.

"Come over here and listen to a story," said the aunt, when the bachelor had looked twice at her and once at the communication cord.

The children moved listlessly towards the aunt's end of the carriage. Evidently her reputation as a story-teller did not rank high in their estimation.

In a low, confidential voice, interrupted at frequent intervals by loud, petulant questions from her listeners, she began an unenterprising and deplorably uninteresting story about a little girl who was good, and made friends with every one on account of her goodness, and was finally saved from a mad bull by a number of rescuers who admired her moral character.

"Wouldn't they have saved her if she hadn't been good?" demanded the bigger of the small girls. It was exactly the question that the bachelor had wanted to ask.

"Well, yes," admitted the aunt lamely, "but I don't think they would have run quite so fast to her help if they had not liked her so much."

"It's the stupidest story I've ever heard," said the bigger of the small girls, with immense conviction.

"I didn't listen after the first bit, it was so stupid," said Cyril.

The smaller girl made no actual comment on the story, but she had long ago recommenced a murmured repetition of her favourite line.

"You don't seem to be a success as a story-teller," said the bachelor suddenly from his corner.

The aunt bristled in instant defence at this unexpected attack.

"It's a very difficult thing to tell stories that children can both understand and appreciate," she said stiffly.

"I don't agree with you," said the bachelor.

"Perhaps *you* would like to tell them a story," was the aunt's retort.

"Tell us a story," demanded the bigger of the small girls.

"Once upon a time," began the bachelor, "there was a little girl called Bertha, who was extraordinarily good."

The children's momentarily-aroused interest began at once to flicker; all stories seemed dreadfully alike, no matter who told them.

"She did all that she was told, she was always truthful, she kept her clothes clean, ate milk puddings as though they were jam tarts, learned her lessons perfectly, and was polite in her manners."

"Was she pretty?" asked the bigger of the small girls.

"Not as pretty as any of you," said the bachelor, "but she was horribly good."

There was a wave of reaction in favour of the story; the word horrible in connection with goodness was a novelty that commended itself. It seemed to introduce a ring of truth that was absent from the aunt's tales of infant life.

"She was so good," continued the bachelor, "that she won several medals for goodness, which she always wore, pinned on to her dress. There was a medal for obedience, another medal for punctuality, and a third for good behaviour. They were large metal medals and they clicked against one another as she walked. No other child in the town where she lived had as many as three medals, so everybody knew that she must be an extra good child."

"Horribly good," quoted Cyril.

"Everybody talked about her goodness, and the Prince of the country got to hear about it, and he said that as she was so very good she might be allowed once a week to walk in his park, which was just outside the town. It was a beautiful park, and no children were ever allowed in it, so it was a great honour for Bertha to be allowed to go there."

"Were there any sheep in the park?" demanded Cyril.

"No," said the bachelor, "there were no sheep."

"Why weren't there any sheep?" came the inevitable question arising out of that answer.

The aunt permitted herself a smile, which might almost have been described as a grin.

"There were no sheep in the park," said the bachelor, "because the Prince's mother had once had a dream that her son would either be killed by a sheep or else by a clock falling on him. For that reason the Prince never kept a sheep in his park or a clock in his palace."

The aunt suppressed a gasp of admiration.

"Was the Prince killed by a sheep or by a clock?" asked Cyril.

"He is still alive, so we can't tell whether the dream will come true," said the bachelor unconcernedly; "anyway, there were no sheep in the park, but there were lots of little pigs running all over the place."

"What colour were they?"

"Black with white faces, white with black spots, black all over, grey with white patches, and some were white all over."

The story-teller paused to let a full idea of the park's treasures sink into the children's imaginations; then he resumed:

"Bertha was rather sorry to find that there were no flowers in the park. She had promised her aunts, with tears in her eyes, that she would not pick any of the kind Prince's flowers, and she had meant to keep her promise, so of course it made her feel silly to find that there were no flowers to pick."

"Why weren't there any flowers?"

"Because the pigs had eaten them all," said the bachelor promptly. "The gardeners had told the Prince that you couldn't have pigs and flowers, so he decided to have pigs and no flowers."

There was a murmur of approval at the excellence of the Prince's decision; so many people would have decided the other way.

"There were lots of other delightful things in the park. There were ponds with gold and blue and green fish in them, and trees with beautiful parrots that said clever things at a moment's notice, and humming birds that hummed all the popular tunes of the day. Bertha walked up and down and enjoyed herself immensely, and thought to herself: 'If I were not so extraordinarily good I should not have been allowed to come into this beautiful park and enjoy all that there is to be seen in it,' and her three medals clinked against one another as she walked and helped to remind her how very good she really was. Just then an enormous wolf came prowling into the park to see if it could catch a fat little pig for its supper."

"What colour was it?" asked the children, amid an immediate quickening of interest.

"Mud-colour all over, with a black tongue and pale grey eyes that gleamed with unspeakable ferocity. The first thing that it saw in the park was Bertha; her pinafore was so spotlessly white and clean that it could be seen from a great distance. Bertha saw the wolf and saw that it was stealing towards her, and she began to wish that she had never been allowed to come into the park. She ran as hard as she could, and the wolf came after her with huge leaps and bounds. She managed to reach a shrubbery of myrtle bushes and she hid herself in one of the thickest of the bushes. The wolf came sniffing among the branches, its black tongue lolling out of its mouth and its pale grey eyes glaring with rage. Bertha was terribly frightened, and thought to herself: 'If I had not been so extraordinarily good I should have been safe in the town at this moment.' However, the scent of the myrtle was so strong that the wolf could not sniff out where Bertha was hiding, and the bushes were so thick that he might have hunted about in them for a long time without catching sight of her, so he thought he might as well go off and catch a little pig instead. Bertha was trembling very much at having the wolf prowling and sniffing so near her, and as she trembled the medal for obedience clinked against the medals for good conduct and punctuality. The wolf was just moving away when he heard the sound of the medals clinking and stopped to listen; they clinked again in a bush quite near him. He dashed into the bush, his pale grey eyes gleaming with ferocity and triumph, and dragged Bertha out and devoured her to the last morsel. All that was left of her were her shoes, bits of clothing, and the three medals for goodness."

"Were any of the little pigs killed?"

"No, they all escaped."

"The story began badly," said the smaller of the small girls, "but it had a beautiful ending."

"It is the most beautiful story that I ever heard," said the bigger of the small girls, with immense decision.

"It is the *only* beautiful story I have ever heard," said Cyril.

A dissentient opinion came from the aunt.

"A most improper story to tell to young children! You have undermined the effect of years of careful teaching."

"At any rate," said the bachelor, collecting his belongings preparatory to leaving the carriage, "I kept them quiet for ten minutes, which was more than you were able to do."

"Unhappy woman!" he observed to himself as he walked down the platform of Templecombe station; "for the next six months or so those children will assail her in public with demands for an improper story!"

A DEFENSIVE DIAMOND

TREDDLEFORD sat in an easeful arm-chair in front of a slumberous fire, with a volume of verse in his hand and the comfortable consciousness that outside the club windows the rain was dripping and pattering with persistent purpose. A chill, wet October afternoon was emerging into a black, wet October evening, and the club smoking-room seemed warmer and cozier by contrast. It was an afternoon on which to be wafted away from one's climatic surroundings, and *The Golden Journey to Samarkand* promised to bear Treddleford

well and bravely into other lands and under other skies. He
had already migrated from London the rain-swept to Bagdad
the Beautiful, and stood by the Sun Gate "in the olden time"
when an icy breath of imminent annoyance seemed to creep
between the book and himself. Amblecope, the man with the
restless, prominent eyes and the mouth ready mobilized for
conversational openings, had planted himself in a neighbouring arm-chair. For a twelvemonth and some odd weeks Treddleford had skilfully avoided making the acquaintance of his
voluble fellow-clubman; he had marvellously escaped from
the infliction of his relentless record of tedious personal
achievements, or alleged achievements, on golf links, turf,
and gaming table, by flood and field and covert-side. Now his
season of immunity was coming to an end. There was no
escape; in another moment he would be numbered among
those who knew Amblecope to speak to—or rather, to suffer
being spoken to.

The intruder was armed with a copy of *Country Life*, not
for purposes of reading, but as an aid to conversational ice-
breaking.

"Rather a good portrait of Throstlewing," he remarked
explosively, turning his large challenging eyes on Treddleford;
"somehow it reminds me very much of Yellowstep, who was
supposed to be such a good thing for the Grand Prix in 1903.
Curious race that was; I suppose I've seen every race for the
Grand Prix for the last—"

"Be kind enough never to mention the Grand Prix in my
hearing," said Treddleford desperately; "it awakens acutely
distressing memories. I can't explain why without going into
a long and complicated story."

"Oh, certainly, certainly," said Amblecope hastily; long and
complicated stories that were not told by himself were abominable in his eyes. He turned the pages of *Country Life* and became spuriously interested in the picture of a Mongolian
pheasant.

"Not a bad representation of the Mongolian variety," he
exclaimed, holding it up for his neighbour's inspection. "They
do very well in some covers. Take some stopping too once

they're fairly on the wing. I suppose the biggest bag I ever made in two successive days—"

"My aunt, who owns the greater part of Lincolnshire," broke in Treddleford, with dramatic abruptness, "possesses perhaps the most remarkable record in the way of a pheasant bag that has ever been achieved. She is seventy-five and can't hit a thing, but she always goes out with the guns. When I say she can't hit a thing, I don't mean to say that she doesn't occasionally endanger the lives of her fellow-guns, because that wouldn't be true. In fact, the chief Government Whip won't allow Ministerial M.P.'s to go out with her; 'We don't want to incur by-elections needlessly,' he quite reasonably observed. Well, the other day she winged a pheasant, and brought it to earth with a feather or two knocked out of it; it was a runner, and my aunt saw herself in danger of being done out of about the only bird she'd hit during the present reign. Of course she wasn't going to stand that; she followed it through bracken and brushwood, and when it took to the open country and started across a ploughed field she jumped on to the shooting pony and went after it. The chase was a long one, and when my aunt at last ran the bird to a standstill she was nearer home than she was to the shooting party; she had left that some five miles behind her."

"Rather a long run for a wounded pheasant," snapped Amblecope.

"The story rests on my aunt's authority," said Treddleford coldly, "and she is local vice-president of the Young Women's Christian Association. She trotted three miles or so to her home, and it was not till the middle of the afternoon that it was discovered that the lunch for the entire shooting party was in a pannier attached to the pony's saddle. Anyway, she got her bird."

"Some birds, of course, take a lot of killing," said Amblecope; "so do some fish. I remember once I was fishing in the Exe, lovely trout stream, lots of fish, though they don't run to any great size—"

"One of them did," announced Treddleford, with emphasis. "My uncle, the Bishop of Southmolton, came across a giant trout in a pool just off the main stream of the Exe near Ugworthy; he tried it with every kind of fly and worm every day for three weeks without an atom of success, and then Fate intervened on his behalf. There was a low stone bridge just over this pool, and on the last day of his fishing holiday a motor van ran violently into the parapet and turned completely over; no one was hurt, but part of the parapet was knocked away, and the entire load that the van was carrying was pitched over and fell a little way into the pool. In a couple of minutes the giant trout was flapping and twisting on bare mud at the bottom of a waterless pool, and my uncle was able to walk down to him and fold him to his breast. The van-load consisted of blotting-paper, and every drop of water in that pool had been sucked up into the mass of spilt cargo."

There was silence for nearly half a minute in the smoking-room, and Treddleford began to let his mind steal back towards the golden road that led to Samarkand. Amblecope, however, rallied, and remarked in a rather tired and dispirited voice:

"Talking of motor accidents, the narrowest squeak I ever had was the other day, motoring with old Tommy Yarby in North Wales. Awfully good sort, old Yarby, thorough good sportsman, and the best—"

"It was in North Wales," said Treddleford, "that my sister met with her sensational carriage accident last year. She was on her way to a garden-party at Lady Nineveh's, about the only garden-party that ever comes to pass in those parts in the course of the year, and therefore a thing that she would have been very sorry to miss. She was driving a young horse that she'd only bought a week or two previously, warranted to be perfectly steady with motor traffic, bicycles, and other common objects of the roadside. The animal lived up to its reputation, and passed the most explosive of motor-bikes with an indifference that almost amounted to apathy. However, I suppose we all draw the line somewhere, and this particular cob drew it at travelling wild beast shows. Of course my sister didn't know that, but she knew it very distinctly when she turned a sharp corner and found herself in a mixed company of camels, piebald horses, and canary-coloured vans. The dog-cart was overturned in a ditch and kicked to splinters, and the cob went home across country. Neither my sister nor the groom was hurt, but the problem of how to get to the Nineveh garden-party, some three miles distant, seemed rather difficult to solve; once there, of course, my sister would easily find some one to drive her home. 'I suppose you wouldn't care for the loan of a couple of my camels?' the showman suggested, in humorous sympathy. 'I would,' said my sister, who had ridden camel-back in Egypt, and she overruled the objections of the groom, who hadn't. She picked out two of the most presentable-looking of the beasts and had them dusted and made as tidy as was possible at short notice, and set out for the Nineveh mansion. You may imagine the sensation that her small but imposing caravan created when she arrived at the hall door. The entire garden-party flocked up to gape. My sister was rather glad to slip down from her camel, and the groom was thankful to scramble down from his. Then young Billy Doulton, of the Dragoon Guards, who has been a lot at Aden and thinks he knows camel-language backwards, thought he would show off by making the beasts kneel down in orthodox fashion. Unfortunately camel words-of-command are not the same all the world over; these were magnificent Turkestan camels, accustomed to stride up the stony terraces of mountain passes, and when Doulton shouted at them they went side by side up the front steps, into the entrance hall, and up the grand staircase. The German governess met them just at the turn of the corridor. The Ninevehs nursed her with devoted attention for weeks, and when I last heard from them she was well enough to go about her duties again, but the doctor says she will alway suffer from Hagenbeck heart.''

Amblecope got up from his chair and moved to another part of the room. Treddleford reopened his book and betook himself once more across

The dragon-green, the luminous, the dark, the serpent-haunted sea.

For a blessed half-hour he disported himself in imagination by the "gay Aleppo-Gate," and listened to the bird-voiced singing-man. Then the world of today called him back; a page summoned him to speak with a friend on the telephone.

As Treddleford was about to pass out of the room he encountered Amblecope, also passing out, on his way to the billiard-room, where, perchance, some luckless wight might be secured and held fast to listen to the number of his attendances at the Grand Prix, with subsequent remarks on Newmarket and the Cambridgeshire. Amblecope made as if to pass out first, but a new-born pride was surging in Treddleford's breast and he waved him back.

"I believe I take precedence," he said coldly; "you are merely the club Bore; I am the club Liar."

THE ELK

TERESA, Mrs. Thropplestance, was the richest and most intractable old woman in the county of Woldshire. In her dealings with the world in general her manner suggested a blend between a Mistress of the Robes and a Master of Foxhounds, with the vocabulary of both. In her domestic circle she comported herself in the arbitrary style that one attributes, probably without the least justification, to an American political Boss in the bosom of his caucus. The late Theodore Thropplestance had left her, some thirty-five years ago, in absolute possession of a considerable fortune, a large landed property, and a gallery full of valuable pictures. In those intervening years she had outlived her son and quarrelled with her elder grandson, who had married without her consent or approval. Bertie Thropplestance, her younger grandson, was the heir-designate to her property, and as such he was a centre of interest and concern to some half-hundred ambitious mothers with daughters of marriageable age. Bertie was an amiable, easy-going young man, who was quite ready to marry any one who was favourably recommended to his notice, but he was not going to waste his time in falling in love with any one who would come under his grandmother's veto. The favourable recommendation would have to come from Mrs. Thropple-stance.

Teresa's house-parties were always rounded off with a plen-tiful garnishing of presentable young women and alert, at-tendant mothers, but the old lady was emphatically discourag-ing whenever any one of her girl guests became at all likely to outbid the others as a possible granddaughter-in-law. It was the inheritance of her fortune and estate that was in question, and she was evidently disposed to exercise and enjoy her pow-ers of selection and rejection to the utmost. Bertie's prefer-ences did not greatly matter; he was of the sort who can be stolidly happy with any kind of wife; he had cheerfully put up with his grandmother all his life, so he was not likely to fret and fume over anything that might befall him in the way of a helpmate.

The party that gathered under Teresa's roof in Christmas week of the year nineteen-hundred-and-something was of smaller proportions than usual, and Mrs. Yonelet, who formed one of the party, was inclined to deduce hopeful augury from this circumstance. Dora Yonelet and Bertie were so obviously made for one another, she confided to the vicar's wife, and if the old lady were accustomed to seeing them about a lot together she might adopt the view that they would make a suitable married couple.

"People soon get used to an idea if it is dangled constantly before their eyes," said Mrs. Yonelet hopefully, "and the more often Teresa sees those young people together, happy in each other's company, the more she will get to take a kindly interest in Dora as a possible and desirable wife for Bertie."

"My dear," said the vicar's wife resignedly, "my own Sybil was thrown together with Bertie under the most romantic cir-cumstances—I'll tell you about it some day—but it made no impression whatever on Teresa; she put her foot down in the most uncompromising fashion, and Sybil married an Indian civilian."

"Quite right of her," said Mrs. Yonelet with vague ap-proval; "it's what any girl of spirit would have done. Still, that was a year or two ago, I believe; Bertie is older now, and so is Teresa. Naturally she must be anxious to see him settled."

The vicar's wife reflected that Teresa seemed to be the one person who showed no immediate anxiety to supply Bertie with a wife, but she kept the thought to herself.

Mrs. Yonelet was a woman of resourceful energy and generalship; she involved the other members of the house-party, the deadweight, so to speak, in all manner of exercises and occupations that segregated them from Bertie and Dora, who were left to their own devisings—that is to say, to Dora's devisings and Bertie's accommodating acquiescence. Dora helped in the Christmas decorations of the parish church, and Bertie helped her to help. Together they fed the swans, till the birds went on a dyspepsia-strike, together they played billiards, together they photographed the village almshouses, and, at a respectful distance, the tame elk that browsed in solitary aloofness in the park. It was "tame" in the sense that it had long ago discarded the least vestige of fear of the human race; nothing in its record encouraged its human neighbours to feel a reciprocal confidence.

Whatever sport or exercise or occupation Bertie and Dora indulged in together was unfailingly chronicled and advertised by Mrs. Yonelet for the due enlightenment of Bertie's grandmother.

"Those two inseparables have just come in from a bicycle ride," she would announce; "quite a picture they make, so fresh and glowing after their spin."

"A picture needing words," would be Teresa's private comment, and as far as Bertie was concerned she was determined that the words should remain unspoken.

On the afternoon after Christmas Day Mrs. Yonelet dashed into the drawing-room, where her hostess was sitting amid a circle of guests and tea-cups and muffin-dishes. Fate had placed what seemed like a trump-card in the hands of the patiently manœuvring mother. With eyes blazing with excitement and a voice heavily escorted with exclamation marks she made a dramatic announcement.

"Bertie has saved Dora from the elk!"

In swift, excited sentences, broken with maternal emotion,

she gave supplementary information as to how the treacherous animal had ambushed Dora as she was hunting for a strayed golf ball, and how Bertie had dashed to her rescue with a stable fork and driven the beast off in the nick of time.

"It was touch and go! She threw her niblick at it, but that didn't stop it. In another moment she would have been crushed beneath its hoofs," panted Mrs. Yonelet.

"The animal is not safe," said Teresa, handing her agitated guest a cup of tea. "I forget if you take sugar. I suppose the solitary life it leads has soured its temper. There are muffins in the grate. It's not my fault; I've tried to get it a mate for ever so long. You don't know of any one with a lady elk for sale or exchange, do you?" she asked the company generally.

But Mrs. Yonelet was in no humour to listen to talk of elk marriages. The mating of two human beings was the subject uppermost in her mind, and the opportunity for advancing her pet project was too valuable to be neglected.

"Teresa," she exclaimed impressively, "after those two young people have been thrown together so dramatically, nothing can be quite the same again between them. Bertie has done more than save Dora's life; he has earned her affection. One cannot help feeling that Fate has consecrated them for one another."

"Exactly what the vicar's wife said when Bertie saved Sybil from the elk a year or two ago," observed Teresa placidly; "I pointed out to her that he had rescued Mirabel Hicks from the same predicament a few months previously, and that priority really belonged to the gardener's boy, who had been rescued in the January of that year. There is a good deal of sameness in country life, you know."

"It seems to be a very dangerous animal," said one of the guests.

"That's what the mother of the gardener's boy said," remarked Teresa; "she wanted me to have it destroyed, but I pointed out to her that she had eleven children and I had only one elk. I also gave her a black silk skirt; she said that though there hadn't been a funeral in her family, she felt as if there had been. Anyhow, we parted friends. I can't offer you a silk skirt, Emily, but you may have another cup of tea. As I have already remarked, there are muffins in the grate."

Teresa closed the discussion, having deftly conveyed the impression that she considered the mother of the gardener's boy had shown a far more reasonable spirit than the parents of other elk-assaulted victims.

"Teresa is devoid of feeling," said Mrs. Yonelet afterwards to the vicar's wife; "to sit there, talking of muffins, with an appalling tragedy only narrowly averted—"

"Of course you know whom she really intends Bertie to marry?" asked the vicar's wife; "I've noticed it for some time. The Bickelbys' German governess."

"A German governess! What an idea!" gasped Mrs. Yonelet.

"She's of quite good family, I believe," said the vicar's wife, "and not at all the mouse-in-the-background sort of person that governesses are usually supposed to be. In fact, next to Teresa, she's about the most assertive and combative personality in the neighbourhood. She's pointed out to my husband all sorts of errors in his sermons, and she gave Sir Laurence a public lecture on how he ought to handle the hounds. You know how sensitive Sir Laurence is about any criticism of his Mastership, and to have a governess laying down the law to him nearly drove him into a fit. She's behaved like that to every one, except, of course, Teresa, and every one has been defensively rude to her in return. The Bickelbys are simply too afraid of her to get rid of her. Now isn't that exactly the sort of woman whom Teresa would take a delight in installing as her successor? Imagine the discomfort and awkwardness in the county if we suddenly found that she was to be the future hostess at the Hall. Teresa's only regret will be that she won't be alive to see it."

"But," objected Mrs. Yonelet, "surely Bertie hasn't shown the least sign of being attracted in that quarter?"

"Oh, she's quite nice-looking in a way, and dresses well, and plays a good game of tennis. She often comes across the park with messages from the Bickelby mansion, and one of these days Bertie will rescue her from the elk, which has become almost a habit with him, and Teresa will say that Fate has consecrated them to one another. Bertie might not be disposed to pay much attention to the consecrations of Fate, but he would not dream of opposing his grandmother."

The vicar's wife spoke with the quiet authority of one who has intuitive knowledge, and in her heart of hearts Mrs. Yonelet believed her.

Six months later the elk had to be destroyed. In a fit of exceptional moroseness it had killed the Bickelbys' German governess. It was an irony of its fate that it should achieve popularity in the last moments of its career; at any rate, it established the record of being the only living thing that had permanently thwarted Teresa Thropplestance's plans.

Dora Yonelet broke off her engagement with an Indian civilian, and married Bertie three months after his grandmother's death—Teresa did not long survive the German governess fiasco. At Christmas time every year young Mrs. Thropplestance hangs an extra large festoon of evergreens on the elk horns that decorate the hall.

"It was a fearsome beast," she observes to Bertie, "but I always feel that it was instrumental in bringing us together."

Which, of course, was true.

"DOWN PENS"

"HAVE you written to thank the Froplinsons for what they sent us?" asked Egbert.

"No," said Janetta, with a note of tired defiance in her voice; "I've written eleven letters today expressing surprise and gratitude for sundry unmerited gifts, but I haven't written to the Froplinsons."

"Some one will have to write to them," said Egbert.

"I don't dispute the necessity, but I don't think the some one should be me," said Janetta. "I wouldn't mind writing

a letter of angry recrimination or heartless satire to some suitable recipient; in fact, I should rather enjoy it, but I've come
to the end of my capacity for expressing servile amiability.
Eleven letters today and nine yesterday, all couched in the
same strain of ecstatic thankfulness: really, you can't expect
me to sit down to another. There is such a thing as writing
oneself out."

"I've written nearly as many," said Egbert, "and I've had
my usual business correspondence to get through too. Besides,
I don't know what it was that the Froplinsons sent us."

"A William the Conqueror calendar," said Janetta, "with
a quotation of one of his great thoughts for every day in the
year."

"Impossible," said Egbert; "he didn't have three hundred
and sixty-five thoughts in the whole of his life, or, if he did,
he kept them to himself. He was a man of action, not of intro-
spection."

"Well, it was William Wordsworth, then," said Janetta;
"I know William came into it somewhere."

"That sounds more probable," said Egbert; "well, let's
collaborate on this letter of thanks and get it done. I'll dictate,
and you can scribble it down. 'Dear Mrs. Froplinson—thank
you and your husband so much for the very pretty calendar
you sent us. It was very good of you to think of us.'"

"You can't possibly say that," said Janetta, laying down
her pen.

"It's what I always do say, and what every one says to
me," protested Egbert.

"We sent them something on the twenty-second," said
Janetta, "so they simply *had* to think of us. There was no
getting away from it."

"What did we send them?" asked Egbert gloomily.

"Bridge-markers," said Janetta, "in a cardboard case, with
some inanity about 'digging for fortune with a royal spade'
emblazoned on the cover. The moment I saw it in the shop
I said to myself 'Froplinsons' and to the attendant 'How
much?' When he said 'Ninepence,' I gave him their address,

jabbed our card in, paid tenpence or elevenpence to cover the postage, and thanked heaven. With less sincerity and infinitely more trouble they eventually thanked me."

"The Froplinsons don't play bridge," said Egbert.

"One is not supposed to notice social deformities of that sort," said Janetta; "it wouldn't be polite. Besides, what trouble did they take to find out whether we read Wordsworth with gladness? For all they knew or cared we might be frantically embedded in the belief that all poetry begins and ends with John Masefield, and it might infuriate or depress us to have a daily sample of Wordsworthian products flung at us."

"Well, let's get on with the letter of thanks," said Egbert.

"Proceed," said Janetta.

" 'How clever of you to guess that Wordsworth is our favourite poet,' " dictated Egbert.

Again Janetta laid down her pen.

"Do you realize what that means?" she asked; "a Wordsworth booklet next Christmas, and another calendar the Christmas after, with the same problem of having to write suitable letters of thankfulness. No, the best thing to do is to drop all further allusion to the calendar and switch off on to some other topic."

"But what other topic?"

"Oh, something like this: 'What do you think of the New Year Honours List? A friend of ours made such a clever remark when he read it.' Then you can stick in any remark that comes into your head; it needn't be clever. The Froplinsons won't know whether it is or isn't."

"We don't even know on which side they are in politics," objected Egbert; "and anyhow you can't suddenly dismiss the subject of the calendar. Surely there must be some intelligent remark that can be made about it."

"Well, we can't think of one," said Janetta wearily; "the fact is, we've both written ourselves out. Heavens! I've just remembered Mrs. Stephen Ludberry. I haven't thanked her for what she sent."

"What did she send?"

"I forget; I think it was a calendar."

There was a long silence, the forlorn silence of those who are bereft of hope and have almost ceased to care.

Presently Egbert started from his seat with an air of resolution. The light of battle was in his eyes.

"Let me come to the writing-table," he exclaimed.

"Gladly," said Janetta. "Are you going to write to Mrs. Ludberry or the Froplinsons?"

"To neither," said Egbert, drawing a stack of notepaper towards him; "I'm going to write to the editor of every enlightened and influential newspaper in the Kingdom. I'm going to suggest that there should be a sort of epistolary Truce of God during the festivities of Christmas and New Year. From the twenty-fourth of December to the third or fourth of January it shall be considered an offence against good sense and good feeling to write or expect any letter or communication that does not deal with the necessary events of the moment. Answers to invitations, arrangements about trains, renewal of club subscriptions, and, of course, all the ordinary everyday affairs of business, sickness, engaging new cooks, and so forth, these will be dealt with in the usual manner as something inevitable, a legitimate part of our daily life. But all the devastating accretions of correspondence, incident to the festive season, these should be swept away to give the season a chance of being really festive, a time of untroubled, unpunctuated peace and good will."

"But you would have to make some acknowledgment of presents received," objected Janetta; "otherwise people would never know whether they had arrived safely."

"Of course, I have thought of that," said Egbert; "every present that was sent off would be accompanied by a ticket bearing the date of dispatch and the signature of the sender, and some conventional hieroglyphic to show that it was intended to be a Christmas or New Year gift; there would be a counterfoil with space for the recipient's name and the date of arrival, and all you would have to do would be to sign and date the counterfoil, add a conventional hieroglyphic indicating heartfelt thanks and gratified surprise, put the thing into an envelope and post it."

"It sounds delightfully simple," said Janetta wistfully, "but people would consider it too cut-and-dried, too perfunctory."

"It is not a bit more perfunctory than the present system," said Egbert; "I have only the same conventional language of gratitude at my disposal with which to thank dear old Colonel Chuttle for his perfectly delicious Stilton, which we shall devour to the last morsel, and the Froplinsons for their calendar, which we shall never look at. Colonel Chuttle knows that we are grateful for the Stilton, without having to be told so, and the Froplinsons know that we are bored with their calendar, whatever we may say to the contrary, just as we know that they are bored with the bridge-markers in spite of their written assurance that they thanked us for our charming little gift. What is more, the Colonel knows that even if we had taken a sudden aversion to Stilton or been forbidden it by the doctor, we should still have written a letter of hearty thanks around it. So you see the present system of acknowledgment is just as perfunctory and conventional as the counterfoil business would be, only ten times more tiresome and brain-racking."

"Your plan would certainly bring the ideal of a Happy Christmas a step nearer realization," said Janetta.

"There are exceptions, of course," said Egbert, "people who really try to infuse a breath of reality into their letters of acknowledgment. Aunt Susan, for instance, who writes: 'Thank you very much for the ham; not such a good flavour as the one you sent last year, which itself was not a particularly good one. Hams are not what they used to be.' It would be a pity to be deprived of her Christmas comments, but that loss would be swallowed up in the general gain."

"Meanwhile," said Janetta, "what *am* I to say to the Froplinsons?"

THE NAME-DAY

ADVENTURES, according to the proverb, are to the adventurous. Quite as often they are to the non-adventurous, to the retiring, to the constitutionally timid. John James Abbleway had been endowed by Nature with the sort of disposition that instinctively avoids Carlist intrigues, slum crusades, the tracking of wounded wild beasts, and the moving of hostile amendments at political meetings. If a mad dog or a Mad Mullah had come his way he would have surrendered the way without hesitation. At school he had unwillingly acquired a thorough knowledge of the German tongue out of deference to the plainly expressed wishes of a foreign-languages master, who, though he taught modern subjects, employed old-fashioned methods in driving his lessons home. It was this enforced familiarity with an important commercial language which thrust Abbleway in later years into strange lands where adventures were less easy to guard against than in the ordered atmosphere of an English country town. The firm that he worked for saw fit to send him one day on a prosaic business errand to the far city of Vienna, and, having sent him there, continued to keep him there, still engaged in humdrum affairs of commerce, but with the possibilities of romance and adventure, or even misadventure, jostling at his elbow. After two and a half years of exile, however, John James Abbleway had embarked on only one hazardous undertaking, and that was of a nature which would assuredly have overtaken him sooner or later if he had been leading a sheltered, stay-at-home existence at Dorking or Huntingdon. He fell placidly in love with a placidly lovable English girl, the sister of one of his commercial colleagues, who was improving her mind by a short trip to foreign parts, and in due course he was formally accepted as the young man she was engaged to. The further step by which she was to become Mrs. John Abbleway was to take place a twelvemonth hence in a town in the English midlands, by which time the firm that employed John James would have no further need for his presence in the Austrian capital.

It was early in April, two months after the installation of Abbleway as the young man Miss Penning was engaged to, when he received a letter from her, written from Venice. She was still peregrinating under the wing of her brother, and as the latter's business arrangements would take him across to Fiume for a day or two, she had conceived the idea that it would be rather jolly if John could obtain leave of absence and run down to the Adriatic coast to meet them. She had looked up the route on the map, and the journey did not appear likely to be expensive. Between the lines of her communication there lay a hint that if he really cared for her—

Abbleway obtained leave of absence and added a journey to Fiume to his life's adventures. He left Vienna on a cold, cheerless day. The flower shops were full of spring blooms, and the weekly organs of illustrated humour were full of spring topics, but the skies were heavy with clouds that looked like cotton-wool that has been kept over long in a shop window.

"Snow comes," said the train official to the station officials; and they agreed that snow was about to come. And it came, rapidly, plenteously. The train had not been more than an hour on its journey when the cotton-wool clouds commenced to dissolve in a blinding downpour of snowflakes. The forest trees on either side of the line were speedily coated with a heavy white mantle, the telegraph wires became thick glistening ropes, the line itself was buried more and more completely under a carpeting of snow, through which the not very powerful engine ploughed its way with increasing difficulty. The Vienna-Fiume line is scarcely the best equipped of the Austrian State railways, and Abbleway began to have serious fears for a breakdown. The train had slowed down to a painful and precarious crawl and presently came to a halt at a spot where the drifting snow had accumulated in a formidable barrier. The engine made a special effort and broke through the obstruction, but in the course of another twenty minutes it was again held up. The process of breaking through was renewed and the train doggedly resumed its way, encountering and surmounting fresh hindrances at frequent intervals. After a standstill of unusually long duration in a particularly deep drift the compartment in which Abbleway was sitting gave a huge jerk and a lurch, and then seemed to remain stationary; it undoubtedly was not moving, and yet he could hear the puffing of the engine and the slow rumbling and jolting of wheels. The puffing and rumbling grew fainter, as though it were dying away through the agency of intervening distance. Abbleway suddenly gave vent to an exclamation of scandalized alarm, opened the window, and peered out into the snowstorm. The flakes perched on his eyelashes and blurred his vision, but he saw enough to help him to realize what had happened. The engine had made a mighty plunge through the drift and had gone merrily forward, lightened of the load of its rear carriage, whose coupling had snapped under the strain. Abbleway was alone, or almost alone, with a derelict railway waggon, in the heart of some Styrian or Croatian forest. In the third-class compartment next to his own he remembered to have seen a peasant woman, who had entered the train at a small wayside station. "With the exception of that woman," he exclaimed dramatically to himself, "the nearest living beings are probably a pack of wolves."

Before making his way to the third-class compartment to acquaint his fellow-traveller with the extent of the disaster Abbleway hurriedly pondered the question of the woman's nationality. He had acquired a smattering of Slavonic tongues during his residence in Vienna, and felt competent to grapple with several racial possibilities.

"If she is Croat or Serb or Bosniak I shall be able to make her understand," he promised himself. "If she is Magyar, heaven help me! We shall have to converse entirely by signs."

He entered the carriage and made his momentous announcement in the best approach to Croat speech that he could achieve.

"The train has broken away and left us!"

The woman shook her head with a movement that might

be intended to convey resignation to the will of heaven, but probably meant noncomprehension. Abbleway repeated his information with variations of Slavonic tongues and generous displays of pantomime.

"Ah," said the woman at last in German dialect, "the train has gone? We are left. Ah, so."

She seemed about as much interested as though Abbleway had told her the result of the municipal elections in Amsterdam.

"They will find out at some station, and when the line is clear of snow they will send an engine. It happens that way sometimes."

"We may be here all night!" exclaimed Abbleway.

The woman looked as though she thought it possible.

"Are there wolves in these parts?" asked Abbleway hurriedly.

"Many," said the woman; "just outside this forest my aunt was devoured three years ago, as she was coming home from market. The horse and a young pig that was in the cart were eaten too. The horse was a very old one, but it was a beautiful young pig, oh, so fat. I cried when I heard that it was taken. They spare nothing."

"They may attack us here," said Abbleway tremulously; "they could easily break in, these carriages are like matchwood. We may both be devoured."

"You, perhaps," said the woman calmly; "not me."

"Why not you?" demanded Abbleway.

"It is the day of Saint Mariä Kleophä, my name-day. She would not allow me to be eaten by wolves on her day. Such a thing could not be thought of. You, yes, but not me."

Abbleway changed the subject.

"It is only afternoon now; if we are to be left here till morning we shall be starving."

"I have here some good eatables," said the woman tranquilly; "on my festival day it is natural that I should have provision with me. I have five good blood-sausages; in the town shops they cost twenty-five heller each. Things are dear in the town shops."

"I will give you fifty heller apiece for a couple of them," said Abbleway with some enthusiasm.

"In a railway accident things become very dear," said the woman; "these blood-sausages are four kronen apiece."

"Four kronen!" exclaimed Abbleway; "four kronen for a blood-sausage!"

"You cannot get them any cheaper on this train," said the woman, with relentless logic, "because there aren't any others to get. In Agram you can buy them cheaper, and in Paradise no doubt they will be given to us for nothing, but here they cost four kronen each. I have a small piece of Emmenthaler cheese and a honey-cake and a piece of bread that I can let you have. That will be another three kronen, eleven kronen in all. There is a piece of ham, but that I cannot let you have on my name-day."

Abbleway wondered to himself what price she would have put on the ham, and hurried to pay her the eleven kronen before her emergency tariff expanded into a famine tariff. As he was taking possession of his modest store of eatables he suddenly heard a noise which set his heart thumping in a miserable fever of fear. There was a scraping and shuffling as of some animal or animals trying to climb up to the footboard. In another moment, through the snow-encrusted glass of the carriage window, he saw a gaunt prick-eared head, with gaping jaw and lolling tongue and gleaming teeth; a second later another head shot up.

"There are hundreds of them," whispered Abbleway; "they have scented us. They will tear the carriage to pieces. We shall be devoured."

"Not me, on my name-day. The holy Mariä Kleophä would not permit it," said the woman with provoking calm.

The heads dropped down from the window and an uncanny silence fell on the beleaguered carriage. Abbleway neither moved nor spoke. Perhaps the brutes had not clearly seen or winded the human occupants of the carriage, and had prowled away on some other errand of rapine.

The long torture-laden minutes passed slowly away.

"It grows cold," said the woman suddenly, crossing over

to the far end of the carriage, where the heads had appeared. "The heating apparatus does not work any longer. See, over there beyond the trees, there is a chimney with smoke coming from it. It is not far, and the snow has nearly stopped. I shall find a path through the forest to that house with the chimney."

"But the wolves!" exclaimed Abbleway; "they may—"

"Not on my name-day," said the woman obstinately, and before he could stop her she had opened the door and climbed down into the snow. A moment later he hid his face in his hands; two gaunt lean figures rushed upon her from the forest. No doubt she had courted her fate, but Abbleway had no wish to see a human being torn to pieces and devoured before his eyes.

When he looked at last a new sensation of scandalized astonishment took possession of him. He had been straitly brought up in a small English town, and he was not prepared to be the witness of a miracle. The wolves were not doing anything worse to the woman than drench her with snow as they gambolled round her.

A short, joyous bark revealed the clue to the situation.

"Are those—dogs?" he called weakly.

"My cousin Karl's dogs, yes," she answered; "that is nis inn, over beyond the trees. I knew it was there, but I did not want to take you there; he is always grasping with strangers. However, it grows too cold to remain in the train. Ah, ah, see what comes!"

A whistle sounded, and a relief engine made its appearance, snorting its way sulkily through the snow. Abbleway did not have the opportunity for finding out whether Karl was really avaricious.

THE LUMBER-ROOM

THE children were to be driven, as a special treat, to the sands at Jagborough. Nicholas was not to be of the party: he was in disgrace. Only that morning he had refused to eat his wholesome bread-and-milk on the seemingly frivolous ground that there was a frog in it. Older and wiser and better people had told him that there could not possibly be a frog in his bread-and-milk and that he was not to talk nonsense; he continued, nevertheless, to talk what seemed the veriest nonsense, and described with much detail the colouration and markings of the alleged frog. The dramatic part of the incident was that there really was a frog in Nicholas' basin of bread-and-milk; he had put it there himself, so he felt entitled to know something about it. The sin of taking a frog from the garden and putting it into a bowl of wholesome bread-and-milk was enlarged on at great length, but the fact that stood out clearest in the whole affair, as it presented itself to the mind of Nicholas, was that the older, wiser and better people had been proved to be profoundly in error in matters about which they had expressed the utmost assurance.

"You said there couldn't possibly be a frog in my bread-and-milk; there *was* a frog in my bread-and-milk," he repeated, with the insistence of a skilled tactician who does not intend to shift from favourable ground.

So his boy-cousin and girl-cousin and his quite uninteresting younger brother were to be taken to Jagborough sands that afternoon and he was to stay at home. His cousins' aunt, who insisted, by an unwarranted stretch of imagination, in styling herself his aunt also, had hastily invented the Jagborough expedition in order to impress on Nicholas the delights that he had justly forfeited by his disgraceful conduct at the breakfast-table. It was her habit, whenever one of the children fell from grace, to improvise something of a festival nature from which the offender would be rigorously debarred; if all the children sinned collectively they were suddenly informed of a circus in a neighbouring town, a circus of unrivalled merit and uncounted elephants, to which, but for their depravity, they would have been taken that very day.

A few decent tears were looked for on the part of Nicholas when the moment for the departure of the expedition arrived. As a matter of fact, however, all the crying was done by his girl-cousin, who scraped her knee rather painfully against the step of the carriage as she was scrambling in.

"How she did howl," said Nicholas cheerfully, as the party drove off without any of the elation of high spirits that should have characterized it.

"She'll soon get over that," said the *soi-disant* aunt; "it will be a glorious afternoon for racing about over those beautiful sands. How they will enjoy themselves!"

"Bobby won't enjoy himself much, and he won't race much either," said Nicholas with a grim chuckle; "his boots are hurting him. They're too tight."

"Why didn't he tell me they were hurting?" asked the aunt with some asperity.

"He told you twice, but you weren't listening. You often don't listen when we tell you important things."

"You are not to go into the gooseberry garden," said the aunt, changing the subject.

"Why not?" demanded Nicholas.

"Because you are in disgrace," said the aunt loftily.

Nicholas did not admit the flawlessness of the reasoning; he felt perfectly capable of being in disgrace and in a gooseberry garden at the same moment. His face took on an expression of considerable obstinacy. It was clear to his aunt that he was determined to get into the gooseberry garden, "only," as she remarked to herself, "because I have told him he is not to."

Now the gooseberry garden had two doors by which it might be entered, and once a small person like Nicholas could slip in there he could effectually disappear from view amid the masking growth of artichokes, raspberry canes, and fruit bushes. The aunt had many other things to do that afternoon, but she spent an hour or two in trivial gardening operations among flower beds and shrubberies, whence she could keep a watchful eye on the two doors that led to the forbidden paradise. She was a woman of few ideas, with immense powers of concentration.

Nicholas made one or two sorties into the front garden, wriggling his way with obvious stealth of purpose towards one or other of the doors, but never able for a moment to evade the aunt's watchful eye. As a matter of fact, he had no intention of trying to get into the gooseberry garden, but it was extremely convenient for him that his aunt should believe that he had; it was a belief that would keep her on self-imposed sentry-duty for the greater part of the afternoon. Having thoroughly confirmed and fortified her suspicions, Nicholas slipped back into the house and rapidly put into execution a plan of action that had long germinated in his brain. By standing on a chair in the library one could reach a shelf on which reposed a fat, important-looking key. The key was as important as it looked; it was the instrument which kept the mysteries of the lumber-room secure from unauthorized intrusion, which opened a way only for aunts and such-like privileged persons. Nicholas had not had much experience of the art of fitting keys into keyholes and turning locks, but for some days past he had practised with the key of the school-room door; he did not believe in trusting too much to luck and accident. The key turned stiffly in the lock, but it turned. The door opened, and Nicholas was in an unknown land, compared with which the gooseberry garden was a stale delight, a mere material pleasure.

Often and often Nicholas had pictured to himself what the lumber-room might be like, that region that was so carefully sealed from youthful eyes and concerning which no questions were ever answered. It came up to his expectations. In the first place it was large and dimly lit, one high window opening on to the forbidden garden being its only source of illumination. In the second place it was a storehouse of unimagined treasures. The aunt-by-assertion was one of those people who think that things spoil by use and consign them to dust and damp by way of preserving them. Such parts of the house as Nicholas knew best were rather bare and cheerless, but here there were wonderful things for the eye to feast on. First and foremost there was a piece of framed tapestry that was evidently meant to be a fire-screen. To Nicholas it was a living, breathing story; he sat down on a roll of Indian hangings, glowing in wonderful colours beneath a layer of dust, and took in all the details of the tapestry picture. A man, dressed in the hunting costume of some remote period, had just transfixed a stag with an arrow; it could not have been a difficult shot because the stag was only one or two paces away from him; in the thickly growing vegetation that the picture suggested it would not have been difficult to creep up to a feeding stag, and the two spotted dogs that were springing forward to join in the chase had evidently been trained to keep to heel till the arrow was discharged. That part of the picture was simple, if interesting, but did the huntsman see, what Nicholas saw, that four galloping wolves were coming in his direction through the wood? There might be more than four of them hidden behind the trees, and in any case would the man and his dogs be able to cope with the four wolves if they made an attack? The man had only two arrows left in his quiver, and he might miss with one or both of them; all one knew about his skill in shooting was that he could hit a large stag at a ridiculously short range. Nicholas sat for many golden minutes revolving the possibilities of the scene; he was inclined to think that there were more than four wolves and that the man and his dogs were in a tight corner.

But there were other objects of delight and interest claiming his instant attention: there were quaint twisted candlesticks in the shape of snakes, and a teapot fashioned like a china duck, out of whose open beak the tea was supposed to come. How dull and shapeless the nursery teapot seemed in comparison! And there was a carved sandal-wood box packed tight with aromatic cotton-wool, and between the layers of cotton-wool were little brass figures, hump-necked bulls, and peacocks and goblins, delightful to see and to handle. Less promising in appearance was a large square book with plain black covers; Nicholas peeped into it, and, behold, it was full of coloured pictures of birds. And such birds! In the garden, and in the lanes when he went for a walk, Nicholas came across a few birds, of which the largest were an occasional magpie or wood-pigeon; here were herons and bustards, kites, toucans, tiger-bitterns, brush turkeys, ibises, golden pheasants, a whole por-trait gallery of undreamed-of creatures. And as he was admiring the colouring of the mandarin duck and assigning a life-history to it, the voice of his aunt in shrill vociferation of his name came from the gooseberry garden without. She had grown suspicious at his long disappearance, and had leapt to the conclusion that he had climbed over the wall behind the sheltering screen of the lilac bushes; she was now engaged in energetic and rather hopeless search for him among the artichokes and raspberry canes.

"Nicholas, Nicholas!" she screamed, "you are to come out of this at once. It's no use trying to hide there; I can see you all the time."

It was probably the first time for twenty years that any one had smiled in that lumber-room.

Presently the angry repetitions of Nicholas' name gave way to a shriek, and a cry for somebody to come quickly. Nicholas shut the book, restored it carefully to its place in a corner, and shook some dust from a neighbouring pile of newspapers over it. Then he crept from the room, locked the door, and replaced the key exactly where he had found it. His aunt was still calling his name when he sauntered into the front garden.

"Who's calling?" he asked.

"Me," came the answer from the other side of the wall; "didn't you hear me? I've been looking for you in the gooseberry garden, and I've slipped into the rain-water tank. Luckily there's no water in it, but the sides are slippery and I can't get out. Fetch the little ladder from under the cherry tree—"

"I was told I wasn't to go into the gooseberry garden," said Nicholas promptly.

"I told you not to, and now I tell you that you may," came the voice from the rain-water tank, rather impatiently.

"Your voice doesn't sound like aunt's," objected Nicholas; "you may be the Evil One tempting me to be disobedient. Aunt often tells me that the Evil One tempts me and that I always yield. This time I'm not going to yield."

"Don't talk nonsense," said the prisoner in the tank; "go and fetch the ladder."

"Will there be strawberry jam for tea?" asked Nicholas innocently.

"Certainly there will be," said the aunt, privately resolving that Nicholas should have none of it.

"Now I know that you are the Evil One and not aunt," shouted Nicholas gleefully; "when we asked aunt for strawberry jam yesterday she said there wasn't any. I know there are four jars of it in the store cupboard, because I looked, and of course you know it's there, but *she* doesn't, because she said there wasn't any. Oh, Devil, you *have* sold yourself!"

There was an unusual sense of luxury in being able to talk to an aunt as though one was talking to the Evil One, but Nicholas knew, with childish discernment, that such luxuries were not to be over-indulged in. He walked noisily away, and it was a kitchenmaid, in search of parsley, who eventually rescued the aunt from the rain-water tank.

Tea that evening was partaken of in a fearsome silence. The tide had been at its highest when the children had arrived at Jagborough Cove, so there had been no sands to play on—a circumstance that the aunt had overlooked in the haste of organizing her punitive expedition. The tightness of Bobby's boots had had disastrous effect on his temper the whole of the afternoon, and altogether the children could not have been said to have enjoyed themselves. The aunt maintained the frozen muteness of one who has suffered undignified and unmerited detention in a rain-water tank for thirty-five minutes. As for Nicholas, he, too, was silent, in the absorption of one who has much to think about; it was just possible, he considered, that the huntsman would escape with his hounds while the wolves feasted on the stricken stag.

FUR

"YOU look worried, dear," said Eleanor.

"I am worried," admitted Suzanne; "not worried exactly, but anxious. You see, my birthday happens next week—"

"You lucky person," interrupted Eleanor; "my birthday doesn't come till the end of March."

"Well, old Bertram Kneyght is over in England just now from the Argentine. He's a kind of distant cousin of my mother's, and so enormously rich that we've never let the relationship drop out of sight. Even if we don't see him or hear from him for years he is always Cousin Bertram when he does turn up. I can't say he's ever been of much solid use to us, but yesterday the subject of my birthday cropped up, and he asked me to let him know what I wanted for a present."

"Now I understand the anxiety," observed Eleanor.

"As a rule when one is confronted with a problem like that," said Suzanne, "all one's ideas vanish; one doesn't seem to have a desire in the world. Now it so happens that I have been very keen on a little Dresden figure that I saw somewhere in Kensington; about thirty-six shillings, quite beyond my means. I was very nearly describing the figure, and giving Bertram the address of the shop. And then it suddenly struck me that thirty-six shillings was such a ridiculously inadequate sum for a man of his immense wealth to spend on a birthday present. He could give thirty-six pounds as easily as you or I could buy a bunch of violets. I don't want to be greedy, of course, but I don't like being wasteful."

"The question is," said Eleanor, "what are his ideas as to present-giving? Some of the wealthiest people have curiously cramped views on that subject. When people grow gradually rich their requirements and standard of living expand in proportion, while their present-giving instincts often remain in the undeveloped condition of their earlier days. Something showy and not-too-expensive in a shop is their only conception of the ideal gift. That is why even quite good shops have their counters and windows crowded with things worth about four shillings that look as if they might be worth seven-and-six, and are priced at ten shillings and labelled 'seasonable gifts.'"

"I know," said Suzanne; "that is why it is so risky to be vague when one is giving indications of one's wants. Now if

I say to him: 'I am going out to Davos this winter, so anything in the travelling line would be acceptable,' he *might* give me a dressing-bag with gold-mounted fittings, but, on the other hand, he might give me Baedeker's *Switzerland*, or *Ski-ing without Tears*, or something of that sort."

"He would be more likely to say: 'She'll be going to lots of dances, a fan will be sure to be useful.' "

"Yes, and I've got tons of fans, so you see where the danger and anxiety lies. Now if there is one thing more than another that I really urgently want it is furs. I simply haven't any. I'm told that Davos is full of Russians, and they are sure to wear the most lovely sables and things. To be among people who are smothered in furs when one hasn't any oneself makes one want to break most of the Commandments."

"If it's furs that you're out for," said Eleanor, "you will have to superintend the choice of them in person. You can't be sure that your cousin knows the difference between silver-fox and ordinary squirrel."

"There are some heavenly silver-fox stoles at Goliath and Mastodon's," said Suzanne, with a sigh; "if I could only inveigle Bertram into their building and take him for a stroll through the fur department!"

"He lives somewhere near there, doesn't he?" said Eleanor. "Do you know what his habits are? Does he take a walk at any particular time of day?"

"He usually walks down to his club about three o'clock, if it's a fine day. That takes him right past Goliath and Mastodon's."

"Let us two meet him accidentally at the street corner tomorrow," said Eleanor; "we can walk a little way with him, and with luck we ought to be able to side-track him into the shop. You can say you want to get a hair-net or something. When we're safely there I can say: 'I wish you'd tell me what you want for your birthday.' Then you'll have everything ready to hand—the rich cousin, the fur department, and the topic of birthday presents."

"It's a great idea," said Suzanne; "you really are a brick.

Come round tomorrow at twenty to three; don't be late, we must carry out our ambush to the minute."

At a few minutes to three the next afternoon the fur-trappers walked warily towards the selected corner. In the near distance rose the colossal pile of Messrs. Goliath and Mastodon's famed establishment. The afternoon was brilliantly fine, exactly the sort of weather to tempt a gentleman of advancing years into the discreet exercise of a leisurely walk.

"I say, dear, I wish you'd do something for me this evening," said Eleanor to her companion; "just drop in after dinner on some pretext or other, and stay on to make a fourth at bridge with Adela and the aunts. Otherwise I shall have to play, and Harry Scarisbrooke is going to come in unexpectedly about nine-fifteen, and I particularly wanted to be free to talk to him while the others are playing."

"Sorry, my dear, no can do," said Suzanne; "ordinary bridge at threepence a hundred, with such dreadfully slow players as your aunts, bores me to tears. I nearly go to sleep over it."

"But I most particularly want an opportunity to talk with Harry," urged Eleanor, an angry glint coming into her eyes.

"Sorry, anything to oblige, but not that," said Suzanne cheerfully; the sacrifices of friendship were beautiful in her eyes as long as she was not asked to make them.

Eleanor said nothing further on the subject, but the corners of her mouth rearranged themselves.

"There's our man!" exclaimed Suzanne suddenly; "hurry!"

Mr. Bertram Kneyght greeted his cousin and her friend with genuine heartiness, and readily accepted their invitation to explore the crowded mart that stood temptingly at their elbow. The plate-glass doors swung open and the trio plunged bravely into the jostling throng of buyers and loiterers.

"Is it always as full as this?" asked Bertram of Eleanor.

"More or less, and autumn sales are on just now," she replied.

Suzanne, in her anxiety to pilot her cousin to the desired haven of the fur department, was usually a few paces ahead of the others, coming back to them now and then if they lingered for a moment at some attractive counter, with the nervous solicitude of a parent rook encouraging its young ones on their first flying expedition.

"It's Suzanne's birthday on Wednesday next," confided Eleanor to Bertram Kneyght at a moment when Suzanne had left them unusually far behind; "my birthday comes the day before, so we are both on the look-out for something to give each other."

"Ah," said Bertram. "Now, perhaps you can advise me on that very point. I want to give Suzanne something, and I haven't the least idea what she wants."

"She's rather a problem," said Eleanor. "She seems to have everything one can think of, lucky girl. A fan is always useful; she'll be going to a lot of dances at Davos this winter. Yes, I should think a fan would please her more than anything. After our birthdays are over we inspect each other's muster of presents, and I always feel dreadfully humble. She gets such nice things, and I never have anything worth showing. You see, none of my relations or any of the people who give me presents are at all well off, so I can't expect them to do anything more than just remember the day with some little trifle. Two years ago an uncle on my mother's side of the family, who had come into a small legacy, promised me a silver-fox stole for my birthday. I can't tell you how excited I was about it, how I pictured myself showing it off to all my friends and enemies. Then just at that moment his wife died, and, of course, poor man, he could not be expected to think of birthday presents at such a time. He has lived abroad ever since, and I never got my fur. Do you know, to this day I can scarcely look at a silver-fox pelt in a shop window or round any one's neck without feeling ready to burst into tears. I suppose if I hadn't had the prospect of getting one I shouldn't feel that way. Look, there is the fan counter, on your left; you can easily slip away in the crowd. Get her as nice a one as you can see—she is such a dear, dear girl."

"Hullo, I thought I had lost you," said Suzanne, making

ner way through an obstructive knot of shoppers. "Where is Bertram?"

"I got separated from him long ago. I thought he was on ahead with you," said Eleanor. "We shall never find him in this crush."

Which turned out to be a true prediction.

"All our trouble and forethought thrown away," said Suzanne sulkily, when they had pushed their way fruitlessly through half a dozen departments.

"I can't think why you didn't grab him by the arm," said Eleanor; "I would have if I'd known him longer, but I'd only just been introduced. It's nearly four now, we'd better have tea."

Some days later Suzanne rang Eleanor up on the telephone.

"Thank you very much for the photograph frame. It was just what I wanted. Very good of you. I say, do you know what that Kneyght person has given me? Just what you said he would—a wretched fan. What? Oh, yes, quite a good enough fan in its way, but still . . ."

"You must come and see what he's given me," came in Eleanor's voice over the 'phone.

"You! Why should he give you anything?"

"Your cousin appears to be one of those rare people of wealth who take a pleasure in giving good presents," came the reply.

"I wondered why he was so anxious to know where she lived," snapped Suzanne to herself as she rang off.

A cloud has arisen between the friendships of the two young women; as far as Eleanor is concerned the cloud has a silver-fox lining.

THE PHILANTHROPIST AND
THE HAPPY CAT

JOCANTHA BESSBURY was in the mood to be serenely and graciously happy. Her world was a pleasant place, and it was wearing one of its pleasantest aspects. Gregory had managed to get home for a hurried lunch and a smoke afterwards in the little snuggery; the lunch had been a good one, and there was just time to do justice to the coffee and cigarettes. Both were excellent in their way, and Gregory was, in his way, an excellent husband. Jocantha rather suspected herself of making him a very charming wife, and more than suspected herself of having a first-rate dressmaker.

"I don't suppose a more thoroughly contented personality is to be found in all Chelsea," observed Jocantha in allusion to herself; "except perhaps Attab," she continued, glancing towards the large tabby-marked cat that lay in considerable ease in a corner of the divan. "He lies there, purring and dreaming, shifting his limbs now and then in an ecstasy of cushioned comfort. He seems the incarnation of everything soft and silky and velvety, without a sharp edge in his composition, a dreamer whose philosophy is sleep and let sleep; and then, as evening draws on, he goes out into the garden with a red glint in his eyes and slays a drowsy sparrow."

"As every pair of sparrows hatches out ten or more young ones in the year, while their food supply remains stationary, it is just as well that the Attabs of the community should have that idea of how to pass an amusing afternoon," said Gregory. Having delivered himself of this sage comment he lit another cigarette, bade Jocantha a playfully affectionate good-bye, and departed into the outer world.

"Remember, dinner's a wee bit earlier tonight, as we're going to the Haymarket," she called after him.

Left to herself, Jocantha continued the process of looking at her life with placid, introspective eyes. If she had not everything she wanted in this world, at least she was very well pleased with what she had got. She was very well pleased, for instance, with the snuggery, which contrived somehow to be cozy and dainty and expensive all at once. The porcelain was rare and beautiful, the Chinese enamels took on wonderful tints in the firelight, the rugs and hangings led the eye through sumptuous harmonies of colouring. It was a room in which one might have suitably entertained an ambassador or an archbishop, but it was also a room in which one could cut out pictures for a scrap-book without feeling that one was scandalizing the deities of the place with one's litter. And as with the snuggery, so with the rest of the house, and as with the house, so with the other departments of Jocantha's life; she really had good reason for being one of the most contented women in Chelsea.

From being in a mood of simmering satisfaction with her lot she passed to the phase of being generously commiserating for those thousands around her whose lives and circumstances were dull, cheap, pleasureless, and empty. Work girls, shop assistants and so forth, the class that have neither the happy-go-lucky freedom of the poor nor the leisured freedom of the rich, came specially within the range of her sympathy. It was sad to think that there were young people who, after a long day's work, had to sit alone in chill, dreary bedrooms because they could not afford the price of a cup of coffee and a sandwich in a restaurant, still less a shilling for a theatre gallery.

Jocantha's mind was still dwelling on this theme when she started forth on an afternoon campaign of desultory shopping; it would be rather a comforting thing, she told herself, if she could do something, on the spur of the moment, to bring a gleam of pleasure and interest into the life of even one or two wistful-hearted, empty-pocketed workers; it would add a good deal to her sense of enjoyment at the theatre that night. She would get two upper circle tickets for a popular play, make her way into some cheap tea-shop, and present the tickets to the first couple of interesting work girls with whom she could casually drop into conversation. She could explain matters by saying that she was unable to use the tickets herself and did not want them to be wasted, and, on the other hand, did not want the trouble of sending them back. On further reflection she decided that it might be better to get only one ticket and give it to some lonely-looking girl sitting eating her frugal meal by herself; the girl might scrape acquaintance with her next-seat neighbour at the theatre and lay the foundations of a lasting friendship.

With the Fairy Godmother impulse strong upon her, Jocantha marched into a ticket agency and selected with immense care an upper circle seat for the "Yellow Peacock," a play that was attracting a considerable amount of discussion and criticism. Then she went forth in search of a tea-shop and philanthropic adventure, at about the same time that Attab sauntered into the garden with a mind attuned to sparrow stalking. In a corner of an A.B.C. shop she found an unoccupied table, whereat she promptly installed herself, impelled by the fact that at the next table was sitting a young girl, rather plain of feature, with tired, listless eyes and a general air of uncomplaining forlornness. Her dress was of poor material, but aimed at being in the fashion, her hair was pretty, and her complexion bad; she was finishing a modest meal of tea and scone, and she was not very different in her way from thousands of other girls who were finishing, or beginning, or continuing their teas in London tea-shops at that exact moment. The odds were enormously in favour of the supposition that she had never seen the "Yellow Peacock"; obviously she supplied excellent material for Jocantha's first experiment in haphazard benefaction.

Jocantha ordered some tea and a muffin, and then turned a friendly scrutiny on her neighbour with a view to catching her eye. At that precise moment the girl's face lit up with sudden pleasure, her eyes sparkled, a flush came into her cheeks, and she looked almost pretty. A young man, whom she greeted with an affectionate "Hullo, Bertie" came up to her table and took his seat in a chair facing her. Jocantha looked hard at the new-comer; he was in appearance a few years younger than herself, very much better looking than Gregory, rather better looking, in fact, than any of the young men of

her set. She guessed him to be a well-mannered young clerk
in some wholesale warehouse, existing and amusing himself
as best he might on a tiny salary, and commanding a holiday
of about two weeks in the year. He was aware, of course, of
his good looks, but with the shy self-consciousness of the
Anglo-Saxon, not the blatant complacency of the Latin or
Semite. He was obviously on terms of friendly intimacy with
the girl he was talking to, probably they were drifting towards
a formal engagement. Jocantha pictured the boy's home, in a
rather narrow circle, with a tiresome mother who always
wanted to know how and where he spent his evenings. He
would exchange that humdrum thraldom in due course for a
home of his own, dominated by a chronic scarcity of pounds,
shillings, and pence, and a dearth of most of the things that
made life attractive or comfortable. Jocantha felt extremely
sorry for him. She wondered if he had seen the "Yellow Peacock"; the odds were enormously in favour of the supposition that he had not. The girl had finished her tea, and would
shortly be going back to her work; when the boy was alone
it would be quite easy for Jocantha to say: "My husband has
made other arrangements for me this evening; would you
care to make use of this ticket, which would otherwise be
wasted?" Then she could come there again one afternoon for
tea, and, if she saw him, ask him how he liked the play. If
he was a nice boy and improved on acquaintance he could be
given more theatre tickets and perhaps asked to come one
Sunday to tea at Chelsea. Jocantha made up her mind that he
would improve on acquaintance, and that Gregory would like
him, and that the Fairy Godmother business would prove far
more entertaining than she had originally anticipated. The boy
was distinctly presentable; he knew how to brush his hair,
which was possibly an imitative faculty; he knew what colour
of tie suited him, which might be intuition; he was exactly the
type that Jocantha admired, which of course was accident.
Altogether she was rather pleased when the girl looked at
the clock and bade a friendly but hurried farewell to her
companion. Bertie nodded "good-bye," gulped down a mouth-
ful of tea, and then produced from his overcoat pocket a

paper-covered book, bearing the title *Sepoy and Sahib, a Tale of the Great Mutiny.*

The laws of tea-shop etiquette forbid that you should offer theatre tickets to a stranger without having first caught the stranger's eye. It is even better if you can ask to have a sugar basin passed to you, having previously concealed the fact that you have a large and well-filled sugar basin on your own table; this is not difficult to manage, as the printed menu is generally nearly as large as the table, and can be made to stand on end. Jocantha set to work hopefully; she had a long and rather high-pitched discussion with the waitress concerning alleged defects in an altogether blameless muffin, she made loud and plaintive inquiries about the tube service to some impossibly remote suburb, she talked with brilliant insincerity to the tea-shop kitten, and as a last resort she upset a milk-jug and swore at it daintily. Altogether she attracted a good deal of attention, but never for a moment did she attract the attention of the boy with the beautifully brushed hair, who was some thousands of miles away in the baking plains of Hindostan, amid deserted bungalows, seething bazaars, and riotous barrack squares, listening to the throbbing of tom-toms and the distant rattle of musketry.

Jocantha went back to her house in Chelsea, which struck her for the first time as looking dull and over-furnished. She had a resentful conviction that Gregory would be uninteresting at dinner, and that the play would be stupid after dinner. On the whole her frame of mind showed a marked divergence from the purring complacency of Attab, who was again curled up in his corner of the divan with a great peace radiating from every curve of his body.

But then he had killed his sparrow.

ON APPROVAL

OF all the genuine Bohemians who strayed from time to time into the would-be-Bohemian circle of the Restaurant Nuremberg, Owl Street, Soho, none was more interesting and more elusive than Gebhard Knopfschrank. He had no friends, and though he treated all the restaurant frequenters as acquaintances he never seemed to wish to carry the acquaintanceship beyond the door that led into Owl Street and the outer world. He dealt with them all rather as a market woman might deal with chance passers-by, exhibiting her wares and chattering about the weather and the slackness of business, occasionally about rheumatism, but never showing a desire to penetrate into their daily lives or to dissect their ambitions.

He was understood to belong to a family of peasant farmers, somewhere in Pomerania; some two years ago, according to all that was known of him, he had abandoned the labours and responsibilities of swine tending and goose rearing to try his fortune as an artist in London.

"Why London and not Paris or Munich?" he had been asked by the curious.

Well, there was a ship that left Stolpmünde for London twice a month, that carried few passengers, but carried them cheaply; the railway fares to Munich or Paris were not cheap. Thus it was that he came to select London as the scene of his great adventure.

The question that had long and seriously agitated the frequenters of the Nuremberg was whether this goose-boy migrant was really a soul-driven genius, spreading his wings to the light, or merely an enterprising young man who fancied he could paint and was pardonably anxious to escape from the monotony of rye bread diet and the sandy, swine-bestrewn plains of Pomerania. There was reasonable ground for doubt and caution; the artistic groups that foregathered at the little restaurant contained so many young women with short hair and so many young men with long hair, who supposed themselves to be abnormally gifted in the domain of music, poetry, painting, or stagecraft, with little or nothing to support the supposition, that a self-announced genius of any sort in their midst was inevitably suspect. On the other hand, there was the ever-imminent danger of entertaining, and snubbing, an angel unawares. There had been the lamentable case of Sledonti, the dramatic poet, who had been belittled and cold-shouldered in the Owl Street hall of judgment, and had been afterwards hailed as a master singer by the Grand Duke Constantine Constantinovitch—"the most educated of the Romanoffs," according to Sylvia Strubble, who spoke rather as one who knew every individual member of the Russian imperial family; as a matter of fact, she knew a newspaper correspondent, a young man who ate borsch with the air of having invented it. Sledonti's *Poems of Death and Passion* were now being sold by the thousand in seven European languages, and were about to be translated into Syrian, a circumstance which made the discerning critics of the Nuremberg rather shy of maturing their future judgments too rapidly and too irrevocably.

As regards Knopfschrank's work, they did not lack opportunity for inspecting and appraising it. However resolutely he might hold himself aloof from the social life of his restaurant acquaintances, he was not minded to hide his artistic performances from their inquiring gaze. Every evening, or nearly every evening, at about seven o'clock, he would make his appearance, sit himself down at his accustomed table, throw a bulky black portfolio on to the chair opposite him, nod round indiscriminately at his fellow-guests, and commence the serious business of eating and drinking. When the coffee stage was reached he would light a cigarette, draw the portfolio over to him, and begin to rummage among its contents. With slow deliberation he would select a few of his more recent studies and sketches, and silently pass them round from table to table, paying especial attention to any new diners who might be present. On the back of each sketch was marked in plain figures the announcement "Price ten shillings."

If his work was not obviously stamped with the hall-mark of genius, at any rate it was remarkable for its choice of an unusual and unvarying theme. His pictures always represented some well-known street or public place in London, fallen into decay and denuded of its human population, in the place of which there roamed a wild fauna, which, from its wealth of exotic species, must have originally escaped from Zoological Gardens and travelling beast shows. "Giraffes drinking at the fountain pools, Trafalgar Square," was one of the most notable and characteristic of his studies, while even more sensational was the gruesome picture of "Vultures attacking dying camel in Upper Berkeley Street." There were also photographs of the large canvas on which he had been engaged for some months, and which he was now endeavouring to sell to some enterprising dealer or adventurous amateur. The subject was "Hyænas asleep in Euston Station," a composition that left nothing to be desired in the way of suggesting unfathomed depths of desolation.

"Of course it may be immensely clever, it may be something epoch-making in the realm of art," said Sylvia Strubble to her own particular circle of listeners, "but, on the other hand, it may be merely mad. One mustn't pay too much attention to the commercial aspect of the case, of course, but still, if some dealer would make a bid for that hyæna picture, or even for some of the sketches, we should know better how to place the man and his work."

"We may all be cursing ourselves one of these days," said Mrs. Nougat-Jones, "for not having bought up his entire portfolio of sketches. At the same time, when there is so much real talent going about, one does not feel like planking down ten shillings for what looks like a bit of whimsical oddity. Now that picture that he showed us last week, 'Sand-grouse roosting on the Albert Memorial,' was very impressive, and of course I could see there was good workmanship in it and breadth of treatment; but it didn't in the least convey the Albert Memorial to me, and Sir James Beanquest tells me that sand-grouse don't roost, they sleep on the ground."

Whatever talent or genius the Pomeranian artist might possess, it certainly failed to receive commercial sanction. The portfolio remained bulky with unsold sketches, and the "Euston

Siesta," as the wits of the Nuremberg nicknamed the large canvas, was still in the market. The outward and visible signs of financial embarrassment began to be noticeable; the half-bottle of cheap claret at dinner-time gave way to a small glass of lager, and this in turn was displaced by water. The one-and-sixpenny set dinner receded from an everyday event to a Sunday extravagance; on ordinary days the artist contented himself with a sevenpenny omelette and some bread and cheese, and there were evenings when he did not put in an appearance at all. On the rare occasions when he spoke of his own affairs it was observed that he began to talk more about Pomerania and less about the great world of art.

"It is a busy time there now with us," he said wistfully; "the schwines are driven out into the fields after harvest, and must be looked after. I could be helping to look after if I was there. Here it is difficult to live; art is not appreciate."

"Why don't you go home on a visit?" some one asked tactfully.

"Ah, it cost money! There is the ship passage to Stolpmünde, and there is money that I owe at my lodgings. Even here I owe a few schillings. If I could sell some of my sketches——"

"Perhaps," suggested Mrs. Nougat-Jones, "if you were to offer them for a little less, some of us would be glad to buy a few. Ten shillings is always a consideration, you know, to people who are not over well off. Perhaps if you were to ask six or seven shillings——"

Once a peasant, always a peasant. The mere suggestion of a bargain to be struck brought a twinkle of awakened alertness into the artist's eyes, and hardened the lines of his mouth.

"Nine schilling, nine pence each," he snapped, and seemed disappointed that Mrs. Nougat-Jones did not pursue the subject further. He had evidently expected her to offer seven-and-fourpence.

The weeks sped by, and Knopfschrank came more rarely to the restaurant in Owl Street, while his meals on those occasions became more and more meagre. And then came a triumphal day, when he appeared early in the evening in a high state of elation, and ordered an elaborate meal that scarcely stopped short of being a banquet. The ordinary resources of the kitchen were supplemented by an imported dish of smoked goosebreast, a Pomeranian delicacy that was luckily procurable at a firm of *delikatessen* merchants in Coventry Street, while a long-necked bottle of Rhine wine gave a finishing touch of festivity and good cheer to the crowded table.

"He has evidently sold his masterpiece," whispered Sylvia Strubble to Mrs. Nougat-Jones, who had come in late.

"Who has bought it?" she whispered back.

"Don't know; he hasn't said anything yet, but it must be some American. Do you see, he has got a little American flag on the dessert dish, and he has put pennies in the music box three times, once to play the 'Star-spangled Banner,' then a Sousa march, and then the 'Star-spangled Banner' again. It must be an American millionaire, and he's evidently got a big price for it; he's just beaming and chuckling with satisfaction."

"We must ask him who has bought it," said Mrs. Nougat-Jones.

"Hush! no, don't. Let's buy some of his sketches, quick, before we are supposed to know that he's famous; otherwise he'll be doubling the prices. I *am* so glad he's had a success at last. I always believed in him, you know."

For the sum of ten shillings each Miss Strubble acquired the drawings of the camel dying in Upper Berkeley Street and of the giraffes quenching their thirst in Trafalgar Square; at the same price Mrs. Nougat-Jones secured the study of roosting sand-grouse. A more ambitious picture, "Wolves and wapiti fighting on the steps of the Athenæum Club," found a purchaser at fifteen shillings.

"And now what are your plans?" asked a young man who contributed occasional paragraphs to an artistic weekly.

"I go back to Stolpmünde as soon as the ship sails," said the artist, "and I do not return. Never."

"But your work? Your career as painter?"

"Ah, there is nossing in it. One starves. Till today I have sold not one of my sketches. Tonight you have bought a few, because I am going away from you, but at other times, not one."

"But has not some American——?"

"Ah, the rich American," chuckled the artist. "God be thanked. He dash his car right into our herd of schwines as they were being driven out to the fields. Many of our best schwines he killed, but he paid all damages. He paid perhaps more than they were worth, many times more than they would have fetched in the market after a month of fattening, but he was in a hurry to get on to Danzig. When one is in a hurry one must pay what one is asked. God be thanked for rich Americans, who are always in a hurry to get somewhere else. My father and mother, they have now so plenty of money; they send me some to pay my debts and come home. I start on Monday for Stolpmünde and I do not come back. Never."

"But your picture, the hyænas?"

"No good. It is too big to carry to Stolpmünde. I burn it."

In time he will be forgotten, but at present Knopfschrank is almost as sore a subject as Sledonti with some of the frequenters of the Nuremberg Restaurant, Owl Street, Soho.

The Toys of Peace

First Collected, 1923

TO
THE 22ND ROYAL FUSILIERS

Thanks are due to the Editors of the *Morning Post*, the *Westminster Gazette*, and the *Bystander* for their amiability in allowing tales that appeared in these journals to be reproduced in the present volume.

THE TOYS OF PEACE

"HARVEY," said Eleanor Bope, handing her brother a cutting from a London morning paper [1] of the 19th of March, "just read this about children's toys, please; it exactly carries out some of our ideas about influence and upbringing."

"In the view of the National Peace Council," ran the extract, "there are grave objections to presenting our boys with regiments of fighting men, batteries of guns, and squadrons of 'Dreadnoughts.' Boys, the Council admits, naturally love fighting and all the panoply of war . . . but that is no reason for encouraging, and perhaps giving permanent form to, their primitive instincts. At the Children's Welfare Exhibition, which opens at Olympia in three weeks' time, the Peace Council will make an alternative suggestion to parents in the shape of an exhibition of 'peace toys.' In front of a specially painted representation of the Peace Palace at The Hague will be grouped, not miniature soldiers but miniature civilians, not guns but ploughs and the tools of industry. . . . It is hoped that manufacturers may take a hint from the exhibit, which will bear fruit in the toy shops."

"The idea is certainly an interesting and very well-meaning one," said Harvey; "whether it would succeed well in practice—"

"We must try," interrupted his sister; "you are coming down to us at Easter, and you always bring the boys some toys, so that will be an excellent opportunity for you to inaugurate the new experiment. Go about in the shops and buy any little toys and models that have special bearing on civilian life in its more peaceful aspects. Of course you must explain the toys to the children and interest them in the new idea. I regret to

[1] An actual extract from a London paper of March 1914.

say that the 'Siege of Adrianople' toy, that their Aunt Susan sent them, didn't need any explanation; they knew all the uniforms and flags, and even the names of the respective commanders, and when I heard them one day using what seemed to be the most objectionable language they said it was Bulgarian words of command; of course it *may* have been, but at any rate I took the toy away from them. Now I shall expect your Easter gifts to give quite a new impulse and direction to the children's minds; Eric is not eleven yet, and Bertie is only nine-and-a-half, so they are really at a most impressionable age."

"There is primitive instinct to be taken into consideration, you know," said Harvey doubtfully, "and hereditary tendencies as well. One of their great-uncles fought in the most intolerant fashion at Inkerman—he was specially mentioned in dispatches, I believe—and their great-grandfather smashed all his Whig neighbours' hothouses when the great Reform Bill was passed. Still, as you say, they are at an impressionable age. I will do my best."

On Easter Saturday Harvey Bope unpacked a large, promising-looking red cardboard box under the expectant eyes of his nephews. "Your uncle has brought you the newest thing in toys," Eleanor had said impressively, and youthful anticipation had been anxiously divided between Albanian soldiery and a Somali camel-corps. Eric was hotly in favour of the latter contingency. "There would be Arabs on horseback," he whispered; "the Albanians have got jolly uniforms, and they fight all day long, and all night too, when there's a moon, but the country's rocky, so they've got no cavalry."

A quantity of crinkly paper shavings was the first thing that met the view when the lid was removed; the most exciting toys always began like that. Harvey pushed back the top layer and drew forth a square, rather featureless building.

"It's a fort!" exclaimed Bertie.

"It isn't, it's the palace of the Mpret of Albania," said Eric, immensely proud of his knowledge of the exotic title; "it's got no windows, you see, so that passers-by can't fire in at the Royal Family."

"It's a municipal dust-bin," said Harvey hurriedly; "you see all the refuse and litter of a town is collected there, instead of lying about and injuring the health of the citizens."

In an awful silence he disinterred a little lead figure of a man in black clothes.

"That," he said, "is a distinguished civilian, John Stuart Mill. He was an authority on political economy."

"Why?" asked Bertie.

"Well, he wanted to be; he thought it was a useful thing to be."

Bertie gave an expressive grunt, which conveyed his opinion that there was no accounting for tastes.

Another square building came out, this time with windows and chimneys.

"A model of the Manchester branch of the Young Women's Christian Association," said Harvey.

"Are there any lions?" asked Eric hopefully. He had been reading Roman history and thought that where you found Christians you might reasonably expect to find a few lions.

"There are no lions," said Harvey. "Here is another civilian, Robert Raikes, the founder of Sunday schools, and here is a model of a municipal wash-house. These little round things are loaves baked in a sanitary bakehouse. That lead figure is a sanitary inspector, this one is a district councillor, and this one is an official of the Local Government Board."

"What does he do?" asked Eric wearily.

"He sees to things connected with his Department," said Harvey. "This box with a slit in it is a ballot-box. Votes are put into it at election times."

"What is put into it at other times?" asked Bertie.

"Nothing. And here are some tools of industry, a wheelbarrow and a hoe, and I think these are meant for hop-poles. This is a model beehive, and that is a ventilator, for ventilating sewers. This seems to be another municipal dust-bin—no, it is a model of a school of art and a public library. This little lead figure is Mrs. Hemans, a poetess, and this is Rowland Hill, who introduced the system of penny postage. This is Sir John Herschel, the eminent astrologer."

"Are we to play with these civilian figures?" asked Eric.

"Of course," said Harvey, "these are toys; they are meant to be played with."

"But how?"

It was rather a poser. "You might make two of them contest a seat in Parliament," said Harvey, "and have an election——"

"With rotten eggs, and free fights, and ever so many broken heads!" exclaimed Eric.

"And noses all bleeding and everybody drunk as can be," echoed Bertie, who had carefully studied one of Hogarth's pictures.

"Nothing of the kind," said Harvey, "nothing in the least like that. Votes will be put in the ballot-box, and the Mayor will count them—the district councillor will do for the Mayor —and he will say which has received the most votes, and then the two candidates will thank him for presiding, and each will say that the contest has been conducted throughout in the pleasantest and most straightforward fashion, and they part with expressions of mutual esteem. There's a jolly game for you boys to play. I never had such toys when I was young."

"I don't think we'll play with them just now," said Eric, with an entire absence of the enthusiasm that his uncle had shown; "I think perhaps we ought to do a little of our holiday task. It's history this time; we've got to learn up something about the Bourbon period in France."

"The Bourbon period," said Harvey, with some disapproval in his voice.

"We've got to know something about Louis the Four-teenth," continued Eric; "I've learnt the names of all the principal battles already."

This would never do. "There were, of course, some battles fought during his reign," said Harvey, "but I fancy the ac-counts of them were much exaggerated; news was very un-reliable in those days, and there were practically no war cor-respondents, so generals and commanders could magnify every little skirmish they engaged in till they reached the proportions of decisive battles. Louis was really famous, now, as a landscape gardener; the way he laid out Versailles was so much admired that it was copied all over Europe."

"Do you know anything about Madame Du Barry?" asked Eric; "didn't she have her head chopped off?"

"She was another great lover of gardening," said Harvey evasively; "in fact, I believe the well-known rose Du Barry was named after her, and now I think you had better play for a little and leave your lessons till later."

Harvey retreated to the library and spent some thirty or forty minutes in wondering whether it would be possible to compile a history, for use in elementary schools, in which there should be no prominent mention of battles, massacres, murderous intrigues, and violent deaths. The York and Lancaster period and the Napoleonic era would, he admitted to himself, present considerable difficulties, and the Thirty Years' War would entail something of a gap if you left it out altogether. Still, it would be something gained if, at a highly impressionable age, children could be got to fix their attention on the invention of calico printing instead of the Spanish Armada or the Battle of Waterloo.

It was time, he thought, to go back to the boys' room, and see how they were getting on with their peace toys. As he stood outside the door he could hear Eric's voice raised in command; Bertie chimed in now and again with a helpful suggestion.

"That is Louis the Fourteenth," Eric was saying, "that one in knee-breeches, that Uncle said invented Sunday schools. It isn't a bit like him, but it'll have to do."

"We'll give him a purple coat from my paintbox by and by," said Bertie.

"Yes, an' red heels. That is Madame de Maintenon, that one he called Mrs. Hemans. She begs Louis not to go on this expedition, but he turns a deaf ear. He takes Marshal Saxe with him, and we must pretend that they have thousands of men with them. The watchword is *Qui vive?* and the answer is *L'état c'est moi*—that was one of his favourite remarks, you know. They land at Manchester in the dead of night, and a Jacobite conspirator gives them the keys of the fortress."

Peeping in through the doorway Harvey observed that the municipal dust-bin had been pierced with holes to accommodate the muzzles of imaginary cannon, and now represented the principal fortified position in Manchester; John Stuart Mill had been dipped in red ink, and apparently stood for Marshal Saxe.

"Louis orders his troops to surround the Young Women's Christian Association and seize the lot of them. 'Once back at the Louvre and the girls are mine,' he exclaims. We must use Mrs. Hemans again for one of the girls; she says 'Never,' and stabs Marshal Saxe to the heart."

"He bleeds dreadfully," exclaimed Bertie, splashing red ink liberally over the façade of the Association building.

"The soldiers rush in and avenge his death with the utmost savagery. A hundred girls are killed"—here Bertie emptied the remainder of the red ink over the devoted building—"and the surviving five hundred are dragged off to the French ships. 'I have lost a Marshal,' says Louis, 'but I do not go back empty-handed.'"

Harvey stole away from the room, and sought out his sister.

"Eleanor," he said, "the experiment—"

"Yes?"

"Has failed. We have begun too late."

LOUISE

"THE tea will be quite cold, you'd better ring for some more," said the Dowager Lady Beanford.

Susan Lady Beanford was a vigorous old woman who had coquetted with imaginary ill-health for the greater part of a lifetime; Clovis Sangrail irreverently declared that she had caught a chill at the Coronation of Queen Victoria and had never let it go again. Her sister, Jane Thropplestance, who was some years her junior, was chiefly remarkable for being the most absent-minded woman in Middlesex.

"I've really been unusually clever this afternoon," she remarked gaily, as she rang for the tea. "I've called on all the people I meant to call on, and I've done all the shopping that I set out to do. I even remembered to try and match that silk for you at Harrod's, but I'd forgotten to bring the pattern with me, so it was no use. I really think that was the only important thing I forgot during the whole afternoon. Quite wonderful for me, isn't it?"

"What have you done with Louise?" asked her sister. "Didn't you take her out with you? You said you were going to."

"Good gracious," exclaimed Jane, "what *have* I done with Louise? I must have left her somewhere."

"But where?"

"That's just it. Where have I left her? I can't remember if the Carrywoods were at home or if I just left cards. If they were at home I may have left Louise there to play bridge. I'll go and telephone to Lord Carrywood and find out."

"Is that you, Lord Carrywood?" she queried over the telephone; "it's me, Jane Thropplestance. I want to know, have you seen Louise?"

" 'Louise,' " came the answer, "it's been my fate to see it three times. At first, I must admit, I wasn't impressed by it, but the music grows on one after a bit. Still, I don't think I want to see it again just at present. Were you going to offer me a seat in your box?"

"Not the opera 'Louise'—my niece, Louise Thropplestance. I thought I might have left her at your house."

"You left cards on us this afternoon, I understand, but I don't think you left a niece. The footman would have been sure to have mentioned it if you had. Is it going to be a fashion to leave nieces on people as well as cards? I hope not; some of these houses in Berkeley Square have practically no accommodation for that sort of thing."

"She's not at the Carrywoods'," announced Jane, returning to her tea; "now I come to think of it, perhaps I left her at the silk counter at Selfridge's. I may have told her to wait there a moment while I went to look at the silks in a better light, and I may easily have forgotten about her when I found

I hadn't your pattern with me. In that case she's still sitting there. She wouldn't move unless she was told to; Louise has no initiative."

"You said you tried to match the silk at Harrod's," interjected the dowager.

"Did I? Perhaps it was Harrod's. I really don't remember. It was one of those places where every one is so kind and sympathetic and devoted that one almost hates to take even a reel of cotton away from such pleasant surroundings."

"I think you might have taken Louise away. I don't like the idea of her being there among a lot of strangers. Supposing some unprincipled person was to get into conversation with her."

"Impossible. Louise has no conversation. I've never discovered a single topic on which she'd anything to say beyond 'Do you think so? I dare say you're right.' I really thought her reticence about the fall of the Ribot Ministry was ridiculous, considering how much her dear mother used to visit Paris. This bread and butter is cut far too thin; it crumbles away long before you can get it to your mouth. One feels so absurd, snapping at one's food in mid-air, like a trout leaping at may-fly."

"I am rather surprised," said the dowager, "that you can sit there making a hearty tea when you've just lost a favourite niece."

"You talk as if I'd lost her in a churchyard sense, instead of having temporarily mislaid her. I'm sure to remember presently where I left her."

"You didn't visit any place of devotion, did you? If you've left her mooning about Westminster Abbey or St. Peter's, Eaton Square, without being able to give any satisfactory reason why she's there, she'll be seized under the Cat and Mouse Act and sent to Reginald McKenna."

"That would be extremely awkward," said Jane, meeting an irresolute piece of bread and butter halfway; "we hardly know the McKennas, and it would be very tiresome having to telephone to some unsympathetic private secretary, describing Louise to him and asking to have her sent back in time for dinner. Fortunately, I didn't go to any place of devotion, though I did get mixed up with a Salvation Army procession. It was quite interesting to be at close quarters with them, they're so absolutely different to what they used to be when I first remember them in the 'eighties. They used to go about then unkempt and dishevelled, in a sort of smiling rage with the world, and now they're spruce and jaunty and flamboyantly decorative, like a geranium bed with religious convictions. Laura Kettleway was going on about them in the lift of the Dover Street Tube the other day, saying what a lot of good work they did, and what a loss it would have been if they'd never existed. 'If they had never existed,' I said, 'Granville Barker would have been certain to have invented something that looked exactly like them.' If you say things like that, quite loud, in a Tube lift, they always sound like epigrams."

"I think you ought to do something about Louise," said the dowager.

"I'm trying to think whether she was with me when I called on Ada Spelvexit. I rather enjoyed myself there. Ada was trying, as usual, to ram that odious Koriatoffski woman down my throat, knowing perfectly well that I detest her, and in an unguarded moment she said: 'She's leaving her present house and going to Lower Seymour Street.' 'I dare say she will, if she stays there long enough,' I said. Ada didn't see it for about three minutes, and then she was positively uncivil. No, I am certain I didn't leave Louise there."

"If you could manage to remember where you *did* leave her, it would be more to the point than these negative assurances," said Lady Beanford; "so far, all that we know is that she is not at the Carrywoods', or Ada Spelvexit's, or Westminster Abbey."

"That narrows the search down a bit," said Jane hopefully; "I rather fancy she must have been with me when I went to Mornay's. I know I went to Mornay's, because I remember meeting that delightful Malcolm What's-his-name there— you know whom I mean. That's the great advantage of people having unusual first names, you needn't try and remember what their other name is. Of course I know one or two other Malcolms, but none that could possibly be described as delightful. He gave me two tickets for the Happy Sunday Evenings in Sloane Square. I've probably left them at Mornay's, but still it was awfully kind of him to give them to me."

"Do you think you left Louise there?"

"I might telephone and ask. Oh, Robert, before you clear the tea-things away I wish you'd ring up Mornay's, in Regent Street, and ask if I left two theatre tickets and one niece in their shop this afternoon."

"A niece, ma'am?" asked the footman.

"Yes, Miss Louise didn't come home with me, and I'm not sure where I left her."

"Miss Louise has been upstairs all the afternoon, ma'am, reading to the second kitchenmaid, who has the neuralgia. I took up tea to Miss Louise at a quarter to five o'clock, ma'am."

"Of course, how silly of me. I remember now, I asked her to read the *Faërie Queene* to poor Emma, to try to send her to sleep. I always get some one to read the *Faërie Queene* to me when I have neuralgia, and it usually sends me to sleep. Louise doesn't seem to have been successful, but one can't say she hasn't tried. I expect after the first hour or so the kitchenmaid would rather have been left alone with her neuralgia, but of course Louise wouldn't leave off till some one told her to. Anyhow, you can ring up Mornay's, Robert, and ask whether I left two theatre tickets there. Except for your silk, Susan, those seem to be the only things I've forgotten this afternoon. Quite wonderful for me."

TEA

JAMES CUSHAT-PRINKLY was a young man who had always had a settled conviction that one of these days he would marry; up to the age of thirty-four he had done nothing to justify that conviction. He liked and admired a great many women collectively and dispassionately without singling out one for especial matrimonial consideration, just as one might admire the Alps without feeling that one wanted any particular peak as one's own private property. His lack of initiative in this matter aroused a certain amount of impatience among the sentimentally minded women-folk of his home circle; his mother, his sisters, an aunt-in-residence, and two or three intimate matronly friends regarded his dilatory approach to the married state with a disapproval that was far from being inarticulate. His most innocent flirtations were watched with the straining eagerness which a group of unexercised terriers concentrates on the slightest movements of a human being who may be reasonably considered likely to take them for a walk. No decent-souled mortal can long resist the pleading of several pairs of walk-beseeching dog-eyes; James Cushat-Prinkly was not sufficiently obstinate or indifferent to home influences to disregard the obviously expressed wish of his family that he should become enamoured of some nice marriageable girl, and when his Uncle Jules departed this life and bequeathed him a comfortable little legacy it really seemed the correct thing to do to set about discovering some one to share it with him. The process of discovery was carried on more by the force of suggestion and the weight of public opinion than by any initiative of his own; a clear working majority of his female relatives and the aforesaid matronly friends had pitched on Joan Sebastable as the most suitable young woman in his range of acquaintance to whom he might propose marriage, and James became gradually accustomed to the idea that he and Joan would go together through the prescribed stages of congratulations, present-receiving, Norwegian or Mediterranean hotels, and eventual domesticity. It was necessary, however, to ask the lady what she thought about the matter; the family had so far conducted and directed the flirtation with ability and discretion, but the actual proposal would have to be an individual effort.

Cushat-Prinkly walked across the Park towards the Sebastable residence in a frame of mind that was moderately complacent. As the thing was going to be done he was glad to feel

that he was going to get it settled and off his mind that afternoon. Proposing marriage, even to a nice girl like Joan, was
a rather irksome business, but one could not have a honeymoon in Minorca and a subsequent life of married happiness
without such preliminary. He wondered what Minorca was
really like as a place to stop in; in his mind's eye it was an
island in perpetual half-mourning, with black or white
Minorca hens running all over it. Probably it would not be
a bit like that when one came to examine it. People who had
been in Russia had told him that they did not remember having seen any Muscovy ducks there, so it was possible that there
would be no Minorca fowls on the island.

His Mediterranean musings were interrupted by the sound
of a clock striking the half-hour. Half-past four. A frown
of dissatisfaction settled on his face. He would arrive at the
Sebastable mansion just at the hour of afternoon tea. Joan
would be seated at a low table, spread with an array of silver
kettles and cream-jugs and delicate porcelain teacups, behind
which her voice would tinkle pleasantly in a series of little
friendly questions about weak or strong tea, how much, if
any, sugar, milk, cream, and so forth. "Is it one lump? I forgot. You do take milk, don't you? Would you like some more
hot water, if it's too strong?"

Cushat-Prinkly had read of such things in scores of novels,
and hundreds of actual experiences had told him that they
were true to life. Thousands of women, at this solemn afternoon hour, were sitting behind dainty porcelain and silver
fittings, with their voices tinkling pleasantly in a cascade of
solicitous little questions. Cushat-Prinkly detested the whole
system of afternoon tea. According to his theory of life a
woman should lie on a divan or couch, talking with incom-
parable charm or looking unutterable thoughts, or merely
silent as a thing to be looked on, and from behind a silken
curtain a small Nubian page should silently bring in a tray
with cups and dainties, to be accepted silently, as a matter of
course, without drawn-out chatter about cream and sugar and
hot water. If one's soul was really enslaved at one's mistress's
feet, how could one talk coherently about weakened tea?

Cushat-Prinkly had never expounded his views on the subject to his mother; all her life she had been accustomed to
tinkle pleasantly at tea-time behind dainty porcelain and silver;
and if he had spoken to her about divans and Nubian pages she
would have urged him to take a week's holiday at the seaside.
Now, as he passed through a tangle of small streets that led
indirectly to the elegant Mayfair terrace for which he was
bound, a horror at the idea of confronting Joan Sebastable at
her tea-table seized on him. A momentary deliverance presented itself; on one floor of a narrow little house at the
noisier end of Esquimault Street lived Rhoda Ellam, a sort of
remote cousin, who made a living by creating hats out of
costly materials. The hats really looked as if they had come
from Paris; the cheques she got for them unfortunately never
looked as if they were going to Paris. However, Rhoda appeared to find life amusing and to have a fairly good time
in spite of her straitened circumstances. Cushat-Prinkly decided to climb up to her floor and defer by half-an-hour or
so the important business which lay before him; by spinning
out his visit he could contrive to reach the Sebastable mansion
after the last vestiges of dainty porcelain had been cleared
away.

Rhoda welcomed him into a room that seemed to do duty
as workshop, sitting-room, and kitchen combined, and to be
wonderfully clean and comfortable at the same time.

"I'm having a picnic meal," she announced. "There's
caviare in that jar at your elbow. Begin on that brown bread-
and-butter while I cut some more. Find yourself a cup; the
teapot is behind you. Now tell me about hundreds of things."

She made no other allusion to food, but talked amusingly
and made her visitor talk amusingly too. At the same time she
cut the bread-and-butter with a masterly skill and produced
red pepper and sliced lemon, where so many women would
merely have produced reasons and regrets for not having any.
Cushat-Prinkly found that he was enjoying an excellent tea
without having to answer as many questions about it as a
Minister for Agriculture might be called on to reply to during
an outbreak of cattle plague.

"And now tell me why you have come to see me," said Rhoda suddenly. "You arouse not merely my curiosity but my business instincts. I hope you've come about hats. I heard that you had come into a legacy the other day, and, of course, it struck me that it would be a beautiful and desirable thing for you to celebrate the event by buying brilliantly expensive hats for all your sisters. They may not have said anything about it, but I feel sure the same idea has occurred to them. Of course, with Goodwood on us, I am rather rushed just now, but in my business we're accustomed to that; we live in a series of rushes—like the infant Moses."

"I didn't come about hats," said her visitor. "In fact, I don't think I really came about anything. I was passing and I just thought I'd look in and see you. Since I've been sitting talking to you, however, a rather important idea has occurred to me. If you'll forget Goodwood for a moment and listen to me, I'll tell you what it is."

Some forty minutes later James Cushat-Prinkly returned to the bosom of his family, bearing an important piece of news.

"I'm engaged to be married," he announced.

A rapturous outbreak of congratulation and self-applause broke out.

"Ah, we knew! We saw it coming! We foretold it weeks ago!"

"I'll bet you didn't," said Cushat-Prinkly. "If any one had told me at lunch-time today that I was going to ask Rhoda Ellam to marry me and that she was going to accept me, I would have laughed at the idea."

The romantic suddenness of the affair in some measure compensated James's women-folk for the ruthless negation of all their patient effort and skilled diplomacy. It was rather trying to have to deflect their enthusiasm at a moment's notice from Joan Sebastable to Rhoda Ellam; but, after all, it was James's wife who was in question, and his tastes had some claim to be considered.

On a September afternoon of the same year, after the honeymoon in Minorca had ended, Cushat-Prinkly came into the drawing-room of his new house in Granchester Square.

Rhoda was seated at a low table, behind a service of dainty porcelain and gleaming silver. There was a pleasant tinkling note in her voice as she handed him a cup.

"You like it weaker than that, don't you? Shall I put some more hot water to it? No?"

THE DISAPPEARANCE OF CRISPINA UMBERLEIGH

IN a first-class carriage of a train speeding Balkanward across the flat, green Hungarian plain, two Britons sat in friendly, fitful converse. They had first foregathered in the cold grey dawn at the frontier line, where the presiding eagle takes on an extra head and Teuton lands pass from Hohenzollern to Habsburg keeping—and where a probing official beak requires to delve in polite and perhaps perfunctory, but always tiresome, manner into the baggage of sleep-hungry passengers. After a day's break of their journey at Vienna the travellers had again foregathered at the trainside and paid one another the compliment of settling instinctively into the same carriage. The elder of the two had the appearance and manner of a diplomat; in point of fact he was the well-connected foster-brother of a wine business. The other was certainly a journalist. Neither man was talkative and each was grateful to the other for not being talkative. That is why from time to time they talked.

One topic of conversation naturally thrust itself forward in front of all others. In Vienna the previous day they had learned of the mysterious vanishing of a world-famous picture from the walls of the Louvre.

"A dramatic disappearance of that sort is sure to produce a crop of imitations," said the Journalist.

"It has had a lot of anticipations, for the matter of that," said the Wine-brother.

"Oh, of course there have been thefts from the Louvre before."

"I was thinking of the spiriting away of human beings rather than pictures. In particular I was thinking of the case of my aunt, Crispina Umberleigh."

"I remember hearing something of the affair," said the Journalist, "but I was away from England at the time. I never quite knew what was supposed to have happened."

"You may hear what really happened if you will respect it as a confidence," said the Wine Merchant. "In the first place I may say that the disappearance of Mrs. Umberleigh was not regarded by the family entirely as a bereavement. My uncle, Edward Umberleigh, was not by any means a weak-kneed individual, in fact in the world of politics he had to be reckoned with more or less as a strong man, but he was unmistakably dominated by Crispina; indeed I never met any human being who was not frozen into subjection when brought into prolonged contact with her. Some people are born to command; Crispina Mrs. Umberleigh was born to legislate, codify, administrate, censor, license, ban, execute, and sit in judgment generally. If she was not born with that destiny she adopted it at an early age. From the kitchen regions upwards every one in the household came under her despotic sway and stayed there with the submissiveness of molluscs involved in a glacial epoch. As a nephew on a footing of only occasional visits she affected me merely as an epidemic, disagreeable while it lasted, but without any permanent effect; but her own sons and daughters stood in mortal awe of her; their studies, friendships, diet, amusements, religious observances, and way of doing their hair were all regulated and ordained according to the august lady's will and pleasure. This will help you to understand the sensation of stupefaction which was caused in the family when she unobtrusively and inexplicably vanished. It was as though St. Paul's Cathedral or the Piccadilly Hotel had disappeared in the night, leaving nothing but an open space to mark where it had stood. As far as was known nothing was troubling her; in fact there was much before her to make life particularly well worth living. The youngest boy had come back from school with an unsatisfactory report, and she was to have sat in judgment on him the very afternoon of the day she disappeared—if it had been he who had vanished in a hurry one could have supplied the motive. Then she was in the middle of a newspaper correspondence with a rural dean in which she had already proved him guilty of heresy, inconsistency, and unworthy quibbling, and no ordinary consideration would have induced her to discontinue the controversy. Of course the matter was put in the hands of the police, but as far as possible it was kept out of the papers, and the generally accepted explanation of her withdrawal from her social circle was that she had gone into a nursing home."

"And what was the immediate effect on the home circle?" asked the Journalist.

"All the girls bought themselves bicycles; the feminine cycling craze was still in existence, and Crispina had rigidly vetoed any participation in it among the members of her household. The youngest boy let himself go to such an extent during his next term that it had to be his last as far as that particular establishment was concerned. The elder boys propounded a theory that their mother might be wandering somewhere abroad, and searched for her assiduously, chiefly, it must be admitted, in a class of Montmartre resort where it was extremely improbable that she would be found."

"And all this while couldn't your uncle get hold of the least clue?"

"As a matter of fact he had received some information, though of course I did not know of it at the time. He got a message one day telling him that his wife had been kidnapped and smuggled out of the country; she was said to be hidden away, in one of the islands off the coast of Norway I think it was, in comfortable surroundings and well cared for. And with the information came a demand for money; a lump sum was to be handed over to her kidnappers and a further sum of £2,000 was to be paid yearly. Failing this she would be immediately restored to her family."

The Journalist was silent for a moment, and then began to laugh quietly.

"It was certainly an inverted form of holding to ransom," he said.

"If you had known my aunt," said the Wine Merchant, "you would have wondered that they didn't put the figure higher."

"I realize the temptation. Did your uncle succumb to it?"

"Well, you see, he had to think of others as well as himself. For the family to have gone back into the Crispina thraldom after having tasted the delights of liberty would have been a tragedy, and there were even wider considerations to be taken into account. Since his bereavement he had unconsciously taken up a far bolder and more initiatory line in public affairs, and his popularity and influence had increased correspondingly. From being merely a strong man in the political world he began to be spoken of as *the* strong man. All this he knew would be jeopardized if he once more dropped into the social position of the husband of Mrs. Umberleigh. He was a rich man, and the £2,000 a year, though not exactly a fleabite, did not seem an extravagant price to pay for the boarding-out of Crispina. Of course, he had severe qualms of conscience about the arrangement. Later on, when he took me into his confidence, he told me that in paying the ransom, or hush-money as I should have called it, he was partly influenced by the fear that if he refused it the kidnappers might have vented their rage and disappointment on their captive. It was better, he said, to think of her being well cared for as a highly valued paying-guest in one of the Lofoden Islands than to have her struggling miserably home in a maimed and mutilated condition. Anyway he paid the yearly instalment as punctually as one pays a fire insurance, and with equal promptitude there would come an acknowledgment of the money and a brief statement to the effect that Crispina was in good health and fairly cheerful spirits. One report even mentioned that she was busying herself with a scheme for proposed reforms in Church management to be pressed on the local pastorate. Another spoke of a rheumatic attack and a journey to a 'cure' on the mainland, and on that occasion an additional eighty pounds was demanded and conceded. Of course it was to the interest of the kidnappers to keep their charge in good health, but the secrecy with which they managed to shroud their arrangements argued a really wonderful organization. If my uncle was paying a rather high price, at least he could console himself with the reflection that he was paying specialists' fees."

"Meanwhile had the police given up all attempts to track the missing lady?" asked the Journalist.

"Not entirely; they came to my uncle from time to time to report on clues which they thought might yield some elucidation as to her fate or whereabouts, but I think they had their suspicions that he was possessed of more information than he had put at their disposal. And then, after a disappearance of more than eight years, Crispina returned with dramatic suddenness to the home she had left so mysteriously."

"She had given her captors the slip?"

"She had never been captured. Her wandering away had been caused by a sudden and complete loss of memory. She usually dressed rather in the style of a superior kind of charwoman, and it was not so very surprising that she should have imagined that she was one, and still less that people should accept her statement and help her to get work. She had wandered as far afield as Birmingham, and found fairly steady employment there, her energy and enthusiasm in putting people's rooms in order counter-balancing her obstinate and domineering characteristics. It was the shock of being patronizingly addressed as 'my good woman' by a curate, who was disputing with her where the stove should be placed in a parish concert hall, that led to the sudden restoration of her memory. 'I think you forget who you are speaking to,' she observed crushingly, which was rather unduly severe, considering she had only just remembered it herself."

"But," exclaimed the Journalist, "the Lofoden Island people! Who had they got hold of?"

"A purely mythical prisoner. It was an attempt in the first place by some one who knew something of the domestic situation, probably a discharged valet, to bluff a lump sum out of Edward Umberleigh before the missing woman turned up; the subsequent yearly instalments were an unlooked-for increment to the original haul.

"Crispina found that the eight years' interregnum had

materially weakened her ascendency over her now grown-up offspring. Her husband, however, never accomplished anything great in the political world after her return; the strain of trying to account satisfactorily for an unspecified expenditure of sixteen thousand pounds spread over eight years sufficiently occupied his mental energies. Here is Belgrad and another custom house."

THE WOLVES OF CERNOGRATZ

"ARE there any old legends attached to the castle?" asked Conrad of his sister. Conrad was a prosperous Hamburg merchant, but he was the one poetically-dispositioned member of an eminently practical family.

The Baroness Gruebel shrugged her plump shoulders.

"There are always legends hanging about these old places. They are not difficult to invent and they cost nothing. In this case there is a story that when any one dies in the castle all the dogs in the village and the wild beasts in the forest howl the night long. It would not be pleasant to listen to, would it?"

"It would be weird and romantic," said the Hamburg merchant.

"Anyhow, it isn't true," said the Baroness complacently; "since we bought the place we have had proof that nothing of the sort happens. When the old mother-in-law died last spring-time we all listened, but there was no howling. It is just a story that lends dignity to the place without costing anything."

"The story is not as you have told it," said Amalie, the grey old governess. Every one turned and looked at her in astonishment. She was wont to sit silent and prim and faded in her place at table, never speaking unless some one spoke to her, and there were few who troubled themselves to make conversation with her. Today a sudden volubility had descended on her; she continued to talk, rapidly and nervously, looking straight in front of her and seeming to address no one in particular.

"It is not when *any one* dies in the castle that the howling is heard. It was when one of the Cernogratz family died here that the wolves came from far and near and howled at the edge of the forest just before the death hour. There were only a few couple of wolves that had their lairs in this part of the forest, but at such a time the keepers say there would be scores of them, gliding about in the shadows and howling in chorus, and the dogs of the castle and the village and all the farms round would bay and howl in fear and anger at the wolf chorus, and as the soul of the dying one left its body a tree would crash down in the park. That is what happened when a Cernogratz died in his family castle. But for a stranger dying here, of course no wolf would howl and no tree would fall. Oh, no."

There was a note of defiance, almost of contempt, in her voice as she said the last words. The well-fed, much-too-well-dressed Baroness stared angrily at the dowdy old woman who had come forth from her usual and seemly position of effacement to speak so disrespectfully.

"You seem to know quite a lot about the von Cernogratz legends, Fräulein Schmidt," she said sharply; "I did not know that family histories were among the subjects you are supposed to be proficient in."

The answer to her taunt was even more unexpected and astonishing than the conversational outbreak which had provoked it.

"I am a von Cernogratz myself," said the old woman, "that is why I know the family history."

"You a von Cernogratz? You!" came in an incredulous chorus.

"When we became very poor," she explained, "and I had to go out and give teaching lessons, I took another name; I thought it would be more in keeping. But my grandfather spent much of his time as a boy in this castle, and my father used to tell me many stories about it, and, of course, I knew all the family legends and stories. When one has nothing left to one but memories, one guards and dusts them with especial care. I little thought when I took service with you that I should one day come with you to the old home of my family. I could wish it had been anywhere else."

There was silence when she finished speaking, and then the Baroness turned the conversation to a less embarrassing topic than family histories. But afterwards, when the old governess had slipped away quietly to her duties, there arose a clamour of derision and disbelief.

"It was an impertinence," snapped out the Baron, his protruding eyes taking on a scandalized expression; "fancy the woman talking like that at our table. She almost told us we were nobodies, and I don't believe a word of it. She is just Schmidt and nothing more. She has been talking to some of the peasants about the old Cernogratz family, and raked up their history and their stories."

"She wants to make herself out of some consequence," said the Baroness; "she knows she will soon be past work and she wants to appeal to our sympathies. Her grandfather, indeed!"

The Baroness had the usual number of grandfathers, but she never, never boasted about them.

"I dare say her grandfather was a pantry boy or something of the sort in the castle," sniggered the Baron; "that part of the story may be true."

The merchant from Hamburg said nothing; he had seen tears in the old woman's eyes when she spoke of guarding her memories—or, being of an imaginative disposition, he thought he had.

"I shall give her notice to go as soon as the New Year festivities are over," said the Baroness; "till then I shall be too busy to manage without her."

But she had to manage without her all the same, for in the cold biting weather after Christmas, the old governess fell ill and kept to her room.

"It is most provoking," said the Baroness, as her guests sat round the fire on one of the last evenings of the dying year; "all the time that she has been with us I cannot remember that she was ever seriously ill, too ill to go about and do her work, I mean. And now, when I have the house full, and she could be useful in so many ways, she goes and breaks down. One is sorry for her, of course, she looks so withered and shrunken, but it is intensely annoying all the same."

"Most annoying," agreed the banker's wife sympathetically; "it is the intense cold, I expect, it breaks the old people up. It has been unusually cold this year."

"The frost is the sharpest that has been known in December for many years," said the Baron.

"And, of course, she is quite old," said the Baroness; "I wish I had given her notice some weeks ago, then she would have left before this happened to her. Why, Wappi, what is the matter with you?"

The small, woolly lapdog had leapt suddenly down from its cushion and crept shivering under the sofa. At the same moment an outburst of angry barking came from the dogs in the castle-yard, and other dogs could be heard yapping and barking in the distance.

"What is disturbing the animals?" asked the Baron.

And then the humans, listening intently, heard the sound that had roused the dogs to their demonstrations of fear and rage; heard a long-drawn whining howl, rising and falling, seeming at one moment leagues away, at others sweeping across the snow until it appeared to come from the foot of the castle walls. All the starved, cold misery of a frozen world, all the relentless hunger-fury of the wild, blended with other forlorn and haunting melodies to which one could give no name, seemed concentrated in that wailing cry.

"Wolves!" cried the Baron.

Their music broke forth in one raging burst, seeming to come from everywhere.

"Hundreds of wolves," said the Hamburg merchant, who was a man of strong imagination.

Moved by some impulse which she could not have explained, the Baroness left her guests and made her way to the narrow, cheerless room where the old governess lay watching the hours of the dying year slip by. In spite of the biting cold of the winter night, the window stood open. With a scandalized exclamation on her lips, the Baroness rushed forward to close it.

"Leave it open," said the old woman in a voice that for all its weakness carried an air of command such as the Baroness had never heard before from her lips.

"But you will die of cold!" she expostulated.

"I am dying in any case," said the voice, "and I want to hear their music. They have come from far and wide to sing the death-music of my family. It is beautiful that they have come; I am the last von Cernogratz that will die in our old castle, and they have come to sing to me. Hark, how loud they are calling!"

The cry of the wolves rose on the still winter air and floated round the castle walls in long-drawn piercing wails; the old woman lay back on her couch with a look of long-delayed happiness on her face.

"Go away," she said to the Baroness; "I am not lonely any more. I am one of a great old family. . . ."

"I think she is dying," said the Baroness when she had rejoined her guests; "I suppose we must send for a doctor. And that terrible howling! Not for much money would I have such death-music."

"That music is not to be bought for any amount of money," said Conrad.

"Hark! What is that other sound?" asked the Baron, as a noise of splitting and crashing was heard.

It was a tree falling in the park.

There was a moment of constrained silence, and then the banker's wife spoke.

"It is the intense cold that is splitting the trees. It is also the cold that has brought the wolves out in such numbers. It is many years since we have had such a cold winter."

The Baroness eagerly agreed that the cold was responsible for these things. It was the cold of the open window, too, which caused the heart failure that made the doctor's ministrations unnecessary for the old Fräulein. But the notice in the newspapers looked very well—

"On December 29th, at Schloss Cernogratz, Amalie von Cernogratz, for many years the valued friend of Baron and Baroness Gruebel."

LOUIS

"IT would be jolly to spend Easter in Vienna this year," said Strudwarden, "and look up some of my old friends there. It's about the jolliest place I know of to be at for Easter—"

"I thought we had made up our minds to spend Easter at Brighton," interrupted Lena Strudwarden, with an air of aggrieved surprise.

"You mean that you had made up your mind that we should spend Easter there," said her husband; "we spent last Easter there, and Whitsuntide as well, and the year before that we were at Worthing, and Brighton again before that. I think it would be just as well to have a real change of scene while we are about it."

"The journey to Vienna would be very expensive," said Lena.

"You are not often concerned about economy," said Strudwarden, "and in any case the trip to Vienna won't cost a bit more than the rather meaningless luncheon parties we usually give to quite meaningless acquaintances at Brighton. To escape from all that set would be a holiday in itself."

Strudwarden spoke feelingly; Lena Strudwarden maintained an equally feeling silence on that particular subject. The set that she gathered round her at Brighton and other South Coast resorts was composed of individuals who might be dull and meaningless in themselves, but who understood the art of flattering Mrs. Strudwarden. She had no intention of foregoing their society and their homage and flinging herself among unappreciative strangers in a foreign capital.

"You must go to Vienna alone if you are bent on going," she said; "I couldn't leave Louis behind, and a dog is always a fearful nuisance in a foreign hotel, besides all the fuss and separation of the quarantine restrictions when one comes back. Louis would die if he was parted from me for even a week. You don't know what that would mean to me."

Lena stooped down and kissed the nose of the diminutive brown Pomeranian that lay, snug and irresponsive, beneath a shawl on her lap.

"Look here," said Strudwarden, "this eternal Louis business is getting to be a ridiculous nuisance. Nothing can be done, no plans can be made, without some veto connected with that animal's whims or convenience being imposed. If you were a priest in attendance on some African fetish you couldn't set up a more elaborate code of restrictions. I believe you'd ask the Government to put off a General Election if you thought it would interfere with Louis's comfort in any way."

By way of answer to this tirade Mrs. Strudwarden stooped down again and kissed the irresponsive brown nose. It was the action of a woman with a beautifully meek nature, who would, however, send the whole world to the stake sooner than yield an inch where she knew herself to be in the right.

"It isn't as if you were in the least bit fond of animals," went on Strudwarden, with growing irritation; "when we are down at Kerryfield you won't stir a step to take the house dogs out, even if they're dying for a run, and I don't think you've been in the stables twice in your life. You laugh at what you call the fuss that's being made over the extermination of plumage birds, and you are quite indignant with me if I interfere on behalf of an ill-treated, over-driven animal on the road. And yet you insist on every one's plans being made subservient to the convenience of that stupid little morsel of fur and selfishness."

"You are prejudiced against my little Louis," said Lena, with a world of tender regret in her voice.

"I've never had the chance of being anything else but prejudiced against him," said Strudwarden; "I know what a jolly responsive companion a doggie can be, but I've never been allowed to put a finger near Louis. You say he snaps at any one except you and your maid, and you snatched him away from old Lady Peterby the other day, when she wanted to pet him, for fear he would bury his teeth in her. All that I ever see of him is the tip of his unhealthy-looking little nose, peeping out from his basket or from your muff, and I occasionally hear his wheezy little bark when you take him for a walk up and down the corridor. You can't expect one to get extravagantly fond of a dog of that sort. One might as well work up an affection for the cuckoo in a cuckoo-clock."

"He loves me," said Lena, rising from the table, and bearing the shawl-swathed Louis in her arms. "He loves only me, and perhaps that is why I love him so much in return. I don't care what you say against him, I am not going to be separated from him. If you insist on going to Vienna you must go alone, as far as I am concerned. I think it would be much more sensible if you were to come to Brighton with Louis and me, but of course you must please yourself."

"You must get rid of that dog," said Strudwarden's sister when Lena had left the room; "it must be helped to some sudden and merciful end. Lena is merely making use of it as an instrument for getting her own way on dozens of occasions when she would otherwise be obliged to yield gracefully to your wishes or to the general convenience. I am convinced that she doesn't care a brass button about the animal itself. When her friends are buzzing round her at Brighton or anywhere else and the dog would be in the way, it has to spend whole days alone with the maid, but if you want Lena to go with you anywhere where she doesn't want to go instantly she trots out the excuse that she couldn't be separated from her dog. Have you ever come into a room unobserved and heard Lena talking to her beloved pet? I never have. I believe she only fusses over it when there's some one present to notice her."

"I don't mind admitting," said Strudwarden, "that I've dwelt more than once lately on the possibility of some fatal accident putting an end to Louis's existence. It's not very easy, though, to arrange a fatality for a creature that spends most of its time in a muff or asleep in a toy kennel. I don't think poison would be any good; it's obviously horribly over-fed, for I've seen Lena offer it dainties at table sometimes, but it never seems to eat them."

"Lena will be away at church on Wednesday morning," said Elsie Strudwarden reflectively; "she can't take Louis with her there, and she is going on to the Dellings for lunch. That will give you several hours in which to carry out your purpose. The maid will be flirting with the chauffeur most of the time, and, anyhow, I can manage to keep her out of the way on some pretext or other."

"That leaves the field clear," said Strudwarden, "but unfortunately my brain is equally a blank as far as any lethal project is concerned. The little beast is so monstrously inactive; I can't pretend that it leapt into the bath and drowned itself, or that it took on the butcher's mastiff in unequal combat and got chewed up. In what possible guise could death come to a confirmed basket-dweller? It would be too suspicious if we invented a Suffragette raid and pretended that they invaded Lena's boudoir and threw a brick at him. We should have to do a lot of other damage as well, which would be rather a nuisance, and the servants would think it odd that they had seen nothing of the invaders."

"I have an idea," said Elsie; "get a box with an air-tight lid, and bore a small hole in it, just big enough to let in an india-rubber tube. Pop Louis, kennel and all, into the box, shut it down, and put the other end of the tube over the gas-bracket. There you have a perfect lethal chamber. You can stand the kennel at the open window afterwards, to get rid of the smell of the gas, and all that Lena will find when she comes home late in the afternoon will be a placidly defunct Louis."

"Novels have been written about women like you," said Strudwarden; "you have a perfectly criminal mind. Let's come and look for a box."

Two mornings later the conspirators stood gazing guiltily at a stout square box, connected with the gas-bracket by a length of india-rubber tubing.

"Not a sound," said Elsie; "he never stirred; it must have been quite painless. All the same I feel rather horrid now it's done."

"The ghastly part has to come," said Strudwarden, turning

off the gas. "We'll lift the lid slowly, and let the gas out by degrees. Swing the door to and fro to send a draught through the room."

Some minutes later, when the fumes had rushed off, he stooped down and lifted out the little kennel with its grim burden. Elsie gave an exclamation of terror. Louis sat at the door of his dwelling, head erect and ears pricked, as coldly and defiantly inert as when they had put him into his execution chamber. Strudwarden dropped the kennel with a jerk, and stared for a long moment at the miracle-dog; then he went into a peal of chattering laughter.

It was certainly a wonderful imitation of a truculent-looking toy Pomeranian, and the apparatus that gave forth a wheezy bark when you pressed it had materially helped the imposition that Lena, and Lena's maid, had foisted on the household. For a woman who disliked animals, but liked getting her own way under a halo of unselfishness, Mrs. Strudwarden had managed rather well.

"Louis is dead," was the curt information that greeted Lena on her return from her luncheon party.

"Louis *dead!*" she exclaimed.

"Yes, he flew at the butcher-boy and bit him, and he bit me too, when I tried to get him off, so I had to have him destroyed. You warned me that he snapped, but you didn't tell me that he was down-right dangerous. I shall have to pay the boy something heavy by way of compensation, so you will have to go without those buckles that you wanted to have for Easter; also I shall have to go to Vienna to consult Dr. Schroeder, who is a specialist on dogbites, and you will have to come too. I have sent what remains of Louis to Rowland Ward to be stuffed; that will be my Easter gift to you instead of the buckles. For Heaven's sake, Lena, weep, if you really feel it so much; anything would be better than standing there staring as if you thought I had lost my reason."

Lena Strudwarden did not weep, but her attempt at laughing was an unmistakable failure.

THE GUESTS

"THE landscape seen from our windows is certainly charming," said Annabel; "those cherry orchards and green meadows, and the river winding along the valley, and the church tower peeping out among the elms, they all make a most effective picture. There's something dreadfully sleepy and languorous about it, though; stagnation seems to be the dominant note. Nothing ever happens here; seedtime and harvest, an occasional outbreak of measles or a mildly destructive thunderstorm, and a little election excitement about once in five years, that is all that we have to modify the monotony of our existence. Rather dreadful, isn't it?"

"On the contrary," said Matilda, "I find it soothing and restful; but then, you see, I've lived in countries where things do happen, ever so many at a time, when you're not ready for them happening all at once."

"That, of course, makes a difference," said Annabel.

"I have never forgotten," said Matilda, "the occasion when the Bishop of Bequar paid us an unexpected visit; he was on his way to lay the foundation-stone of a mission-house or something of the sort."

"I thought that out there you were always prepared for emergency guests turning up," said Annabel.

"I was quite prepared for half a dozen bishops," said Matilda, "but it was rather disconcerting to find out after a little conversation that this particular one was a distant cousin of mine, belonging to a branch of the family that had quarrelled bitterly and offensively with our branch about a Crown Derby dessert service; they got it, and we ought to have got it, in some legacy, or else we got it and they thought they ought to have it, I forget which; anyhow, I know they behaved disgracefully. Now here was one of them turning up in the odour of sanctity, so to speak, and claiming the traditional hospitality of the East."

"It was rather trying, but you could have left your husband to do most of the entertaining."

"My husband was fifty miles up-country, talking sense, or what he imagined to be sense, to a village community that fancied one of their leading men was a were-tiger."

"A what tiger?"

"A were-tiger; you've heard of were-wolves, haven't you, a mixture of wolf and human being and demon? Well, in those parts they have were-tigers, or think they have, and I must say that in this case, so far as sworn and uncontested evidence went, they had every ground for thinking so. However, as we gave up witchcraft prosecutions about three hundred years ago, we don't like to have other people keeping on our discarded practices; it doesn't seem respectful to our mental and moral position."

"I hope you weren't unkind to the Bishop," said Annabel.

"Well, of course he was my guest, so I had to be outwardly polite to him, but he was tactless enough to rake up the incidents of the old quarrel, and to try to make out that there was something to be said for the way his side of the family had behaved; even if there was, which I don't for a moment admit, my house was not the place in which to say it. I didn't argue the matter, but I gave my cook a holiday to go and visit his aged parents some ninety miles away. The emergency cook was not a specialist in curries; in fact, I don't think cooking in any shape or form could have been one of his strong points. I believe he originally came to us in the guise of a gardener, but as we never pretended to have anything that could be considered a garden he was utilized as assistant goatherd, in which capacity, I understand, he gave every satisfaction. When the Bishop heard that I had sent away the cook on a special and unnecessary holiday, he saw the inwardness of the manœuvre, and from that moment we were scarcely on speaking terms. If you have ever had a Bishop with whom you were not on speaking terms staying in your house, you will appreciate the situation."

Annabel confessed that her life-story had never included such a disturbing experience.

"Then," continued Matilda, "to make matters more complicated, the Gwadlipichee overflowed its banks, a thing it did every now and then when the rains were unduly prolonged, and the lower part of the house and all the out-buildings were submerged. We managed to get the ponies loose in time, and the syce swam the whole lot of them off to the nearest rising ground. A goat or two, the chief goatherd, the chief goat-herd's wife, and several of their babies came to anchorage in the verandah. All the rest of the available space was filled up with wet, bedraggled-looking hens and chickens; one never really knows how many fowls one possesses till the servants' quarters are flooded out. Of course, I had been through some-thing of the sort in previous floods, but never before had I had a houseful of goats and babies and half-drowned hens, supplemented by a Bishop with whom I was hardly on speaking terms."

"It must have been a trying experience," commented Anna-bel.

"More embarrassments were to follow. I wasn't going to let a mere ordinary flood wash out the memory of that Crown Derby dessert service, and I intimated to the Bishop that his large bedroom, with a writing table in it, and his small bath-room, with a sufficiency of cold-water jars in it, was his share of the premises, and that space was rather congested under the existing circumstances. However, at about three o'clock in the afternoon, when he had awakened from his midday sleep, he made a sudden incursion into the room that was normally the drawing-room, but was now dining-room, storehouse, saddle-room, and half a dozen other temporary premises as well. From the condition of my guest's costume he seemed to think it might also serve as his dressing-room.

" 'I'm afraid there is nowhere for you to sit,' I said coldly; 'the verandah is full of goats.'

" 'There is a goat in my bedroom,' he observed with equal coldness, and more than a suspicion of sardonic reproach.

" 'Really,' I said, 'another survivor! I thought all the other goats were done for.'

" 'This particular goat is quite done for,' he said; 'it is being devoured by a leopard at the present moment. That is why I left the room; some animals resent being watched while they are eating.'

"The leopard, of course, was easily explained; it had been hanging round the goat-sheds when the flood came, and had clambered up by the outside staircase leading to the Bishop's bath-room, thoughtfully bringing a goat with it. Probably it found the bath-room too damp and shut-in for its taste, and transferred its banqueting operations to the bedroom while the Bishop was having his nap."

"What a frightful situation!" exclaimed Annabel; "fancy having a ravening leopard in the house, with a flood all round you."

"Not in the least ravening," said Matilda; "it was full of goat, had any amount of water at its disposal if it felt thirsty, and probably had no more immediate wish than a desire for uninterrupted sleep. Still, I think any one will admit that it was an embarrassing predicament to have your only available guest-room occupied by a leopard, the verandah choked up with goats and babies and wet hens, and a Bishop with whom you were scarcely on speaking terms planted down in your only sitting-room. I really don't know how I got through those crawling hours, and of course meal-times only made matters worse. The emergency cook had every excuse for sending in watery soup and sloppy rice, and as neither the chief goatherd nor his wife were expert divers, the cellar could not be reached. Fortunately the Gwadlipichee subsides as rapidly as it rises, and just before dawn the syce came splashing back, with the ponies only fetlock deep in water. Then there arose some awkwardness from the fact that the Bishop wished to leave sooner than the leopard did, and as the latter was ensconced in the midst of the former's personal possessions there was an obvious difficulty in altering the order of departure. I pointed out to the Bishop that a leopard's habits and tastes are not those of an otter, and that it naturally preferred walking to wading, and that in any case a meal of an entire goat, washed down with tub-water, justified a certain amount of repose; if I had had guns fired to frighten the animal away, as the Bishop suggested, it would probably merely have left the bedroom to come into the already overcrowded drawing-room. Altogether it was rather a relief when they both left. Now, perhaps, you can understand my appreciation of a sleepy countryside where things don't happen."

THE PENANCE

OCTAVIAN RUTTLE was one of those lively cheerful individuals on whom amiability had set its unmistakable stamp, and, like most of his kind, his soul's peace depended in large measure on the unstinted approval of his fellows. In hunting to death a small tabby cat he had done a thing of which he scarcely approved himself, and he was glad when the gardener had hidden the body in its hastily dug grave under a lone oak tree in the meadow, the same tree that the hunted quarry had climbed as a last effort towards safety. It had been a distasteful and seemingly ruthless deed, but circumstances had demanded the doing of it. Octavian kept chickens; at least he kept some of them; others vanished from his keeping, leaving only a few bloodstained feathers to mark the manner of their going. The tabby cat from the large grey house that stood with its back to the meadow had been detected in many furtive visits to the hen-coops, and after due negotiation with those in authority at the grey house a sentence of death had been agreed on: "The children will mind, but they need not know," had been the last word on the matter.

The children in question were a standing puzzle to Octavian; in the course of a few months he considered that he should have known their names, ages, the dates of their birthdays, and have been introduced to their favourite toys. They remained, however, as non-committal as the long blank wall that shut them off from the meadow, a wall over which their three heads sometimes appeared at odd moments. They had parents in India—that much Octavian had learned in the neighbourhood; the children, beyond grouping themselves garment-wise into sexes, a girl and two boys, carried their life-story no further on his behoof. And now it seemed he was engaged in something which touched them closely, but must be hidden from their knowledge.

The poor helpless chickens had gone one by one to their doom, so it was meet that their destroyer should come to a violent end, yet Octavian felt some qualms when his share of the violence was ended. The little cat, headed off from its wonted tracks of safety, had raced unfriended from shelter to shelter, and its end had been rather piteous. Octavian walked through the long grass of the meadow with a step less jaunty than usual. And as he passed beneath the shadow of the high blank wall he glanced up and became aware that his hunting had had undesired witnesses. Three white set faces were looking down at him, and if ever an artist wanted a threefold study of cold human hate, impotent yet unyielding, raging yet masked in stillness, he would have found it in the triple gaze that met Octavian's eye.

"I'm sorry, but it had to be done," said Octavian, with genuine apology in his voice.

"Beast!"

The answer came from three throats with startling intensity.

Octavian felt that the blank wall would not be more impervious to his explanations than the bunch of human hostility that peered over its coping; he wisely decided to withhold his peace overtures till a more hopeful occasion.

Two days later he ransacked the best sweet-shop in the neighbouring market town for a box of chocolates that by its size and contents should fitly atone for the dismal deed done under the oak tree in the meadow. The two first specimens that were shown him he hastily rejected; one had a group of chickens pictured on its lid, the other bore the portrait of a tabby kitten. A third sample was more simply bedecked with a spray of painted poppies, and Octavian hailed the flowers of forgetfulness as a happy omen. He felt distinctly more at ease with his surroundings when the imposing package had been sent across to the grey house, and a message returned to say that it had been duly given to the children. The next morning he sauntered with purposeful steps past the long blank wall on his way to the chicken-run and piggery that stood at the bottom of the meadow. The three children were perched at their accustomed look-out, and their range of sight did not seem to concern itself with Octavian's presence. As he became depressingly aware of the aloofness of their gaze he also noted a strange variegation in the herbage at his feet; the greensward for a considerable space around was strewn and speckled with a chocolate-coloured hail, enlivened here and there with gay tinsel-like wrappings or the glistening mauve of crystallized violets. It was as though the fairy paradise of a greedy-minded child had taken shape and substance in the vegetation of the meadow. Octavian's blood-money had been flung back at him in scorn.

To increase his discomfiture the march of events tended to shift the blame of ravaged chicken-coops from the supposed culprit who had already paid full forfeit; the young chicks were still carried off, and it seemed highly probable that the cat had only haunted the chicken-run to prey on the rats which harboured there. Through the flowing channels of servant talk the children learned of this belated revision of verdict, and Octavian one day picked up a sheet of copy-book paper on which was painstakingly written: "Beast. Rats eated your chickens." More ardently than ever did he wish for an opportunity for sloughing off the disgrace that enwrapped him, and earning some happier nickname from his three unsparing judges.

And one day a chance inspiration came to him. Olivia, his two-year-old daughter, was accustomed to spend the hour from high noon till one o'clock with her father while the nurse-maid gobbled and digested her dinner and novelette. About the same time the blank wall was usually enlivened by the presence of its three small wardens. Octavian, with seeming carelessness of purpose, brought Olivia well within hail of the watchers and noted with hidden delight the growing interest that dawned in that hitherto sternly hostile quarter. His little Olivia, with her sleepy placid ways, was going to succeed where he, with his anxious well-meant overtures, had so signally failed. He brought her a large yellow dahlia, which she grasped tightly in one hand and regarded with a stare of benevolent boredom, such as one might bestow on amateur classical dancing performed in aid of a deserving charity. Then he turned shyly to the group perched on the wall and asked with affected carelessness, "Do you like flowers?" Three solemn nods rewarded his venture.

"Which sorts do you like best?" he asked, this time with a distinct betrayal of eagerness in his voice.

"Those with all the colours, over there." Three chubby arms pointed to a distant tangle of sweet-pea. Child-like, they had asked for what lay farthest from hand, but Octavian trotted off gleefully to obey their welcome behest. He pulled and plucked with unsparing hand, and brought every variety of tint that he could see into his bunch that was rapidly becoming a bundle. Then he turned to retrace his steps, and found the blank wall blanker and more deserted than ever, while the foreground was void of all trace of Olivia. Far down the meadow three children were pushing a go-cart at the utmost speed they could muster in the direction of the piggeries; it was Olivia's go-cart and Olivia sat in it, somewhat bumped and shaken by the pace at which she was being driven, but apparently retaining her wonted composure of mind. Octavian stared for a moment at the rapidly moving group, and then started in hot pursuit, shedding as he ran sprays of blossom from the mass of sweet-pea that he still clutched in his hands. Fast as he ran the children had reached the piggery before he could overtake them, and he arrived just in time to see Olivia, wondering but unprotesting, hauled and pushed up to the roof of the nearest sty. They were old buildings in some need of repair, and the rickety roof would certainly not have borne Octavian's weight if he had attempted to follow his daughter and her captors on their new vantage ground.

"What are you going to do with her?" he panted. There was no mistaking the grim trend of mischief in those flushed but sternly composed young faces.

"Hang her in chains over a slow fire," said one of the boys. Evidently they had been reading English history.

"Frow her down and the pigs will d'vour her, every bit 'cept the palms of her hands," said the other boy. It was also evident that they had studied Biblical history.

The last proposal was the one which most alarmed Octavian, since it might be carried into effect at a moment's notice; there had been cases, he remembered, of pigs eating babies.

"You surely wouldn't treat my poor little Olivia in that way?" he pleaded.

"You killed our little cat," came in stern reminder from three throats.

"I'm very sorry I did," said Octavian, and if there is a standard of measurement in truths Octavian's statement was assuredly a large nine.

"We shall be very sorry when we've killed Olivia," said the girl, "but we can't be sorry till we've done it."

The inexorable child-logic rose like an unyielding rampart before Octavian's scared pleadings. Before he could think of any fresh line of appeal his energies were called out in another direction. Olivia had slid off the roof and fallen with a soft, unctuous splash into a morass of muck and decaying straw. Octavian scrambled hastily over the pigsty wall to her rescue, and at once found himself in a quagmire that engulfed his feet. Olivia, after the first shock of surprise at her sudden drop through the air, had been mildly pleased at finding herself in close and unstinted contact with the sticky element that oozed around her, but as she began to sink gently into the bed of slime a feeling dawned on her that she was not after all very happy, and she began to cry in the tentative fashion of the normally good child. Octavian, battling with the quagmire, which seemed to have learned the rare art of giving way at all points without yielding an inch, saw his daughter slowly disappearing in the engulfing slush, her smeared face further distorted with the contortions of whimpering wonder, while from their perch on the pigsty roof the three children looked down with the cold unpitying detachment of the Parcæ Sisters.

"I can't reach her in time," gasped Octavian, "she'll be choked in the muck. Won't you help her?"

"No one helped our cat," came the inevitable reminder.

"I'll do anything to show you how sorry I am about that," cried Octavian, with a further desperate flounder, which carried him scarcely two inches forward.

"Will you stand in a white sheet by the grave?"

"Yes," screamed Octavian.

"Holding a candle?"

"An' saying, 'I'm a miserable Beast'?"

Octavian agreed to both suggestions.

"For a long, long time?"

"For half an hour," said Octavian. There was an anxious ring in his voice as he named the time-limit; was there not the precedent of a German king who did open-air penance for several days and nights at Christmas-time clad only in his shirt? Fortunately the children did not appear to have read German history, and half an hour seemed long and goodly in their eyes.

"All right," came with threefold solemnity from the roof, and a moment later a short ladder had been laboriously pushed across to Octavian, who lost no time in propping it against the low pigsty wall. Scrambling gingerly along its rungs he was able to lean across the morass that separated him from his slowly foundering offspring and extract her like an unwilling cork from its slushy embrace. A few minutes later he was listening to the shrill and repeated assurances of the nursemaid that her previous experience of filthy spectacles had been on a notably smaller scale.

That same evening when twilight was deepening into darkness Octavian took up his position as penitent under the lone oak tree, having first carefully undressed the part. Clad in a zephyr shirt, which on this occasion thoroughly merited its name, he held in one hand a lighted candle and in the other a watch, into which the soul of a dead plumber seemed to have passed. A box of matches lay at his feet and was resorted to on the fairly frequent occasions when the candle succumbed to the night breezes. The house loomed inscrutable in the middle distance, but as Octavian conscientiously repeated the formula of his penance he felt certain that three pairs of solemn eyes were watching his moth-shared vigil.

And the next morning his eyes were gladdened by a sheet of copy-book paper lying beside the blank wall, on which was written the message "Un-Beast."

THE PHANTOM LUNCHEON

"THE Smithly-Dubbs are in Town," said Sir James. "I wish you would show them some attention. Ask them to lunch with you at the Ritz or somewhere."

"From the little I've seen of the Smithly-Dubbs I don't think I want to cultivate their acquaintance," said Lady Drakmanton.

"They always work for us at election times," said her husband; "I don't suppose they influence very many votes, but they have an uncle who is on one of my ward committees, and another uncle speaks sometimes at some of our less important meetings. Those sort of people expect some return in the shape of hospitality."

"Expect it!" exclaimed Lady Drakmanton; "the Misses Smithly-Dubb do more than that; they almost demand it. They belong to my club, and hang about the lobby just about lunch-time, all three of them, with their tongues hanging out of their mouths and the six-course look in their eyes. If I were to breathe the word 'lunch' they would hustle me into a taxi and scream 'Ritz' or 'Dieudonné's' to the driver before I knew what was happening."

"All the same, I think you ought to ask them to a meal of some sort," persisted Sir James.

"I consider that showing hospitality to the Smithly-Dubbs is carrying Free Food principles to a regrettable extreme," said Lady Drakmanton; "I've entertained the Joneses and the Browns and the Snapheimers and the Lubrikoffs, and heaps of others whose names I forget, but I don't see why I should inflict the society of the Misses Smithly-Dubb on myself for a solid hour. Imagine it, sixty minutes, more or less, of unrelenting gobble and gabble. Why can't *you* take them on, Milly?" she asked, turning hopefully to her sister.

"I don't know them," said Milly hastily.

"All the better; you can pass yourself off as me. People say that we are so alike that they can hardly tell us apart, and I've only spoken to these tiresome young women about twice in my life, at committee-rooms, and bowed to them in the club. Any of the club page-boys will point them out to you; they're always to be found lolling about the hall just before lunch-time."

"My dear Betty, don't be absurd," protested Milly; "I've got some people lunching with me at the Carlton tomorrow, and I'm leaving Town the day afterwards."

"What time is your lunch tomorrow?" asked Lady Drakmanton reflectively.

"Two o'clock," said Milly.

"Good," said her sister; "the Smithly-Dubbs shall lunch with me tomorrow. It shall be rather an amusing lunch-party. At least, I shall be amused."

The last two remarks she made to herself. Other people did not always appreciate her ideas of humour. Sir James never did.

The next day Lady Drakmanton made some marked variations in her usual toilet effects. She dressed her hair in an unaccustomed manner, and put on a hat that added to the transformation of her appearance. When she had made one or two minor alterations she was sufficiently unlike her usual smart self to produce some hesitation in the greeting which the Misses Smithly-Dubb bestowed on her in the club lobby. She responded, however, with a readiness which set their doubts at rest.

"What is the Carlton like for lunching in?" she asked breezily.

The restaurant received an enthusiastic recommendation from the three sisters.

"Let's go and lunch there, shall we?" she suggested, and in a few minutes' time the Smithly-Dubb mind was contemplating at close quarters a happy vista of baked meats and approved vintage.

"Are you going to start with caviare? I am," confided Lady Drakmanton, and the Smithly-Dubbs started with caviare. The subsequent dishes were chosen in the same ambitious spirit, and by the time they had arrived at the wild duck course it was beginning to be a rather expensive lunch.

The conversation hardly kept pace with the brilliancy of the menu. Repeated references on the part of the guests to the local political conditions and prospects in Sir James's constituency were met with vague "ahs" and "indeeds" from Lady Drakmanton, who might have been expected to be specially interested.

"I think when the Insurance Act is a little better understood it will lose some of its present unpopularity," hazarded Cecilia Smithly-Dubb.

"Will it? I dare say. I'm afraid politics don't interest me very much," said Lady Drakmanton.

The three Miss Smithly-Dubbs put down their cups of Turkish coffee and stared. Then they broke into protesting giggles.

"Of course, you're joking," they said.

"Not me," was the disconcerting answer; "I can't make head or tail of these bothering old politics. Never could, and never want to. I've quite enough to do to manage my own affairs, and that's a fact."

"But," exclaimed Amanda Smithly-Dubb, with a squeal of bewilderment breaking into her voice, "I was told you spoke so informingly about the Insurance Act at one of our social evenings."

It was Lady Drakmanton who stared now. "Do you know," she said, with a scared look around her, "rather a dreadful thing is happening. I'm suffering from a complete loss of memory. I can't even think who I am. I remember meeting you somewhere, and I remember you asking me to come and lunch with you here, and that I accepted your kind invitation. Beyond that my mind is a positive blank."

The scared look was transferred with intensified poignancy to the faces of her companions.

"*You* asked *us* to lunch," they exclaimed hurriedly. That seemed a more immediately important point to clear up than the question of identity.

"Oh, no," said the vanishing hostess, "*that* I do remember about. You insisted on my coming here because the feeding was so good, and I must say it comes up to all you said about it. A very nice lunch it's been. What I'm worrying about is, who on earth am I? I haven't the faintest notion."

"You are Lady Drakmanton," exclaimed the three sisters in chorus.

"Now, don't make fun of me," she replied crossly. "I happen to know her quite well by sight, and she isn't a bit like me. And it's an odd thing you should have mentioned her, for it so happens she's just come into the room. That lady in black, with the yellow plume in her hat, there over by the door."

The Smithly-Dubbs looked in the indicated direction, and the uneasiness in their eyes deepened into horror. In outward appearance the lady who had just entered the room certainly came rather nearer to their recollection of their Member's wife than the individual who was sitting at table with them.

"Who *are* you, then, if that is Lady Drakmanton?" they asked in panic-stricken bewilderment.

"That is just what I don't know," was the answer; "and you don't seem to know much better than I do."

"You came up to us in the club—"

"In what club?"

"The New Didactic, in Calais Street."

"The New Didactic!" exclaimed Lady Drakmanton with an air of returning illumination; "thank you so much. Of course, I remember now who I am. I'm Ellen Niggle, of the Ladies' Brass-polishing Guild. The Club employs me to come now and then and see to the polishing of the brass fittings. That's how I came to know Lady Drakmanton by sight; she's very often in the Club. And you are the ladies who so kindly asked me out to lunch. Funny how it should all have slipped my memory, all of a sudden. The unaccustomed good food and wine must have been too much for me; for the moment I really couldn't call to mind who I was. Good gracious," she broke off suddenly, "it's ten past two; I should be at a polishing job in Whitehall. I must scuttle off like a giddy rabbit. Thanking you ever so."

She left the room with a scuttle sufficiently suggestive of the animal she had mentioned, but the giddiness was all on the side of her involuntary hostesses. The restaurant seemed to be spinning round them, and the bill when it appeared did nothing to restore their composure. They were as nearly in tears as it is permissible to be during the luncheon hour in a really good restaurant. Financially speaking, they were well able to afford the luxury of an elaborate lunch, but their ideas on the subject of entertaining differed very sharply, according to the circumstances of whether they were dispensing or receiving hospitality. To have fed themselves liberally at their own expense was, perhaps, an extravagance to be deplored, but, at any rate, they had had something for their money; to have drawn an unknown and socially unremunerative Ellen Niggle into the net of their hospitality was a catastrophe that they could not contemplate with any degree of calmness.

The Smithly-Dubbs never quite recovered from their unnerving experience. They have given up politics and taken to doing good.

A BREAD AND BUTTER MISS

"STARLING CHATTER and Oakhill have both dropped back in the betting," said Bertie van Tahn, throwing the morning paper across the breakfast table.

"That leaves Nursery Tea practically favourite," said Odo Finsberry.

"Nursery Tea and Pipeclay are at the top of the betting at

present," said Bertie, "but that French horse, Le Five O'Clock, seems to be fancied as much as anything. Then there is White-bait, and the Polish horse with a name like some one trying to stifle a sneeze in church; they both seem to have a lot of support."

"It's the most open Derby there's been for years," said Odo.

"It's simply no good trying to pick the winner on form," said Bertie; "one must just trust to luck and inspiration."

"The question is whether to trust to one's own inspiration, or somebody else's. *Sporting Swank* gives Count Palatine to win, and Le Five O'Clock for a place."

"Count Palatine—that adds another to our list of perplexities. Good morning, Sir Lulworth; have you a fancy for the Derby by any chance?"

"I don't usually take much interest in turf matters," said Sir Lulworth, who had just made his appearance, "but I always like to have a bet on the Guineas and the Derby. This year, I confess, it's rather difficult to pick out anything that seems markedly better than anything else. What do you think of Snow Bunting?"

"Snow Bunting?" said Odo, with a groan, "there's another of them. Surely, Snow Bunting has no earthly chance?"

"My housekeeper's nephew, who is a shoeing-smith in the mounted section of the Church Lads' Brigade, and an authority on horseflesh, expects him to be among the first three."

"The nephews of housekeepers are invariably optimists," said Bertie; "it's a kind of natural reaction against the professional pessimism of their aunts."

"We don't seem to get much further in our search for the probable winner," said Mrs. de Claux; "the more I listen to you experts the more hopelessly befogged I get."

"It's all very well to blame us," said Bertie to his hostess; "*you* haven't produced anything in the way of an inspiration."

"My inspiration consisted in asking you down for Derby week," retorted Mrs. de Claux; "I thought you and Odo between you might throw some light on *the* question of the moment."

Further recriminations were cut short by the arrival of Lola

Pevensey, who floated into the room with an air of gracious apology.

"So sorry to be so late," she observed, making a rapid tour of inspection of the breakfast dishes.

"Did you have a good night?" asked her hostess with perfunctory solicitude.

"Quite, thank you," said Lola; "I dreamt a most remarkable dream."

A flutter, indicative of general boredom, went round the table. Other people's dreams are about as universally interesting as accounts of other people's gardens, or chickens, or children.

"I dreamt about the winner of the Derby," said Lola.

A swift reaction of attentive interest set in.

"Do tell us what you dreamt," came in a chorus.

"The really remarkable thing about it is that I've dreamt it two nights running," said Lola, finally deciding between the allurements of sausages and kedgeree; "that is why I thought it worth mentioning. You know, when I dream things two or three nights in succession, it always means something; I have special powers in that way. For instance, I once dreamed three times that a winged lion was flying through the sky and one of his wings dropped off, and he came to the ground with a crash; just afterwards the Campanile at Venice fell down. The winged lion is the symbol of Venice, you know," she added for the enlightenment of those who might not be versed in Italian heraldry. "Then," she continued, "just before the murder of the King and Queen of Servia I had a vivid dream of two crowned figures walking into a slaughter-house by the banks of a big river, which I took to be the Danube; and only the other day——"

"Do tell us what you've dreamt about the Derby," interrupted Odo impatiently.

"Well, I saw the finish of the race as clearly as anything; and one horse won easily, almost in a canter, and everybody cried out 'Bread and Butter wins! Good old Bread and Butter.' I heard the name distinctly, and I've had the same dream two nights running."

"Bread and Butter," said Mrs. de Claux, "now, whatever horse can that point to? Why—of course; Nursery Tea!"

She looked round with the triumphant smile of a successful unraveller of mystery.

"How about Le Five O'Clock?" interposed Sir Lulworth.

"It would fit either of them equally well," said Odo; "can you remember any details about the jockey's colours? That might help us."

"I seem to remember a glimpse of lemon sleeves or cap," but I can't be sure," said Lola, after due reflection.

"There isn't a lemon jacket or cap in the race," said Bertie, referring to a list of starters and jockeys; "can't you remember anything about the appearance of the horse? If it were a thick-set animal, thick bread and butter would typify Nursery Tea; and if it were thin, of course, it would mean Le Five O'Clock."

"That seems sound enough," said Mrs. de Claux; "do think, Lola dear, whether the horse in your dream was thin or stoutly built."

"I can't remember that it was one or the other," said Lola; "one wouldn't notice such a detail in the excitement of a finish."

"But this was a symbolic animal," said Sir Lulworth; "if it were to typify thick or thin bread and butter, surely it ought to have been either as bulky and tubby as a shire cart-horse, or as thin as a heraldic leopard."

"I'm afraid you are rather a careless dreamer," said Bertie resentfully.

"Of course, at the moment of dreaming I thought I was witnessing a real race, not the portent of one," said Lola; "otherwise I should have particularly noticed all helpful details."

"The Derby isn't run till tomorrow," said Mrs. de Claux; "do you think you are likely to have the same dream again tonight? If so, you can fix your attention on the important detail of the animal's appearance."

"I'm afraid I shan't sleep at all tonight," said Lola pathetically; "every fifth night I suffer from insomnia, and it's due tonight."

"It's most provoking," said Bertie; "of course, we can back both horses, but it would be much more satisfactory to have all our money on the winner. Can't you take a sleeping-draught, or something?"

"Oakleaves, soaked in warm water and put under the bed, are recommended by some," said Mrs. de Claux.

"A glass of Benedictine, with a drop of eau-de-Cologne—" said Sir Lulworth.

"I have tried every known remedy," said Lola, with dignity; "I've been a martyr to insomnia for years."

"But now we are being martyrs to it," said Odo sulkily; "I particularly want to land a big coup over this race."

"I don't have insomnia for my own amusement," snapped Lola.

"Let us hope for the best," said Mrs. de Claux soothingly; "tonight may prove an exception to the fifth-night rule."

But when breakfast time came round again Lola reported a blank night as far as visions were concerned.

"I don't suppose I had as much as ten minutes' sleep, and, certainly, no dreams."

"I'm so sorry, for your sake in the first place, and ours as well," said her hostess; "do you think you could induce a short nap after breakfast? It would be so good for you—and you *might* dream something. There would still be time for us to get our bets on."

"I'll try if you like," said Lola; "it sounds rather like a small child being sent to bed in disgrace."

"I'll come and read the *Encyclopædia Britannica* to you if you think it will make you sleep any sooner," said Bertie obligingly.

Rain was falling too steadily to permit of outdoor amusement, and the party suffered considerably during the next two hours from the absolute quiet that was enforced all over the house in order to give Lola every chance of achieving slumber. Even the click of billiard balls was considered a possible factor of disturbance, and the canaries were carried down to the gardener's lodge, while the cuckoo clock in the hall was muffled under several layers of rugs. A notice, "Please do not Knock or Ring," was posted on the front door at Bertie's suggestion, and guests and servants spoke in tragic whispers as though the dread presence of death or sickness had invaded the house. The precautions proved of no avail: Lola added a sleepless morning to a wakeful night, and the bets of the party had to be impartially divided between Nursery Tea and the French Colt.

"So provoking to have to split our bets," said Mrs. de Claux, as her guests gathered in the hall later in the day, waiting for the result of the race.

"I did my best for you," said Lola, feeling that she was not getting her due share of gratitude; "I told you what I had seen in my dreams, a brown horse, called Bread and Butter, winning easily from all the rest."

"What?" screamed Bertie, jumping up from his seat, "a *brown* horse! Miserable woman, you never said a word about it's being a brown horse."

"Didn't I?" faltered Lola. "I thought I told you it was a brown horse. It was certainly brown in both dreams. But I don't see what colour has got to do with it. Nursery Tea and Le Five O'Clock are both chestnuts."

"Merciful Heaven! Doesn't brown bread and butter with a sprinkling of lemon in the colours suggest anything to you?" raged Bertie.

A slow, cumulative groan broke from the assembly as the meaning of his words gradually dawned on his hearers.

For the second time that day Lola retired to the seclusion of her room; she could not face the universal looks of reproach directed at her when Whitebait was announced winner at the comfortable price of fourteen to one.

BERTIE'S CHRISTMAS EVE

IT was Christmas Eve, and the family circle of Luke Steffink, Esq., was aglow with the amiability and random mirth which the occasion demanded. A long and lavish dinner had been partaken of, waits had been round and sung carols, the house-party had regaled itself with more carolling on its own account, and there had been romping which, even in a pulpit reference, could not have been condemned as ragging. In the midst of the general glow, however, there was one black unkindled cinder.

Bertie Steffink, nephew of the aforementioned Luke, had early in life adopted the profession of ne'er-do-weel; his father had been something of the kind before him. At the age of eighteen Bertie had commenced that round of visits to our Colonial possessions, so seemly and desirable in the case of a Prince of the Blood, so suggestive of insincerity in a young man of the middle-class. He had gone to grow tea in Ceylon and fruit in British Columbia, and to help sheep to grow wool in Australia. At the age of twenty he had just returned from some similar errand in Canada, from which it may be gathered that the trial he gave to these various experiments was of the summary drum-head nature. Luke Steffink, who fulfilled the troubled rôle of guardian and deputy-parent to Bertie, deplored the persistent manifestation of the homing instinct on his nephew's part, and his solemn thanks earlier in the day for the blessing of reporting a united family had no reference to Bertie's return.

Arrangements had been promptly made for packing the youth off to a distant corner of Rhodesia, whence return would be a difficult matter; the journey to this uninviting destination was imminent, in fact a more careful and willing traveller would have already begun to think about his packing. Hence Bertie was in no mood to share in the festive spirit which displayed itself around him, and resentment smouldered within him at the eager, self-absorbed discussion of social plans for the coming months which he heard on all sides. Beyond depressing his uncle and the family circle generally by singing "Say au revoir, and not good-bye," he had taken no part in the evening's conviviality.

Eleven o'clock had struck some half-hour ago, and the elder Steffinks began to throw out suggestions leading up to that process which they called retiring for the night.

"Come, Teddie, it's time you were in your little bed, you know," said Luke Steffink to his thirteen-year-old son.

"That's where we all ought to be," said Mrs. Steffink.

"There wouldn't be room," said Bertie.

The remark was considered to border on the scandalous; everybody ate raisins and almonds with the nervous industry of sheep feeding during threatening weather.

"In Russia," said Horace Bordenby, who was staying in the house as a Christmas guest, "I've read that the peasants believe that if you go into a cow-house or stable at midnight on Christmas Eve you will hear the animals talk. They're supposed to have the gift of speech at that one moment of the year."

"Oh, *do* let's *all* go down to the cow-house and listen to what they've got to say?" exclaimed Beryl, to whom anything was thrilling and amusing if you did it in a troop.

Mrs. Steffink made a laughing protest, but gave a virtual consent by saying, "We must all wrap up well, then." The idea seemed a scatterbrained one to her, and almost heathenish, but it afforded an opportunity for "throwing the young people together," and as such she welcomed it. Mr. Horace Bordenby was a young man with quite substantial prospects, and he had danced with Beryl at a local subscription ball a sufficient number of times to warrant the authorized inquiry on the part of the neighbours whether "there was anything in it." Though Mrs. Steffink would not have put it in so many words, she shared the idea of the Russian peasantry that on this night the beast might speak.

The cow-house stood at the junction of the garden with a small paddock, an isolated survival, in a suburban neighbourhood, of what had once been a small farm. Luke Steffink was complacently proud of his cow-house and his two cows; he felt that they gave him a stamp of solidity which no number of Wyandottes or Orpingtons could impart. They even seemed to link him in a sort of inconsequent way with those patriarchs who derived importance from their floating capital of flocks and herds, he-asses and she-asses. It had been an anxious and momentous occasion when he had had to decide definitely between "the Byre" and "the Ranch" for the naming of his villa residence. A December midnight was hardly the moment he would have chosen for showing his farm-building to visitors, but since it was a fine night, and the young people were anxious for an excuse for a mild frolic, Luke consented to chaperon the expedition. The servants had long since gone to bed, so the house was left in charge of Bertie, who scornfully declined to stir out on the pretext of listening to bovine conversation.

"We must go quietly," said Luke, as he headed the procession of giggling young folk, brought up in the rear by the shawled and hooded figure of Mrs. Steffink; "I've always laid stress on keeping this a quiet and orderly neighbourhood."

It was a few minutes to midnight when the party reached the cow-house and made its way in by the light of Luke's stable lantern. For a moment every one stood in silence, almost with a feeling of being in church.

"Daisy—the one lying down—is by a shorthorn bull out of a Guernsey cow," announced Luke in a hushed voice, which was in keeping with the foregoing impression.

"Is she?" said Bordenby, rather as if he had expected her to be by Rembrandt.

"Myrtle is—"

Myrtle's family history was cut short by a little scream from the women of the party.

The cow-house door had closed noiselessly behind them and the key had turned gratingly in the lock; then they heard Bertie's voice pleasantly wishing them good night and his footsteps retreating along the garden path.

Luke Steffink strode to the window; it was a small square opening of the old-fashioned sort, with iron bars let into the stonework.

"Unlock the door this instant," he shouted, with as much air of menacing authority as a hen might assume when screaming through the bars of a coop at a marauding hawk. In reply to his summons the hall-door closed with a defiant bang.

A neighbouring clock struck the hour of midnight. If the cows had received the gift of human speech at that moment they would not have been able to make themselves heard. Seven or eight other voices were engaged in describing Bertie's present conduct and his general character at a high pressure of excitement and indignation.

In the course of half an hour or so everything that it was permissible to say about Bertie had been said some dozens of times, and other topics began to come to the front—the extreme mustiness of the cow-house, the possibility of it catching fire, and the probability of it being a Rowton House for the vagrant rats of the neighbourhood. And still no sign of deliverance came to the unwilling vigil-keepers.

Towards one o'clock the sound of rather boisterous and undisciplined carol-singing approached rapidly, and came to a sudden anchorage, apparently just outside the garden-gate. A motor-load of youthful "bloods," in a high state of conviviality, had made a temporary halt for repairs; the stoppage, however, did not extend to the vocal efforts of the party, and the watchers in the cow-shed were treated to a highly unauthorized rendering of "Good King Wenceslas," in which the adjective "good" appeared to be very carelessly applied.

The noise had the effect of bringing Bertie out into the garden, but he utterly ignored the pale, angry faces peering out at the cow-house window, and concentrated his attention on the revellers outside the gate.

"Wassail, you chaps!" he shouted.

"Wassail, old sport!" they shouted back; "we'd jolly well drink y'r health, only we've nothing to drink it in."

"Come and wassail inside," said Bertie hospitably; "I'm all alone, and there's heaps of 'wet.'"

They were total strangers, but his touch of kindness made them instantly his kin. In another moment the unauthorized version of King Wenceslas, which, like many other scandals, grew worse on repetition, went echoing up the garden path; two of the revellers gave an impromptu performance on the way by executing the staircase waltz up the terraces of what Luke Steffink, hitherto with some justification, called his rock-garden. The rock part of it was still there when the waltz had been accorded its third encore. Luke, more than ever like a cooped hen behind the cow-house bars, was in a position to realize the feelings of concert-goers unable to countermand the call for an encore which they neither desire nor deserve.

The hall door closed with a bang on Bertie's guests, and the sounds of merriment became faint and muffled to the weary watchers at the other end of the garden. Presently two ominous pops, in quick succession, made themselves distinctly heard.

"They've got at the champagne!" exclaimed Mrs. Steffink.

"Perhaps it's the sparkling Moselle," said Luke hopefully.

Three or four more pops were heard.

"The champagne *and* the sparkling Moselle," said Mrs. Steffink.

Luke uncorked an expletive which, like brandy in a temperance household, was only used on rare emergencies. Mr. Horace Bordenby had been making use of similar expressions under his breath for a considerable time past. The experiment of "throwing the young people together" had been prolonged beyond a point when it was likely to produce any romantic result.

Some forty minutes later the hall door opened and disgorged a crowd that had thrown off any restraint of shyness that might have influenced its earlier actions. Its vocal efforts in the direction of carol-singing were now supplemented by instrumental music; a Christmas-tree that had been prepared for the children of the gardener and other household retainers had yielded a rich spoil of tin trumpets, rattles, and drums. The life-story of King Wenceslas had been dropped, Luke was thankful to notice, but it was intensely irritating for the chilled prisoners in the cow-house to be told that it was "a hot time in the old town tonight," together with some accurate but entirely superfluous information as to the imminence of Christmas morning. Judging by the protests which began to be shouted from the upper windows of neighbouring houses, the sentiments prevailing in the cow-house were heartily echoed in other quarters.

The revellers found their car, and, what was more remarkable, managed to drive off in it, with a parting fanfare of tin trumpets. The lively beat of a drum disclosed the fact that the master of the revels remained on the scene.

"Bertie!" came in an angry, imploring chorus of shouts and screams from the cow-house window.

"Hullo." cried the owner of the name, turning his rather errant steps in the direction of the summons; "are you people still there? Must have heard everything cows got to say by this time. If you haven't, no use waiting. After all, it's a Russian legend, and Russian Chrismush Eve not due for 'nother fortnight. Better come out."

After one or two ineffectual attempts he managed to pitch the key of the cow-house door in through the window. Then, lifting his voice in the strains of "I'm afraid to go home in the dark," with a lusty drum accompaniment, he led the way back to the house. The hurried procession of the released that followed in his steps came in for a good deal of the adverse comment that his exuberant display had evoked.

It was the happiest Christmas Eve he had ever spent. To quote his own words, he had a rotten Christmas.

FOREWARNED

ALETHIA DEBCHANCE sat in a corner of an otherwise empty railway carriage, more or less at ease as regarded body, but in some trepidation as to mind. She had embarked on a social adventure of no little magnitude as compared with the accustomed seclusion and stagnation of her past life. At the age of twenty-eight she could look back on nothing more eventful than the daily round of her existence in her aunt's house at Webblehinton, a hamlet four and a half miles distant from a country town and about a quarter of a century removed from modern times. Their neighbours had been elderly and few, not much given to social intercourse, but helpful or politely sympathetic in times of illness. Newspapers of the ordinary kind were a rarity; those that Alethia

saw regularly were devoted exclusively either to religion or
to poultry, and the world of politics was to her an unheeded
unexplored region. Her ideas on life in general had been acquired through the medium of popular respectable novel-
writers, and modified or emphasized by such knowledge as
her aunt, the vicar, and her aunt's housekeeper had put at
her disposal. And now, in her twenty-ninth year, her aunt's
death had left her, well provided for as regards income,
but somewhat isolated in the matter of kith and kin and
human companionship. She had some cousins who were on
terms of friendly, though infrequent, correspondence with
her, but as they lived permanently in Ceylon, a locality about
which she knew little, beyond the assurance contained in the
missionary hymn that the human element there was vile,
they were not of much immediate use to her. Other cousins
she also possessed, more distant as regards relationship,
but not quite so geographically remote, seeing that they lived
somewhere in the Midlands. She could hardly remember ever
having met them, but once or twice in the course of the last
three or four years they had expressed a polite wish that she
should pay them a visit; they had probably not been unduly
depressed by the fact that her aunt's failing health had prevented her from accepting their invitation. The note of condolence that had arrived on the occasion of her aunt's death
had included a vague hope that Alethia would find time in
the near future to spend a few days with her cousins, and after
much deliberation and many hesitations she had written to propose herself as a guest for a definite date some weeks ahead.
The family, she reflected with relief, was not a large one;
the two daughters were married and away, there was only
old Mrs. Bludward and her son Robert at home. Mrs. Bludward was something of an invalid, and Robert was a young
man who had been at Oxford and was going into Parliament.
Further than that Alethia's information did not go; her imagination, founded on her extensive knowledge of the people
one met in novels, had to supply the gaps. The mother was
not difficult to place; she would either be an ultra-amiable old
lady, bearing her feeble health with uncomplaining fortitude,

and having a kind word for the gardener's boy and a sunny smile for the chance visitor, or else she would be cold and peevish, with eyes that pierced you like a gimlet, and an un-reasoning idolatry of her son. Alethia's imagination rather inclined her to the latter view. Robert was more of a prob-lem. There were three dominant types of manhood to be taken into consideration in working out his classification; there was Hugo, who was strong, good, and beautiful, a rare type and not very often met with; there was Sir Jasper, who was utterly vile and absolutely unscrupulous; and there was Nevil, who was not really bad at heart, but had a weak mouth and usually required the life-work of two good women to keep him from ultimate disaster. It was probable, Alethia considered, that Robert came into the last category, in which case she was cer-tain to enjoy the companionship of one or two excellent women, and might possibly catch glimpses of undesirable ad-venturesses or come face to face with reckless admiration-seek-ing married women. It was altogether an exciting prospect, this sudden venture into an unexplored world of unknown human beings, and Alethia rather wished that she could have taken the vicar with her; she was not, however, rich or important enough to travel with a chaplain, as the Marquis of Moyston-cleugh always did in the novel she had just been reading, so she recognized that such a proceeding was out of the question.

The train which carried Alethia towards her destination was a local one, with the wayside station habit strongly developed. At most of the stations no one seemed to want to get into the train or to leave it, but at one there were several market folk on the platform, and two men, of the farmer or small cattle-dealer class, entered Alethia's carriage. Apparently they had just foregathered, after a day's business, and their conversa-tion consisted of a rapid exchange of short friendly inquiries as to health, family, stock, and so forth, and some grumbling remarks on the weather. Suddenly, however, their talk took a dramatically interesting turn, and Alethia listened with wide-eyed attention.

"What do you think of Mister Robert Bludward, eh?"
There was a certain scornful ring in the question.

"Robert Bludward? An out-an'-out rotter, that's what he is. Ought to be ashamed to look any decent man in the face. Send him to Parliament to represent us—not much! He'd rob a poor man of his last shilling, he would."

"Ah, that he would. Tells a pack of lies to get our votes, that's all that he's after, damn him. Did you see the way the *Argus* showed him up this week? Properly exposed him, hip and thigh, I tell you."

And so on they ran, in their withering indictment. There could be no doubt that it was Alethia's cousin and prospective host to whom they were referring; the allusion to a Parliamentary candidature settled that. What could Robert Bludward have done, what manner of man could he be, that people should speak of him with such obvious reprobation?

"He was hissed down at Shoalford yesterday," said one of the speakers.

Hissed! Had it come to that? There was something dramatically biblical in the idea of Robert Bludward's neighbours and acquaintances hissing him for very scorn. Lord Hereward Stranglath had been hissed, now Alethia came to think of it, in the eighth chapter of *Matterby Towers*, while in the act of opening a Wesleyan bazaar, because he was suspected (unjustly as it turned out afterwards) of having beaten the German governess to death. And in *Tainted Guineas* Roper Squenderby had been deservedly hissed, on the steps of the Jockey Club, for having handed a rival owner a forged telegram, containing false news of his mother's death, just before the start for an important race, thereby ensuring the withdrawal of his rival's horse. In placid Saxon-blooded England people did not demonstrate their feelings lightly and without some strong compelling cause. What manner of evildoer was Robert Bludward?

The train stopped at another small station, and the two men got out. One of them left behind him a copy of the *Argus*, the local paper to which he had made reference. Alethia pounced on it, in the expectation of finding a cultured literary endorsement of the censure which these rough farming men had expressed in their homely, honest way. She had not far to look; "Mr. Robert Bludward, Swanker," was the title of one of the principal articles in the paper. She did not exactly know what a swanker was, probably it referred to some unspeakable form of cruelty, but she read enough in the first few sentences of the article to discover that her cousin Robert, the man at whose house she was about to stay, was an unscrupulous, unprincipled character, of a low order of intelligence, yet cunning withal, and that he and his associates were responsible for most of the misery, disease, poverty, and ignorance with which the country was afflicted; never, except in one or two of the denunciatory Psalms, which she had always supposed to have been written in a spirit of exaggerated Oriental imagery, had she read such an indictment of a human being. And this monster was going to meet her at Derrelton Station in a few short minutes. She would know him at once; he would have the dark beetling brows, the quick, furtive glance, the sneering, unsavoury smile that always characterized the Sir Jaspers of this world. It was too late to escape; she must force herself to meet him with outward calm.

It was a considerable shock to her to find that Robert was fair, with a snub nose, merry eye, and rather a schoolboy manner. "A serpent in duckling's plumage," was her private comment; merciful chance had revealed him to her in his true colours.

As they drove away from the station a dissipated-looking man of the labouring class waved his hat in friendly salute. "Good luck to you, Mr. Bludward," he shouted; "you'll come out on top! We'll break old Chobham's neck for him."

"Who was that man?" asked Alethia quickly.

"Oh, one of my supporters," laughed Robert; "a bit of a poacher and a bit of a pub-loafer, but he's on the right side."

So these were the sort of associates that Robert Bludward consorted with, thought Alethia.

"Who is the person he referred to as old Chobham?" she asked.

"Sir John Chobham, the man who is opposing me," answered Robert; "that is his house away there among the trees on the right."

So there was an upright man, possibly a very Hugo in character, who was thwarting and defying the evildoer in his nefarious career, and there was a dastardly plot afoot to break his neck! Possibly the attempt would be made within the next few hours. He must certainly be warned. Alethia remembered how Lady Sylvia Broomgate, in *Nightshade Court,* had pretended to be bolted with by her horse up to the front door of a threatened county magnate, and had whispered a warning in his ear which saved him from being the victim of foul murder. She wondered if there was a quiet pony in the stables on which she would be allowed to ride out alone. The chances were that she would be watched. Robert would come spurring after her and seize her bridle just as she was turning in at Sir John's gates.

A group of men that they passed in a village street gave them no very friendly looks, and Alethia thought she heard a furtive hiss; a moment later they came upon an errand-boy riding a bicycle. He had the frank open countenance, neatly brushed hair and tidy clothes that betoken a clear conscience and a good mother. He stared straight at the occupants of the car, and, after he had passed them, sang in his clear, boyish voice:

"We'll hang Bobby Bludward on the sour apple tree."

Robert merely laughed. That was how he took the scorn and condemnation of his fellow-men. He had goaded them to desperation with his shameless depravity till they spoke openly of putting him to a violent death, and he laughed.

Mrs. Bludward proved to be of the type that Alethia had suspected, thin-lipped, cold-eyed, and obviously devoted to her worthless son. From her no help was to be expected. Alethia locked her door that night, and placed such ramparts of furniture against it that the maid had great difficulty in breaking in with the early tea in the morning.

After breakfast Alethia, on the pretext of going to look at an outlying rose-garden, slipped away to the village through which they had passed on the previous evening. She remembered that Robert had pointed out to her a public reading-room, and here she considered it possible that she might meet

Sir John Chobham, or some one who knew him well and would carry a message to him. The room was empty when she entered it; a *Graphic*, twelve days old, a yet older copy of *Punch*, and one or two local papers lay upon the central table, the other tables were stacked for the most part with chess and draughts-boards, and wooden boxes of chessmen and dominoes. Listlessly she picked up one of the papers, the *Sentinel*, and glanced at its contents. Suddenly she started, and began to read with breathless attention a prominently printed article, headed "A Little Limelight on Sir John Chobham." The colour ebbed away from her face, a look of frightened despair crept into her eyes. Never, in any novel that she had read, had a defence-less young woman been confronted with a situation like this. Sir John, the Hugo of her imagination, was, if anything, rather more depraved and despicable than Robert Bludward. He was mean, evasive, callously indifferent to his country's interests, a cheat, a man who habitually broke his word, and who was responsible, with his associates, for most of the poverty, misery, crime, and national degradation with which the country was afflicted. He was also a candidate for Parliament, it seemed, and as there was only one seat in this particular locality, it was obvious that the success of either Robert or Sir John would mean a check to the ambitions of the other, hence, no doubt, the rivalry and enmity between these other-wise kindred souls. One was seeking to have his enemy done to death, the other was apparently trying to stir up his supporters to an act of "Lynch law." All this in order that there might be an unopposed election, that one or other of the candidates might go into Parliament with honeyed eloquence on his lips and blood on his heart. Were men really so vile?

"I must go back to Webblehinton at once," Alethia informed her astonished hostess at lunch-time; "I have had a telegram. A friend is very seriously ill, and I have been sent for."

It was dreadful to have to concoct lies, but it would be more dreadful to have to spend another night under that roof.

Alethia reads novels now with even greater appreciation than before. She has been herself in the world outside Webblehinton, the world where the great dramas of sin and villainy are played unceasingly. She had come unscathed through it, but what might have happened if she had gone unsuspectingly to visit Sir John Chobham and warn him of his danger? What indeed! She had been saved by the fearless outspokenness of the local Press.

THE INTERLOPERS

IN a forest of mixed growth somewhere on the eastern spurs of the Carpathians, a man stood one winter night watching and listening, as though he waited for some beast of the woods to come within the range of his vision, and, later, of his rifle. But the game for whose presence he kept so keen an outlook was none that figured in the sportsman's calendar as lawful and proper for the chase; Ulrich von Gradwitz patrolled the dark forest in quest of a human enemy.

The forest lands of Gradwitz were of wide extent and well stocked with game; the narrow strip of precipitous woodland that lay on its outskirt was not remarkable for the game it harboured or the shooting it afforded, but it was the most jealously guarded of all its owner's territorial possessions. A famous lawsuit, in the days of his grandfather, had wrested it from the illegal possession of a neighbouring family of petty landowners; the dispossessed party had never acquiesced in the judgment of the Courts, and a long series of poaching affrays and similar scandals had embittered the relationships between the families for three generations. The neighbour feud had grown into a personal one since Ulrich had come to be head of his family; if there was a man in the world whom he detested and wished ill to it was Georg Znaeym, the inheritor of the quarrel and the tireless game-snatcher and raider of the disputed border-forest. The feud might, perhaps, have died down or been compromised if the personal ill-will of the two men had not stood in the way; as boys they had thirsted for one another's blood, as men each prayed that misfortune might fall on the other, and this wind-scourged winter night Ulrich had banded together his foresters to watch the dark forest, not in quest of four-footed quarry, but to keep a look-out for the prowling thieves whom he suspected of being afoot from across the land boundary. The roebuck, which usually kept in the sheltered hollows during a storm-wind, were running like driven things tonight, and there was movement and unrest among the creatures that were wont to sleep through the dark hours. Assuredly there was a disturbing element in the forest, and Ulrich could guess the quarter from whence it came.

He strayed away by himself from the watchers whom he had placed in ambush on the crest of the hill, and wandered far down the steep slopes amid the wild tangle of under-growth, peering through the tree-trunks and listening through the whistling and skirling of the wind and the restless beating of the branches for sight or sound of the marauders. If only on this wild night, in this dark, lone spot, he might come across Georg Znaeym, man to man, with none to witness—that was the wish that was uppermost in his thoughts. And as he stepped round the trunk of a huge beech he came face to face with the man he sought.

The two enemies stood glaring at one another for a long silent moment. Each had a rifle in his hand, each had hate in his heart and murder uppermost in his mind. The chance had come to give full play to the passions of a lifetime. But a man who has been brought up under the code of a restraining civil-ization cannot easily nerve himself to shoot down his neigh-bour in cold blood and without word spoken, except for an offence against his hearth and honour. And before the mo-ment of hesitation had given way to action a deed of Nature's own violence overwhelmed them both. A fierce shriek of the storm had been answered by a splitting crash over their heads, and ere they could leap aside a mass of falling beech tree had thundered down on them. Ulrich von Gradwitz found himself stretched on the ground, one arm numb beneath him and the other held almost as helplessly in a tight tangle of forked branches, while both legs were pinned beneath the fallen mass. His heavy shooting-boots had saved his feet from being crushed to pieces, but if his fractures were not as serious as they might have been, at least it was evident that he could not move from his present position till some one came to release him. The descending twigs had slashed the skin of his face, and he had to wink away some drops of blood from his eyelashes before he could take in a general view of the disaster. At his side, so near that under ordinary circumstances he could almost have touched him, lay Georg Znaeym, alive and struggling, but obviously as helplessly pinioned down as himself. All round them lay a thick-strewn wreckage of splintered branches and broken twigs.

Relief at being alive and exasperation at his captive plight brought a strange medley of pious thank-offerings and sharp curses to Ulrich's lips. Georg, who was nearly blinded with the blood which trickled across his eyes, stopped his struggling for a moment to listen, and then gave a short, snarling laugh.

"So you're not killed, as you ought to be, but you're caught, anyway," he cried; "caught fast. Ho, what a jest, Ulrich von Gradwitz snared in his stolen forest. There's real justice for you!"

And he laughed again, mockingly and savagely.

"I'm caught in my own forest-land," retorted Ulrich. "When my men come to release us you will wish, perhaps, that you were in a better plight than caught poaching on a neighbour's land, shame on you."

Georg was silent for a moment; then he answered quietly:

"Are you sure that your men will find much to release? I have men, too, in the forest tonight, close behind me, and *they* will be here first and do the releasing. When they drag me out from under these damned branches it won't need much clumsiness on their part to roll this mass of trunk right over on the top of you. Your men will find you dead under a fallen beech tree. For form's sake I shall send my condolences to your family."

"It is a useful hint," said Ulrich fiercely. "My men had orders to follow in ten minutes' time, seven of which must have gone by already, and when they get me out—I will remember the hint. Only as you will have met your death poaching on my lands I don't think I can decently send any message of condolence to your family."

"Good," snarled Georg, "good. We fight this quarrel out to the death, you and I and our foresters, with no cursed interlopers to come between us. Death and damnation to you, Ulrich von Gradwitz."

"The same to you, Georg Znaeym, forest-thief, game-snatcher."

Both men spoke with the bitterness of possible defeat before them, for each knew that it might be long before his men would seek him out or find him; it was a bare matter of chance which party would arrive first on the scene.

Both had now given up the useless struggle to free themselves from the mass of wood that held them down; Ulrich limited his endeavours to an effort to bring his one partially free arm near enough to his outer coat-pocket to draw out his wine-flask. Even when he had accomplished that operation it was long before he could manage the unscrewing of the stopper or get any of the liquid down his throat. But what a Heaven-sent draught it seemed! It was an open winter, and little snow had fallen as yet, hence the captives suffered less from the cold than might have been the case at that season of the year; nevertheless, the wine was warming and reviving to the wounded man, and he looked across with something like a throb of pity to where his enemy lay, just keeping the groans of pain and weariness from crossing his lips.

"Could you reach this flask if I threw it over to you?" asked Ulrich suddenly; "there is good wine in it, and one may as well be as comfortable as one can. Let us drink, even if tonight one of us dies."

"No, I can scarcely see anything; there is so much blood caked round my eyes," said Georg, "and in any case I don't drink wine with an enemy."

Ulrich was silent for a few minutes, and lay listening to the weary screeching of the wind. An idea was slowly forming and growing in his brain, an idea that gained strength every time that he looked across at the man who was fighting so grimly against pain and exhaustion. In the pain and languor

that Ulrich himself was feeling the old fierce hatred seemed
to be dying down.

"Neighbour," he said presently, "do as you please if your
men come first. It was a fair compact. But as for me, I've
changed my mind. If my men are the first to come you shall
be the first to be helped, as though you were my guest. We
have quarrelled like devils all our lives over this stupid strip
of forest, where the trees can't even stand upright in a breath
of wind. Lying here tonight, thinking, I've come to think
we've been rather fools; there are better things in life than
getting the better of a boundary dispute. Neighbour, if you
will help me to bury the old quarrel I—I will ask you to be
my friend."

Georg Znaeym was silent for so long that Ulrich thought,
perhaps, he had fainted with the pain of his injuries. Then he
spoke slowly and in jerks.

"How the whole region would stare and gabble if we rode
into the market-square together. No one living can remember
seeing a Znaeym and a von Gradwitz talking to one another
in friendship. And what peace there would be among the for-
ester folk if we ended our feud tonight. And if we choose
to make peace among our people there is none other to interfere, no interlopers from outside. . . . You would come and
keep the Sylvester night beneath my roof, and I would come
and feast on some high day at your castle. . . . I would
never fire a shot on your land, save when you invited me as a
guest; and you should come and shoot with me down in the
marshes where the wildfowl are. In all the countryside there
are none that could hinder if we willed to make peace. I never
thought to have wanted to do other than hate you all my life,
but I think I have changed my mind about things too, this
last half-hour. And you offered me your wine-flask. . . . Ulrich von Gradwitz, I will be your friend."

For a space both men were silent, turning over in their
minds the wonderful changes that this dramatic reconciliation
would bring about. In the cold, gloomy forest, with the wind
tearing in fitful gusts through the naked branches and whistling round the tree-trunks, they lay and waited for the help

that would now bring release and succour to both parties. And each prayed a private prayer that his men might be the first to arrive, so that he might be the first to show honourable attention to the enemy that had become a friend.

Presently, as the wind dropped for a moment, Ulrich broke silence.

"Let's shout for help," he said; "in this lull our voices may carry a little way."

"They won't carry far through the trees and undergrowth," said Georg, "but we can try. Together, then."

The two raised their voices in a prolonged hunting call.

"Together again," said Ulrich a few minutes later, after listening in vain for an answering halloo.

"I heard something that time, I think," said Ulrich.

"I heard nothing but the pestilential wind," said Georg hoarsely.

There was silence again for some minutes, and then Ulrich gave a joyful cry.

"I can see figures coming through the wood. They are following in the way I came down the hillside."

Both men raised their voices in as loud a shout as they could muster.

"They hear us! They've stopped. Now they see us. They're running down the hill towards us," cried Ulrich.

"How many of them are there?" asked Georg.

"I can't see distinctly," said Ulrich; "nine or ten."

"Then they are yours," said Georg; "I had only seven out with me."

"They are making all the speed they can, brave lads," said Ulrich gladly.

"Are they your men?" asked Georg. "Are they your men?" he repeated impatiently as Ulrich did not answer.

"No," said Ulrich with a laugh, the idiotic chattering laugh of a man unstrung with hideous fear.

"Who are they?" asked Georg quickly, straining his eyes to see what the other would gladly not have seen.

"*Wolves.*"

QUAIL SEED

"THE outlook is not encouraging for us smaller businesses," said Mr. Scarrick to the artist and his sister, who had taken rooms over his suburban grocery store. "These big concerns are offering all sorts of attractions to the shopping public which we couldn't afford to imitate, even on a small scale—reading-rooms and play-rooms and gramophones and Heaven knows what. People don't care to buy half a pound of sugar nowadays unless they can listen to Harry Lauder and have the latest Australian cricket scores ticked off before their eyes. With the big Christmas stock we've got in we ought to keep half a dozen assistants hard at work, but as it is my nephew Jimmy and myself can pretty well attend to it ourselves. It's a nice stock of goods, too, if I could only run it off in a few weeks' time, but there's no chance of that—not unless the London line was to get snowed up for a fortnight before Christmas. I did have a sort of idea of engaging Miss Luffcombe to give recitations during afternoons; she made a great hit at the Post Office entertainment with her rendering of 'Little Beatrice's Resolve.'"

"Anything less likely to make your shop a fashionable shopping centre I can't imagine," said the artist, with a very genuine shudder; "if I were trying to decide between the merits of Carlsbad plums and confected figs as a winter dessert it would infuriate me to have my train of thought entangled with little Beatrice's resolve to be an Angel of Light or a girl scout. No," he continued, "the desire to get something thrown in for nothing is a ruling passion with the feminine shopper, but you can't afford to pander effectively to it. Why not appeal to another instinct, which dominates not only the woman shopper but the male shopper—in fact, the entire human race?"

"What is that instinct, sir?" said the grocer.

．　　．　　．　　．　　．　　．　　．

Mrs. Greyes and Miss Fritten had missed the 2.18 to Town, and as there was not another train till 3.12 they thought that

502

they might as well make their grocery purchases at Scarrick's. It would not be sensational, they agreed, but it would still be shopping.

For some minutes they had the shop almost to themselves, as far as customers were concerned, but while they were debating the respective virtues and blemishes of two competing brands of anchovy paste they were startled by an order, given across the counter, for six pomegranates and a packet of quail seed. Neither commodity was in general demand in that neighbourhood. Equally unusual was the style and appearance of the customer; about sixteen years old, with dark olive skin, large dusky eyes, and thick, low-growing, blue-black hair, he might have made his living as an artist's model. As a matter of fact he did. The bowl of beaten brass that he produced for the reception of his purchases was distinctly the most astonishing variation on the string bag or marketing basket of suburban civilization that his fellow-shoppers had ever seen. He threw a gold piece, apparently of some exotic currency, across the counter, and did not seem disposed to wait for any change that might be forthcoming.

"The wine and figs were not paid for yesterday," he said; "keep what is over of the money for our future purchases."

"A very strange-looking boy?" said Mrs. Greyes interrogatively to the grocer as soon as his customer had left.

"A foreigner, I believe," said Mr. Scarrick, with a shortness that was entirely out of keeping with his usually communicative manner.

"I wish for a pound and a half of the best coffee you have," said an authoritative voice a moment or two later. The speaker was a tall, authoritative-looking man of rather outlandish aspect, remarkable among other things for a full black beard, worn in a style more in vogue in early Assyria than in a London suburb of the present day.

"Has a dark-faced boy been here buying pomegranates?" he asked suddenly, as the coffee was being weighed out to him.

The two ladies almost jumped on hearing the grocer reply with an unblushing negative.

"We have a few pomegranates in stock," he continued, "but there has been no demand for them."

"My servant will fetch the coffee as usual," said the purchaser, producing a coin from a wonderful metal-work purse. As an apparent afterthought he fired out the question: "Have you, perhaps, any quail seed?"

"No," said the grocer, without hesitation, "we don't stock it."

"What will he deny next?" asked Mrs. Greyes under her breath. What made it seem so much worse was the fact that Mr. Scarrick had quite recently presided at a lecture on Savonarola.

Turning up the deep astrachan collar of his long coat, the stranger swept out of the shop, with the air, as Miss Fritten afterwards described it, of a Satrap proroguing a Sanhedrim. Whether such a pleasant function ever fell to a Satrap's lot she was not quite certain, but the simile faithfully conveyed her meaning to a large circle of acquaintances.

"Don't let's bother about the 3.12," said Mrs. Greyes; "let's go and talk this over at Laura Lipping's. It's her day."

When the dark-faced boy arrived at the shop next day with his brass marketing bowl there was quite a fair gathering of customers, most of whom seemed to be spinning out their purchasing operations with the air of people who had very little to do with their time. In a voice that was heard all over the shop, perhaps because everybody was intently listening, he asked for a pound of honey and a packet of quail seed.

"More quail seed!" said Miss Fritten. "Those quails must be voracious, or else it isn't quail seed at all."

"I believe it's opium, and the bearded man is a detective," said Mrs. Greyes brilliantly.

"I don't," said Laura Lipping; "I'm sure it's something to do with the Portuguese Throne."

"More likely to be a Persian intrigue on behalf of the ex-Shah," said Miss Fritten; "the bearded man belongs to the Government Party. The quail seed is a countersign, of course;

Persia is almost next door to Palestine, and quails come into the Old Testament, you know."

"Only as a miracle," said her well-informed younger sister; "I've thought all along it was part of a love intrigue."

The boy who had so much interest and speculation centred on him was on the point of departing with his purchases when he was waylaid by Jimmy, the nephew-apprentice, who, from his post at the cheese and bacon counter, commanded a good view of the street.

"We have some very fine Jaffa oranges," he said hurriedly, pointing to a corner where they were stored, behind a high rampart of biscuit tins. There was evidently more in the remark than met the ear. The boy flew at the oranges with the enthusiasm of a ferret finding a rabbit family at home after a long day of fruitless subterranean research. Almost at the same moment the bearded stranger stalked into the shop, and flung an order for a pound of dates and a tin of the best Smyrna halva across the counter. The most adventurous housewife in the locality had never heard of halva, but Mr. Scarrick was apparently able to produce the best Smyrna variety of it without a moment's hesitation.

"We might be living in the Arabian Nights," said Miss Fritten excitedly.

"Hush! Listen," beseeched Mrs. Greyes.

"Has the dark-faced boy, of whom I spoke yesterday, been here today?" asked the stranger.

"We've had rather more people than usual in the shop today," said Mr. Scarrick, "but I can't recall a boy such as you describe."

Mrs. Greyes and Miss Fritten looked round triumphantly at their friends. It was, of course, deplorable that any one should treat the truth as an article temporarily and excusably out of stock, but they felt gratified that the vivid accounts they had given of Mr. Scarrick's traffic in falsehoods should receive confirmation at first hand.

"I shall never again be able to believe what he tells me about the absence of colouring matter in the jam," whispered an aunt of Mrs. Greyes tragically.

The mysterious stranger took his departure; Laura Lipping distinctly saw a snarl of baffled rage reveal itself behind his heavy moustache and upturned astrachan collar. After a cautious interval the seeker after oranges emerged from behind the biscuit tins, having apparently failed to find any individual orange that satisfied his requirements. He, too, took his departure, and the shop was slowly emptied of its parcel and gossip laden customers. It was Emily Yorling's "day," and most of the shoppers made their way to her drawing-room. To go direct from a shopping expedition to a tea-party was what was known locally as "living in a whirl."

Two extra assistants had been engaged for the following afternoon, and their services were in brisk demand; the shop was crowded. People bought and bought, and never seemed to get to the end of their lists. Mr. Scarrick had never had so little difficulty in persuading customers to embark on new experiences in grocery wares. Even those women whose purchases were of modest proportions dawdled over them as though they had brutal, drunken husbands to go home to. The afternoon had dragged uneventfully on, and there was a distinct buzz of unpent excitement when a dark-eyed boy carrying a brass bowl entered the shop. The excitement seemed to have communicated itself to Mr. Scarrick; abruptly deserting a lady who was making insincere inquiries about the home life of the Bombay duck, he intercepted the newcomer on his way to the accustomed counter and informed him, amid a death-like hush, that he had run out of quail seed.

The boy looked nervously round the shop, and turned hesitatingly to go. He was again intercepted, this time by the nephew, who darted out from behind his counter and said something about a better line of oranges. The boy's hesitation vanished; he almost scuttled into the obscurity of the orange corner. There was an expectant turn of public attention towards the door, and the tall, bearded stranger made a really effective entrance. The aunt of Mrs. Greyes declared afterwards that she found herself subconsciously repeating "The Assyrian came down like a wolf on the fold" under her breath, and she was generally believed.

The newcomer, too, was stopped before he reached the counter, but not by Mr. Scarrick or his assistant. A heavily veiled lady, whom no one had hitherto noticed, rose languidly from a seat and greeted him in a clear, penetrating voice.

"Your Excellency does his shopping himself?" she said.

"I order the things myself," he explained; "I find it difficult to make my servants understand."

In a lower, but still perfectly audible, voice the veiled lady gave him a piece of casual information.

"They have some excellent Jaffa oranges here." Then with a tinkling laugh she passed out of the shop.

The man glared all round the shop, and then, fixing his eyes instinctively on the barrier of biscuit tins, demanded loudly of the grocer: "You have, perhaps, some good Jaffa oranges?"

Every one expected an instant denial on the part of Mr. Scarrick of any such possession. Before he could answer, however, the boy had broken forth from his sanctuary. Holding his empty brass bowl before him he passed out into the street. His face was variously described afterwards as masked with studied indifference, overspread with ghastly pallor, and blazing with defiance. Some said that his teeth chattered, others that he went out whistling the Persian National Hymn. There was no mistaking, however, the effect produced by the encounter on the man who had seemed to force it. If a rabid dog or a rattlesnake had suddenly thrust its companionship on him he could scarcely have displayed a greater access of terror. His air of authority and assertiveness had gone, his masterful stride had given way to a furtive pacing to and fro, as of an animal seeking an outlet for escape. In a dazed perfunctory manner, always with his eyes turning to watch the shop entrance, he gave a few random orders, which the grocer made a show of entering in his book. Now and then he walked out into the street, looked anxiously in all directions, and hurried back to keep up his pretence of shopping. From one of these sorties he did not return; he had dashed away into the dusk, and neither he nor the dark-faced boy nor the veiled lady were seen again

by the expectant crowds that continued to throng the Scarrick
establishment for days to come.

.   .   .   .

"I can never thank you and your sister sufficiently," said the
grocer.

"We enjoyed the fun of it," said the artist modestly, "and
as for the model, it was a welcome variation on posing for
hours for 'The Lost Hylas.' "

"At any rate," said the grocer, "I insist on paying for the
hire of the black beard."

CANOSSA

DEMOSTHENES PLATTERBAFF, the eminent Un-
rest Inducer, stood on his trial for a serious offence, and
the eyes of the political world were focussed on the jury. The
offence, it should be stated, was serious for the Government
rather than for the prisoner. He had blown up the Albert Hall
on the eve of the great Liberal Federation Tango Tea, the
occasion on which the Chancellor of the Exchequer was expected to propound his new theory: "Do partridges spread infectious diseases?" Platterbaff had chosen his time well; the
Tango Tea had been hurriedly postponed, but there were
other political fixtures which could not be put off under any
circumstances. The day after the trial there was to be a by-
election at Nemesis-on-Hand, and it had been openly announced in the division that if Platterbaff were languishing
in gaol on polling day the Government candidate would be
"outed" to a certainty. Unfortunately, there could be no doubt
or misconception as to Platterbaff's guilt. He had not only
pleaded guilty, but had expressed his intention of repeating his
escapade in other directions as soon as circumstances permitted;
throughout the trial he was busy examining a small model of
the Free Trade Hall in Manchester. The jury could not possibly find that the prisoner had not deliberately and intentionally blown up the Albert Hall; the question was: Could they
find any extenuating circumstances which would permit of an

acquittal? Of course any sentence which the law might feel compelled to inflict would be followed by an immediate pardon, but it was highly desirable, from the Government's point of view, that the necessity for such an exercise of clemency should not arise. A headlong pardon, on the eve of a by-election, with threats of a heavy voting defection if it were withheld or even delayed, would not necessarily be a surrender, but it would look like one. Opponents would be only too ready to attribute ungenerous motives. Hence the anxiety in the crowded Court, and in the little groups gathered round the tape-machines in Whitehall and Downing Street and other affected centres.

The jury returned from considering their verdict; there was a flutter, an excited murmur, a death-like hush. The foreman delivered his message:

"The jury find the prisoner guilty of blowing up the Albert Hall. The jury wish to add a rider drawing attention to the fact that a by-election is pending in the Parliamentary division of Nemesis-on-Hand."

"That, of course," said the Government Prosecutor, springing to his feet, "is equivalent to an acquittal?"

"I hardly think so," said the Judge coldly: "I feel obliged to sentence the prisoner to a week's imprisonment."

"And may the Lord have mercy on the poll," a Junior Counsel exclaimed irreverently.

It was a scandalous sentence, but then the Judge was not on the Ministerial side in politics.

The verdict and sentence were made known to the public at twenty minutes past five in the afternoon; at half-past five a dense crowd was massed outside the Prime Minister's residence lustily singing, to the air of "Trelawney":

> "And should our Hero rot in gaol,
>   For e'en a single day,
> There's Fifteen Hundred Voting Men
>   Will vote the other way."

"Fifteen hundred," said the Prime Minister, with a shudder; "it's too horrible to think of. Our majority last time wa only a thousand and seven."

"The poll opens at eight tomorrow morning," said the Chief Organizer; "we must have him out by 7 a.m."

"Seven-thirty," amended the Prime Minister; "we must avoid any appearance of precipitancy."

"Not later than seven-thirty, then," said the Chief Organizer; "I have promised the agent down there that he shall be able to display posters announcing 'Platterbaff is Out,' before the poll opens. He said it was our only chance of getting a telegram 'Radprop is In' tonight."

At half-past seven the next morning the Prime Minister and the Chief Organizer sat at breakfast, making a perfunctory meal, and awaiting the return of the Home Secretary, who had gone in person to superintend the releasing of Platterbaff. Despite the earliness of the hour, a small crowd had gathered in the street outside, and the horrible menacing Trelawney refrain of the "Fifteen Hundred Voting Men" came in a steady, monotonous chant.

"They will cheer presently when they hear the news," said the Prime Minister hopefully. "Hark! They are booing some one now! That must be McKenna."

The Home Secretary entered the room a moment later, disaster written on his face.

"He won't go!" he exclaimed.

"Won't go? Won't leave gaol?"

"He won't go unless he has a brass band. He says he never has left prison without a brass band to play him out, and he's not going to go without one now."

"But surely that sort of thing is provided by his supporters and admirers?" said the Prime Minister; "we can hardly be supposed to supply a released prisoner with a brass band. How on earth could we defend it on the Estimates?"

"His supporters say it is up to us to provide the music," said the Home Secretary; "they say we put him in prison, and it's our affair to see that he leaves it in a respectable manner. Anyway, he won't go unless he has a band."

The telephone squealed shrilly; it was a trunk call from Nemesis.

"Poll opens in five minutes. Is Platterbaff out yet? In Heaven's name, why——"

The Chief Organizer rang off.

"This is not a moment for standing on dignity," he observed bluntly; "musicians must be supplied at once. Platterbaff must have his band."

"Where are you going to find the musicians?" asked the Home Secretary wearily; "we can't employ a military band; in fact, I don't think he'd have one if we offered it, and there aren't any others. There's a musicians' strike on, I suppose you know."

"Can't you get a strike permit?" asked the Organizer.

"I'll try," said the Home Secretary, and went to the telephone.

Eight o'clock struck. The crowd outside chanted with an increasing volume of sound:

"Will vote the other way."

A telegram was brought in. It was from the central committee rooms at Nemesis. "Losing twenty votes per minute," was its brief message.

Ten o'clock struck. The Prime Minister, the Home Secretary, the Chief Organizer, and several earnest helpful friends were gathered in the inner gateway of the prison, talking volubly to Demosthenes Platterbaff, who stood with folded arms and squarely planted feet, silent in their midst. Golden-tongued legislators whose eloquence had swayed the Marconi Inquiry Committee, or at any rate the greater part of it, expended their arts of oratory in vain on this stubborn unyielding man. Without a band he would not go; and they had no band.

A quarter-past ten, half-past. A constant stream of telegraph boys poured in through the prison gates.

"Yamley's factory hands just voted you can guess how," ran a despairing message, and the others were all of the same tenor. Nemesis was going the way of Reading.

"Have you any band instruments of an easy nature to

play?" demanded the Chief Organizer of the Prison Governor; "drums, cymbals, those sort of things?"

"The warders have a private band of their own," said the Governor, "but of course I couldn't allow the men themselves—"

"Lend us the instruments," said the Chief Organizer.

One of the earnest helpful friends was a skilled performer on the cornet, the Cabinet Ministers were able to clash cymbals more or less in tune, and the Chief Organizer had some knowledge of the drum.

"What tune would you prefer?" he asked Platterbaff.

"The popular song of the moment," replied the Agitator after a moment's reflection.

It was a tune they had all heard hundreds of times, so there was no difficulty in turning out a passable imitation of it. To the improvised strains of "I didn't want to do it" the prisoner strode forth to freedom. The words of the song had reference, it was understood, to the incarcerating Government and not to the destroyer of the Albert Hall.

The seat was lost, after all, by a narrow majority. The local Trade Unionists took offence at the fact of Cabinet Ministers having personally acted as strike-breakers, and even the release of Platterbaff failed to pacify them.

The seat was lost, but Ministers had scored a moral victory They had shown that they knew when and how to yield.

THE THREAT

SIR LULWORTH QUAYNE sat in the lounge of his favourite restaurant, the Gallus Bankiva, discussing the weaknesses of the world with his nephew, who had lately returned from a much-enlivened exile in the wilds of Mexico. It was that blessed season of the year when the asparagus and the plover's egg are abroad in the land, and the oyster has not yet withdrawn into its summer entrenchments, and Sir Lulworth and his nephew were in that enlightened after-dinner mood when politics are seen in their right perspective, even the politics of Mexico.

"Most of the revolutions that take place in this country nowadays," said Sir Lulworth, "are the product of moments of legislative panic. Take, for instance, one of the most dramatic reforms that has been carried through Parliament in the lifetime of this generation. It happened shortly after the coal strike, of unblessed memory. To you, who have been plunged up to the neck in events of a more tangled and tumbled description, the things I am going to tell you of may seem of secondary interest, but after all we had to live in the midst of them."

Sir Lulworth interrupted himself for a moment to say a few kind words to the liqueur brandy he had just tasted, and then resumed his narrative.

"Whether one sympathizes with the agitation for female suffrage or not one has to admit that its promoters showed tireless energy and considerable enterprise in devising and putting into action new methods for accomplishing their ends. As a rule they were a nuisance and a weariness to the flesh, but there were times when they verged on the picturesque. There was the famous occasion when they enlivened and diversified the customary pageantry of the Royal progress to open Parliament by letting loose thousands of parrots, which had been carefully trained to scream 'Votes for women,' and which circled round his Majesty's coach in a clamorous cloud of green, and grey and scarlet. It was really rather a striking episode from the spectacular point of view; unfortunately, however, for its devisers, the secret of their intentions had not been well kept, and their opponents let loose at the same moment a rival swarm of parrots, which screeched 'I *don't* think' and other hostile cries, thereby robbing the demonstration of the unanimity which alone could have made it politically impressive. In the process of recapture the birds learned a quantity of additional language which unfitted them for further service in the Suffragette cause; some of the green ones were secured by ardent Home Rule propagandists and trained to disturb the serenity of Orange meetings by pessimistic reflections on Sir Edward Carson's destination in the life to come. In fact, the bird in politics is a factor that seems to have come to stay; quite recently, at a political gathering held in a dimly lighted place of worship, the congregation gave a respectful hearing for nearly ten minutes to a jackdaw from Wapping, under the impression that they were listening to the Chancellor of the Exchequer, who was late in arriving."

"But the Suffragettes," interrupted the nephew; "what did they do next?"

"After the bird fiasco," said Sir Lulworth, "the militant section made a demonstration of a more aggressive nature; they assembled in force on the opening day of the Royal Academy Exhibition and destroyed some three or four hundred of the pictures. This proved an even worse failure than the parrot business; every one agreed that there were always far too many pictures in the Academy Exhibition, and the drastic weeding out of a few hundred canvases was regarded as a positive improvement. Moreover, from the artists' point of view it was realized that the outrage constituted a sort of compensation for those whose works were persistently 'skied,' since out of sight meant also out of reach. Altogether it was one of the most successful and popular exhibitions that the Academy had held for many years. Then the fair agitators fell back on some of their earlier methods; they wrote sweetly argumentative plays to prove that they ought to have the vote, they smashed windows to show that they must have the vote, and they kicked Cabinet Ministers to demonstrate that they'd better have the vote, and still the coldly reasoned or unreasoned reply was that they'd better not. Their plight might have been summed up in a perversion of Gilbert's lines—

> " 'Twenty voteless millions we,
>   Voteless all against our will,
>   Twenty years hence we shall be
>   Twenty voteless millions still.'

And of course the great idea for their master-stroke of strategy came from a masculine source. Lena Dubarri, who was the captain-general of their thinking department, met Waldo Orpington in the Mall one afternoon, just at a time when the fortunes of the Cause were at their lowest ebb. Waldo Orpington is a frivolous little fool who chirrups at drawing-room concerts and can recognize bits from different composers without referring to the programme, but all the same he occasionally has ideas. He didn't care a twopenny fiddlestring about the Cause, but he rather enjoyed the idea of having his finger in the political pie. Also it is possible, though I should think highly improbable, that he admired Lena Dubarri. Anyhow, when Lena gave a rather gloomy account of the existing state of things in the Suffragette world, Waldo was not merely sympathetic but ready with a practical suggestion. Turning his gaze westward along the Mall, towards the setting sun and Buckingham Palace, he was silent for a moment, and then said significantly, 'You have expended your energies and enterprise on labours of destruction; why has it never occurred to you to attempt something far more terrific?'

" 'What do you mean?' she asked him eagerly.

" 'Create.'

" 'Do you mean create disturbances? We've been doing nothing else for months,' she said.

"Waldo shook his head, and continued to look westward along the Mall. He's rather good at acting in an amateur sort of fashion. Lena followed his gaze, and then turned to him with a puzzled look of inquiry.

" 'Exactly,' said Waldo, in answer to her look.

" 'But—how can we create?' she asked; 'it's been done already.'

" 'Do it *again*,' said Waldo, 'and again and again—'

"Before he could finish the sentence she had kissed him. She declared afterwards that he was the first man she had ever kissed, and he declared that she was the first woman who had ever kissed him in the Mall, so they both secured a record of a kind.

"Within the next day or two a new departure was noticeable in Suffragette tactics. They gave up worrying Ministers and Parliament and took to worrying their own sympathizers and supporters—for funds. The ballot-box was temporarily forgotten in the cult of the collecting-box. The daughters of the horseleech were not more persistent in their demands, the financiers of the tottering *ancien régime* were not more desperate in their expedients for raising money than the Suffragist workers of all sections at this juncture, and in one way and another, by fair means and normal, they really got together a very useful sum. What they were going to do with it no one seemed to know, not even those who were most active in collecting work. The secret on this occasion had been well kept. Certain transactions that leaked out from time to time only added to the mystery of the situation.

" 'Don't you long to know what we are going to do with our treasure hoard?' Lena asked the Prime Minister one day when she happened to sit next to him at a whist drive at the Chinese Embassy.

" 'I was hoping you were going to try a little personal bribery,' he responded banteringly, but some genuine anxiety and curiosity lay behind the lightness of his chaff; 'of course I know,' he added, 'that you have been buying up building sites in commanding situations in and around the Metropolis. Two or three, I'm told, are on the road to Brighton, and another near Ascot. You don't mean to fortify them, do you?'

" 'Something more insidious than that,' she said; 'you could prevent us from building forts; you can't prevent us from erecting an exact replica of the Victoria Memorial on each of those sites. They're all private property, with no building restrictions attached.'

" 'Which memorial?' he asked; 'not the one in front of Buckingham Palace? Surely not that one?'

" 'That one,' she said.

" 'My dear lady,' he cried, 'you can't be serious. It is a beautiful and imposing work of art—at any rate, one is getting accustomed to it, and even if one doesn't happen to admire it one can always look in another direction. But imagine what life would be like if one saw that erection confronting one wherever one went. Imagine the effect on people with tired, harassed nerves who saw it three times on the way to Brighton and three times again on the way back. Imagine seeing it dominate the landscape at Ascot, and trying to keep your eye off it on the Sandwich golf-links. What have your countrymen done to deserve such a thing?'

" 'They have refused us the vote,' said Lena bitterly.

"The Prime Minister always declared himself an opponent of anything savouring of panic legislation, but he brought a Bill into Parliament forthwith and successfully appealed to both Houses to pass it through all its stages within the week. And that is how we got one of the most glorious measures of the century."

"A measure conferring the vote on women?" asked the nephew.

"Oh, dear, no. An act which made it a penal offence to erect commemorative statuary anywhere within three miles of a public highway."

EXCEPTING MRS. PENTHERBY

IT was Reggie Bruttle's own idea for converting what had threatened to be an albino elephant into a beast of burden that should help him along the stony road of his finances. "The Limes," which had come to him by inheritance without any accompanying provision for its upkeep, was one of those pretentious, unaccommodating mansions which none but a man of wealth could afford to live in, and which not one wealthy man in a hundred would choose on its merits. It might easily languish in the estate market for years, set round with notice-boards proclaiming it, in the eyes of a sceptical world, to be an eminently desirable residence.

Reggie's scheme was to turn it into the headquarters of a prolonged country-house party, in session during the months from October till the end of March—a party consisting of young or youngish people of both sexes, too poor to be able to do much hunting or shooting on a serious scale, but keen on getting their fill of golf, bridge, dancing, and occasional theatre-going. No one was to be on the footing of a paying guest, but every one was to rank as a paying host; a committee would look after the catering and expenditure, and an informal sub-committee would make itself useful in helping forward the amusement side of the scheme.

As it was only an experiment, there was to be a general agreement on the part of those involved in it to be as lenient and mutually helpful to one another as possible. Already a promising nucleus, including one or two young married couples, had been got together, and the thing seemed to be fairly launched.

"With good management and a little unobtrusive hard work, I think the thing ought to be a success," said Reggie, and Reggie was one of those people who are painstaking first and optimistic afterwards.

"There is one rock on which you will unfailingly come to grief, manage you never so wisely," said Major Dagberry cheerfully; "the women will quarrel. Mind you," continued this prophet of disaster, "I don't say that some of the men won't quarrel too, probably they will; but the women are bound to. You can't prevent it; it's in the nature of the sex. The hand that rocks the cradle rocks the world, in a volcanic sense. A woman will endure discomforts, and make sacrifices, and go without things to an heroic extent, but the one luxury she will not go without is her quarrels. No matter where she may be, or how transient her appearance on a scene, she will instal her feminine feuds as assuredly as a Frenchman would concoct soup in the waste of the Arctic regions. At the commencement of a sea voyage, before the male traveller knows half a dozen of his fellow-passengers by sight, the average woman will have started a couple of enmities, and laid in material for one or two more—provided, of course, that there are sufficient women aboard to permit quarrelling in the plural. If there's no one else she will quarrel with the stewardess. This experiment of yours is to run for six months; in less than five weeks there will be war to the knife declaring itself in half a dozen different directions."

"Oh, come, there are only eight women in the party; they won't all pick quarrels quite so soon as that," protested Reggie.

"They won't all originate quarrels, perhaps," conceded the Major, "but they will all take sides, and just as Christmas is upon you, with its conventions of peace and good will, you will find yourself in for a glacial epoch of cold, unforgiving hostility, with an occasional Etna flare of open warfare. You can't help it, old boy; but, at any rate, you can't say you were not warned."

The first five weeks of the venture falsified Major Dagberry's prediction and justified Reggie's optimism. There were of course, occasional small bickerings, and the existence of certain jealousies might be detected below the surface of everyday intercourse; but, on the whole, the womenfolk got on remarkably well together. There was, however, a notable exception. It had not taken five weeks for Mrs. Pentherby to get herself cordially disliked by the members of her own sex; five days had been amply sufficient. Most of the women declared that they had detested her the moment they set eyes on her; but that was probably an afterthought.

With the menfolk she got on well enough, without being of the type of woman who can only bask in male society; neither was she lacking in the general qualities which make an individual useful and desirable as a member of a co-operative community. She did not try to "get the better of" her fellow-hosts by snatching little advantages or cleverly evading her just contributions; she was not inclined to be boring or snobbish in the way of personal reminiscence. She played a fair game of bridge, and her card-room manners were irreproachable. But wherever she came in contact with her own sex the light of battle kindled at once; her talent for arousing animosity seemed to border on positive genius.

Whether the object of her attentions was thick-skinned or sensitive, quick-tempered or good-natured, Mrs. Pentherby managed to achieve the same effect. She exposed little weaknesses, she prodded sore places, she snubbed enthusiasms, she was generally right in a matter of argument, or, if wrong, she somehow contrived to make her adversary appear foolish and opinionated. She did, and said, horrible things in a matter-of-fact innocent way, and she did, and said, matter-of-fact innocent things in a horrible way. In short, the unanimous feminine verdict on her was that she was objectionable.

There was no question of taking sides, as the Major had anticipated; in fact, dislike of Mrs. Pentherby was almost a bond of union between the other women, and more than one threatening disagreement had been rapidly dissipated by her obvious and malicious attempts to inflame and extend it; and the most irritating thing about her was her successful assumption of unruffled composure at moments when the tempers of her adversaries were with difficulty kept under control. She made her most scathing remarks in the tone of a tube conductor announcing that the next station is Brompton Road—the measured, listless tone of one who knows he is right, but is utterly indifferent to the fact that he proclaims.

On one occasion Mrs. Val Gwepton, who was not blessed with the most reposeful of temperaments, fairly let herself go, and gave Mrs. Pentherby a vivid and truthful *résumé* of her opinion of her. The object of this unpent storm of accumulated animosity waited patiently for a lull, and then remarked quietly to the angry little woman—

"And now, my dear Mrs. Gwepton, let me tell you something that I've been wanting to say for the last two or three minutes, only you wouldn't give me a chance; you've got a hairpin dropping out on the left side. You thin-haired women always find it difficult to keep your hairpins in."

"What can one do with a woman like that?" Mrs. Val demanded afterwards of a sympathizing audience.

Of course, Reggie received numerous hints as to the unpopularity of this jarring personality. His sister-in-law openly tackled him on the subject of her many enormities. Reggie listened with the attenuated regret that one bestows on an earthquake disaster in Bolivia or a crop failure in Eastern Turkestan, events which seem so distant that one can almost persuade oneself they haven't happened.

"That woman has got some hold over him," opined his sister-in-law darkly; "either she is helping him to finance the show, and presumes on the fact, or else, which Heaven forbid, he's got some queer infatuation for her. Men do take the most extraordinary fancies."

Matters never came exactly to a crisis. Mrs. Pentherby, as a source of personal offence, spread herself over so wide an area that no one woman of the party felt impelled to rise up and declare that she absolutely refused to stay another week in the same house with her. What is everybody's tragedy is nobody's tragedy. There was ever a certain consolation in comparing notes as to specific acts of offence. Reggie's sister-in-law had the added interest of trying to discover the secret bond which blunted his condemnation of Mrs. Pentherby's long catalogue of misdeeds. There was little to go on from his manner towards her in public, but he remained obstinately unimpressed by anything that was said against her in private.

With the one exception of Mrs. Pentherby's unpopularity, the house-party scheme was a success on its first trial, and there was no difficulty about reconstructing it on the same lines for another winter session. It so happened that most of the women of the party, and two or three of the men, would not be available on this occasion, but Reggie had laid his plans well ahead and booked plenty of "fresh blood" for the new departure. It would be, if anything, rather a larger party than before.

"I'm so sorry I can't join this winter," said Reggie's sister-in-law, "but we must go to our cousins in Ireland; we've put them off so often. What a shame! You'll have none of the same women this time."

"Excepting Mrs. Pentherby," said Reggie demurely.

"Mrs. Pentherby! *Surely*, Reggie, you're not going to be so idiotic as to have that woman again! She'll set all the women's backs up just as she did this time. What *is* this mysterious hold she's got over you?"

"She's invaluable," said Reggie; "she's my official quarreller."

"Your—what did you say?" gasped his sister-in-law.

"I introduced her into the house-party for the express purpose of concentrating the feuds and quarrelling that would otherwise have broken out in all directions among the women.

kind. I didn't need the advice and warning of sundry friends to foresee that we shouldn't get through six months of close companionship without a certain amount of pecking and sparring, so I thought the best thing was to localize and sterilize it in one process. Of course, I made it well worth the lady's while, and as she didn't know any of you from Adam, and you don't even know her real name, she didn't mind getting herself disliked in a useful cause."

"You mean to say she was in the know all the time?"

"Of course she was, and so were one or two of the men, so she was able to have a good laugh with us behind the scenes when she'd done anything particularly outrageous. And she really enjoyed herself. You see, she's in the position of poor relation in a rather pugnacious family, and her life has been largely spent in smoothing over other people's quarrels. You can imagine the welcome relief of being able to go about saying and doing perfectly exasperating things to a whole houseful of women—and all in the cause of peace."

"I think you are the most odious person in the whole world," said Reggie's sister-in-law. Which was not strictly true; more than anybody, more than ever she disliked Mrs. Pentherby. It was impossible to calculate how many quarrels that woman had done her out of.

MARK

AUGUSTUS MELLOWKENT was a novelist with a future; that is to say, a limited but increasing number of people read his books, and there seemed good reason to suppose that if he steadily continued to turn out novels year by year a progressively increasing circle of readers would acquire the Mellowkent habit, and demand his works from the libraries and bookstalls. At the instigation of his publisher he had discarded the baptismal Augustus and taken the front name of Mark.

"Women like a name that suggests some one strong and

silent, able but unwilling to answer questions. Augustus merely suggests idle splendour, but such a name as Mark Mellowkent, besides being alliterative, conjures up a vision of some one strong and beautiful and good, a sort of blend of Georges Carpentier and the Reverend What's-his-name."

One morning in December Augustus sat in his writing-room, at work on the third chapter of his eighth novel. He had described at some length, for the benefit of those who could not imagine it, what a rectory garden looks like in July; he was now engaged in describing at greater length the feelings of a young girl, daughter of a long line of rectors and arch-deacons, when she discovers for the first time that the postman is attractive.

"Their eyes met, for a brief moment, as he handed her two circulars and the fat wrapper-bound bulk of the *East Essex News*. Their eyes met, for the merest fraction of a second, yet nothing could ever be quite the same again. Cost what it might she felt that she must speak, must break the intolerable, unreal silence that had fallen on them. 'How is your mother's rheumatism?' she said."

The author's labours were cut short by the sudden intrusion of a maidservant.

"A gentleman to see you, sir," said the maid, handing a card with the name Caiaphas Dwelf inscribed on it; "says it's important."

Mellowkent hesitated and yielded; the importance of the visitor's mission was probably illusory, but he had never met any one with the name Caiaphas before. It would be at least a new experience.

Mr. Dwelf was a man of indefinite age; his high, narrow forehead, cold grey eyes, and determined manner bespoke an unflinching purpose. He had a large book under his arm, and there seemed every probability that he had left a package of similar volumes in the hall. He took a seat before it had been offered him, placed the book on the table, and began to address Mellowkent in the manner of an "open letter."

"You are a literary man, the author of several well-known books—"

"I am engaged on a book at the present moment—rather busily engaged," said Mellowkent pointedly.

"Exactly," said the intruder; "time with you is a commodity of considerable importance. Minutes, even, have their value."

"They have," agreed Mellowkent, looking at his watch.

"That," said Caiaphas, "is why this book that I am introducing to your notice is not a book that you can afford to be without. *Right Here* is indispensable for the writing man; it is no ordinary encyclopædia, or I should not trouble to show it to you. It is an inexhaustible mine of concise information—"

"On a shelf at my elbow," said the author, "I have a row of reference books that supply me with all the information I am likely to require."

"Here," persisted the would-be salesman, "you have it all in one compact volume. No matter what the subject may be which you wish to look up, or the fact you desire to verify, *Right Here* gives you all that you want to know in the briefest and most enlightening form. Historical reference, for instance; career of John Huss, let us say. Here we are: 'Huss, John, celebrated religious reformer. Born 1369, burned at Constance 1415. The Emperor Sigismund universally blamed.'"

"If he had been burnt in these days every one would have suspected the Suffragettes," observed Mellowkent.

"Poultry-keeping, now," resumed Caiaphas, "that's a subject that might crop up in a novel dealing with English country life. Here we have all about it: 'The Leghorn as egg-producer. Lack of maternal instinct in the Minorca. Gapes in chickens, its cause and cure. Ducklings for the early market, how fattened.' There, you see, there it all is, nothing lacking."

"Except the maternal instinct in the Minorca, and that you could hardly be expected to supply."

"Sporting records, that's important too; now how many men, sporting men even, are there who can say off-hand what horse won the Derby in any particular year? Now it's just a little thing of that sort—"

"My dear sir," interrupted Mellowkent, "there are at least

four men in my club who can not only tell me what horse
won in any given year, but what horse ought to have won and
why it didn't. If your book could supply a method for protecting one from information of that sort, it would do more
than anything you have yet claimed for it."

"Geography," said Caiaphas imperturbably; "that's a thing
that a busy man, writing at high pressure, may easily make a
slip over. Only the other day a well-known author made the
Volga flow into the Black Sea instead of the Caspian; now,
with this book—"

"On a polished rose-wood stand behind you there reposes a
reliable and up-to-date atlas," said Mellowkent; "and now I
must really ask you to be going."

"An atlas," said Caiaphas, "gives merely the chart of the
river's course, and indicates the principal towns that it passes.
Now *Right Here* gives you the scenery, traffic, ferry-boat
charges, the prevalent types of fish, boatmen's slang terms,
and hours of sailing of the principal river steamers. It gives
you—"

Mellowkent sat and watched the hard-featured, resolute,
pitiless salesman, as he sat doggedly in the chair wherein he
had installed himself, unflinchingly extolling the merits of his
undesired wares. A spirit of wistful emulation took possession
of the author. Why could he not live up to the cold stern name
he had adopted? Why must he sit here weakly and listen to this
weary, unconvincing tirade? Why could he not be Mark
Mellowkent for a few brief moments, and meet this man on
level terms?

A sudden inspiration flashed across him.

"Have you read my last book, *The Cageless Linnet?*" he
asked.

"I don't read novels," said Caiaphas tersely.

"Oh, but you ought to read this one, every one ought to,"
exclaimed Mellowkent, fishing the book down from a shelf;
"published at six shillings, you can have it at four-and-six.
There is a bit in chapter five that I feel sure you would like,
where Emma is alone in the birch copse waiting for Harold
Huntingdon—that is the man her family want her to marry.

She really wants to marry him too, but she does not discover that till chapter fifteen. Listen: 'Far as the eye could stretch rolled the mauve and purple billows of heather, lit up here and there with the glowing yellow of gorse and broom, and edged round with the delicate greys and silver and green of the young birch trees. Tiny blue and brown butterflies fluttered above the fronds of heather, revelling in the sunlight, and overhead the larks were singing as only larks can sing. It was a day when all Nature—' "

"In *Right Here* you have full information on all branches of Nature study," broke in the book-agent, with a tired note sounding in his voice for the first time; "forestry, insect life, bird migration, reclamation of waste lands. As I was saying, no man who has to deal with the varied interests of life—"

"I wonder if you would care for one of my earlier books, *The Reluctance of Lady Cullumpton*," said Mellowkent, hunting again through the bookshelf; "some people consider it my best novel. Ah, here it is. I see there are one or two spots on the cover, so I won't ask more than three-and-ninepence for it. Do let me read you how it opens:

" 'Beatrice Lady Cullumpton entered the long, dimly lit drawing-room, her eyes blazing with a hope that she guessed to be groundless, her lips trembling with a fear that she could not disguise. In her hand she carried a small fan, a fragile toy of lace and satinwood. Something snapped as she entered the room; she had crushed the fan into a dozen pieces.'

"There, what do you think of that for an opening? It tells you at once that there's something afoot."

"I don't read novels," said Caiaphas sullenly.

"But just think what a resource they are," exclaimed the author, "on long winter evenings, or perhaps when you are laid up with a strained ankle—a thing that might happen to any one; or if you were staying in a house-party with persistent wet weather and a stupid hostess and insufferably dull fellow-guests, you would just make an excuse that you had letters to write, go to your room, light a cigarette, and for three-and-ninepence you could plunge into the society of Beatrice Lady Cullumpton and her set. No one ought to travel without one or two of my novels in their luggage as a stand-by. A friend of mine said only the other day that he would as soon think of going into the tropics without quinine as of going on a visit without a couple of Mark Mellowkents in his kit-bag. Perhaps sensation is more in your line. I wonder if I've got a copy of *The Python's Kiss*."

Caiaphas did not wait to be tempted with selections from that thrilling work of fiction. With a muttered remark about having no time to waste on monkey-talk, he gathered up his slighted volume and departed. He made no audible reply to Mellowkent's cheerful "Good morning," but the latter fancied that a look of respectful hatred flickered in the cold, grey eyes.

THE HEDGEHOG

A "MIXED DOUBLE" of young people were contesting a game of lawn tennis at the Rectory garden party; for the past five-and-twenty years at least mixed doubles of young people had done exactly the same thing on exactly the same spot at about the same time of year. The young people changed and made way for others in the course of time, but very little else seemed to alter.

The present players were sufficiently conscious of the social nature of the occasion to be concerned about their clothes and appearance, and sufficiently sport-loving to be keen on the game. Both their efforts and their appearance came under the four-fold scrutiny of a quartet of ladies sitting as official spectators on a bench immediately commanding the court. It was one of the accepted conditions of the Rectory garden party that four ladies, who usually knew very little about tennis and a great deal about the players, should sit at that particular spot and watch the game. It had also come to be almost a tradition that two ladies should be amiable, and that the other two should be Mrs. Dole and Mrs. Hatch-Mallard.

"What a singularly unbecoming way Eva Jonelet has taken to doing her hair in," said Mrs. Hatch-Mallard; "it's ugly

hair at the best of times, but she needn't make it look ridiculous
as well. Some one ought to tell her."

Eva Jonelet's hair might have escaped Mrs. Hatch-Mallard's
condemnation if she could have forgotten the more glaring
fact that Eva was Mrs. Dole's favourite niece. It would, perhaps, have been a more comfortable arrangement if Mrs.
Hatch-Mallard and Mrs. Dole could have been asked to the
Rectory on separate occasions, but there was only one garden
party in the course of the year, and neither lady could have
been omitted from the list of invitations without hopelessly
wrecking the social peace of the parish.

"How pretty the yew trees look at this time of year," interposed a lady with a soft, silvery voice that suggested a chinchilla muff painted by Whistler.

"What do you mean by this time of year?" demanded Mrs.
Hatch-Mallard. "Yew trees look beautiful at all times of the
year. That is their great charm."

"Yew trees never look anything but hideous under any circumstances or at any time of year," said Mrs. Dole, with the
slow, emphatic relish of one who contradicts for the pleasure
of the thing. "They are only fit for graveyards and cemeteries."

Mrs. Hatch-Mallard gave a sardonic snort, which, being
translated, meant that there were some people who were better
fitted for cemeteries than for garden parties.

"What is the score, please?" asked the lady with the chinchilla voice.

The desired information was given her by a young gentleman in spotless white flannels, whose general toilet effect suggested solicitude rather than anxiety.

"What an odious young cub Bertie Dykson has become!"
pronounced Mrs. Dole, remembering suddenly that Bertie was
rather a favourite with Mrs. Hatch-Mallard. "The young
men of today are not what they used to be twenty years ago."

"Of course not," said Mrs. Hatch-Mallard; "twenty years
ago Bertie Dykson was just two years old, and you must expect some difference in appearance and manner and conversation between those two periods."

"Do you know," said Mrs. Dole confidentially, "I shouldn't be surprised if that was intended to be clever."

"Have you any one interesting coming to stay with you, Mrs. Norbury?" asked the chinchilla voice hastily; "you generally have a house-party at this time of year."

"I've got a most interesting woman coming," said Mrs. Norbury, who had been mutely struggling for some chance to turn the conversation into a safe channel; "an old acquaintance of mine, Ada Bleek——"

"What an ugly name," said Mrs. Hatch-Mallard.

"She's descended from the de la Bliques, an old Huguenot family of Touraine, you know."

"There weren't any Huguenots in Touraine," said Mrs. Hatch-Mallard, who thought she might safely dispute any fact that was three hundred years old.

"Well, anyhow, she's coming to stay with me," continued Mrs. Norbury, bringing her story quickly down to the present day; "she arrives this evening and she's highly clairvoyante, a seventh daughter of a seventh daughter, you know, and all that sort of thing."

"How very interesting," said the chinchilla voice; "Exwood is just the right place for her to come to, isn't it? There are supposed to be several ghosts there."

"That is why she was so anxious to come," said Mrs. Norbury; "she put off another engagement in order to accept my invitation. She's had visions and dreams, and all those sort of things, that have come true in a most marvellous manner, but she's never actually seen a ghost, and she's longing to have that experience. She belongs to that Research Society, you know."

"I expect she'll see the unhappy Lady Cullumpton, the most famous of all the Exwood ghosts," said Mrs. Dole; "my ancestor, you know, Sir Gervase Cullumpton, murdered his young bride in a fit of jealousy while they were on a visit to Exwood. He strangled her in the stables with a stirrup leather, just after they had come in from riding, and she is seen sometimes at dusk going about the lawns and the stable yard, in a long green habit, moaning and trying to get the thong from round her throat. I shall be most interested to hear if your friend sees—"

"I don't know why she should be expected to see a trashy, traditional apparition like the so-called Cullumpton ghost, that is only vouched for by house-maids and tipsy stable-boys, when my uncle, who was the owner of Exwood, committed suicide there under the most tragical circumstances, and most certainly haunts the place."

"Mrs. Hatch-Mallard has evidently never read *Popple's County History*," said Mrs. Dole icily, "or she would know that the Cullumpton ghost has a wealth of evidence behind it—"

"Oh, Popple!" exclaimed Mrs. Hatch-Mallard scornfully; "any rubbishy old story is good enough for him. Popple, indeed! Now my uncle's ghost was seen by a Rural Dean, who was also a Justice of the Peace. I should think that would be good enough testimony for any one. Mrs. Norbury, I shall take it as a deliberate personal affront if your clairvoyante friend sees any other ghost except that of my uncle."

"I dare say she won't see anything at all; she never has yet, you know," said Mrs. Norbury hopefully.

"It was a most unfortunate topic for me to have broached," she lamented afterwards to the owner of the chinchilla voice; "Exwood belongs to Mrs. Hatch-Mallard, and we've only got it on a short lease. A nephew of hers has been wanting to live there for some time, and if we offend her in any way she'll refuse to renew the lease. I sometimes think these garden parties are a mistake."

The Norburys played bridge for the next three nights till nearly one o'clock; they did not care for the game, but it reduced the time at their guest's disposal for undesirable ghostly visitations.

"Miss Bleek is not likely to be in a frame of mind to see ghosts," said Hugo Norbury, "if she goes to bed with her brain awhirl with royal spades and no trumps and grand slams."

"I've talked to her for hours about Mrs. Hatch-Mallard's uncle," said his wife, "and pointed out the exact spot where he killed himself, and invented all sorts of impressive details, and I've found an old portrait of Lord John Russell and put it in her room, and told her that it's supposed to be a picture of the uncle in middle age. If Ada does see a ghost at all it certainly ought to be old Hatch-Mallard's. At any rate, we've done our best."

The precautions were in vain. On the third morning of her stay Ada Bleek came down late to breakfast, her eyes looking very tired, but ablaze with excitement, her hair done anyhow, and a large brown volume hugged under her arm.

"At last I've seen something supernatural!" she exclaimed, and gave Mrs. Norbury a fervent kiss, as though in gratitude for the opportunity afforded her.

"A ghost!" cried Mrs. Norbury, "not really!"

"Really and unmistakably!"

"Was it an oldish man in the dress of about fifty years ago?" asked Mrs. Norbury hopefully.

"Nothing of the sort," said Ada; "it was a white hedgehog."

"A white hedgehog!" exclaimed both the Norburys, in tones of disconcerted astonishment.

"A huge white hedgehog with baleful yellow eyes," said Ada; "I was lying half asleep in bed when suddenly I felt a sensation as of something sinister and unaccountable passing through the room. I sat up and looked round, and there, under the window, I saw an evil, creeping thing, a sort of monstrous hedgehog, of a dirty white colour, with black, loathsome claws that clicked and scraped along the floor, and narrow, yellow eyes of indescribable evil. It slithered along for a yard or two, always looking at me with its cruel, hideous eyes, then, when it reached the second window, which was open, it clambered up the sill and vanished. I got up at once and went to the window; there wasn't a sign of it anywhere. Of course, I knew it must be something from another world, but it was not till I turned up Popple's chapter on local traditions that I realized what I had seen."

She turned eagerly to the large brown volume and read:
" 'Nicholas Herison, an old miser, was hung at Batchford in 1763 for the murder of a farm lad who had accidentally dis-

covered his secret hoard. His ghost is supposed to traverse the countryside, appearing sometimes as a white owl, sometimes as a huge white hedgehog.'"

"I expect you read the Popple story overnight, and that made you *think* you saw a hedgehog when you were only half awake," said Mrs. Norbury, hazarding a conjecture that probably came very near the truth.

Ada scouted the possibility of such a solution of her apparition.

"This must be hushed up," said Mrs. Norbury quickly; "the servants——"

"Hushed up!" exclaimed Ada, indignantly; "I'm writing a long report on it for the Research Society."

It was then that Hugo Norbury, who is not naturally a man of brilliant resource, had one of the really useful inspirations of his life.

"It was very wicked of us, Miss Bleek," he said, "but it would be a shame to let it go further. That white hedgehog is an old joke of ours; stuffed albino hedgehog, you know, that my father brought home from Jamaica, where they grow to enormous size. We hide it in the room with a string on it, run one end of the string through the window; then we pull it from below and it comes scraping along the floor, just as you've described, and finally jerks out of the window. Taken in heaps of people; they all read up Popple and think it's old Harry Nicholson's ghost; we always stop them from writing to the papers about it, though. That would be carrying matters too far."

Mrs. Hatch-Mallard renewed the lease in due course, but Ada Bleek has never renewed her friendship.

THE MAPPINED LIFE

"THESE Mappin Terraces at the Zoological Gardens are a great improvement on the old style of wild-beast cage," said Mrs. James Gurtleberry, putting down an illustrated paper; "they give one the illusion of seeing the animals in their natural surroundings. I wonder how much of the illusion is passed on to the animals?"

"That would depend on the animal," said her niece; "a jungle-fowl, for instance, would no doubt think its lawful jungle surroundings were faithfully reproduced if you gave it a sufficiency of wives, a goodly variety of seed food and ants' eggs, a commodious bank of loose earth to dust itself in, a convenient roosting tree, and a rival or two to make matters interesting. Of course there ought to be jungle-cats and birds of prey and other agencies of sudden death to add to the illusion of liberty, but the bird's own imagination is capable of inventing those—look how a domestic fowl will squawk an alarm note if a rook or wood-pigeon passes over its run when it has chickens."

"You think, then, they really do have a sort of illusion, if you give them space enough—"

"In a few cases only. Nothing will make me believe that an acre or so of concrete enclosure will make up to a wolf or a tiger-cat for the range of night prowling that would belong to it in a wild state. Think of the dictionary of sound and scent and recollection that unfolds before a real wild beast as it comes out from its lair every evening, with the knowledge that in a few minutes it will be hieing along to some distant hunting ground where all the joy and fury of the chase awaits it; think of the crowded sensations of the brain when every rustle, every cry, every bent twig, and every whiff across the nostrils means something, something to do with life and death and dinner. Imagine the satisfaction of stealing down to your own particular drinking spot, choosing your own particular tree to scrape your claws on, finding your own particular bed of dried grass to roll on. Then, in the place of all that, put a concrete promenade, which will be of exactly the same dimensions whether you race or crawl across it, coated with stale, unvarying scents and surrounded with cries and noises that have ceased to have the least meaning or interest. As a substitute for a narrow cage the new enclosures are excellent, but I should think they are a poor imitation of a life of liberty."

"It's rather depressing to think that," said Mrs. Gurtleberry; "they look so spacious and so natural, but I suppose a good deal of what seems natural to us would be meaningless to a wild animal."

"That is where our superior powers of self-deception come in," said the niece; "we are able to live our unreal, stupid little lives on our particular Mappin terrace, and persuade ourselves that we really are untrammelled men and women leading a reasonable existence in a reasonable sphere."

"But good gracious," exclaimed the aunt, bouncing into an attitude of scandalized defence, "we are leading reasonable existences! What on earth do you mean by trammels? We are merely trammelled by the ordinary decent conventions of civilized society."

"We are trammelled," said the niece, calmly and pitilessly, "by restrictions of income and opportunity, and above all by lack of initiative. To some people a restricted income doesn't matter a bit, in fact it often seems to help as a means for getting a lot of reality out of life; I am sure there are men and women who do their shopping in little back streets of Paris, buying four carrots and a shred of beef for their daily sustenance, who lead a perfectly real and eventful existence. Lack of initiative is the thing that really cripples one, and that is where you and I and Uncle James are so hopelessly shut in. We are just so many animals stuck down on a Mappin terrace, with this difference in our disfavour, that the animals are there to be looked at, while nobody wants to look at us. As a matter of fact there would be nothing to look at. We get colds in winter and hay-fever in summer, and if a wasp happens to sting one of us, well, that is the wasp's initiative, not ours; all we do is to wait for the swelling to go down. Whenever we do climb into local fame and notice, it is by indirect methods; if it happens to be a good flowering year for magnolias the neighbourhood observes, 'Have you seen the Gurtleberrys' magnolia? It is a perfect mass of flowers,' and we go about telling people that there are fifty-seven blossoms as against thirty-nine the previous year."

"In Coronation year there were as many as sixty," put in the aunt; "your uncle has kept a record for the last eight years."

"Doesn't it ever strike you," continued the niece relentlessly, "that if we moved away from here or were blotted out of existence our local claim to fame would pass on automatically to whoever happened to take the house and garden? People would say to one another, 'Have you seen the Smith-Jenkins' magnolia? It is a perfect mass of flowers,' or else, 'Smith-Jenkins tells me there won't be a single blossom on their magnolia this year; the east winds have turned all the buds black.' Now if, when we had gone, people still associated our names with the magnolia tree, no matter who temporarily possessed it, if they said, 'Ah, that's the tree on which the Gurtleberrys hung their cook because she sent up the wrong kind of sauce with the asparagus,' that would be something really due to our own initiative, apart from anything east winds or magnolia vitality might have to say in the matter."

"We should never do such a thing," said the aunt. The niece gave a reluctant sigh.

"I can't imagine it," she admitted. "Of course," she continued, "there are heaps of ways of leading a real existence without committing sensational deeds of violence. It's the dreadful little everyday acts of pretended importance that give the Mappin stamp to our life. It would be entertaining, if it wasn't so pathetically tragic, to hear Uncle James fuss in here in the morning and announce, 'I must just go down into the town and find out what the men there are saying about Mexico. Matters are beginning to look serious there.' Then he patters away into the town, and talks in a highly serious voice to the tobacconist, incidentally buying an ounce of tobacco; perhaps he meets one or two others of the world's thinkers and talks to them in a highly serious voice, then he patters back here and announces with increased importance, 'I've just been talking to some men in the town about the condition of affairs in Mexico. They agree with the view that I have formed, that things there will have to get worse before they get better.' Of course nobody in the town cared in the least little bit what his views about Mexico were or whether he had any. The tobacconist wasn't even fluttered at his buying the ounce of tobacco; he knows that he purchases the same quantity of the same sort of tobacco every week. Uncle James might just as well have lain on his back in the garden and chattered to the lilac tree about the habits of caterpillars."

"I really will not listen to such things about your uncle," protested Mrs. James Gurtleberry angrily.

"My own case is just as bad and just as tragic," said the niece dispassionately; "nearly everything about me is conventional make-believe. I'm not a good dancer, and no one could honestly call me good-looking, but when I go to one of our dull little local dances I'm conventionally supposed to 'have a heavenly time,' to attract the ardent homage of the local cavaliers, and to go home with my head awhirl with pleasurable recollections. As a matter of fact, I've merely put in some hours of indifferent dancing, drunk some badly made claret cup, and listened to an enormous amount of laborious light conversation. A moonlight hen-stealing raid with the merry eyed curate would be infinitely more exciting; imagine the pleasure of carrying off all those white Minorcas that the Chibfords are always bragging about. When we had disposed of them we could give the proceeds to a charity, so there would be nothing really wrong about it. But nothing of that sort lies within the Mappined limits of my life. One of these days somebody dull and decorous and undistinguished will 'make himself agreeable' to me at a tennis party, as the saying is, and all the dull old gossips of the neighbourhood will begin to ask when we are to be engaged, and at last we shall be engaged, and people will give us butter-dishes and blotting-cases and framed pictures of young women feeding swans. Hullo, Uncle, are you going out?"

"I'm just going down to the town," announced Mr. James Gurtleberry, with an air of some importance: "I want to hear what people are saying about Albania. Affairs there are beginning to take on a very serious look. It's my opinion that we haven't seen the worst of things yet."

In this he was probably right, but there was nothing in the immediate or prospective condition of Albania to warrant Mrs. Gurtleberry in bursting into tears.

FATE

REX DILLOT was nearly twenty-four, almost good-looking and quite penniless. His mother was supposed to make him some sort of an allowance out of what her creditors allowed her, and Rex occasionally strayed into the ranks of those who earn fitful salaries as secretaries or companions to people who are unable to cope unaided with their correspondence or their leisure. For a few months he had been assistant editor and business manager of a paper devoted to fancy mice, but the devotion had been all on one side, and the paper disappeared with a certain abruptness from club reading-rooms and other haunts where it had made a gratuitous appearance. Still, Rex lived with some air of comfort and well-being, as one can live if one is born with a genius for that sort of thing, and a kindly Providence usually arranged that his week-end invitations coincided with the dates on which his one white dinner-waistcoat was in a laundry-returned condition of dazzling cleanness. He played most games badly, and was shrewd enough to recognize the fact, but he had developed a marvellously accurate judgment in estimating the play and chances of other people, whether in a golf match, billiard handicap, or croquet tournament. By dint of parading his opinion of such and such a player's superiority with a sufficient degree of youthful assertiveness he usually succeeded in provoking a wager at liberal odds, and he looked to his week-end winnings to carry him through the financial embarrassments of his mid-week existence. The trouble was, as he confided to Clovis Sangrail, that he never had enough available or even prospective cash at his command to enable him to fix the wager at a figure really worth winning.

"Some day," he said, "I shall come across a really safe thing, a bet that simply can't go astray, and then I shall put it up for all I'm worth, or rather for a good deal more than I'm worth if you sold me up to the last button."

"It would be awkward if it didn't happen to come off," said Clovis.

543

"It would be more than awkward," said Rex; "it would be a tragedy. All the same, it would be extremely amusing to bring it off. Fancy awaking in the morning with about three hundred pounds standing to one's credit. I should go and clear out my hostess's pigeon-loft before breakfast out of sheer good-temper."

"Your hostess of the moment mightn't have a pigeon-loft," said Clovis.

"I always choose hostesses that have," said Rex; "a pigeon-loft is indicative of a careless, extravagant, genial disposition, such as I like to see around me. People who strew corn broadcast for a lot of feathered inanities that just sit about cooing and giving each other the glad eye in a Louis Quatorze manner are pretty certain to do you well."

"Young Strinnit is coming down this afternoon," said Clovis reflectively; "I dare say you won't find it difficult to get him to back himself at billiards. He plays a pretty useful game, but he's not quite as good as he fancies he is."

"I know one member of the party who can walk round him," said Rex softly, an alert look coming into his eyes; "that cadaverous-looking Major who arrived last night. I've seen him play at St. Moritz. If I could get Strinnit to lay odds on himself against the Major the money would be safe in my pocket. This looks like the good thing I've been watching and praying for."

"Don't be rash," counselled Clovis, "Strinnit may play up to his self-imagined form once in a blue moon."

"I intend to be rash," said Rex quietly, and the look on his face corroborated his words.

"Are you all going to flock to the billiard-room?" asked Teresa Thundleford, after dinner, with an air of some disapproval and a good deal of annoyance. "I can't see what particular amusement you find in watching two men prodding little ivory balls about on a table."

"Oh, well," said her hostess, "it's a way of passing the time, you know."

"A very poor way, to my mind," said Mrs. Thundleford;

"now I was going to have shown all of you the photographs
I took in Venice last summer."

"You showed them to us last night," said Mrs. Cuvering
hastily.

"Those were the ones I took in Florence. These are quite
a different lot."

"Oh, well, some time tomorrow we can look at them. You
can leave them down in the drawing-room, and then every
one can have a look."

"I should prefer to show them when you are all gathered
together, as I have quite a lot of explanatory remarks to make,
about Venetian art and architecture, on the same lines as my
remarks last night on the Florentine galleries. Also, there are
some verses of mine that I should like to read you, on the
rebuilding of the Campanile. But, of course, if you all prefer
to watch Major Latton and Mr. Strinnit knocking balls about
on a table—"

"They are both supposed to be first-rate players," said the
hostess.

"I have yet to learn that my verses and my art *causerie* are
of second-rate quality," said Mrs. Thundleford with acerbity.
"However, as you all seem bent on watching a silly game,
there's no more to be said. I shall go upstairs and finish some
writing. Later on, perhaps, I will come down and join
you."

To one, at least, of the onlookers the game was anything
but silly. It was absorbing, exciting, exasperating, nerve-stretch-
ing, and finally it grew to be tragic. The Major with the St.
Moritz reputation was playing a long way below his form,
young Strinnit was playing slightly above his, and had all the
luck of the game as well. From the very start the balls seemed
possessed by a demon of contrariness; they trundled about
complacently for one player, they would go nowhere for the
other.

"A hundred and seventy, seventy-four," sang out the youth
who was marking. In a game of two hundred and fifty up it
was an enormous lead to hold. Clovis watched the flush of ex-

citement die away from Dillot's face, and a hard white look take its place.

"How much have you got on?" whispered Clovis. The other whispered the sum through dry, shaking lips. It was more than he or any one connected with him could pay; he had done what he had said he would do. He had been rash.

"Two hundred and six, ninety-eight."

Rex heard a clock strike ten somewhere in the hall, then another somewhere else, and another, and another; the house seemed full of striking clocks. Then in the distance the stable clock chimed in. In another hour they would all be striking eleven, and he would be listening to them as a disgraced outcast, unable to pay, even in part, the wager he had challenged.

"Two hundred and eighteen, a hundred and three." The game was as good as over. Rex was as good as done for. He longed desperately for the ceiling to fall in, for the house to catch fire, for anything to happen that would put an end to that horrible rolling to and fro of red and white ivory that was jostling him nearer and nearer to his doom.

"Two hundred and twenty-eight, a hundred and seven."

Rex opened his cigarette-case; it was empty. That at least gave him a pretext to slip away from the room for the purpose of refilling it; he would spare himself the drawn-out torture of watching that hopeless game played out to the bitter end. He backed away from the circle of absorbed watchers and made his way up a short stairway to a long, silent corridor of bedrooms, each with a guest's name written in a little square on the door. In the hush that reigned in this part of the house he could still hear the hateful click-click of the balls; if he waited for a few minutes longer he would hear the little outbreak of clapping and buzz of congratulation that would hail Strinnit's victory. On the alert tension of his nerves there broke another sound, the aggressive, wrath-inducing breathing of one who sleeps in heavy after-dinner slumber. The sound came from a room just at his elbow; the card on the door bore the announcement. "Mrs. Thundleford." The door was just slightly ajar; Rex pushed it open an inch or two more and looked in. The august Teresa had fallen asleep over an illustrated guide to Florentine art-galleries; at her side, somewhat dangerously near the edge of the table, was a reading-lamp. If Fate had been decently kind to him, thought Rex, bitterly, that lamp would have been knocked over by the sleeper and would have given them something to think of besides billiard matches.

There are occasions when one must take one's Fate in one's hands. Rex took the lamp in his.

"Two hundred and thirty-seven, one hundred and fifteen." Strinnit was at the table, and the balls lay in good position for him; he had a choice of two fairly easy shots, a choice which he was never to decide. A sudden hurricane of shrieks and a rush of stumbling feet sent every one flocking to the door. The Dillot boy crashed into the room, carrying in his arms the vociferous and somewhat dishevelled Teresa Thundleford; her clothing was certainly not a mass of flames, as the more excitable members of the party afterwards declared, but the edge of her skirt and part of the table-cover in which she had been hastily wrapped were alight in a flickering, half-hearted manner. Rex flung his struggling burden on to the billiard table, and for one breathless minute the work of beating out the sparks with rugs and cushions and playing on them with soda-water syphons engrossed the energies of the entire company.

"It was lucky I was passing when it happened," panted Rex; "some one had better see to the room. I think the carpet is alight."

As a matter of fact the promptitude and energy of the rescuer had prevented any great damage being done, either to the victim or her surroundings. The billiard table had suffered most, and had to be laid up for repairs; perhaps it was not the best place to have chosen for the scene of salvage operations; but then, as Clovis remarked, when one is rushing about with a blazing woman in one's arms one can't stop to think out exactly where one is going to put her.

THE BULL

TOM YORKFIELD had always regarded his half-brother, Laurence, with a lazy instinct of dislike, toned down, as years went on, to a tolerant feeling of indifference. There was nothing very tangible to dislike him for; he was just a blood-relation, with whom Tom had no single taste or interest in common, and with whom, at the same time, he had had no occasion for quarrel. Laurence had left the farm early in life, and had lived for a few years on a small sum of money left him by his mother; he had taken up painting as a profession, and was reported to be doing fairly well at it, well enough, at any rate, to keep body and soul together. He specialized in painting animals, and he was successful in finding a certain number of people to buy his pictures. Tom felt a comforting sense of assured superiority in contrasting his position with that of his half-brother; Laurence was an artist-chap, just that and nothing more, though you might make it sound more important by calling him an animal painter; Tom was a farmer, not in a very big way, it was true, but the Helsery farm had been in the family for some generations, and it had a good reputation for the stock raised on it. Tom had done his best, with the little capital at his command, to maintain and improve the standard of his small herd of cattle, and in Clover Fairy he had bred a bull which was something rather better than any that his immediate neighbours could show. It would not have made a sensation in the judging-ring at an important cattle show, but it was as vigorous, shapely, and healthy a young animal as any small practical farmer could wish to possess. At the King's Head on market days Clover Fairy was very highly spoken of, and Yorkfield used to declare that he would not part with him for a hundred pounds; a hundred pounds is a lot of money in the small farming line, and probably anything over eighty would have tempted him.

It was with some especial pleasure that Tom took advantage of one of Laurence's rare visits to the farm to lead him

down to the enclosure where Clover Fairy kept solitary state
—the grass widower of a grazing harem. Tom felt some of
his old dislike for his half-brother reviving; the artist was becoming more languid in his manner, more unsuitably turned-
out in attire, and he seemed inclined to impart a slightly patronizing tone to his conversation. He took no heed of a flourishing
potato crop, but waxed enthusiastic over a clump of yellow-
flowering weed that stood in a corner by a gateway, which
was rather galling to the owner of a really very well weeded
farm; again, when he might have been duly complimentary
about a group of fat, black-faced lambs, that simply cried
aloud for admiration, he became eloquent over the foliage
tints of an oak copse on the hill opposite. But now he was
being taken to inspect the crowning pride and glory of Helsery; however grudging he might be in his praises, however
backward and niggardly with his congratulations, he would
have to see and acknowledge the many excellencies of that
redoubtable animal. Some weeks ago, while on a business journey to Taunton, Tom had been invited by his half-brother to
visit a studio in that town, where Laurence was exhibiting one
of his pictures, a large canvas representing a bull standing
knee-deep in some marshy ground; it had been good of its
kind, no doubt, and Laurence had seemed inordinately pleased
with it; "the best thing I've done yet," he had said over and
over again, and Tom had generously agreed that it was fairly
life-like. Now, the man of pigments was going to be shown
a real picture, a living model of strength and comeliness, a
thing to feast the eyes on, a picture that exhibited new pose
and action with every shifting minute, instead of standing
glued into one unvarying attitude between the four walls of
a frame. Tom unfastened a stout wooden door and led the
way into a straw-bedded yard.

"Is he quiet?" asked the artist, as a young bull with a curly
red coat came inquiringly towards them.

"He's playful at times," said Tom, leaving his half-brother
to wonder whether the bull's ideas of play were of the catch-
as-catch-can order. Laurence made one or two perfunctory
comments on the animal's appearance and asked a question or

so as to his age and such-like details; then he coolly turned the talk into another channel.

"Do you remember the picture I showed you at Taunton?" he asked.

"Yes," grunted Tom; "a white-faced bull standing in some slush. Don't admire those Herefords much myself; bulky-looking brutes, don't seem to have much life in them. Daresay they're easier to paint that way; now, this young beggar is on the move all the time, aren't you, Fairy?"

"I've sold that picture," said Laurence, with considerable complacency in his voice.

"Have you?" said Tom; "glad to hear it, I'm sure. Hope you're pleased with what you've got for it."

"I got three hundred pounds for it," said Laurence.

Tom turned towards him with a slowly rising flush of anger in his face. Three hundred pounds! Under the most favourable market conditions that he could imagine his prized Clover Fairy would hardly fetch a hundred, yet here was a piece of varnished canvas, painted by his half-brother, selling for three times that sum. It was a cruel insult that went home with all the more force because it emphasized the triumph of the patronizing, self-satisfied Laurence. The young farmer had meant to put his relative just a little out of conceit with himself by displaying the jewel of his possessions, and now the tables were turned, and his valued beast was made to look cheap and insignificant beside the price paid for a mere picture. It was so monstrously unjust; the painting would never be anything more than a dexterous piece of counterfeit life, while Clover Fairy was the real thing, a monarch in his little world, a personality in the countryside. After he was dead, even, he would still be something of a personality; his descendants would graze in those valley meadows and hillside pastures, they would fill stall and byre and milking-shed, their good red coats would speckle the landscape and crowd the market-place; men would note a promising heifer or a well-proportioned steer, and say: "Ah, that one comes of good old Clover Fairy's stock." All that time the picture would be hanging, lifeless and unchanging, beneath its dust and varnish, a

chattel that ceased to mean anything if you chose to turn it
with its back to the wall. These thoughts chased themselves
angrily through Tom Yorkfield's mind, but he could not put
them into words. When he gave tongue to his feelings he put
matters bluntly and harshly.

"Some soft-witted fools may like to throw away three hundred pounds on a bit of paintwork; can't say as I envy them
their taste. I'd rather have the real thing than a picture of
it."

He nodded towards the young bull, that was alternately
staring at them with nose held high and lowering its horns
with a half-playful, half-impatient shake of the head.

Laurence laughed a laugh of irritating, indulgent amusement.

"I don't think the purchaser of my bit of paintwork, as you
call it, need worry about having thrown his money away. As
I get to be better known and recognized my pictures will go
up in value. That particular one will probably fetch four hundred in a sale-room five or six years hence; pictures aren't a
bad investment if you know enough to pick out the work of
the right men. Now you can't say your precious bull is going
to get more valuable the longer you keep him; he'll have his
little day, and then, if you go on keeping him, he'll come
down at last to a few shillingsworth of hoofs and hide, just
at a time, perhaps, when *my* bull is being bought for a big
sum for some important picture gallery."

It was too much. The united force of truth and slander
and insult put over heavy a strain on Tom Yorkfield's powers
of restraint. In his right hand he held a useful oak cudgel,
with his left he made a grab at the loose collar of Laurence's
canary-coloured silk shirt. Laurence was not a fighting man;
the fear of physical violence threw him off his balance as completely as overmastering indignation had thrown Tom off his,
and thus it came to pass that Clover Fairy was regaled with
the unprecedented sight of a human being scudding and
squawking across the enclosure, like the hen that would per-
sist in trying to establish a nesting-place in the manger. In
another crowded happy moment the bull was trying to jerk

Laurence over his left shoulder, to prod him in the ribs while still in the air, and to kneel on him when he reached the ground. It was only the vigorous intervention of Tom that induced him to relinquish the last item of his programme.

Tom devotedly and ungrudgingly nursed his half-brother to a complete recovery from his injuries, which consisted of nothing more serious than a dislocated shoulder, a broken rib or two, and a little nervous prostration. After all, there was no further occasion for rancour in the young farmer's mind; Laurence's bull might sell for three hundred, or for six hundred, and be admired by thousands in some big picture gallery, but it would never toss a man over one shoulder and catch him a jab in the ribs before he had fallen on the other side. That was Clover Fairy's noteworthy achievement, which could never be taken away from him.

Laurence continues to be popular as an animal artist, but his subjects are always kittens or fawns or lambkins—never bulls.

MORLVERA

THE Olympic Toy Emporium occupied a conspicuous frontage in an important West End street. It was happily named Toy Emporium, because one would never have dreamed of according it the familiar and yet pulse-quickening name of toyshop. There was an air of cold splendour and elaborate failure about the wares that were set out in its ample windows; they were the sort of toys that a tired shop-assistant displays and explains at Christmas-time to exclamatory parents and bored, silent children. The animal toys looked more like natural history models than the comfortable, sympathetic companions that one would wish, at a certain age, to take to bed with one, and to smuggle into the bath-room. The mechanical toys incessantly did things that no one could want a toy to do more than half a dozen times in its lifetime; it was a merciful reflection that in any right-minded nursery the lifetime would certainly be short.

Prominent among the elegantly dressed dolls that filled an entire section of the window frontage was a large hobble-skirted lady in a confection of peach-coloured velvet, elaborately set off with leopard-skin accessories, if one may use such a conveniently comprehensive word in describing an intricate feminine toilette. She lacked nothing that is to be found in a carefully detailed fashion-plate—in fact, she might be said to have something more than the average fashion-plate female possesses; in place of a vacant, expressionless stare she had character in her face. It must be admitted that it was bad character, cold, hostile, inquisitorial, with a sinister lowering of one eyebrow and a merciless hardness about the corners of the mouth. One might have imagined histories about her by the hour, histories in which unworthy ambition, the desire for money, and an entire absence of all decent feeling would play a conspicuous part.

As a matter of fact, she was not without her judges and biographers, even in this shop-window stage of her career. Emmeline, aged ten, and Bert, aged seven, had halted on the way from their obscure back street to the minnow-stocked water of St. James's Park, and were critically examining the hobble-skirted doll, and dissecting her character in no very tolerant spirit. There is probably a latent enmity between the necessarily under-clad and the unnecessarily over-dressed, but a little kindness and good-fellowship on the part of the latter will often change the sentiment to admiring devotion; if the lady in peach-coloured velvet and leopard skin had worn a pleasant expression in addition to her other elaborate furnishings, Emmeline at least might have respected and even loved her. As it was, she gave her a horrible reputation, based chiefly on a second-hand knowledge of gilded depravity derived from the conversation of those who were skilled in the art of novelette reading; Bert filled in a few damaging details from his own limited imagination.

"She's a bad lot, that one is," declared Emmeline, after a long unfriendly stare; "'er 'usbind 'ates 'er."

"'E knocks 'er abart," said Bert with enthusiasm.

"No, 'e don't, cos 'e's dead; she poisoned 'im slow and

gradual, so that nobody didn't know. Now she wants to marry a lord, with 'eaps and 'eaps of money. 'E's got a wife already, but she's going to poison 'er, too."

"She's a bad lot," said Bert with growing hostility.

" 'Er mother 'ates her, and she's afraid of 'er, too, cos she's got a serkestic tongue; always talking serkesms, she is. She's greedy, too; if there's fish going, she eats 'er own share and 'er little girl's as well, though the little girl is dellikit."

"She 'ad a little boy once," said Bert, "but she pushed 'im into the water when nobody wasn't looking."

"No, she didn't," said Emmeline, "she sent 'im away to be kep' by poor people, so 'er 'usbind wouldn't know where 'e was. They ill-treat 'im somethink cruel."

"Wot's 'er nime?" asked Bert, thinking that it was time that so interesting a personality should be labelled.

" 'Er nime?" said Emmeline, thinking hard, " 'er nime's Morlvera." It was as near as she could get to the name of an adventuress who figured prominently in a cinema drama. There was silence for a moment while the possibilities of the name were turned over in the children's minds.

"Those clothes she's got on ain't paid for, and never won't be," said Emmeline; "she thinks she'll get the rich lord to pay for 'em, but 'e won't. 'E's given 'er jools, 'underds of pounds' worth."

" 'E won't pay for the clothes," said Bert with conviction. Evidently there was some limit to the weak good nature of wealthy lords.

At that moment a motor carriage with liveried servants drew up at the emporium entrance; a large lady, with a pene-trating and rather hurried manner of talking, stepped out, followed slowly and sulkily by a small boy, who had a very black scowl on his face and a very white sailor suit over the rest of him. The lady was continuing an argument which had probably commenced in Portman Square.

"Now, Victor, you are to come in and buy a nice doll for your cousin Bertha. She gave you a beautiful box of soldiers on your birthday, and you must give her a present on hers."

"Bertha is a fat little fool," said Victor, in a voice that

was as loud as his mother's and had more assurance in it.

"Victor, you are not to say such things. Bertha is not a fool, and she is not in the least fat. You are to come in and choose a doll for her."

The couple passed into the shop, out of view and hearing of the two back-street children.

"My, he is in a wicked temper," exclaimed Emmeline, but both she and Bert were inclined to side with him against the absent Bertha, who was doubtless as fat and foolish as he had described her to be.

"I want to see some dolls," said the mother of Victor to the nearest assistant; "it's for a little girl of eleven."

"A fat little girl of eleven," added Victor by way of supplementary information.

"Victor, if you say such rude things about your cousin, you shall go to bed the moment we get home, without having any tea."

"This is one of the newest things we have in dolls," said the assistant, removing a hobble-skirted figure in peach-coloured velvet from the window; "leopard-skin toque and stole, the latest fashion. You won't get anything newer than that anywhere. It's an exclusive design."

"Look!" whispered Emmeline outside; "they've bin and took Morlvera."

There was a mingling of excitement and a certain sense of bereavement in her mind; she would have liked to gaze at that embodiment of overdressed depravity for just a little longer.

"I 'spect she's going away in a kerridge to marry the rich lord," hazarded Bert.

"She's up to no good," said Emmeline vaguely.

Inside the shop the purchase of the doll had been decided on.

"It's a beautiful doll, and Bertha will be delighted with it," asserted the mother of Victor loudly.

"Oh, very well," said Victor sulkily; "you needn't have it stuck into a box and wait an hour while it's being done up into a parcel. I'll take it as it is, and we can go round to Manchester Square and give it to Bertha, and get the thing done with. That will save me the trouble of writing, 'For dear Bertha, with Victor's love,' on a bit of paper."

"Very well," said his mother, "we can go to Manchester Square on our way home. You must wish her many happy returns of tomorrow, and give her the doll."

"I won't let the little beast kiss me," stipulated Victor.

His mother said nothing; Victor had not been half as troublesome as she had anticipated. When he chose he could really be dreadfully naughty.

Emmeline and Bert were just moving away from the window when Morlvera made her exit from the shop, very carefully held in Victor's arms. A look of sinister triumph seemed to glow in her hard, inquisitorial face. As for Victor, a certain scornful serenity had replaced the earlier scowls; he had evidently accepted defeat with a contemptuous good grace.

The tall lady gave a direction to the footman and settled herself in the carriage. The little figure in the white sailor suit clambered in beside her, still carefully holding the elegantly garbed doll.

The car had to be backed a few yards in the process of turning. Very stealthily, very gently, very mercilessly Victor sent Morlvera flying over his shoulder, so that she fell into the road just behind the retrogressing wheel. With a soft, pleasant-sounding scrunch the car went over the prostrate form, then it moved forward again with another scrunch. The carriage moved off and left Bert and Emmeline gazing in scared delight at a sorry mess of petrol-smeared velvet, sawdust, and leopard skin, which was all that remained of the hateful Morlvera. They gave a shrill cheer, and then raced away shuddering from the scene of so much rapidly enacted tragedy.

Later that afternoon, when they were engaged in the pursuit of minnows by the waterside in St. James's Park, Emmeline said in a solemn undertone to Bert—

"I've bin finking. Do you know oo 'e was? 'E was 'er little boy wot she'd sent away to live wiv poor folks. 'E come back and done that."

SHOCK TACTICS

ON a late spring afternoon Ella McCarthy sat on a green-painted chair in Kensington Gardens, staring listlessly at an uninteresting stretch of park landscape, that blossomed suddenly into tropical radiance as an expected figure appeared in the middle distance.

"Hullo, Bertie!" she exclaimed sedately, when the figure arrived at the painted chair that was the nearest neighbour to her own, and dropped into it eagerly, yet with a certain due regard for the set of its trousers; "hasn't it been a perfect spring afternoon?"

The statement was a distinct untruth as far as Ella's own feelings were concerned; until the arrival of Bertie the afternoon had been anything but perfect.

Bertie made a suitable reply, in which a questioning note seemed to hover.

"Thank you ever so much for those lovely handkerchiefs," said Ella, answering the unspoken question; "they were just what I've been wanting. There's only one thing spoilt my pleasure in your gift," she added, with a pout.

"What was that?" asked Bertie anxiously, fearful that perhaps he had chosen a size of handkerchief that was not within the correct feminine limit.

"I should have liked to have written and thanked you for them as soon as I got them," said Ella, and Bertie's sky clouded at once.

"You know what mother is," he protested; "she opens all my letters, and if she found I'd been giving presents to any one there'd have been something to talk about for the next fortnight."

"Surely, at the age of twenty—" began Ella.

"I'm not twenty till September," interrupted Bertie.

"At the age of nineteen years and eight months," persisted Ella, "you might be allowed to keep your correspondence private to yourself."

"I ought to be, but things aren't always what they ought

to be. Mother opens every letter that comes into the house, whoever it's for. My sisters and I have made rows about it time and again, but she goes on doing it."

"I'd find some way to stop her if I were in your place," said Ella valiantly, and Bertie felt that the glamour of his anxiously deliberated present had faded away in the disagreeable restriction that hedged round its acknowledgment.

"Is anything the matter?" asked Bertie's friend Clovis when they met that evening at the swimming-bath.

"Why do you ask?" said Bertie.

"When you wear a look of tragic gloom in a swimming-bath," said Clovis, "it's especially noticeable from the fact that you're wearing very little else. Didn't she like the handkerchiefs?"

Bertie explained the situation.

"It is rather galling, you know," he added, "when a girl has a lot of things she wants to write to you and can't send a letter except by some roundabout, underhand way."

"One never realizes one's blessings while one enjoys them," said Clovis; "now I have to spend a considerable amount of ingenuity inventing excuses for not having written to people."

"It's not a joking matter," said Bertie resentfully: "you wouldn't find it funny if your mother opened all your letters."

"The funny thing to me is that you should let her do it."

"I can't stop it. I've argued about it——"

"You haven't used the right kind of argument, I expect. Now, if every time one of your letters was opened you lay on your back on the dining-table during dinner and had a fit, or roused the entire family in the middle of the night to hear you recite one of Blake's 'Poems of Innocence,' you would get a far more respectful hearing for future protests. People yield more consideration to a mutilated mealtime or a broken night's rest, than ever they would to a broken heart."

"Oh, dry up," said Bertie crossly, inconsistently splashing Clovis from head to foot as he plunged into the water.

It was a day or two after the conversation in the swimming-bath that a letter addressed to Bertie Heasant slid into the letter-box at his home, and thence into the hands of his mother. Mrs. Heasant was one of those empty-minded individuals to whom other people's affairs are perpetually interesting. The more private they are intended to be the more acute is the interest they arouse. She would have opened this particular letter in any case; the fact that it was marked "private," and diffused a delicate but penetrating aroma, merely caused her to open it with headlong haste rather than matter-of-course deliberation. The harvest of sensation that rewarded her was beyond all expectations.

"Bertie, carissimo," it began, "I wonder if you will have the nerve to do it: it will take some nerve, too. Don't forget the jewels. They are a detail, but details interest me.

"Yours as ever,
"CLOTILDE.

"Your mother must not know of my existence. If questioned swear you never heard of me."

For years Mrs. Heasant had searched Bertie's correspondence diligently for traces of possible dissipation or youthful entanglements, and at last the suspicions that had stimulated her inquisitorial zeal were justified by this one splendid haul. That any one wearing the exotic name "Clotilde" should write to Bertie under the incriminating announcement "as ever" was sufficiently electrifying, without the astounding allusion to the jewels. Mrs. Heasant could recall novels and dramas wherein jewels played an exciting and commanding rôle, and here, under her own roof, before her very eyes as it were, her own son was carrying on an intrigue in which jewels were merely an interesting detail. Bertie was not due home for another hour, but his sisters were available for the immediate unburdening of a scandal-laden mind.

"Bertie is in the toils of an adventuress," she screamed; "her name is Clotilde," she added, as if she thought they had better know the worst at once. There are occasions when more harm than good is done by shielding young girls from a knowledge of the more deplorable realities of life.

By the time Bertie arrived his mother had discussed every possible and improbable conjecture as to his guilty secret; the girls limited themselves to the opinion that their brother had been weak rather than wicked.

"Who is Clotilde?" was the question that confronted Bertie almost before he had got into the hall. His denial of any knowledge of such a person was met with an outburst of bitter laughter.

"How well you have learned your lesson!" exclaimed Mrs. Heasant. But satire gave way to furious indignation when she realized that Bertie did not intend to throw any further light on her discovery.

"You shan't have any dinner till you've confessed everything," she stormed.

Bertie's reply took the form of hastily collecting material for an impromptu banquet from the larder and locking himself into his bedroom. His mother made frequent visits to the locked door and shouted a succession of interrogations with the persistence of one who thinks that if you ask a question often enough an answer will eventually result. Bertie did nothing to encourage the supposition. An hour had passed in fruitless one-sided palaver when another letter addressed to Bertie and marked "private" made its appearance in the letter-box. Mrs. Heasant pounced on it with the enthusiasm of a cat that has missed its mouse and to whom a second has been unexpectedly vouchsafed. If she hoped for further disclosures assuredly she was not disappointed.

"So you have really done it!" the letter abruptly commenced; "Poor Dagmar. Now she is done for I almost pity her. You did it very well, you wicked boy, the servants all think it was suicide, and there will be no fuss. Better not touch the jewels till after the inquest.

"CLOTILDE."

Anything that Mrs. Heasant had previously done in the way of outcry was easily surpassed as she raced upstairs and beat frantically at her son's door.

"Miserable boy, what have you done to Dagmar?"

"It's Dagmar now, is it?" he snapped; "it will be Geraldine next."

"That it should come to this, after all my efforts to keep you at home of an evening," sobbed Mrs. Heasant; "it's no use you trying to hide things from me; Clotilde's letter betrays everything."

"Does it betray who she is?" asked Bertie. "I've heard so much about her, I should like to know something about her home-life. Seriously, if you go on like this I shall fetch a doctor; I've often enough been preached at about nothing, but I've never had an imaginary harem dragged into the discussion."

"Are these letters imaginary?" screamed Mrs. Heasant. "What about the jewels, and Dagmar, and the theory of suicide?"

No solution of these problems was forthcoming through the bedroom door, but the last post of the evening produced another letter for Bertie, and its contents brought Mrs. Heasant that enlightenment which had already dawned on her son.

"DEAR BERTIE," it ran; "I hope I haven't distracted your brain with the spoof letters I've been sending in the name of a fictitious Clotilde. You told me the other day that the servants, or somebody at your home, tampered with your letters, so I thought I would give any one that opened them something exciting to read. The shock might do them good.

"Yours,
"CLOVIS SANGRAIL."

Mrs. Heasant knew Clovis slightly, and was rather afraid of him. It was not difficult to read between the lines of his successful hoax. In a chastened mood she rapped once more at Bertie's door.

"A letter from Mr. Sangrail. It's all been a stupid hoax. He wrote those other letters. Why, where are you going?"

Bertie had opened the door; he had on his hat and overcoat.

"I'm going for a doctor to come and see if anything's the

matter with you. Of course it was all a hoax, but no person in his right mind could have believed all that rubbish about murder and suicide and jewels. You've been making enough noise to bring the house down for the last hour or two."

"But what was I to think of those letters?" whimpered Mrs. Heasant.

"I should have known what to think of them," said Bertie; "if you choose to excite yourself over other people's correspondence it's your own fault. Anyhow, I'm going for a doctor."

It was Bertie's great opportunity, and he knew it. His mother was conscious of the fact that she would look rather ridiculous if the story got about. She was willing to pay hush-money.

"I'll never open your letters again," she promised.

And Clovis has no more devoted slave than Bertie Heasant.

THE SEVEN CREAM JUGS

"I SUPPOSE we shall never see Wilfrid Pigeoncote here now that he has become heir to the baronetcy and to a lot of money," observed Mrs. Peter Pigeoncote regretfully to her husband.

"Well, we can hardly expect to," he replied, "seeing that we always choked him off from coming to see us when he was a prospective nobody. I don't think I've set eyes on him since he was a boy of twelve."

"There was a reason for not wanting to encourage his acquaintanceship," said Mrs. Peter. "With that notorious failing of his he was not the sort of person one wanted in one's house."

"Well, the failing still exists, doesn't it?" said her husband; "or do you suppose a reform of character is entailed along with the estate?"

"Oh, of course, there is still that drawback," admitted the wife, "but one would like to make the acquaintance of the future head of the family, if only out of mere curiosity. Besides, cynicism apart, his being rich *will* make a difference in the way people will look at his failing. When a man is absolutely wealthy, not merely well-to-do, all suspicion of sordid motive naturally disappears; the thing becomes merely a tiresome malady."

Wilfrid Pigeoncote had suddenly become heir to his uncle, Sir Wilfrid Pigeoncote, on the death of his cousin, Major Wilfrid Pigeoncote, who had succumbed to the after-effects of a polo accident. (A Wilfrid Pigeoncote had covered himself with honours in the course of Marlborough's campaigns, and the name Wilfrid had been a baptismal weakness in the family ever since.) The new heir to the family dignity and estates was a young man of about five-and-twenty, who was known more by reputation than by person to a wide circle of cousins and kinsfolk. And the reputation was an unpleasant one. The numerous other Wilfrids in the family were distinguished one from another chiefly by the names of their residences or professions, as Wilfrid of Hubbledown, and young Wilfrid the Gunner, but this particular scion was known by the ignominious and expressive label of Wilfrid the Snatcher. From his late schooldays onward he had been possessed by an acute and obstinate form of kleptomania; he had the acquisitive instinct of the collector without any of the collector's discrimination. Anything that was smaller and more portable than a sideboard, and above the value of ninepence, had an irresistible attraction for him, provided that it fulfilled the necessary condition of belonging to some one else. On the rare occasions when he was included in a country-house party, it was usual and almost necessary for his host, or some member of the family, to make a friendly inquisition through his baggage on the eve of his departure, to see if he had packed up "by mistake" any one else's property. The search usually produced a large and varied yield.

"This is funny," said Peter Pigeoncote to his wife, some half-hour after their conversation; "here's a telegram from Wilfrid, saying he's passing through here in his motor, and would like to stop and pay us his respects. Can stay for the night if it doesn't inconvenience us. Signed 'Wilfrid Pigeoncote.' Must be the Snatcher; none of the others have a motor. I suppose he's bringing us a present for the silver wedding."

"Good gracious!" said Mrs. Peter, as a thought struck her; "this is rather an awkward time to have a person with his failing in the house. All those silver presents set out in the drawing-room, and others coming by every post; I hardly know what we've got and what are still to come. We can't lock them all up; he's sure to want to see them."

"We must keep a sharp look-out, that's all," said Peter reassuringly.

"But these practised kleptomaniacs are so clever," said his wife apprehensively, "and it will be so awkward if he suspects that we are watching him."

Awkwardness was indeed the prevailing note that evening when the passing traveller was being entertained. The talk flitted nervously and hurriedly from one impersonal topic to another. The guest had none of the furtive, half-apologetic air that his cousins had rather expected to find; he was polite, well-assured, and, perhaps, just a little inclined to "put on side." His hosts, on the other hand, wore an uneasy manner that might have been the hallmark of conscious depravity. In the drawing-room, after dinner, their nervousness and awkwardness increased.

"Oh, we haven't shown you the silver-wedding presents," said Mrs. Peter suddenly, as though struck by a brilliant idea for entertaining the guest; "here they all are. Such nice, useful gifts. A few duplicates, of course."

"Seven cream jugs," put in Peter.

"Yes, isn't it annoying," went on Mrs. Peter; "seven of them. We feel that we must live on cream for the rest of our lives. Of course, some of them can be changed."

Wilfrid occupied himself chiefly with such of the gifts as were of antique interest, carrying one or two of them over to the lamp to examine their marks. The anxiety of his hosts at these moments resembled the solicitude of a cat whose newly born kittens are being handed round for inspection.

"Let me see; did you give me back the mustard-pot? This is its place here," piped Mrs. Peter.

"Sorry. I put it down by the claret-jug," said Wilfrid, busy with another object.

"Oh, just let me have that sugar-sifter again," asked Mrs. Peter, dogged determination showing through her nervousness. "I must label it who it comes from before I forget."

Vigilance was not completely crowned with a sense of victory. After they had said "Good night" to their visitor, Mrs. Peter expressed her conviction that he had taken something.

"I fancy, by his manner, that there was something up," corroborated her husband. "Do you miss anything?"

Mrs. Peter hastily counted the array of gifts.

"I can only make it thirty-four, and I think it should be thirty-five," she announced. "I can't remember if thirty-five includes the Archdeacon's cruet-stand that hasn't arrived yet."

"How on earth are we to know?" said Peter. "The mean pig hasn't brought us a present, and I'm hanged if he shall carry one off."

"Tomorrow, when he's having his bath," said Mrs. Peter excitedly, "he's sure to leave his keys somewhere, and we can go through his portmanteau. It's the only thing to do."

On the morrow an alert watch was kept by the conspirators behind half-closed doors, and when Wilfrid, clad in a gorgeous bath-robe, had made his way to the bath-room, there was a swift and furtive rush by two excited individuals towards the principal guest-chamber. Mrs. Peter kept guard outside, while her husband first made a hurried and successful search for the keys, and then plunged at the portmanteau with the air of a disagreeably conscientious Customs official. The quest was a brief one; a silver cream jug lay embedded in the folds of some zephyr shirts.

"The cunning brute," said Mrs. Peter; "he took a cream jug because there were so many; he thought one wouldn't be missed. Quick, fly down with it and put it back among the others."

Wilfrid was late in coming down to breakfast, and his manner showed plainly that something was amiss.

"It's an unpleasant thing to have to say," he blurted out presently, "but I'm afraid you must have a thief among your servants. Something's been taken out of my portmanteau. It was a little present from my mother and myself for your silver wedding. I should have given it to you last night after dinner, only it happened to be a cream jug, and you seemed annoyed at having so many duplicates, so I felt rather awkward about giving you another. I thought I'd get it changed for something else, and now it's gone."

"Did you say it was from your *mother* and yourself?" asked Mr. and Mrs. Peter almost in unison. The Snatcher had been an orphan these many years.

"Yes, my mother's at Cairo just now, and she wrote to me at Dresden to try and get you something quaint and pretty in the old silver line, and I pitched on this cream jug."

Both the Pigeoncotes had turned deadly pale. The mention of Dresden had thrown a sudden light on the situation. It was Wilfrid the Attaché, a very superior young man, who rarely came within their social horizon, whom they had been entertaining unawares in the supposed character of Wilfrid the Snatcher. Lady Ernestine Pigeoncote, his mother, moved in circles which were entirely beyond their compass or ambitions, and the son would probably one day be an Ambassador. And they had rifled and despoiled his portmanteau! Husband and wife looked blankly and desperately at one another. It was Mrs. Peter who arrived first at an inspiration.

"How dreadful to think there are thieves in the house! We keep the drawing-room locked up at night, of course, but anything might be carried off while we are at break-fast."

She rose and went out hurriedly, as though to assure herself that the drawing-room was not being stripped of its silverware, and returned a moment later, bearing a cream jug in her hands.

"There are eight cream jugs now, instead of seven," she cried; "this one wasn't there before. What a curious trick of memory, Mr. Wilfrid! You must have slipped downstairs with it last night and put it there before we locked up, and forgotten all about having done it in the morning."

"One's mind often plays one little tricks like that," said Mr. Peter, with desperate heartiness. "Only the other day I went into the town to pay a bill, and went in again next day, having clean forgotten that I'd——"

"It is certainly the jug that I brought for you," said Wilfrid, looking closely at it; "it was in my portmanteau when I got my bath-robe out this morning, before going to my bath, and it was not there when I unlocked the portmanteau on my return. Some one had taken it while I was away from the room."

The Pigeoncotes had turned paler than ever. Mrs. Peter had a final inspiration.

"Get me my smelling-salts, dear," she said to her husband; "I think they're in the dressing-room."

Peter dashed out of the room with glad relief; he had lived so long during the last few minutes that a golden wedding seemed within measurable distance.

Mrs. Peter turned to her guest with confidential coyness.

"A diplomat like you will know how to treat this as if it hadn't happened. Peter's little weakness; it runs in the family."

"Good Lord! Do you mean to say he's a kleptomaniac, like Cousin Snatcher?"

"Oh, not exactly," said Mrs. Peter, anxious to whitewash her husband a little greyer than she was painting him. "He would never touch anything he found lying about, but he can't resist making a raid on things that are locked up. The doctors have a special name for it. He must have pounced on your portmanteau the moment you went to your bath, and taken the first thing he came across. Of course, he had no motive for taking a cream jug; we've already got *seven*, as you know——not, of course, that we don't value the kind gift you and your mother—— Hush, here's Peter coming."

Mrs. Peter broke off in some confusion, and tripped out to meet her husband in the hall.

"It's all right," she whispered to him; "I've explained everything. Don't say anything more about it."

"Brave little woman," said Peter, with a gasp of relief; "I could never have done it."

. . . .

Diplomatic reticence does not necessarily extend to family affairs. Peter Pigeoncote was never able to understand why Mrs. Consuelo van Bullyon, who stayed with them in the spring, always carried two very obvious jewel-cases with her to the bath-room, explaining them to any one she chanced to meet in the corridor as her manicure and face-massage set.

THE OCCASIONAL GARDEN

"DON'T talk to me about town gardens," said Elinor Rapsley; "which means, of course, that I want you to listen to me for an hour or so while I talk about nothing else. 'What a nice-sized garden you've got,' people said to us when we first moved here. What I suppose they meant to say was what a nice-sized site for a garden we'd got. As a matter of fact, the size is all against it; it's too large to be ignored altogether and treated as a yard, and it's too small to keep giraffes in. You see, if we could keep giraffes or reindeer or some other species of browsing animal there we could explain the general absence of vegetation by a reference to the fauna of the garden: 'You can't have wapiti *and* Darwin tulips, you know, so we didn't put down any bulbs last year.' As it is, we haven't got the wapiti, and the Darwin tulips haven't survived the fact that most of the cats of the neighbourhood hold a parliament in the centre of the tulip bed; that rather forlorn-looking strip that we intended to be a border of alternating geranium and spiræa has been utilized by the cat-parliament as a division lobby. Snap divisions seem to have been rather frequent of late, far more frequent than the geranium blooms are likely to be. I shouldn't object so much to ordinary cats, but I do complain of having a congress of vegetarian cats in my garden; they must be vegetarians, my dear, because, whatever ravages they may commit among the sweet-pea seedlings, they never seem to touch the sparrows; there are always just as many adult sparrows in the garden on Saturday as there were on Monday, not to mention newly fledged additions. There seems to have been an irreconcilable difference of opinion between sparrows and Providence since the beginning of time as to whether a crocus looks best standing upright with its roots in the earth or in a recumbent posture with its stem neatly severed; the sparrows always have the last word in the matter, at least in our garden they do. I fancy that Providence must have originally intended to bring in an amending Act, or whatever it's called, providing either for a less destructive sparrow or a more indestructible crocus. The one consoling point about our garden is that it's not visible from the drawing-room or the smoking-room, so unless people are dining or lunching with us they can't spy out the nakedness of the land. That is why I am so furious with Gwenda Pottingdon, who has practically forced herself on me for lunch on Wednesday next; she heard me offer the Paulcote girl lunch if she was up shopping on that day, and, of course, she asked if she might come too. She is only coming to gloat over my bedraggled and flowerless borders and to sing the praises of her own detestably over-cultivated garden. I'm sick of being told that it's the envy of the neighbourhood; it's like everything else that belongs to her— her car, her dinner-parties, even her headaches, they are all superlative; no one else ever had anything like them. When her eldest child was confirmed it was such a sensational event, according to her account of it, that one almost expected questions to be asked about it in the House of Commons, and now she's coming on purpose to stare at my few miserable pansies and the gaps in my sweet-pea border, and to give me a glowing, full-length description of the rare and sumptuous blooms in her rose-garden."

"My dear Elinor," said the Baroness, "you would save yourself all this heart-burning and a lot of gardener's bills, not to mention sparrow anxieties, simply by paying an annual subscription to the O.O.S.A."

"Never heard of it," said Elinor; "what is it?"

"The Occasional-Oasis Supply Association," said the Baroness; "it exists to meet cases exactly like yours, cases of back-yards that are of no practical use for gardening purposes, but are required to blossom into decorative scenic backgrounds at stated intervals, when a luncheon or dinner-party is contemplated. Supposing, for instance, you have people coming to lunch at one-thirty; you just ring up the Association at about ten o'clock the same morning, and say, 'Lunch garden.' That is all the trouble you have to take. By twelve forty-five your yard is carpeted with a strip of velvety turf, with a hedge of lilac or red may, or whatever happens to be in season, as a background, one or two cherry trees in blossom, and clumps of heavily flowered rhododendrons filling in the odd corners; in the foreground you have a blaze of carnations or Shirley poppies, or tiger lilies in full bloom. As soon as the lunch is over and your guests have departed the garden departs also, and all the cats in Christendom can sit in council in your yard without causing you a moment's anxiety. If you have a bishop or an antiquary or something of that sort coming to lunch you just mention the fact when you are ordering the garden, and you get an old-world pleasaunce, with clipped yew hedges and a sun-dial and hollyhocks, and perhaps a mulberry tree, and borders of sweet-williams and Canterbury bells, and an old-fashioned beehive or two tucked away in a corner. Those are the ordinary lines of supply that the Oasis Association undertakes, but by paying a few guineas a year extra you are entitled to its emergency E.O.N. service."

"What on earth is an E.O.N. service?"

"It's just like a conventional signal to indicate special cases like the incursion of Gwenda Pottingdon. It means you've got some one coming to lunch or dinner whose garden is alleged to be 'the envy of the neighbourhood.'"

"Yes," exclaimed Elinor, with some excitement, "and what happens then?"

"Something that sounds like a miracle out of the Arabian Nights. Your backyard becomes voluptuous with pomegranate and almond trees, lemon groves, and hedges of flowering cactus, dazzling banks of azaleas, marble-basined fountains, in which chestnut-and-white pond-herons step daintily amid exotic water-lilies, while golden pheasants strut about on alabaster terraces. The whole effect rather suggests the idea that Providence and Norman Wilkinson have dropped mutual jealousies and collaborated to produce a background for an open-air Russian Ballet; in point of fact, it is merely the background to your luncheon party. If there is any kick left in Gwenda Pottingdon, or whoever your E.O.N. guest of the moment may be, just mention carelessly that your climbing putella is the only one in England, since the one at Chatsworth died last winter. There isn't such a thing as a climbing putella, but Gwenda Pottingdon and her kind don't usually know one flower from another without prompting."

"Quick," said Elinor, "the address of the Association."

Gwenda Pottingdon did not enjoy her lunch. It was a simple yet elegant meal, excellently cooked and daintily served, but the piquant sauce of her own conversation was notably lacking. She had prepared a long succession of eulogistic comments on the wonders of her town garden, with its unrivalled effects of horticultural magnificence, and, behold, her theme was shut in on every side by the luxuriant hedge of Siberian berberis that formed a glowing background to Elinor's bewildering fragment of fairyland. The pomegranate and lemon trees, the terraced fountain, where golden carp slithered and wriggled amid the roots of gorgeous-hued irises, the banked masses of exotic blooms, the pagoda-like enclosure, where Japanese sand-badgers disported themselves, all these contributed to take away Gwenda's appetite and moderate her desire to talk about gardening matters.

"I can't say I admire the climbing putella," she observed shortly, "and anyway it's not the only one of its kind in England; I happen to know of one in Hampshire. How gardening is going out of fashion. I suppose people haven't the time for it nowadays."

Altogether it was quite one of Elinor's most successful luncheon parties.

It was distinctly an unforeseen catastrophe that Gwenda should have burst in on the household four days later at lunch-time and made her way unbidden into the dining-room.

"I thought I must tell you that my Elaine has had a water-colour sketch accepted by the Latent Talent Art Guild; it's to be exhibited at their summer exhibition at the Hackney Gallery. It will be the sensation of the moment in the art world— Hullo, what on earth has happened to your garden? It's not there!"

"Suffragettes," said Elinor promptly; "didn't you hear about it? They broke in and made hay of the whole thing in about ten minutes. I was so heartbroken at the havoc that I had the whole place cleared out; I shall have it laid out again on rather more elaborate lines.

"That," she said to the Baroness afterwards, "is what I call having an emergency brain."

THE SHEEP

THE enemy had declared "no trumps." Rupert played out his ace and king of clubs and cleared the adversary of that suit; then the Sheep, whom the Fates had inflicted on him for a partner, took the third round with the queen of clubs, and, having no other club to lead back, opened another suit. The enemy won the remainder of the tricks—and the rubber.

"I had four more clubs to play; we only wanted the odd trick to win the rubber," said Rupert.

"But I hadn't another club to lead you," exclaimed the Sheep, with his ready, defensive smile.

"It didn't occur to you to throw your queen away on my king and leave me with the command of the suit," said Rupert, with polite bitterness.

"I suppose I ought to have—I wasn't certain what to do. I'm awfully sorry," said the Sheep.

Being awfully and uselessly sorry formed a large part of his occupation in life. If a similar situation had arisen in a subsequent hand he would have blundered just as certainly, and he would have been just as irritatingly apologetic.

Rupert stared gloomily across at him as he sat smiling and

fumbling with his cards. Many men who have good brains for business do not possess the rudiments of a card-brain, and Rupert would not have judged and condemned his prospective brother-in-law on the evidence of his bridge play alone. The tragic part of it was that he smiled and fumbled through life just as fatuously and apologetically as he did at the card-table. And behind the defensive smile and the well-worn expressions of regret there shone a scarcely believable but quite obvious self-satisfaction. Every sheep of the pasture probably imagines that in an emergency it could become terrible as an army with banners—one has only to watch how they stamp their feet and stiffen their necks when a minor object of suspicion comes into view and behaves meekly. And probably the majority of human sheep see themselves in imagination taking great parts in the world's more impressive dramas, forming swift, unerring decisions in moments of crisis, cowing mutinies, allaying panics, brave, strong, simple, but, in spite of their natural modesty, always slightly spectacular.

"Why in the name of all that is unnecessary and perverse should Kathleen choose this man for her future husband?" was the question that Rupert asked himself ruefully. There was young Malcolm Athling, as nice-looking, decent, level-headed a fellow as any one could wish to meet, obviously her very devoted admirer, and yet she must throw herself away on this pale-eyed, weak-mouthed embodiment of self-approving ineptitude. If it had been merely Kathleen's own affair Rupert would have shrugged his shoulders and philosophically hoped that she might make the best of an undeniably bad bargain. But Rupert had no heir; his own boy lay underground somewhere on the Indian frontier, in goodly company. And the property would pass in due course to Kathleen and Kathleen's husband. The Sheep would live there in the beloved old home, rearing up other little Sheep, fatuous and rabbit-faced and self-satisfied like himself, to dwell in the land and possess it. It was not a soothing prospect.

Towards dusk on the afternoon following the bridge experience Rupert and the Sheep made their way homeward after a day's mixed shooting. The Sheep's cartridge bag was nearly empty, but his game bag showed no signs of overcrowd-ing. The birds he had shot at had seemed for the most part as impervious to death or damage as the hero of a melodrama. And for each failure to drop his bird he had some explanation or apology ready on his lips. Now he was striding along in front of his host, chattering happily over his shoulder, but obviously on the look-out for some belated rabbit or wood-pigeon that might haply be secured as an eleventh-hour addi-tion to his bag. As they passed the edge of a small copse a large bird rose from the ground and flew slowly towards the trees, offering an easy shot to the oncoming sportsmen. The Sheep banged forth with both barrels, and gave an exultant cry.

"Hooray! I've shot a thundering big hawk."

"To be exact, you've shot a honey-buzzard. That is the hen bird of one of the few pairs of honey-buzzards breeding in the United Kingdom. We've kept them under the strictest preser-vation for the last four years; every gamekeeper and village gun loafer for twenty miles round has been warned and bribed and threatened to respect their sanctity, and egg-snatching agents have been carefully guarded against during the breed-ing season. Hundreds of lovers of rare birds have delighted in seeing their snap-shotted portraits in *Country Life*, and now you've reduced the hen bird to a lump of broken feathers."

Rupert spoke quietly and evenly, but for a moment or two a gleam of positive hatred shone in his eyes.

"I say, I'm so sorry," said the Sheep, with his apologetic smile. "Of course I remember hearing about the buzzards, but somehow I didn't connect this bird with them. And it was such an easy shot—"

"Yes," said Rupert; "that was the trouble."

Kathleen found him in the gun-room smoothing out the feathers of the dead bird. She had already been told of the catastrophe.

"What a horrid misfortune," she said sympathetically.

"It was my dear Robbie who first discovered them the last time he was home on leave. Don't you remember how excited he was about them? Let's go and have some tea."

Both bridge and shooting were given a rest for the next

two or three weeks. Death, who enters into no compacts with
party whips, had forced a Parliamentary vacancy on the neighbourhood at the least convenient season, and the local partisans
on either side found themselves immersed in the discomforts
of a mid-winter election. Rupert took his politics seriously
and keenly. He belonged to that type of strangely but rather
happily constituted individuals which these islands seem to
produce in a fair plenty; men and women who for no personal profit or gain go forth from their comfortable firesides
or club card-rooms to hunt to and fro in the mud and rain
and wind for the capture or tracking of a stray vote here and
there on their party's behalf—not because they think they
ought to, but because they want to. And his energies were welcome enough on this occasion, for the seat was a closely disputed possession, and its loss or retention would count for
much in the present position of the Parliamentary game. With
Kathleen to help him, he had worked his corner of the constituency with tireless, well-directed zeal, taking his share of
the dull routine work as well as of the livelier episodes. The
talking part of the campaign wound up on the eve of the poll
with a meeting in a centre where more undecided votes were
supposed to be concentrated than anywhere else in the division.
A good final meeting here would mean everything. And the
speakers, local and imported, left nothing undone to improve
the occasion. Rupert was down for the unimportant task of
moving the complimentary vote to the chairman which should
close the proceedings.

"I'm so hoarse," he protested, when the moment arrived;
"I don't believe I can make my voice heard beyond the platform."

"Let me do it," said the Sheep; "I'm rather good at that sort
of thing."

The chairman was popular with all parties, and the Sheep's
opening words of complimentary recognition received a round
of applause. The orator smiled expansively on his listeners and
seized the opportunity to add a few words of political wisdom
on his own account. People looked at the clock or began to
grope for umbrellas and discarded neck-wraps. Then, in the

midst of a string of meaningless platitudes, the Sheep delivered himself of one of those blundering remarks which
travel from one end of a constituency to the other in half an
hour, and are seized on by the other side as being more potent
on their behalf than a ton of election literature. There was a
general shuffling and muttering across the length and breadth
of the hall, and a few hisses made themselves heard. The Sheep
tried to whittle down his remark, and the chairman unhesitat-
ingly threw him over in his speech of thanks, but the damage
was done.

"I'm afraid I lost touch with the audience rather over that
remark," said the Sheep afterwards, with his apologetic smile
abnormally developed.

"You lost us the election," said the chairman, and he proved
a true prophet.

A month or so of winter sport seemed a desirable pick-me-up
after the strenuous work and crowning discomfiture of the
election. Rupert and Kathleen hied them away to a small
Alpine resort that was just coming into prominence, and thither
the Sheep followed them in due course, in his rôle of husband-
elect. The wedding had been fixed for the end of March.

It was a winter of early and unseasonable thaws, and the
far end of the local lake, at a spot where swift currents flowed
into it, was decorated with notices, written in three languages,
warning skaters not to venture over certain unsafe patches.
The folly of approaching too near these danger spots seemed to
have a natural fascination for the Sheep.

"I don't see what possible danger there can be," he protested, with his inevitable smile, when Rupert beckoned him
away from the proscribed area; "the milk that I put out on
my window-sill last night was frozen an inch deep."

"It hadn't got a strong current flowing through it," said
Rupert; "in any case, there is not much sense in hovering
round a doubtful piece of ice when there are acres of good
ice to skate over. The secretary of the ice-committee has
warned you once already."

A few minutes later Rupert heard a loud squeal of fear, and
saw a dark spot blotting the smoothness of the lake's frozen

surface. The Sheep was struggling helplessly in an ice-hole of his own making. Rupert gave one loud curse, and then dashed full tilt for the shore; outside a low stable building on the lake's edge he remembered having seen a ladder. If he could slide it across the ice-hole before the Sheep went under the rescue would be comparatively simple work. Other skaters were dashing up from a distance, and, with the ladder's help, they could get him out of his death-trap without having to trust themselves on the margin of rotten ice. Rupert sprang on to the surface of lumpy, frozen snow, and staggered to where the ladder lay. He had already lifted it when the rattle of a chain and a furious outburst of growls burst on his hearing, and he was dashed to the ground by a mass of white and tawny fur. A sturdy young yard-dog, frantic with the pleasure of performing his first piece of active guardian service, was ramping and snarling over him, rendering the task of regaining his feet or securing the ladder a matter of considerable difficulty. When he had at last succeeded in both efforts he was just by a hair's-breadth too late to be of any use. The Sheep had definitely disappeared under the ice-rift.

Kathleen Athling and her husband stay the greater part of the year with Rupert, and a small Robbie stands in some danger of being idolized by a devoted uncle. But for twelve months of the year Rupert's most inseparable and valued companion is a sturdy tawny and white yard-dog.

THE OVERSIGHT

"IT'S like a Chinese puzzle," said Lady Prowche resentfully, staring at a scribbled list of names that spread over two or three loose sheets of notepaper on her writing-table. Most of the names had a pencil mark running through them.

"What is like a Chinese puzzle?" asked Lena Luddleford briskly; she rather prided herself on being able to grapple with the minor problems of life.

"Getting people suitably sorted together. Sir Richard likes me to have a house party about this time of year, and gives me a free hand as to whom I should invite; all he asks is that it should be a peaceable party, with no friction or unpleasantness."

"That seems reasonable enough," said Lena.

"Not only reasonable, my dear, but necessary. Sir Richard has his literary work to think of; you can't expect a man to concentrate on the tribal disputes of Central Asian clansmen when he's got social feuds blazing under his own roof."

"But why should they blaze? Why should there be feuds at all within the compass of a house party?"

"Exactly; why should they blaze or why should they exist?" echoed Lady Prowche. "The point is that they always do. We have been unlucky; persistently unlucky, now that I come to look back on things. We have always got people of violently opposed views under our roof, and the result has been not merely unpleasantness but explosion."

"Do you mean people who disagree on matters of political opinion and religious views?" asked Lena.

"No, not that. The broader lines of political or religious difference don't matter. You can have Church of England and Unitarian and Buddhist under the same roof without courting disaster; the only Buddhist I ever had down here quarrelled with everybody, but that was on account of his naturally squabblesome temperament; it had nothing to do with his religion. And I've always found that people can differ profoundly about politics and meet on perfectly good terms at breakfast. Now, Miss Larbor Jones, who was staying here last year, worships Lloyd George as a sort of wingless angel, while Mrs. Walters, who was down here at the same time, privately considers him to be—an antelope, let us say."

"An antelope?"

"Well, not an antelope exactly, but something with horns and hoofs and tail."

"Oh, I see."

"Still, that didn't prevent them from being the chummiest of mortals on the tennis court and in the billiard-room. They did quarrel finally, about a lead in a doubled hand of no trumps, but that of course is a thing that no amount of judicious guest-grouping could prevent. Mrs. Walters had got king, knave, ten, and seven of clubs——"

"You were saying that there were other lines of demarcation that caused the bother," interrupted Lena.

"Exactly. It is the minor differences and side-issues that give so much trouble," said Lady Prowche; "not to my dying day shall I forget last year's upheaval over the Suffragette question. Laura Henniseed left the house in a state of speechless indignation, but before she had reached that state she had used language that would not have been tolerated in the Austrian Reichsrath. Intensive bear-gardening was Sir Richard's description of the whole affair, and I don't think he exaggerated."

"Of course the Suffragette question is a burning one, and lets loose the most dreadful ill-feeling," said Lena; "but one can generally find out beforehand what people's opinions——"

"My dear, the year before it was worse. It was Christian Science. Selina Goobie is a sort of High Priestess of the Cult, and she put down all opposition with a high hand. Then one evening, after dinner, Clovis Sangrail put a wasp down her back, to see if her theory about the non-existence of pain could be depended on in an emergency. The wasp was small, but very efficient, and it had been soured in temper by being kept in a paper cage all the afternoon. Wasps don't stand confinement well, at least this one didn't. I don't think I ever realized till that moment what the word 'invective' could be made to mean. I sometimes wake in the night and think I still hear Selina describing Clovis's conduct and general character. That was the year that Sir Richard was writing his volume on *Domestic Life in Tartary*. The critics all blamed it for a lack of concentration."

"He's engaged on a very important work this year, isn't he?" asked Lena.

"*Land-tenure in Turkestan*," said Lady Prowche; "he is just at work on the final chapters and they require all the concentration he can give them. That is why I am so very anxious not to have any unfortunate disturbance this year. I have taken every precaution I can think of to bring non-conflicting and harmonious elements together; the only two people I am not quite easy about are the Atkinson man and Marcus Popham. They are the two who will be down here longest together, and if they are going to fall foul of one another about any burning question, well, there will be more unpleasantness."

"Can't you find out anything about them? About their opinions, I mean."

"Anything? My dear Lena, there's scarcely anything that I haven't found out about them. They're both of them moderate Liberal, Evangelical, mildly opposed to female suffrage, they approve of the Falconer Report, and the Stewards' decision about Craganour. Thank goodness in this country we don't fly into violent passions about Wagner and Brahms and things of that sort. There is only one thorny subject that I haven't been able to make sure about, the only stone that I have left unturned. Are they unanimously anti-vivisectionist or do they both uphold the necessity for scientific experiment? There has been a lot of correspondence on the subject in our local newspapers of late, and the vicar is certain to preach a sermon about it; vicars are dreadfully provocative at times. Now, if you could only find out for me whether these two men are divergently for or against—"

"I!" exclaimed Lena; "how am I to find out? I don't know either of them to speak to."

"Still, you might discover, in some roundabout way. Write to them, under an assumed name, of course, for subscriptions to one or other cause—or, better still, send a stamped typewritten reply postcard, with a request for a declaration for or against vivisection; people who would hesitate to commit themselves to a subscription will cheerfully write Yes or No on a prepaid postcard. If you can't manage it that way, try and meet them at some one's house and get into argument on the subject. I think Milly occasionally has one or other of them at her at-homes; you might have the luck to meet both of them there the same evening. Only it must be done soon. My invitations ought to go out by Wednesday or Thursday at the latest, and today is Friday."

"Milly's at-homes are not very amusing, as a rule," said Lena; "and one never gets a chance of talking uninterruptedly to any one for a couple of minutes at a time; Milly is one of those restless hostesses who always seem to be trying to see how you look in different parts of the room, in fresh grouping effects. Even if I got to speak to Popham or Atkinson I couldn't plunge into a topic like vivisection straight away. No, I think the postcard scheme would be more hopeful and decidedly less tiresome. How would it be best to word them?"

"Oh, something like this: 'Are you in favour of experiments on living animals for the purpose of scientific research—Yes or No?' That is quite simple and unmistakable. If they don't answer it will at least be an indication that they are indifferent about the subject, and that is all I want to know."

"All right," said Lena, "I'll get my brother-in-law to let me have them addressed to his office, and he can telephone the result of the plebiscite direct to you."

"Thank you ever so much," said Lady Prowche gratefully, "and be sure to get the cards sent off as soon as possible."

On the following Tuesday the voice of an office clerk, speaking through the telephone, informed Lady Prowche that the postcard poll showed unanimous hostility to experiments on living animals.

Lady Prowche thanked the office clerk, and in a louder and more fervent voice she thanked Heaven. The two invitations, already sealed and addressed, were immediately dispatched; in due course they were both accepted. The house party of the halcyon hours, as the prospective hostess called it, was auspiciously launched.

Lena Luddleford was not included among the guests, having previously committed herself to another invitation. At the opening day of a cricket festival, however, she ran across Lady Prowche, who had motored over from the other side of the county. She wore the air of one who is not interested in cricket and not particularly interested in life. She shook hands limply with Lena, and remarked that it was a beastly day.

"The party, how has it gone off?" asked Lena quickly.

"Don't speak of it!" was the tragical answer; "why do I always have such rotten luck?"

"But what has happened?"

"It has been awful. Hyænas could not have behaved with greater savagery. Sir Richard said so, and he has been in countries where hyænas live, so he ought to know. They actually came to blows!"

"Blows?"

"Blows and curses. It really might have been a scene from one of Hogarth's pictures. I never felt so humiliated in my life. What the servants must have thought!"

"But who were the offenders?"

"Oh, naturally the very two that we took all the trouble about."

"I thought they agreed on every subject that one could violently disagree about—religion, politics, vivisection, the Derby decision, the Falconer Report; what else was there left to quarrel about?"

"My dear, we were fools not to have thought of it. One of them was Pro-Greek and the other Pro-Bulgar."

HYACINTH

"THE new fashion of introducing the candidate's children into an election contest is a pretty one," said Mrs. Panstreppon; "it takes away something from the acerbity of party warfare, and it makes an interesting experience for the children to look back on in after years. Still, if you will listen to my advice, Matilda, you will not take Hyacinth with you down to Luffbridge on election day."

"Not take Hyacinth!" exclaimed his mother; "but why not? Jutterly is bringing his three children, and they are going to drive a pair of Nubian donkeys about the town, to emphasize the fact that their father has been appointed Colonial Secretary. We are making the demand for a strong Navy a special feature in *our* campaign, and it will be particularly appropriate to have Hyacinth dressed in his sailor suit. He'll look heavenly."

"The question is, not how he'll look, but how he'll behave. He's a delightful child, of course, but there is a strain of unbridled pugnacity in him that breaks out at times in a really alarming fashion. You may have forgotten the affair of the little Gaffin children; I haven't."

"I was in India at the time, and I've only a vague recollection of what happened; he was very naughty, I know."

"He was in his goat-carriage, and met the Gaffins in their perambulator, and he drove the goat full tilt at them and sent the perambulator spinning. Little Jacky Gaffin was pinned down under the wreckage, and while the nurse had her hands full with the goat Hyacinth was laying into Jacky's legs with his belt like a small fury."

"I'm not defending him," said Matilda, "but they must have done something to annoy him."

"Nothing intentionally, but some one had unfortunately told him that they were half French——their mother was a Duboc, you know——and he had been having a history lesson that morning, and had just heard of the final loss of Calais by the English, and was furious about it. He said he'd teach the little toads to go snatching towns from us, but we didn't know at the time that he was referring to the Gaffins. I told him afterwards that all bad feeling between the two nations had died out long ago, and that anyhow the Gaffins were only half French, and he said that it was only the French half of Jacky that he had been hitting; the rest had been buried under the perambulator. If the loss of Calais unloosed such fury in him, I tremble to think what the possible loss of the election might entail."

"All that happened when he was eight; he's older now and knows better."

"Children with Hyacinth's temperament don't know better as they grow older; they merely know more."

"Nonsense. He will enjoy the fun of the election, and in any case he'll be tired out by the time the poll is declared, and the new sailor suit that I've had made for him is just in the

right shade of blue for our election colours, and it will exactly
match the blue of his eyes. He will be a perfectly charming
note of colour."

"There is such a thing as letting one's æsthetic sense override
one's moral sense," said Mrs. Panstreppon. "I believe you
would have condoned the South Sea Bubble and the persecu-
tion of the Albigenses if they had been carried out in effective
colour schemes. However, if anything unfortunate should happen down at Luffbridge, don't say it wasn't foreseen by one
member of the family."

The election was keenly but decorously contested. The
newly appointed Colonial Secretary was personally popular,
while the Government to which he adhered was distinctly un-
popular, and there was some expectancy that the majority of
four hundred, obtained at the last election, would be altogether wiped out. Both sides were hopeful, but neither could
feel confident. The children were a great success; the little
Jutterlys drove their chubby donkeys solemnly up and down
the main streets, displaying posters which advocated the claims
of their father on the broad general grounds that he was their
father, while as for Hyacinth, his conduct might have served
as a model for any seraph-child that had strayed unwittingly
on to the scene of an electoral contest. Of his own accord,
and under the delighted eyes of half a dozen camera operators,
he had gone up to the Jutterly children and presented them
with a packet of butterscotch; "we needn't be enemies because
we're wearing the opposite colours," he said with engaging
friendliness, and the occupants of the donkey-cart accepted his
offering with polite solemnity. The grown-up members of
both political camps were delighted at the incident—with the
exception of Mrs. Panstreppon, who shuddered.

"Never was Clytemnestra's kiss sweeter than on the night
she slew me," she quoted, but made the quotation to herself.

The last hour of the poll was a period of unremitting
labour for both parties; it was generally estimated that not
more than a dozen votes separated the candidates, and every
effort was made to bring up obstinately wavering electors. It
was with a feeling of relaxation and relief that every one

heard the clocks strike the hour for the close of the poll. Exclamations broke out from the tired workers, and corks flew out from bottles.

"Well, if we haven't won, we've done our level best." "It has been a clean, straight fight, with no rancour." "The children were quite a charming feature, weren't they?"

The children? It suddenly occurred to everybody that they had seen nothing of the children for the last hour. What had become of the three little Jutterlys and their donkey-cart, and, for the matter of that, what had become of Hyacinth? Hurried, anxious embassies went backwards and forwards between the respective party headquarters and the various committee-rooms, but there was blank ignorance everywhere as to the whereabouts of the children. Every one had been too busy in the closing moments of the poll to bestow a thought on them. Then there came a telephone call at the Unionist Women's Committee-rooms, and the voice of Hyacinth was heard demanding when the poll would be declared.

"Where are you, and where are the Jutterly children?" asked his mother.

"I've just finished having high-tea at a pastry-cook's," came the answer; "and they let me telephone. I've had a poached egg and a sausage roll and four meringues."

"You'll be ill. Are the little Jutterlys with you?"

"Rather not. They're in a pigsty."

"A pigsty? Why? What pigsty?"

"Near the Crawleigh Road. I met them driving about a back road, and told them they were to have tea with me, and put their donkeys in a yard that I knew of. Then I took them to see an old sow that had got ten little pigs. I got the sow into the outer sty by giving her bits of bread, while the Jutterlys went in to look at the litter, then I bolted the door and left them there."

"You wicked boy, do you mean to say you've left those poor children there alone in the pigsty?"

"They're not alone, they've got ten little pigs in with them; they're jolly well crowded. They were pretty mad at being shut in, but not half as mad as the old sow is at being shut out from her young ones. If she gets in while they're there she'll bite them into mincemeat. I can get them out by letting a short ladder down through the top window, and that's what I'm going to do *if we win*. If their blighted father gets in, I'm just going to open the door for the sow, and let her do what she dashed well likes to them. That's why I want to know when the poll will be declared."

Here the narrator rang off. A wild stampede and a frantic sending-off of messengers took place at the other end of the telephone. Nearly all the workers on either side had disappeared to their various club-rooms and public-house bars to await the declaration of the poll, but enough local information could be secured to determine the scene of Hyacinth's exploit. Mr. John Ball had a stable yard down near the Crawleigh Road, up a short lane, and his sow was known to have a litter of ten young ones. Thither went in headlong haste both the candidates, Hyacinth's mother, his aunt (Mrs. Panstreppon), and two or three hurriedly summoned friends. The two Nubian donkeys, contentedly munching at bundles of hay, met their gaze as they entered the yard. The hoarse savage grunting of an enraged animal and the shriller note of thirteen young voices, three of them human, guided them to the sty, in the outer yard of which a huge Yorkshire sow kept up a ceaseless raging patrol before a closed door. Reclining on the broad ledge of an open window, from which point of vantage he could reach down and shoot the bolt of the door, was Hyacinth, his blue sailor-suit somewhat the worse for wear, and his angel smile exchanged for a look of demoniacal determination.

"If any of you come a step nearer," he shouted, "the sow will be inside in half a jiffy."

A storm of threatening, arguing, entreating expostulation broke from the baffled rescue party, but it made no more impression on Hyacinth than the squealing tempest that raged within the sty.

"If Jutterly heads the poll I'm going to let the sow in. I'll teach the blighters to win elections from us."

"He means it," said Mrs. Panstreppon; "I feared the worst when I saw that butterscotch incident."

"It's all right, my little man," said Jutterly, with the duplicity to which even a Colonial Secretary can sometimes stoop, "your father has been elected by a large majority."

"Liar!" retorted Hyacinth, with the directness of speech that is not merely excusable, but almost obligatory, in the political profession; "the votes aren't counted yet. You won't gammon me as to the result, either. A boy that I've palled with is going to fire a gun when the poll is declared; two shots if we've won, one shot if we haven't."

The situation began to look critical. "Drug the sow," whispered Hyacinth's father.

Some one went off in the motor to the nearest chemist's shop and returned presently with two large pieces of bread, liberally dosed with narcotic. The bread was thrown deftly and unostentatiously into the sty, but Hyacinth saw through the manœuvre. He set up a piercing imitation of a small pig in Purgatory, and the infuriated mother ramped round and round the sty; the pieces of bread were trampled into slush.

At any moment now the poll might be declared. Jutterly flew back to the Town Hall, where the votes were being counted. His agent met him with a smile of hope.

"You're eleven ahead at present, and only about eighty more to be counted; you're just going to squeak through."

"I mustn't squeak through," exclaimed Jutterly hoarsely. "You must object to every doubtful vote on our side that can possibly be disallowed. I must *not* have the majority."

Then was seen the unprecedented sight of a party agent challenging the votes on his own side with a captiousness that his opponents would have hesitated to display. One or two votes that would have certainly passed muster under ordinary circumstances were disallowed, but even so Jutterly was six ahead with only thirty more to be counted.

To the watchers by the sty the moments seemed intolerable. As a last resort some one had been sent for a gun with which to shoot the sow, though Hyacinth would probably draw the bolt the moment such a weapon was brought into the yard. Nearly all the men were away from their homes, however, on election night, and the messenger had evidently gone far afield in his search. It must be a matter of minutes now to the declaration of the poll.

A sudden roar of shouting and cheering was heard from the direction of the Town Hall. Hyacinth's father clutched a pitchfork and prepared to dash into the sty in the forlorn hope of being in time.

A shot rang out in the evening air. Hyacinth stooped down from his perch and put his finger on the bolt. The sow pressed furiously against the door.

"Bang!" came another shot.

Hyacinth wriggled back, and sent a short ladder down through the window of the inner sty.

"Now you can come up, you unclean little blighters," he sang out; "my daddy's got in, not yours. Hurry up, I can't keep the sow waiting much longer. And don't you jolly well come butting into any election again where I'm on the job."

In the reaction that set in after the deliverance furious recriminations were indulged in by the lately opposed candidates, their women folk, agents, and party helpers. A recount was demanded, but failed to establish the fact that the Colonial Secretary had obtained a majority. Altogether the election left a legacy of soreness behind it, apart from any that was experienced by Hyacinth in person.

"It is the last time I shall let him go to an election," exclaimed his mother.

"There I think you are going to extremes," said Mrs. Panstreppon; "if there should be a general election in Mexico I think you might safely let him go there, but I doubt whether our English politics are suited to the rough and tumble of an angel-child."

THE IMAGE OF THE LOST SOUL[1]

THERE were a number of carved stone figures placed at intervals along the parapets of the old Cathedral; some of them represented angels, others kings and bishops, and nearly all were in attitudes of pious exaltation and composure. But one figure, low down on the cold north side of the building, had neither crown, mitre, nor nimbus, and its face was hard and bitter and downcast; it must be a demon, declared the fat blue pigeons that roosted and sunned themselves all day on the ledges of the parapet; but the old belfry jackdaw, who was an authority on ecclesiastical architecture, said it was a lost soul. And there the matter rested.

One autumn day there fluttered on to the Cathedral roof a slender, sweet-voiced bird that had wandered away from the bare fields and thinning hedgerows in search of a winter roosting-place. It tried to rest its tired feet under the shade of a great angel-wing or to nestle in the sculptured folds of a kingly robe, but the fat pigeons hustled it away from wherever it settled, and the noisy sparrow-folk drove it off the ledges. No respectable bird sang with so much feeling, they cheeped one to another, and the wanderer had to move on.

Only the effigy of the Lost Soul offered a place of refuge. The pigeons did not consider it safe to perch on a projection that leaned so much out of the perpendicular, and was, besides, too much in the shadow. The figure did not cross its hands in the pious attitude of the other graven dignitaries, but its arms were folded as in defiance and their angle made a snug resting-place for the little bird. Every evening it crept trustfully into its corner against the stone breast of the image, and the darkling eyes seemed to keep watch over its slumbers. The lonely bird grew to love its lonely protector, and during the day it would sit from time to time on some rain-shoot or other abutment and trill forth its sweetest music in grateful thanks for its nightly shelter. And, it may have been the work of wind and weather, or some other influence, but the wild drawn face

[1] Written in 1891.

seemed gradually to lose some of its hardness and unhappiness. Every day, through the long monotonous hours, the song of his little guest would come up in snatches to the lonely watcher, and at evening, when the vesper-bell was ringing and the great grey bats slid out of their hiding-places in the belfry roof, the bright-eyed bird would return, twitter a few sleepy notes, and nestle into the arms that were waiting for him. Those were happy days for the Dark Image. Only the great bell of the Cathedral rang out daily its mocking message, "After joy . . . sorrow."

The folk in the verger's lodge noticed a little brown bird flitting about the Cathedral precincts, and admired its beautiful singing. "But it is a pity," said they, "that all that warbling should be lost and wasted far out of hearing up on the parapet." They were poor, but they understood the principles of political economy. So they caught the bird and put it in a little wicker cage outside the lodge door.

That night the little songster was missing from its accustomed haunt, and the Dark Image knew more than ever the bitterness of loneliness. Perhaps his little friend had been killed by a prowling cat or hurt by a stone. Perhaps . . . perhaps he had flown elsewhere. But when morning came there floated up to him, through the noise and bustle of the Cathedral world, a faint heart-aching message from the prisoner in the wicker cage far below. And every day, at high noon, when the fat pigeons were stupefied into silence after their midday meal and the sparrows were washing themselves in the street-puddles, the song of the little bird came up to the parapets—a song of hunger and longing and hopelessness, a cry that could never be answered.

The pigeons remarked, between mealtimes, that the figure leaned forward more than ever out of the perpendicular.

One day no song came up from the little wicker cage. It was the coldest day of the winter, and the pigeons and sparrows on the Cathedral roof looked anxiously on all sides for the scraps of food which they were dependent on in hard weather.

"Have the lodge-folk thrown out anything on to the dust-heap?" inquired one pigeon of another which was peering over the edge of the north parapet.

"Only a little dead bird," was the answer.

There was a crackling sound in the night on the Cathedral roof and a noise as of falling masonry. The belfry jackdaw said the frost was affecting the fabric, and as he had experienced many frosts it must have been so. In the morning it was seen that the Figure of the Lost Soul had toppled from its cornice and lay now in a broken mass on the dust-heap outside the verger's lodge.

"It is just as well," cooed the fat pigeons, after they had peered at the matter for some minutes; "now we shall have a nice angel put up there. Certainly they will put an angel there."

"After joy . . . sorrow," rang out the great bell.

THE PURPLE OF THE BALKAN KINGS [1]

LUITPOLD WOLKENSTEIN, financier and diplomat on a small, obtrusive, self-important scale, sat in his favoured café in the world-wise Habsburg capital, confronted with the *Neue Freie Presse* and the cup of cream-topped coffee and attendant glass of water that a sleek-headed piccolo had just brought him. For years longer than a dog's lifetime sleek-headed piccolos had placed the *Neue Freie Presse* and a cup of cream-topped coffee on his table; for years he had sat at the same spot, under the dust-coated, stuffed eagle, that had once been a living, soaring bird on the Styrian mountains, and was now made monstrous and symbolical with a second head grafted on to its neck and a gilt crown planted on either dusty skull. Today Luitpold Wolkenstein read no more than the first article in his paper, but he read it again and again.

"The Turkish fortress of Kirk Kilisseh has fallen. . . .

[1] This and the following tale were written during the Balkan war.

The Serbs, it is officially announced, have taken Kumanovo.
. . . The fortress of Kirk Kilisseh lost, Kumanovo taken by
the Serbs, these are tidings for Constantinople resembling
something out of Shakespeare's tragedies of the kings. . . .
The neighbourhood of Adrianople and the Eastern region,
where the great battle is now in progress, will not reveal merely
the future of Turkey, but also what position and what influence the Balkan States are to have in the world."

For years longer than a dog's lifetime Luitpold Wolkenstein had disposed of the pretensions and strivings of the Balkan
States over the cup of cream-topped coffee that sleek-headed
piccolos had brought him. Never travelling farther eastward
than the horse-fair at Temesvar, never inviting personal risk
in an encounter with anything more potentially desperate than
a hare or partridge, he had constituted himself the critical ap-
praiser and arbiter of the military and national prowess of the
small countries that fringed the Dual Monarchy on its Danube
border. And his judgment had been one of unsparing contempt
for small-scale efforts, of unquestioning respect for the big
battalions and full purses. Over the whole scene of the Balkan
territories and their troubled histories had loomed the commanding magic of the words "the Great Powers"—even more imposing in their Teutonic rendering, "Die Grossmächte."

Worshipping power and force and money-mastery as an
elderly nerve-ridden woman might worship youthful physical
energy, the comfortable, plump-bodied café-oracle had jested
and gibed at the ambitions of the Balkan kinglets and their
peoples, had unloosed against them that battery of strange
lip-sounds that a Viennese employs almost as an auxiliary language to express the thoughts when his thoughts are not complimentary. British travellers had visited the Balkan lands and
reported high things of the Bulgarians and their future, Russian officers had taken peeps at their army and confessed "this
is a thing to be reckoned with, and it is not we who have
created it, they have done it by themselves." But over his cups
of coffee and his hour-long games of dominoes the oracle had
laughed and wagged his head and distilled the worldly wisdom
of his caste. The Grossmächte had not succeeded in stifling

the roll of the war-drum, that was true; the big battalions of the Ottoman Empire would have to do some talking, and then the big purses and big threatenings of the Powers would speak and the last word would be with them. In imagination Luitpold heard the onward tramp of the red-fezzed bayonet bearers echoing through the Balkan passes, saw the little sheep-skin-clad mannikins driven back to their villages, saw the augustly chiding spokesmen of the Powers dictating, adjusting, restoring, settling things once again in their allotted places, sweeping up the dust of conflict, and now his ears had to listen to the war-drum rolling in quite another direction, had to listen to the tramp of battalions that were bigger and bolder and better skilled in war-craft than he had deemed possible in that quarter; his eyes had to read in the columns of his ac-customed newspaper a warning to the Grossmächte that they had something new to learn, something new to reckon with, much that was time-honoured to relinquish. "The Great Powers will have no little difficulty in persuading the Balkan States of the inviolability of the principle that Europe cannot permit any fresh partition of territory in the East without her approval. Even now, while the campaign is still undecided, there are rumours of a project of fiscal unity, extending over the entire Balkan lands, and further of a constitutional union in imitation of the German Empire. That is perhaps only a political straw blown by the storm, but it is not possible to dis-miss the reflection that the Balkan States leagued together com-mand a military strength with which the Great Powers will have to reckon. . . . The people who have poured out their blood on the battlefields and sacrificed the available armed men of an entire generation in order to encompass a union with their kinsfolk will not remain any longer in an attitude of dependence on the Great Powers or on Russia, but will go their own ways. . . . The blood that has been poured forth today gives for the first time a genuine tone to the purple of the Balkan Kings. The Great Powers cannot overlook the fact that a people that has tasted victory will not let itself be driven back again within its former limits. Turkey has lost today not only Kirk Kilisseh and Kumanovo, but Macedonia also"

Luitpold Wolkenstein drank his coffee, but the flavour had somehow gone out of it. His world, his pompous, imposing, dictating world, had suddenly rolled up into narrower dimensions. The big purses and the big threats had been pushed unceremoniously on one side; a force that he could not fathom, could not comprehend, had made itself rudely felt. The august Cæsars of Mammon and armament had looked down frowningly on the combat, and those about to die had *not* saluted, had no intention of saluting. A lesson was being imposed on unwilling learners, a lesson of respect for certain fundamental principles, and it was not the small struggling States who were being taught the lesson.

Luitpold Wolkenstein did not wait for the quorum of domino players to arrive. They would all have read the article in the *Freie Presse*. And there are moments when an oracle finds its greatest salvation in withdrawing itself from the area of human questioning.

THE CUPBOARD OF THE YESTERDAYS

"WAR is a cruelly destructive thing," said the Wanderer, dropping his newspaper to the floor and staring reflectively into space.

"Ah, yes, indeed," said the Merchant, responding readily to what seemed like a safe platitude; "when one thinks of the loss of life and limb, the desolated homesteads, the ruined——"

"I wasn't thinking of anything of the sort," said the Wanderer; "I was thinking of the tendency that modern war has to destroy and banish the very elements of picturesqueness and excitement that are its chief excuse and charm. It is like a fire that flares up brilliantly for a while and then leaves everything blacker and bleaker than before. After every important war in South-East Europe in recent times there has been a shrinking of the area of chronically disturbed territory, a stiffening of frontier lines, an intrusion of civilized monotony. And imagine what may happen at the conclusion of this war if the Turk should really be driven out of Europe."

"Well, it would be a gain to the cause of good government, I suppose," said the Merchant.

"But have you counted the loss?" said the other. "The Balkans have long been the last surviving shred of happy hunting-ground for the adventurous, a playground for passions that are fast becoming atrophied for want of exercise. In old bygone days we had the wars in the Low Countries always at our doors, as it were; there was no need to go far afield into malaria-stricken wilds if one wanted a life of boot and saddle and licence to kill and be killed. Those who wished to see life had a decent opportunity for seeing death at the same time."

"It is scarcely right to talk of killing and bloodshed in that way," said the Merchant reprovingly; "one must remember that all men are brothers."

"One must also remember that a large percentage of them are younger brothers; instead of going into bankruptcy, which is the usual tendency of the younger brother nowadays, they gave their families a fair chance of going into mourning. Every bullet finds a billet, according to a rather optimistic proverb, and you must admit that nowadays it is becoming increasingly difficult to find billets for a lot of young gentlemen who would have adorned, and probably thoroughly enjoyed, one of the old-time happy-go-lucky wars. But that is not exactly the burden of my complaint. The Balkan lands are especially interesting to us in these rapidly moving days because they afford us the last remaining glimpse of a vanishing period of European history. When I was a child one of the earliest events of the outside world that forced itself coherently under my notice was a war in the Balkans; I remember a sunburnt, soldierly man putting little pin-flags in a war-map, red flags for the Turkish forces and yellow flags for the Russians. It seemed a magical region, with its mountain passes and frozen rivers and grim battlefields, its drifting snows, and prowling wolves; there was a great stretch of water that bore the sinister but engaging name of the Black Sea—nothing that I ever learned before or after in a geography lesson made the same impression on me as that strange-named inland sea, and I don't think its magic has ever faded out of my imagination. And there was a battle called Plevna that went on and on with varying fortunes for what seemed like a great part of a lifetime; I remember the day of wrath and mourning when the little red flag had to be taken away from Plevna —like other maturer judges, I was backing the wrong horse, at any rate the losing horse. And now today we are putting little pin-flags again into maps of the Balkan region, and the passions are being turned loose once more in their playground."

"The war will be localized," said the Merchant vaguely; "at least every one hopes so."

"It couldn't wish for a better locality," said the Wanderer; "there is a charm about those countries that you find nowhere else in Europe, the charm of uncertainty and landslide, and the little dramatic happenings that make all the difference between the ordinary and the desirable."

"Life is held very cheap in those parts," said the Merchant.

"To a certain extent, yes," said the Wanderer. "I remember a man at Sofia who used to teach me Bulgarian in a rather inefficient manner, interspersed with a lot of quite wearisome gossip. I never knew what his personal history was, but that was only because I didn't listen; he told it to me many times. After I left Bulgaria he used to send me Sofia newspapers from time to time. I felt that he would be rather tiresome if I ever went there again. And then I heard afterwards that some men came in one day from Heaven knows where, just as things do happen in the Balkans, and murdered him in the open street, and went away as quietly as they had come. You will not understand it, but to me there was something rather piquant in the idea of such a thing happening to such a man; after his dulness and his long-winded small-talk it seemed a sort of brilliant *esprit d'escalier* on his part to meet with an end of such ruthlessly planned and executed violence."

The Merchant shook his head; the piquancy of the incident was not within striking distance of his comprehension.

"I should have been shocked at hearing such a thing about any one I had known," he said.

"The present war," continued his companion, without stopping to discuss two hopelessly divergent points of view, "may be the beginning of the end of much that has hitherto survived the resistless creeping-in of civilization. If the Balkan lands are to be finally parcelled out between the competing Christian Kingdoms and the haphazard rule of the Turk banished to beyond the Sea of Marmora, the old order, or disorder if you like, will have received its death-blow. Something of its spirit will linger perhaps for a while in the old charmed regions where it bore sway; the Greek villagers will doubtless be restless and turbulent and unhappy where the Bulgars rule, and the Bulgars will certainly be restless and turbulent and unhappy under Greek administration, and the rival flocks of the Exarchate and Patriarchate will make themselves intensely disagreeable to one another wherever the opportunity offers; the habits of a lifetime, of several lifetimes, are not laid aside all at once. And the Albanians, of course, we shall have with us still, a troubled Moslem pool left by the receding wave of Islam in Europe. But the old atmosphere will have changed, the glamour will have gone; the dust of formality and bureaucratic neatness will slowly settle down over the time-honoured landmarks; the Sanjak of Novi Bazar, the Muersteg Agreement, the Komitadje bands, the Vilayet of Adrianople, all those familiar outlandish names and things and places, that we have known so long as part and parcel of the Balkan Question, will have passed away into the cupboard of yesterdays, as completely as the Hansa League and the wars of the Guises.

"They were the heritage that history handed down to us, spoiled and diminished no doubt, in comparison with yet earlier days that we never knew, but still something to thrill and enliven one little corner of our Continent, something to help us to conjure up in our imagination the days when the Turk was thundering at the gates of Vienna. And what shall we have to hand down to our children? Think of what their news from the Balkans will be in the course of another ten or fifteen years. Socialist Congress at Uskub, election riot at Monastir, great dock strike at Salonika, visit of the Y.M.C.A. to Varna. Varna—on the coast of that enchanted sea! They will drive out to some suburb for tea, and write home about it as the Bexhill of the East.

"War is a wickedly destructive thing."

"Still, you must admit—" began the Merchant. But the Wanderer was not in the mood to admit anything. He rose impatiently and walked to where the tape-machine was busy with the news from Adrianople.

FOR THE DURATION OF THE WAR [1]

THE Rev. Wilfrid Gaspilton, in one of those clerical migrations inconsequent-seeming to the lay mind, had removed from the moderately fashionable parish of St. Luke's, Kensingate, to the immoderately rural parish of St. Chuddock's, somewhere in Yondershire. There were doubtless substantial advantages connected with the move, but there were certainly some very obvious drawbacks. Neither the migratory clergyman nor his wife were able to adapt themselves naturally and comfortably to the conditions of country life. Beryl, Mrs. Gaspilton, had always looked indulgently on the country as a place where people of irreproachable income and hospitable instincts cultivated tennis-lawns and rose-gardens and Jacobean pleasaunces, wherein selected gatherings of interested week-end guests might disport themselves. Mrs. Gaspilton considered herself as distinctly an interesting personality, and from a limited standpoint she was doubtless right. She had indolent dark eyes and a comfortable chin, which belied the slightly plaintive inflection which she threw into her voice at suitable intervals. She was tolerably well satisfied with the smaller advantages of life, but she regretted that Fate had not seen its way to reserve for her some of the ampler successes for which

[1] Written at the Front.

she felt herself well qualified. She would have liked to be the centre of a literary, slightly political salon, where discerning satellites might have recognized the breadth of her outlook on human affairs and the undoubted smallness of her feet. As it was, Destiny had chosen for her that she should be the wife of a rector, and had now further decreed that a country rectory should be the background to her existence. She rapidly made up her mind that her surroundings did not call for exploration: Noah had predicted the Flood, but no one expected him to swim about in it. Digging in a wet garden or trudging through muddy lanes were exertions which she did not propose to undertake. As long as the garden produced asparagus and carnations at pleasingly frequent intervals Mrs. Gaspilton was content to approve of its expense and otherwise ignore its existence. She would fold herself up, so to speak, in an elegant, indolent little world of her own, enjoying the minor recreations of being gently rude to the doctor's wife and continuing the leisurely production of her one literary effort, *The Forbidden Horse-pond*, a translation of Baptiste Lepoy's *L'Abreuvoir interdit*. It was a labour which had already been so long drawn-out that it seemed probable that Baptiste Lepoy would drop out of vogue before her translation of his temporarily famous novel was finished. However, the languid prosecution of the work had invested Mrs. Gaspilton with a certain literary dignity, even in Kensingate circles, and would place her on a pinnacle in St. Chuddock's, where hardly any one read French, and assuredly no one had heard of *L'Abreuvoir interdit*.

The Rector's wife might be content to turn her back complacently on the country; it was the Rector's tragedy that the country turned its back on him. With the best intention in the world and the immortal example of Gilbert White before him, the Rev. Wilfrid found himself as bored and ill at ease in his new surroundings as Charles II would have been at a modern Wesleyan Conference. The birds that hopped across his lawn hopped across it as though it were their lawn, and not his, and gave him plainly to understand that in their eyes he was infinitely less interesting than a garden worm or the rectory cat. The hedgeside and meadow flowers were equally

uninspiring; the lesser celandine seemed particularly unworthy
of the attention that English poets had bestowed on it, and the
Rector knew that he would be utterly miserable if left alone
for a quarter of an hour in its company. With the human inhabitants of his parish he was no better off; to know them
was merely to know their ailments, and the ailments were
almost invariably rheumatism. Some, of course, had other
bodily infirmities, but they always had rheumatism as well.
The Rector had not yet grasped the fact that in rural cottage
life not to have rheumatism is as glaring an omission as not
to have been presented at Court would be in more ambitious
circles. And with all this dearth of local interest there was
Beryl shutting herself off with her ridiculous labours on *The
Forbidden Horsepond*.

"I don't see why you should suppose that any one wants to
read Baptiste Lepoy in English," the Reverend Wilfrid remarked to his wife one morning, finding her surrounded with
her usual elegant litter of dictionaries, fountain pens, and
scribbling paper; "hardly any one bothers to read him now in
France."

"My dear," said Beryl, with an intonation of gentle weariness, "haven't two or three leading London publishers told
me they wondered no one had ever translated *L'Abreuvoir
interdit*, and begged me——"

"Publishers always clamour for the books that no one has
ever written, and turn a cold shoulder on them as soon as
they're written. If St. Paul were living now they would pester
him to write an Epistle to the Esquimaux, but no London publisher would dream of reading his Epistle to the Ephesians."

"Is there any asparagus anywhere in the garden?" asked
Beryl; "because I've told cook——"

"Not anywhere in the garden," snapped the Rector, "but
there's no doubt plenty in the asparagus-bed, which is the usual
place for it."

And he walked away into the region of fruit trees and
vegetable beds to exchange irritation for boredom. It was
there, among the gooseberry bushes and beneath the medlar

trees, that the temptation to the perpetration of a great literary fraud came to him.

Some weeks later the *Bi-Monthly Review* gave to the world, under the guarantee of the Rev. Wilfrid Gaspilton, some fragments of Persian verse, alleged to have been unearthed and translated by a nephew who was at present campaigning somewhere in the Tigris valley. The Rev. Wilfrid possessed a host of nephews, and it was, of course, quite possible that one or more of them might be in military employ in Mesopotamia, though no one could call to mind any particular nephew who could have been suspected of being a Persian scholar.

The verses were attributed to one Ghurab, a hunter, or, according to other accounts, warden of the royal fishponds, who lived, in some unspecified century, in the neighbourhood of Karmanshah. They breathed a spirit of comfortable, even-tempered satire and philosophy, disclosing a mockery that did not trouble to be bitter, a joy in life that was not passionate to the verge of being troublesome.

> "A Mouse that prayed for Allah's aid
> Blasphemed when no such aid befell:
> A Cat, who feasted on that mouse,
> Thought Allah managed vastly well.
>
> Pray not for aid to One who made
> A set of never-changing Laws,
> But in your need remember well
> He gave you speed, or guile—or claws.
>
> Some laud a life of mild content:
> Content may fall, as well as Pride.
> The Frog who hugged his lowly Ditch
> Was much disgruntled when it dried.
>
> 'You are not on the Road to Hell,'
> You tell me with fanatic glee:
> Vain boaster, what shall that avail
> If Hell is on the road to thee?
>
> A Poet praised the Evening Star,
> Another praised the Parrot's hue:
> A Merchant praised his merchandise,
> And he, at least, praised what he knew."

It was this verse which gave the critics and commentators some clue as to the probable date of the composition; the parrot, they reminded the public, was in high vogue as a type of elegance in the days of Hafiz of Shiraz; in the quatrains of Omar it makes no appearance.

The next verse, it was pointed out, would apply to the political conditions of the present day as strikingly as to the region and era for which it was written—

> "A Sultan dreamed day-long of Peace,
> The while his Rivals' armies grew:
> They changed his Day-dreams into sleep
> —The Peace, methinks, he never knew."

Woman appeared little, and wine not at all in the verse of the hunter-poet, but there was at least one contribution to the love-philosophy of the East—

> "O Moon-faced Charmer, with Star-drownèd Eyes,
> And cheeks of soft delight, exhaling musk,
> They tell me that thy charm will fade; ah well,
> The Rose itself grows hue-less in the Dusk."

Finally, there was a recognition of the Inevitable, a chill breath blowing across the poet's comfortable estimate of life—

> "There is a sadness in each Dawn,
> A sadness that you cannot rede,
> The joyous Day brings in its train
> The Feast, the Loved One, and the Steed.
>
> Ah, there shall come a Dawn at last
> That brings no life-stir to your ken,
> A long, cold Dawn without a Day,
> And ye shall rede its sadness then."

The verses of Ghurab came on the public at a moment when a comfortable, slightly quizzical philosophy was certain to be welcome, and their reception was enthusiastic. Elderly colonels, who had outlived the love of truth, wrote to the papers to say that they had been familiar with the works of Ghurab in Afghanistan, and Aden, and other suitable localities a quarter of a century ago. A Ghurab-of-Karmanshah Club sprang into existence, the members of which alluded to each other as

Brother Ghurabians on the slightest provocation. And to the flood of inquiries, criticisms, and requests for information, which naturally poured in on the discoverer, or rather the discloser, of this long-hidden poet, the Rev. Wilfrid made one effectual reply: Military considerations forbade any disclosures which might throw unnecessary light on his nephew's movements.

After the war the Rector's position will be one of unthinkable embarrassment, but for the moment, at any rate, he has driven *The Forbidden Horsepond* out of the field.

The Square Egg

First Collected, 1924

Thanks are due to the Editors of the *Morning Post*, the *Westminster Gazette*, and the *Bystander* for their courtesy in allowing tales that appeared in these journals to be reproduced in this volume.

Thanks are also due to the Editor of the *Outlook*.

THE SQUARE EGG

(A BADGER'S-EYE VIEW OF THE WAR MUD IN THE TRENCHES)

ASSUREDLY a badger is the animal that one most resembles in this trench warfare, that drab-coated creature
of the twilight and darkness, digging, burrowing, listening;
keeping itself as clean as possible under unfavourable circumstances, fighting tooth and nail on occasion for possession of a
few yards of honeycombed earth.

What the badger thinks about life we shall never know,
which is a pity, but cannot be helped; it is difficult enough to
know what one thinks about, oneself, in the trenches. Parliament, taxes, social gatherings, economies, and expenditure, and
all the thousand and one horrors of civilization seem immeasurably remote, and the war itself seems almost as distant
and unreal. A couple of hundred yards away, separated from
you by a stretch of dismal untidy-looking ground and some
strips of rusty wire-entanglement, lies a vigilant, bullet-spit-
ting enemy; lurking and watching in those opposing trenches
are foemen who might stir the imagination of the most slug-
gish brain, descendants of the men who went to battle under
Moltke, Blücher, Frederick the Great, and the Great Elector,
Wallenstein, Maurice of Saxony, Barbarossa, Albert the Bear,
Henry the Lion, Witekind the Saxon. They are matched
against you there, man for man and gun for gun, in what is
perhaps the most stupendous struggle that modern history has
known, and yet one thinks remarkably little about them. It
would not be advisable to forget for the fraction of a second
that they are there, but one's mind does not dwell on their
existence; one speculates little as to whether they are drinking
warm soup and eating sausage, or going cold and hungry,
whether they are well supplied with copies of the *Meggendor-*

fer Blätter and other light literature or bored with unutterable weariness.

Much more to be thought about than the enemy over yonder or the war all over Europe is the mud of the moment, the mud that at times engulfs you as cheese engulfs a cheesemite. In Zoological Gardens one has gazed at an elk or bison loitering at its pleasure more than knee-deep in a quagmire of greasy mud, and one has wondered what it would feel like to be soused and plastered, hour-long, in such a muck-bath. One knows now. In narrow-dug support-trenches, when thaw and heavy rain have come suddenly atop of a frost, when everything is pitch-dark around you, and you can only stumble about and feel your way against streaming mud walls, when you have to go down on hands and knees in several inches of soup-like mud to creep into a dug-out, when you stand deep in mud, lean against mud, grasp mud-slimed objects with mud-caked fingers, wink mud away from your eyes, and shake it out of your ears, bite muddy biscuits with muddy teeth, then at least you are in a position to understand thoroughly what it feels like to wallow—on the other hand the bison's idea of pleasure becomes more and more incomprehensible.

When one is not thinking about mud one is probably thinking about *estaminets*. An *estaminet* is a haven that one finds in agreeable plenty in most of the surrounding townships and villages, flourishing still amid roofless and deserted houses, patched up where necessary in rough-and-ready fashion, and finding a new and profitable tide of customers from among the soldiers who have replaced the bulk of the civil population. An *estaminet* is a sort of compound between a wine-shop and a coffee-house, having a tiny bar in one corner, a few long tables and benches, a prominent cooking stove, generally a small grocery store tucked away in the back premises, and always two or three children running and bumping about at inconvenient angles to one's feet. It seems to be a fixed rule that *estaminet* children should be big enough to run about and small enough to get between one's legs. There must, by the way, be one considerable advantage in being a child in a war-zone village; no one can attempt to teach it tidiness. The wearisome maxim, "A place for everything and everything in its proper place," can never be insisted on when a considerable part of the roof is lying in the backyard, when a bedstead from a neighbour's demolished bedroom is half buried in the beetroot pile, and the chickens are roosting in a derelict meat-safe because a shell has removed the top and sides and front of the chicken-house.

Perhaps there is nothing in the foregoing description to suggest that a village wine-shop, frequently a shell-nibbled building in a shell-gnawed street, is a paradise to dream about, but when one has lived in a dripping wilderness of unrelieved mud and sodden sandbags for any length of time one's mind dwells on the plain-furnished parlour with its hot coffee and *vin ordinaire* as something warm and snug and comforting in a wet and slushy world. To the soldier on his trench-to-billets migration the wine-shop is what the tavern rest-house is to the caravan nomad of the East. One comes and goes in a crowd of chance-foregathered men, noticed or unnoticed as one wishes; amid the khaki-clad, be-putteed throng of one's own kind one can be as unobtrusive as a green caterpillar on a green cabbage leaf; one can sit undisturbed, alone or with one's own friends, or if one wishes to be talkative and talked to one can readily find a place in a circle where men of divers variety of cap badges are exchanging experiences, real or improvised.

Besides the changing throng of mud-stained khaki there is a drifting leaven of local civilians, uniformed interpreters, and men in varying types of foreign military garb, from privates in the Regular Army to Heaven-knows-what in some intermediate corps that only an expert in such matters could put a name to, and, of course, here and there are representatives of that great army of adventurer purse-sappers, that carries on its operations uninterruptedly in time of peace or war alike, over the greater part of the earth's surface. You meet them in England and France, in Russia and Constantinople; probably they are to be met with also in Iceland, though on that point I have no direct evidence.

In the *estaminet* of the Fortunate Rabbit I found myself

sitting next to an individual of indefinite age and nondescript uniform, who was obviously determined to make the borrowing of a match serve as a formal introduction and a banker's reference. He had the air of jaded jauntiness, the equipment of temporary amiability, the aspect of a foraging crow, taught by experience to be wary and prompted by necessity to be bold; he had the contemplative downward droop of nose and moustache and the furtive sidelong range of eye—he had all those things that are the ordinary outfit of the purse-sapper the world over.

"I am a victim of the war," he exclaimed after a little preliminary conversation.

"One cannot make an omelette without breaking eggs," I answered, with the appropriate callousness of a man who had seen some dozens of square miles of devastated country-side and roofless homes.

"Eggs!" he vociferated, "but it is precisely of eggs that I am about to speak. Have you ever considered what is the great drawback in the excellent and most useful egg—the ordinary, everyday egg of commerce and cookery?"

"Its tendency to age rapidly is sometimes against it," I hazarded; "unlike the United States of North America, which grow more respectable and self-respecting the longer they last, an egg gains nothing by persistence; it resembles your Louis the Fifteenth, who declined in popular favour with every year he lived—unless the historians have entirely misrepresented his record."

"No," replied the Tavern Acquaintance seriously, "it is not a question of age. It is the shape, the roundness. Consider how easily it rolls. On a table, a shelf, a shop counter, perhaps, one little push, and it may roll to the floor and be destroyed. What catastrophe for the poor, the frugal!"

I gave a sympathetic shudder at the idea; eggs here cost 6 sous apiece.

"Monsieur," he continued, "it is a subject I had often pondered and turned over in my mind, this economical malformation of the household egg. In our little village of Verchey-les-Torteaux, in the Department of the Tarn, my aunt has a small dairy and poultry farm, from which we drew a modest income. We were not poor, but there was always the necessity to labour, to contrive, to be sparing. One day I chanced to notice that one of my aunt's hens, a hen of the mop-headed Houdan breed, had laid an egg that was not altogether so round-shaped as the eggs of other hens; it could not be called square, but it had well-defined angles. I found out that this particular bird always laid eggs of this particular shape. The discovery gave a new stimulus to my ideas. If one collected all the hens that one could find with a tendency to lay a slightly angular egg and bred chickens only from those hens, and went on selecting and selecting, always choosing those that laid the squarest egg, at last, with patience and enterprise, one would produce a breed of fowls that laid only square eggs."

"In the course of several hundred years one might arrive at such a result," I said; "it would more probably take several thousands."

"With your cold Northern conservative slow-moving hens that might be the case," said the Acquaintance impatiently and rather angrily; "with our vivacious Southern poultry it is different. Listen. I searched, I experimented, I explored the poultry-yards of our neighbours, I ransacked the markets of the surrounding towns, wherever I found a hen laying an angular egg I bought her; I collected in time a vast concourse of fowls all sharing the same tendency; from their progeny I selected only those pullets whose eggs showed the most marked deviation from the normal roundness. I continued, I persevered. Monsieur, I produced a breed of hens that laid an egg which could not roll, however much you might push or jostle it. My experiment was more than a success; it was one of the romances of modern industry."

Of that I had not the least doubt, but I did not say so.

"My eggs became known," continued the *soi-disant* poultry-farmer; "at first they were sought after as a novelty, something curious, bizarre. Then merchants and housewives began to see that they were a utility, an improvement, an advantage over the ordinary kind. I was able to command a sale for my wares at a price considerably above market rates. I began to make money. I had a monopoly. I refused to sell any of my 'square-layers,' and the eggs that went to market were carefully sterilized, so that no chickens should be hatched from them. I was in the way to become rich, comfortably rich. Then this war broke out, which has brought misery to so many. I was obliged to leave my hens and my customers and go to the Front. My aunt carried on the business as usual, sold the square eggs, the eggs that I had devised and created and perfected, and received the profits; can you imagine it, she refuses to send me one centime of the takings! She says that she looks after the hens, and pays for their corn, and sends the eggs to market, and that the money is hers. Legally, of course, it is mine; if I could afford to bring a process in the Courts I could recover all the money that the eggs have brought in since the war commenced, many thousands of francs. To bring a process would only need a small sum; I have a lawyer friend who would arrange matters cheaply for me. Unfortunately I have not sufficient funds in hand; I need still about eighty francs. In war-time, alas! it is difficult to borrow."

I had always imagined that it was a habit that was especially indulged in during war-time, and said so.

"On a big scale, yes, but I am talking of a very small matter. It is easier to arrange a loan of millions than of a trifle of eighty or ninety francs."

The would-be financier paused for a few tense moments. Then he recommenced in a more confidential strain.

"Some of you English soldiers, I have heard, are men with private means: is it not so? It is perhaps possible that among your comrades there might be some one willing to advance a small sum——you yourself, perhaps——it would be a secure and profitable investment, quickly repaid——"

"If I get a few days' leave I will go down to Verchey-les-Torteaux and inspect the square-egg hen-farm," I said gravely, "and question the local egg-merchants as to the position and prospects of the business."

The Tavern Acquaintance gave an almost imperceptible shrug to his shoulders, shifted in his seat, and began moodily to roll a cigarette. His interest in me had suddenly died out,

but for the sake of appearances he was bound to make a perfunctory show of winding up the conversation he had so
laboriously started.

"Ah, you will go to Verchey-les-Torteaux and make inquiries about our farm. And if you find that what I have told
you about the square eggs is true, Monsieur, what then?"

"I shall marry your aunt."

BIRDS ON THE WESTERN FRONT

CONSIDERING the enormous economic dislocation
which the war operations have caused in the regions
where the campaign is raging, there seems to be very little corresponding disturbance in the bird life of the same districts.
Rats and mice have mobilized and swarmed into the fighting
line, and there has been a partial mobilization of owls, particularly barn owls, following in the wake of the mice, and making laudable efforts to thin out their numbers. What success
attends their hunting one cannot estimate; there are always
sufficient mice left over to populate one's dug-out and make
a parade-ground and race-course of one's face at night. In
the matter of nesting accommodation the barn owls are well
provided for; most of the still intact barns in the war zone are
requisitioned for billeting purposes, but there is a wealth of
ruined houses, whole streets and clusters of them, such as can
hardly have been available at any previous moment of the
world's history since Nineveh and Babylon became humanly
desolate. Without human occupation and cultivation there can
have been no corn, no refuse, and consequently very few mice,
and the owls of Nineveh cannot have enjoyed very good hunting; here in Northern France the owls have desolation and
mice at their disposal in unlimited quantities, and as these birds
breed in winter as well as in summer, there should be a goodly
output of war owlets to cope with the swarming generations
of war mice.

Apart from the owls one cannot notice that the campaign

is making any marked difference in the bird life of the country-side. The vast flocks of crows and ravens that one expected to find in the neighbourhood of the fighting line are non-existent, which is perhaps rather a pity. The obvious explanation is that the roar and crash and fumes of high explosives have driven the crow tribe in panic from the fighting area; like many obvious explanations, it is not a correct one. The crows of the locality are not attracted to the battlefield, but they certainly are not scared away from it. The rook is normally so gun-shy and nervous where noise is concerned that the sharp banging of a barn door or the report of a toy pistol will sometimes set an entire rookery in commotion; out here I have seen him sedately busy among the refuse heaps of a battered village, with shells bursting at no great distance, and the impatient-sounding, snapping rattle of machine-guns going on all round him; for all the notice that he took he might have been in some peaceful English meadow on a sleepy Sunday afternoon. Whatever else German frightfulness may have done it has not frightened the rook of North-Eastern France; it has made his nerves steadier than they have ever been before, and future generations of small boys, employed in scaring rooks away from the sown crops in this region, will have to invent something in the way of super-frightfulness to achieve their purpose. Crows and magpies are nesting well within the shell-swept area, and over a small beech-copse I once saw a pair of crows engaged in hot combat with a pair of sparrow-hawks, while considerably higher in the sky, but almost directly above them, two Allied battle-planes were engaging an equal number of enemy aircraft.

Unlike the barn owls, the magpies have had their choice of building sites considerably restricted by the ravages of war; the whole avenues of poplars, where they were accustomed to construct their nests, have been blown to bits, leaving nothing but dreary-looking rows of shattered and splintered trunks to show where once they stood. Affection for a particular tree has in one case induced a pair of magpies to build their bulky, domed nest in the battered remnants of a poplar of which so little remained standing that the nest looked almost bigger

than the tree; the effect rather suggested an archiepiscopal en-
thronement taking place in the ruined remains of Melrose
Abbey. The magpie, wary and suspicious in his wild state, must
be rather intrigued at the change that has come over the erstwhile fearsome not-to-be-avoided human, stalking everywhere
over the earth as its possessor, who now creeps about in screened
and sheltered ways, as chary of showing himself in the open
as the shyest of wild creatures.

The buzzard, that earnest seeker after mice, does not seem
to be taking any war risks, at least I have never seen one out
here, but kestrels hover about all day in the hottest parts of
the line, not in the least disconcerted, apparently, when a
promising mouse-area suddenly rises in the air in a cascade of
black or yellow earth. Sparrow-hawks are fairly numerous,
and a mile or two back from the firing line I saw a pair of
hawks that I took to be red-legged falcons, circling over the
top of an oak-copse. According to investigations made by Russian naturalists, the effect of the war on bird life on the Eastern
front has been more marked than it has been over here. "During the first year of the war rooks disappeared, larks no longer
sang in the fields, the wild pigeon disappeared also." The sky-
lark in this region has stuck tenaciously to the meadows and
crop-lands that have been seamed and bisected with trenches
and honeycombed with shell-holes. In the chill, misty hour of
gloom that precedes a rainy dawn, when nothing seemed alive
except a few wary waterlogged sentries and many scuttling
rats, the lark would suddenly dash skyward and pour forth a
song of ecstatic jubilation that sounded horribly forced and
insincere. It seemed scarcely possible that the bird could carry
its insouciance to the length of attempting to rear a brood in
that desolate wreckage of shattered clods and gaping shell-
holes, but once, having occasion to throw myself down with
some abruptness on my face, I found myself nearly on the
top of a brood of young larks. Two of them had already been
hit by something, and were in rather a battered condition, but
the survivors seemed as tranquil and comfortable as the average nestling.

At the corner of a stricken wood (which has had a name

made for it in history, but shall be nameless here), at a moment when lyddite and shrapnel and machine-gun fire swept
and raked and bespattered that devoted spot as though the artillery of an entire Division had suddenly concentrated on it,
a wee hen-chaffinch flitted wistfully to and fro, amid splintered and falling branches that had never a green bough left
on them. The wounded lying there, if any of them noticed the
small bird, may well have wondered why anything having
wings and no pressing reason for remaining should have chosen
to stay in such a place. There was a battered orchard alongside
the stricken wood, and the probable explanation of the bird's
presence was that it had a nest of young ones whom it was
too scared to feed, too loyal to desert. Later on, a small flock
of chaffinches blundered into the wood, which they were doubtless in the habit of using as a highway to their feeding-grounds;
unlike the solitary hen-bird, they made no secret of their desire to get away as fast as their dazed wits would let them.
The only other bird I ever saw there was a magpie, flying
low over the wreckage of fallen tree-limbs; "one for sorrow," says the old superstition. There was sorrow enough in
that wood.

The English gamekeeper, whose knowledge of wild life
usually runs on limited and perverted lines, has evolved a sort
of religion as to the nervous debility of even the hardiest game
birds; according to his beliefs a terrier trotting across a field
in which a partridge is nesting, or a mouse-hawking kestrel
hovering over the hedge, is sufficient cause to drive the distracted bird off its eggs and send it whirring into the next
county.

The partridge of the war zone shows no signs of such sensitive nerves. The rattle and rumble of transport, the constant
coming and going of bodies of troops, the incessant rattle of
musketry and deafening explosions of artillery, the night-long
flare and flicker of star-shells, have not sufficed to scare the
local birds away from their chosen feeding grounds, and to all
appearances they have not been deterred from raising their
broods. Gamekeepers who are serving with the colours might
seize the opportunity to indulge in a little useful nature study.

THE GALA PROGRAMME

AN UNRECORDED EPISODE IN ROMAN HISTORY

IT was an auspicious day in the Roman Calendar, the birth-day of the popular and gifted young Emperor Placidus Superbus. Every one in Rome was bent on keeping high festival, the weather was at its best, and naturally the Imperial Circus was crowded to its fullest capacity. A few minutes before the hour fixed for the commencement of the spectacle a loud fanfare of trumpets proclaimed the arrival of Cæsar, and amid the vociferous acclamations of the multitude the Emperor took his seat in the Imperial Box. As the shouting of the crowd died away an even more thrilling salutation could be heard in the near distance, the angry, impatient roaring and howling of the beasts caged in the Imperial menagerie.

"Explain the programme to me," commanded the Emperor, having beckoned the Master of the Ceremonies to his side.

That eminent official wore a troubled look.

"Gracious Cæsar," he announced, "a most promising and entertaining programme has been devised and prepared for your august approval. In the first place there is to be a chariot contest of unusual brilliancy and interest; three teams that have never hitherto suffered defeat are to contend for the Herculaneum Trophy, together with the purse which your Imperial generosity has been pleased to add. The chances of the competing teams are accounted to be as nearly as possible equal, and there is much wagering among the populace. The black Thracians are perhaps the favourites—"

"I know, I know," interrupted Cæsar, who had listened to exhaustive talk on the same subject all the morning; "what else is there on the programme?"

"The second part of the programme," said the Imperial Official, "consists of a grand combat of wild beasts, specially selected for their strength, ferocity, and fighting qualities. There will appear simultaneously in the arena fourteen Nubian

617

lions and lionesses, five tigers, six Syrian bears, eight Persian panthers, and three North African ditto, a number of wolves and lynxes from the Teutonic forests, and seven gigantic wild bulls from the same region. There will also be wild swine of unexampled savageness, a rhinoceros from the Barbary coast, some ferocious man-apes, and a hyæna, reputed to be mad."

"It promises well," said the Emperor.

"It *promised* well, O Cæsar," said the official dolorously, "it promised marvellously well; but between the promise and the performance a cloud has arisen."

"A cloud? What cloud?" queried Cæsar, with a frown.

"The Suffragetæ," explained the official; "they threaten to interfere with the chariot race."

"I'd like to see them do it!" exclaimed the Emperor indignantly.

"I fear your Imperial wish may be unpleasantly gratified," said the Master of the Ceremonies; "we are taking, of course, every possible precaution, and guarding all the entrances to the arena and the stables with a triple guard; but it is rumoured that at the signal for the entry of the chariots five hundred women will let themselves down with ropes from the public seats and swarm all over the course. Naturally no race could be run under such circumstances; the programme will be ruined."

"On my birthday," said Placidus Superbus, "they would not dare to do such an outrageous thing."

"The more august the occasion, the more desirous they will be to advertise themselves and their cause," said the harassed official; "they do not scruple to make riotous interference even with the ceremonies in the temples."

"Who *are* these Suffragetæ?" asked the Emperor. "Since I came back from my Pannonian expedition I have heard of nothing else but their excesses and demonstrations."

"They are a political sect of very recent origin, and their aim seems to be to get a big share of political authority into their hands. The means they are taking to convince us of their fitness to help in making and administering the laws consist of wild indulgence in tumult, destruction, and defiance of all authority. They have already damaged some of the most historically valuable of our public treasures, which can never be replaced."

"Is it possible that the sex which we hold in such honour and for which we feel such admiration can produce such hordes of Furies?" asked the Emperor.

"It takes all sorts to make a sex," observed the Master of the Ceremonies, who possessed a certain amount of worldly wisdom; "also," he continued anxiously, "it takes very little to upset a gala programme."

"Perhaps the disturbance that you anticipate will turn out to be an idle threat," said the Emperor consolingly.

"But if they should carry out their intention," said the official, "the programme will be utterly ruined."

The Emperor said nothing.

Five minutes later the trumpets rang out for the commencement of the entertainment. A hum of excited anticipation ran through the ranks of the spectators, and final bets on the issue of the great race were hurriedly shouted. The gates leading from the stables were slowly swung open, and a troop of mounted attendants rode round the track to ascertain that everything was clear for the momentous contest. Again the trumpets rang out, and then, before the foremost chariot had appeared, there arose a wild tumult of shouting, laughing, angry protests, and shrill screams of defiance. Hundreds of women were being lowered by their accomplices into the arena. A moment later they were running and dancing in frenzied troops across the track where the chariots were supposed to compete. No team of arena-trained horses would have faced such a frantic mob; the race was clearly an impossibility. Howls of disappointment and rage rose from the spectators, howls of triumph echoed back from the women in possession. The vain efforts of the circus attendants to drive out the invading horde merely added to the uproar and confusion; as fast as the Suffragetæ were thrust away from one portion of the track they swarmed on to another.

The Master of the Ceremonies was nearly delirious from

rage and mortification. Placidus Superbus, who remained calm and unruffled as ever, beckoned to him and spoke a word or two in his ear. For the first time that afternoon the sorely tried official was seen to smile.

A trumpet rang out from the Imperial Box; an instant hush fell over the excited throng. Perhaps the Emperor, as a last resort, was going to announce some concession to the Suffragetæ.

"Close the stable gates," commanded the Master of the Ceremonies, "and open all the menagerie dens. It is the Imperial pleasure that the second portion of the programme be taken first."

It turned out that the Master of the Ceremonies had in no wise exaggerated the probable brilliancy of this portion of the spectacle. The wild bulls were really wild, and the hyæna reputed to be mad thoroughly lived up to its reputation.

THE INFERNAL PARLIAMENT

IN an age when it has become increasingly difficult to accomplish anything new or original, Bavton Bidderdale interested his generation by dying of a new disease. "We always knew he would do something remarkable one of these days," observed his aunts; "he has justified our belief in him." But there is a section of humanity ever ready to refuse recognition to meritorious achievement, and a large and influential school of doctors asserted their belief that Bidderdale was not really dead. The funeral arrangements had to be held over until the matter was settled one way or the other, and the aunts went provisionally into half-mourning.

Meanwhile, Bidderdale remained in Hell as a guest pending his reception on a more regular footing. "If you are not really supposed to be dead," said the authorities of that region, "we don't want to seem in an indecent hurry to grab you. The theory that Hell is in serious need of population is a thing of the past. Why, to take your family alone, there are any number of Bidderdales on our books, as you may discover later. It is part of our system that relations should be encouraged to live together down here. From observations made in another world we have abundant evidence that it promotes the ends we have in view. However, while you are a guest we should like you to be treated with every consideration and be shown anything that specially interests you. Of course, you would like to see our Parliament?"

"Have you a Parliament in Hell?" asked Bidderdale in some surprise.

"Only quite recently. Of course we've always had chaos, but not under Parliamentary rules. Now, however, that Parliaments are becoming the fashion, in Turkey and Persia, and I suppose before long in Afghanistan and China, it seemed rather ostentatious to stand outside the movement. That young Fiend just going by is the Member for East Brimstone; he'll be delighted to show you over the institution."

"You will just be in time to hear the opening of a debate," said the Member, as he led Bidderdale through a spacious outer lobby, decorated with frescoes representing the fall of man, the discovery of gold, the invention of playing cards, and other traditionally appropriate subjects. "The Member for Nether Furnace is proposing a motion 'that this House do arrogantly protest to the legislatures of earthly countries against the wrongful and injurious misuse of the word "fiendish," in application to purely human misdemeanours, a misuse tending to create a false and detrimental impression concerning the Infernal Regions.' "

A feature of the Parliament Chamber itself was its enormous size. The space allotted to Members was small and very sparsely occupied, but the public galleries stretched away tier on tier as far as the eye could reach, and were packed to their utmost capacity.

"There seems to be a very great public interest in the debate," exclaimed Bidderdale.

"Members are excused from attending the debates if they so desire," the Fiend proceeded to explain; "it is one of their most highly valued privileges. On the other hand, constituents are compelled to listen throughout to all the speeches. After all, you must remember, we are in Hell."

Bidderdale repressed a shudder and turned his attention to the debate.

"Nothing," the Fiend-Orator was observing, "is more deplorable among the cultured races of the present day than the tendency to identify fiendhood, in the most sweeping fashion, with all manner of disreputable excesses, excesses which can only be alleged against us on the merest legendary evidence. Vices which are exclusively or predominatingly human are unblushingly described as inhuman, and, what is even more contemptible and ungenerous, as fiendish. If one investigates such statements as 'inhuman treatment of pit ponies' or 'fiendish cruelties in the Congo,' so frequently to be heard in our brother Parliaments on earth, one finds accumulative and indisputable evidence that it is the human treatment of pit ponies and Congo natives that is really in question, and that no authenticated case of fiendish agency in these atrocities can be substantiated. It is, perhaps, a minor matter for complaint," continued the orator, "that the human race frequently pays us the doubtful compliment of describing as 'devilish funny' jokes which are neither funny nor devilish."

The orator paused, and an oppressive silence reigned over the vast chamber.

"What is happening?" whispered Bidderdale.

"Five minutes Hush," explained his guide; "it is a sign that the speaker was listened to in silent approval, which is the highest mark of appreciation that can be bestowed in Pandemonium. Let's come into the smoking-room."

"Will the motion be carried?" asked Bidderdale, wondering inwardly how Sir Edward Grey would treat the protest if it reached the British Parliament; an *entente* with the Infernal Regions opened up a fascinating vista, in which the Foreign Secretary's imagination might hopelessly lose itself.

"Carried? Of course not," said the Fiend; "in the Infernal Parliament all motions are necessarily lost."

"In earthly Parliaments nowadays nearly everything is

found," said Bidderdale, "including salaries and travelling expenses."

He felt that at any rate he was probably the first member of his family to make a joke in Hell.

"By the way," he added, "talking of earthly Parliaments, have you got the Party system down here?"

"In Hell? Impossible. You see we have no system of rewards. We have specialized so thoroughly on punishments that the other branch has been entirely neglected. And besides, Government by delusion, as you practise it in your Parliament, would be unworkable here. I should be the last person to say anything against temptation, naturally, but we have a proverb down here 'in baiting a mouse-trap with cheese, always leave room for the mouse.' Such a party-cry, for instance, as your 'ninepence for fourpence' would be absolutely inoperative; it not only leaves no room for the mouse, it leaves no room for the imagination. You have a saying in your country, I believe, 'there's no fool like a damned fool'; all the fools down here are, necessarily, damned, but—you wouldn't get them to nibble at ninepence for fourpence."

"Couldn't they be scolded and lectured into believing it, as a sort of moral and intellectual duty?" asked Bidderdale.

"We haven't all your facilities," said the Fiend; "we've nothing down here that exactly corresponds to the Master of Elibank."

At this moment Bidderdale's attention was caught by an item on a loose sheet of agenda paper: "Vote on account of special Hells."

"Ah," he said, "I've often heard the expression 'there is a special Hell reserved for such-and-such a type of person.' Do tell me about them."

"I'll show you one in course of preparation," said the Fiend, leading him down the corridor. "This one is designed to accommodate one of the leading playwrights of your nation. You may observe scores of imps engaged in pasting notices of modern British plays into a huge press-cutting book, each under the name of the author, alphabetically arranged. The book will contain nearly half a million notices, I suppose, and it will form the sole literature supplied to this specially doomed individual."

Bidderdale was not altogether impressed.

"Some dramatic authors wouldn't so very much mind spending eternity poring over a book of contemporary press-cuttings," he observed.

The Fiend, laughing unpleasantly, lowered his voice.

"The letter 'S' is missing."

For the first time Bidderdale realized that he was in Hell.

THE ACHIEVEMENT OF THE CAT

IN the political history of nations it is no uncommon experience to find States and peoples which but a short time since were in bitter conflict and animosity with each other, settled down comfortably on terms of mutual goodwill and even alliance. The natural history of the social developments of species affords a similar instance in the coming-together of two once warring elements, now represented by civilized man and the domestic cat. The fiercely waged struggle which went on between humans and felines in those far-off days when sabre-toothed tiger and cave lion contended with primeval man, has long ago been decided in favour of the most fitly equipped combatant—the Thing with a Thumb—and the descendants of the dispossessed family are relegated today, for the most part, to the waste lands of jungle and veld, where an existence of self-effacement is the only alternative to extermination. But the *felis catus*, or whatever species was the ancestor of the modern domestic cat (a vexed question at present), by a master-stroke of adaptation avoided the ruin of its race, and "captured" a place in the very keystone of the conqueror's organization. For not as a bond-servant or dependent has this proudest of mammals entered the human fraternity; not as a slave like the beasts of burden, or a humble camp-follower like the dog. The cat is domestic only as far as suits its own ends; it will not be kennelled or harnessed nor suffer any dictation as to its goings out or comings in. Long contact with the human race has developed in it the art of diplomacy, and no Roman Cardinal of mediæval days knew better how to ingratiate himself with his surroundings than a cat with a saucer of cream on its mental horizon. But the social smoothness, the purring innocence, the softness of the velvet paw may be laid aside at a moment's notice, and the sinuous feline may disappear, in deliberate aloofness, to a world of roofs and chimney-stacks, where the human element is distanced and disregarded. Or the innate savage spirit that helped its survival in the bygone days of tooth and claw may be summoned forth from beneath the sleek exterior, and the torture-instinct (common alone to human and feline) may find free play in the death-throes of some luckless bird or rodent. It is, indeed, no small triumph to have combined the untrammelled liberty of primeval savagery with the luxury which only a highly developed civilization can command; to be lapped in the soft stuffs that commerce has gathered from the far ends of the world; to bask in the warmth that labour and industry have dragged from the bowels of the earth; to banquet on the dainties that wealth has bespoken for its table, and withal to be a free son of nature, a mighty hunter, a spiller of life-blood. This is the victory of the cat. But besides the credit of success the cat has other qualities which compel recognition. The animal which the Egyptians worshipped as divine, which the Romans venerated as a symbol of liberty, which Europeans in the ignorant Middle Ages anathematized as an agent of demonology, has displayed to all ages two closely blended characteristics—courage and self-respect. No matter how unfavourable the circumstances, both qualities are always to the fore. Confront a child, a puppy, and a kitten with a sudden danger; the child will turn instinctively for assistance, the puppy will grovel in abject submission to the impending visitation, the kitten will brace its tiny body for a frantic resistance. And disassociate the luxury-loving cat from the atmosphere of social comfort in which it usually contrives to move, and observe it critically under the adverse conditions of civilization—that civilization which can impel a man to the degradation of clothing himself in tawdry ribald garments and capering mountebank dances in the streets for the earning of the few coins that keep him on the respectable, or non-criminal, side of society. The cat of the slums and alleys, starved, outcast, harried, still keeps amid the prowlings of its adversity the bold, free, panther-tread with which it paced of yore the temple courts of Thebes, still displays the self-reliant watchfulness which man has never taught it to lay aside. And when its shifts and clever managings have not sufficed to stave off inexorable fate, when its enemies have proved too strong or too many for its defensive powers, it dies fighting to the last, quivering with the choking rage of mastered resistance, and voicing in its death-yell that agony of bitter remonstrance which human animals, too, have flung at the powers that may be; the last protest against a destiny that might have made them happy— and has not.

THE OLD TOWN OF PSKOFF

RUSSIA at the present crisis of its history not unnaturally suggests to the foreign mind a land pervaded with discontent and disorder and weighed down with depression, and it is certainly difficult to point to any quarter of the Imperial dominions from which troubles of one sort or another are not reported. In the *Novoe Vremya* and other papers a column is now devoted to the chronicling of disorders as regularly as a British news-sheet reports sporting events. It is the more agreeable therefore occasionally to make the acquaintance of another phase of Russian life where the sombreness of political mischance can be momentarily lost sight of or disbelieved in. Perhaps there are few spots in European Russia where one so thoroughly feels that one has passed into a new and unfamiliar atmosphere as the old town of Pskoff, once in its day a very important centre of Russian life. To the average modern Russian a desire to visit Pskoff is an inexplicable mental freak on the part of a foreigner who wishes to see something of the country he is living in; Petersburg, Moscow, Kieff, perhaps, and Nijni-Novgorod, or the Finnish watering-places if you want a country holiday, but why Pskoff? And thus happily an aversion to beaten tracks and localities where inspection is invited and industriously catered for turns one towards the old Great Russian border town, which probably gives as accurate a picture as can be obtained of a mediæval Russian burgh, untouched by Mongol influence, and only slightly affected by Byzantine-imported culture.

The little town has ample charm of situation and structure, standing astride of a bold scarp of land wedged into the fork of two rivers, and retaining yet much of the long lines of ramparts and towers that served for many a hundred years to keep out Pagan Lithuanians and marauding Teuton knights. The powers of Darkness were as carefully guarded against in those old days as more tangible human enemies, and from out of thick clusters of tree-tops there still arise the white walls and green roofs of many churches, monasteries, and bell-towers, quaint and fantastic in architecture, and delightfully harmonious in colouring. Steep winding streets lead down from the rampart-girt heart of the town to those parts which lie along the shores of the twin rivers, and two bridges, one a low, wide, wooden structure primitively planted on piles, give access to the further banks, where more towers and monasteries, with other humbler buildings, continue the outstraggling span of the township. On the rivers lie barges with high masts painted in wonderful bands of scarlet, green, white, and blue, topped with gilded wooden pennons figured somewhat like a child's rattle, and fluttering strips of bunting at their ends. Up in the town one sees on all sides quaint old doorways, deep archways, wooden gable-ends, railed staircases, and a crowning touch of pleasing colour in the sage green or dull red of the roofs. But it is strangest of all to find a human population in complete picturesque harmony with its rich old-world setting. The scarlet or blue blouses that are worn by the working men in most Russian towns give way here to a variety of gorgeous-tinted garments, and the women-folk are similarly gay in their apparel, so that streets and wharves and market-place glow with wonderfully effective groupings of colour. Mulberry, orange, dull carmine, faded rose, hyacinth purple, greens, and lilacs and rich blues mingle their hues on shirts and shawls, skirts and breeches and waistbands. Nature competing with Percy Anderson was the frivolous comment that came to one's mind, and certainly a mediæval crowd could scarcely have been more effectively staged. And the business of a town in which it seemed always market day went forward with an air of contented absorption on the part of the inhabitants. Strings of primitively fashioned carts went to and from the riverside, the horses wearing their bits for the most part hung negligently under the chin, a fashion that prevails in many parts of Russia and Poland.

Quaint little booths line the sides of some of the steeper streets, and here wooden toys and earthenware pottery of strange local patterns are set out for sale. On the broad market-place women sit gossiping by the side of large baskets of strawberries, one or two long-legged foals sprawl at full stretch under the shade of their parental market carts, and an extremely contented pig pursues his leisurely way under the guardianship of an elderly dame robed in a scheme of orange, mulberry, and white that would delight the soul of a colourist. A stalwart peasant strides across the uneven cobbles, leading his plough-horse, and carrying on his shoulder a small wooden plough, with iron-tipped shares, that must date back to some stage of agriculture that the West has long left behind. Down in the buoyant waters of the Velikaya, the larger of the two rivers, youths and men are disporting themselves and staider washerwomen are rinsing and smacking piles of many-hued garments. It is pleasant to swim well out into the stream of the river, and, with one's chin on a level with the wide stretch of water, take in a "trout's-eye view" of the little town, ascending in tiers of wharfage, trees, grey ramparts, more trees, and clustered roofs, with the old cathedral of the Trinity poised guardian-like above the crumbling walls of the Kremlin. The cathedral, on closer inspection, is a charming specimen of genuine old Russian architecture, full of rich carvings and aglow with scarlet pigment and gilded scrollwork, and stored with yet older relics or pseudo-relics of local hero-saints and hero-princes who helped in their day to make the history of the Pskoff Commonwealth. After an hour or two spent among these tombs and ikons and memorials of dead Russia, one feels that some time must elapse before one cares to enter again the drearily magnificent holy places of St. Petersburg, with their depressing *nouveau riche* atmosphere, their price-list tongued attendants, and general lack of historic interest.

The heart knoweth its own bitterness, and maybe the Pskoffskie, amid their seeming contentment and self-absorption, have their own hungerings for a new and happier era of national life. But the stranger does not ask to see so far; he is thankful to have found a picturesque and apparently well-contented corner of a weary land, a land "where distress seems like a bird of passage that has hurt its wing and cannot fly away."

CLOVIS ON THE ALLEGED
ROMANCE OF BUSINESS

"IT is the fashion nowadays," said Clovis, "to talk about the romance of Business. There isn't such a thing. The romance has all been the other way, with the idle apprentice, the truant, the runaway, the individual who couldn't be bothered with figures and book-keeping and left business to look after itself. I admit that a grocer's shop is one of the most romantic and thrilling things that I have ever happened on, but the romance and thrill are centred in the groceries, not the grocer. The citron and spices and nuts and dates, the barrelled anchovies and Dutch cheeses, the jars of *caviar* and the chests of tea, they carry the mind away to Levantine coast towns and tropic shores, to the Old World wharfs and quays of the Low Countries, to dusty Astrachan and far Cathay; if the grocer's apprentice has any romance in him it is not a business education he gets behind the grocer's counter, it is a standing invitation to dream and to wander, and to remain poor.

As a child such places as South America and Asia Minor were brought painstakingly under my notice, the names of their principal rivers and the heights of their chief mountain peaks were committed to my memory, and I was earnestly enjoined to consider them as parts of the world that I lived in; it was only when I visited a large well-stocked grocer's shop that I realized that they certainly existed. Such galleries of romance and fascination are not bequeathed to us by the business man; he is only the dull custodian, who talks glibly of Spanish olives and Rangoon rice, a Spain that he has never known or wished to know, a Rangoon that he has never imagined or could imagine. It was the unledgered wanderer, the careless-hearted seafarer, the aimless outcast, who opened up new trade routes, tapped new markets, brought home samples or cargoes of new edibles and unknown condiments. It was they who brought the glamour and romance to the threshold of business life, where it was promptly reduced to pounds, shillings, and pence; invoiced, double-entried, quoted, written-off, and so forth; most of those terms are probably wrong, but a little inaccuracy sometimes saves tons of explanation.

"On the other side of the account there is the industrious apprentice, who grew up into the business man, married early and worked late, and lived, thousands and thousands of him, in little villas outside big towns. He is buried by the thousand in Kensal Green and other large cemeteries; any romance that was ever in him was buried prematurely in shop and warehouse and office. Whenever I feel in the least tempted to be business-like or methodical or even decently industrious I go to Kensal Green and look at the graves of those who died in business."

THE COMMENTS OF MOUNG KA

MOUNG KA, cultivator of rice and philosophic virtues, sat on the raised platform of his cane-built house by the banks of the swiftly flowing Irrawaddy. On two sides of the house there was a bright-green swamp, which stretched away to where the uncultivated jungle growth began. In the bright-green swamp, which was really a rice-field when you looked closely at it, bitterns and pond-herons and elegant cattle-egrets stalked and peered with the absorbed air of careful and conscientious reptile-hunters, who could never forget that, while they were undoubtedly useful, they were also distinctly decorative. In the tall reed growth by the riverside grazing buffaloes showed in patches of dark slaty blue, like plums fallen amid long grass, and in the tamarind trees that shaded Moung Ka's house the crows, restless, raucous-throated, and much-too-many, kept up their incessant afternoon din, saying over and over again all the things that crows have said since there were crows to say them.

Moung Ka sat smoking his enormous green-brown cigar, without which no Burmese man, woman, or child seems really complete, dispensing from time to time instalments of worldly information for the benefit and instruction of his two companions. The steamer which came up-river from Mandalay thrice a week brought Moung Ka a Rangoon news-sheet, in which the progress of the world's events was set forth in telegraphic messages and commented on in pithy paragraphs. Moung Ka, who read these things and retailed them as occasion served to his friends and neighbours, with philosophical additions of his own, was held in some esteem locally as a political thinker; in Burma it is possible to be a politician without ceasing to be a philosopher.

His friend Moung Thwa, dealer in teakwood, had just returned down-river from distant Bhamo, where he had spent many weeks in dignified, unhurried chaffering with Chinese merchants; the first place to which he had naturally turned his steps, bearing with him his betel-box and fat cigar, had been the raised platform of Moung Ka's cane-built house under the tamarind trees. The youthful Moung Shoogalay, who had studied in the foreign schools at Mandalay and knew many English words, was also of the little group that sat listening to Moung Ka's bulletin of the world's health and ignoring the screeching of the crows.

There had been the usual preliminary talk of timber and

the rice market and sundry local matters, and then the wider and remoter things of life came under review.

"And what has been happening away from here?" asked Moung Thwa of the newspaper reader.

"Away from here" comprised that considerable portion of the world's surface which lay beyond the village boundaries.

"Many things," said Moung Ka reflectively, "but principally two things of much interest and of an opposite nature. Both, however concern the action of Governments."

Moung Thwa nodded his head gravely, with the air of one who reverenced and distrusted all Governments.

"The first thing, of which you may have heard on your journeyings," said Moung Ka, "is an act of the Indian Government, which has annulled the not-long-ago accomplished partition of Bengal."

"I heard something of this," said Moung Thwa, "from a Madrassi merchant on the boat journey. But I did not learn the reasons that made the Government take this step. Why was the partition annulled?"

"Because," said Moung Ka, "it was held to be against the wishes of the greater number of the people of Bengal. Therefore the Government made an end of it."

Moung Thwa was silent for a moment. "Is it a wise thing the Government has done?" he asked presently.

"It is a good thing to consider the wishes of a people," said Moung Ka. "The Bengalis may be a people who do not always wish what is best for them. Who can say? But at least their wishes have been taken into consideration, and that is a good thing."

"And the other matter of which you spoke?" questioned Moung Thwa, "the matter of an opposite nature."

"The other matter," said Moung Ka, "is that the British Government has decided on the partition of Britain. Where there has been one Parliament and one Government there are to be two Parliaments and two Governments, and there will be two treasuries and two sets of taxes."

Moung Thwa was greatly interested at this news.

"And is the feeling of the people of Britain in favour of

this partition?" he asked. "Will they not dislike it, as the people of Bengal disliked the partition of their Province?"

"The feeling of the people of Britain has not been consulted, and will not be consulted," said Moung Ka; "the Act of Partition will pass through one Chamber where the Government rules supreme, and the other Chamber can only delay it a little while, and then it will be made into the Law of the Land."

"But is it wise not to consult the feeling of the people?" asked Moung Thwa.

"Very wise," answered Moung Ka, "for if the people were consulted they would say 'No,' as they have always said when such a decree was submitted to their opinion, and if the people said 'No' there would be an end of the matter, but also an end of the Government. Therefore, it is wise for the Government to shut its ears to what the people may wish."

"But why must the people of Bengal be listened to and the people of Britain not listened to?" asked Moung Thwa; "surely the partition of their country affects them just as closely. Are their opinions too silly to be of any weight?"

"The people of Britain are what is called a Democracy," said Moung Ka.

"A Democracy?" questioned Moung Thwa. "What is that?"

"A Democracy," broke in Moung Shoogalay eagerly, "is a community that governs itself according to its own wishes and interests by electing accredited representatives who enact its laws and supervise and control their administration. Its aim and object is government of the community in the interests of the community."

"Then," said Moung Thwa, turning to his neighbour, "if the people of Britain are a Democracy—"

"I never said they were a Democracy," interrupted Moung Ka placidly.

"Surely we both heard you!" exclaimed Moung Thwa.

"Not correctly," said Moung Ka; "I said they are what is called a Democracy."

Biography of Saki

BY

ETHEL M. MUNRO

Saki's drawings, scattered through the biography, have, many of them, no connection with the text. They are given as examples of his whimsical humour.   E. M. M.

BIOGRAPHY OF SAKI

MY earliest recollection of Hector, my younger brother, was in the nursery at home, where, with my elder brother, Charlie, we had been left alone. Hector seized the long-handled hearth brush, plunged it into the fire, and chased Charlie and me round the table, shouting, "I'm God! I'm going to destroy the world!"

The "world" tore round and round the all-too-inadequate table, not daring to leave it to dash for the door, while Hector, his face lit with impish glee and the flare from the brush, enjoyed to the full his self-imposed divinity. Our yells brought Aunt Augusta on the scene, and we all got a dressing down.

The nursery looked on to a field, where appeared various farm animals that served as models for Hector's sketches—models that he kept in his head, for I never saw him drawing from life until years later.

Broadgate Villa, in the village of Pilton, near Barnstaple, North Devon, was the house my father took for us, after our mother's death, before leaving for India. Here his mother, and his two sisters, Charlotte and Augusta, were installed to look after us.

I think Hector must have been about two when we arrived there. He was born in Akyab, Burma, where my father was stationed, on December 18, 1870, and christened Hector Hugh. He was a delicate child, in fact the family doctor at Barnstaple, whom the grown-ups looked upon as an oracle, declared that the three of us would never live to grow up. Probably children not so highly strung and excitable *would* have succumbed, because, judged by modern methods, our bringing up was quite wrong. The house was too dark, verandas kept much of the sunlight out, the flower and vegetable gardens were surrounded by high walls and a hedge, and on rainy days we were kept indoors.

Also fresh air was feared, especially in winter; we slept in

rooms with windows shut and shuttered, with only the door
open on to the landing to admit stale air. All hygienic ideas
were to Aunt Augusta, the Autocrat, "choc rot," a word of
her own invention.

Then we should have had more country walks than we ever
got, there were lovely fields and woods quite handy, but Aunt
Augusta wanted shops and gossip—also she was afraid of
cows.

Fortunately, there were the three of us, and we lived a life
of our own, in which the grown-ups had no part, and to which
we admitted only animals and a favourite uncle, Wellesley,
who stayed with us about once a year.

Our pleasures were of the very simplest—other children
hardly came into our lives—once a year, at Christmas, we
went to a children's party, where we were not allowed to eat
any attractive, exciting-looking food, "for fear of consequences," and in *case* the party might have done us harm,
Granny gave us hot brandy and water on our return.

Also, once a year, in the summer, the child of some friend
visiting the neighbourhood would come to play with us. "So
good a boy," we would be told, "he always does what he is
bid."

From that moment a look of deep purpose settled on Hector's face, and on the day when the good Claud arrived an
entirely busy and happy time for Hector was the result.

He saw to it that Claud did all the things we must never
do, the easier to accomplish since his mother would be indoors
tongue-wagging with Granny and the aunts. Poor Claud really
was a good child, with no inclination to be anything else, but
under Hector's ruthless tuition, backed up by Charlie, he put
in a breathless day of bad deeds.

And when Aunt Tom (Charlotte she was never called),
after the visitors' departure, remarked, "Claud is not the good
child I imagined him to be," Hector felt it was the end of a
perfect day.

But by ourselves we had not the scope for naughty deeds—
it was, "Don't play on the grass," from one aunt, and "Children, you're not to play on the gravel," from the other.

The front garden, with its grass slopes under the elm-trees where the rooks lived, was the only outdoor place we had to play in, the kitchen garden being considered too tempting a place, with its fruit trees. Therefore the boys had to get into it, by hook or by crook.

So much has been said, in reviews of Hector's books, about the cruelty element in them, an element which, personally, I cannot see, that an account of the aunts' characters may perhaps throw some light on the environment of his early years.

Our grandmother, a gentle, dignified old lady, was entirely overruled by her turbulent daughters, who hated each other with a ferocity and intensity worthy of a bigger cause. How it was they were not consumed by the strength of their feelings I don't know. I once asked a friend of the family what had started the antagonism.

"Jealousy," she said; "when your Aunt Tom, who was fifteen years older than Augusta, returned from a long visit to Scotland, where she had been much admired, and spoilt, and found the little sister growing up, also pretty and admired, she became intensely jealous of her—from that time they have always quarrelled."

Aunt Tom was the most extraordinary woman I have ever known—perhaps a reincarnation of Catherine of Russia. What she meant to know or do, that she did. She had no scruples, never saw when she was hurting people's feelings, was possessed of boundless energy and had not a day's real illness until she was seventy-six.

Her religious convictions would fit into any religion ever invented. She took us regularly to Pilton Church on Sunday mornings. For a long time I was struck by her familiarity with the Psalms, which she apparently repeated without looking at her book, but one day I discovered she was merely murmuring, without saying a word at all, and had put on her long-distance glasses in order to take good stock of the congregation and its clothes. A walk back after church with various neighbours provided material for a dramatic account to Granny (not that she was interested) of the doings of the neighbourhood. Whatever Aunt Tom did was dramatic, and whatever story she repeated, she embroidered. No use to try to get to the end before she intended you should. Without any sense of humour whatever, she was the funniest story-teller I've ever met. She was a colossal humbug, and never knew it.

The other aunt, Augusta, is the one who, more or less, is depicted in "Sredni Vashtar" ("Chronicles of Clovis"). She was the autocrat of Broadgate—a woman of ungovernable temper, of fierce likes and dislikes, imperious, a moral coward, possessing no brains worth speaking of, and a primitive disposition. Naturally the last person who should have been in charge of children.

But the character of the aunt in "The Lumber Room" is Aunt Augusta to the life. "It was her habit, whenever one of the children fell from grace, to improvise something of a festival nature from which the offender would be rigorously debarred; if all the children sinned collectively they were suddenly informed of a circus in a neighbouring town, a circus of unrivalled merit and uncounted elephants, to which, but for their depravity, they would have been taken that very day. . . . She was a woman of few ideas, with immense powers of concentration. . . . Tea that evening was partaken of in a fearsome silence."

Well do I remember those "fearsome silences!" Nothing could be said, because it was certain to sound silly, in the vast gloom. With Aunt Tom alone we should have fared much better—she adored Hector as long as he kept off the flower-beds and out of the kitchen garden—but as we could not obey both aunts (I believe each gave us orders which she knew were contrary to those issued by the other), we found it better for ourselves, in the end, to obey Aunt Augusta.

Our best time was during some pitched battle in their internecine warfare, "with Aunt calling to Aunt like mastodons bellowing across primeval swamps;" [1] we lived our little lives, criticized our "elders and betters" and rejoiced exceedingly when Aunt Augusta went to bed for a whole day with a headache.

This gave us more scope, and we became more venturesome

[1] P. G. Wodehouse.

—Hector always the most daring—even exploring the top story because it was forbidden ground, and contained a mysterious room, the original of "The Lumber Room" in "Beasts and Super-Beasts."

Aunt Augusta's religion was not elastic; it was definite and High Church and took her into Barnstaple on Sunday evenings. Neither aunt permitted her religion to come between her and her ruling passion, which was, to outwit the other. What they squabbled about never seemed to be of much importance. If Aunt Tom came back from Barnstaple market bearing reports of poultry she had bought at 2s. 6d., Aunt Augusta would know no peace until she had seen a far fatter bird at 2s. 4d. and announced it.

Then a row began—more or less intense, according to the length of time that had elapsed since the last one. Fighting probably relieved their tremendous energy. They never swore, so we heard no bad words. One good effect the quarrelling certainly had on us—it looked so ugly, we never copied them—never in our lives have we three had a row.

The aunts' outside interests lay in politics and the gossip of Pilton. Gardening kept Aunt Tom more or less sane, and making yards of useless embroidery had a soothing influence on Aunt Augusta. From morning to night, whether the jobbing gardener were there or not, Aunt Tom would be busy and dirty. Both aunts were exceedingly loyal to their friends, who, in their eyes, could do no wrong, and very generous to the poor.

They did not care at all for animals, but luckily did not interfere with our pets, whom we adored—they were the only young things we had to play with.

Hector had a curious dislike of rooks; I had a pet young one, and used to feed it with bread and milk; if he took the spoon he dropped it as it opened its beak. This dislike lasted all his life.

We had charming cats, who gave us all the affection the grown-ups did not know how to show. Tortoises, rabbits, doves, guinea-pigs and mice were other pets we had for a time, but cats and cocks and hens were always with us.

There was a most intelligent Houdan cock, who was Hector's shadow; he fed out of his hand and loved being petted. Unhappily he got something wrong with one leg, and had to be destroyed. I believe a "Vet." would have cured him, but this would have been considered a sinful extravagance. No one but myself knew what Hector felt at the loss of the bird. We had early learnt to hide our feelings—to show enthusiasm or emotion were sure to bring an amused smile to Aunt Augusta's face. It was a hateful smile, and I cannot imagine why it hurt, but it did; among ourselves we called it "the meaning smile."

Of course there were lots of days on which life went smoothly, but, with an autocrat like herself, the most unexpected little things would upset her.

Both aunts were guilty of mental cruelty: we often longed for revenge with an intensity I suspect we inherited from our Highland ancestry. The following episode has already appeared somewhere, years after it happened. I told it to a friend of Hector's, who said he should make it into a story.

We always had plenty of good food, but, of course, plain, and except on our birthdays we never got roast duck, of which we were very fond. Sometimes a friend coming from a distance would be asked to lunch, and then roast duck would be the chief dish. Before the guest arrived Aunt Augusta would tell the three of us that at lunch she should ask us which we would have—roast duck or cold beef, and we were to answer, "Cold beef, please."

Well, on one occasion there were a couple of ducks, which Aunt Augusta was carving, and cold beef, which Granny had before her. All the grown-ups had had their plates filled, and Aunt Augusta turned to us. Hector and I gave the dutiful replies, but Charlie, on her left, was evidently so overcome by the sight and smell of the birds that he replied, "Roast duck, please."

Aunt Augusta glowered at him.

"What did you say?" she asked, with furious eyes, and kicked him under the table.

"Oh, cold beef, please," said Charlie, hurriedly.

"What extraordinary children, to prefer cold beef to duck!" remarked the visitor, and the children did not enlighten her.

Charlie really came off worst—Aunt Augusta never liked him, and positively used to enjoy whipping him. Hector and I escaped whipping, being considered too delicate. Fortunately for Charlie, he went to school when he was eight, and so got away from her malign influence. In her queer way she was fond of Hector and me, but being such an unlovable character, we extended only a lukewarm sort of liking to her.

With the best will in the world we could not be really naughty, for there simply was not the scope. Three children with three grown-ups to manage them are really handicapped from the outset.

Granny we were very fond of; she was always very gentle with us, but appallingly strict on Sunday. No toys, no books except Sunday books, Dr. Watts's ghastly catechism, a collect and piece of a hymn to be learnt and repeated to her, stories read to us from "Peep of Day," and church, of course, in the morning. But at church we saw people and other children.

In the afternoons we had a church service among ourselves, the grown-ups must have been sleeping the Sabbath sleep. Preaching was the favourite part of the game and was a solemn affair, listened to with deep attention, far deeper than the preacher in church ever got, but there had to be three sermons in rapid succession—we all had something to say.

It also, in summer, was the favourite day for the boys to attempt, generally successfully, to get into the kitchen garden. Not every afternoon did the aunts sleep, so either that or to make a marauding expedition into the store-room via the greenhouse, and equally forbidden ground, was naturally the only thing to be done.

On one occasion they emerged from the latter with a jar of tamarinds, and got it safely into the night nursery, where there was a large trunk in which Aunt Augusta kept spare clothes. They ate what they wanted and put the jar in the trunk between folds of a black silk dress. The jar contained a lot of juice, very sticky, and in the eating much was smeared over the sides. However, the black silk absorbed a lot.

And then Aunt Augusta had occasion to open that trunk! Broadgate resounded to her bellowings, and the row was frightful. In a former life she must have been a dragon. No

MISSIONARY SUNDAY

"OH WE Whose lives are lighted With Wisdom from on High —"

toys allowed for two days, disgrace for all of us, and, of course, nothing to do. But mercifully we had fertile brains, and Hector was never nonplussed for occupation. Aunt Tom sometimes read to us—*Robinson Crusoe, Masterman Ready,* and the two *Alice's*, which we loved, *Sandford and Merton* we refused to listen to.

"*Johnnykin and the Goblins*," a very little-known book, had always fascinated Hector. Being a Celt, I suppose it was natural he should be fond of goblins and nature spirits—he was certainly a Puck himself to the end of his life.

Pilton was a sort of Cranford; there were about ten families, most of them without children, so we got to know grownups well and to be quite at ease in their society. When we did see children, it was in a crowd at a Christmas party. Aunt Augusta always went with us, and sometimes left us with the other children while she departed to gossip with the grownups. Hector leapt at the opportunity and the nearest boy, and was soon in the ecstasies of a fight.

Then Aunt Augusta would look in and in a restrained fury drag him off to be tidied. But his blood was up and any threat as to subsequent punishment was ignored. It was not that he was pugnacious—he was a very sweet-tempered child, but his high spirits had to have some outlet, and life at Broadgate was very monotonous. At the same party he had to be restrained from dashing on to the stage to rescue a man who was being threatened by another.

At this time he was an extremely fair child—very pink and white skin, blue-grey eyes with long black lashes, and flaxen hair. In his teens he began to get darker. Those who only knew him in his London days cannot understand that he could ever have been fair.

From about seven years old he was a keen politician. There was a most exciting election in Barnstaple, when Lord Portsmouth's son, a Radical, was elected. We were taken to the town to hear the poll declared, and had seats in a window opposite "The Golden Lion." The sights we saw were far too thrilling, and Hector was in a fever of excitement and furious at the result of the poll. He remained Conservative all his life.

He showed no signs of a writing talent as a boy with the exception of contributions to *The Broadgate Paper* which we ran. Drawing animals was his favourite occupation; he

Golf in the Wild West

I. A cautious approach.—

2. Bunkers

never copied—just drew things out of his head. One rainy day in the holidays we had nothing to do, so we settled to have a Picture Exhibition that afternoon. Hector would be about eight then. We set to work to paint the pictures, of which many were still wet at the time the show opened. The grown-ups knew what we had planned, yet they never troubled to attend and praise our efforts, so we had to be audience and judges as well. With great solemnity and perfect justice Hector's pictures were awarded the prize, an old copy I had of *Æsop's Fables*.

Once in four years my father came home on leave (he was then a major in the Bengal Staff Corps, and Inspector-General of the Burma Police), and for six weeks we had a glorious time.

He took us for picnics, and to the houses of friends who had farmyards, where Hector rode the pigs, climbed haystacks with Charlie and arrived home rakish and buttonless, but in unquenchable spirits, snapping his fingers (figuratively, of course) at Aunt Augusta.

We did not fear her when Papa was about. The wonder was we did not fear God with every inducement to do so. It was patent that our characters were fatally attractive to Him, and when we went a bit too far we were told that He sent a thunderstorm as a warning that we had better be careful.

I think Aunt Augusta must have mesmerized us—the look in her dark eyes, added to the fury in her voice, and the uncertainty as to the punishment, used to make me shiver. She had the strange characteristic of being unable to be just annoyed at anything, she had to be so angry that she would work herself into a passion. After all, we fared better than a splendid retriever she had, who was kept chained up in an outhouse of the back-yard for years, with nothing to look at, eating his heart out. He was taken out for a walk perhaps twice in the year (until my father came home) and frightened Aunt Augusta with his obstreperous delight. He died of tumours when he was about eight.

Uncle Wellesley, our only civilian uncle, was a great favourite with us. He only came about once a year, and took

3. Lofted.   HM

4. one up and one to follow.   HM.

Hector on fishing and sketching expeditions. We never had a dull moment when he was home; in a letter I found lately, written to his mother, he said (*à propos* of Aunt Augusta's complaint of our behaviour), "the children are never naughty with me, because I take the trouble to amuse them."

Hector began lessons with a daily governess we had; our history lessons were read aloud, each taking a page. All went well until we reached Cromwell's time.

5. "Dead"

"You must take the Roundheads' part," he said to me.

"But I would rather be Royalist," I objected.

"We can't both be Royalists, so you must be Roundhead."

(The odd thing is that, from being forced into it, I have remained Roundhead ever since.) So we began the period of the Civil Wars with great delight—it soon became exciting —Hector would gloat over a victory of his side, even rising up in his chair to hurl abuse at the Roundheads, which naturally I wouldn't stand, so I abused back; the governess, being a fool, at last stopped the concerted history lesson, but she couldn't stop us; we only waited until she was off, got down the histories and took the battles at a gallop, going through all the gamut of emotions from depression to exultation, according to the fortune of war. History then and ever after-

wards became his favourite study, and as he had a wonderful
memory his knowledge of European history from its beginning was remarkable. He was also very keen on natural history. When he was about nine he had brain-fever: the aunts
nursed him most carefully; we had only to be ill, and everything was changed at Broadgate, scoldings were things of the
past. This illness delayed his going to school. We went much
too seldom to visit my mother's people in Kent. They were
much more our sort than the home aunts. My grandfather,
Rear-Admiral Mercer, was full of fun, and his daughters
were young and lively, and they let us do lots of things we
could never do at home. Grandpapa was very fond of practical jokes, which fondness his grandchildren inherited in full
measure.

Two or three London visits, and, very seldom, two weeks
by the sea, completed our outings.

Hector was rather a favourite with old ladies, with whom
he made himself quite at home. Aunt Tom took us once to
see a very charming old lady, whose daughter (not a chicken)
was then away on a round of visits. In a pause in the conversation Hector approached our hostess and, in a most courtly
manner, proceeded:

"And so I hear, Mrs. Simpson, that Miss Janet is away
in Scotland, enjoying all kinds of debauchery."

There was an astonished pause, every one laughed, and Aunt
Tom exclaimed:

"That dreadful Roman history! That's where he picks up
these extraordinary expressions!"

It was quite true—we had a remarkable, unexpurgated history with novel and lengthy words which needed airing, and
this seemed to be a good occasion to have one out.

My father chose a resident governess for me before his last
departure for Burma; she was to teach Hector as well until
he was strong enough for school (he was then twelve). It
would be a great change for us to have a new-comer in the
house, and we gravely discussed the situation.

"After all," said Hector, "we have only the grown-ups'
word for it that she is a *real* governess, but how are we to

know? We must put a pea under her mattress, and see how she sleeps."

In one of Hans Andersen's tales, an unknown Princess was

The was a young girl called O'brien
Who sang Sunday-school hymns to a lion,
Of this lady there's some
In the lion's tum-tum,
And the rest is an angel in Zion.

admitted on a wild night into a royal castle and given a bed consisting of twenty mattresses and twenty feather beds, after the Queen had thoughtfully put a pea under the lot. If she slept well, she was an impostor; if badly, that proved her royalty. She slept atrociously.

So before the pseudo-governess arrived we put a dried pea under her mattress, and next morning asked her anxiously how she had slept.

"Very well indeed, thank you," she replied, with a pleased surprise at our solicitude.

"Ah, then, you can't be a *real* governess," said Hector, greatly disappointed, and told her what we had done.

She was, however, a real companion, and took us for the walks we loved and explored the whole countryside. She, like Uncle Wellesley, never found us naughty, because she took the trouble to amuse us. However, Aunt Augusta was afraid of her; we did not know it at the time, but she thought Miss J.'s dark eyes were trying to mesmerize her, so, on the day she left for the holidays, after only one term with us, Aunt Augusta, who had not the nerve to do it herself, got Granny, who was then dying, to dismiss her. The following term we had no governess; Granny died, and we had a very sad time.

Another governess arrived for the next term, chosen by Aunt Augusta, and Hector soon after that was considered strong enough to go to school.

He went to Exmouth, where Charlie had preceded him, and was very happy there.

It was on returning to school after the holidays that Aunt Augusta gave a sample of mental cruelty. Some petty naughtiness had angered her the day before his return to school, so she sent him back without any pocket-money. As each boy had to bank his allowance for the whole term with one of the masters, Hector's ordeal may be imagined when he had to confess he had none.

Charlie, who had not yet returned to Charterhouse, and I planned what we could do to help Hector. We settled to sell our books—Christmas and birthday presents from friends of the family. So we did, secretly, to a second-hand bookseller for quite a nice sum, and sent a postal order to Hector. Charlie then wrote to Papa, telling him what we had done, and the latter's letter to Aunt Augusta, blaming her for her action, was the first news she had of the affair. There was a row.

At fifteen Hector went to Bedford Grammar School and was there for two years. His school reports used to be, "Plenty of ability, but little application." In his Easter holidays he went bird-nesting with some of our neighbours, and made the beginning of a collection which he added to in our Heanton days. This collection is now in the Bideford Museum.

ELISHA AND THE MOCKING CHILDREN

Two bears came forth from their cubless den—
Their cubless den, for their cubs were robbed—
And hunted about in search of men
Till they came to the spot where the Prophet was mobbed.
For men must hunt, tho' bears will fret,
And a cub will command a good price as a pet
And money is always consoling.

Thirty-two corpses lay stretched on the sward,
Thirty-two corpses, or possibly more,
For the bears were too busy their bag to record
And the Saint didn't stay to attend to the score.

My father, who had now retired, took us both to Normandy, our first trip abroad. We had some amusing young playmates, French and Russian, and enjoyed to the hilt the novelty and fascination of life at Etretat, with no aunts to mar our delight: the bathing would certainly have shocked them.

Our second trip abroad was a more educational one, to Germany. We had a lengthy stay in Dresden, Charlie joining us, and my father first began to feel what it was like to look after strictly brought up children! Although Hector was then eighteen, he was still a boy, with no intention of growing up. One effect of the strict Broadgate *régime* was that he developed late—he remained and looked a boy long after he was in the twenties. We stayed in a Dresden pension run by a German lady, where the other guests were Americans.

On the flat beneath us was a girls' school, all of them ugly. One day, when my father was out, the boys made a weird figure of his bathing costume, stuffed out with paper and clothes, with a sponge for a face, and a rakish-looking hat. This they lowered into the balcony below. The schoolmistress happened to be giving dinner to a pastor, and to them, instead of to the girls, was vouchsafed this appalling vision.

When the boys thought enough time had elapsed, they swiftly drew up the figure. Swiftly, also, a note of complaint arrived for our landlady, who, being a German, saw no fun in the affair, not even with the figure sprawling at her feet. It was the convulsive laughter of a hitherto rather unbending American woman (in fact, the only time we ever knew her to laugh) that thawed her, and a note of apology was sent—insincere, as the school ma'am must have guessed, from the shouts of laughter above.

A "Lohengrin" night at the opera resulted in a sketch in which Hector depicted Lohengrin suffering from sea-sickness, while the swan turns round and gazes at him in astonishment. A German who saw it begged him to send it to the *Fliegende Blätter*, but he never bothered to do it. He took long walks by himself in the parks to observe bird-life, and would stop Germans and draw in the gravel path the sort of bird he wanted, and ask if it were to be found. They would then write the bird's name in the gravel, and tell him where to get further information.

He routed out, in some obscure corner, an old man who sold birds' eggs, and from him bought a model of the Great Auk's egg, and insisted on coming home in a cab, for the greater safety of the egg.

Charlie left us to go to a crammer's (he was trying for the Army), and we then began a strenuous tour, beginning with Berlin. At the Palace of Sans Souci at Potsdam we searched for the graves of Frederick the Great's chargers and favourite dogs, and refused to go over the Palace until a park-keeper could be found who knew where they were buried.

We saw an immense number of picture galleries in Berlin, Munich, etc., and were impressed by the love of German artists for St. Sebastian (the arrow-stuck saint), so we started bets on the gallery which would have the most: Berlin won.

Nuremberg delighted Hector—then and always he loved old towns; in later days Pskoff more than fulfilled his dream of what a mediæval town should be. Prague was another delight, particularly Wallenstein's castle, where I had to engage our guide in talk while Hector cut a hair from the tail of Wallenstein's charger. In one room high up, formerly a council chamber, we were shown the window from which obstreperous councillors were thrown; we leant out while my father hung on to us, to see the depth they had to fall. This is the one described in "Karl-Ludwig's Window," in this book.

It was on our way to Prague that we saw snow-capped mountains for the first time, a never-to-be-forgotten experience. Any Celt will know the sort of awesome thrill one gets.

Fortunately, Innsbruck was the last place on our tour, for we were fagged out, and on arriving at Davos, where we were to spend several months, we lay low for a week, drank much milk and took stock of our fellow-guests at the Hôtel Belvedere.

And then we let ourselves go!

My father was soon nicknamed "the Hen that hatched out ducklings," and some middle-aged, self-sacrificing men tried to be extra fathers to us, but it was no use. Swiss air and freedom went to our heads—nothing but an avalanche would have stopped us.

Tennis, paper-chases, riding, dancing, climbing, searching for marmots on the high reaches, occupied our bodies, and lectures on all manner of learned subjects and painting lessons kept our brains busy. Professor Meyer, a painter of birds of prey, was a teacher after our own hearts. He understood that we *had* to play some wild game before settling down to work. Usually we got to his flat before he was ready for us, and crept into his bedroom; presently a search began, and before he knew where he was he found himself in the midst of a pillow-fight—that or a wild scrimmage round the studio, and then we settled down, first eating some excellent cakes he fetched hot from the kitchen.

Hector learnt pastel from him, and did a very good picture of an eagle, life-size, bringing a seagull to her young ones.

John Addington Symonds had a house at Davos; he and Hector played chess together, and found they had a taste for heraldry in common.

The winter was even more fascinating than the summer—we were tobogganing all day, sometimes at night as well, and "tailed" behind sleighs to far-off runs, picnicking in the sun and snow. Charlie and Uncle Wellesley came out, and the bigger indoor entertainments began, fancy dress and domino balls, sheet and pillow-case dances, theatricals, etc. No better "coming-out" could any young thing desire, it was certainly the happiest winter we three had ever spent. Davos in those days was a friendly, jolly place, not at all fashionable.

We left it in April and went to stay at Schloss Salenstein, on the Swiss side of Lake Constance, the home of some very charming people whom we met at Davos.

Then to England, where we took a house, absurdly large for us, at Heanton, four miles from Barnstaple, also four miles from the aunts. Occasionally they came to visit us, one at a time, but were not encouraged to stay long. On the whole we were far too kind to them—so much water had flowed under the bridge since Broadgate days, and we were now topdogs and they knew it. Moreover, they had mellowed a bit, and Aunt Tom especially was devoted to Hector. She was such an original character we had to forgive her much, simply because of her unusualness. We were certainly blessed in our near relatives in one respect, we had not one who could be called dull!

"GILLIE"

Charlie, having failed, unfortunately, for the Army, being the only one of us with bad sight, left for the Burma Police. At Heanton we had for the first time a dog of our own, a fox-terrier, who accompanied Hector on all his explorings. Toby, our cat, we brought from Broadgate; she was delighted to have us back, also to find so many hares in the field at the bottom of the garden, but unhappily through them she met her death from some beast of a keeper; her kitten had the same fate, and we were too sad to have another cat.

It was while roaming the country-side that Hector got to know the Devon character so well. The incidents in "The

Blood-Feud of Toad-Water" really happened; our rector knew the people. There was also a witch in our neighbourhood who had uncanny powers, but we never met her.

For two years we lived at Heanton, studying under my father's direction, then left it for a season in town. Then back to Davos for the winter.

We had no more painting lessons there; our old friend had died the year before. We soon got together a "Push," of which Hector was the leading spirit, and on one or two occasions we literally painted the place red and blue with Aspinall's enamel. There was a very pious hotel, the Hôtel des Iles, which received Hector's most artistic efforts. Six of us one night kept guard while he painted devils in every stage of intoxication on its pure walls.

The theatricals were on a more ambitious scale than two years previously. Hector took the part of the old lawyer in "Two Roses"; I heard an old colonel say he had created the part.

We had curling for the first time that winter, a game my father and Hector played a great deal, and some exciting toboggan races. But the event that set the seal on our activities was the gorgeous hoax we played on the Hôtel des Iles. It had committed the unforgivable crime in Hector's eyes of being mean.

The four English hotels at Davos (the Hôtel des Iles was one) at the beginning of the winter season elected each an Amusement Committee, which provided the various entertainments, dances, etc., for the season, sending round the hat for the funds, and it was the custom for each hotel to invite the guests of the others to the weekly dances, concerts, etc.

The Hôtel des Iles was the only one that invited no one to anything—the fault, of course, of the guests, not of the proprietor. They collected the money and—spent it on a dinner to themselves!

This, naturally, we could not stand, so the "Push," at the end of the winter season, decided they should give an entertainment that would be talked about. Hector, whose writing was not known there, wrote the invitations.

"The Hôtel des Iles requests the pleasure of the company of the Hôtel Belvedere's visitors on 20th March.

" 'Box and Cox.'

"LE PETIT HOTEL."

This last, we heard, was an improper play, and was chosen to attract the foreigners.

These invitations were sent to the English hotels and to some of the visitors at the Kurhaus. We picked out Russian princes, German barons, Italian counts, etc., and we left out the distant chalets, so that no one should be put to any expense in hiring sleighs. I wanted to stay and see the fun, but Hector said he had not the nerve to look innocent. The replies, we stated on the invitations, should be sent to two men who, we knew, had left the Hôtel des Iles, and naturally were forwarded on to them.

As the Hôtel des Iles people were so unco' guid and kept so much to themselves, they did not mix in the life of Davos and so knew nothing of the excitement their invitation caused.

A Scottish girl, one of our "Push," sent us a thrilling account of the evening. The English hotels were warned in time, not so the people at the Kurhaus, who arrived in strength.

Then there was pandemonium, and a babel of imprecations assailed the chaste ears of the innocent inmates. "I know who did it," shouted an irascible man, and rushing home for a horsewhip he hurled himself into the room of a guiltless American. I mean he was not one of the "Push." Fortunately explanations were satisfactory, and no one was whipped. I believe the authorship of the hoax was never guessed. We heard long afterwards a rumour that early next winter the Hôtel des Iles gave a concert to which everybody was invited and no one turned up!

We went to stay with Aunt Tom at Pilton, that spring of 1893, and in June Hector left for a post my father had got for him in Burma, in the Military Police.

Charlie met him on arrival and they both stopped in Rangoon with the Deputy Inspector-General of Police.

Hector was in Burma only thirteen months and had seven fevers in the time. He got a lot of enjoyment from the animal life surrounding him—to be on a horse was one great delight, and to be at close quarters with wild animals was another.

He also, as his letters show, appreciated the good qualities and resourcefulness of the Burmese servants; whether other masters have found them so all-round useful I do not know, but Hector had the gift of attracting willing service wherever he was. The Burman is fond of animals, particularly little animals, and saw nothing extraordinary in a tiger-cat as a pet. I have quoted, in the following letters, almost exclusively the bits dealing with animals, because they are the most characteristic of him.

SINGU, *June 5th,* —93.

MY DEAR E.

The heat during the last few days has been scorching, and I have been quite knocked off my legs in consequence. . . . This is a dreadfully noisy place when one is not feeling well; there are the children: the little brats have a remarkably good time of it, they are never whacked or scolded, and they take a deliberate pleasure in howling at the slightest opportunity; you never heard such yells, they throw all their little heathen souls—if they have any—into the performance. I should like to spank them for ever, stopping, of course, for meal times. . . . Then during the night, the frogs and owls and lizards have necessarily lots to say to each other, and whenever my pony hears another neigh she whinnies back, and being a mare always insists on having the last word. As to the dogs they go on at intervals during the twenty-four hours, like the Cherubim which rest not day or night. Have you ever seen a dog bark and yawn at the same time? I did the other day and nearly had a fit; it reminded me of a person saying the responses in church. The most welcome noise of all is the whistle of the steam-boat, especially when it brings the English mail. . . . I am agreeably surprised with my servants, they are quick, resourceful, seem honest, and are genuinely attached to their master's interests; of course they are more or less stupid, they are human beings. . . . I had quite a nursery establishment last week; I found a little house-squirrel which had just left its nest, on my verandah; it is like a large dormouse, silver grey with a mauve grey tail, and orange buff underneath; it lives upon milk, and is very tame and snoomified. . . . Then there was a duckling; I thought of putting it with the squirrel, but the latter looks upon everything as meant to be eaten and the duck had broad views on the same subject, so I thought they had better live in single blessedness. As the squirrel occupied the only empty biscuit tin the duck had to go into the waste-paper basket where it was quite happy.

SINGU, 17.6.93.

I am rather excité over a pony I have unearthed with zebra markings on its legs; Darwin believed that the horse, ass, zebra, quagga and hemonius were all evolved from an equine animal striped like the zebra but differently constructed, and in his book on the descent of domestic animals he attached great importance to some zebra-like markings which he observed on an Exmoor pony; so my discovery may be of some interest. . . . This is a disappointing place as far as the flora is concerned; I have not seen any decent flowers or shrubs, except a kind of magnolia which is common here. . . .

Aunt Tom's first letter was full of her grievances—so interesting to read; really if Providence persecuted me in the way it does her, I should be too proud to go to Heaven. Her complaint of loneliness amused me. If she is lonely in a place with 13,000 inhabitants it's her own fault. My boy continues to give satisfaction in regard to cooking, the way he serves chicken up as beefsteak borders on the supernatural.

I amuse myself by painting, when the midges are not too troublesome. I am doing a picture of the coronation of Albert II, Archduke of Austria, in 1437; not a proper picture but a sort of heraldic procession like you would see in old tapestries. The arch-bishop of Trèves looks very smart on a fiery bay; I shall never forget the trouble I had to find his arms at the Brit. Museum.

MWÉHINTHA OUTPOST, 26.7.93.

I meant to have written to you last mail, but Mr. Carey arrived by the boat and paid me a long visit—it was a relief to have some one human to talk to—and I had to get ready for going out in the district; you see I have taken to district visiting in my old age. The place is so inundated that no pony can get out so I had to go by boat. . . . The Maid of Sker is charmed with her new quarters, she sees so much more life than formerly, and instead of having to thump on the earth floor when she wants anything, she can now rap her fore hoofs against the wooden partitions, which makes fifty times as much noise and ensures a prompt attendance. . . . There are most charming birds here now the rains are on, egrets, bitterns, pelicans, storks, pond-herons, etc. Shwepyi (the 1st guard on my route) is a great stronghold of these birds, as in the dry weather there are 2 large lakes there and in the rains it is all one big swamp; so when I arrived there last night I determined to make a hurried excursion next morning before leaving for this place. Accordingly I went forth this morning in a small sort of canoe with my boy and two men to row. We saw lots of pelicans and other birds but no nests, as most of them don't breed till August. As we were getting back, a Malay spotted dove flew up from a nest in a tree, which hung just over us. I sent one man up to get the eggs but he could not get at it, so I gave it a prod with an oar. There was a yell from the men and as I stood back I saw an enormous snake rise "long and slowly" from the nest and glide into the branches. The man in the tree came down with the agility of three apes. It was a monster snake and looked very venomous. . . . As we were coming here in the big boat we passed a tree on which were several nests with darters sitting on them (the darter is a sort of cross between a gannet and a cormorant), a frightful tree to climb, but one of the natives ran up it like a cat and brought me down a lot of eggs and some young birds for them (the natives) to eat; fancy eating unfledged cormorants—oo-ah! When I got here I found the stockade was ankle deep in water; I had to be dragged up to the guard house in a small boat, which had to be carefully led rour various shallows; it was like the swan scene in Lohengrin.

Owl and oaf thou art, not to see "Woman of no importance" and "Second Mrs. T." The plays of the season; what would I not give to be able to see them!

For the last three days I have been at this place (can't remember the name, but it's six miles from Mandalay) where a high festival is being held in honour of two local deities of great repute, called the Nats. Their history is briefly this: they were two brothers who were ordered by the king to build a temple here, which they did, but omitted two bricks, for which reason the king killed them, in the impulsive way these Eastern monarchs have. After they were dead they seemed to think they had gone rather cheap and they made themselves so unpleasant about it that the king gave them permission to become deities, and built them a temple, and here they are, don't you know. Just that. The original temple with the vacant places for the missing bricks is still here; this is not an orthodox Buddhist belief but the Nats are held in great esteem in Upper Burma and parts of China, and this show is held here every year in their honour. The whole thing is so new to me that I will describe it at some length. Of course I had to come here as the presence of a European officer is necessary to keep order, and twenty-five police had to be drafted here. No martyr ever suffered so much on account of religion as I have. When I arrived the Nats were being escorted to the river to bathe, accompanied by unearthly music which sent the pony I was riding spinning round like a weathercock in a whirlwind. Then I came to where the chief show is held and to my horror I found a solitary chair had been placed on an elevated platform for my especial use, to which I was conducted with great ceremony; I am not sure the orchestra did not try to strike up the National Anthem. I inquired wildly for Carey, but was told he was with his wife somewhere. I was in terror lest they might expect a speech, and how could I get up and tell this people, replete with the learning of centuries of Eastern civilization, "this animal will eat rice"? Fortunately the sparring commenced at once and was very absorbing to watch; two men fight with hands and legs and go for each other like cats, the one who draws blood first wins. I was quite disappointed to see them stop as soon as one was scratched. I had hoped (such is our fallen nature) that they would fight to the death and was trying hurriedly to remember whether you turned your thumbs up or down for mercy. Some of the encounters were very exciting, but I had to preserve a calm dignity befitting the representative of Great Britain and Ireland, besides which my chair was in rather a risky position and required careful sitting. Noblesse oblige. Then Carey came and told me that he had got quarters in the monastery grounds . . . and had got me a house adjoining the show-place. Not only does it adjoin the building, but it forms part of it and opens on to the arena! The hours of performance are from 10 a.m. to 3 p.m., and from 8 p.m. to 6 a.m. There are two bands. During performances my dining-room is a sort of dress-circle, so I have to get my meals when I can. As to sleep, it's not kept on the premises, while the heat is so great that you could boil an egg on an iceberg. There are also smells. The acting is not up to much but the audience are evidently charmed with it. I go to bed at ten, finding two hours quite enough, but when I get up at 5.30 the audience are applauding as vigorously as ever. Then I am worried to death by princesses; some of the native magistrates' wives are relatives of the ex-king and fancy themselves accordingly. One old lady, who carries enough jewels for twenty ordinary princesses, takes an annoying interest in me and is always pressing me to partake of various fruits at all hours of the day. She asked me, through Mrs. Carey, how old I was, and then told me I was too tall for my age, obligingly showing me the height I ought to be. It reminded me of another royal lady's dictum "All persons above a mile high to leave the Court." I told her that in this damp climate one must allow something for shrinkage, and she did not press the matter.

It is no sinecure to keep order with this huge mob of mixed nationalities, and I shall be glad when it is all over.

SINGU,
6 *Sept.*, 93.

. . . I found the tiger-kitten quite wild; pretended it had never seen me before, so I had to go through the ceremony of introduction again. I soon made it tame again, and we have great games together. It has not learnt how to drink properly yet and immerses its nose in the milk, then it gets mad with the saucer and shakes it, which sends the milk all over its paws, upon which it swears horribly. I have another queer creature in the shape of a young darter (same species of bird as the self-hatching one) which I saw sitting on the river bank en route for here; the men rowed to shore and just picked it up and put it in the boat where it sat as if it didn't care a twopenny damn. What blasé birds those darters are. Then there is the

Problem: To seat two inside.

crow-brought chicken which was carried here by a crow and rescued by the syce; crows often run off with one's chickens but it is not often they add to your poultry. I feel quite like the prophet Elijah (or was it Elisha?) who was boarded by ravens. Milk is scarce now, but the kitten has to have some of my scanty store, while the ponies feel very annoyed if they don't get a bit of bread now and then; I believe I am rather expected to share my sardines with the darter, but I draw the line there! The Burmans have not collected any eggs for me yet; my boy says the birds are "too much upstairs living." Frightfully thrilling! . . .

The kitten throws off the cat and assumes the tiger when it is fed; I have to throw it its food (generally the head of a chicken) and then bolt; it is making the day hideous with its growling now, as I gave it the head and wing, and it is trying to eat both at once.

MADAYA, 15.9.93.

A day or two before I left (headquarters) I was enjoying my midday tub, when my boy came and announced that a big bear had been caught and was being brought up to me; I implored him not to do anything so rash but he went away saying "Master bringing, yes." The bathroom is comparatively small and I knew that if a large bear were introduced there would be unpleasantness. I hastily forgave my enemies and tried to say my prayers, but the only one I could remember was the prayer for fine weather. As it happened my boy meant bird when he said bear, having caught a large sort of buzzard which naturalists have dignified with the name of hawk-eagle; so I left off praying for fine weather and unforgave my enemies forthwith. The bird has fine plumage but a very sinister expression; when I go near it, it opens its mouth, elevates its crest and glares at me with baleful eyes.

OHNMIN, 17.9.93.

I left Madaya yesterday. . . . My new pony I have called "Microbe" on account of his diminutive size. Poor little neglected beast, he looked on so modestly and wistfully when the mare was being given her corn and he was so charmed and thankful when he found he was going to have some too: and when he had a plantain brought him for dessert he began to think with "Mrs. Erlynne" that the world was "an intensely amusing place." . . . At Yenetha my bullock cart had to be stopped, as two bears were walking along the path in front; I was on ahead, so missed seeing them. It is ever thus. . . . The *Mandalay Herald* had an article on the Toungbein Pwé, in which it said, "Many Europeans graced the proceedings with their presence, but the one who was most generally noticed and admired was a police-officer in full khaki uniform." This is rather rough on me, as I was the only European in uniform there.

HÔTEL DE FRANCE,
MANDALAY,
24 *Oct.*, 93.

. . . The tiger-kitten has had a nice cage made for it, with an upstair apartment to sleep in, but every afternoon it comes out into my room for an hour or two and has fine romps. It would make a nice pet for you but it would be an awful trouble sending it—it might die—and it won't be safe when it grows up. It goes into lovely tiger attitudes, when it thinks I'm looking.

. . . Tell Mrs. Byrne there is no immediate danger of my marrying a Burmese wife; there was a woman at Singu—ugly as a Fury—who, I think, had great hopes, but my boy, always ready to save me trouble, married her himself; he had one wife already, but that was a trifle. I impress upon him that he may have as many as he likes, within reasonable limits, but no babies. To this rule there is no exception. When I was out in the district if a child howled in any neighbouring hut men were sent at once to stop it; if it wouldn't stop it was conducted out of earshot; wouldn't you like to do that with English brats! How rabid the mothers would get!

HÔTEL DE FRANCE,
MANDALAY,
30 *Oct.*, 93.

. . . An old lady came to the hotel last week, one of those people with a tongue and a settled conviction that they can manage everybody's affairs. She had the room next to mine—connected by a door—and I was rather astonished when the proprietor came that evening, and with great nervousness, said that there was an old lady in the next room and er—she was rather er—fidgety old lady and er—er—er—there was a door connecting our rooms. I was quite mystified as to what he was driving at but I answered languidly that the door was locked on my side and there was a box against it, so she could not possibly break in. The proprietor collapsed and retired in confusion; I afterwards remembered that the "cub" had spent a large portion of the afternoon pretending that this door was a besieged city, and it was a battering ram. And it does throw such vigour into its play. I met the old lady at dinner and was greeted with an icy stare which was refreshing in such a climate. That night the kitten broke out in a new direction; as soon as I went up to bed it began to roar; "and still the wonder grew, so small a throat could give so large a mew." The more

I tried to comfort it the more inconsolable it grew. The situation was awful—in my room a noise like the lion-house at
4 p.m., while on the other side of the door rose the beautiful
Litany of the Church of England. Then I heard the rapid
turning of leaves, she was evidently searching for Daniel to
gain strength from the perusal of the lion's den story; only
she couldn't find Daniel so fell back upon the Psalms of David.
As for me, I fled, and sent my boy to take the cage down to the
stable. When I came back I heard words in the next room
that never came out of the Psalms; words such as no old lady
ought to use; but then it is annoying to be woken out of your
first sleep by a rendering of "Jamrach's Evening Hymn." She
left. The beast has behaved fairly well since, except that it eat
up a handkerchief. . . . It also insisted on taking tea with
me yesterday and sent my cup flying into my plate, trying
meanwhile to hide itself in the milk jug to prove an alibi. I am
getting as bad as Aunt Charlotte with her perpetual cats, but
I have seen very few human beings as yet, every one being
away, as this is a sort of holiday time. . . .

MANDALAY,
1 Feb., 94.

. . . I had a delightful petition brought me by a native in
my guard who had got a Burman clerk to write it for him;
he wanted to resign the police and his reasons were that his
father and mother had died after him and that his uncle was
generously ill. I hear you have a Persian kitten; of course I,
who have the untameable carnivora of the jungle roaming in
savage freedom through my rooms, cannot feel any interest
in mere domestic cats, but I am not intolerant and I have no
objection to your keeping one or two. My beast does not show
any signs of getting morose; it sleeps on a shelf in its cage
all day but comes out after dinner and plays the giddy goat
all over the place. I should like to get another wild cat to chum
with it, there are several species in Burma: the jungle-cat, the
bay-cat, the lesser leopard-cat, the tiger-cat, marbled cat,
spotted wild-cat, and rusty-spotted cat; the latter, I have read,
make delightful pets.

I hope you have no more bother with servants; my boy gives me notice about once a month but I never think of accepting it; if he doesn't know a good master I know a good servant, to paraphrase an old remark. He has a great idea of my consequence and of his own reflected importance; I sent him to a village with a message, and Beale A.S.P., who was expecting some fowls from that place, asked if they had been sent by him; he told me he should never forget the tone in which he said "I am Mr. Munro's boy!" Civis Romanus sum.

MANDALAY,
7 *Feb.*, 94.

. . . The men who bring grass carry it in two bundles thus:

the other day just as my grass man was bringing the fodder into the stable the mare came up from behind and catching

hold of the hind bundle gave it a violent jerk, which brought the whole bag of tricks to the ground. I luckily had no stays on or they would certainly have burst.

MANDALAY, 11.2.94.

I went to watch a game of polo last week; I long to play, and I am told that Gordon, of the military police, would mount any one who cared to play, but at present I can scarcely find time to go and look on, much less go in for it regularly. . . .

I am very interested in watching the vultures which congregate in great numbers just here; there are three kinds, 2 brown and 1 black; the latter is a fine bird and very much cock of the walk; whenever one comes to a carcase the brown birds have to leave off eating and wait till he's finished, trying to look as if they weren't in the least hungry. Usually only one eats at a time at a small carcase, but this morning there was a regular Rugby scrimmage over a particularly "ripe" pariah puppy, about 14 birds struggling for the choice morsel. Among the vultures I was astonished to see a lovely black eagle (Neopus Malayensis) but just as I got my field-glasses to bear on him, off he flew.

MANDALAY,
30 *March*, 94.

. . . My boy has just got me some crows' eggs; the Burmans don't quite approve of my taking them as they have an idea that the spirits of their grandmothers turn into crows, but I cannot be expected to respect the eggs of other people's grandmothers. Some absurd owls built themselves a nest inside my roof, which was a rash thing to do; of course I promptly took care of their eggs for them. Where would one find English servants who, besides cooking one's food and bottle-washing generally, hunted for birds' eggs and routed out police cases (my boy is of more use to me that way than any of my police men, and is invaluable in the witness box, as he will swear not only to what he saw, but to what he thinks I should like him to have seen)? Fancy saying to an English cook "Dinner at 7 sharp, and I've three guests coming; and, by the way, just see if the buzzard's nest in the high elm has any eggs in it; and while you're about it find out if there is any gambling going on in the Red Lion, etc., etc." Pedrica would have wept scalding tears at such requests.

MAYMYO,
23.4.94.

I am still delighted with this place, it is delightfully cool and we have whist every night and dine and breakfast in each other's houses rather more frequently than in our own; not much work to do, and a fair amount of sport to be had. . . . I heard a good story of some police officer to whom one of the Petty Burman princelings wrote an official letter, styling himself as usual "Lord of a 100 elephants," etc., etc. The police officer in reply called himself Lord of 1 pony, a half-bred terrier, 3 puppies, 13 fowls, and 1 duck. The princeling kicked up no end of a row.

My goose has hatched out a brood of goslings in spite of 40 miles' transit in a jolting bullock cart.

MAYMYO,
26.5.94.

Don't count your chickens after they're hatched; it's quite as fatal as it was to number one's subjects in David's time. I was writing to Mr. Lamb out in the jungle last week and telling him what gentlemanly geese and ducks I had and how they multiplied exceedingly and waxed fat, etc., when a confounded messenger rode up with the following letter from the Head Constable:

"Your syce report that 2 goose and 2 gooseling, duck 3, hen 1, died yesterday with deceased. Syce weeping tears,
"Your obedient servant, etc.
"P.S. I saw them lying dead and ordered them to dry in the sun."

English's poultry are dying too; he has just built a swagger fowl house so I wrote and told him that he was like the Rich Fool who built bigger barns, not that I wished to suggest for a moment that he was rich.

In the summer months Hector got malaria very badly, and in August had to resign and come home, to my great delight. He told me that while lying in bed, feeling wretchedly ill, in some hotel, he heard footsteps passing in the corridor and called out. A German, a visitor like himself, and a stranger to Hector, came in and asked what was the matter? Hector told him he wanted a servant to bring him something to drink; the German stood and argued that it was not his business and he could not attend to sick people, neither should he give a message to any one, and then departed. Of course he may have been mad, or madder than usual. It was some time after that Hector attracted the attention of a servant passing by and got what he wanted.

My father went to meet him in London and found he was too ill to travel down to Devon at once, so they stopped in town for a time, a nurse was engaged, and he gradually got better.

When he did arrive home, although looking ghastly ill, he lost no time in getting well, and soon bought a horse for the hunting season. But the fevers had weakened him so much that he could not last out a whole day's hunting until quite the end of the season.

However, we had some lovely times out together, in the hilly country between Devon and Cornwall, and these were priceless opportunities for Hector to study Devon types.

We had settled down at Westward Ho, in those days a gay and jolly place, and separated by eleven miles from the aunts.

A fox terrier, some Persian cats, and Agag, a jackdaw, with a passion for bathing, were our pets at that time. Hector shared that passion—not that they bathed together, but, wherever water was, he was not happy unless he was in it. We thought of keeping bears, but there were difficulties in the way, how to get them, chiefly. If a merchant travelling in wild animals had come our way, he would not have passed our gates in vain.

In the summer, in addition to sea-bathing and riding, there was tennis, a game Hector loved more than any other, and we had lots of fun on our sporting "putting" green, but apart from putting he never played golf.

Not more than three miles from Westward Ho there lived another witch, known personally to our housemaid, whose brother had been uncivil to her one day, and who was punished by a plague of creeping things all over him, which only left him next morning; but she is not the original of the witch in Hector's stories.

In 1896, Hector left for London, to earn his living by writing. Some Devon friends introduced him to Sir Francis Gould (then Carruthers Gould), who launched him in the literary world. He wrote for the *Westminster Gazette* political satires, called "Alice in Westminster," illustrated by Carruthers Gould, and afterwards published in book form, as *The Westminster Alice.*

In these sketches all the characters are public men, chiefly Cabinet Ministers, portrayed as the animals, etc., in *Alice in Wonderland.*

These were followed in 1902 by the *Not So Stories,* also political satires.

The Munro clan has always been composed of fighters and writers. Our grandfather, a colonel in the Indian Army, had a great compliment paid him by the Marquis Wellesley of his day, who said that he wrote purely classical language. His writing was entirely, I believe, on Indian politics. Aunt Tom told us this—she always said Hector had inherited his grandfather's gift. At any rate, he wrote naturally and never went through a literary correspondence course. My mother's mother was a very clever woman, and she, through her mother, belonged to the Macnab clan. So Hector was Celtic on both sides of his family.

To me, his strongest characteristics were—whimsicality, keen sense of humour, love of animals, and pride in being Highland. There are people who think that to be fond of animals means domestic animals only; to include wild ones shows madness. Well—Hector must have been raving! It is possible to get a good deal more out of madness than sane people have any conception of!

Another characteristic was his indifference to money. His attitude to business is shown in "Clovis on the Romance of Business," in this volume.

I have kept, unfortunately, very few of his letters written from town. Some, in fact, I destroyed as soon as read, because my father insisted on reading any letters his sons ever wrote, and Hector and I sometimes had plans which we did not divulge to him at once.

Here is an extract from one written when he was chumming with a friend, one Tocke.

My Dear E.

The duck was a bird of great parts and as tender as a good man's conscience when confronted with the sins of others. Truly a comfortable bird. Tockling is looking well and is in better health and spirits generally, and everything in the garden's lovely. Except the "Cambridgeshire" which we all came a cropper over. We put our underclothing on the wrong horse and are now praying for a mild Winter.

Sometimes when I left Westward Ho for a short visit, he came down to "understudy" me, chiefly in looking after the animals, and to see that Aunt Tom, who made a bee line for our house as soon as she knew I had started, did not have everything at sixes and sevens before I came back. This is one from home:

Aunt Tom came on a visit the day Ker left, but I am still understudying your place. She is horrified at the rapidity of my marketing (which has been so far successful), but I pointed out to her that it was doubtful economy to spend an hour trying to save a few halfpennies on the price of vegetables when other people spent pounds to snatch a short time by the seaside—and the quicker I marketed the sooner I got back. Of course she was not converted to my view. . . . On Wednesday we drove to Bucks and met a menagerie, so with two other traps we turned into a field to let it pass. Bertie and I went in on both nights to see the beasts, and made friends with the young trainer, who was quite charming, and had sweet little lion cubs (born in the first coronation week) taken out of their cage and put into our arms, also seductive little wolf-puppies which you would have loved.

He spent much time in the British Museum Reading Room getting material for his book, *The Rise of the Russian Empire*. This was published in 1900, his only entirely serious book, tracing the beginnings of Russian history to the time of Peter the Great.

A friend writes that he is sorry the book is so little known, "for it is better written and more interesting than Rambaud's *History of Russia*, which I fancy is still the most widely read book on this subject."

Hector himself had not a great opinion of the book. He was charmed with the remark of our coachman who asked for the loan of it. I don't know how much of it he read, but one day he said to Hector, "I've read your book, sir, and I must say I shouldn't care to have written it myself."

Hector said it was the biggest compliment he had ever had.

The *Bookman* considered he had provided "an historical outline of no little value."

In August 1901 he had the experience of going to Edinburgh with Aunt Tom. At one time I wished that she had invited me too, but not after reading the following account.

EDINBURGH, 17.8.01.

MY DEAR E.

Travelling with Aunt Tom is more exciting than motorcarring. We had four changes and on each occasion she expected the railway company to bring our trunks round on a tray to show that they really had them on the train. Every 10 minutes or so she was prophetically certain that her trunk, containing among other things "poor mother's lace," would never arrive at Edinburgh. There are times when I almost wish Aunt Tom had never had a mother. Nothing but a merciful sense of humour brought me through that intermittent unstayable outpour of bemoaning. And at Edinburgh, sure enough, her trunk was missing!

It was in vain that the guard assured her that it would come on in the next train, half-an-hour later; she denounced the vile populace of Bristol and Crewe, who had broken open her box and were even then wearing the maternal lace. I said no one wore lace at 8 o'clock in the morning and persuaded her to get some breakfast in the refreshment-room while we waited for the alleged train. Then a worse thing befel—no baps! There were lovely French rolls but she demanded of the terrified waiter if he thought we had come to Edinburgh to eat bread!

In the midst of our bapless breakfast I went out and lit upon her trunk and got a wee bit laddie to carry it in and lay it at her very feet. Aunt Tom received it with faint interest and complained of the absence of baps.

Then we spent a happy hour driving from one hostelry to another in search of rooms, Aunt Tom reiterating the existence of a Writer to the Signet who went away and let his rooms 30 years ago, and ought to be doing it still. "Anyhow," she said, "we are seeing Edinburgh," much as Moses might have informed the companions of his 40 years' wanderings that they were seeing Asia. Then we came here, and she took rooms after scolding the manageress, servants and entire establishment nearly out of their senses because everything was not to her liking. I hurriedly explained to everybody that my aunt was tired and upset after a long journey, and disappointed at not getting the rooms she had expected; after I had comforted two chambermaids and the boots, who were crying quietly in corners, and coaxed the hotel kitten out of the waste-paper basket, I went to get a shave and a wash—when I came back Aunt Tom was beaming on the whole establishment and saying she should recommend the hotel to all her friends. "You can easily manage these people," she remarked at lunch, "if you only know the way to their hearts." She told the manageress that I was frightfully particular. I believe we are to be here till Tuesday morning, and then go into rooms· the hotel people have earnestly recommended a lot to us.

Aunt Tom really is marvellous; after 16 hours in the train without a wink of sleep, and an hour spent in hunting for rooms, her only desire is to go out and see the shops. She says it was a remarkably comfortable journey; personally I have never known such an exhausting experience.

y. a. b.

H. H. Munro.

I told Hector once that Aunt Tom's character should be immortalized in some story.

"I shall write about her some day," he said, "but not until after her death."

She died in 1915 when he was learning to be a soldier, and has only appeared sketchily in his stories; "The Sex That Doesn't Shop," is chiefly about her.

Somewhere before 1902 Hector had a severe attack of double pneumonia in London. After his recovery he seemed to be much stronger than he had ever been before and continued so for the rest of his life.

In 1902 he was in the Balkans as correspondent for the *Morning Post*, a part of the world that had always attracted him.

To find a horse to ride, a river to bathe in and a game of tennis or bridge, were his first considerations after work had been seen to.

SOPHIA, 7.1.03.

Have been elected a visiting member of the Union Club, which is the social hub of the local universe; the English vice-consul and I fell into each other's arms when we each discovered that the other played Bridge. I have voluminous discussions in French with some of the leaders in the Bulgarian Parliament; I don't mean to say the discussions take place there; mercifully neither can criticize the other's accent.

Don't get humpy with L. B.; it is part of his nature to do odd things and he will never be otherwise. I can imagine him walking out of Heaven and saying, "This place is run by the Jews." And at heart he is friendly.

Wyntour sent me a tiny silver crucifix to keep off vampires, which up to the present it has done.

USKUB, 20.4.03.

This is the most delightfully outlandish and primitive place I have ever dared to hope for. Rustchuk was elegant and up-to-date in comparison. The only hotel in the place is full; I am in the other. A small ragged boy swooped on my things and marched before me like a pillar of dust, while two blind beggars came behind with suggestions of charitable performances on my part. Then I was walked upstairs and offered the alternative of sharing a bedroom with a Turk or a nicer bedroom with two Turks.

I pleaded a lonely and morose disposition and was at last given a room without carpet, stove, or wardrobe, but also without Turks. The only person on the "hotel" staff that I can converse with is a boy who speaks Bulgarian with a stutter. The country round is "apart"; lovely rolling hills and huge snow-capped mountains, and storks nesting in large communities; everything wild and open and full of life. There are two magpies who seem to have some idea of living in this room with me.

SALONIQUE, 9.5.03.

There is a "Young Turk," if you know what that means, staying in this hotel, very interesting and amusing. He has learnt and forgotten a little English, but the other day in the midst of a political discussion in French he took our breath away by starting off at a great rate "Twinkle, twinkle, little star," and went on with more of it than I had ever heard before. It's a funny world.

There is rather a nice Turkish dish one gets here, a cross between a junket and a cream cheese, eaten with sugar.

In the stampede here the other day when the attempt was made on the Telegraph Office I picked up a tiny kitten that was in danger of being trampled on and put it into a place of safety.

There was a highly coloured account of our adventure with the piquet in the *Neue Freie Presse*.

This refers to his experience when "held up" as a dynamiter—he sent the following account to the *Morning Post*:

SALONICA RAILWAY STATION,
April 30, 1903.
(MIDNIGHT.)

The reports which reached Uskub on Wednesday night and this morning of sinister doings at Salonica, of attempts to dynamite the line to Constantinople, and of the Ottoman Bank having been blown up, tempered by a cheerful official optimism that parts of the bank were still standing, prompted an immediate move towards the scene of disturbance.

In company with an American newspaper representative, whose last act in Uskub was to snapshot almost the entire Consular Body, which had turned out to see our departure, I started south by the train leaving at two o'clock in the afternoon along a line dotted throughout its length by frequent picquets, patrols, and small camps of railway guards. Before the train, slightly overdue, drew into the dark and apparently deserted terminal station the news was passed along by obviously demoralized officials that the town was in a state of siege, and that no one could be allowed to leave the station that night.

The first duty of a correspondent is to correspond, and a town in the throes of a revolutionary outbreak seemed to offer more attractions than a railway station tenanted with herded humans.

In the hope of slipping out by a side exit we therefore picked up our valises and made for an apparent outlet some five hundred yards distant across a waste of inconveniently overgrown grass. As a slight precaution against being mistaken for prowling Komitniki we turned down the collars of our overcoats so as to display the white collar, if not of a blameless life, at least of a business that did not call for concealment.

About four hundred yards of the distance had been covered when a frantic challenge in Turkish brought us to a standstill, and five armed and agitated figures sprang forward in the starlight and began to interrogate us at a distance, which they seemed disinclined to lessen. As five triggers had clicked and five rifles were covering us we dropped our valises and "up-handed," but without reassuring our questioners, who seemed to be possessed of a panic which might more reasonably have been displayed on our part.

Neither of us knew a word of Turkish, and Bulgarian was obviously unsuited to the occasion. Never in my study of that tongue have its words come so readily and persistently to my lips, and every French sentence I began become entangled with the phraseology of the debarred language.

The men had reached a point whence they were unwilling to approach nearer, and for a minute or two they took deliberate aim from a ridiculously easy range in a state of excitement which was unpleasant to witness from our end of the barrels.

At last two lowered their rifles, and after stalking round us with elaborate caution managed to secure our hands with a rope or sash-cord, which was hurriedly produced from somewhere. The operation would have been shorter if they had not tried to hold their rifles at our heads at the same time. When it was safely accomplished the statement that I was "Inglesi effendi" and the demand for our Consuls allayed their suspicions to a certain extent, but nothing would induce them to pick up my valise until the light of day should show its real nature, and it is still lying out on the waste land, where, if it explodes violently, no great harm will be done.

Arrived at the railway waiting-room, where the accumulation of apparently several trainloads was gathered in philosophic discomfort, the horrified officials flocked to release us with a haste which made the untying process almost as long as the binding.

The explanations on both sides had to be accepted for the moment, and two loud explosions in the distance made us feel that we had gained our security none too soon.

According to the information, doubtless panic-coloured, which was given us in nervous scraps by non-Turkish railway officials, the town is in a condition which makes it dangerous to venture into the streets, the Ottoman Bank is in ruins, the Colombo and other hotels have been damaged by bombs, and many persons have been killed and wounded.

The exits of the station are closed until daylight. On my asking the members of the picquet why they had not fired they answered that they had only hesitated on seeing our collars, which made them doubt if we were Bulgarian desperadoes.

In the spring of 1904, he was in Warsaw, corresponding for the *Morning Post*. His experiences with young men in Poland and Russia were always the same—he could not get them to be energetic.

WARSAW, 19.6.04.

The American Consul has a schoolboy nephew staying with him, who goes to swimbath every day with me, and afterwards we play tennis, he, I, Consul and an Irish girl. Poles of my own age are pleasant enough, but it is impossible to get them to do anything; on the most scorching days nothing will induce them to join my amphibious afternoons in the Vistula; they agree to come, with every sign of nervous depression, but return presently beaming to say they have remembered they have got a cold and it would be dangerous, etc. . . .

P.S.—A 14 year old Polish kid belonging to the house has constituted himself my valet and carries on my toilet every day with extreme minuteness, besides doing most of my shopping. On a hot day I can thoroughly recommend a syphon of soda-water turned on between the shoulder-blades.

1.8.04.

The amateur valet continues to be amusing. Nearly all the time I have known him he has gone every night to sleep at his aunt's house on the other side of the river, in consequence of a row with his mother. I asked him when matters were going to be smoothed over between him and his hen parent and he said he didn't intend to be reconciled, he only got tea in the morning at home, while at his aunt's house there was always chocolate. After that I realized that the matter was beyond even the healing touch of time; what is home and a mother where no chocolate is?

I have got some more coins, old Russian, Polish, Bohemian, etc., going back to 1300, from a man here who has an immense collection. I fairly took his breath away when he started on mediæval history, as he found I knew rather more about the old lines of east-European princes than he did, and an Englishman is expected to be profoundly ignorant of such things.

Have you thought of getting a wolf instead of a hound? There would be no license to pay and at first it could feed largely on the smaller Inktons, with biscuits sometimes for a change. You would have to train it to distinguish the small Vernon boys from other edible sorts, or else Cook would be coming with trembling lip nigh upon breakfast-time to say there was no milk in the house. Also you and Aunt Tom could do marketing in comfort. Think it over.

The poorer people here have nice feudal ways and kiss your hand on the least provocation. The Russian officers, whatever their private sentiments may be, have not the atrocious manners of the Prussians, which I believe cannot be matched anywhere in Europe. . . . I heard from T——; I had mentioned to her that I had had enough of bad news this year, which I have in one way and another, and she observes that she didn't know that I had experienced misfortune of any sort lately. I suppose it is impossible for her to realize what the loss of that little dog means to you and me. I keep dreaming that he is found, and then comes the waking disappointment. Of course it's worse for you because he was always with you.

In 1904 *Reginald* was published, having first appeared in the *Westminster Gazette*. The characters in the various stories are all imaginary. Reginald is a type composed of several young men, studied during his years of town life; Hector told me that more than one of his acquaintances considered himself the original. Some friends wrote him that the identity of the duchess had been established. He wrote me from Petersburg:

Thanks for your letter and the cuttings. The *Athenæum* consoled me for Aunt Tom's remark that it was a pity the book had been published as, after the *Alice*, people would expect it to be clever and of course be disappointed. The "of course" was terribly crushing but I am able to sit up now and take a little light nourishment.

He was settled in Petersburg in the autumn and had a delightful two years there. I joined him in the winter: with the exception of Davos it was the most perfect time abroad we had ever had together. He always lunched at the Hôtel de France, which was quite a club for journalists; the food was good, and there were generally interesting people to be met there; moreover, being close to the Nevsky Prospekt, it was the hub of Petersburg.

It was to be a very exciting place for us, the day of Father Gapon's attempt, with his legion of followers, to reach the Winter Palace to present his petition to the Tsar. Knowing that there was likely to be trouble, Hector settled that we must go early to the Hôtel de France that Sunday, which by its close proximity to the Palace was the best centre from which to watch events. We were joined at the hotel by a Polish friend and lunched quickly.

Hector and the Pole then went out to scout, leaving me in the smoking-room to watch the street and the archway leading to the Winter Palace.

They soon returned at a trot with a lot of others, troops being in possession of the Palace Square, allowing no one to enter it. The Nevsky Prospekt at this time (between one and two) was the favourite promenade of Russians, as Church Parade in Hyde Park is with us.

The crowds were curious to see what was going on in the Square, but soon came scampering back, being driven by Cossacks, who were using their whips freely. A second time they tried, and this time the Cossacks charged them with drawn swords. Hector and the Pole had gone out by another exit to the Moïka Embankment, and a page presently came to fetch me to them. Here we waited for something to happen. Meanwhile the troops in the Palace Square had fired on the deputation arriving by the bridge, and here there was great slaughter.

Thinking nothing would happen on our side of the hotel, I went in, and immediately soldiers arrived on the scene and fired three volleys. Hector and his friend pressed themselves flat against a doorway; a bullet whizzed past Hector's head and lodged a foot off in the wall.

By 2.50 the Palace Square was cleared of people and the corpses and wounded were being collected. As Hector had to get all the information he could, he took a sleigh to go to another part of the city where the fighting was reported to be severe. He got his news, wired to the *Post* and returned to take me to another hotel, where we dined with one of Reuter's men, who appeared to think the Revolution had begun.

The next two days were very exciting, the Cossacks were doing some killing on their own account, and murdered some unfortunate students merely because they had called out insults to them. They were an evil-looking lot, pronounced Mongolian type, with criminal faces. Hector scowled so at them as they passed, we being in a sleigh going slowly along rather empty streets, that I hurriedly tried to draw his attention to something on the opposite side of the road, seeing that they were scowling worse at us.

For two nights we had to get back to the flat before dark because the electricians had struck and the lampless streets were not safe. Hector went out to forage and had to run the hardest he knew in one street, an officer shouting that his men would shoot any one remaining in that street in two minutes' time. (Fact was, all Petersburg had nerves at that time.) He returned with eggs, sweet biscuits, smoked tongue and Bessarabian wine, snatching them up just as the shops, in a panic, were closing. Better dinner have I never tasted, with excitement as a sauce.

Hardly had we finished our meal when excited Russians, friends of Hector's, dashed in and gave us the news of the latest Cossack atrocities, pacing up and down the room all the time. It was more exciting than any play. On the second evening, after telling us harrowing tales of searching hospitals for his friend, whom at last he found dead, one Russian calmly invited us to go to the opera with him that night! It was such a jump from horrors to frivolity that I could hardly keep grave, especially as Hector was making signs to me, behind the man's back, to refuse.

Hector was the only foreign correspondent whom General Trépoff, Governor of Petersburg, did not send for. The others had given to their papers very high figures for the casualties, and Hector, from information supplied by his spies, put the number of dead at about 1500.

When the excitement had simmered down we did a lot of sight-seeing, and tried to "do" the Winter Palace in one afternoon, but it was too vast. The evening generally saw us at the telegraph office where Hector sent off his report and where we met the other journalists doing the same thing. We both noticed the extraordinary slackness and inertia of Russian men and boys of all classes. This is Hector's impression of men in Russian towns:

ST. PETERSBURG,
August 29, 1905.

The inquiry which has been going on in the columns of the *Morning Post* into the existence and causes of physical deterioration might be extended if Russia were brought within the scope of the discussion to a study of physical stagnation in the life of a nation. Such a study would open out interesting speculations as to the political consequences which such stagnation is likely to have on the immediate future of the race in question.

One of the most striking discoveries which one makes in the course of a residence in this country is the all-prevailing inertia of the stalwart and seemingly lusty Russian race, an inertia that appears to be common to all classes, and to spring from no particular accident of circumstance, unless the long Russian winter can be held partly responsible. I have before alluded to the impression of convalescents out for an airing produced by the heavily overcoated, aimlessly lounging soldiers and sailors off duty in the streets of the capital; the officers, in spite of their brilliant and imposing uniforms, do not succeed much better in imparting a tone of dash and vigour to their surroundings.

A young officer stationed in a town drives from his quarters to his club, from his club to his restaurant, back to his club and so forth, and that represents about the sum of his non-professional exertions; by driving it must not be supposed that he climbs into a high dogcart and steers a spirited pony through the streets. If he possesses a private carriage it takes the form of a roomy, well-cushioned brougham or victoria drawn by a pair of heavy, long-maned, flowing-tailed horses and driven by a fat, bearded coachman swathed in thick quilted garments into the semblance of a huge human sack. In this conveyance he takes the air if the weather should be sufficiently tempting. The daily routine of an old lady at Bath with a taste for cards would not be very widely different, except that she would perhaps go less often to church and never to parade or café chantant.

Brave, charming, and good-natured as the Russian officer is universally acknowledged to be by those who know him, he has certainly no compelling impulse towards the recreations of saddle and greensward, and one contrasts wonderingly the unceasing outdoor programme of an Indian military station under the enervating influence of a tropical atmosphere. One senior officer, probably not of Russian stock, may be seen at times taking horse exercise in the streets of St. Petersburg, and I believe that a letter addressed to this city, "to the General who rides," would find him without difficulty.

With the younger generation of the military caste it is the same story. In the spacious grounds attached to one of the cadet headquarters in St. Petersburg one may find on a late summer evening the youths of the British and German colonies vigorously engaged in football practice or in the milder activities of lawn tennis, while the cadets walk sedately along the gravel paths or find an outlet for their superfluous energies in the game of gorodki, somewhat resembling ninepins.

In civilian walks of life the same stagnation has universal sway; among peasant agriculturists in the country districts and among certain classes of townsfolk there are of course seasons and occasions when energy is a matter of necessity, but when that compulsion of circumstance is removed or non-existent the Russian relapses naturally into an atmosphere of congenial torpidity.

In every Russian town of any size there are thousands or hundreds of well-built, healthy-looking men, ranging from eighteen years upwards, but mostly in the prime of early manhood, who occupy the posts of door-keepers and yard-keepers, and whose most laborious functions consist of a little sweeping and wood-chopping, an occasional errand, and sometimes escorting an over-drunken wayfarer to his destination. For the rest of their time they sleep, or gossip by the hour over sweetened concoctions of weak tea, or play mild baby games with their children or any friendly dog or kitten that comes their way. And in their peaked caps, gay shirts, and high Blücher boots, they convey the impression of a sort of Prætorian Guard in undress.

Probably the custom of dressing nearly every male civilian, from small errand-boys to postmen and such minor officials, in high military boots is responsible for many of our earliest notions of the Russians as a stern, truculent warrior breed. An army, it has been said, marches on its stomach; the Russians for several generations have lived on their boots. If an average British boy were put at an early age into such boots he would become a swashbuckling terror to his family and neighbourhood, and in due course would rove abroad and found an Empire, or at any rate die of a tropical disease. A Russian would not feel impelled by the same influence further than the nearest summer garden.

Hector had a very good little servant at his rooms, but after I left there was a change, and a girl arrived who helped herself to food. Hector and a friend who was chumming with him then noticed that mince-pies were irresistible to her, so one day they opened those that were left over and put mustard underneath the mince-meat. After that nothing was touched, and everything was understood!

From Petersburg Hector went to Paris, in 1906, found himself an *appartement*, and sought for an original servant. One after another he inspected at a Registry Office—all were correct and probably excellent, but not original. At last one offered who gave the desired impression, one Marcellin, and an invaluable valet he proved, with a taste for cooking and an imperturbable temper. Hector attended the French Chamber a good deal and suffered from the closeness of the atmosphere; this probably gave him an attack of "intermittent something, which people insist is influenza, all the symptoms being absent; it might as well be snake-bite."

In addition to writing for the *Morning Post* he wrote some articles in French for a French paper, but not regularly, I think. He had an amusing time in Paris, made many friends (he had a gift for friendship), and having an intelligent interest in food, the only one of our family so gifted, appreciated the restaurants there. But not all the American tourists whom he met had the same appreciation. I think they were chiefly people from *very* country parts. "I seem fated," he wrote once, "to learn the inmost yearnings of American stomachs; was dining at Constan's one night when an elderly American lady was leaving the restaurant after her dinner, and informing the busy manager in a high scream which grew higher and higher as she neared the door: 'I like *roast lamb*. My sister likes *roast lamb*. At the Grand hô-tel Godknowswhere we had some roast lamb that was *real good*. Yes, we both like *roast lamb*.' Then the Roumanian orchestra struck up, so I never knew what her little son's feelings were towards roast lamb."

My father became very ill in May, 1907, and we wired for Hector. The incident in *The Unbearable Bassington* of the little black dog happened to himself. He was playing bridge at a friend's flat and saw the dog, which only appeared to people when bad news was on the way to them. So far he had only heard that my father was ill, the next morning he got the wire to come home, and arrived two days before he died.

A very close friendship existed between the two. Hector told me afterwards that writing for the papers had lost much of its incentive since he had lost his most appreciative reader (my father).

Later in the summer he invited me to stay with him in

Normandy. We lit upon Pourville because it was small and unfashionable (I don't know what it is like now) and picturesque.

We settled ourselves at a newly opened little hotel whose landlady possessed a temperament. Hector chose the hotel; he had an unerring instinct for a place a little out of the ordinary. Next door to our caravanserai was a post-office which sold odds and ends as well as stamps. Choosing some picture post-cards one day I asked how much they were and was answered from behind the counter by Hector, who sold them to me, and some stamps to another customer, suggesting further outlay on his part on various goods, the owner looking on and beaming.

We bathed in the mornings, explored the countryside in the afternoons and sometimes watched the play at the Casino in the evenings, studying types all the time. The place, Pourville, was thick with types; one of them was the original of "The Soul of Laploshka," in "Reginald in Russia." We found he had a reputation for meanness, and in the fulness of time Hector played a hoax on him; if there were a crime on which he had no pity it was meanness, and this man had apparently plenty of money, so there was no shadow of excuse for him.

In September Hector returned to Paris, and next year, 1908, was settled in London. He bought a charming cottage on the Surrey Hills, where I was his tenant; as it was only twenty-three miles from London he could come down whenever he liked. With Logie, my Dandy, and Ho, the black Persian, and a garden that we planned and made ourselves, we had the most delightful home.

In this garden was a bed planted with May-flowering tulips; we were both of us tulip mad. One night at supper I set fire to the lamp by swinging it to release the oil.

We stood gazing at the flames, wondering what to do.

"Earth is the best thing," said Hector, and dashed into the garden.

A friend, supping with us, who had more sense than either of us, seized the hearth-rug and extinguished the lamp under it. When Hector at last appeared I said to him, "You've been a long time fetching that earth."

"Well," he said, "the tulip bed came first, and of course I couldn't disturb *that*, so I had to go farther on to the cabbage plot."

One summer we had rather a sunless period and I was deploring the effect on the garden. "We will invoke Apollo's aid tonight, round a bonfire," said Hector.

So, with a guest who was with us, we draped sheets round us to look more Grecian and therefore more pleasing to Apollo, while we craved the boon of sunshine. The next day there was a brilliant sun and every day after for three weeks.

In London Hector lived at 97 Mortimer Street, where he did all his writing, and spent his evenings chiefly at his club, the "Cocoa Tree," playing Bridge.

In the summer of 1909, I think it was, the Russian dancers, Nijinsky Karsavina, and the others, first came to London. Hector and his friend of Petersburg days, Mr. Reynolds, gave an "At Home" at a friend's studio, "to meet the dancers." No one to be invited who could not speak French, that being the only foreign language the Russians understood.

It was a *succès fou*, sixty people turned up eager to meet the novelties. The Russians up to that time had been nowhere and were delighted at their first glimpse of English social life and also at being greeted in Russian by their hosts.

I found Nijinsky and another man peering eagerly under a table.

"What is it?" I asked.

"C'est le diable," cried Nijinsky, and out walked an Aberdeen terrier.

He had never seen the breed before from the way he gazed at it. He told me he was surprised not to see bulldogs about. "In Russia we heard that every Englishman walks out accompanied by a bulldog."

We finished that day, a few of us, by dining at the "Gourmets," beloved of Hector and myself. We always dined at some Italian restaurant, because I liked the food, but the "Gourmets" was our favourite. An air of gaiety met us at the door and an air of gaiety we took in with us. It is haunted ground for me now and I never go there. The Café Royal was another favourite place—generally we wound up there. And one New Year's Eve we had hilarious revels with some friends at Gambrinus, dancing afterwards. Hector had thoughtfully provided himself with one of those toys, new at that time, which imitate a dog growling. I think ours *must* have been the liveliest table!

"Foreigners must be puzzled by all this," said he; "I'm sure they never make as much noise themselves."

It was on another New Year's Eve that, meeting a party of strangers, he insisted on seizing hands and dancing "Here we go round the mulberry bush" in Oxford Circus. He could throw himself into whatever he was doing at the moment as though no other kind of life existed; this characteristic he certainly inherited from his mother's family, whose vitality and youngness were uncommon.

Tapestry painting he was very keen on; he painted a large canvas when staying with me, "A Boar-hunt in the Middle Ages"; the background looked exactly as though it were faded needlework. But he did a much better one, which when I saw it for the first time I took for an old French tapestry he had bought in Paris which I had never seen. I wish I knew where it is now; he lent it to a friend who died, and of course his people did not know the ownership of the tapestry and probably gave it away.

In going over Hector's papers I came across a pencilled fragment on "the Garden of Eden." Eve is depicted as a very stubborn, even mule-like character. The serpent simply cannot get her to eat the forbidden fruit. She does not see that any good will come of it, and she is placidly happy in her limited knowledge.

"'The Serpent elaborated all the arguments and inducements that he had already brought forward, and improvised some new ones, but Eve's reply was unfailingly the same. Her mind was made up. The Serpent gave a final petulant wriggle of its coils and slid out of the landscape with an unmistakable air of displeasure.

"'You haven't tasted the Forbidden Fruit, I suppose?' said

a pleasant but rather anxious voice at Eve's shoulder a few minutes later. It was one of the Archangels who was speaking.

" 'No,' said Eve placidly, 'Adam and I went into the matter very thoroughly last night and we came to the conclusion that we should be rather ill-advised in eating the fruit of that tree; after all, there are heaps of other trees and vegetables for us to feed on.'

" 'Of course it does great credit to your sense of obedience,' said the Archangel, with an entire lack of enthusiasm in his voice, 'but it will cause considerable disappointment in some quarters. There was an idea going about that you might be persuaded by specious arguments into tasting the Forbidden Fruit.'

" 'There *was* a Serpent here speaking about it the last few days,' said Eve; 'he seemed rather huffed that we didn't follow his advice, but Adam and I went into the whole matter last night and we came to t—'

" 'Yes, yes,' said the Archangel in an embarrassed voice, 'a very praiseworthy decision, of course. At the same time, well, it's not exactly what every one anticipated. You see Sin has got to come into the world, somehow.'

" 'Yes?' said Eve, without any marked show of interest.

" 'And you are practically the only people who *can* introduce it.'

" 'I don't know anything about that,' said Eve placidly; 'Adam and I have got to think of our own interests. We went very thoroughly—'

" 'You see,' said the Archangel, 'the most elaborate arrangements have been foreordained on the assumption that you *would* yield to temptation. No end of pictures of the Fall of Man are destined to be painted and a poet is going one day to write an immortal poem called "Paradise L—" '

" 'Called what?' asked Eve as the Archangel suddenly pulled himself up.

" ' "Paradise Life." It's all about you and Adam eating the Forbidden Fruit. If you don't eat it I don't see how the poem can possibly be written.' "

"Eve is still dogged—says she has no appetite for more fruit.

"'I had some figs and plantains and half a dozen medlars early this morning, and mulberries and a few mangosteens in the middle of today, and last night Adam and I feasted to repletion on young asparagus and parsley-tops with a sauce of pomegranate juice; and yesterday morning—'

"'I must be going,' said the Archangel, adding rather sulkily, 'If I should see the Serpent would it be any use telling him to look round again—?'

"'Not in the least,' said Eve. Her mind was made up.

. . . .

"'The trouble is,' said the Archangel as he folded his wings in a serener atmosphere and recounted his Eden experiences, 'there is too great a profusion of fruit in that garden; there isn't enough temptation to hunger after one special kind. Now if there was a partial crop failure—' The idea was acted on. Blight, mildew and caterpillars and untimely frosts worked havoc among trees and bushes and herbs; the plantains withered, the asparagus never sprouted, the pineapples never ripened, radishes were worm-eaten before they were big enough to pick. The Tree of Knowledge alone flaunted itself in undiminished luxuriance.

"'We shall have to eat it after all,' said Adam, who had breakfasted sparsely on some mouldy tamarinds and the rind of yesterday's melon.

"'We were told not to, and we're not going to,' said Eve stubbornly. Her mind was made up on the point—"

How she eventually succumbed I don't know. Hector had a special detestation for this type of character, stubborn, placid, unimaginative, like the awful, good child in ".The Story Teller," who is from life, though we never knew her as a child. We tried to change her by playing a few hoaxes off on her—but she had been in the mould too long.

In the summers Hector and I tried various out-of-the-way seaside places, and in one very hot spell we bathed in what he considered an ideal way—we spent the day in the sea with intervals on land, Logie guarding our clothes and food-basket.

Charlie was at this time with his wife and child in Dublin, where he was Governor of Mountjoy Prison, having left the Burma Police service; though stronger than Hector, the climate rather told on him. Hector and I spent Christmas with them one year and next summer we were all together again on the Donegal coast at Innishowen, where, the house being just on the sea, he had as much bathing as he wanted. In London, swimming-baths helped to keep him fit.

All this time he was writing sketches for the *Morning Post*, the *Bystander*, and the *Westminster Gazette*, and some political sketches, illustrated by "Pat," for the *Daily Express*.

In 1910 *Reginald in Russia* was published, a further collection of Reginald's doings; "Judkin of the Parcels" and "The Soul of Laploshka" are from characters he knew.

In 1912 *The Chronicles of Clovis* appeared, Clovis being an irrepressible young man, something after the style of "Reginald," and this year he wrote his first novel, *The Unbearable Bassington*. The chief character is taken from life, but the original, so far, has not had a tragic ending; many of the other characters are also real people, in fact some of the reviews kindly gave clues as to the originals.

There is, as Mr. Reynolds said in his Memoir to *The Toys of Peace*, a little bit of autobiography in the account of the loneliness Comus felt when exiled to Africa. Opinion varied very much about the book—one friend, whom Hector asked for a candid opinion, said it was unbalanced, this Hector rather thought himself. The Press was pretty unanimously enthusiastic, the *Observer* calling it "one of the wittiest books, not only of the year but of the decade," and another paper pronounced it "clever to distraction."

Beasts and Super-Beasts, another collection of short stories, was published in 1914, and late in 1913, *When William Came*. Hector wrote part of it while staying with me near Rye, and in order to get absolute quiet spent hours writing in a wood near, while Logie hunted rabbits.

Many of the characters in that too are from life—one of them, the most sympathetic, the lady of Torywood, being that of a well-known London Conservative hostess, for whom

Hector had a great admiration. Lord Roberts wrote him a most appreciative note, which pleased him tremendously.

The story is an account of the conditions of English life after a successful invasion by the Germans. Two women friends, to whom I lent it during the war, got as far as the middle and dared not finish it, they were more than half afraid that William might come.

Hector chose the name "Saki" from the cup-bearer in the "Rubáiyát" of Omar Khayyám.

> "Yon rising Moon that looks for us again—
> How oft hereafter will she wax and wane;
> How oft hereafter rising look for us
> Through this same Garden—and for *one* in vain!
>
> And when like her, oh, Sákí, you shall pass
> Among the Guests Star-scatter'd on the Grass,
> And in your joyous errand reach the spot
> Where I made One—turn down an empty Glass!"

He loved Persian poetry and Eastern stories; Flecker's "The Golden Journey to Samarkand" was an especial favourite.

For one who knew him only through his books Mr. S. P. B. Mais has an uncanny insight into his character. He wrote of him: "Munro's understanding of children can only be explained by the fact that he was in many ways a child himself: his sketches betray a harshness, a love of practical jokes, a craze for animals of the most exotic breeds, a lack of mellow geniality that hint very strongly at the child in the man. Manhood has but placed in his hands a perfect sense of irony and withheld all other adult traits.

"In 'The Mappined Life' we get for the first time near to the secret of a genius who did not unlock his heart. Here at last, behind the child, the buffoon, the satirist, the eclectic, the aristocrat, the elegant man of the world, we can trace the features of one who discovered that the only way to make life bearable was to laugh at it.

"Meredith would have acclaimed him as a true master of the Comic: posterity will acknowledge him as one of our great writers."

But a friend of Hector's, a man who knew him well,

summed him up best of all, I think, in the following words: "The elusive charm of the man-in-himself—this charm, being the perfume of personality, was even more subtly, strongly felt in his conversation than in anything he ever wrote. We who loved him as the kindliest of companions who was utterly incapable of boring a fellow-creature—man or dog or woman or cat or child of any age you like—always felt the keen sense of honour and strength of purpose and stark simplicity which were his essential qualities. As a companion he was an unfailing antidote to boredom. He loved to make an impracticable jest practical in action. On the way to a mixed dinner we rehearsed an elaborate quarrel which was to lead, by nice gradations of invective, to threats of personal violence. Saki worked out the idea with a sure sense of the theatre, and the crisis came (just before the arrival of the port) when another Scot—the kind who develops a 'mither' in moments of exaltation—had his hand on my shoulder, and was imploring me not to mind what Saki said, for he didn't mean it. He didn't."

In the spring of 1914 he was writing "Potted Parliament" for the *Outlook*, and attended the House regularly for his data. These are some of his characteristic remarks:

"An army moves at the rate of its slowest unit, it is the fate of a Coalition to move at the rate of its most headlong section."

"Mr. Lloyd George expressed unstinted approval of his various taxation schemes; the spectacle of the Chancellor of the Exchequer approving of all his works is almost as familiar as the companion picture of the Chancellor of the Exchequer finding words to express his loathing of the private lives and family histories of his opponents."

"The member for North Carnarvonshire always gives me the impression of one who in his long-ago youth heard the question-half of a very good riddle, and has spent the remainder of his life in the earnest expectation of hearing some one disclose the answer. Even when such politely wearisome speakers as Reginald McKenna are in possession of the House one can see Mr. William Jones, with a happy smile of strained expectancy on his face, listening intently to every syllable that falls from the orator's lips; one of these days, one feels sure, he will give a wild scream of joy and rush away to apply for the Chiltern Hundreds, with his life's desire at last achieved."

"The Scotsman is sometimes accused of being 'slow in the uptake'; he likes to enjoy the full flavour of a joke before he chuckles at it; the 'bubble-and-squeak' brigade on the Ministerial benches like to giggle before they have heard the point —and with regard to some of their own humour there is a good deal to be said for the arrangement."

"Conversations and suggestions with regard to the Amending Bill are supposed to be welcome in Ministerial circles at the present moment. There is one suggestion that has occurred to me that seems so eminently practical that I know it will have no chance of being considered. The Protestants of the North of Ireland regard the prospect of being governed by a Nationalist Parliament with a horror and alarm that is admitted to be genuine; on the other hand, the members representing Protestant Wales have again and again, by an overwhelming vote, recorded their opinion that a Nationalist Parliament would be a tolerant, fair-minded, pleasant, peaceful, and sweetly reasonable body, from which no safeguards need be exacted, and from which no oppression need be apprehended. The Welsh members and their constituents seem as firmly rooted in their championship of a Dublin Parliament as the Ulster Protestants are resolute in their opposition to it. Therefore why not exclude Ulster and include Wales in a Hiberno-Cambrian Parliament. . . . The Nationalists have not been able to win Ulster, but they have always been able to win Wales."

"The political situation has lost none of its gravity, but the House of Commons has lost touch with the political situation. In the House of Lords, which is not at present sitting, a measure is to be introduced on which the hopes and fears of the peacemakers are centred. Lord Haldane announces that he knows the details of this measure, and that therefore his lips are sealed; everybody else's lips are sealed for a precisely opposite reason. . . ."

"The Home Rule Amending Bill passed its third reading in the Upper House. Crewe was dignified, correct, and dispassionate, suggesting to one's mind an archangel who regarded the Creation of the World as a risky and unnecessary experiment but had no intention of saying so. . . ."

"One of the most exasperating features of the House of Commons is its resemblance to an over-crowded kitchen-range. Pots that are at boiling-point have to be set aside to simmer while others take their place."

The next "Potted Parliament" is the last he wrote.

Monday, *August* 3, 1914.

For one memorable and uncomfortable hour the House of Commons had the attention of the nation and most of the world concentrated on it. Grey's speech, when one looked back at it, was a statesman-like utterance, delivered in excellent manner, dignified and convincing. To sit listening to it, in uncertainty for a long time as to what line of policy it was going to announce, with all the accumulated doubts and suspicions of the previous forty-eight hours heavy on one's mind, was an experience that one would not care to repeat often in a lifetime. Men who read it as it was spelled out jerkily on the tape-machines, letter by letter, told me that the strain of uncertainty was even more cruel; and I can well believe it. When the actual tenor of the speech became clear, and one knew beyond a doubt where we stood, there was only room for one feeling; the miserable tension of the past two days had been removed, and one discovered that one was slowly recapturing the lost sensation of being in a good temper. Redmond's speech was the dramatic success of the occasion; it obviously isolated the action of the Labour members and the few, but insistent, Radicals who were clamorous against the war, but one hardly realized at the moment with what feelings of dismay and discouragement it would be read in Berlin.

Of the men who rose in melancholy succession to counsel a standing aloof from the war, a desertion of France, a humble submission to the will of Potsdam in the matter of Belgium's neutrality, one wishes to speak fairly. Many of them are men who have gloatingly threatened us with class war-fare in this country—warfare in which rifles and machine-guns should be used to settle industrial disputes; they have seemed to take a ghoulish pleasure in predicting a not-far-distant moment when Britons shall range themselves in or-ganized combat, not against an aggressive foreign enemy, but against their own kith and kin. Never have they been more fluent with these hints and incitements than during the pres-ent Session; if a crop of violent armed outbreaks does not spring up one of these days in this country it will not be for lack of sowing of seed. Now these men read us moral lectures on the wickedness of war. One is sometimes assured that every man has at least two sides to his character; so one may chari-tably assume that an honest Quaker-like detestation of war and bloodshed is really the motive which influences at the present moment some of these men who have harped so assiduously on the idea—one might almost say the ideal—of armed col-lision between the classes. There are other men in the anti-war party who seem to be obsessed with the idea of snatching commercial advantages out of the situation, regardless of other considerations which usually influence men of honour. The Triple Entente, after all, is no new thing; even if the nature of its obligations was not clearly defined or well understood, at least it was perfectly well known that there were obliga-tions; it was perfectly well known that the people of the other countries involved in its scope believed that there were obligations—at the very least a sentimental sympathy. And this is how the *Daily News* writes of our possible and desirable action at this crisis:

"If we remained neutral we should be, from the commer-cial point of view, in precisely the same position as the United States. We should be able to trade with all the belligerents (so far as the war allows of trade with them); we should be able to capture the bulk of their trade in neutral mar-kets."

There seems to be some confusion of mind in these circles of political thought between a nation of shop-keepers and a nation of shoplifters.

If these men are on the side of the angels, may I always have a smell of brimstone about me.

Hector wired to me when war was declared; his next wire, "Enrolled," is the most exciting and delightful I have ever received. The account of his early days as a Tommy at Shepherd's Bush is given by a comrade of his, at the end of this biography. Hector told a friend that, having written *When William Came*, he ought to go half-way to meet him.

Once in training he had very little time for writing: the following is from Horsham.

29th Nov., 14.

MY DEAR ETHEL,

The Board of Education is now taking over the teaching arrangements for the troops, and from next week onwards I shall have to teach 4 hours a week. Of course the Board wanted us to *begin* by teaching German grammar, but the other fellows and myself flatly refused, pointing out that a class of tired men simply wouldn't listen to a lot of dry rules about an unknown language. . . . Lady C. sent me two dictionaries and her mother has sent me a lovely lot of chocolates and acid drops which I am distributing among the men, especially some of the poorer ones who can't afford much. It makes an enormous difference when one is marching to have something in one's mouth to suck. We did about 23 miles on Thursday, most of it at a very quick rate and a lot of it over difficult ground, and I was glad to find I was not stiff or tired next day. . . . Do you remember Capt. C. of B.T.? He has written to ask me if I would like a commission in the Argyll and Sutherland Highlanders; he is Major in the —th Battalion. . . . I would not accept it, as I should have so much to learn that it would be a case of beginning all over again and I might never see service at all. The 3½ months' training that I have had will fit me to be a useful infantry soldier and I should be a very indifferent officer. Still it is nice to have had the offer.

In January, 1915, Hector and I had to hurry down to Barnstaple: Aunt Tom had died suddenly of a stroke.

It was a frightfully sad time, especially for Hector. Although exasperating, she had a tremendous love for him and he felt the loss of so virile a character.

He only had a few days' leave and had to hurry back to Horsham.

A. COMPANY,
22nd BATTALION, ROYAL FUSILIERS,
HORSHAM, SUSSEX.

Mar. 5th, 15.

MY DEAR ETHEL,

We have been here for eight days and most of us find the life very jolly, though of course there are a lot of extra fatigues to be done. Yesterday I was hut orderly (there are 30 of us in a hut) and I found that drawing rations, cleaning the hut, washing plates, cups, etc., kept me busy from a quarter to 6 a.m. till 5.30 p.m. with hasty intervals for meals. We have a good deal of fun, with skirmishing raids at night with neighbouring huts, and friendly games of footer; it is like being boy and man at the same time. All the same I wish we could count on going away soon; it is a poor game to be waiting when others are bearing the brunt and tasting the excitement of real warfare. . . . I have done 3 days digging in water-logged trenches; it sounds a formidable job, but I am a good digger and like the work of draining off the water. . . . A youth I know, about 22, in the pink of health as far as I know, wrote asking if I would use my influence with the papers I wrote for to get him an engagement at Daly's or some other London theatre (I don't know how he imagined it was to be done!) as he wanted to study voice-production in Town and it was really rather important. You may imagine the perfectly horrible reply he got.

April 2nd, 15.

. . . We have a lot of fun in our hut and never seem too tired to indulge in sport or ragging; the work is hard some

days but it is not incessant like it was in the K.E.H. I was
O.C.'s orderly on a field-day on Wednesday and was jumping brooks and scrambling up slippery banks and through
thickets with a pack on my back that I should scarcely have
thought myself capable of carrying at all a few months ago,
and I came home quite fit.

The following pages contain an account that Hector sent
to *The Bystander*, in June, 1915, describing his life as a corporal. It was accompanied by a snapshot of himself in his
shirt-sleeves, carrying a bucket, but his expression is so severe
and unlike him that I have not included it.

A leading French newspaper a few years ago published an
imaginary account of the difficulties experienced by Noah in
mobilizing birds and beasts and creeping things for embarka-
tion in the Ark. The arctic animals were the chief embarrassment; the polar bears persistently ate the seals long before
the consignment had reached the rendezvous, and while a
fresh supply was being sent for certain South American in-
sects, which only live for a few hours, had to be kept alive
by artificial respiration. When everything seemed at length
to have been got ready, and the last bale of hay and the last
hundredweight of bird-seed had been taken on board, some
one asked, with cold reproach, "I suppose you know you've
forgotten the Australian animals?"

The job of Company Orderly Corporal resembles in some
respects the labours of Noah; one can never safely flatter oneself at any given moment that one has got to a temporary
end of it. When one has drawn the milk and doled out the
margarine, and distributed the letters and parcels, and seen
to the whereabouts of migratory tea-pails and flat-pans and
paraded defaulters and off-duty men under the cold scrutiny
of the canteen sergeant—and disentangled recruits from messes
to which they do not belong—and induced unwilling hut-
orderlies to saddle themselves with buckets full of unpeeled
potatoes which they neither desire nor deserve—and has begun
to think that the moment has arrived in which one may in-

dulge in a cigarette and read a letter—then some detestably thoughtful friend will sidle up to one and say, "I suppose you know there's the watercress waiting at the cook-house?"

There are at least two distinct styles in use by those who hold the office of Company Orderly Corporal. One is to stalk at the head of one's hut-orderlies like a masterful rainproof hen on a wet day, followed by a melancholy string of wish-they-had-never-been-hatched chickens; the other is to rush about in a demented fashion, as though one had invented the science of modern camp organization and had forgotten most of the details.

There are certain golden rules to be observed by the C.O.C. who wishes to make a success of his job.

Cultivate an indifference to human suffering; if Heaven intended hut-orderlies to be happy you have received no instructions on the point.

Develop your imagination; if the officer of the day remarks on the paleness of a joint of meat, hazard the probable explanation that the beast it was cut from was fed on Sicilian clover, which fattens quickly, but gives a pale appearance; there may be no such thing as Sicilian clover, but one-half of the world believes what the other half invents. At any rate, you will get credit for unusual intelligence.

Be kind to those who live in cook-houses.

It has been said that "great men are lovable for their mistakes"; do not imagine for a moment that this applies, even in a minor degree, to Company Orderly Corporals. If you make the mistake of forgetting to draw the Company's butter till the Company's tea is over, no one will love you or pretend to love you.

A gifted woman writer has observed "it is an extravagance to do anything that some one else can do better." Be extravagant.

Of all the labours that fall to the lot of C.O.C. the most formidable is the distribution of the post-bag. There are about seven men in every hut who are expecting important letters that never seem to reach them, and there are always individuals who glower at you and tell you that they invariably get a letter from home on Tuesday; by Thursday they are firmly con-vinced that you have set all their relations against them. There was one young man in Hut 3 whose reproachful looks got on my nerves to such an extent that at last I wrote him a letter from his Aunt Agatha, a letter full of womanly counsel and patient reproof, such as any aunt might have been proud to write. Possibly he hasn't got an Aunt Agatha; anyhow, the reproachful look has been replaced by a puzzled frown.

TIDWORTH CAMP, HANTS.
10.10.15.

MY DEAR E.,

. . . We have been doing field operations this last week, sleeping out under the stars, and luckily having fine weather. The villages we moved through, particularly Amport and Abbot's Ann, are about the most beautiful I have seen any-where, and the villagers the most friendly, running out to give us basketfuls of apples. There is some prospect of us going to Serbia, which I should like; I told one rather timorous youth that the forests there swarmed with wolves, which came and pounced on men on outpost duty. I do hope it won't be Gallipoli.

TIDWORTH. *Nov. 7th,* 15.

After the long months of preparation and waiting we are at last on the eve of departure and there is a good prospect of our getting away this week. It seems almost too good to be true that I am going to take an active part in a big European war. I fear it will be France, not the Balkans, but there is no knowing where one may find oneself before the war is over; anyhow, I shall keep up my study of the Servian language. I expect at first we shall be billeted in some French town.

It was France, and France all the time of his service. He again was offered a commission, and again refused. One day, so one of his comrades told me, Hector was washing potatoes when a General came along who had last met him in his own house at Bridge.

"What on earth are you doing here, Munro?" he asked, and tried to persuade him to accept another job, a softer one, but also farther from the fighting line. But he was genuinely attached to his comrades, and quite determined to get to close quarters with the Boche.

His letters from the front were chiefly descriptions of things he wanted sent out to him, but he managed to write some sketches for the *Morning Post* and the *Westminster Gazette*, two being in this volume, and "For the Duration of the War" in *The Toys of Peace*.

The following are extracts from letters he wrote to me, and one to Charlie (who was trying to get temporarily released from his job of governing Mountjoy Prison, and have a go at the fighting himself; but he did not succeed).

Dec. 19th, 15.

MY DEAR ETHEL,

. . . I came away yesterday to the nearest town for 2 weeks' attendance at a mixed officers' and n.c.o.s' instruction class; 2 officers, a sergeant and myself, are the only ones from my battalion; it seems likely to be interesting and I don't suppose I should miss any lively fighting. I had a longish way to march, with all my possessions on my back, my overcoat in addition being twice its normal weight through soaked-in mud, so I was glad enough to get to my billet, especially as I had had very little sleep for the previous 3 or 4 nights. . . . At a village where we were quartered for a few days' rest there was a dog in a farmyard, chained always to a kennel without any floor, and only sharp cobblestones to lie on. I gave it a lot of straw from my own bed allowance, much to the astonishment of the farm-folk.

25.12.15.

Am spending a quaint Christmas in a quaint town. The battalion is in the trenches.

> "While Shepherds watched their flocks by night
>   All seated on the ground
> A high-explosive shell came down
>   And mutton rained around."

The above is my adaptation of a Christmas carol. Most things here are at semi-famine prices: the French have been saying all their lives *la vie coûte chère* and now it really does.

Feb. 8, 16.

. . . We are holding a rather hot part of the line and I must say I have enjoyed it better than any we have been in. There is not much dug-out accommodation so I made my bed (consisting of overcoat and waterproof sheet) on the fire-step of the parapet; on Sunday night, while I was on my round looking up the sentries, a bomb came into the trench, riddled the overcoat and sheet and slightly wounded a man sleeping on the other side of the trench. I assumed that no 2 bombs would fall exactly in the same spot, so remade the bed and had a good sleep. . . . Got some chocolates from Reynolds and his book [1] with a very charming dedication to myself. . . . A lot of owls come to the trenches; they must have a good time as there is a large selection of ruined buildings to accommodate them and hordes of mice to prey on.

March 11, 16.

. . . For the moment, in a spasm between trenches, we are in a small village where I have found excellent Burgundy, but we leave this oasis in a few hours. . . . We are having plenty of snow, but my blood must be in very good condition as I go out on night watches without any wrapping up and don't feel cold. . . . Our line is so close to the Germans in some places that one can talk to them: one of them called out to me that the war would soon be over, so I said "in about 3 years' time," whereat there was a groan from him and his comrades.

20 May, 16.

. . . We are for the moment in a very picturesque hill-top village, where we have been twice before; I had a boisterous welcome from elderly farm-wives, yard dogs and other friends. . . . I am in very good health and spirits; the fun and adventure of the whole thing and the good comradeship

[1] *My Slav Friends.*

of some of one's companions make it jolly, and one attaches an enormous importance to little comforts such as a cup of hot tea at the right moment.

In June, 1916, Hector came back on short leave: Charlie and I hurried to London and all three put up at the Richelieu (now Dean) Hotel. It was a breathless time, with friends and relatives coming to see him, theatres, the Academy and shopping. He showed signs of wear and tear, but was in great spirits and was discussing his project of going out to Siberia when the war was over, with a friend and having a little farm there.

"I could never settle down again to the tameness of London life," he told me. This idea appealed strongly to me—I saw myself bringing up the rear with all the things he would find on arrival he ought to have brought and had not. It would have been a remarkable life, wild animals beyond the dreams of avarice, at our very doors, and, before long, inside them.

This delightful time in town passed with lightning swiftness, and the day came for us to see him off at Victoria, Charlie and I and a friend, never thinking it was the last time we should see him. Such an appalling idea never entered my head, nor even that he might be wounded. So we were quite gay; in any case we should have sent him off in good spirits.

Not being allowed to stand nearer the troop train than the outside edge of the platform, what we had to say had to be shouted. And the last words I called out to him were, "Kill a good few for me!" I believe he did—he was never, though, to have the satisfaction of a bayonet charge, which was his ambition.

A letter I had from him in July was full of depression because of a "most melancholy post-bag," telling of the death of a friend. "Equally sad was a letter from Lady L——, sending me a pathetic message of greeting from S—— Macnaughtan (the author), who is slowly dying, the doctors giving no hope. Her journey to Russia seems to have overtaxed her strength and she never would spare herself. . . . Three men of my section were hit by a shell yesterday, and one, a dear, faithful, illiterate old sort, who used to make tea for me and do other little services, was killed outright, so I am not feeling at my gayest, but luckily there is a good deal to take the mind off unhappy things."

In September he was promoted to Lance-Sergeant, and late in the month was down with malaria. He wrote to Charlie from hospital, full of impatience at being laid up, and feeling very lonely among strangers.

"I keep thinking of the boys all the time: when one is sharing dangers they don't seem big, but when one is in safety and the others in the front line all sorts of catastrophes seem possible and probable."

The following account is from a comrade in the 22nd Royal Fusiliers who was with him through all his training, and service in France, Mr. W. R. Spikesman:

Saki's humour, wit and gift of satire, never malicious, are well known to his readers of *Reginald, Bassington,* and *When William Came,* etc., but the generosity and sincerity of purpose only probably imagined by a few outside those who knew him personally.

Of his country and his service to his country there can be no doubt of his sincerity, as he was one of the first to enlist; despite the age limit; which recalls August 2nd, 1914, a Saturday night. We had spent the afternoon swimming at baths; tea, a walk in the Green Park; these places were often visited by him; then after dinner a short visit to the Cocoa Tree Club. On leaving his Club we passed the Geographical Society's Club, where a dinner or an address was being given in honour of Sir E. Shackleton, who was then, shortly, after long and extensive preparation, about to start for the South Pole. It recalled to his mind *When William Came* and he was keenly sorry for "S," who was leaving England and civilization, where communication of current events could not reach him. It seemed so tragic to him. Then the excitement watching the changing posters of the newsboys and the motley cries and loud opinions of passers-by. We parted early that evening, being unable to settle down to anything definite.

It was not until early September of 1914 that I saw him again. I had been rejected four times previously, but by luck I managed to enlist, and from that time until the end we were always, if possible, together or knew where to find each other.

Knowing Hector as I did in peace time, many thoughts crossed my mind, how would he like the discipline, the early rising, etc., but I never knew him to be late for any parade of any description or at any time. He quickly settled down to a life so entirely different from that which he had left, like so many others, but to me there was a difference. He saw the beginning of a titanic struggle, he had visited the Continent and other parts of the globe and knew the French, Germans, Austrians, and Russians well, as will be seen from previous chapters of this book, and he intended to play his part, and that part was to be as big a part as he could attain. It is remembered that he repeatedly refused the offers of a commission, as he wanted to know a soldier's duties before he felt justified in expecting a soldier to obey a command given by a superior officer, so he determined to be a soldier first. I remember in this connection that he was one of the first to volunteer, and was chosen to form the first "wiring party" of A Company in our maiden trench visit in November, 1915, at Vermelles.

From the White City to Horsham and Roffey, where a very thorough and sound training began, he was just like a fine, healthy boy, full of life, fun, and devilment, but with the main purpose always in view; and here I must digress as an amusing incident is recalled.

Out of a hut of thirty fellows, two only were known to have returned to camp, during our occupation of about four months, perfectly sober. To even things up Hector decided that it was up to us two to be like the rest. At the time of this decision Cyril Winterscale, then Captain, who was home from the Front, convalescent, promised to visit him at Roffey; the result was a good dinner and talk and farewells about

11.30 p.m., leaving just time to get back to camp without having to "wake the guard." We were perfectly sober and in our right minds, but two "drunks" were expected in No. 2 Hut, ours, and the fellows got what they expected. We explained the next morning that it was a "rag" and cited the sergt.-major, whom we had passed on our way back to camp, as a witness, but the story was discredited. I think the fellows could not understand what the sergt.-major was doing out just before midnight, and sober too.

Time passed and we left Horsham for Clipstone, and after a short time went to Tidworth for "firing" and the final touches. Up till this time there was a certain straining of nerves and anxiety, wondering if the war would cease before the battalion got out, but eventually, on 15th November, 1915, we left England for France, arriving the same night. It was a fine crossing, but St. Martin's Camp, Boulogne, was a good example of what was to come, a long, dreary march, fully equipped and tired, up steep hills to reach a snow-covered plateau, and into tents which were wet both sides.

At the beginning Hector showed great fortitude, for then, as afterwards, it did not matter what the circumstances were, he thought first of those who were under him, he was a corporal at this time, before ministering to his own needs. I got the biggest "slating" from him on this subject at a later date. Briefly the circumstances were these: I was attached to Coy. H.Q. as well as having charge of a section of No. 1 Platoon, Hector's, to wit, and thought that after a heavy march and arriving at "billets" Coy. H.Q. had first call on me, my section second call, but in the middle of a street of a small mining town, Hersin Coupigny, he soon gave me to understand that I was wrong. Again his splendid character was shown, he would with justification lose his temper, but after having said his say with no little heat perhaps there was an end to it. There was not the slightest trace of "littleness" in anything he did or thought, if one can judge by his spoken thoughts, which were many, as numerous times we spent discussing people and things in general.

His consideration for others was most marked in his actions.

especially in the trenches. To those who know the life, this point will be appreciated, but to the uninitiated a little explanation is necessary.

An N.C.O. has numerous duties to perform, tours or patrols with or without an officer, and a two-, three-, or even perhaps four-hour patrol of this particular duty properly performed is a heavy task, especially in such parts of the line as Givenchy, and one was ready for his relief. It was so often necessary to spend five or ten minutes rousing one's relief and a further five minutes in handing over reports, and the situation is excusable perhaps, especially if the day had been a "jumpy" one and the only rest you had got was disturbed by a rough hand or foot which belonged to a person who demanded "What in the name, etc." did one mean by keeping a fellow waiting? Hector realized that if "resters" were kept they must be like time-tables, I mean artillery, not railway time-tables, absolutely adhered to, so in consequence he was always waiting to meet or going to meet his prior relief. On one occasion his punctuality saved his life, at Givenchy—the home of grenades and "Minnies." Awaking a quarter of an hour before his tour, he immediately aroused himself by taking a short prowl and a stretch, and within two minutes of leaving the firing step a grenade fell into the bay on to his ground sheet, on which he had been lying. One knows of many narrow escapes, but few happening because of that fixed idea of being just.

As the war seemed to be one of "duration," it was necessary to think of something besides war, so Hector hit upon the brilliant idea of forming a Club. The battalion was at Ham-en-Artois about April, 1916, and I think it was seeing a pig killed and fancying something different from "bully" that suggested it. It was at this place that the Back Kitchen Club was formed. Pork was purchased and a search was made throughout the village to find some one who would prepare a meal for the evening's enjoyment. We soon found a dear old French-woman who kept a small epicerie, and after listening patiently to her long story of the vicissitudes of the war and how she had suffered, she took us into her kitchen and showed us a most elaborate "kitchen stove or kitchener," most beautifully polished and in the finest condition, with the exception of a crack in one of the top plates, which, with tears in her eyes, she explained was caused by a piece of shell, German. She was retreating from "Mons," where she had lived for a few years till war broke up her home; the stove was one of the things she managed to get away. Here, of course, was a splendid opportunity, and Hector explained his mission. The pork was left and we were told to call at 7.30 p.m. sharp. On our arrival we were told to go to the back kitchen, and found the dear lady there to receive us with the words "Messieurs, bon appétit," and a splendidly cooked dinner of pork, roast potatoes, green peas ("packet peas") and the usual dressing that goes with pork laid on the table. She then told us that as long as we remained at Ham or were ever on a visit, the back kitchen was at our disposal. There and then I took down a card advertising "Chocolat Ménier" and reversing it wrote the words "The Back Kitchen Club" and four signatures followed, Hector, the founder, coming first. This card was seen about a year later by some one we knew, and it is my hope that it still hangs there. Hector, after we had dined, then enumerated a few rules which were never departed from. Because of the spirit of this Club, the Rules as given out on that night are worthy of note:

Membership not to exceed nine, and to replace members "passing on" the unanimous approval of all existing members of a name chosen.

On all days, when possible, without departing from military discipline, the members to meet to partake of an evening meal, however frugal.

When free, "out of the line," all members to take dinner, which consisted of "omelettes, salad, meat and wine, together at some house or estaminet," duty being accepted only as an excuse for non-attendance.

All parcels received from home by members to be common property of the Club.

In the event of any member or members being "broke,"

their share of expenses to be paid by the member with the most ready money available, or by two or more jointly.

The conduct of all members to be beyond reproach.

Needless to say, these rules were never broken during Hector's time. It was hoped to continue the Club in London after the war, but the moving spirit having "passed on" there is little likelihood of this happening.

The battalion moved on from one field of battle to another, and many more heavy marches were experienced, and although fatigued at times to breaking point, Hector always showed that same dogged spirit, and on a fifteen-mile march in the heat of a very hot July day, full pack and ammunition, I remember him finishing up plus another rifle, that of a much younger man of his platoon.

Delville Wood in August, 1916, is vivid in my memory because of the terrible "gunfire" experienced, and the undaunted bravery and courage of "Saki." Just imagine a wood, the trees battered to splintered stumps, trenches about two feet deep, no definite trench line, troops from many battalions in isolated knots having during the attack become disintegrated, looking for "leaders," ready to attach themselves to any officer as long as they had some one to command them, a terrific fire from enemy heavy batteries (I remember one shell which fell to my right killing 16 men) and so many dead.

Hector on this occasion even surprised me, who had always tried to emulate some one worth while; he stood and gave commands to frightened men, in such a cool, fine manner that I saw many backs stiffen, and he was responsible for the organization of a strong section, giving them a definite "front" to face, and a reassuring word of advice.

Still another move, and a winter to face, but about October, 1916, malaria, a fever that had attacked him in India when a boy, sent Hector to the M.O., who asked no question but immediately sent him to the Base. It was a big miss, and I felt just lonely and I know was severely "told off" by my friends for being such a misery, but if I had seen the results of the next "do," I would have borne a longer miss. Unfortunately, it has been known for men to go sick for the purpose of missing something, many did not go sick who should have done, especially if it was a question of "over the top." News travelled, and although the attack on Beaumont Hamel was a sure thing, the date was uncertain, but Hector heard it at the Base and I saw him again about the 11th November. He looked a very sick man and should have been in bed, but I knew his thoughts and the reason for his being fit. We were in position by 3 a.m. on 13th November, 1916, left of Beaumont Hamel in front of "Pendant Copse" and the Quadrilateral, and remained till the early morning of the 14th November, when we left our front line to "flank out" on the left of our advanced line, the troops on the left, through the marsh-like conditions of the ground (men had sunk in mud to their stomachs), being unable to come up.

It was a very dark winter morning, but after much excitement we were hailed by voices and a figure rose to the top of the trenches in front of us and shouting greetings to the Company Commander (one Capt. Roscoe, one of the finest of fellows, who was killed in February, 1917) engaged him in conversation. A number of the fellows sank down on the ground to rest, and Hector sought a shallow crater, with the lip as a back-rest. I heard him shout, "Put that bloody cigarette out," and heard the snip of a rifle-shot. Then an immediate command to get into the trenches. It was some time later, about an hour, when a fellow came to me and said, "So they got your friend." My feelings then I cannot describe, but I knew I had lost something inestimable, the friendship of a man whose ideas and thoughts I tried to emulate, some one whom I loved for his being just "Saki."

In writing all I have cared to tell of Hector's life, it has been impossible not to have a good deal of my own life in the picture. We were such chums. I have not touched upon his social life, visits to country-house parties, etc., because they would not be of interest to the general reader.

The softer, sympathetic side of him never, I think, appeared in his writings, except, perhaps, in "The Image of the Lost Soul." He had a tremendous sympathy for young men struggling to get on, and in practical ways helped many a lame dog.

ETHEL M. MUNRO.

INDEX OF TITLES

MODERN LIBRARY GIANTS

A series of sturdily bound and handsomely printed, full-sized library editions of books formerly available only in expensive sets. These volumes contain from 600 to 1,400 pages each.

THE MODERN LIBRARY GIANTS REPRESENT A
SELECTION OF THE WORLD'S GREATEST BOOKS